# God's Little Soldier

# God's Little Soldier

Kiran Nagarkar

HarperCollins *Publishers* India
*a joint venture with*
The India Today Group
New Delhi

HarperCollins *Publishers* India
*a joint venture with*
The India Today Group

First published in India in 2006 by
HarperCollins *Publishers* India

**Second impression 2006**



ISBN: 81-7223-633-6



**HarperCollins *Publishers***
1A Hamilton House, Connaught Place, New Delhi 110001, India
77-85 Fulham Palace Road, London W6 8JB, United Kingdom
Hazelton Lanes, 55 Avenue Road, Suite 2900, Toronto, Ontario M5R 3L2
*and* 1995 Markham Road, Scarborough, Ontario M1B 5M8, Canada
25 Ryde Road, Pymble, Sydney, NSW 2073, Australia
31 View Road, Glenfield, Auckland 10, New Zealand
10 East 53rd Street, New York NY 10022, USA

Typeset in 11/13.5 Sabon
Nikita Overseas Pvt. Ltd.

Printed and bound at
Thomson Press (India) Ltd.

*Zia*

# 1

One of Zia's earliest memories was of a concert at their home, Firdaus. His aunt Zubeida pushed her chin out in the direction of the dais and said, 'Satan, that's what he is.'

Zia was supposed to have been in bed. He could barely keep his eyes open but he was not about to sleep. Abbajaan and Ammi had allowed his brother Amanat to stay up all night on the paltry excuse that he was older. Zia would show them. Not only Amanat, but his father, mother and the entire audience of invitees would be dead to the world by three or four in the morning and he would still be keeping vigil.

'Just look at them, men and women mingling shamelessly,' Zubeida Khaala muttered as she tried to pat Zia to sleep by bringing both her hands down like thunderclaps to his head and chest. 'Decent women don't throw off the pallus of their saris and expose their breasts. They should sit in the zenana. Or wear a burkha when they have company.'

On any other day this pummelling would have rendered Zia unconscious within minutes. But not today.

'I'm not sleepy,' Zia said sitting up in his bed. 'I'm not.'

'You are a wilful child, Zia. I should be punishing you but I have a soft heart and you are taking advantage of me.' Zubeida Khaala took a deep breath and clenched her jaws firmly to say no. 'All right. Five minutes is all you have to watch the disgraceful spectacle outside. After that it's back to bed and, as penance, Zubeida Khaala won't be singing any lullabies for you tonight.'

Zia threw aside the light cotton quilt and ran to the door. He left it slightly ajar and plonked himself down on the carpet. His aunt made a show of being uninterested while she straightened the pillow and the coverlet but then quickly settled down behind him.

Ustad Rehmat Khan was rumbling like a gathering storm from the centre of a makeshift raised platform. On his left sat the tabalchi chewing paan and looking bored, while the sarangi player on the right stayed just a fraction behind the Khan Sahib's voice and reproduced it note for note. Behind the singer sat a man who looked like a weaker and shorter version of the Ustad. He strummed the four strings of the tanpura pretending that he was not actually there, in the hope that his father would not ask him to pitch in. But every now and then the Ustad Sahib would grunt and the young man would essay a few feeble notes.

Zia preferred not to look at Ustad Rehmat but the sheer tonnage of the man was a gravitational force that couldn't be denied. He was not a man, he was a mountain; Kanchenjunga with a twirled moustache. He didn't reach the ceiling but that didn't matter. It felt as though his six-inch Kashmiri cap was scraping it. He wore a knee-length midnight blue sherwani. The top three buttons, as well as the clasp of the collar and the bottom three buttons, were open. There were patches of sweat under his armpits, and he kept dabbing his face with a green silk kerchief the size of a scarf. He sat cross-legged. Below his trouser legs were magenta socks. The elastic had come undone and they wilted outwards. He had a voice like a giant drill burrowing a tunnel some three hundred feet below the ground; nothing could resist it. If he had wanted it to, it could have swept the earth from under them, leaving them to fall into the fiery pits of jehannum that Zubeida Khaala said were reserved for sinners and non-believers.

Even with his mouth shut, Ustad Sahib would have seemed sinister. But it was what he was doing with his eyes and mouth and tongue and hands that struck terror into Zia's heart. The Ustad's index finger shot up suddenly and pointed at the hub of the vast lit flower of the chandelier. His left eyebrow arched dangerously and the eyeballs disappeared. His mouth went around itself in circles with the lips opened wider than the tops of his socks while his tongue flapped inside like a red fish gasping for air. The other hand went up and retrieved the first one. Mesmerized by the disharmony and violence of the spectacle, Zia's eyes too vanished sideways, his mouth was agape and his tongue vibrated in tandem with the singer's. Ustad Rehmat's head dived down as his right hand sliced and chopped the five notes he was playing with into an intricate taan that zigzagged and skittered, shimmered and somersaulted. At least a hundred and fifty other people, maybe two hundred, sitting on the carpets and durries around the dais, in the doorways, and the length of the verandah in front of the house, watched him, awestruck.

It was the month of December. The tide must have been rising for a cool breeze had begun to blow. The wet patches in the Ustad's armpits were now drying up slowly, leaving behind outlines of how far they had earlier spread.

The tempo increased. The Ustad's voice was a thunderbolt one minute, falsetto the next. It moved from register to register keeping the audience off balance. The tabalchi too had got into the spirit of things. He was smashing the tabla and dugga with the flats of his hands. A few more wallops and the taut leather would split open and his hands would disappear. Now the Ustad was out of control. You couldn't make out whether he was smiling or crying, or both. His hands flailed, his eyes rolled, his ears twitched and his jaw seemed dislocated, but he continued regardless.

That was when Zubeida Khaala took the name of the hated one.

'Satan, that's what he is.'

'Is singing forbidden, Khaalajaan?'

'Yes,' Zubeida hissed. 'Unless it is in praise of Allah.'

'Maybe he is praising the Almighty.'

'No, he is not.'

'How can you tell? You can't make out a word of what he is saying.'

'Don't blaspheme. I know in my heart of hearts.'

'Is that what makes the Ustad, Satan?'

'Not the Ustad, you fool. He's only the handyman of Satan.'

'Then who's Satan?'

'Your father. Yes, your father. He's the very image of the evil one. We'll all burn in hell for eternity because of him.'

Zia knew then that he had lost his Abbajaan forever and ever. His aunt was right: Abbajaan was Satan, for only he could pretend to be so gentle, funny, loving and affectionate, toiling for the wellbeing of his family while all the time planning its downfall. But he, Zia

Khan, would not shirk his duty. Wasn't he the anointed one? Zubeida Khaala had always told him so. And now it was his duty to expose this devil that paraded as his father. Let Abbajaan try his tricks again, let him buy a gift for his birthday, it was next month, he would refuse it. But that would not suffice. Devil that Abba was, he bought presents for the whole family, including Zubeida Khaala, even when it wasn't anyone's birthday. Just for the pleasure of seeing the delight on their faces, he said. Pleasure, that was the key word. Pleasure is how Satan entices and entraps gullible fools. Abbajaan would come to kiss him goodnight with Ammi but he, Zia, would turn away. That would hurt Ammijaan but there was no helping it. He was, after all, doing it for a good cause; a greater cause than any other. The Almighty would understand and be proud of him.

Zia would make a list of all the things that gave his father joy, and would dissociate himself from them. It was going to be difficult. His father enjoyed small things, medium things, big things. He was such a crass man he even enjoyed doing absolutely nothing. He thought it fun to watch his incipient paunch go up and down as he lay flat on his back in bed. He would place a marble on his navel and take bets with his sons and wife about whether it would roll to the left or right or go backwards or forwards to his chin. He had names for all three of them. Ammijaan was the love of his life, Amanat was the joy of his life and Zia was the light of his life.

There he was, Satan. His eyes were closed and he was lost in Rehmat Sahib's song. Next to him sat Son of Satan, Zia's mortal enemy, Amanat. The 'joy' would be going out of their lives, Zia would make sure of that.

'Sin away, Satan,' Zubeida said aloud. 'It's a songster today. Next thing you know he will be bringing nautch girls from the kotha to this house.'

If he had a choice, Zia would infinitely have preferred nautch girls to this Rehmat Khan's singing. They would have worn bells on their ankles as all dancers did. They would have whirled around till their feet were a giddy blur.

Zubeida Khaala had once taken him to a Hindi movie and had asked him to close his eyes when a woman in hot pants, along with fifty other girls in skimpy skirts, had danced to the most enchanting song he had ever heard. 'Rumba ho, ho. Sumba ho, ho.' He had covered his face with his hands and watched the disco dancing through the gaps between the fingers. He'd felt strange in his chest. His heart had taken on the rhythm of the song. One slow beat followed by two quick knocks on the rib cage. Slow ho, ho; slow ho ho. He had danced for weeks to Rumba ho, ho. Sumba ho ho. He had taught Abbajaan how to disco. And Abbajaan had got Ammi out of the kitchen, rewound the tape and made her dance. He had even dragged Zubeida Khaala out of her room. She had been furious with him but his father simply laughed and forced her to shuffle her feet a bit. The only one who had sat still and watched them was Amanat because he had had an attack. But then when had he not?

'Is Abbajaan really going to get nautch girls? Wouldn't that be fun? So much better than this man braying.'

'Over my dead body.' Zubeida thumped Zia on the head. 'If I don't look out for you, you'll be Satan's next recruit and victim. Get into bed, this minute.'

## 2

On Sunday afternoons, Abba and Ammi went to the races. Sometimes though, Amanat would stop Ammi from going. It was always touch and go with him. He would be sick all night long, be fine in the morning and then suddenly, when Ammi and Abba were getting dressed, or better still, just stepping into the old Bentley, he would have an asthmatic attack. One look at him and Ammi would be back out of the car.

'You go ahead, Zafar. I want to be with the children.'

Ammijaan must have been a fine actress. Never, never did her face show disappointment or rancour. Not even two or five days later would she snap at Amanat or obliquely make some sarcastic comment about him to Zia.

Abba was not such a bad performer either but sometimes as his wife got out, his hand would stretch towards her for the briefest moment as though to stop her from deserting him.

'Shagufta, you know I'm not that keen on the races.'

Ammi would laugh. 'Liar.'

But it was true. Cards and races were a fix for her. Come 4.30 in the afternoon, she would start to get restless. It was time to go to the card room at the Willingdon Club. After lunch on Sunday, she was as nervous as the colts and horses who would be racing that day.

'Go on, Zafar, Amanat needs me.'

Zia despised Amanat for ruining his parents' outings. His elder brother was a spoilsport. Zia prayed that his brother would never change. On the days when he was well and their parents were at the racecourse, Zia shut his eyes tight and willed his brother to be sick, dreadfully, irrecoverably sick, so that one of the servants would have to take a cab, rush to the Permanent Members' Enclosure and get Ammi back. Maybe, get both Ammi and Abbajaan back, so that Abba could be with Amanat and Zia would have his mother all to himself.

An attack was always reason enough for Amanat not to play with Zia. 'Cricket?' Zia was willing to be generous: 'You bat, I'll bowl.'

This would represent no mean sacrifice on Zia's part. Frankly, he would have to be a shade beyond desperate to make such an offer. He was without doubt the world's greatest batsman. Whether he was playing with his brother, his parents, any of the servants or with a team of boys from the neighbourhood, he never got out.

Cricket, like everything else in life, was all about numbers. Other people added runs to their score, Zia took a different view of the matter. If he hit a boundary, his score went up fourfold. Since he mostly hit sixes, his score escalated in multiples of six. Some day, preferably sooner rather than later, they would have to rewrite the rules of the game just for him. Fours and sixes were small change to Zia. They did not do justice to his game. His power play and technique were so extraordinary, his shots were more like tens and twenties.

Zia has a way with numbers. He can square and cube any figure, whether it's five digits or fifteen, and just as easily calculate the square or cube root, even if it means entering decimal territory. Go ahead, test him. 6 x 6, that's easy, anybody can tell you it's 36. 36 x 36? Need some help with the answer? Before you can hit the second key on the calculator, Zia will tell you it's 1,296. Now cube that. Don't bother to say Jack and the rest of it. 2,176,782,336. You think Zia's bluffing? Go ahead. Use the calculator. Are you finally convinced that he is not making it all up? Zia can zip and unzip through arithmetic with barely a trace of conscious thought and yet he believes that what he excels at is cricket.

Amanat had been up the whole night and was still gasping for air. He looked ravaged but he kept going. He did everything the doctors told him to without complaint or fuss. He took his inhalers, stretched out his arm for the lab technician to shove the needle in his vein and draw blood, he swallowed his pills, breathed through the oxygen mask, got relief for a few hours and then went back to his panting. He did not lose his temper when he was sick. He did not become moody. You could sit up all night with him and pray to Allah to cure him. You could gently, gently run your hand over his back, as Abba did, to relieve his spasms. And yet all the while you knew that whatever you did was more to ease your conscience than to help him. If Abba, Ammi or even the doctors had had the guts, they would have admitted that they hated Amanat because he made them feel so helpless.

'How about a game of Trade?' Zia tried again.

'Baby later,' Amanat blurted between two attempts to swallow all the air in the universe.

'You always say maybe later and your later never comes.'

'Bromise.'

'No, now. Not promises. Where's Ammijaan? She can be the third player.'

Amanat had the makings of a great stammerer when he had an attack. He could go on mercilessly until Zia wanted to slit his throat and end his agony.

'Ba, ba, ba – '

'Babababa black sheep. Stop it, Amanat.'

'Huddy and pot potter.'

Honey and hot water, Zia should have known. When Amanat had a spasm, Ammijaan went to the kitchen, heated a glass of water, added two tablespoons of honey and brought it over to Amanat. It made no difference that Amanat was bucking and rearing with a manic cough. That didn't faze Ammi. She stood there smiling amiably, full of understanding.

'I am in no hurry, sweetheart. You take your time.'

Sweetheart always did take his time; he had little choice since he was ricocheting all over the place. Ammi's patience may have been infinite but it was the mute pleading in her eyes that would make Amanat capitulate. The outcome was always the same. Amanat would say yes, open his mouth, the spoon would dock next to it and the hot honey water would spill over his starched white kurta, onto the mattress, onto the carpet, onto Ammi, onto the floor. Ammi never gave up. There'd be a growing sticky-sweet puddle on the mattress and Amanat would smell like a honeycomb. And then, one could never tell whether he did it deliberately or the violence of the attack was the cause of it, the glass would go for a toss and lie shattered on the floor.

'Never mind son, never mind. Don't take it to heart, it's not your fault,' Ammi would try to reassure her elder son but without much conviction.

Amanat, even at that early age, was too much of a gentleman. And like all gentlemen, was a seasoned hypocrite. He did not tell his mother that yes, indeed, it was not his fault; quite the contrary, the broken glass was the result of her cussed insistence on feeding him when he was so volatile.

There were three systems of medicine in the Khan household, all of them operating simultaneously. Ammijaan's honey series. Honey and water, honey and eggs, honey and brandy, honey and fresh lime juice, honey and toast, honey and curds.

Abbajaan, meanwhile, was willing to stake his honour, his name and reputation on one single medicine: Vicks Vaporub. Rub it gently into the chest at night, cover the body with a blanket, and not just your average cough, he assured you, but bronchitis, pneumonia, whooping cough and emphysema would all have fled by the next morning. Rub it on your forehead if you had a headache, around your nostrils if you wanted to get rid of a cold. Drop dollops of it in boiling water and inhale twice a day, and even the most chronic sinuses would clear up and stay cleared. Amanat shuddered at the sight of Abbajaan proceeding towards him with an economy jar of Vaporub. He disliked any contact with unguents and oils and poultices and pastes, but Abba's Vicks, he loathed. And yet, goody-goody that he was, he suffered Abba's ministrations in silence.

It fell, however, to Zubeida Khaala to administer the final solution for all of mankind's and womankind's and childkind's maladies. It was literally a solution. Sometimes she mixed soap in it, sometimes Epsom Salts, but most of the time she just warmed clear, clean water and poured it into the white enamel can with its midnight blue border, its ten-foot red rubber tube and black nozzle. She held the can at waist level in her left hand and the nozzle over her head in her right.

By this time Amanat was already lying, pyjamas down, on his side on a durrie on the floor, his lower leg stretched out while the one above was pulled up at the knee all the way to his chin. He had undergone the procedure six or seven dozen times and yet the fool was petrified and terror stricken. He who never asked for pity, looked piteously at his aunt. But Zubeida Khaala did not falter or relent. She was not doing this because she was a monster who got pleasure from the pain of others, or because she enjoyed it, she assured Amanat. Her motives were the most noble and pure. The heart of all human troubles, ailments and misfortunes lay in the alimentary canal. The remedy was simple. Flush the evil out. If possible every day. Abbajaan called her Florence Nightingale with the enema, and she certainly practised what she preached. Come morning, sometimes at night too, she took the black nozzle and flushed herself clean. When she was through with it, unclogged and washed, she felt virtuous and looked it. There was a luminous halo around her face. Perhaps elsewhere too.

Amanat, bloody fool that he was, did not ever ask Zubeida Khaala, a.k.a. Florence of the enema, to explain why the treatment that she said cured brain tumours, stomatitis, elephantiasis, encephalitis, leprosy, insomnia, multiple sclerosis, loss of hair, burst appendix, hepatitis ABCD and E, skin disorders, each and every variety of cancer including leukemia, and every other disease known to man and woman, could not relieve his breathlessness and asthma and allergies.

Perhaps he was wiser than his years and there was good reason for his silence. For Zubeida Khaala had always told him his troubles were unreal, that they were only in his mind.

'Ammi, Amanat won't play Trade with me,' Zia complained to his mother.

'Don't be selfish, Amanat. Why won't you play with your brother? Oh.' Ammi looked at her desperately-seeking-air son and realized her mistake. 'He's a little unwell, Zia. Nothing that honey and hot water won't cure though. Just wait a while.'

Zia wandered into the garden, the lawn in front of the house and the more substantial one at the back. He walked up the stairs to Abbajaan's studio above the garage. Sculpting was Zafar Khan's hobby but Zia thought he spent more time here than at the Khan Architects' office. His excuse was that he got his best ideas for his architectural projects while he was carving out a torso in marble or welding scrap iron for a forty-foot-high pole-vaulting athlete for the new stadium in Delhi. With his eyes closed, Zia ran his hands over the varying textures of the sculpted figures, feeling he had entered the chill, translucent marble or become as hard and unyielding as the steel. But then he withdrew his hand as though it had been singed. He had once again forgotten Zubeida Khaala's injunction and wandered into Satan's den of sin. Islam, she had warned him, forbade all graven images.

The house was a little over a hundred years old and stood on a ridge of land that jutted into the sea. There was something marvellous about this location. Once you were there, it was impossible to tell that you were in Bombay, downtown Bombay. Just a couple of hundred metres away, however, and you would suddenly be in the midst of traffic, cars, taxis, speeding BEST buses, the occasional cyclists, and the trucks that were allowed to ply their way only between 9 p.m. and 6 a.m. The structure had been designed as a separate guesthouse, the main bungalow being the property to the left where the land recessed sharply, and where a five-storey luxury apartment block now stood. Zafar's grandfather, the building contractor, had bought the guesthouse and called it Firdaus, the Islamic paradise. He had made some changes and added to it but Abba had almost completely reinvented the place. If it had been possible, Zafar Khan would have built the house in the middle of the ocean. Even as it stood now, he had tried to blur the distinction between without and within. He'd used a lot of glass, but as he never tired of saying, beauty is function and proportion. He wanted the sea inside his house but he also wanted the window to frame the view of the rocks, ocean, sun, sky and moon as an ever-changing picture.

The only language Zafar Khan seemed to speak was architecture, and he could be a bit of a bore. But not for Amanat. Amanat could never have enough of Abbajaan.

'Can you imagine how graceless a woman or man would look without a neck, with the head sunk between the shoulders? That's how the earlier Islamic domes were. They had little or no neck. Then the Mughals came on the scene and got the neck just right, so you could see the beautiful dome of Humayun's tomb even from a distance.'

Willy-nilly, not only Zia and the rest of the family, but even the servants could hold forth on cross-ventilation or the difference between the Roman and the Gothic arch.

The tide was out now and the black rocks were exposed. Zia had thought of clambering down and wading into the water, but there was a drop of seven feet and the rocks were jagged and it was difficult to get a foothold. He wondered what their bungalow looked like from the sea. Would he be able to see inside his room? The gold, copper, silver, bronze discs of the mobile at the window? The bedspread with Peter Pan trying to catch his shadow? His cricket set?

He saw his mother on the phone in the drawing room. The honey and hot water libation must have failed once again, for Ammijaan, he was almost sure, was calling the family physician. Dr Patwardhan had warned the Khan family that the only way to treat Amanat's asthma, when it did not respond to the regular medication, was to take quick, decisive action. Or else...

Dr Patwardhan did not elaborate.

Dr Patwardhan, Zia felt, was much given to exaggeration. Amanat had often been rushed to hospital but how come he always came back? Surely if it was a case of 'or else...', to quote the doctor himself, Amanat would not have returned, or at least not alive.

Ammijaan had taken her own sweet time today, since Dr Patwardhan hated to be disturbed on a Sunday. Zia's guess was that she had followed up the honey treatment with Abbajaan's Vaporub, and that only when that had also failed had she got on the phone to the GP. It would now be up to Dr Patwardhan to ease Amanat's agony. Permanently, if Zia had his way.

Dr Patwardhan's Ambassador pulled in at the side of the house. The doctor got out, followed by a Pomeranian and a poodle. From the other side emerged Sagari, with two pups in her arms, a Dalmatian and a pariah.

'Don't allow them to come into the house, Sagari,' the doctor told his daughter as she let the pups go. 'Zubeida Auntie doesn't care for dogs.'

The dogs, maybe they were bitches, Zia hadn't observed them at close quarters, barked at each other, barked at the sky, the sea, the apartment block next door, the grass, the glass windows, the sun, the trees.

Sagari adjusted the two bows that held two pony tails atop her head like a pair of black Pekingese ears. She took out a yellow plastic hairbrush from the gold lamé lady's purse on her arm, ran it through her hair and then fluffed it out expertly. She snapped open a compact and tried on a quarter smile, a half smile, a three-quarter smile, then the full one. She practised the half smile again; it required some fine-tuning. She patted down her dress and sucked in her cheeks like an actress. 'Like' is the wrong word. She was an actress. Wrong again. A child superstar. She was the mascot of a detergent, Saffa Saffa, and of a fruit-flavoured concentrate called Rasleela, contains-no-fruit-juice-or-fruit-pulp. Within a year it had overtaken all the other juice powders put together.

Seven children, ages one to seven, sit at a long table facing the camera. The first six are sucking their thumbs. The seventh, none other than Sagari, is sipping a coloured drink with the name Rasleela printed on the glass. Sagari turns to her six companions, switches on a simpering quarter smile and says, 'Oh, grow up. Try Rasleela. It's a sweetheart of a drink.' Hearts with arrows pop out of the glass of Rasleela.

'Oh, grow up' soon became a cult slogan. Not just school kids, but college kids and their parents were telling each other to oh, grow up. The next thing you knew, Sagari was advising Miss India, the most popular cricketer in the country, the Indian chess champion and Bollywood's biggest celluloid star, all of them sucking their thumbs, to 'Oh, grow up'.

There she was, this creature of dreams and delight for whom Zia longed every time he saw her on TV, which was at least four times a day. Yet he could not move from where he had taken shelter.

'Oh look, your friend Zia's behind the rain tree,' Dr Patwardhan told his daughter.

'I know,' she said, 'he's hiding. He won't be able to speak or come out from behind the tree for a while. He's in love with me.'

Dr Patwardhan went into the house. Sagari played with the four dogs, as though she was shooting an ad for dog food, pointedly ignoring Zia.

Did you hear what she said? 'He's in love with me.' Zia didn't even know that she existed. There was no creature on earth, fish, animal, reptile, bird, crustacean or human whom he hated with as much passion as Sagari. He saw her fall into the sea below and crack her skull and spill her brains like egg yolk on the black rocks. He wasn't sure whether he wanted her to die or not. The neck should certainly be broken. She would beg and plead with him to pick her up in his strong arms and would tell him she was sorry, abjectly sorry, for having been so arrogant. The truth was, she was madly, wildly, hopelessly in love with him. She was crazy about him the way in foreign movies those shameless actresses were about their heroes. Like them she would also wear off-the-shoulder blouses and kiss him on the lips and profess her love for him in public. No, it wouldn't do to have her dead if she was going to make that confession. He would have to gather up her splattered brains and put them back. Instead he wanted her on her knees, the neck broken, the head flapping around in the wind that had begun to blow in from the sea.

She was a witch, that's what she was, and a mind-reader. How else could she know he was dying to be with her or predict with such accuracy how he was going to behave?

'Oh, grow up, Zia,' Sagari said languorously as she stretched out on the lawn, and looked up at a cloud pretending to be a white camel. 'I can't wait here all evening for you to come and play with me.'

And all the cares were lifted off Zia's shoulders; the long, thick rusted iron nails that had held him rooted to the ground under the rain tree flew up into the air and joy rose in him like the tide that was sweeping across the black rocks.

'Your mother's asked us to stay on for dinner tonight,' Sagari told Zia. 'That way Papa can make sure Amanat can get a good night's rest.'

'Really?' He leapt up.

Zia pelted the dogs with pebbles and rolled on the lawn with them. His relationship with dogs was ambivalent to say the least. He loved them because Sagari loved them. He hated them because Zubeida Khaala hated them and said they were no good. Sagari kissed them on the mouth, she fed them, she bathed them, dried their fur with a hair dryer, brushed their coats. He had questioned his aunt a hundred times about why she thought dogs were fit only to be despised, but she didn't seem too keen on answering. 'They are unclean,' she had told him brusquely. 'Don't you believe your aunt, or are you suggesting that you doubt the wisdom of Islam?'

'Will you be staying the night with us?' Zia asked casually.

'Do you want me to?'

What an absurd question. 'Yes. If you sleep in my room and not in Amanat's.'

'I'll have to ask Papa.'

'Let's pick flowers.' Sagari let go of the dogs and took Zia's hand in hers.

Flowers? Did Sagari really expect to pick flowers from his garden? He would not give her permission. They were his flowers. From his garden. He plucked three deep burgundy rosebuds. 'May I put them in your hair?'

It was beginning to dawn on him that where his heart was, now there were fields of roses that stretched all the way to infinity. His whole body and head were flooded with love of Sagari. He was willing to give her his house, his garden, his father's telescope, his prayer rug, his life and now the roses from his heart.

'What a lovely thought, Zia.' She kissed him on his cheek. 'But these are for the dancing Ganesh.'

'Ganesh?' Zia couldn't seem to focus because of the intense seismic activity on his cheek. 'Which Ganesh?'

'The one in the window. There's no other, is there?'

'Why would you want to put flowers on him?'

'Because he's a god, silly.'

Zia felt faint. There was a crackling sound in his head. His brain was jammed with static. It was an objet d'art, his father had told him and Amanat, an exquisite piece of sculpture from the Tanjavur kingdom. Maybe so, but it was a sin to place flowers in front of an idol and worship it. Sin. Sin. Sin. The words rang like a gong in his head.

Zia looked at his companion, the beauteous princess, the darling of millions, the witch of Rasleela. What spell had she cast on him that, even as he called her idolater, he put his hand in hers and pressed the bell without letting go so that Yaqub, the servant, opened the door yelling at him to stop that infernal noise and keep the dogs out, and Zia giggled and raced past him romping through the house with Sagari until he was standing in front of the dancing Ganesh from Tanjavur with Sagari pouring flowers at the feet of the auspicious god, the god his Hindu friends Rajan and Kumar invoked before starting a new term, and here is Sagari joining her palms and closing her eyes and saying a prayer and laying her head at the feet of the god and everything she does, Zia does too, except that he says his own Islamic prayers before bringing his head to rest on the dancing feet of Ganesh and he is aware without looking behind that his aunt is watching him, with incredulous eyes, and so is his God whom he has shamelessly betrayed.

'Zia, Zia-ul Haq, dictator of Pakistan and master of all he surveys, archrival and nemesis of the Bhutto family, son of Zafar and my sister Shagufta, jewel and hope of India, where art thou?' Altaaf Mamoo. Who else would call out so many variations of his name? His uncle Altaaf was standing in the drawing room with Abbajaan. 'Behold the heavenly houri, of "oh, grow up" fame. What incredible fortune that one gets to see not one but two *id ke chand* simultaneously.'

Altaaf Mamoo had a nickname for everybody: Amanat, Abba, Ammi, Zubeida Khaala, the servants, Dr Patwardhan, the barber, the driver, the gardener, the paanwallah; film stars, singers and rock stars, politicians, prime ministers and presidents. But most of all, he had a name for his favourite Zia, a name for almost every occasion. However low Zia felt, Altaaf Mamoo could cheer him up. Altaaf Mamoo was executive director at the family firm, Khan Builders, but he was never too busy. He had a slow, lazy manner. Nothing seemed to bother him. Even if something terrible was happening, he could make you laugh. It was difficult, no, it was impossible, to be angry with him.

Ammijaan adored her only brother. She loved his insouciant ways, his impeccable dress sense, his casual take-it-or-leave-it attitude, his fey humour that found it ill-bred to take anything too seriously. He had a secret life and it was exciting and amusing to wonder about it.

Altaaf swept the children off the ground, one in each arm, and asked his brother-in-law, who had just walked in, 'Zafar mian, isn't it time we got Prince Zia and Princess Sagari married?'

For some inexplicable reason, Zia Khan blushed and pretended to be angry with his most, mostest, more than mostest favourite uncle on earth, Altaaf Mamoo.

'Yes, what an excellent idea. That's the only way we'll be able to keep her with us.' Abba turned to Zia. 'How is your brother, son? Is he feeling better?'

'Yes, he's perfectly fine.'

'Oh? Then Ammijaan needn't have stayed at home with him.'

Zia realized he had gone a bit too far.

'Let's go and take a look at Amanat, shall we?'

Abbajaan, Altaaf Mamoo and Sagari were still on the staircase landing when Zia darted into his mother's room. He couldn't have chosen a worse moment to enter. Ammi was cradling Amanat's head in her lap, making all kinds of solicitous noises and pleading with the doctor.

'Does the poor boy have to be given another injection? He's a child, why does he have to suffer so?'

'Ma, I want that injection.' Amanat was, as usual, making a big production of breathing as if he had invented it.

'Does he really need it, Pat?' Ammi asked again.

'Ma, I want that injection.' He said it again.

Dr Patwardhan did not bother to reply.

The whole family was gathered round the bed now. Outside, the dogs were barking forlornly for their mistress.

'Dogs?' Zubeida Khaala asked in dire alarm, breaking the silence in the room. She turned on Sagari: 'Did you bring them with you?'

Sagari switched on the three-quarter smile. 'You have nothing to fear. They are in the garden.'

Dr Patwardhan rubbed the flattened crook of Amanat's arm with a spirit swab. He had a choice of four engorged veins. The needle pressed down on the one to the extreme right and pierced the flesh. The doctor pulled back the plunger. This was the moment Zia hated. He could have closed his eyes or turned his head away as Sagari had done. Instead he watched mesmerized as the blood burst in like an explosive charge. Crimson smoke rose in wisps, then curled and clouded the fluid inside the syringe. Abba was leaning over and fanning Altaaf who had fainted.

Zia saw the princess Sagari leave the group of spectators. She walked to the bed, the handbag in her hand motionless as though becalmed by her seriousness. She bent down over Amanat as her father withdrew the needle, pressed the cotton swab into the crook of Amanat's arm and kissed his forehead.

Dr Pat gazed fondly at his daughter. 'Look at her, Zafar. She wants to become a vet, but I'm going to make her a star, a star on the big screen. You watch, she'll be even bigger than Nargis or Audrey Hepburn.'

## 3

Zia had to make up to Zubeida Khaala for his terrible betrayal. He'd have been willing to move both the mountain and the Prophet but he had no idea whether that would have any effect on his aunt. Ever since he could remember, she had told him that it was his destiny to become a waalee, a saint who could perform wondrous miracles: cure the sick, bring light to the blind and speech to the mute. Mohammed was the last and greatest prophet of all; greater than Moses to whom God Himself gave the tablets with the Ten Commandments. Yes, greater than Jesus, whom the foolish Christians held to be the son of God, when he was only a fine and loving prophet and nothing more. It was Mohammed who had given the world the gift of Islam. Islam: the act of surrendering, the surrender of the true believer to the One and Only God who is Allah. It is this same verb Islam, his aunt had told him, which is the source of the word Muslim.

But the Prophet Mohammed, peace be upon Him, had come and gone. And now so many of his people were losing their way. It was not to the One and Only that they offered obeisance and obedience, but to Satan and Mammon. Oh, mankind was adrift, perhaps the universe itself was rudderless. Zubeida Khaala was not talking about the covers of magazines where young women flaunted their breasts as though they were Bukhara peaches for sale and wore skirts that barely reached the fork of their legs, but about her own people. Many of them did not pray five times a day. Some of them did not even know their prayers. A great many hardly ever went to the mosque. The women had lost all sense of decency and went about without covering their faces and bodies. She herself had almost given up going out because her sister and Zia's father would not allow her to wear a black burkha. 'The unbelievers love this fleeting life too well, and thus prepare for themselves a heavy day of doom...' Zubeida Khaala quoted from the Koran. 'The righteous shall surely dwell in bliss. But the wicked shall burn in Hell-fire on Judgement Day: they shall not escape.'

Even well-known Muslims seemed unable to sustain unflawed faith. Her favourite playback singer from Hindi films was Rafi. Do you know what Rafi's first name was? It was the name of the Prophet. God had given him the wondrous gift of a mellifluous voice that earned him hundreds of thousands of rupees a year. And to what use was he putting it when he was not crooning love songs to heroines? Singing hymns and praises to heathen gods like Rama, Krishna-Kanhaiyya and Shiva.

It was Zia's vocation, Zubeida Khaala had determined, to bring back to Islam those who had strayed. His voice would be a thunderous indictment in the ears and consciences of those who had become casual about Allah or had turned their backs upon Him altogether. His own faith would be like a beacon to sinners. Yes, he would bring back the lost souls of Islam. In due course, he would convert the pagans and idolaters and increase the tribe of the Prophet. And Allah had chosen her, the meek and submissive Zubeida, to mould and guide the little boy into a great pir and saint. That was her mission.

'You will not remember this, Zia,' Zubeida Khaala had told him many times, 'but we almost lost you twice. First at the time of your birth, and then soon after that to the devil in the form of a woman who tried to snatch your soul from Islam. But I stood firm, and Allah, the compassionate and merciful, saved you.'

'Can the devil be a woman?' Zia asked.

'He can be anything, a snake, a sin, a temptation.'

'Who was the woman?' Zia asked in a whisper, lest she was around.

'Never you mind. All you need to know is that great battles were fought over you.'

And now Zia had let Zubeida Khaala down.

He wanted to make amends. He was willing to pay any price, undergo any punishment, offer any sacrifice to win back his aunt.

He didn't know what the terms of reparation were and what would move the stone that passed for Khaalajaan's heart. How had he lost her? She might be strict but she was also the most caring person he had known. She had very little money and whatever she had she was constantly giving to beggars, to a servant for his son's eye operation or to the driver to send his daughter to school. It did not matter whether the person was a Hindu, Christian or Muslim.

All these years, everybody had said that she lived only for Zia. But all that had changed now. There was not a word of recrimination or remonstrance from her. Instead, Zubeida Khaala was especially civil with him. The equation between aunt and nephew had undergone a subtle though radical change.

There had always been two camps in the Khan household, the Amanat camp and the Zia camp. The rules were simple and clear enough. If you were not a hundred per cent with Zia and did not demonstrate your fealty to him on an hourly basis, make that a minute by minute basis, you were against him. Abbajaan, there were no two ways about it, was a traitor. He didn't just believe in universal love, he practised it. All creatures, animals, plant and sea life were equal in his eyes. He was as fond of Sagari's dog as he was of Amanat, which was fine with Zia, but what was intolerable was that he could speak of Amanat and Zia in the same breath; worse still, treat them as if they were equals. The case of Ammi was a little different. Zia had a feeling that for all her talk of fair play, he was his mother's favourite. And yet she had clearly cast her lot with the Amanat faction. She spent twice as much time with Amanat as she did with Zia. He couldn't quite figure out Altaaf Mamoo. Altaaf was at ease with both camps, though Zia suspected that he belonged to neither. The only camp he looked out for was his own.

Zubeida Khaala was Ammi and Altaaf Mamoo's sister. Not much else was known about her because she was as much a fact of life as Abbajaan or Amanat. She was there, full stop. Altaaf Mamoo was the only one who sometimes talked about Zubeida Khaala but it was always behind her back and, as was his way, you could never tell whether he was being serious or making it all up.

Zubeida had two friends during her childhood in Lahore: her sister Shagufta and Dorothea, the daughter of the assistant postmaster.

She was eleven when she went with them to see a Hindi movie called *Deedar* at the Plaza. When the film ended, the three friends could not move from their seats. Their eyes were red and swollen. They had endured a devastating experience that had seared them. They were branded for life. What, oh what was the point of life? Why not just end it here and now?

Of the two heroes in *Deedar,* one left them cold. The other was Dilip Kumar whose real name was Yusuf Khan. Blind since childhood, he regains his sight after surgery but gouges out his eyes when he discovers that the woman he loves belongs to another, the very surgeon who has given him back his eyesight. All three girls knew then that there would never be another man in their lives except Dilip Kumar.

But Shagufta and Dorothea were fickle. When they grew up, they laughed at their childish infatuation and fell in love with other men. Not Zubeida. A hurricane called Dilip Kumar had taken residence in Zubeida's heart and was wreaking havoc with it. She had little idea why it had chosen her as the locus of its fury, nor did she know how to deal with it. She felt victimized and battered. What unnerved her even more was her own response. She did not seem to resent the intrusion. Her reactions were far more complicated. She wondered if it was possible to enjoy extreme suffering. Was the nature of agony half pain, half pleasure? It couldn't be. But then why was she not keen on ridding herself of this incubus, which was not only causing pandemonium in her heart, but every now and then alighted on her neck and sometimes materialized inside her throat, seeming to strangle her.

Despite the cataclysmic upheavals in her heart, she found she was indifferent to her own condition. The only thing she wanted to do was to give her eyesight to Dilip, or Yusuf Khan as she preferred to call him, who had once again become eyeless. She was brimming with giving. Her heart, limbs, body, brains, mind, spirit, soul, they were all Dilip's for the asking. Even if he didn't ask, she was his. And the more she gave, the more abundant and richer she would become.

Zubeida had no intention of getting married to anyone except the matinée idol, but her mother thought she was being childish and arranged a fine match for her. The groom was an officer with the Indian Administrative Service, a prize catch by any standard. His career path was a steep gradient. It went up and up and up.

When Zubeida and he got married, he was sent to the chief minister's secretariat in Bombay, an almost unheard of posting for someone so young. The high life, the prestige, the prospect of one day becoming the wife of the most powerful bureaucrat in the country, all of it left Zubeida cold. She hated the sterile enticements of the terminally snobbish, cutthroat and incestuous club called the IAS. The marriage was, as might be expected, a brief and unhappy one.

Zubeida left a short note for her husband telling him that she did not see any point prolonging the dreariness and pain of a loveless coupling. She was leaving behind all the jewellery and gifts that his parents had given her and would be sending him the divorce papers. In a P.S. she laid the blame for the marriage not working out upon herself and on the Indian custom of the parents choosing partners for their children.

Zubeida was once again free to devote herself to the man she had chosen when she was eleven.

## 4

War. Zia would have to declare holy war upon his brother. The rat had tried to steal Sagari from him and now he had insidiously curried favour with Zia's one and only friend, ally, guide task-master; his lodestar, his inspired instructor: Zubeida Khaala. Amanat had cast a spell on Khaalajaan, enticed her with his illness, his good nature, his quiet, unassuming ways. That is the way the devil works, Zubeida Khaala should have known this. He's a subtle one, the devil is. Hadn't she herself told Zia that if austerity, other-worldliness, the martyrdom of illness appeal to you, so be it, he will assume all these and, come what may, engineer your fall.

To arms, my friends, to arms. Zia would rescue his aunt from the Great Tempter. What better weapon can you conjure against the devil than the name and word of God Himself? All these years Zubeida Khaala had only taught Zia the salaat, those limited prayers that children are supposed to say during the five daily namaazes.

These, obviously, were not going to be enough. He had to raise the stakes.

Zia tried, God knows Zia tried his utmost. He learnt almost half the Koran in English to win over his aunt, to elicit just one word of encouragement from her. Even an affectionate glance would have done. No, that is not true. He was not Amanat. He would not settle for pale gestures. He wanted his Zubeida Khaala back, not this recent, vapid creature, but the one he had known before his tragic idolatrous error, the one who loved him fiercely and scolded him brutally, the one who stood by him regardless of whether Amanat was sick or dying, whether Ammijaan and Abba were on his side or not; the one person who had recognized his fate and future and made him aware of it, the one human being who was certain that he was going to lead his people back to the light of Allah.

Ramzaan was a difficult month. The family, barring Zubeida, went about its business normally. Or at least they tried to. Ammijaan, Abba and Amanat went to work, to the club or to school just as they always did. They had tea, ate lunch and dinner, drank water and burped silently. Zia's routine too was undisturbed, except that he was aware that when he turned eleven, he would join Zubeida Khaala in the fasting and prayers. That had been the original secret plan between him and his aunt. How things would pan out now that the Zia–Zubeida equation had changed so drastically, only time would tell.

Zubeida did her chores, sent the children to school and then kept as much to herself as possible. Ramzaan was a month of prayer and introspection. She was subdued, almost saintly in her patience, for that was also an injunction of the Faith. Hardly anybody would presume to eat in her presence when she was fasting. But the curious thing was that the rest of the family felt just as guilty when she was in her own room and they happened to bite into a biscuit or swallow a mouthful of water. She herself did not eat from sunrise until the sun had set. She did not drink anything, no tea, coffee or water. Any free moment she had, she read from the Holy Book.

Zia pondered a long time over the matter of fasting. Fasting, he knew, required truly superhuman fortitude. He relished his food, the tandoori chicken, tangdi kebabs and bund gosht, the sherbets and the bhajjyas and kachoris, not to mention the whole incredible range of sweets that the cook and Zubeida Khaala put on the table at meal times and as snacks for tea, especially on festival days. But it was not so much the thought of deprivation that gave him pause as the discipline of it: a full thirty days of keeping your most natural of instincts at bay. Might as well ask him not to breathe. And yet what repelled him most was the rancid smell in Zubeida Khaala's mouth as the day progressed and her fluid levels began to fall. Would his mouth too smell fetid and acrimonious? It didn't matter now. It was a small sacrifice. The prayers and the recitations from the Koran had failed. He would have to up the ante. He would undertake a fast that would break Zubeida Khaala's adamantine heart. He was a mere child but he was not about to ask for any special favours, handicaps or the affectionate, easy-going, patronizing children's version of a fast. He would go the whole hog, match the severity of Zubeida's abstinence. No solids, no liquids, not even his own saliva.

It was going to be a trifle difficult. There was no way either his father or Ammi would let him fast. As a rule Abba did not interfere with the way in which Zubeida Khaala brought up the children, especially Zia, but on occasion his parents had long and heated discussions with Zubeida about it. They were both on the same side, but because they were ineffectual in front of Zubeida's inflexibility, they always ended up feeling aggrieved and helpless.

'Show me,' she would say, 'where I have done wrong. Have I taught the children something that embarrasses you?'

It was rarely anything that specific and Abbajaan and Ammi would begin to back down against her counter-offensive. But this would only be the beginning.

'Are you ashamed? Ashamed of your own religion?' she would ask.

'No one said anything of the kind,' Shagufta would mutter in a huff.

'Then why don't you want Zia to know the meaning of Islam and the teachings of the Prophet, may peace be upon Him?'

'It's not that. You always give him a one-sided picture. Zia hardly ever gets to see and understand that different people have different faiths and different points of view.'

'You think right is wrong, Zafar, and wrong can be right?'

'Don't twist words, Zubeida, just to score a point.' Abba had had this argument many times and could never make any headway. 'I just want the children to realize that whichever religion people belong to, Hinduism, Christianity or Islam, they are God's children.'

'So they are, so they are,' Zubeida Khaala would nod her head vigorously.

Abbajaan would then heave a sigh of relief.

'That's why it's up to each of us to choose the right God,' Zubeida said.

In the matter of fasting, however, both Zafar and Shagufta were firm. A couple of years ago, Zubeida Khaala had devised a wonderful children's fasting plan for Ramzaan. It was cleverly worked out so that at the outset you hardly noticed that some things had been dropped from your meals and yet by the end of the month you had graduated to missing out an entire meal.

'No,' Ammijaan was a trifle brusque.

'Why not? A little bit of discipline and deprivation won't do them any harm.' Zubeida was at her most amiably reasonable.

'The discipline of the body and mind is a fine idea, so long as it's not overdone.'

'As you can see from my plan, there's no drastic fasting at all.'

'And so long,' Shagufta had not finished, 'as the fasting plan lasts a week at a time and does not occur in the month of Ramzaan.'

'But that is ridiculous. There is a specific significance to fasting during Ramzaan.'

'Then it's not discipline you are after but a religious duty.' Zafar's powder too was dry and ready.

'And what is wrong with that?'

'Two things. You introduced the idea under the guise of discipline when what you had in mind was a theological consideration. Secondly, I think God is merciful and compassionate as the Koran tells us. Why would He want us to prove our love for Him by starving ourselves every day for a whole month?'

'Shame on you, Zafar. How can you distort the love of the faithful for God into something so cynical? You'll regret the folly of your words.'

'Nevertheless, no fasting for the children. Is that understood? They can decide whether they want to fast or not once they are grown up.'

It was obvious then that Zia would have to get around his father's fiat by a tortuous route. He would eat his meals with the rest of the family, come back to his own room, get into the bathroom, shove his middle finger deep into his throat and move it back and forth until he succeeded in his resolve. He was a wilful child and, however painful it was, he stuck to his plan. Within a few days, he had merely to put the finger on the tip of his tongue and an entire breakfast or lunch would tumble out.

Ironically, Zia's fasting proved to be even more severe than Zubeida Khaala's. Ramzaan permitted a believer two meals so long as they were consumed after sunset and before sunrise. This meant that Zubeida Khaala had dinner as well as a substantial breakfast. With Zia things were a little different. Dinner was the only meal he retained in his belly. When Zubeida Khaala woke up before dawn to have breakfast, Zia was very much asleep. Since the rest of his family had breakfast later, Zia had no alternative but to visit the bathroom after his morning repast and throw up. Little wonder then that within a week his eyes were bright and unusually dilated while his weight was falling rapidly.

It was towards the end of the second week of Ramzaan that Zia realized that his monumental starvation and dehydration were in vain. He had passed out in class and was sent home. The teacher had forced him to drink a solution of water, salt, sugar and lemon juice. It tasted like ambrosia but the moment he was alone he knew he would have to reverse the natural order of things.

Ammi settled him on a divan in the drawing room and brought him a Hardy Boys mystery. She propped up a pillow under his head, kissed his forehead, said it was nothing serious, just the heat, and left for the club. Just the heat, what was she talking about? And how could she go to the club when he might die any minute? Now, if it were Amanat who was ill, more likely just pretending to be ill, cheap shot, he would withdraw that, she would not have rushed off. She would have been only too happy to stay behind, nurse him and keep him company.

It was while he was lying down commiserating with himself about his lot, and the stepson treatment given to him by his own mother, that it dawned on him that he had got himself into an untenable position. His family, Abba, Ammijaan and Amanat, were unaware of his stupendous sacrifice. As a matter of fact his parents would have been horrified to learn that he was keeping the roza. And then it hit him. That woman sitting there on the leather couch with an Urdu newspaper spread out in front of her, that woman who studiously ignored him while she pretended to be reading, he wanted to grip her shoulders and shake her till every vertebra in her backbone was misaligned. He wanted to scream at her: 'Why do you think my stomach is upset? Why do you think I spend so much time in the bathroom? Can you make a guess why I am starving myself to death and my legs are so shaky that I can barely stand on my feet?'

But how was she to know? He looked at the statue of the dancing Ganesh, the one that had got him into such grievous trouble, and asked himself again, how in God's name was that woman to guess what he was up to? The truth was that she was so wrapped up in herself and in the punishment she was meting out to him, she had forgotten that he was even alive. If only someone would tell that hard-hearted, no, that heartless woman what she had put him through. Because he was not about to do it, no way. He was too proud to ask for her pity.

Oh, the folly, the folly of his undertaking. And the futility of it.

What was she muttering? What did she read in the paper that so incensed her?

'If only someone would rid us of these Hindu dogs, they won't leave us in peace even during the holy month of Ramzaan. The police just stand by while they deliberately take out a procession to disrupt our prayer meetings.'

At the corner of the Firdaus lane and Nepean Sea Road, tucked away almost into the pleat of Glitterati, 'Designer Tailors to the Rich and Famous', was Bajrang Paan Beedi Shop. The owner of Glitterati had tried every possible way, both legal and extra-legal, to get rid of the paan-beedi shop, which ruined the chic façade of his establishment. People said that he had first tried to buy Bajrang off, then bribed the municipal authorities to evict him and the Nepean Sea Road police to close him down by claiming that his shop was a traffic hazard. He had even got the local mafia don to threaten him. Nothing worked.

Lucknow paanwallahs come in only one size. Extra large with an extra paunch. It is an occupational hazard. There is zero mobility in the job once you've washed, dried and polished the large brass plate and all the small and big containers for the various masalas that go into a paan. You are seated cross-legged on your cushion-throne at eight in the morning and do not get up, except to have a meal and go to the loo, till you close shop at midnight or later. In between, the extent of your movements is limited to swivelling around to reach out for cigarettes, paan masala or envelopes. Bajrang is five-feet eleven and wiry. Almost every paan-beedi shop owner in South Bombay has a fulsome, handlebar moustache. Not Bajrang. Paanwallahs are gregarious: business demands that they be affable. Bajrang is silent to the point of being surly and yet he has an almost constant stream of clients. Handcart pullers and taxi drivers eat his paans, those astringent betel leaves, and so do most of the patrons of Glitterati. After 9 p.m. there's a long line of cars waiting outside his shop. Ammijaan and Zubeida Khaala are also regular customers. The cook picks up their paans on his way back from the market every day and puts them in the fridge.

Bajrang was Zia's friend.

Anytime Zia stirred out and wandered off into the lane adjoining his house, he'd go and watch Bajrang work. There were times when Zia was undecided about whether he should become like Altaaf Mamoo or a paanwallah. No museum could compare with Bajrang's paan shop. There were stacks and stacks of cigarette packets and cartons, imported and local, over thirty varieties of betel nut and chewing tobacco, jars of sticky rose preserves with slivers of micro-thin silver foil, seven brands of beedis, a choice of every betel leaf known to man, an ice box in which fat paans sat atop slabs of ice for special customers. But the centre of gravity, the thirty-ring circus and the magnetic field of all this activity converged in and around the large brass plate with a diameter of twenty-four inches and the row upon row of glistening golden brass boxes arranged in it.

In the mornings when Zia waits for the school bus to pick him up (Amanat is often unwell and either misses school or goes late), Bajrang is lighting joss sticks and praying to the silver image of Ganesh in the tiny recessed altar at the dead centre of the niche that is his shop, and to his namesake, the flying Bajrang Bali with the Drongiri mountain on the palm of his left hand. The only communication between Zia and the paanwallah at this hour is a toffee placed in the middle of the empty brass plate and, very occasionally, a pencil sharpener, a whistle or a multicoloured top.

Zia says, 'Thank you.' Bajrang ignores him. Until the school bus arrives, Zia plays with Sher, Bajrang's pariah dog. It is Bajrang's dog only because Bajrang was the one who baptized him. Otherwise, he belongs to anyone who will pat him and feed him. He is called tiger because even a low-decibel cracker or the screeching of a car's brakes sends Sher bleating and scurrying under the platform where Bajrang sits.

Bajrang calls Zia Chhote Nawab. If there are no customers around, the two of them play a game. Zia points his index finger from one box to another and Bajrang identifies the contents without pause or stumble. Fresh grated coconut, fenugreek seeds, super-thin shredded areca nuts, chewing tobacco number 47, cloves, saffron paste, cardamoms, scented tobacco, rose water, raisins, shilajeet. Every once in a while Zia will say 'show me' and Bajrang will uncap the lid and lower the box for Zia to confirm the rapid-fire identification. Only once in all these years has Bajrang gone wrong and that was because a policeman instigated by the Glitterati owner asked him just then to produce his licence.

Three days before the end of Ramzaan, Zia decided to bring things to a head. He woke up certain that he had finally found a way to win back his aunt. Her stone-heart would crack and cave in and crumble and welcome him back and, far more importantly, she would realize that he was and would always be the sole hope of Islam, its latter-day saviour. She would beg him, yes, Zubeida Khaala would go down on her knees and beg him to let bygones be bygones.

He brushed his teeth and bathed. He had breakfast (Amanat had had a bad night and was still asleep, and Abbajaan was reading the paper), he pocketed the knife next to Amanat's plate, went back to his room, did the Open Sesame routine by shoving his middle finger down his throat, slung his school bag around his shoulders backpack fashion, kissed Ammi who was upstairs with Amanat, said goodbye to Abbajaan, went across to Zubeida Khaala, smiled and said 'Khuda Hafiz, Zubeida Khaala', did not wait for her to ignore him, opened the door and walked with determined step to the Bajrang Paan Beedi shop. A flute with a red string tied to it was waiting diagonally for him on the brass plate while Bajrang prayed and Sher yawned. Down, down with Hindu dogs, Zia hissed, as he bent down and plunged the knife into Sher's flank. For a second, a long, long second that

Zia would never be able to forget or get rid of, both Bajrang Paanwallah and Sher looked at him uncomprehendingly.

Then, all of a sudden, Sher leapt up yelping and yowling in pain. He took a whole chunk of Zia's exposed thigh in his mouth and didn't let go of it till Bajrang had broken off his prayers and with almost superhuman force loosened Sher's jaw and pulled him away.

For the next forty-eight hours Zia seemed to be fluctuating between semi-consciousness and delirium. He said over and over again without much conviction, 'I'm your friend, I am. Bajrang Paanwallah, Sher, don't turn your back on me.' Sometimes he said, 'Zubeida Khaala, please tell Bajrang Paanwallah and Sher that I did it for you.'

Dr Patwardhan took one look at him and said, 'This boy is severely undernourished and dehydrated. Zafar, has the boy been keeping the roza and fasting?'

'No,' Zafar told him. 'Both Shagufta and I don't. How could the children?' Then his confidence seemed to waver. He looked at Zubeida.

She stared back at him. 'How would I know? I didn't ask him to.'

Shagufta called up the school and spoke to Zia's class teacher. No, he didn't go to the toilet during class but he'd been a little dull and yet overwrought, she didn't know how to explain it.

Dr Patwardhan peered inside Zia's throat. It was red and swollen. He put Zia on a glucose-saline drip. 'I think he's been eating with you and making himself throw up after.'

To be on the safe side Zia was given three anti-rabies injections and Sher was kept under observation.

When Zia regained consciousness and began to recover, Abbajaan brought Bajrang Paanwallah and Sher to meet him.

'Why don't you say sorry to them, son?' Abba asked Zia gently.

Zia turned his face away.

'No, no, please, Zafar Sahib.' Bajrang Paanwallah did not want to embarrass father or son. 'It's a bad day best forgotten. I'm just relieved to find that Chhote Nawab and Sher are both recovered.'

# 5

Later on, when Zia had become a young man, he was unable to understand why first Freud and then all his readers, followers, patients and critics made such a fuss about the mother-son thing or Oedipus Complex, as the father of psychoanalysis called it in his pretentious fashion. It was not just his father, Abbajaan, he'd be willing to kill. He would have killed anyone who stood between him and his mother. Yes, he would commit fratricide, genocide, patricide and whatever other 'cides' it took to keep rivals away from his mother. Zia loved Ammijaan. In truth, that was a pretty tepid description of his feelings for her. She was, to borrow from Abbajaan's endearments for his family, the light, love and joy of his life. As she could be the despair and distraction of his waking and sleeping moments. When he was not with her, he felt orphaned. Amanat took Zia's mother away from him all the time. Amanat did not have to ask or beg for her or demand her presence. She would run to him, stroke his back and nurse him. Sometimes Zia thought that his older brother was the centre of her life, her reason and her passion, her sole concern and preoccupation. And then he was willing to kill that sick, dastardly brother of his. And yet in his heart he knew she was his and his alone. Amanat was duty; he, Zia, was her happiness, her slave, her delight, her world.

He knew every lipstick, mascara, kohl pencil, rouge, perfume and cologne on her dressing table. There were times when he even put lipstick on his lips and kohl under his eyes. Zubeida Khaala disapproved of Ammijaan letting him play with her saris and cosmetics and said these were women's things and not something a boy should be interested in. 'It's the work of the devil. You'll become a homosexual or a hijra and end up in jehannum.'

The long English word he didn't know and the first Hindi one, he wished he didn't. He was going to the club one evening with Altaaf Mamoo to pick up his mother when the car stopped at the Haji Ali traffic lights. A man dressed as a woman sidled up to his window, spread out his hands and brought them together like cymbals. Zia had never heard a clap sound so hard and tight and unyielding. He felt his head was caught between the man-woman's hands as he-she clapped again. Zia's eyes, nose, cheekbones, ears, brains were crushed into fine powder and were falling like snow from the pair of taut hands.

'Give me money, little prince.' The man-woman smiled archly but there was something peremptory about that harsh male voice. 'God will give you back a thousandfold.'

Whoever the person was, he-she-it couldn't seem to stand still. It kept gyrating in half-circles, all the time looking coyly at Zia. It had kohl under its eyes, and was wearing golden earrings. The face was clean-shaven but there was a blue shadow across the cheeks and chin. It had a receding forehead and its hair was tied in a little knot at the back.

'I don't have any money,' Zia whispered as he shrank into his seat.

It picked up its falling pallu and slapped it against its left shoulder. It laughed scornfully, opening wide its paan-red mouth. The teeth were stained and there were bits of betel nut stuck on the long, livid tongue.

'Got a car all to yourself and you telling me you've got no money?' The cheap, yellow plastic zari on the border of the sari shone acridly as the sun went down behind the mosque of Haji Ali half a mile into the sea.

Why weren't the traffic lights changing? Why was Altaaf Mamoo smiling stupidly and enjoying the man-woman's antics instead of driving away?

'Shame on you for lying. Give me the watch or I'll break the whole hand off.' One more clap and it had put its arm in all the way and the bony fingers with magenta nails were pinching Zia's cheek and then the hand was grabbing Zia, pulling at his watch and trying to yank him whole out of the car window and Altaaf laughed as Zia screamed in terror: 'Let go of me, leave me alone. Mamoo get rid of this thing. Start the car, roll up the window, free me, free me.' And all the while, it was smiling.

The lights changed and the cars behind were honking away and his uncle Altaaf was cackling as the car pulled out and the hand let go.

Zia was still shaking, his body twitching when Ammijaan got into the car and kissed him on the cheek. He withdrew from her.

'What's the matter, my love? Why are you angry with Ammi?'

'Oh, don't pay him any heed,' Altaaf tittered. 'He just wants attention because a hijra asked him for some money and touched him.'

Altaaf was Ammijaan's one and only and absolute favourite brother. She could never get angry with him but she became quiet now and her body turned rigid. 'Did you find it amusing, Altaaf?' her voice was low and soft.

'Yes, very. Our brave and indomitable President Zia was hugely rattled,' Altaaf recalled in good humour. 'He thought the eunuch would really take him away.'

'Would you find it just as funny – ' there was a metallic edge to Ammijaan's voice that Zia had never heard before and he understood then that there was much about his mother he did not know ' – would you find it just as uproarious if I told Zafar that you've missed not one, but two meetings with the minister for roads and transportation? And that he should start looking for a professional to take over as CEO of Khan Builders? Or shall I tell Rehana that you were not with us for dinner on Tuesday, but were cooing with the American deputy consul general's wife?'

Zia watched Ammi get dressed and make herself up before she went to the club. She had her back to him. Her sari was a lake on the floor that she pulled up vertically and, with swift, sure movements, tucked around the waist of her petticoat. And now came the miracle, as a five-metre-long piece of cloth was moulded and fitted around her body without a single stitch or pin. All it took to tailor the garment precisely and perfectly was sixty seconds of time. The lake diminished. One end of the sari was thrown carelessly over the left shoulder while the rest of it she pleated with breathtaking speed into accordion folds and secured at the navel into the petticoat. A pull here and a tug there and the sari was draped.

There was only one person who was as crazy about Ammijaan as Zia was. His father. Sometimes Zia thought Abbajaan loved her even more than he did. Amanat, Abba; Zia would have to get rid of them.

Almost every day he discovered new enemies. His father rarely entertained his clients at the club or in restaurants. He gave parties at Firdaus where he could show off his home and his queen. Zia wanted his mother to be the centre of gravity at every dinner, to see her make a silent entry (she was always late) and watch everybody in the room arrange themselves in concentric ripples around her. And yet as the party warmed up and one of the guests monopolized her or paid her a compliment, Zia wanted to strangle the man.

The visitors he resented most were the ones who came to stay. Of course some of the guests made a fuss of the children. But you could almost always be sure that there was an ulterior motive. The gifts they gave were to fob off Zia and Amanat so that they could take Ammijaan out for lunch or to a concert or anywhere away from the children. There was also the other kind of guest, the kind who for no known reason was actually fond of the Khan children, the rasping, air-grasping, wheezing Amanat and his younger brother Zia who pretended to be shy to the point of being deaf-mute. An extreme example of this kind was the Antonia woman.

Antonia and Zia's father had been friends since the time Abbajaan had been an architecture student in England. She now taught in Cambridge, and the Khans spent a couple of nights at her home whenever they went to England. Whoever Mr Antonia was, Zia had never seen him. But there was a daughter called Vivian who was about Zia's age. She was a sullen and prickly creature, given to inexplicable fits of rage. Her vocabulary seemed limited to the word 'no'. Do you want to go for a walk with us? No. How about an ice cream? No. A swim maybe? You could show Zia how to do the backstroke. No.

'Where do you keep your father?' Zia had asked Vivian, and surprise, surprise, she had managed to string together a dozen words.

'Mum keeps him locked in a cupboard in the basement. And if you don't look out, she'll lock you up too and no one will ever find you again.'

'What utter drivel.' It was uncanny how within minutes of being with the monosyllabic Vivian, Zia began to sound like his own idea of a resident of Cambridge. 'Aunt Antonia loves me. She calls me "Little Miracle".'

Zia had no idea why he had quoted the name his English aunt had for him, since he hated it, but some demon must have persuaded him to remind Vivian of it. The words 'Little Miracle' had a catastrophic effect on her. He had pressed some hidden button and Mount Vivian erupted like Etna, which they had once visited on the way to England. Vivian's body coordination was staggering. While she beat a tattoo on the floor with her head, her arms and feet pounded the ground and her screeching seemed to chip the paint off the wall.

'That's enough, Vivian,' Aunt Antonia had called out from the dining table before going back to her conversation with Abba.

Zia had felt a twinge of sympathy for Vivian. The intensity of her unhappiness bothered him but Aunt Antonia was strangely unmoved by it. Her way of dealing with her daughter's tantrums was to ignore them.

Aunt Antonia, like Ammi's club friends, thought of Zia as a mathematical prodigy. Zia wondered whether people mistook him for a circus animal, one of those dogs wearing fake spectacles who did all kinds of tricks with numbers. He could never say when someone at a party would quiz him about fractions or ask him to give an instant answer to an algebraic equation. Sure, he had a talent for maths, but he was not Aunt Antonia's Little Miracle. He was special, yes, very special, as Zubeida Khaala told him often, but for altogether different reasons. He was Zia, the light. He was going to light the path to Allah and bring errant souls back into the righteous fold.

Zia had the feeling that the two aunts couldn't stand each other, though taking care never to show it. It was as though they were fighting over him without ever mentioning his name. Zia was hardly averse to being anybody's favourite but Aunt Antonia had no finesse. He found her affection and attention stifling.

Aunt Antonia came to India every summer to work with a Catholic charity based in Delhi but she always made it a point to stop over in Bombay to meet the Khan family. She brought gifts for both Amanat and Zia but there was no mistaking who got the lion's share. There was one present Aunt Antonia gave Zia around this time that had a lasting effect on him. It was a diary bound in burgundy calf-leather with Zia Khan written in gold lettering in the lower right-hand corner.

7th February: My name is Zia Khan. I am seven years old today. Allah is my God. Islam is my flag. And the Prophet is my Guide.

Zubeida Khaala has told me that I'm chosen to be a waalee and lead my people to the light of Allah. She says I must be a good boy with good thoughts, only then can I be a waalee.

Amanat is my brother. He's older than I. He's always sick. Abbajaan and I call him 1001 because he tells me as many stories as Scheherazade told the king. I get angry with him when he's not well because then he doesn't tell me a story before I go to sleep.

Last night as a birthday treat 1001 told me a new story.

What happened was this: on Sunday morning Raj was sucking on a green-sour tamarind when he swallowed a whole seed. He put his fingers in his throat and tried to pull it out, but it had already gone down into his stomach. Just then his mother shouted at him to stop fooling around and do his homework. That was the problem with Mama, he thought: whatever you were doing, she wanted you to stop that and do your homework. Well, he better get down to it unless he wanted to be scolded and told 'No playtime tomorrow'.

Ten days later, he noticed something strange when he looked at the mirror. There were two dainty green leaves growing out of his head. Another two weeks and the sapling had grown by three inches and there were now forty-seven leaves. Raj plucked a leaf and put it in his mouth. No two ways about it. It was a tamarind tree. The next morning Raj felt something strange on his head. He climbed out of his bed and looked in the mirror. There was a baby cardinal sitting on top of the tree.

The diary habit would stay with Zia for life.

The night of Vivian's tantrum, Zia stole out of his bedroom and lingered on the stairs to gather the courage to unbolt the door to the basement.

'What are you doing out of bed in the middle of the night?'

Trust Amanat not to leave Zia alone. Kept a hawk's eye on him all the time. Zia should have returned the compliment and asked him, 'And what about you?' but he was relieved to see his brother. He had watched a couple of minutes of *The Poltergeist* the day before on TV and was sure that the ghost was waiting to pounce on him from behind the sofa. He had even heard it skulking behind the basement door, and the curtain had shivered against the moonlight when all the windows were closed.

'I want to go to the basement.'

'Basement? Why do you want to go down there?'

'Vivian said Aunt Antonia kept her husband locked in a cupboard there.'

Amanat burst out laughing. 'Vivian said her father had been locked in the basement?'

'Stop repeating everything I say.'

'But Mr Booth-Langston has been dead for years. He died in a plane crash.'

## 6

Zubeida Khaala and Zia could have told Abbajaan quite some time ago that he had it coming. Allah gives Satan a long, a very, very long rope to hang himself by. But at some time or other His patience runs out and then there's no escaping the wrath and retribution of God.

That's exactly what happened. Abbajaan woke up one morning and discovered that he had lost everything: the house, the garden, the car, the servants, the furniture, the business, the friends; everything that three earlier generations had built through sheer grit, daring and hard work was gone.

Zafar's father had headed a thriving family construction business. He had taken it for granted that his son would join Khan Builders but Zafar had had little interest in contracting and construction. He had wanted to be an architect, to design bridges, hospitals, aerodromes, homes and cities. Zafar's father had been patient. He had loved his son and had hoped that history would not repeat itself. Father and son would make a team, instead of being wary and suspicious of each other as he and his own father had been. Architecture and construction are, after all, first cousins. Thank God, at least Zafar didn't go into films or become a Kathak dancer. The Khans had been wealthy for two generations; now they were also highly educated. Zafar studied architecture in England and got a first in his finals. Zafar's father couldn't stop boasting about how well his son had done and how many prizes he had won. But it was soon evident that father and son took a different view of their work. The father had waited all these years to break into the high-rise builders' club. Now, on the strength of his foreign-returned son's world-class designs, the reclaimed land of Nariman Point and Cuffe Parade would become showpieces for Khan Builders. But Zafar had different ideas. He wanted to change the world. The last thing the city of Bombay needed, he said, was skyscrapers. Zia was familiar with Abbajaan's spiel. He was going to design housing and total environments, whatever that phrase meant, for the poor. His idea was to tear down the chawls of Bombay and transform them into homes for the chawl tenants, built around a central common area with utilities like playgrounds, schools and markets; to give each family space, light and air. He wanted to design and landscape public spaces. Architecture, he was always saying, is the source of human dignity, the basis of a civic society.

Zafar set up his own company, Khan Architects. His father was angry and disappointed. All his hopes had been in vain. No point raging against a foolish young son, he told himself. It's merely a matter of time before he sees reason and sense. Instead of his son, he teamed up with a young Delhi architect. The project was a five-star hotel at Cuffe Parade and the building was to be thirty-two storeys high.

They were laying the slab for the seventeenth storey when the cable of the materials trolley in which Zafar's father was riding, broke. His death brought about what all his powers of persuasion could not: Zafar completed the five-star hotel project. Khan Builders and Khan Architects were now both Abbajaan's but there was never any doubt about where his heart lay.

Abbajaan had been head of the family business for fifteen years when disaster struck at one of his favourite projects. For decades there had been talk of building an expressway along the western seafront of Bombay to relieve the mounting congestion. The scheme had its share of critics and defenders but finally it got a partial okay. It was decided to relieve the inhuman face of urbanization by creating public spaces parallel to the new motorway. Zafar Khan was called in to design a promenade and pavilions alongside the Nepean Sea Road section as a pilot project. It was Abbajaan's kind of assignment. His designs were so airy, so serene and full of subtle echoes from India's Mughal past, it would be one of the most beautiful and tranquil public spaces in the country. There was, however, one proviso. Khan Builders would get the contract only on the condition that four of the minor prefabricated spans were to be subcontracted to the revenue minister's son.

Zia was too young to understand what was going on, but everything seemed to happen at one and the same time. The first calamity was headline news in all three English papers to which the Khans subscribed: *The Times of India*, *The Indian Express* and *The Economic*

*Times*. 'Under-construction Flyover Collapses'. 'Flyover Falls at Midnight'. 'New Overbridge Caves In'. Every subhead mentioned Khan Builders.

The house itself fell into a profound silence as though there had been a death in the family. No one spoke at breakfast except Zia who said he didn't want to go to school. Then the press arrived. Abba told them he had no comment for the moment. He wanted to have all the facts before he made a statement.

'What facts?' The journalists had him cornered. 'Are you trying to tell us you don't know what's going on in your own project?'

'This is a big project and a lot of people and companies are involved. Just be patient for a day till we get to the bottom of things.'

'Khan Builders was willing to take all the profits. Now when it comes to taking the blame you start looking for scapegoats.'

'Twenty-four hours, that's all I am asking for. We'll have a clearer picture then.'

'A man is dead and you want twenty-four hours? You planning to bolt the country in that time?'

Abba tried to call Altaaf Mamoo, executive director of Khan Builders, in St Moritz where he had gone skiing. The resort said no one called Altaaf Syed had checked in. Abba told Ammijaan to phone their common friends abroad and trace him, and he left for the Khan Builders office. He called home every hour and then every half-hour to check whether Ammi had located Altaaf. When he came home late at night he looked ashen.

'Have you seen the eveningers?' Shagufta asked him.

'No,' Abba said, 'I've been caught up in other things.'

'Well, you should. They are screaming for your blood.' She spread the papers on the coffee table. '"Flyover builder ignorant of what goes on in his company." "Khan Builders looking for scapegoat." "Builder remorseless at death and tragedy."'

'I didn't go to Khan Architects today but to Khan Builders, Shagufta,' Abba told his wife. 'The revenue minister's son was supposed to carry out the standard series of stress tests on the prefabricated concrete spans in the presence of the city engineers. He didn't.' Abbajaan tried to calm Ammi down.

'I'm not interested in your technical abracadabra.'

'There's something terribly wrong, Shagufta. I can't make sense of anything.'

'Nothing I'm sure that can't be sorted out when Altaaf comes back,' Ammijaan said.

Zafar looked at his wife as though she were speaking some alien tongue. 'I doubt if he plans to come back. At least not in the near future.'

'Oh, stop exaggerating, Zafar.' Ammi was surprisingly short with Abbajaan. 'You don't have to dramatize things and bring my brother into it merely because you've been careless.'

The bell rang some time around two at night. The police had come to take Abba into custody.

'On what charges?' he asked again and again.

'Criminal negligence and manslaughter. Stop wasting time.'

'But one of the Marathi newspapers said the body had been lying there covered in a white sheet from the previous evening. You know how beggars will collect money from passers-by for a funeral, when one of their own dies, and then vanish.'

'Tell that to the judge tomorrow. Now shut up and come along with us.'

Ammijaan called one of their friends who was a lawyer. The lawyer spoke to the police inspector in charge. 'Why at night? That's highly unusual.' 'Don't ask me, Mr Phadnis. I'm not the one who issued the orders. I'm merely doing my duty. There's an apprehension that the party may try to leave the country. Some very big parties, don't ask me to name them, are putting a lot of pressure.'

The matter was heard in the late afternoon of the next day. The second-degree manslaughter charges were dropped and the criminal negligence charge was changed to a civil one: damage to public property and serious irregularities in safety procedures.

A week later an emergency meeting of the National Institute of Architects, with barely the quorum present, suspended Zafar Khan's licence to practise architecture. There were worse things to come but nothing seemed to touch Abba after that.

Zia was confused about what was going on. Was his father guilty of the flyover collapsing? He must have been, even if Ammi had assured the children that he was not. Why else would the police have come for him at night and taken him away? The least Abba could have done was to protest his innocence. Zia's schoolmates were sure that Abba was guilty. Their parents had told them he was. But then how had he got out of prison? His friends had something to say about that too. Zafar Khan, they said, with certainty, was out only temporarily. No question about it, he'd be going back soon, and for good.

So what was new? Hadn't Zubeida Khaala always said Abba was Satan and would come to a bad end? Allah works in strange and quiet ways. He watches, lets you carry on as though everything's hunky-dory, and then one day, when you've convinced yourself that He is blind and doesn't care what happens on earth, yes, when you least expect it, He strikes you down. Abba didn't merely skip prayers, he never said them, ever. His family had followed his example. They drank, they even ate pork, though not at home because the servants got upset, they did not keep the roza during Ramzaan, they had graven images in the house and they had no thought for tomorrow. Now tomorrow had arrived and there was hell to pay. The Almighty had decided it was payback time.

Zia knew that one should feel nothing but righteous happiness when the will of Allah came to pass. He was happy, oh, he rejoiced, and yet he did not know why there was a constant ache in his heart. Every moment Abba was at home, he would try to hold his hand or, at least, keep him in sight. He had taken to calling Abba at the office every hour and asking him what time he would be back home. Once or twice he had woken up at night, Zubeida Khaala had been fast asleep, as usual with her mouth open, and slipped out and gone to his parents' room. Amanat was already there sleeping between the two and it was a bit of a squeeze, but Zia didn't mind it, he just curled up in Abba's arms.

He tried to talk things over with his brother.

'Leave me alone,' Amanat said, but Zia knew he didn't mean it.

'What's going to happen?' Zia asked.

'About what?'

'To Abbajaan.'

'Nothing.'

'They said in school that he would be sent back to jail and would never ever come back.'

'You believe them?'

'I don't know. Do you?'

'No.' But Amanat didn't sound so sure.

'Why are they taking Abbajaan's licence away?'

'Because they don't want Abba to design any more buildings, bridges, hospitals, aerodromes, till he's found not guilty.'

'What will Abba do if he can't draw and design? He doesn't know anything else.'

'How would I know?' Amanat turned viciously upon his brother, but when Zia started to leave, he said, 'Let's play cricket. You bat, I'll bowl.'

Ammijaan was becoming more and more frantic about Altaaf Mamoo. Abba had endless meetings with bankers and spent most of the day, and sometimes part of the night, in Altaaf Mamoo's office at Khan Builders. Ammi spent at least an hour every day on the phone trying to get through to her brother in St Moritz or the other places his itinerary had mentioned. Some of the people she called were getting a little impatient with her. They had had no news, and hadn't they said they would get back to her the moment they knew anything?

What had happened to him? Had he been in an accident? Perhaps he had fallen ill and was in some hospital dying. Maybe he had returned to India and the taxi driver had done something to him on his way home from the airport. He couldn't just disappear, could he? She went and met the police. They were not terribly interested in this Altaaf Syed. Besides, they had no jurisdiction beyond Bombay city limits. She took up the matter with Indian embassies abroad. They were sympathetic but ineffective.

'I'm going to Delhi,' she told Zafar while the family was at dinner. 'I want to see the external affairs minister to get him to make enquiries about Altaaf.'

Zafar put his hand on his wife's shoulder. 'Yes, do go. It will be a good change for you too.'

'I'm not going for a "change",' Ammi said tersely. 'I'm going to look for my brother who may well be dead.'

'He's all right,' Abba said. 'He just wants to be left alone, I think.'

'How would you know?'

'You know he's right, Shagufta. Altaaf's taken all the money and gone,' Zubeida Khaala suddenly intruded upon their conversation. 'Neither of us would admit it, but didn't you always suspect that he would let us down one day?'

Ammi was silent for a minute. She certainly had not expected her sister to side with Zafar. But she got her emotions under control, then whispered something barely audible: 'If only you had not abdicated all responsibility, Zafar, and had kept an eye on what was going on, things would never have come to this pass.'

In the end Ammi did not go to Delhi. Her phone calls to places abroad also ceased. Altaaf was not coming back. Abba's trips to banks grew longer and more frequent. The final blow fell two months later. Abbajaan came home one evening and called the children into his study.

'There are going to be some changes in the way we live. We have to leave this house and move to a new place in the heart of the city. The two of you will be going to a new school. We have two days to move. So help Ammijaan and Zubeida Khaala to pack up your things.'

Two days later the bankers came to take possession of the house. The clerks had already checked every item against the sixty-page inventory that had been made of all the furniture, paintings, silver and other goods. Finally the signatures were on the papers and it was time to leave. The children, Zubeida Khaala and Ammijaan were already sitting in the Bentley when Abbajaan came over and said, 'The car is no longer ours. We have to take a taxi.'

Ammijaan looked at her husband and turned her face away.

'How could you do this to us, Zafar?'

# 7

The new Khan home was a flat on the third floor of a building called Suleiman Mansion on S.V.P. Road, named after the 'Iron Man of India' Sardar Vallabhbhai Patel, though hardly anyone remembers that. In the heart of Bhendi Bazaar, the mansion was a seven-storeyed block of one, two and three-room apartments. Like every other building on S.V.P. Road, the ground floor was taken up by shops. Suleiman Mansion had a kite shop with thousands of kites in all sizes, shapes and colours, and manja so sharp that it didn't merely cut kite after kite from its moorings, it could sever a man's throat clean; it also had a barber's shop, a grocer, a Chinese dentist, a driving school and a shop with hundreds of TVs lined along the walls all tuned in to the same channel, so that you were in Emperor Akbar's sheesh mahal where every tiny mirror reproduced the same image. The building was a mini-universe that catered to every need. Zubeida Khaala said that from the day you were born till the day you died, you would hardly ever need to step out.

The top floor was divided into two wings. On the left was an Ismaili family that owned two leather goods shops, one in Chamar Alley and a fancy one on Colaba Causeway. They were followers of the Aga Khan. On the right were the Sunni Muslims who had a tin factory in the suburbs. They were going through a lean period because galvanized iron buckets and drums were being replaced by plastic containers. The two neighbours would not exchange the time of day. If the Gelanis were going down in the lift, the Sheikhs preferred to use the stairs.

The fifth and sixth floors had seven Dawoodi Bohra families. The men were always in white. They wore loose polyester-cotton sherwanis that reached below the knees, narrow polyester-cotton trousers, a white cap, and always covered their feet in white socks. They considered it disrespectful to Allah to expose their feet. Their women wore ankle-length skirts and a hooded, cape-like garment over their salwar-kameez. Dawoodi Bohra homes in Suleiman Mansion all displayed a portrait of the elderly head of the sect, Syedna Mohammed Buhranuddin. Between the third and the fourth floor there were four Suleimani Bohras, two Ahmediyas, one Ismaili and two Sunni families. There were no families on the first floor. It was a maternity home.

All these years Zia had known that there were different kinds of people in the world with different religions. There were Hindus, Christians, Parsis, Sikhs, Buddhists, Neo-Buddhists and then, of course, there were the true believers, the followers of Allah and His prophet Mohammed, peace be upon Him. But the bitterness and hostility in the block came as a revelation to Zia. He learned that Muslims came in all shades and hues, and that some of them hated each other as much as Hindus and Muslims seemed to.

Zia asked Zubeida Khaala how they could all be true believers and yet be such enemies. She said that some were true believers but the others were false believers.

'How can that be?' Zia asked. 'The false believers too believe in the One and Only God and His prophet, Mohammed.'

'Because they've gone astray,' she stressed each word, 'and cannot tell right from wrong. And you'd better watch your tongue, it's roiling like Satan's tail. All this wild talk and an idle mind is what makes people go astray. You say your prayers, do as the Holy Book says and follow what your parents teach you,' she corrected herself, 'what your khaala teaches you, and you'll always be God's little soldier.'

Still unable to grasp the chasms that separated the different residents of the mansion from each other, he asked Ammijaan where they themselves stood in the spectrum of Islam.

'We are Muslims, isn't that enough?' she asked him.

It was not. He wanted to narrow the field, own a label that he could hang on to. Ammi was not very forthcoming.

'Why don't you ask Khaalajaan? I thought she was your mentor in spiritual matters.'

'She says we are nobodies and belong nowhere since we have turned our back upon Allah.'

Ammijaan snorted. 'Quite the contrary, Allah appears to have turned His back on us.'

Zia was still waiting. 'You haven't answered my question.'

'I don't know the answer and I don't care, sweetheart, so long as I have you and Amanat and my family.'

At Suleiman Mansion, Zia had discovered a world every bit as new and intriguing as the continent that confronted Columbus. It was going to be a while before he could take it all in. His parents were not much help. Ammijaan lay in bed, sometimes for the whole day. She was not so much ill-humoured as listless. It was difficult to get through to her. Abba kept an impassive face and left the house by 8.30 in the morning trying to look for work. He took an egg sandwich with him and a portfolio of his drawings. By the time he returned, it was 7.30 or 8 in the evening. Sometimes he worked at home late into the night on a rare freelance assignment, but he was always up by six the next morning.

Amanat, Zia and Zubeida Khaala shared a room, and for some reason the brothers were getting along much better than ever before, but Amanat had to miss school far more these days and always had a lot of catching up to do. He liked to go for walks with Zia but all the dust, and the strange smells of spices from the three grocers' shops nearby, and the chemical effluents from the tyre-retreading outlet and the leather-curing units made him breathless. So he preferred to sit at home and read. That left Zubeida Khaala and Zia to explore the new world.

Zubeida Khaala was the most intrepid member of the family. She took Zia along with her every day to scout the alien terrain, the wild jungle full of tigers, hippos, mad elephants and polar bears. Walk five minutes down Amin Lane, make it nine, and you are at the Jumma Masjid. This may be the best known mosque in Bombay, but there's a mosque within hailing distance from any point in Bhendi Bazaar. Zubeida Khaala often took Zia for a private prayer to the Dawoodi mosque attached to the marble mausoleum of the late Syedna Taher Saifuddin Sahib.

'But we are not Dawoodi Bohras,' he protested.

'A mosque is a mosque. And any holy man's blessings bring one nearer to Allah. Now shut up and pray.'

Just a lane or two beyond the mausoleum of the late Syedna was a place that aroused the most intense and contrary feelings in Zia: curiosity, fear, fascination and unease for starters. Chor Bazaar. The Thieves' Market. He was not quite sure what exactly the word underworld meant, but he was convinced Chor Bazaar was it.

Zubeida was aware that Zia was afraid to venture anywhere near Chor Bazaar. If the best way to teach a person to swim is to throw him into water, then the most effective means to kill Zia's fear of Chor Bazaar, she thought, would be to take him shopping there. Within minutes he would realize what an exciting place it was.

Zubeida, who knew Zia's mind and the way he thought almost better than he himself did, had for once got him wrong. He was filled with trepidation, his heart beat unevenly and the palms of his hands and the soles of his feet were cold but sweaty. His head was bent and his eyes were focused between his shoes. Khaalajaan had his right hand firmly in hers, so there was no point trying to make a run for it, and besides, they were already there. He could feel with his feet that they had crossed the point of no return, they were in the netherworld, the place he knew he had to avoid at all costs; a land of disorder and debris and all the rejected, useless, broken, dilapidated things that had stopped working. This was the turf of the thieves, of all the millions of things that had been stolen from their owners and orphaned, never never to find their way back. There were phantom shapes moving all around him. Someone had kicked a lame beggar; a group of teenagers was fiddling with the lock of a car, the alarm went off, they had got the door open and switched off the alarm, you could hear a police siren, but they had already driven off; a woman's hand was resting on the window of a bus, the bus started and a man on a motorcycle sliced off the woman's wedding ring finger, and the blood was dripping into Zia's eyes. His eyes were still glued to the ground and all he could see were other shod feet. There were voices all around, whispering his name as though it were a sibilant knife with which they aimed to slit his throat: Zia, Zia. Zia, Zia.

'Look up, Zia,' his aunt told him twice. He ignored her. His only hope was not to see anything. Because if his eyes met anybody else's, he was doomed.

A handcart came between aunt and nephew and then the hands were linked again, but it was not Zubeida Khaala's hand. Zia wanted to tell the man there was no need to do that really, he was not going to scream, he knew he had been kidnapped and would never see Ammijaan, Abba, Amanat and Zubeida Khaala ever again.

It took Zubeida two hours to locate Zia. He had no idea how he'd got lost, and was standing outside a warehouse-like shop crammed with old furniture when Khaalajaan found him. He still would not look up.

But in a matter of weeks Zia was completely at home in Suleiman Mansion. He missed the sea, and everybody was in each other's hair in the apartment, but frankly he loved that. All these years he had had to play by himself, or with Amanat when he was well, which was almost never. Now it didn't matter what Amanat's health was like. Zia had scores of neighbours' children to play with. They were either in his house or he was in theirs, or they were all on the terrace playing cricket. Even on the rare occasions when he was alone, he was never bored or lost for things to do. He had merely to step on to the balcony or peer out of a window and he would be caught in a vortex of frantic activity. Spread all around him was the busiest, the most crowded, the most intriguing, the most fascinating, the most compelling, just the most most most most most most thoroughfare in the whole world. If Bajrang Paanwallah's brass thali was a thirty-ring circus, Bhendi Bazaar was a thousand-ring one. No, that was too pallid a comparison. This was the Milky Way and a hundred other galaxies weaving in and out of each other. The street never took a rest. It was perpetual motion. It was romance, it was danger, it was adventure; it was a maze, it was a ghetto, it was one endless marketplace; it was anarchy, it was impatience, it was frenzy, it was a planning disaster (Abba's phrase); it was hotchpotch and hocus-pocus, and it was ecstasy. You could either love it, as Zia did, or be confounded and lump it as Amanat did. Nowhere else on earth were your senses assailed so relentlessly. Nowhere else in the universe was there such a brew of accents, languages, dress codes; so many smells and scents, so many varieties of light, such a crush of people per square centimetre of air and space. And that was just on ordinary weekdays.

Everything in Bhendi Bazaar mesmerized Zia. But there was one place that stood apart from all the others. The Durbar-e-Akbar Attar Shop. It was a seedy place with dim lighting and a couple of cadaverous salesmen with kohl in their eyes and three teeth between the two of them. The metal blades of the prehistoric fans had been twisted and wrung till they looked like oars ploughing through becalmed seas of air. On three sides of the shop there were teak cupboards with glass fronts floor-to-ceiling. Each displayed, or rather kept in the dark, hundreds, maybe thousands of tiny, mysterious, smoky and glazed coloured bottles and jars with glass and cork stoppers.

In the evenings, as the electric bulbs swayed on long wires in the draughts generated by the slow, lugubrious movement of the ancient fans, the vials of attar picked up the feeble light and twinkled like distant stars, and the Durbar-e-Akbar turned into a living, breathing firmament that expanded and contracted with the pendulum movement of the lights. Business seemed to pick up as the sun went down. Young and old men, some with bracelets of flowers wrapped around their wrists, thrust forward the backs of their hands while the salesmen brought out bottles, one by one, from the cupboards, and rubbed on an infinitesimal quantum of the attar with the glass stick of the stopper.

Zia saw a customer raise his hand to his nose and inhale deeply. The scent went to his head (as it went to Zia's even though he watched from outside) and he seemed to go into a trance. The salesman with the lone black tooth at the centre of his lower jaw adjusted his crocheted cap and spat a mouthful of tobacco juice into a spittoon.

The young customer opened his eyes and shook his head. 'Almost there, mian, but not quite.'

The old man smiled and seemed to take the 'no' as a personal challenge.

'Ama, we can certainly get you there but first you must tell us where you wish to go. Your destination or manzil is the key to everything. Jannat, paradise itself, is not beyond our reach once we know your objective. Is it the very first encounter with a houri? Do you wish to cast a spell upon the apparition? Or is it enchantment you are after, perchance arousal? Is it to be a seduction? Is it a parting, albeit hopefully, a brief one? Is it a reconciliation? Or do you wish to wrest the divine vision from someone else's arms? Tell us the disease you suffer from and we'll give you the remedy. Or is it that you prefer the disease, my prince, to the cure?'

What were these guys talking about? How had the young man, with a red scarf of polyester filament that shone like a mirror, and a garland of sparse and wilting mogras around his wrist, become a prince? Zia had no idea how they had jumped from attars to houris to diseases that were preferable to cures. He understood that there was some kind of encoding behind all that imagery, and that they circled around and recycled the same keywords, but he didn't know how to crack the code. One thing was certain, from now on, Urdu couplet upon couplet would be the only form of dialogue. Soon the two of them would be talking to each other as long-lost soul mates, and the customer would reveal the innermost secrets of his heart.

The salesman would now draw a second bar on the customer's hand and then a third, and sometimes, if there was still no satisfaction, he followed up with a fourth and a fifth. How a young man could tell one fragrance from the others by now was beyond Zia. But what intrigued him most was how the salesman knew which attar was in which of the tens of thousands of bottles.

Then one day, the Durbar-e-Akbar closed down without notice. The place was covered in brown tarpaulin and no one was allowed to enter. There was talk that a bakery and a car showroom were opening up in the premises. Zia heard from a friend on the fifth floor, Salim, who had got the news from a one hundred and seven per cent reliable source, that a disco-dancing school was coming up in the same spot.

The shroud was finally lifted on the seventh of December but that only deepened the mystery. The new establishment was called The Perfumed Garden, and it still sold attars, and was owned by the same family, except that now the owner's daughter, who had studied and worked in Paris and was supposed to be something called a 'nose', was in charge of operations. Was it the same shop or was it a new one? Whatever the truth of the matter, the place was unrecognizable. It didn't belong to Bhendi Bazaar or to Nepean Sea Road where Zia used to live. The Perfumed Garden was so incongruous, it might as well have come from Pluto. It had a cool, chill air that had nothing to do with the fact that it was air-conditioned. It was full of light and any time the padded black steel, gold-studded door was opened, you could hear the strains of the sarod, sitar or santoor.

Scattered on the sands of the big display window, which was set deep inside the façade of the shop to avoid sunlight, lay sealed bottles of foreign perfumes: Joy, Miss Dior, Je Reviens, Ma Griffe, Chanel No. 5. Seven ebony hands rose from the miniature seashore. Zia was sure that the outstretched hands were an urgent call for help from people who were drowning. A little more time and they would go under. But they always remained afloat, mutely pleading with Zia to rescue them. Zia would try to put them out of his mind but his eyes always returned to the black palms on which rested vials of jade, garnet, amethyst, amber, agate and jasper set in gold filigree and studded with emeralds, rubies, diamonds and sapphires. In the centre of the window was a plaque. 'Dear customer,' it read. 'Welcome to The Perfumed Garden. You are familiar with the finest and most expensive perfumes from abroad. The attars in the vials are some of the rarest in the world and a thousandfold more expensive. The Mughal emperors, connoisseurs of the art of attars, used these very perfumes. They knew that only a fool would put a price on the priceless.'

Bhendi Bazaar was perhaps the most conservative Muslim locality in Bombay. The majority of the women there moved about in burkhas. Imagine the shock and sensation when it was discovered that the three salespersons in ivory trousers, bows, tails and short-cropped hair were not men but women. Months after the shop was reopened, people would stand outside waiting to get a glimpse of them any time the door opened and a customer, usually a foreigner, walked in or out. Zia's new friends had all the dope on the transvestite-like creatures. They were snake-women from the Amazon. Their breasts had been chopped off and they ate newborn babies raw with red chillies and salt. They knew several languages, English, French, Italian, German and Spanish. They didn't just sit behind the marble counters and guide you through the maze of attars in the shop, they were responsible for valet-parking the cars of the customers. They might look soft and feminine but they were all kung-fu black belters who could disarm and lethally pin down any unwelcome intruder. Do you know how strong they were? A customer's car had stalled one evening in the middle of the traffic. You won't believe this but Ahmed, Zia's Ismaili friend from the seventh floor, had seen it with his own eyes, the three saleswomen had simply picked up the Cadillac, raised it over their heads and deposited it in the courtyard where the cars of the visitors to The Perfumed Garden were parked.

Of late, Zia had taken to saluting the foreigners as they came out of the shop. It had started out as a lark but they apparently took him to be a child-usher employed for the purpose, and would almost always tip him. He had tried to pass off their francs, liras, pesos and pence as rupees at the tuck shop in school, and even to the peanut and ice-candy vendors, but had always been caught out. He was called a thief and a cheat (the peanut guy had whacked him on the head too) and the sold goods had been taken back. Now Zia would put on an Esperanto accent, at least he thought it was a universal foreign intonation: 'Outside mooney no ghood. Only rupees, pleece.'

Zia made sure that none of his friends from Suleiman Mansion was around when he was cadging tips, since he did not wish to forsake his monopoly. But retribution came, as always, from another quarter: Zubeida Khaala. She caught Zia in the act and her shock was so great, she was unable to utter a word. Corporal punishment was not her style, but she wished to make a point that would also be a deterrent for life. It seemed to Zia that she was trying to unscrew his ear anticlockwise.

'Beggar,' Zubeida Khaala hissed. 'I could never have imagined that my own blood would sink so low as to go begging on the streets. Return the money to the lady this instant and apologize to her.'

'She doesn't understand English,' Zia blurted, despite the geyser of pain emanating from his ear. There was no way he was going to give in. This was, after all, a matter of his honour. If anybody should fall on her knees and express contrition, it was Zubeida Khaala, who had humiliated Zia not merely in public, but in front of a foreigner.

'But I do.' Zubeida Khaala held on to his ear. 'I'm waiting.'

Alarmed by this merciless child abuse, of which not a single passer-by seemed to take notice, Zia's foreign patroness spoke volubly in an alien tongue to Zubeida Khaala and tried to dislodge her grip from the piece of cartilage.

'You stay out of this,' Zubeida snapped at her as she gave a further turn to Zia's ear.

Zia was beginning to grasp that honour was a highly dispensable virtue. Like many a realist before him, he ditched it. We'll never know whether it was pain that made Zia open his palm and drop the coins to the ground instead of handing them over, or just plain cussedness.

'Apologize,' Zubeida's voice had risen ominously.

'*Main aap se maafi maangta hun.*' Zia caved in, but he did it in his mother tongue, Hindustani, which he was sure the lady would not understand.

Zia may have had the last word when he brought things to an unsatisfactory closure that day, but Zubeida Khaala had successfully put an end to his foreign coin collection.

Then one day Zia found a white card on the road. It was impossible, even absurd, but a light perfume rose from it. He closed his eyes and held the ivory card to his nose and inhaled deeply. It reminded him of the time when the Khans had gone for a holiday in the mountains above Nainital. Their car had had a punctured tyre. Abba was fixing it with Amanat's help while Ammijaan and he wandered into a field next to the road. You could see the lake and the boats sailing on it but Zia himself seemed to be in the middle of an ocean that was bobbing and swaying in the wind. Its colour was lilac and its scent was lilac and both he and his mother were overtaken by a lilac madness as they ran wildly about, unmindful of the grass and flowers they were crushing.

How could a card, blank on one side and delicately embossed on the other, give off such a gentle but continuous scent? He opened his eyes. 'The Perfumed Garden,' the card read. 'Parfumiers since 1570. First to Emperor Akbar. And now to you.' Below were the address and telephone number of the shop.

He hid the card under the newspaper that lined the shelf on which his shirts, shorts and underwear were stacked in the closet. Every night, and sometimes during the day when no one was around, he would open the cupboard, take out the card and hold it close to his nose. Had Emperor Akbar really held one, or maybe all of those precious vials in the window of The Perfumed Garden, in his own hands? How could such fragile bottles survive for four hundred years? It no longer made any difference whether Zia was awake or sleeping, he was always standing in front of the long display window of The Perfumed Garden. The call of the ebony hands had now become urgent. They were waving frantically to him. There were secrets that those hands alone held. Come what may, he had to unravel them. If only his own hands were like Superman's X-ray vision, he could have penetrated through walls of concrete or steel plate. If only he could smash the glass.

At seven one evening, Zubeida took Zia along with her to the patch of open ground behind Jumma Masjid. She had heard that a fine maulvi from Lucknow preached there during Muharram. Thousands of people had gathered, all of them waiting for the man of God.

'Let's go home,' Zia told Zubeida Khaala. 'I can't see and I can't breathe.'

'Just a few minutes and everybody will sit down and you'll feel much better.'

'No, I want to go home now,' Zia insisted. 'I feel funny with so many people and so much noise and so many smells.'

The crowd suddenly quietened. All those who were standing put a kerchief or a piece of cloth on the ground and sat down. A tall, handsome man with a trim black beard climbed on to the dais. He looked like a prince. He had not uttered a word but his very presence and the few steps he had taken had silenced everybody.

'Language and the human mind are peculiar things,' the maulvi spoke in a clear voice. 'They can be precise and yet so obviously imprecise and wrong. You've all heard the words "sons and daughters", "fathers and mothers". These words confuse me. In truth, I do not understand them. What awful and horrible folly leads us to think that we are the children of our parents. Our fathers and mothers like to believe they gave birth to us and so have proprietorial rights over us. They think that it is their duty to protect and nurse their children till the children in turn can nurse and protect them.

'How misguided we all are. There is no such thing as my children and your children. Your parents and my parents. There is nobody on earth who is step and foster either. For one simple reason. And that is because we are all the children of just one Father, the great and good Almighty Himself. You are all my brothers and sisters because the same blood flows in our veins and those of the One we call Father. It is He, in His infinite love, who begot us all.'

Zia's mind had almost immediately become a mere vessel, a vessel as large as this preacher's infinity. This man, this maulvi, was his first revelation. He was torched by a light, the light of Allah Himself, which this man on the dais had directed towards him.

'I'm going to talk to you about two brothers today. You know them well. Every year during Muharram, you remember them and shed tears for them. Then Muharram is over and you forget about them. How can you forget your flesh and blood? For if after today you cast them into the darkness of oblivion in your mind, then I'll say this to you, that the sacrifice of Hassan and Hussein has been in vain. On the other hand, if you remember as I am about to remember them, then you'll realize one immortal truth. Like your brothers Hassan and Hussein so many centuries ago, you too can show your Father that you will sacrifice anything, yes, even your lives, to defend the honour of your Allah and to bring greater glory to His name.

'My brothers...'

And then he told the story of the grandsons of the Prophet, the children of his daughter Fatima and his son-in-law Ali, of how Hassan was poisoned, and the great and valiant fight Hussein put up against the enemies of the true faith. He spoke of Hussein's torture, slaughter and quartering. Zia had heard the story of the sacrifice of Hassan and Hussein a hundred times before and yet when the young maulvi told it, it was as though this was the very first time he had heard the names of the Prophet's grandsons.

For the next few weeks Zia was awash with fraternal love. 'I will embrace not just Amanat,' he wrote in his diary, 'but the coolie in his red tunic at Victoria Terminus and the leper (he cancelled the last word as going a little too far and opted for something a mite less ambitious), the beggar on the street as my brother. I swear to unite all the brothers and sisters of the planet in the name of Allah. I will not tolerate any dissent.'

The image of the maulvi kept coming back to him, tall and manly and astride a steed. He had a sword in his hand and he was urging ten thousand warriors to charge against the heathen hordes. Zia was right behind him, for he was the maulvi's right-hand man. Suddenly the maulvi was no longer there and his ten thousand warriors had retreated into the distance. Now Zia was alone against the pagan armies. The maulvi's words kept ringing in his ears. 'If your brothers Hassan and Hussein could sacrifice their lives for Allah, you too, Zia, can ride forth and redeem your people by becoming a martyr for them.' And a chorus of ten thousand men and women beat their breasts and wailed. They sobbed heart-rendingly as they lashed themselves. Their voices were rising hysterically when Zia woke up. The moaning and sighing, he discovered, was no dream. From the balcony he saw processions of mourners carrying paper replicas of the mausoleums of Hassan and Hussein, and all around them were men stripped to the waist who were, he couldn't believe his eyes, flogging themselves with whips, strands of knotted cords on wooden handles, and other strange instruments. There was a low continuous hum of groaning and grieving that flared up from time to time in a crescendo of inconsolable sorrow. Zia cringed every time a whip cracked and a long snake wound itself around the torso of a man. There was so much agony on the road, yet he was aware of an ecstasy in the pain and the suffering.

He went into the bathroom and retched.

Amanat is now monopolizing his parents almost full-time but Zia has become a shade more tolerant. If the maulvi was right, then Zia must consider Amanat his brother. This is difficult but Zia will not shirk his duty. He forces himself to think kindly of Amanat. After all, his new preceptor has taught him that Allah too is merciful. Amanat's travails have become worse, much worse, since the family moved to Suleiman Mansion and he and Zia were enrolled in a school called St Paul's English Academy near Dockyard Road. To begin with, he got acute sinusitis. The combination of an extremely severe and brittle asthma and the total blocking of the nasal passages would have put paid to the most rugged of mountain climbers. Not brother Amanat, though. He was on antibiotics for months, his sinuses were punctured and drained time and again. He sat hunched up during the day and he sat hunched over the whole night with Abbajaan to keep him company. Anybody with even an iota of humanity would, at least for the sake of his parents and his young brother, have got better. Not Amanat, though. He got worse. There was immovable greenish yellow snot frozen in his brains, in his ears, behind his cheeks and in his nose. He couldn't hear, he couldn't eat, of course he couldn't breathe, and when he tried to say something it came out as baby talk, bebabebababebe, phephaphepahephephe. This was when he decided to have typhoid. His fever shot up to 105° and he became delirious. He was sandwiched between icepacks, over his head and at his feet. It took him seventeen days to recover and to start walking around the house, and another seven days to engineer a relapse. Even as he was blasted by Typhoid, Part II, his other ailments did not betray him. Both his asthma and the acute sinusitis stuck with him through that time.

Amanat has never heard the word 'enough'. His temperature shoots up again. This time even the consultants are at a loss. It is Dr Patwardhan, who, a long time ago, had worked as an intern in the Arthur Road Infectious Diseases Hospital, and had then done a three-year stint as a houseman and registrar there, who puts his finger on the elusive infection. Amanat now has nasal diphtheria.

There's some kind of routine and schedule to Amanat's sick days. By 1 or 1.30 p.m. at the very latest, he's in such bad shape, Ammi has to take him by bus to Dr Patwardhan's rooms. Dr Pat gives him an injection and Amanat is back by 4 p.m. By 9 p.m., he is in a state again and this time Abba accompanies him. Often, Dr Patwardhan drives them back home around 11. He gives Amanat an IV and begs him not to wake him up first thing in the morning. Amanat winces but, needless to say, is at Dr Patwardhan's door at 7.30 a.m. the next day, in need of his morning fix.

From his standard sitting posture, the weight of his breathing upon his arms and hands, Amanat watches his father, mother, brother and aunt. They look washed out but pretend that everything's fine. He knows money's tight, and there's almost always tension in the air.

It is clear to him that he must have done something terrible before he was born, something so abhorrent that no one, not even his parents, can put a name to it, or even dares mention it. How else can he explain his condition? His crime is so heinous that there is no forgiveness or pardon for it. He's overwhelmed by the weight of his guilt even though he has no idea what he's guilty of. He has a sense that his illness, the spasms that clutch and squeeze his lungs and leave him gasping, is a visitation from a god from another planetary system. He would like to sink his nails and fingers deep into his chest, rip it open and flash-flood his lungs with this incredible and rare substance called air of which all those around him, the ones who are normal and healthy, are blissfully unaware. He sees the look of helplessness in his parents' eyes; he hates himself for what he's done to them and he hates them for not being able to put him out of his misery.

Like a drug addict with acute withdrawal symptoms, his only hope is the needle and the manna passing through it into his body. Ammijaan and the others are always talking about what a brave lad he is taking all those injections. What ignoramuses they are. If he could, he would stab himself with deriphylline or whatever it took, a hundred times a day.

Over the years he'll formulate a personal theology and metaphysic that will be the underpinning of his life. The medicine man is his god. He'll pray to him and wait for the second coming three times a day. But he also begins to understand a strange truth: this god is not all-powerful; the salvation Dr Patwardhan promises is at best transient.

Amanat has a unique if warped insight into people. He knows secrets about the healthy that they themselves would never admit to. Friends, acquaintances, even strangers feel responsible for his sickness. They are well meaning and will do anything to get off the hook. 'Six months, a year at the most and his asthma will be a thing of the past,' they told Abba and Ammijaan when he was four. They were still saying it when he turned seven. Good people that they are, they don't give up.

Amanat is a considerate child and polite to a fault. But sometimes he gets impatient. 'I'm nine going on ten.' They are unperturbed. 'Ten, that's the turning point. You watch, that's when the allergies and asthma will disappear, once and for all.' Amanat likes to believe that it is the same impulse, this feeling of guilt, and not pure viciousness, that makes some people tell him it's all in his head.

Abba and Ammi have always considered babas, gurus and faith healers suspect. And yet every now and then, in moments of desperation when Amanat has had a crisis and does not respond to treatment, Abbajaan and Ammi cave in. They take Amanat along with some friend or acquaintance to meet a god-man. It's a wonder there is so much suffering and sickness in the world considering everybody, the vegetable vendor, Ammijaan's club friends, the old driver's wife and Zubeida Khaala's acquaintances know a holy man who has cured a nephew or a friend's daughter when everyone's given up hope.

There are variations in the modalities of the cure: at times the guru produces holy ash from the palm of his hand and applies it to the patient's forehead, or offers the root of some medicinal plant from the Himalayas. One swami merely passes a healing hand over the sick person's head, and the ailing man, woman or child is completely cured and given a new lease of life. If you see him today, they are sure to add, you wouldn't believe that he had almost breathed his last just a couple of months ago. When Ammi or Abba seem reluctant or not altogether convinced, there's one sure way of guilt-tripping them. It's up to you, they shrug their shoulders. Nobody's holding a gun to your head. But would you rather that Amanat suffer to the end of his life? Or God forbid, have his life cut short? Besides, and this is always the trump card, what harm will it do?

Oh yes, Amanat could tell them when he grows up, great and incalculable harm. It cripples the patient as no ailment can. But at the moment, Amanat too has succumbed to hope and gone along. When he doesn't get any better, he knows whose fault it is. His faith is flawed, he does not believe enough or it's because he skipped a whole verse from the hundred and eleven shlokas he's supposed to recite every night. But there is worse to follow. He has become a creature of superstition. He will cross the road only on amber, stop at every seventh step, look at the sun first thing when he wakes up or else... The more gurus he sees, the more dos and don'ts he has to observe. As if that isn't bad enough, he concocts some more of his own.

There is one other lasting gift the gurus have bestowed upon him: he has learnt to live in fear, perpetual fear.

Later on he'll ask himself: Why bother, why bother to go to such lengths to fight for a breath of air? There are times when he thinks it's not worth it. And yet what he can't reconcile with this sense of futility is his greed, his obscene greed for the obvious pleasures of life. Anything he wants, he wants obsessively, whether it is to attend a classical music concert by Mallikarjun Mansoor or see *Gone with the Wind*.

Gradually he's able to distil a watertight maxim from his own experience. If you like it or want it badly, you can't have it. It's a little extreme but he's not asking anybody else to subscribe to it. And he's found that it's almost always true, and makes his disappointments a little more bearable. But there is a fervent side to all this: if he can make-believe, or at least make the fates believe, that he doesn't really care, they might just let him get what he wants.

There was no one in The Perfumed Garden. One of the saleswomen was absent that day and the other two had gone for lunch. The door to the office was slightly ajar but whoever was there was evidently busy checking the order books. Zia looked around, not much pedestrian traffic either. He took out his father's snap-off cutter from his pocket. It had a series of sharp blades with which you could cut almost anything. He slipped out the angled edge of the blade, locked it in position and was about to cut a six-inch square from the corner of the glass pane when he felt a hand light upon his shoulder and a woman's voice whisper in his ear.

'Drop the blade. Or else...'

The cutter clattered to the pavement. Zia was rooted to the ground, his body frozen in terror. He forced himself to turn his gaze. Sheets of sweat were pouring down his forehead, eyes and body, and he couldn't tell for sure whether the snake was forty or fifty feet long. It had a beaded pattern on its body, black onyxes interlocked with emeralds and topazes.

'You are the boa constrictor woman.' There was awe and wonder in Zia's voice as he looked at the daughter of the owner of The Perfumed Garden. 'You eat children whole and wrap yourself around a tree or pillar till every bone in their bodies is broken and crushed.'

'Then you know what's going to happen to you. I'm going to break your fingers, your hands, your arms, your ribs, your hips, your legs and your peepee thing. But first you'll tell me what you were planning to steal after you had cut through the glass, you thief.'

'I'm not a thief,' Zia said with asperity. 'All I wanted to do was touch Emperor Akbar's perfume bottle.'

'A likely story.' The talons had dug deep into Zia's shoulders and tightened their grip. His friend Salim, who was his chief source of information on snakes, had not mentioned that some of them had long, bony claws. 'How would you know which one is Akbar's?'

'Then it's true, they really belonged to the Mughal emperors?'

'So what? What's the big deal?'

Zia had nothing but contempt for the woman's ignorance.

'Come on, tell me,' she goaded him.

'Have you been to Fatehpur Sikri? Or the Red Fort that Akbar built?'

'No, where are they?'

Zia was not sure whether she was pulling his leg. 'You don't know anything about Akbar?'

The woman shook her head.

'Abbajaan says he was the greatest king of our country. He conquered three-quarters of India. He had the navratnas or the nine jewels at his court. Tansen, the singer, was one of them, and Birbal and Abul Fazl. He loved architecture and he was a great builder. He built a whole new city called Fatehpur Sikri. Abba explained everything to us when we went there.'

'What does your father do?'

'My father, he's, he's a – oh nothing, just a draughtsman.'

He looked suddenly out of sorts and she changed the subject. 'I knew you were up to something. You've been coming here every day after school for weeks.'

'How did you know?'

'I can see everything. I have a third eye.'

'Where? Show me.'

'I'm hungry. I haven't eaten for days.' She felt his arms and cheeks. 'I prefer my meals younger and chubbier but I guess you'll have to do.' She picked up the snap-off cutter without letting go of Zia. 'Let's step inside. I need to sit quietly when I eat.'

'No.' Zia tried to wriggle free, but she held him tightly and steered him in.

'What is your name?' the snake woman asked him as she made him sit in one of the silk-upholstered recesses. Her face was close to his. She had startling eyes, they seemed green one moment and then dark and smoky blue. She had thrown a red scarf around her neck and head and it framed her face like a hood.

'If you can stop staring at me, maybe you'll find a moment to tell me your name.'

'Zia Khan. What's yours?'

'Aminara. Aminara Mirza. Are you comfortable? Don't shake your head. Say yes or no.'

'Yes.'

'You sure? You want some water? Are you hungry? Do you want to go to the loo?'

What was she up to? Why was she suddenly being so kind?

'No.'

'Good. Then you've got no reason to fidget. I suggest you sit absolutely still. Rock still. Even if the heavens fall upon you.'

She left him and walked into her office. Zia suddenly had an uncontrollable desire to fidget. He realized he was terribly hungry; his throat was parched and he needed to drink twenty-three litres of water. And if he didn't go to the loo right that moment, he would be sitting in a pool of pee. But now the heavens began to fall just as Aminara had said. There was a sudden thunderous sound as though thick steel plates were grinding against each other. Now he would never escape. What a fool he had been to think that she was concerned about him. The steel panels had come down over the main door and the display window.

'Don't even bother to think of escaping, Zia Khan. Everything's bolted and shut.'

How did she know what he was up to even when she couldn't see him? She was a witch, that's what she was.

'Close your eyes.'

'What are you going to do to me? Ammijaan and Abba will miss me.'

'You should have thought of that before you decided to break into the shop.'

He should have listened to Zubeida Khaala and stayed away from The Perfumed Garden. What was Amanat going to do without him? Zia didn't seem to have any control over his trembling body. Even his teeth were stammering away of their own accord. He had a test in arithmetic tomorrow. If he didn't turn up they would fail him.

There was a snaky hissing sound. She was slithering on the floor. Oh god, she was sitting right beside him now. She held his palm and slipped something cold into it.

'Open your eyes.'

The jasper vial was sitting in his hand. It had felt chill to the touch for a split second and then it was like a dark green fire scorching his flesh. He could not take his eyes off it. He knew it was not real. Neither was Aminara nor the fact that he was seated inside The Perfumed Garden. It was all a dream and he did not want it to end.

'Is this the one?' You could barely hear Zia.

'Yes,' Aminara nodded.

'The same one that Emperor Akbar held in his hand?'

'Yes,' Aminara said softly.

Everything seemed to slow down. The water flowing from the fountain in the corner, the hands of the watch on Aminara's wrist, Zia's very breath, all were held in suspended animation. He felt his hand stretch right back four hundred years and touch Akbar.

Aminara took the vial from his palm, gently, very gently unplugged the stopper, then rubbed it on Zia's wrist. A fragrance as light as Ammijaan's dhaka mull sent a shiver of pleasure up Zia's spine. It was an azure breeze that floated away and kept coming back. It was so insubstantial, it was nothing but the memory of a perfume.

'What is its name?'

'The Emperor called it Mirage.'

He was at the padded steel door when he said to Aminara, 'I'm never going to wash my hands or have a shower again.'

# 8

What more could one ask of life? One Sunday, after they had been at Suleiman Mansion a few months, Sagari came over. Zia was unsure of himself. He had not seen Sagari for almost a year now. What was she going to think of their changed and straitened circumstances? What if she wanted to see their school uniform, dirty khaki-coloured shirts and shorts with a grubby red tie, which St Paul's English Academy insisted they wore? But Sagari walked in and he forgot his trepidation, his anxieties and all the questions to which he had not found the right evasive answers.

Sagari was no longer the most popular child model in the country. She had branched out into the movies and had become an even bigger star. Four of her films had already been released. Two had celebrated silver jubilees all over India and the other two had managed to break even only because of her. Zia had seen all four of them but his favourite was *Sona aur Mona* which was in its forty-ninth week. Sagari played both the twins, Sona and Mona. Sona was lively, vivacious and full of mischief while Mona was serious, studious and timid. There were lots of very funny mix-ups, and then some wicked people kidnap the twins and terrorize them, but they don't know who they are up against. The twins outwit them and bring the estranged parents together again. You can't imagine how beautifully she danced and mimicked all the superstars, Raj Kapoor, Dev Anand, Rajesh Khanna, Amitabh Bachchan. When the villain started to torture her sister, she quickly snatched the whip from him and cracked it till he was rolling on the ground pleading for mercy. She could do card tricks, open out the whole deck in the air like an accordion and fold it like a Chinese fan. Oh, she could do anything, absolutely anything. Zia was sure she could have flown if she'd wanted to. He was crazy about her, and so were ninety million other children and their parents.

Zia had been waiting for her on the balcony from seven in the morning. He had rushed to open the door every time the bell rang. The milkman, the newspaperman who came to collect his monthly dues, the maid who cleaned the dishes and washed their clothes, a man who sold joss sticks, and his friends from the floor above asking him to play cricket. When the bell rang, around 11.40, his enthusiasm hadn't waned but he was getting impatient and irritable. There was a fat girl with dark glasses, Afro hair and shabby, shapeless clothes at the door.

'Yes?' Zia was short with her.

'Do you sell pariah dogs with gold-capped teeth here?' She had funny teeth.

'This is not a kennel,' Zia snapped as he closed the door but she pushed it back before the latch caught.

'Oh, grow up, Zia.'

He could have died. Sagari came in and took off her dark glasses, her wig and the awful baggy clothes. He reached out and touched her hand. She was there all right. More real to him at that moment than his brother, his parents or even himself.

'I had to come camouflaged,' she said shyly. 'I didn't want to attract attention.'

When Sagari had made herself comfortable (she no longer drank Rasleela, only fresh coconut water), Zia suggested that he take her to the world's most expensive perfume shop.

'If we don't have it,' he repeated The Perfumed Garden legend, 'it's not worth having.'

Sagari smiled and shook her head.

'Why not? From there we'll go to the Chinese dentist's and hear a hundred and twenty dentures chattering.'

Again Sagari shook her head and said, 'I don't want to attract attention.'

What was she talking about? All Zia wanted to do was to show her his favourite haunts. And...and well, he wouldn't mind impressing the Perfumed Gardeners, his neighbours, the principal and staff and peons of St Paul's English Academy, and all the boys who had been sniggering behind his back because his father was a criminal and had been to jail and lost all his money. In one single stroke his shameful past would be wiped out, and no one would ever again dare to pass snide remarks or look pitifully at him or whisper to their children to go and play somewhere else, as Ammi's friends at Nepean Sea Road had done, and they would all beg him to introduce them to Sagari, and they would look at him in awe and point out to each other and to strangers that his name was Zia Khan and he was Sagari's friend, her best friend, her boyfriend.

'Then what shall we do?' Zia was disappointed but he was not one to give up so easily. He would wait a while and then, on one pretext or another, take her down. Damn, if only it had been a weekday and the road crowded and St Paul's open.

'Let's play Trade. I haven't played it since the last time we were together.'

'You know I'll win.'

'I can always beat Amanat.'

Amanat was strangely quiet and aloof. Sagari tried to draw him, but although he hadn't had an attack that morning, he was not forthcoming. She went over to where he was sitting with a book in his hand, not reading a word but surreptitiously following her every move and word, till Sagari took the book away.

'Come, I promise not to cheat.'

'Liar, you would cheat even on oath.' He was happy to be coerced. 'And what about him, he'll cheat even if he's winning.'

'I never cheat. I'm just a better investor than either of you.'

Zubeida Khaala came out of the bedroom where Abbajaan and Ammi had retreated. Zia was sure she had come to tell them to lower their voices. The room quietened down.

'Is it true that you are acting in a film with Yusuf Khan?' she asked Sagari in a whisper.

'No, I'm not.'

'I mean with Dilip Kumar.'

'Yes, I am. In *Lal Dariya*. You know him?'

'Not really.' Amanat could have sworn Zubeida Khaala blushed. 'May I come and watch a shooting when you are working with him? Just once?'

There was awe in Zubeida Khaala's voice and a note of wistfulness that bordered on the obsequious.

'Yes, any time.'

'Can I come too?' Zia didn't want to be left out.

'Yes, of course, and Amanat also. And Shagufta Auntie and Zafar Uncle.'

'God bless you.' Zubeida Khaala put her hand on Sagari's head. 'I'm very grateful to you.'

The game gathered momentum. Sagari counted her money while Zia purchased the hottest real estate in Bombay, Malabar Hill. He had already bought Byculla, Bandra, Victoria Terminus and Ballard Estate. Life couldn't have been better. He was singing a song from *Sona aur Mona* and keeping the beat slapping his knee. It was

Amanat's turn and, Allah be praised, he landed himself in jail. Sagari couldn't restrain her joy. She joined in Zia's song and flung the dice. A clean twelve. She skipped eleven places in a triumphant hurry and landed at Nariman Point, one station ahead of jail. It was the most wanted reclaimed land in the country, all the commercial skyscrapers were going up there. Amanat decided to be a spoilsport and said he wanted to count up to twelve from her earlier position once again.

'Go ahead, go right ahead,' Sagari sang, to the same tune from *Sona aur Mona*. 'Won't make a difference. Nariman Point, here I come.'

'Quite the contrary.' It was Amanat's turn to sing. 'You are in jail with me.'

Sagari counted. Amanat had got it wrong.

'I hate your films,' Amanat hissed. 'You are a precocious brat and a pain in the hindquarters.'

This was so unexpected, Sagari couldn't seem to understand his words.

'What's precocious?' she asked.

'I don't know. But that's what you are. You always talk like someone four times your age.' Even as he was saying it, Amanat looked aghast. What had come over him?

'No, she's not,' Zia screamed at him. 'She's wonderful. She's fantastic. You are just jealous and upset that you are losing and she and I are winning. Shame on you. If I could I would see *Sona aur Mona* and *Maya and Jackie* every day.'

'I, I didn't mean it,' Amanat stammered. 'I swear to you I didn't mean it.'

'Yes, you meant it, every word you said,' Sagari told him, perhaps a little too virtuously.

'No, no,' Amanat tried to contradict Sagari but he knew it was no use and ran out of the room.

Zia should have gone with Zubeida Khaala and Amanat to see the shooting of Sagari's film but there was once again a change in his fortunes and he was no longer in Bombay. A few weeks after Sagari's visit, Abbajaan had spoken to him at the dinner table. He was smiling.

'I've got some good news for you, Zia.'

What good news could Abbajaan give Zia after he had lost Firdaus? None of the family ever referred to their old home. There seemed to be a tacit agreement amongst the Khans that Firdaus should be a taboo word. But the more Zia tried not to think of it, the more it seemed to intrude upon him. He finished his homework; his friend Salim took him out after sunset to eat at one of the hundreds of food stalls that had erupted on the pavements of Bhendi Bazaar during Ramzaan; he quarrelled and made up with Amanat at least thrice a day, but he could not get rid of Firdaus. There were times when he thought that the only thing he wanted of life was to return to his old house. Firdaus was for him precisely what the name meant. Paradise. He now knew what Adam and Eve must have felt when they were driven out of their home. But Zia had not committed any sin or disobeyed God. Abba alone should have been thrown out and perhaps Altaaf Mamoo with him. Zia wanted to swear out loud, and yell at the world looking at the sky as Amitabh Bachchan did in his movies, that he would not rest till he had repossessed Firdaus.

Zia no longer trusted his father. What Abba thought of as good news might not look so good to him.

'You are going to a boarding school that many people consider the finest in the country.'

Zia was right to have been suspicious. This didn't at all sound like good news.

'But I have only been in St Paul's for a year.'

Amanat had stopped eating and was watching his father.

'Forget St Paul's.' Ammijaan was obviously party to this new school business. 'This school is British. It has swimming, riding, mountain climbing, carpentry, bird-watching and anything else you may want to do.'

'No studies?' Zia asked. Best not to get carried away. It sounded like too much of a good thing.

'I'm afraid they are not that advanced yet,' Abbajaan took over from his wife. 'But they have highly trained teachers from all over the world. And they let you do your own experiments in physics and chemistry and do projects on cinema and racing cars. Oh, and I forgot, they have a theatre department and they teach you music.'

'I hate acting in plays and becoming a butterfly or a cake.'

'We'll tell them to give you a starring role just like Sagari.'

'You haven't told me the name of the school.'

'It's called New Eden and it's in Coonoor, right next to Ooty,' Ammi piped up. 'Do you remember we spent a summer vacation there? There was mist everywhere in the mornings and we went boating in the afternoons. You said you wouldn't mind staying there forever.'

It was a little unusual to hear Ammijaan and Abba playing a duet these days. They hardly ever exchanged a harsh word, but Ammi had of late disowned Abba, and didn't talk much to him unless there was little choice, and even then it was Abba who always made the effort to draw her in.

'I don't know, maybe I won't like it any more.'

Ammijaan laughed. It was her old amused, half-believing, half-incredulous titter. 'It's only three years since we went there. It couldn't have changed that much, become a desert or a colony of slaves.'

Zia laughed as Ammijaan stretched out her hand and mussed his hair.

'What about Amanat?' he asked.

'How can we send Amanat?' Abba interjected before Ammijaan could answer. 'His health won't permit it.'

New Eden was certainly beginning to look like an interesting proposition. Imagine Amanat at St Paul's and he, Zia, at some fancy school run by foreigners.

'And anyway, we can't let both of you abandon us old people.' Ammi turned her charm on Amanat. 'We need at least one of you to take care of us.'

'I can take care of you, Ammi.' Zia sensed that he was being left out.

'Of course you can. I was only half-joking. You know the doctors won't let Amanat out of their sight.'

'I thought we were poor,' Amanat cornered his father.

Abbajaan smiled lamely. 'Let's say we are not rich.'

'So how will you pay for this school?' Zia's elder brother was not about to let go of the subject.

'Don't worry your little head about it,' said Ammijaan soothingly.

But I do, I do, Amanat wanted to yell at his parents. He wondered if they took him to be a fool. Since the Khans had moved to Suleiman

Mansion and Amanat's health had got worse, Dr Pat had been after Abba to send the boy out of Bombay for a change of climate, to improve his health. Did they really expect Amanat to buy that story about wanting at least one of their children with them? Why not just come out in the open and say there was money for Zia but not for him? And then he was stricken with guilt and instantly contrite. How could he think such terrible thoughts about his parents? Was there ever a more ungrateful son than him? Abbajaan was always in debt because of him and his marathon ailments. Though it had to be admitted that Ammijaan was far better at putting his father in the red than he was.

'There's one other thing that I should have mentioned.' Abba got back to hard-selling New Eden. 'They don't do the SSC exam there at the end of school. You do something called the International Baccalaureate. Which means if you do well, you can join almost any university abroad directly.'

'Will Amanat go back to Christ Church School?'

Abbajaan looked discomfited.

'We'll have to see,' Ammijaan said. 'They hardly ever allow anyone to join in the middle of the year since all their classes are full.'

The prospect of seeing Dilip Kumar in the flesh instead of on the screen or in the film glossies unnerved Zubeida. It might even have unbalanced her a bit. She could not sleep, she lost her appetite, she became absent-minded and edgy. She spent hours and hours deciding on what to wear for the occasion, changing her mind every five minutes. Ammijaan made matters worse by putting her entire wardrobe at her disposal.

Amanat was a little ashamed of this aunt who had fallen in love with a Hindi matinée idol. He told Ammijaan that he would rather not go with his aunt to watch a middle-aged actor shooting some utterly rubbishy film with Sagari. Ammijaan gathered Amanat in her arms and looked at him indulgently.

'Of course, you needn't,' she said, 'and I wouldn't dream of forcing you because I love you dearly. You are a gentle and good-natured boy, Amanat, but sometimes I think that's just a front. At heart, you are a snob and you sit in judgement upon the whole world and I believe hardly anybody finds favour with you.' She patted his cheek and smiled. 'Do you think your illness makes you a superior being? And how can you like anybody, Amanat, if you dislike yourself so much?'

Amanat loved Ammi as most children love their mothers. But he had always thought of her as lightweight stuff. And yet she had been more perspicacious than almost anybody he knew. He was hurt and livid with her. But he couldn't sustain his anger. She had only told him innocently what she thought of him without worrying that she would cripple him psychologically. She knew that he would get over the shock of confronting the truth and, sometime, begin to accept it.

'What is important to Zubeida Khaala,' she added, 'may not carry much weight with Abbajaan, me or you, but that doesn't make it any less important.'

Sagari was to pick them up at eight in the morning but Zubeida Khaala got ready at six. Amanat could feel a low tremor running through her as she took his hand in hers and they walked down the stairs. Sagari was a little confused when she saw him and his companion. 'I thought you were coming with Zu – ' she said, 'it is Zubeida Auntie. I didn't recognize you.' Amanat knew that his aunt had waited a lifetime to be with this man, but he had no patience with her. She had regressed to the age she had been when she first saw the Dilip Kumar movie that changed her life.

The shooting was to start at 9.30 but the great actor was still missing at 11.30. By that time Zubeida Khaala was no longer able to hide her disquiet. Sagari explained that the big stars did not think it seemly to appear on time and it was Dilipji's custom to come two or three hours late. But that didn't assuage Zubeida's fears. Sagari did not seem to notice Zubeida's trepidation. She introduced her guests to the director of the film, ordered soft drinks and eats every half an hour, and taught Zubeida and Amanat a card game called Bluff.

At 12.30 there was a commotion and a flurry of action. It was as though a fire alarm had gone off in the studio and everybody on the set rushed around. There was tension in the air and even Amanat, an unwilling and reluctant spectator, was galvanized and felt part of this vast enterprise. Sagari annotated the proceedings every now and then. The courtroom set was abuzz with people. An overhead crane moved eerily like the Loch Ness monster, while gigantic floods and other lights were positioned along with cutters and reflectors. The carpenters changed the angle of the dock in which Dilipji would stand; trolley tracks were laid and the camera set-up readied. The sound recordist fixed a tiny mike in the collar of Sagari's dress while the make-up man worked on her face. People shouted and swore across the set and the director went into Dilipji's room for a consultation.

'He's rewriting the dialogue and perhaps the script too,' Sagari smiled as she got a new set of eyelashes. 'If he could, he would rewrite every scene to have no one but him facing the camera.'

'Does that mean he's going to write you out of the script?' Amanat asked.

'I think he would like to, but just now he needs me more than I need him. Don't look so surprised. He's not so bad once he's fixed the script to suit himself and got the camera to frame him as he wants.'

Amanat looked sneakily at Zubeida Khaala. Was she disillusioned with the greatest tragedian of the Indian screen? Had he begun to fall from his pedestal? She seemed unperturbed by Sagari's offhand revelations. He doubted if she had heard any of them. She had stood in front of the multiple mirrors in Sagari's dressing room for a minute, dabbed her face with a little make-up and then gone back to her seat. Now the teenage trepidation had disappeared. She had become still, though not in a stony, obtrusive way.

What was going on in her mind? Amanat wondered. Was she thinking about what she would say to Dilipji? Was she programming the meeting, her gestures, the look in her eyes, where he would sit, what he would say, his questions and her answers? Would she pour out her heart and life to him? Would she take off with him without saying bye? Was she planning to imprint everything that happened on her memory so that she could replay it again and again later in life? Or was all that concentrated energy turning her into a black hole whose gravitational force would suck in the actor until nothing of him was left?

Amanat's disjointed musings were suddenly cut short. Dilipji was at the door.

'Sagari, my pet, why have you been ignoring – ?' he stopped when he realized that Sagari had company.

The man was past his prime and was putting on weight, but he certainly had an aura about him. It was a mix of charm, polish, self-assurance and the knowledge that he was almost irresistible. He was not far off the mark. Amanat found himself putting up a brave fight against this spell, knowing all the while that it was pointless.

'Have I?' Sagari answered gaily. 'I've been waiting for the great lover for the last two and a half, or is it three and a half hours, Amanat?' The prima donna in Sagari was in full control of the situation.

'I'm contrite. I beg your pardon,' the actor smiled. 'I was held up at the last minute.'

'Liar.' Sagari had decided it was not worth pursuing the matter.

'Aren't you going to introduce me to your friends?'

'This is Zubeida Auntie.'

Dilipji did an adaab but looked a trifle puzzled. 'I know this sounds like a song from one of our Hindi movies, but why do I feel I've seen you before?'

Zubeida smiled, a whisper of a smile. It confused the actor even more.

'And this is my friend, Amanat.'

'Friend? Am I to understand that this is the competition? Am I about to be displaced from your heart, Sagari? Or is it that I've already been thrown out on the road, bag and baggage?' He turned to Amanat. 'What a fine name you have.'

Amanat blushed at the compliment as though he had invented his own name.

'Do you know how lucky you are to have such a beautiful woman for your mother?'

Amanat wanted to hurt this man who thought he was god's gift to humankind. He had no reason to dislike him and yet he did. He would have liked to scratch his mouth to see whether there was blood behind the skin of his lips or just smiling wax.

'She's not my mother.' It seemed that the thespian was still having silent converse with Zubeida, but the spell was broken. 'She's just my aunt.'

Amanat had no idea why he inserted the word 'just' in that sentence.

'Camera ready,' the megaphone boomed, 'please call Dilipji and Sagariji.'

'It's been lovely meeting the two of you. Do come again.' Dilipji turned to leave when Sagari stopped him.

'Aren't you going to autograph your picture for my aunt?'

'Why, of course, would she care for one?'

Dilipji sat down and asked for his briefcase. When it came, he took out a photograph printed on matt-finished paper and signed it. He got up and went over to Zubeida. He bowed and gave her the picture.

'Just a memento of your visit.'

Zubeida too had something for him. He looked nonplussed as he held the gift in his hand. It was a picture of her with her signature.

He looked up at her. 'I... I... I don't know how to thank you.' He did an adaab and went to the door. Then as an afterthought he came back. 'It's been a pleasure talking to you. *Khuda hafiz*.'

Zubeida Khaala had not said a word all that morning.

# 9

All through school, Amanat wrote twice a week to his younger brother. Zia averaged a letter once a month.

Dear 1001,

You wrote only once last week.

Tell Ammi I'm okay. Zubeida Khaala will be pleased to know that I did well in her favourite subject, geography. My horse at school, Dare Devil, took a fall and has injured his leg. I'm nursing it every day and praying to Allah to make him well.

My friends want to read your letters before I get a chance to go over them. They've asked me to tell you that they want more stories about Gagan, the flying boy. Last Saturday we counted the letters you sent me this year: 85 so far.

You didn't finish the tamarind story. What happened to the baby cardinal?

Your affectionate brother,
Zia

Zia studied at New Eden for eight years. He was ten when Nandini Devi visited New Eden and catapulted him to star status in the school.

Nandini Devi was an Indian institution. She had, the headmaster informed the students, travelled around the country and all over the world. She was a maths wizard. They called her the human computer. She went to schools, colleges and universities to demonstrate her superhuman skills. Multiplication, division, equations, she could do them all in her head and faster than a computer. She'll show you that maths is not dull, not dull at all, he said. It's dramatic, thrilling and fun. He was sure she would inspire the boys and girls at New Eden to take a more active interest in the subject.

Nandini Devi's arrival was greeted with cynicism, superciliousness and a lack of interest bordering on the uncouth. Mathematics was bad enough, but a performing mathematician, and that too a woman? The students would rather have been given a dose of castor oil. They made it a point to let Nandini Devi know that they were in the assembly hall under duress. They yawned, they talked amongst themselves, they were bored.

Nandini was unfazed. She was a big woman, with a big bosom from which her voice seemed to reverberate. Within minutes she had the students enthralled. She didn't have a sales pitch about mathematics; what she put on was a major production. Riddles, puzzles, conundrums; the great mathematicians, their follies, the problems they had solved. The astounding and astonishing ways in which the rarefied and abstruse theories and equations of pure maths found use and application in things we would not remotely connect with the subject. Clouds, rain, the heights of trees, air currents, tides, she converted everything to the magic and mystery of numbers.

It was an exhilarating performance. She took a break of fifteen minutes and started on the second half of her presentation. There was only one mistake she made. She should never have looked to the audience for answers, even as a mere formality or theatrical gimmick.

'27 x 27?' she asked. No one hazarded a guess and she didn't expect anyone to either. '729,' she said.

Abba had told Zia that in the old days, at least in the vernacular schools, they taught tables up to thirty and then moved on to tables of a quarter, half, three-quarters, one and a quarter, and one and a half. At New Eden, the furthest they went was to twelve times twelve.

'729 x 27 x 27 x 27?' She looked around for an answer in the auditorium. '14,348,907. Anybody wants to check to see if I have got it wrong by a digit or two? Come on, get out your calculators.'

Barring one of the teachers, there were only two students who had brought their pocket calculators.

'Any mistake?' she asked. 'None? Okay then, now it's your turn to put me on the mat. Multiplication, division, cube roots, square roots, decimal points. Don't go above seven numbers. Your calculators won't be able to cope with them.'

Since nobody would start the ball rolling, the senior maths teacher asked the first question.

'137 squared?'

'18,769.'

'137 cubed?' one of the girls decided to plunge in.

'Anybody? Anybody wants to take a guess?' Nandini Devi asked perfunctorily and was about to give the answer herself when someone at the back said something.

'2,571,353.' The voice broke the number into three parts.

'Would you repeat that please?'

Zia obliged and Nandini Devi wrote the answer on the blackboard.

'Congratulations. I believe you've got it right. Very good. Very good.' Nandini Devi had the right mix of lofty tolerance and a patronizing air. 'You want to try the square root of 22,401,289?'

Zia answered even as she was writing the number on the blackboard. '4,733.'

'Do you have a calculator there, young man?' Nandini Devi laughed but there was an uneasy edge to her voice. 'No cheating, no cheating.'

Zia stood up and said, 'Next.'

'4,733 cubed.' Nandini Devi spoke reluctantly as if she would rather not know the answer.

'106,025,300,837.'

Nandini Devi wrote the numbers slowly, turned around and stared at Zia. One of the students with a calculator yelled, 'He's right, he's right.'

The entire hall switched its attention to Zia. A final-year student threw some decimal figures at him.

'793,645.39 ÷ 11.394759?'

Zia waited for Nandini Devi to answer.

'It's for you, not me.' Her voice was sharp.

'69,650.03735.'

'So much for the easy stuff.' Nandini Devi's smile was a bit forced. 'Now how about some simultaneous equations?'

She called Zia up to the stage. He wasn't quite sure whether to go or not. But the boys and girls of New Eden were rooting for him. They were chanting Zia, Zia, Zia, as though this were a rugby match, and the honour of the school were at stake.

Simultaneous, quadratic and vector equations, integral and differential calculus, Nandini hauled him through every possible variation since the introduction of numbers. She put a spin on even the simplest problem and tried to catch him off-guard. Everything she flung at Zia, he fielded with assurance and panache. He was neither ruffled nor defiant, but watched patiently while she grew more and more agitated. She had come to New Eden to be the star, and here she was spending all her energy and efforts trying to intimidate, unnerve and push over a little boy. Zia looked at his teachers and the headmaster and realized that they had smelt blood; they had identified with him and were baying for him to give the coup de grace. He looked into Nandini Devi's eyes; there was something desperate in them. She needed to vanquish him, grind him into the earth, if she wanted to come out of this encounter with her self-respect intact. He had nothing to lose and she...she certainly had made up her mind that she would stake everything on this boy: it was all or nothing for her.

What was the matter with him? Why was he playing along? It had been a mere game for him when he had, unbeknownst to himself, piped up with an answer to her first question. He had lost interest a long time ago, while Nandini Devi kept egging him on. They should have wound up by 12 and gone for lunch. Now it was past 12.30. She asked him some question about logarithmic functions but he was not listening.

He looked blankly at Nandini Devi and said, 'I don't know.'

There was no mistaking the disappointment of the students and teachers. They didn't for one moment believe that he couldn't give the answer, and they were furious with him for having let them down, though, God knows, he hadn't asked them to put their faith in him. But it was worth it just to see the relief on Nandini Devi's face.

'I knew it, I just knew that you were improvising, that this was your lucky day. But I also knew,' she seemed ready to hug him till the last breath had been squeezed out of him, 'that your lucky streak couldn't last forever. I'll tell you something little boy, and take my advice. Never take on a pro, or you'll always end up losing.'

Zia was now the school's hero number one. In the past, only sportsmen had been stars at New Eden. Now the balance seemed to tip towards brains. But there was something else. For the first time, Zia began to understand the actual game plan that Allah had for him. Hadn't He left clues right from the beginning? From Christ Church to St Paul's English Academy, from the bungalow on Nepean Sea Road to Suleiman Mansion, He had tested Zia and taught him not to be affected either by adversity or good fortune. Faith in Allah was all that mattered. Why else had he been taught such a bitter lesson when he had laid flowers at the feet of the elephant god? And why had he, and not Amanat, been pulled out of St Paul's and sent to perhaps the most exclusive and expensive school in the country?

If all this were not proof enough, did you see how Allah, glory be to Him, had blessed him with a unique gift? He could still recall the incredulity and wonder in the eyes of his fellow-students. They had not been fooled, not one of them, when he told Nandini that he didn't know the answer to the last question. Of course he knew it, he just wasn't interested.

God's hand was not just guiding him; He had chosen the occasion with unerring insight and resounding success. Think of the care with which He had arranged every single aspect of what transpired that day in the assembly hall. New Eden had never invited a maths wizard till then. When they did, they chose a Hindu woman of forty-five or fifty. It was the story of David and Goliath again. The numbers and the solutions had come to him as though someone was telling him exactly what to say. A boy of ten had vanquished and humiliated Nandini Devi, and then, because Allah is all-merciful, He had saved her face by making Zia pretend that he didn't know the answer. And where was the battlefield located? In the heart of Christendom where the missionary teachers made a point of deviously suggesting that Christianity was better than all other religions. Well, what did Nandini Devi and all the Christian missionaries have to say now?

It was time to proclaim his fealty to Allah and sing His praises.

Two hours before the wake-up bell, Zia slipped out of the dorm and took the first bus to Coimbatore. He had been to Coimbatore many times but never to the state transport bus station. It was crowded and hardly anybody spoke anything but Tamil. He finally located some of his own brethren. You could always recognize the devout by the caps they wore, and if they were not educated and well-off, then by the checked lungis. Zia soon found his way to a big Shia mosque.

Today was the day of maatam, the grief and grieving over the loss of the Prophet's grandsons, especially Hussein. It was Zia's very first visit to a mosque alone. He felt a sense of awe. The floor was covered with durries. Zia sat in the second row; there were twenty-seven more behind him. In his own row there were seventy men sitting, or rather kneeling next to each other. They were close and yet each man's space was inviolate.

The power of mass prayer was a revelation to Zia. He discovered that his prayers had more body and weight and rapture when he was amongst the believers in the mosque. There were no rich or poor, no great or small, no mathematical geniuses or Little Miracles in the temple of God. You could feel Allah descend upon the faithful as they knelt down in unison, the soles of their feet turned upwards, hands conjoined as they prayed using the very language in which the archangel had spoken to the Prophet. At the end of the prayers, Zia was aware of an intense bond with his fellow-men. The words of the maulvi whom he had heard years ago in Bombay came back to him: Allah was their father and all those in the mosque were Zia's blood brothers.

He was ready now to enter a new phase of life and to take on the responsibilities of adulthood. He took off his shirt and vest along with the others, folded them carefully and left them with the caretaker. The procession of mourners was about to set off when Zia joined it. In front, a man was leading a handsome white horse decked in gold embroidery, with a saddle covered in white silk. The horse was riderless. It was symbolic of Hussein's mount, which returned home alone after his master's martyrdom. There were at least a dozen tazias, replicas of Hussein's mausoleum. Some were thin and rickety and a little tacky, but a few of them were exquisitely built around a framework of cane, with the walls and dome made of silk. A couple of them even reproduced the intricate tracery of the original.

The people around were beginning to chant 'Ya Hassan, ya Hussein'. It was a soft, slow invocation, almost a sigh. Some of the older people first called upon Hassan and Hussein's father. 'Ya Ali, ya Ali,' they said again and again, and then began to weep for Hussein. Soon the whole road was resounding with lamentation. It was heart-rending, this cry, and the recalling of the terrible martyrdom. It was as though the people in the procession would not cease till Hussein himself appeared. And when he did not come or answer, and their grief knew no bounds, they slowly started to scourge themselves. Ya Hussein, ya Hussein. What a fearsome price did this grandson of the Prophet pay for his stubborn faith. Ya Hussein, ya Hussein.

The young Zia unwrapped the flail he had bought from a stall near the mosque. There were several varieties: leather thongs, whips, steel chains, jangling knives. Zia had chosen a zanzeer. It was perhaps the deadliest of the lot. It had a wooden handle and seven chains ending with stunted S-shaped steel blades. They had finely ground, paper-thin sharp edges on both sides. 'Ya Hussein, ya Hussein,' he too wailed, for the treacherously butchered son of Fatima and Ali, as he swung the zanzeer in the air and flicked it backwards. The blades bit into his back and the blood rose slowly and filled the contours of each cut. Ya Hussein, ya Hussein. The zanzeer went back and scooped out light slivers of flesh. He felt a piercing pain and the blood splattered on his back and on those around him. Ya Hussein, ya Hussein. Tears rose in Zia's eyes, and now he was using the wooden handle as a swivel. The chained blades swept to the left and drew long deep tracks on his back. '*Hai dost, hai dost.*' Alas my friend, alas my friend, Zia wept for Hussein. With a twist of his wrist, the chains and blades flicked the other way. They jangled to the right and caught in his flesh, tearing it. The blood flowed freely now. 'Ya Hussein, ya Hussein,' the other flagellants called out sorrowfully. There were hundreds of them and more were joining in every minute. The crowds on the street were four and five deep and there was no room to move. Cameras flashed in all directions and people wept and wailed as though their sons or mothers had died.

And now Zia had got the rhythm right. What he had in his hand was neither a scourge nor a zanzeer. It was a fan made of the softest, most precious feathers in the world. He was no longer lashing out erratically, and his step and swing were not those of a drunkard any more. Ya Hussein, ya Hussein. Oh, the terrible tragedy of it. The blades dug deeper, twisted and turned and tried to claw in, wanting to hold on as a lover clutches his beloved's hand when she insists on going home. '*Hai dost, hai dost.*' Zia no longer cried for his lost friend. He was no longer aware of this world; he was in the grip of a mysterious tranquillity even as his body danced and the crowds stopped to watch, as this whirring, flashing, zipping, arching, pirouetting, weightless and bodiless genie leapt up and floated forever in the air, the zanzeer swishing in and out of his flesh, left to right and right to left. It was no longer moving front to back and back to front. It seemed to go clean through his chest and out. Ribbons of his skin fluttered in the air. 'Ya Hussein, ya Hussein.' He was in a trance and on a trip of his own. And now even Hussein was forgotten, and this was only between him and his God. It was a rapture and an ecstasy that he did not want to end.

By the time Zia got back to New Eden and crawled into bed, it was 12.30 at night. He had managed to slip in unobserved, but by four o'clock, the entire dorm was aware that he was back. He learnt later from his friend Roy Cambray that he had been delirious, running a temperature of 104.5°. The doctor had been called, and Zia was transferred to the school sickbay. He had to be sedated before his vest and shirt could be cut off. Classes were held as usual but the atmosphere was tense and nobody was paying much attention to their books. The question foremost in everyone's mind was whether anyone on campus was safe any longer. On the day Zia disappeared, the headmaster had informed the police, and they had been on the lookout for him at bus and train stations and even at Coimbatore airport. Now the boy had come back with his body in shreds. The younger students huddled together and some began to cry and wanted to be taken home.

The headmaster, Zia's dorm parent and the senior police inspector from Ooty conferred in the headmaster's office. Had the boy been kidnapped? Who could have brutalized Zia in such a terrible fashion?

Had he been sexually abused and assaulted? Where had they taken him? And why had they let him go? It was a miracle the boy had survived at all. The police inspector was keen to talk to Zia and question him about anything that he remembered of the previous day, but he was in no condition to communicate with anyone.

It was close to 10.30 in the morning, and the meeting was about to break up, when the peon brought in the papers from Coimbatore. There was a large picture of Zia on the front page of *The Hindu*. That week Zia would be on the cover of *Time*. He was up in the air, his right hand holding the handle of the zanzeer stretched across his bare chest. Two of the blades were almost embedded in his flesh while the others were a steel blur. Zia's head was flung back, his mouth was slightly open and his eyes were closed, one couldn't make out whether in pain or pleasure, like the woman in the *Playboy* centre spread Roy had shown him. *Time* called it 'The Agony and the Ecstasy of Islam'. The photographer had obviously chatted with the boy after the flagellation, for his name was quoted and so was that of New Eden.

The school authorities informed Zia's parents that the boy was no longer welcome there and said they would appreciate it if he could be taken home as soon as he had recovered. But then, at the last minute, when Zafar Khan had arrived to pick up his son, they seemed to have a change of heart. Zia was allowed to stay on at the school on the condition that he would observe no more Muslim rituals.

When Zia went home to Bombay for the summer holidays, he found that his mother had moved out. She had told Amanat prior to leaving that she was fed up with being ill-treated by Zafar, and with living cooped up in that tiny, claustrophobic flat in Bhendi Bazaar, and so she was staying with some friends called Barrett on Malabar Hill. Nicholas Barrett was head of First Federal Bank of America, and had a five-bedroom penthouse overlooking the Arabian Sea. Ammijaan, or was it Amanat, hinted that Bombay's climate didn't suit Mrs Barrett and that she spent most of the year in Florida.

Nicholas Barrett didn't have much to say to Zia but he was pleasant enough and often enquired about Zia's studies and New Eden, which, it appeared, thanks to *Time* magazine, everybody knew about. Zia had no problem understanding why Ammijaan had moved to the Barrett place. He himself would have done the same. It was the closest thing you could find to their old house on Nepean Sea Road. Not half as big as Firdaus, nor a bungalow, but what it lacked in space and seclusion, it made up for with its height and its air of exclusivity. Every room had a view of the sea, and you could see Ammijaan's hand in the quiet splendour of the interiors.

Zia spent more than three-quarters of his holidays with Ammijaan. Sometimes Amanat came to visit but he was always an oddball and preferred to go home to Suleiman Mansion to sleep. It was nothing short of amazing what a change of environment could do for the human soul. Ammijaan was a completely different woman in her new residence. She was once more her aristocratic, easy old self; the colour had come back to her cheeks; she could make people laugh and, more to the point, she could herself laugh again. She had once more started going to the club and every Sunday she went to the races. And because she got so much pleasure from life, she made Zia's holidays much more fun. He travelled in an air-conditioned car, he slept in an air-conditioned bedroom and now he could even invite his New Eden friends over.

Amanat hadn't changed much, except that he had grown very tall. But he was as thin as ever, so thin that sometimes you saw him and sometimes you didn't. He was still his sick self, missing school more often than attending it. He thought that Zia had acquired something like an upper-crust British accent, not the instant hue his speech had taken on when he had been with Aunt Antonia's daughter, Vivian, but something deeper and more lasting. Amanat could not decipher whether he felt absurdly proud of his brother or resentful and envious.

Zia is going to be even taller than his brother and had inherited his mother's fair looks. With his New Eden accent he's often taken to be a foreigner. He has a whole new wardrobe. He wears flannels, a blazer and a tie, and has different pairs of shoes for different sports. He goes riding, swimming and bird-watching, and canoeing in the rapids. He uses words like 'tosh', 'cockup' and 'canticle'. His friends have cars with names like Alpha Romeo, Lamborghini and Lotus. He thinks the people from Suleiman Mansion, and by implication Abbajaan, Amanat and even Zubeida Khaala, rather common. There were times when Amanat, too, saw things in this light.

Abba must have been doing a little better in life, for there was a phone at home now, and Amanat had a radio-cassette player.

Zubeida Khaala took care of the house and, whenever possible, she and Zia went around Bhendi Bazaar and visited all the mosques and Zia's favourite haunts.

By the time Zia was in his second-to-last year at New Eden, he had three steady girlfriends: Mary-Ann, Laajwanti and Yvonne. The three of them hated each other but not enough to give up Zia.

Yvonne was two years senior to Zia, but she had taken to failing her finals almost as though she wanted him to catch up with her and be in the same class. He did not pretend to like Laajwanti or Mary-Ann more than Yvonne or the other way round. They had stopped asking him to choose one of them because he always gave them the same answer: 'But I like you all so much.' Sometimes it appeared that he was playing one against the others, an indication of at least moderate interest on his part. At other times it was as though he didn't care.

He had several friends among the boys now. They marvelled at his ability to carry on with three women simultaneously and wouldn't have minded changing places with him. But they found it difficult to get to the bottom of Zia.

Roy Cambray was his closest friend. Roy was an extrovert and an outdoors person. He liked poaching chickens and ducks from the neighbouring estates and setting traps for rabbits and birds. He was a good shot and he took Zia hunting in the woods to kill partridges and pigeons with his air gun, and taught Zia how to barbecue them over a pit. He represented the school at rugby, hockey and tennis, while the only sport that Zia played for his school was cricket.

Roy's choice of a steady girlfriend was, to say the least, a little ironic, if not odd. Sarah Roberts was the school's most strident feminist. She seemed to have an acute distaste for men, especially the sporting variety, with their male bonding and macho camaraderie. She was just as critical of her own sex when they didn't stand up for their rights and allowed men to dominate them. She couldn't quite make up her mind who was the greater criminal: Zia, that feckless rat who took women for granted, or his three girlfriends, who had no pride, let alone the sense of sisterhood that would have made them ditch him a long time ago.

Sarah, Roy and Zia made a strange trinity on the rare occasions they were together. At the school dance, annual days, or in the school parliament where all three belonged to the same party, Sarah was pointedly cool and withering, while Zia was a master at ignoring her barbs and insults. She often asked Roy why he was friends with that slimy M (M for Muslim; Sarah was not aware of her own bigotry) and was incensed when Roy said that he had no idea, he just was, that's all. If Roy felt caught between his two favourite people, he didn't seem to mind it.

Zia did not go out of his way to be popular but he was there when you needed him. He would help anyone with maths, physics, history or any other subject, and if one of his classmates was in a spot, he would even write an essay for him. He had no problem holding his answer paper at an angle if a friend wished to peek at it. But far more valuable to his peers was his facility with signatures. He could do Donald Bradman, Madhuri Dixit, Indira Gandhi, Winston Churchill, Madonna or Pelé for your autograph book. When Roy and Sarah wanted to take in a movie in Ooty or go boating on the lake, Zia scribbled the signature of the dorm parent or the dean, and they got a pass for an afternoon out.

And then, in his final year, Sarah Roberts was found to be pregnant. In time she revealed that Roy was not the father. Zia was. Nobody could fathom how, when and where the two antagonists had got together. Not just got together but started a baby. Had Sarah set out to conquer the enemy but instead had ended up being seduced? How could Zia have betrayed his friend and pulled off such a coup? For the boys at New Eden, Zia was once again a hero. His girlfriends were devastated at being ditched but were delighted that Sarah Roberts had got her comeuppance. The only one who seemed strangely indifferent to the whole affair was Roy.

Zia's and Sarah's parents were called and told to take the children away. Sarah Roberts went back to the States and Zia was about to go back to Bombay when he got a reprieve. Nobody could understand how. There were only three months to the final exams and he was allowed to sit the International Baccalaureate.

# 10

Sometime in September or October of his last year at New Eden, Zafar Khan had sent Zia an application form for Cambridge. This was before the scandal of Sarah Roberts's pregnancy had shaken the school and made Zia persona non grata. Zia was none too keen on filling up the form and gathering all the certificates and recommendations, but the headmaster had summoned him to his office twice, and when he realized that Zia was dragging his feet, had ordered him not to leave his ante-room till the entire application was complete. Why the man should take a personal interest in Zia's career and not in anybody else's was as inexplicable as his decision to allow Zia to appear for his finals.

Zia returned to Bombay after the exams, meaning to go straight to the penthouse on Malabar Hill. But Ammijaan and Nicholas Barrett appeared to have forgotten the date and time of his arrival. The silver Mercedes, with its impenetrable windowpanes, was nowhere to be seen at the station. Zia was not a little put out, but many of the New Eden boys from Bombay lived on Peddar Road or Malabar Hill and their cars had certainly turned up.

Roy offered to drop him off. It was a little awkward to be talking to him again after what had happened, but since Roy seemed willing to forget, or at least was willing not to hold the past against him, Zia accepted the ride. When Zia got out, Roy said something about keeping in touch and that he would give him a ring. Of course this couldn't be true but Zia was grateful to Roy for having the decency to be polite when all he needed to have said was goodbye.

Zia took the lift up to the seventeenth floor, walked up the last flight to the penthouse and rang the bell. The cook opened the door. He was a bad actor and tried to pretend that he was not taken aback. Zia started to walk in but the cook would not budge.

'Where's my mother?'

'Not here.'

'Mr Barrett, where is he?'

'Gone to office.'

'Let me phone him.' Zia attempted to enter again but he had the feeling that he was being thwarted without being actually physically restrained.

'I don't think so. Not a good idea.'

'Why? Has my mother gone out of town?'

'No. Maybe.'

'What's "maybe" about it? It is either no or yes. Where is she?'

'Gone home.'

It was as though Ammijaan had never left. She certainly didn't ever mention Nicholas Barrett, his penthouse or the intervening six years. Zia wondered why he had been so apprehensive about coming home. Nothing had changed. Abba and Ammi continued to pretend that everything was fine. They did not mention the SOS sent to Abbajaan by the headmaster to come to New Eden and escort his fornicating son back to Bombay. Abba had not said a word about the previous SOS either. After the Muharram flagellation he, along with Zubeida Khaala, had nursed Zia through the appalling setbacks of the sepsis from the mangling of his back, without a word of recrimination.

But Khaalajaan seemed to have drifted into a strange world all her own. That night, she had run her hand across Zia's scars and said, 'How much prickly heat you've got on your back. You must take better care of yourself.' She had then looked at him, touched his face softly and said in an almost inaudible whisper, 'How grand and handsome you've grown. May the evil eye never get close to you.' And then suddenly she had added, 'You mustn't let any harm come to the unborn baby or her mother. It's your seed. Now that you've planted it, you must take good care of it.' Zia had looked at her puzzled, though he did not dwell on it. The old bond between aunt and nephew had long since grown tenuous.

Amanat, Zia had always known, was far too private a person ever to broach such a sensitive subject as Sarah Roberts, unless Zia himself brought it up. Since Amanat would not bare his heart like a eunuch picking up his skirt at the slightest provocation, those who didn't care for him called him secretive, dodgy and slippery. Amanat was discreet, close-mouthed (not a chink there, only a blank, purchaseless smooth wall that would reveal nothing), noninterfering and wary of trespassing on the solitude of others. Which is not to say he didn't have an opinion. Don't ever make the mistake of asking him to be candid. If he feels you are a friend and that he owes it to you to be honest, he may just come clean. God help you then.

Abbajaan had now set up a kind of folding office in the drawing room. After his licence had been suspended, he had worked out an arrangement with another architectural firm. He did most of the designing for slave wages while they took the credit and the fees. Amanat had been assisting Abbajaan now for the past five or six years. He had a natural talent for drawing and his draughtsmanship was superb. Amanat had never had any doubts about what he was going to be when he grew up: he would be an architect and join his father. Together they would change the face of architecture in India. But Abba's suspension had burnt his son perhaps even more than himself.

Instead of studying architecture, Amanat took his B.A. in, of all subjects, English literature. At the end of it, he said he had wasted his time usefully.

'What's that supposed to mean?' Zia asked him. 'Are you being smart-arsed, talking for effect?'

Amanat had looked blank. 'No. I didn't get anything concrete out of it but I suspect it has a slow-release effect, something which accumulates over the years, and only then do you become aware of it.'

Amanat next turned his attention to learning a trade. Once again his choice of a profession was so far-fetched and alien to his personality that for a while everybody thought he was joking. He had decided to study industrial design in Ahmedabad.

When Zia got back from New Eden, Amanat came down to Bombay for the summer vacation. His health was still a persistent problem but he was a young man now and eager to assert his independence. Industrial design in India, he was convinced, was in its Neolithic phase. Frankly, he said, it was worse than that: design and function were not antagonistic in India, they were simply unaware of each other's existence. Amanat was sure that he was being brain-damaged by the course. Every morning, as he sat tying his shoelaces, he seemed to be praying for the courage to overcome a severe case of vacillation. Abbajaan kept telling him to forget the course and join him, but Amanat was determined to get a degree after his name, so that he could look for work. He'd have, according to his own estimate, the rest of his life to unlearn what was being taught.

Zia was convinced that Amanat and he were not siblings at all. A genetic test would easily establish this. The facts were there for everyone to see. The older Khan had zero self-esteem. He really believed that he had nothing to say on any subject. Now try and square this with the fact that he could be singularly arrogant and opinionated. He perpetually sat astride every contradiction you could think of. He was the shyest of people and yet he could put even a nervous porcupine at ease. Roy and he had barely known each other a week or two, but they were closer than Zia had ever been to Roy in all these years.

Zia could have died of shame the day Roy turned up at Suleiman Mansion. Zia had not given his Bhendi Bazaar address to any of his schoolmates and had always met them at the Barrett penthouse. Now Roy had discovered Zia's double life. He wanted to say he was not in, even though he himself had opened the door. Good manners and politeness were one thing, but to turn up in person at the home of the man who had betrayed you was in frightful taste. Amanat was working at the drawing board. Well, he could entertain Roy. Zia went into the bedroom. He had no idea what droll or ridiculous things Amanat was saying, but Roy was guffawing like a horse with whooping cough, and he stayed on for dinner.

Zia wondered whether Roy had no sense of vengeance. He was that most pitiable of creatures, a fool and a simpleton. Sometimes Zia suspected that Roy was biding his time, waiting to slit Zia's throat or eviscerate him. He felt contempt for Roy but was also on his guard. If the man had had any self-respect, he would never have come looking for Zia. Zia's name might have been under a cloud in the last few months at New Eden, but he also knew that, amongst their peers, the one who was the object of ridicule was Roy.

He should have joined his parents in New York but he had kept postponing his departure. He was staying with the American consul general, who happened to be a friend of his father's, but Zia was willing to bet that, given half a chance, he would have moved in with the Khans for good.

Roy was still ensconced at Suleiman Mansion when Zia left for Cambridge. Fortunately, in a couple of weeks Roy himself would head for Harvard and, in Zia's mind, he would become nothing more than a memory.

# 11

'You were heralded as the next Ramanujan. Instead, Dr Haddington tells me that he has already had two meetings with you about your performance, or rather the lack of it, and that your Director of Studies has spoken to you on several occasions, but you continue to evince no interest in your studies.'

It was the beginning of the second term. The Master of Emmanuel College was sitting with Zia, his Director of Studies, Stanley Pierce, and the Senior Tutor, Alfred Haddington, in the library of the Master's home. The place could just as well have been a set for a BBC Inspector Morse serial, though that would have needed to be in Oxford, not Cambridge. Perhaps all the thousands of volumes, neatly arranged behind glass doors in oak cupboards that reached to the ceiling, were just spines with embossed titles. Michael Laughton was an economist and all his own eleven titles were lined up under 'L'. Had the Master really read even a quarter of the books on his shelves? Mrs Laughton brought in tea and scones. Was she his second wife? Zia wondered. She seemed much younger than her husband, and was unlike the dowdy large-framed creatures that were the wives of most dons at Cambridge. Dr Haddington said, 'Hello Rachel,' and complimented her on what sounded like a rare disease to Zia, but turned out to be some plant, like hydrangea or chrysanthemum.

The Master introduced Zia. 'This is Zia Khan, Rachel. Khan, my wife. Khan is from India. The word is that he's going to reinvent maths and make Newton sit up in his grave.'

Zia shook hands with her and didn't bother to disown the Master's nonsense. Damn Aunt Antonia and her big mouth. She was always grossly inflating Zia's mathematical dexterity. He wished Rachel Laughton would stay and talk about her garden with Dr Haddington or about the trouble she was having toilet-training one of the dogs that was yapping outside, but she was obviously an expert in the art of making a quick, courteous exit.

'I'm sorry, Mr Khan, but your great talent will be lost on me. I have trouble just checking my change at Sainsbury's.' Mrs Laughton laughed and excused herself.

'What has gone wrong, Khan?' The Master was not about to let the tea or his wife interrupt him. 'Are you unhappy at Emmanuel?'

'No, sir.'

'Are you homesick? Missing your parents?'

'No, sir.'

'Your fellow-students say that you don't go carousing or pub-crawling with them. Yet you are rarely ever present for lectures. You don't hand in your work, nor do you show up to discuss it. Dr Haddington recommended that you see a counsellor and even fixed an appointment for you, but you did not show up.'

Zia would not look the Master, the Senior Tutor or Stanley Pierce in the eye, nor did he say anything. The Master of Emmanuel wondered if Khan held his silence because he had made a statement instead of formulating a question. It was an odd pause. Zia was not defiant or hostile, nor did he give the impression of being unable to communicate.

'Is algebraic geometry not to your liking, Khan?' This time Dr Laughton made sure there was no ambiguity about his expecting a reply, but Zia had run out of monosyllabic answers.

The Master tried again: 'Are you upset that you are at Emmanuel when, let's face it, most of the maths students prefer Trinity?'

Quite the contrary, Zia was sure he would have detested Trinity. That's where all the pure math geniuses congregated. Aunt Antonia and Dr Laughton were old friends, which was how Zia found himself in Emmanuel. It was the only good turn Aunt Antonia had done him.

Zia wondered what Stanley Pierce and Alfred Haddington were doing at this meeting. They had not contributed a word, though Zia was their baby, so to speak. Perhaps they were there only to confirm facts or reinforce a point of view just in case the Master was in need of such assistance. In fairness to them though, Zia would have to admit that both his Director of Studies and the Senior Tutor were spent men. They were good people, ever willing to help, but Zia had drained them of words, effort and will. Alfred Haddington, especially, had gone out of his way to rouse Zia out of his apathy. He had taken him to movies and plays, invited him to his home for tea and dinner, asked him to baby-sit his nine- and eleven-year-old daughters to make Zia feel part of the family, or make him feel put upon and elicit some response. But to no avail.

'Khan,' Dr Laughton spoke again, 'do you realize that it is more than a little unusual, even irregular, for the Master of Emmanuel, or any other college, to take time from his myriad academic and administrative duties, not to mention research, to humour an undergraduate who appears to have no interest in his studies?'

Yes, Zia was aware of it. He could see that dear Aunt Antonia had been meddling in his affairs and had pressurized Dr Laughton into seeing him.

'It's still a while to your first-year exams. With your talent you will manage to get through them, but I imagine with only a disappointing first. If, however, you continue to be as cavalier as you've been so far, please understand that we'll be left with no choice but to send you down. You are a valuable student of this college. Emmanuel places a great deal of faith in your ability to contribute to its intellectual and academic reputation. Do not disappoint us, Khan.'

Zia could not get used to the alarm. It was now a little over a month that it had been going off at four in the morning, but he still woke up with a terrible start. It was always the same. He was in a desert. He had been walking for days, maybe weeks. The sands leapt and blazed fearfully like firestorms on the sun. But curiously enough, he was neither thirsty nor afraid, just cold. It was the chill of loneliness, a thermocol insulation that dulled his senses and prevented him from feeling anything. His mind, which had always been full of ideas and plans, had been anaesthetized. Not a thought stirred in his head. The depression had left him bereft of desire and all motivation. Perhaps he had died.

He would have parted with his God for just a moment of company. He knew the desert was never deserted. All kinds of creatures and living things were there. If he could come across an ant or a cactus, it would warm his heart and give him hope.

Zia walked to the door without switching on the light. His right foot got caught in something. Maybe it was the blanket or one of his woollen vests, shirts, underpants or scarves lying on the floor. He tried to kick it off. When he didn't succeed, he tried to peel it off with the other foot and now both his feet were trapped in it and he was falling over. His head hit the corner of the heavy wooden bed and he was in a rage and cursing violently in Urdu. He got up and almost ripped the piece of clothing that had felled him. It was a T-shirt that he must have flung in the pile of dirty clothes four, maybe five weeks previously. He was glad that he had located it though. He had nothing to wear; he had already reworn most of his unlaundered clothes twice or thrice over. Zia, in a variation of the ascetic life, no longer washed himself or his clothes. He smelt like an airtight room full of Edam cheese.

There was not a soul in sight as he walked down St Andrews Street. The city had obviously died the previous night. But frankly, even if there had been a hundred thousand people screaming for help out there he couldn't have seen or heard them. A steel-wool mist was packed tightly between the blurred moon and the ground. An icicle wind blew across Parker's Piece. It tore at him, slipped inside his trouser legs, groped at his crotch, ferreted in his armpits and careened into his lungs.

How he loathed this job. He had gone out for a walk one morning around five because he couldn't sleep, and had been struck by the filth and litter on the road. He was convinced that all tourists should be banned from Cambridge. It was not their town and so they simply didn't care if they shat all over the place. The pair of sweepers on this beat must have gone for a cup of tea, for they had leaned their brooms against a hedge and left their carts nearby. Zia had finished cleaning up half the street when one of them came running towards him.

'What the hell do you think you are doing?'

'I would have thought even a fool could tell that I was cleaning up the mess on the road.'

'It's my street. And that's my broom.' Then he added with surprising formality, 'If you don't have a work permit, you can't take a job here.'

'Sure I can,' Zia contradicted him, 'I'm doing it for free.'

The next morning Zia was at work before the others got there. He had bought himself his own heavy-duty broom. In time the rest of the crew shrugged their shoulders and smiled. There was no dearth of weirdos in Cambridge. Every second fellow, tutor or don was a nutcase. Now there was one more. Besides, it turned out Zia was a manic worker and was always willing to fill in for anyone who reported sick or wanted to take the day off. Over the next few months Zia developed a rapport with the sweeper who had yelled at him on that first day. His name was Gordon Bowers.

Zia told himself that he didn't need the job, and that even if he were starving, he would rather die than have to wake up at four in the morning to clean up other people's debris, not to mention their dog shit. He had said this to himself every morning, and every morning he had gone back to the grind. Zia's attitude to the work was perverse: the more he abhorred his new-found métier, the more meticulous he became. No Marlborough packet, no Wrigley's wrapper, no Kodak Gold plastic canister, no Molson, Guinness, Lowenbrau, Heineken or Beck's can, no McDonald's or Burger King container, no dry or fresh sperm-filled condom, no kebab or fish-and-chips bag, no nacho, potato chip, cheese stick, no Coke or Pepsi bottle could escape his eye. This was the enemy, the original sin, the evil cornucopia of human waste on which the whole of mankind would choke and die. You cleared and cleaned up the mess on the roads and the pavements, in the alleys and the gutters, across the parks and the commons; you forced it into sacks; you pressed and squeezed it into neat five-foot cubes; you loaded it on to the garbage trucks; and then you chanced to look down and what you saw was flash floods of refuse and litter and garbage rising all around you.

There is only one purpose to life; only one ontological, epistemological, teleological end to and reason for creation: shit. What you eat, you shit. The more you consume, the more you shit. That is it, tortillas, shepherd's pie, doner kebabs or gyros as the Greeks call them, photographic films, computers, cars and car exhausts, woollens, synthetics, everything equals everything. There is not a grain of excess in the universe. All is accounted for. Yes, whoever sat up there in the sky was first, last, middle and sideways an accountant.

And who clears all the detritus in the universe? It is the sweepers of the world who must continually clean up the shit of human kind and canine kind and one other kind that is the nemesis, the diabolical and true Satan for Zia Khan. The other kind so beloved of nature lovers like Wordsworth, Kalidasa, Shelley, Keats and a hundred others who should have been forced to be sweepers before they were allowed to write a word about the joys of creation, the other kind, or rather the most unkind: the trees on this damned planet, earth.

It was during his first autumn that Zia realized why the American term for it was far more appropriate. Was there ever a more apt name for a season, or the human condition, than the fall? There is nothing, absolutely nothing, in the chronicles of mankind's suffering as great, as fallen, as symbolic and symptomatic, as overwhelming as fall, with or without the definite article.

Cambridge in October. Zia wasn't buying the crap about the saffron and copper and burnished burgundy and all the other ravishing autumn colours on the trees. Have you ever had to wade through roads knee-deep in leaves in Cambridge? No? And why do you think you can walk, proceed, make headway and reach whatever assignation or destination you may have on your mind? Because Zia Khan and his mates have been breaking their backs, hands, legs and fingers trying to clear the roads for the likes of you. At the last count, from one beech alone, Khan swept, collected and piled up a hundred and seventeen billion, seven hundred and ninety-three million, five hundred and ninety-four thousand, nine hundred and seventeen leaves. There are a million and a half deciduous trees in the city of Cambridge. That, of course, does not include the three hundred thousand saplings planted annually by the Friends of Trees Society in Cambridge, nor the propensity of the trees to propagate themselves almost as fast as the denizens of the Indian subcontinent.

Autumn had indeed exacted a terrible price from Zia. It seemed to him that Allah, too, had taken a fall. Zia didn't bother to pray these days. Allah had ceased to matter to him any more.

Now Zia stood outside the University Arms Hotel trying to pierce through the steel wool but only getting more and more entangled in it. There was no sight of Gordon Bowers, his team-mate, senior sweeper, friend and mentor. In his seventeen years at the job, Bowers had never missed a day and he wasn't ever late. What had happened to him?

Gordon Bowers was a history graduate from Exeter city. He had thought he would take a break, earn some money, travel and then get back to his studies. He was passing through Cambridge when someone relieved him of whatever little cash he had. He could have asked his parents for money. Instead he took up a job with the Cambridge City Council. It was temporary employment; all he wished was to earn enough to get out. After the second year, he didn't pretend to want to leave any more. He was made permanent. He was neither happy nor unhappy.

Four years later, Bowers was offered a supervisorship. He would never again have to be out on the roads by five in the morning, except to make the occasional random check. He could also take a few exams and keep moving up, perhaps even become one of the senior bureaucrats in the Cambridge municipality. Gordon refused. He had taken a course on the history of Cambridge and become a part-time guide to the city.

'Why haven't you married, Mr Bowers?' Zia had asked him once.

'I thought I would. I certainly didn't plan against it. But it just hasn't seemed to happen. Now, I don't know. It's probably too late for me, and besides, with two jobs, I don't get much time for myself, let alone for anyone else.'

'Too late, Mr Bowers? Thirty-five or thereabouts can't be too late. Just the prime of your life.'

'You should talk, Mr Khan. Not even twenty and look what you're up to. A fine Cambridge education you're getting working as a sweeper, and sweeper without pay at that, while your father's paying something exorbitant in fees. I fear this depression of yours will take a toll. Under special circumstances, they allow you to change your subject. How about it? How about giving yourself and Cambridge a chance, Mr Khan?'

Zia had switched off the moment Bowers turned his attention to him.

'I'm sorry, Mr Khan. I didn't mean to interfere. Do you have any idea what that painted cock is doing above the bishop's statue?'

Zia and Gordon Bowers had been sweeping outside the gate-tower of Jesus College. Bowers waited for an answer but Zia didn't even bother to look up and see what his companion was referring to. Bowers refused to take offence.

'That, my friend, is a bit of a visual pun. The founder's name was Bishop John Alcock and the cock in the golden orb above him is supposed to be, I wouldn't bet my life on it though, an allusion to the Bishop's surname. Did you know that Jesus College was where Laurence Sterne, the inspiration for your compatriot Salman Rushdie, studied? Coleridge was there too. John Milton studied under an old mulberry tree with beehives in the Fellows' Garden at Christ's College. John Harvard, the founder of Harvard College, studied at your college, Mr Khan.' Bowers was always spilling out the nuggets of information and trivia which he used to grab the attention of tourists.

Where the hell was Gordon Bowers? Zia stood at the Unversity Arms Hotel for a few more minutes and then walked over to Hobbs

Pavilion. Still no sign of the man. He walked back to the hotel and peered down Regent Terrace. Only in England would a straight road have three, four or five names. How could St Andrews Street be Hobson and Regent Streets within five minutes of each other and without a single turn to the left or right? There was Gordon next to the postbox. He must have been at work for at least ten minutes, he had already cleared quite a bit of Regent Street. What clean strokes; when he had finished sweeping, you could eat off the road.

'Good morning, Mr Khan. Bit of a nip in the air.'

How could you ever take these Brits seriously? The wind was bellowing and whooshing and bleating, trying to ruin all the work Bowers had already put in, scattering the piles of leaves that should have been standing like well-behaved yellow mini-mountains, and all he had to say was, a bit of a nip in the air.

Zia spotted a gold ring glinting in a pile soggy leaves and handed it to Bowers.

'Don't you ever look up, Mr Khan? Forget all the history, what about the present?'

'Don't see much point.'

'The present, the latest moment, freshly made by the good Lord himself, perfectly etched and in mint condition, is waiting to catch your attention, to entice you, to show you that cumulous cloud up there scudding through on an urgent appointment, challenging you to name the hundred and seven kinds of blue in the sky, to disagree with Wittgenstein, to improve upon Derrida, to compress the chip to a pinhead, to go punting on the Cam, to come home from a May ball in evening dress at dawn with a lady on your arm.

'Ah, look up, Mr Khan. Catch the moment and catch your life, lest it pass you by.'

Zia was not ungrateful for the interest Bowers took in him. Only if someone paid him attention could he be sure that he was alive. But there was no way he could respond. Bowers had not reported on Zia to anyone, for fear that the boy might end up doing himself harm. He merely asked him to look up, but Zia had lost the sky. And everything at and above eye-level. His world came into focus only when he looked down.

'Why don't you dump this work if you hate it so much?' Bowers asked him. 'You're not that penurious, are you?'

Dump the job? How could he? As long as he had it, he had every reason to catch up on sleep all day and not go to supervisions or lectures where he would have to study that most barren of subjects, pure maths.

Maths had been his lot since childhood. He had never been Zia Khan, but a genius, a child prodigy, the Little Miracle. He was going to be Newton II and he was going to solve Fermat's Last Theorem. The first few weeks at Cambridge, he'd attended lectures regularly. After that, try as he might, he couldn't. He had developed a pathological aversion to pure maths. It had not taken him long to discover that the only thing pure about pure maths was its self-absorption. It was sufficient unto itself. Nothing else mattered. Nothing else existed beyond its throttling confines. There was no point to it. None whatsoever.

Zia couldn't afford to give up his sweeping work. So long as he was a city sweeper, he could keep Cambridge and its education system at bay. The work was his lifeline; it was the only way he could carry on. It made no difference that he absolutely hated sweeping leaves.

'Does the wind get any colder in winter, Mr Bowers?'

'Only occasionally, but I assure you there are compensations. For one thing, the trees will have all shed their leaves soon and the roads will be much less work.'

Zia was taken aback by this news. He hadn't quite worked out that as a consequence of fall, winter would be bare.

'Tell me about this season, this wonderful thing called winter, Mr Bowers.'

A few weeks before the end of the summer term, Zia received a letter from the administrative office of Emmanuel. It was a notice asking him to explain why, in the light of his consistent absence from lectures and supervisions, his unwillingness to submit any work, and repeated warnings from the college authorities, he should be allowed to sit for his first-year exams. An appointment with the Master of Emmanuel in his office was fixed for 11.30 on the morning of the twenty-third of April. A copy of the letter was sent to Zia's guardian, Dr Antonia Booth-Langston. Zia held the piece of paper and stared at it incredulously. He could not believe his good luck. He kissed the paper as if it were a missive from the Prophet Himself. If he could have, he would have fallen on his knees, wept tears of joy and gone around Cambridge praising Allah for His great and all-encompassing mercy. He had not thought about what he would do once he had seen the Master and offered no explanation whatsoever, so that there would be no question of his staying on in Cambridge. Would he go back to India? How would he show his face to Ammijaan, Abba, Amanat and Zubeida Khaala? How would he look his father, and especially Amanat, in the eye when such huge sums of money had been spent on him to no purpose at all?

There was, of course, the minor problem of Aunt Antonia, that old family friend, Doctor of Theology, one of the most influential and respected academics in Cambridge, and Zia Khan's local guardian. She had written to Abba and Ammijaan when Zia had been accepted at Cambridge telling them that she would have liked Zia to stay at her place. It would have been a home to him and he would have had her daughter Vivian, who was close to him in age, as company. But since University rules forbade undergraduates to live outside college, at least for the first year, she would make it a point to have Zia over for meals as often as possible and to be with him whenever he needed her.

Antonia Booth-Langston was not one to shirk her duties. She had absolutely insisted that Zia spend weekends with her and her daughter, Vivian. He did go in the beginning, but his guardian's unflagging interest in him soon got him down.

'What's the maths faculty like?'

'Okay, I guess.'

'Can you follow what's going on in class?'

Zia nodded. It was an Indian nod. It could mean yes or no and sometimes both.

'I could talk to the head of the maths department, what's his name, Dr Pitt?'

'I'm okay, really. If I need help in some area, I'll let you know.'

'What are you studying just now?'

'Do you really want me to tell you, Aunt Antonia? It will all be Greek and Latin to you.'

'That should be no problem,' Aunt Antonia said tartly. 'I know both of them well.'

If the mother was difficult, Vivian was impossible. She had never been fun as a child when she visited India with her mother. Now she was sullen and utterly charmless. She had taken an instant dislike to Zia. Her mother seemed to be close to him and that was reason enough to hate him. When Antonia had asked her to show Zia around town or to take him with her to parties, she made it clear that he was a drag and she didn't fancy escorting him.

To Zia's relief, the Doctor of Theology was invited to take up a teaching engagement at Princeton for three months, upon which Zia's visits ceased overnight. When she came back, he refused to respond to her invitations. Aunt Antonia took it upon herself to call on him in his rooms. He was mostly not in, and if he happened to be there, he pretended he wasn't. Fortunately she was always short of time. She was one of the foremost authorities on the Early Christian Fathers and a Senior Fellow in the Faculty of Divinity. She was always speaking at theological conferences and seminars, and was the author of five books. But her first love, as Vivian said mockingly, was Jesus, and it was her vocation (again, quote Vivian) to light the lamp of God on the five continents. Now that a copy of the official letter from Emmanuel had been sent to her, Zia could expect the visits again. She was going to confront him and make his life difficult by asking all sorts of uncomfortable questions, but one thing he was sure of: she could do nothing because it was too late.

Too late, too late, too late, the joyous words pealed like an anthem of victory in his mind. How quickly the last twelve days had passed. The Doctor of Theology had come by thrice but luck had been on Zia's side. He had been out. She had left notes for him with the words 'Important', 'Urgent' and 'Extremely Urgent' written in a bold hand, warning him of the dire consequences that would follow if he did not keep his appointment with the Master of Emmanuel.

Zia was standing at the window when he saw his guardian making her way towards his room in South Court, the drab 1960s building about which everyone complained and felt sniffy, but which Zia hardly noticed. She had a murderous expression on her face, well, at least as close to murder as a practising Catholic and world-renowned Professor of Divinity could get. He still had two hours before his meeting with the Master of Emmanuel but he knew when he was beaten. Before Aunt Antonia could bludgeon him into submission, Zia thought it prudent to fly.

He could hear Aunt Antonia imperiously ordering his ghost to open the door as he raced on light feet to the terrace and escaped from the far end of the building.

There was no point wandering around. He might run into his guardian hound again, the redoubtable Booth-Langston. All he had to do was get the meeting with the Master of Emmanuel over and he would be through with Cambridge forever.

Damn, there was Gordon Bowers waving out to him from across the street. Don't, Gordon, don't call out my name. Just ignore me. I haven't seen you and you haven't seen me either. Just go away.

'Mr Khan, where have you been for the past week?'

A tourist bus came between Bowers and Zia. Bowers was still yelling.

Zia slipped into Christ's College, ran to the entrance of the nearest building and took the stairs in great, long strides. From the balcony on the first floor, he could see Bowers entering the building. A lecture was in progress in a classroom on the first floor. It was his only chance to escape his friend. He opened the door, God Almighty, what a mess he had landed himself in. Dr Michael Laughton looked up from the blackboard, where he had been writing an equation on the effects of market turbulence, and was on the verge of saying something withering, but restrained himself.

'Please take a seat, Khan. You are ten minutes late. Or are you an hour and twenty-five minutes early?'

Flight was no longer possible. The hall was full and Zia had to make his way to the back to get a seat. What was the Master of Emmanuel doing at Christ's College? And anyway, he thought Masters didn't usually lecture. Damn, how could he have forgotten that Dr Laughton was scheduled to give the Paul Samuelson Memorial Lecture this year? All Zia could think of was how he was going to get through the next hour and twenty-three, correction, twenty-two minutes. Laughton in class sounded, looked and was very different from Laughton at home reading the Riot Act to him in tones of barely veiled irritation. Zia had to admit he had an impressive, sonorous, old-world voice.

Laughton spoke in long, intricately crafted periods, balanced clause upon clause upon clause, and developed his argument in a magisterial series of complex propositions. It was incredible, the grand vistas and perspectives that he was opening up through his words. Slowly the complexion of the landscape changed from peace to war. All the markets of the world were embroiled in a hundred, a thousand battle-scenarios. One market force reacting to another and conflicting with the next. With the flick of a word or a sentence, Laughton was opening new fronts. There was the clash of titanic economies here and the muted, almost inaudible susurrus of tiny third-world monetary systems. Who would have thought of current world economics with its famines, capitalist greed, globalization and dying communist models as sheer nerve-rattling drama, a hundred times more gripping and breathtaking than any thriller? The Master of Emmanuel, it was clear, was an anachronism. His subject was statistics and yet he could only compute an economic or fiscal phenomenon in terms of its human cost.

'I'm going to end with a puzzle and not an inspiring peroration,' he said. 'Academic economics, despite all its talk to the contrary, is not interested in human suffering, or perhaps human happiness either. Often, it would seem, though there are worthy exceptions, its only interest is in the market.

'When you are lying on the beach on the Cote d'Azur or playing darts in a pub in Devon, you may want to ask yourself if it's possible that a micro-event far far away in a micro-country like Sierra Leone could bring about an upheaval, perhaps even a crash, on the major stock exchanges of the world. What kind of statistical model do you build to account for a reversal of fortunes where an inconsequential country can shake and unnerve the big brother economies?'

## 12

Zia did not turn up for his appointment with Dr Michael Laughton. Instead, he headed for his room. Edmond Drummer, Head Porter at Emmanuel, was waiting for him.

'I am sorry to inform you, Mr Khan, that you may find on your return to your room that you have been highly reduced in circumstance.' Drummer smirked happily. 'Your guardian, Dr Antonia Booth-Langston, has walked away with all your laundry, which I take to mean that you are left without any clothes. It showed a stout heart to enter your hole, but Dr Langston is a valiant lady. I have been told to direct you to her house on the chance you might show up who knows when.'

'I don't mean to be rude, but are you finished, Mr Drummer? Because I'm in a bit of hurry.'

'I'm sure you are, Mr Khan. I wouldn't dream of delaying your progress out of Emmanuel and the mother institution, Cambridge itself.'

'I'm much beholden to you.'

Zia went up to his room. Fortunately Aunt Antonia had not taken his notebooks, pens and library card to be washed along with the rest. He had planned to take a shower before going to the library, but what the hell, another fortnight of not bathing couldn't do his person or health any more damage than they had undergone already. And just in case he needed to buy anything, starting from underpants or whatever, he wasn't exactly badly off. He had saved most of his allowance for nearly a year.

Zia went to the library and stayed there. In the next nine days he returned to Emmanuel only to go to Hall for breakfast and dinner, or to his rooms to sleep, and that was because the library was not open all twenty-four hours.

'Oh, it's you,' the secretary to the Master of Emmanuel said to Zia when he introduced himself. 'I'm afraid you are ten days too late. I was just typing out a letter to you.'

'Would you give these papers to Dr Laughton?'

'Perhaps I have not made myself clear. As far as we are concerned, you are a closed chapter. Now if you'll allow me to get back to my work.'

'I think he may find them amusing, perhaps even interesting.'

'When he wants to be amused, Mr Khan, he goes to the cinema or reads *Gargantua and Pantagruel*.'

'I'm sure you are right, but will you give him the papers nevertheless? Let him decide whether he wants to read them or not.'

Zia showered for an hour and a half, and got into the clothes he had picked up at Arthur Shepherd's: a pin-striped three-piece Barbour suit in charcoal grey and a Pringle cashmere pullover. The clothes were not his style, that's if you had known him at New Eden or even as a child. He'd liked strong colours then, and had dressed flamboyantly; but he would now find it difficult to get back to those clothes. He felt different. He understood why most religions had the concept of a second birth, when a child's mind was formed and he had reached a certain stage of understanding and self-awareness. It was a break with the past, a coming into your own, into adulthood.

For as long as he could remember, he had mouthed the first lines of the Koran without having a clue to what they meant. Now the truth of the words struck him and his heart was filled with gratitude. Allah was indeed merciful and compassionate. He had given Zia a second life. Inshallah, he would prove himself worthy.

He caught the train to Peterborough and went to the Abubakr Siddiq Islamic Centre and Mosque on Mawson Road. He had no idea what had made him forsake his God. No, that was not true, the act of forsaking is a conscious decision. However terrible, it still has the merit of involvement of the self, of a willing, of leading your life where you want it to go. What he had done was infinitely and unforgivably worse. He had let go of Allah. He had forgotten Him. Yes, he, Zia Khan, had done the unthinkable: he had turned his back on Allah. And look what had happened to him. He was less than the lowliest creature that crawls the earth. For six months, he had been at sea, tossed and driven to desperation. He'd been barely aware of himself or the world without. He had sunk into an abyss of loneliness and depression from which he had never expected to climb back. He had forgotten God, but praise be to Allah, Allah had not forgotten him.

He prostrated himself in the house of God. Allahu Akbar, Allahu Akbar. God is great, God is great, he spoke the words of the azan. I bear witness that there is no God but Allah. I bear witness that Mohammed is His Messenger. Come for prayers. Come towards fulfilment. God is great, God is great.

What wonderful words they were. What is the mystery, the magic and the power of words? How can mere words be so potent and healing? It occurred to Zia with a terrible sense of urgency that mankind had lost sight of the Word. How we abuse and debase this greatest gift of God, this instrument with which we explore and unravel the universe, ourselves and even God Himself. The Word is the mother of all inventions. The wheel, the zero, the steam engine, the computer, penicillin, they are all the prodigious miracles of the Word. In the beginning was the Word. Would the end too be a word? And what word would that be? Would it be a joyous word or one that destroyed? Is a wordless world happiness or terror? He realized that he was being silly. He was trying to negotiate the absence of words, the primordial silence, with words. Perhaps that's what death was.

Zia had read the Koran in English many times. He never ceased to marvel at how such a small book managed to encompass all of life for all time. And yet he knew that the Koran he read was not the Word of God. For the Word of God was in Arabic, and any translation, however literal, was at best an attenuation of God's voice, and however well-meaning, a tampering with the Word.

He spoke to the maulana at the makeshift mosque near Cambridge railway station. Maulana Rizvi had come recently from Pakistan on a tourist visa. He was barely thirty, but his azan, learning and enunciation of the Word had already earned him the reputation of being one of the most inspired teachers of Islam. The maulana interviewed Zia for an hour. Zia, he realized, might be brash, but he was also blessed with humility. He promised to teach Zia the Koran in Arabic.

Zia was sitting at his table reading *Challenges of the Marketplace* when there was a light tapping on the door and the author of the book he was reading walked in.

The Master pulled up a chair next to Zia.

'I'll get directly to the point. You have disregarded the rules of the University. You have neither been regular in your supervisions, nor have you done any work. Nor have you participated in the academic or social life of this community. You turned up ten days late for your appointment with me, and then left a folder of seventy pages with my secretary with the instruction that I might find it edifying to labour through them.

'I've spent a good part of the day, against my better judgement, trying to make sense of the half-baked, undigested and occasionally bizarre theories you outline in your monograph on the three statistical models. The absence of logical development is breathtaking. Is it intellectual temerity, I keep asking myself, or sheer ignorance of basic economic principles that made you attempt on a wing and half a prayer, a new paradigm for the dynamics of market economics?

'You've tried my patience, Khan, and I've run out of it.'

'I understand, Dr Laughton,' Zia spoke softly. 'I'm sorry that I put you in such an untenable position. If you will give me till the end of this week, I will vacate my rooms, sign the forms and complete all the formalities necessary to leaving Emmanuel.'

'Kindly hear me out, Khan, without interrupting me.' Dr Laughton seemed weary but he had come to some kind of decision. 'Am I to understand that you wish to abandon your studies in maths and move to economics?'

'That is what I would have liked to do. I may be naturally good at pure maths but I find it pointless. Till I attended your lecture by accident, I didn't know how exciting statistical modelling can be when applied to economics.'

'If, on the basis of your ridiculous monograph, I organize for you to switch to economics next year, will you give me your word that from now on you'll attend supervisions regularly, that you'll do all your work, and that you'll turn up for your maths exams and get a bloody first?'

# 13

It took Zia two days to clean his room. Airing it proved more difficult. It had the unwashed smell of waiting rooms at railway stations or Salvation Army dormitories. It seemed odd that he hadn't asphyxiated himself with his own malodour. He had the carpet shampooed at his own expense, kept the windows open, and the rain flat-angled like a frisbee across his bed and on to his writing table, but there was no getting rid of the armpit odours. He had tried every air-freshener available at the local Boots but nothing seemed to work.

When he thought his room was habitable, at least to the point where he didn't gag, Zia looked at some of the mail he had tossed on his table all these months. He had been wrong about Roy Cambray.

It looked as though he was stuck with him even though he lived on another continent.

Dear Zia,

Am having a great time here in Harvard though I sometimes forget that I have been given admission to this place to play football and not rugby.

What's up with you? Have you been punting and playing cricket or are you up to your eyeballs in work?

I hope you will visit me soon. I could easily transfer my frequent-flyer miles to you. My parents are rarely in New York and we could get down to some serious fun.

Why don't you write to me once in a while? If I don't get an answer to this letter, beware, you might force me to come over and straighten you out.

Amanat wrote last week. He's started getting the odd design assignment. We should go down and see him. I miss being at Suleiman Mansion.

Roy

Zia stepped into the Porter's Lodge to check whether Dr Riemenschneider had left a message confirming tomorrow's supervision, and stepped right out again when he saw Aunt Antonia sitting on a bench in the corner. His instant reaction was to take off, when he asked himself why he would want to run away from her now. Her head was bent down and her chin dug deep into her chest. You could never call Aunt Antonia frail, but she looked as though she was about to crumple up like one of the ancient parchments she so often studied. Zia was relieved that she had not noticed him trying to make a quick getaway. She looked up as he went over to say hello.

'How are you, Aunt Antonia?'

'I want to have a word with you.'

Nothing had changed. He should have known better. Aunt Antonia was not about to let him off that easily for his unforgivable behaviour.

'Shall we go to my room?'

Zia was not sure she had registered his words. She appeared to be troubled by something and started walking towards the stairs. He squared his shoulders and followed her to his room. She was entitled to a temper tantrum and it was best to get it over with.

'How can love be so blind that it believes it knows best what's good for others?' She went and sat on the bed, though Zia had pulled out a chair for her. 'I was so sure pure maths was your vocation, and I wasn't prepared to listen, though there was no dearth of signs that you would rather be doing something else. What would you have done if you had been sent down from Cambridge in disgrace? Maybe you would have given up studies altogether, taken to drugs. Who knows? All because of my blasted self-righteousness. How can I ever forgive myself?'

It was as though she had been talking to herself and she was wrung out by the enormity of her hubris and the havoc it had nearly wrought. Zia could no longer dislike her, hate was perhaps the more precise word for his former feelings, and he wanted to make peace.

'You are being far too harsh on yourself,' he told her.

She shook her head. 'There's no room for kindness here. The truth is, that was my conviction and you would have had to suffer the consequences.'

'I had no idea what I wanted to read instead of maths, either. It was the hand of Allah that led me to Dr Laughton's lecture that day.'

Aunt Antonia made the sign of the cross. 'Little Miracle, if you only knew how good the Lord has been to you and me.'

She got up and put a key ring with a couple of keys on it on his writing table. 'These are for the front door to the house. You don't have to come, but if you feel like it, the room next to Vivian's is yours.'

Abbajaan wrote to Zia every week and gave him news of the family. They were affectionate letters and full of good cheer. Sometimes he made wry comments about the art scene in Bombay or talked about some quaint building he had seen on his way to work. Once he wrote an impromptu monograph on Christopher Wren's chapel at Pembroke. He had an amazing memory – how many years was it since he had visited Cambridge? – and he could remember niches and gables and cornices and would sketch them to make a point. There was rarely anything overtly emotional in Abba's letters and yet when Zia got around to reading them, he felt a closeness to his father that he had not experienced when he was at school.

There was always a paragraph in Abba's letters about Ammijaan and a line about Zubeida Khaala. Zubeida now spent half the day in the mosque and the other half at home, praying or gazing at the pictures of her actor from a scrapbook. She herself wrote the same letter once a month, regardless of what month it was.

My dear Zia,

How are you, my child? Are you wearing enough sweaters and woollen underwear and keeping warm? They say now there's something called thermal underwear. It is like a sheath of heat against your body. Go to a shop and buy one. No, buy two. One you can wash and the other you will wear.

Are you praying, my little boy? Pray five times a day and Allah will keep you out of harm's way. Are you going to the mosque on Fridays? Make friends with the mullah. And read the Koran every day. It cleanses your soul.

I am well. Look after yourself.

Love,

Zubeida Khaala

P.S. Ammijaan sends you her love.

Ammijaan wrote only once in a while. She said she wanted to write every week but what was the point since Abbajaan would have given Zia all the news anyway. She was going to write him a long letter one of these days telling him about all the ladies from the club who had wanted to marry him when he was a child because he was so good looking. But right now she was in a hurry because she had to get to the club. Take care, Zia, don't get engaged to all the girls in Cambridge simultaneously.

Amanat's missives, as usual, were something of a conundrum. Zia couldn't tell what they were about. He didn't even know if they could be called letters; more like essays, stray thoughts and miscellaneous jottings. They could be short or they could be extended monologues. Often there was no logical progression from one point to the next, and if you weren't used to the switches, you could get lost or lose patience. The only good thing about them was that Amanat did not usually expect a reply.

A couple of weeks later Zia decided to take up Aunt Antonia's offer, more as a way of showing her that he bore her no animus than to establish a base in her home. At the last minute he thought he should take something along as a peace offering. Flowers, of course, were out – they reminded him of his days as a sweeper. He could have taken a bottle of Scotch but he knew Aunt Antonia didn't drink. He went to Heffers and got her a book.

'For me?' Aunt Antonia seemed as surprised as she was pleased. 'What is it?'

She lifted the glossy blue rosette the saleswoman had stuck at the corner, and then carefully peeled the three bits of transparent tape so that the wrapping paper was undamaged. She smiled sheepishly when she caught Zia staring at her folding the paper neatly.

'The children in the orphanages in Johannesburg, or anywhere else for that matter, think the wrapping paper is the gift. *Indian Cooking in 30 Minutes Flat*, what a marvellous idea. Maybe one of these days I'll cook you a lovely Indian meal.'

'That'll be the day,' Vivian said derisively. 'So far Mum's cooking skills extend from half-cooked spaghetti to burnt shepherd's pie.'

'That's not true, Vivian.' It was odd to hear Aunt Antonia pleading for her daughter's approval. 'I make a nice couscous, you said so yourself yesterday, and last Christmas everybody complimented me on the turkey.'

'Don't tell me you actually believed them, Mother.'

Zia could see that Vivian was in fine fettle. 'I rather like Aunt Antonia's shepherd's pie,' he said.

'You make a fine lackey, Zia.' Vivian turned her attention to him. 'No wonder Mum loves you as if you were her own son.'

Over the next few months Zia would get the hang of how to handle this moody creature. Ignore her, stay out of her way, do not under any circumstances show any interest in her. Vivian's bite was worse than her bark. He had often been its victim, almost always unprovoked. In one thing and one thing alone Zia sympathized with her. She was doing a degree in physics but she seemed to rival Zia's former inertia. Something was amiss, something had gone wrong a long time ago with Vivian. Zia did not know what it was and he had no interest in it either.

Cambray Park, 'the Park' to family members, was an hour's drive from Cambridge. Zia did not know what to expect of the place. Did the Cambrays own something like Dunrobin Castle? Was it on the lines of the English Garden in Munich? The Georgian house was imposing in its isolation and yet had a friendly air once you got to know it from the inside. There were portraits of Roy's ancestors everywhere, along with Turners and a not insubstantial collection of post-impressionists, besides contemporary art. Zia's room was on the second floor and he had a fairly good view of the Cambray estate. He didn't like what he saw: trees and more trees, followed by more trees, until the eye finally gave up looking for the horizon.

'I thought you said the Cambrays lost all their land and money in the thirties.'

Zia and Roy were taking what Roy called a walk, one of those English euphemisms for trudging cross-country and not stopping till you dropped dead.

'Not all, just half.'

'If this is penury, may all the wretched of the earth suffer from it.'

'My father's been working at reviving the Cambray fortunes since he left the diplomatic service.'

'What does he do?'

'Oh, this and that.'

'Maybe he could teach me "this and that",' Zia suggested.

'Maybe he will one of these days,' said Roy but he went no further, apparently disinclined to discuss the subject.

Zia lay inert on the lawns in the Park. The green pile was seventy feet deep and he was suspended in the middle. Zia was sure it had been fed on anabolic steroids of the kind that Olympic athletes take on the sly. Each blade was fat with sap and had been polished and waxed till it looked as though it had been trucked out of Madame Tussaud's.

He fought against the pull and suction of the grass and turned on his side exhausted. The Georgian house looked two-dimensional, as in a Kangra miniature. He must ask Roy which George the Georgian referred to, perhaps the one who peed purple and went mad. Mrs Cambray was standing as still as a leafless tree in winter, framed in the white window of her bedroom. For a moment Zia wondered if she was staring at him, but she had no inkling that he was beached on the lawns without the energy or breath to call for help.

Deirdre was an event. She and her diplomat-husband would arrive at Zia's school like royalty. They never came by themselves. There was always some celebrity musician, physicist or high-flying banker with them. They came bearing gifts for the school, the teachers, the headmaster and Roy's close friends like Zia.

Deirdre was one of those artists whose persona had outstripped her promise. She had been touted as a prima ballerina in the making. She possessed, the critics had said, the technical virtuosity of Pavlova, Dame Margot Fonteyn's grace and an understanding of the irrational workings of the human mind, not to mention an emotional charge all her own. People talked of an electric blue glow emanating from her. Often it seemed that with the intensity of her portrayal of Giselle or Eurydice she would burn out in front of the audience in a fiery nebula. Her finest moment had come when Bob Fosse choreographed her as the Virgin Mary. Audiences had wept when Deirdre clutched the dead Saviour in her arms, rocking silently till the curtain came down.

Deirdre never did manage to catch fire thereafter. What had gone wrong? Did her creative springs run dry, or did the brilliance of her talent consume the dancer? Perhaps her finest moment had really been her marriage to James Cambray. Deirdre's legend could only grow once her career had been nipped so prematurely in the bud.

Sometimes Zia thought that Roy would have liked to disown his parents. Frankly, he looked so unlike them, it wouldn't have been hard to imagine that they were unrelated. Perhaps he was really an adopted child. Roy's father, James Cambray, was barely five feet four. He had a cherubic face, and like many a compulsively gregarious person, it was impossible to get close to him. As to the mother, she had the figure of a waif, and the contours of her face were sharply etched, but there was something regal about her. Or maybe it was the fact that she was so often in the gaze of the camera that made her every gesture as studied and slow as an opium-eater's.

Roy, by contrast, was six feet one and had an athlete's body ready to spring into action without notice. He fought shy of any kind of attention and was at his ease only on the field in the midst of ten other football players from his team. He liked Zia because Zia had no interest in his parents or their fancy friends.

Where was Roy anyway? He should have got back from his game of tennis, squash or the seventy miles he seemed to run every day to keep himself in shape. Zia looked at the bedroom window again. Deirdre was still ethereal and distant but the Virgin mouth had become tight and she had the look of a trapped animal.

Zia had seen that look in her eyes when the Cambrays had swept into New Eden a couple of years before he graduated. They were accompanied by a guru of sorts who wore a lungi, a long white kurta, and had an angavastram thrown around his neck. On his forehead were drawn the three horizontal ashen lines of a Shiva devotee. He was six foot three or four and towered over the landscape like some fake Godzilla. He had large eyes and you were never quite sure whether he was looking past you beyond the horizon or staring into the darkest secrets of your soul. But it was his lips that seemed to have a life of their own. They were a livid pink and resembled nothing so much as a woman's genitalia.

What had Deirdre been doing with the Neanderthal man? She'd seemed to fear him and yet was in his thrall. It was as though she had become a marionette and he could pull her any way he wanted.

Then something strange had happened. The man had walked over to Zia and had placed a hand on his shoulder. Zia had wanted to grab the hand, rip the arm off and fling it into one of the coffee estates a couple of hundred miles away. But he'd been unable to move, aware that the holy man was enjoying his discomfiture.

'So you are the one who wants to save the world?' He said the words so softly, Zia wasn't sure he had spoken. 'The question is, young man, who's going to save the world from you?'

James Cambray's car slithered past soundlessly and came to a halt. Zia looked up. Deirdre had stepped back from the window into the shadows but not soon enough.

'Deirdre,' James Cambray called out to her softly as the chauffeur opened the door.

Silence. Cambray Senior waited for a minute and then called out again without raising his voice. 'I know you are still there, Deirdre.'

Deirdre appeared at the window, her eyes glittering and her mouth ajar with a stiff, synthetic smile.

'You've been drinking,' James said, shaking his head sadly.

'No, I haven't. I was sleeping.'

'I thought you would be dressed and ready by now.'

'I'm running the water for a long hot bath. Come and join me.'

'We have to go for dinner.'

'No, we don't.'

'This is business, Deirdre.' A note of pleading had crept into James's voice.

'Everything's business for you and I hate business.'

Zia sensed he was no longer alone. Roy was standing at the edge of the lawns where the ground dipped steeply and the wood started. He was gazing intently at his mother and father, unaware that Zia was around.

'I know, darling, but some things leave us no choice. We have to do them whether we like it or not.'

'How much time do I have?'

'Fifteen minutes, twenty at the outside.'

'Half an hour.'

'I'll get ready and call the ambassador. I'll tell him we're caught in a traffic jam.'

'I hear Dr Laughton has asked you to help with the new book that he's writing on three-dimensional statistical modelling,' Aunt Antonia said, as she, Vivian and Zia played Scrabble one evening.

Where, he wondered, does Aunt Antonia get all this gossip from? How and when does she find the time? She worked till twelve or one at night and was up by six; she was forever consulting some nineteen-hundred-year-old scrap of papyrus, researching the minutes of the Second Ecumenical Council, or preparing for her lectures and her speaking engagements; and during vacations and sabbaticals, trying to bring God, education and medical care to the tribes of darkest Africa and the natives of Asia and Latin America. And yet she always had the latest titbit on the bureaucratic wrangles between the town and the University; on the feisty, petty and deadly manoeuvring for grants and research scholarships; on breaking news about the cuts the government was instituting in grants to the humanities department.

'Nothing of any consequence really. Something like proofreading,' said Zia.

Vivian was looking glassily at the Scrabble board and every now and then lifting those demon-eyes to give him a comprehensive once-over.

'Modesty, I'll grant you, is a fine quality, Zia, but not at the cost of the truth. Some of the more intricate or, as you people say, far-out variations are yours, I believe.'

Couldn't be Dr Laughton slopping this information all over the Doctor of Divinity since he had been out of town for ten days now. Must be Riemenschneider, his economics tutor. Or Edmund Drummer, Head Porter, who had undergone a radical change of heart. He was now a born-again Zia fanatic. His evangelical zeal for Mr Khan often bordered on sycophancy. Zia could just hear him laying it on thick.

'Finished a year's economics in two months flat and is now helping the Master with his book. Just outstanding. Going to make a name for Emmanuel, that boy.'

'Ugh. I could puke,' Vivian muttered.

'Pregnant again, dear?' Zia whispered.

Vivian got up and left.

Zia prayed five times a day. If he was out and unable to keep his prayer timings, he asked God's forgiveness and prayed when he returned to his room or whenever he got a bit of privacy. He went to the mosque in Cambridge every Friday but it was cramped, and on sacred days and other important occasions, he preferred going to the Peterborough mosque. Whenever he thought of Allah, there were tears in his eyes. Zia Khan had been reborn because Allah had picked up a foolish and erring man and given him a second chance. The Master of Emmanuel was of course right. Zia had had a smattering of economics and it had only been a dilettante's rashness that led him to write the seventy-page disquisition that he could now see was mostly incomprehensible gibberish. He would have to work long, hard hours merely to come level with the other students. But there was something more, something far more relevant. He had got a taste of that hybrid creature called statistical economics and he was hooked. He wanted to study every moment he could. He wished to get the basics right quickly, so he could take off on his own and explore this new world of numbers attached to reality.

Zia wanted to show Allah that he would do anything, absolutely anything to be worthy of Him. 'Give me a sign, oh Lord of Creation, give me a sign. Ask any sacrifice, be it my life, and I will not hesitate to lay it down for you.'

He liked going to the Peterborough mosque even though it was far away. He would wait there after prayers when it grew quiet, and he seemed to feel the presence of the Almighty almost physically. He stayed on folded knees for half an hour, sometimes an hour, at times even longer.

There was one memorable occasion at Peterborough when a group of qawwals from Lucknow called Ghulam-e-Allah sang in the courtyard. They looked almost like Indian villagers who had turned up on the wrong continent. They cleared their throats endlessly and the leader told the audience about all the places they had visited on their way to England. He cited the names of patrons in Nairobi, Dar-es-Salaam and Cape Town as though everybody was familiar with them, and quoted the wonderful things they had said about his troupe.

It was a summer night and the moon cast the singers and the accompanists in sterling silver. They seemed unreal, frieze-like. But then they started singing and it was clear that these were simple, artless folk who, when they narrated all the wonderful things that were said about them in Africa or elsewhere, were really praising Allah. Their voices and their song were the bounty of Allah.

As always, it took a few minutes for Zia to adjust to the words and the intonation, not because they spoke an alien language or their accent was unfamiliar, but because these were passionate love songs. The lovers would vault over stone walls, break down doors, brook no opposition from their parents, their village elders or even the king. They would walk the desert, they would trudge through the snow, they would drink themselves to oblivion, they would cheat and kill and break their word, make friends with their enemies, all to get a glimpse of their beloved. It should have sounded banal, instead it sounded worshipful and ecstatic. For who else was the beloved but God Himself?

The mosque in Peterborough proved to be a propitious discovery in other ways too. Zia met various people there, some of them expatriate Indian industrialists and entrepreneurs from African countries who had been kicked out overnight by one dictator or another and had had to make a fresh start in England. They set up new lines of business, worked twice as hard as before, and were in a hurry to make good in their new adopted country. Zia was soon doing their books and advising them on how to raise capital and manage their funds. He made a fair amount of money himself, though it was a pittance compared to what he could have earned if he had had a work permit.

He wrote to Amanat telling him he would pay his tuition fees if he came to London and joined Abba's architecture school. Amanat said that he was overwhelmed by Zia's generous offer but he'd been done with the subject since the day Abbajaan's licence was revoked.

As in New Eden, Zia routinely assisted any of his fellow-students who had difficulties in the maths course. He didn't stop there though. If one of the foreign students was having trouble paying tuition fees, Zia would help out. Now on weekends he also gave free maths classes in the Peterborough mosque for the children of the congregation.

## 14

Zia rang the bell, and when no one answered, opened the door with his key. Aunt Antonia was bound to be back any minute. Vivian, on the other hand, had probably fled when she heard that they were having company. He lay down on the sofa in the drawing room and picked up the book of physics lying on the floor. It had big, small and medium question marks like hot-air balloons drawn all down the margins and even on the body of the text. Wherever there were problems and equations to be solved, the question marks were grouped in clusters or stood in long queues. The equations were not very difficult and Zia amused himself working them out. He was half way through when Vivian snatched the book from his hands.

'I didn't know you were at home.' Zia looked at her in surprise.

'I didn't know you were at home either. But of course the keys of the kingdom have been given to the Prince of Khan.'

She stood with her left arm bent at the elbow, hand on hip, and her chin thrust forward. She must have been playing darts in her room for she had three feathered missiles in her right palm. Little wonder physics had no interest for her, her vocation was darts. She played darts in her room, she played darts at the pub, and when she was bored, she cleaned her fingernails with them.

For the first time, Zia noticed her arms. They were black and blotchy, and in places the skin was riddled with pus. He realized she usually wore long-sleeved shirts.

'Never seen white female flesh?' she flared up again.

'Please, Vivian.' Zia thought it wise to scotch the possibility of an outburst.

The phone rang but neither moved. The answering machine came on and Aunt Antonia's voice said that she was held up at a meeting but would try to hurry back. In the meantime they were to have dinner.

'So now we are feeling superior to the dumb white blond?'

'Vivian, I can help you...'

'Don't you dare patronize me.' She covered the scars with the palms of her hands. 'What I do with my body and myself is my business. You can try your Good Samaritan stuff on someone else.'

'Will you hear me out? I can help you with the maths in the physics. There's nothing to it. Once you get the hang of it, you'll solve the problems with your eyes closed.'

'Why don't you shove it?'

Zia wanted to tell Vivian to be a little more innovative with her language. But he knew better; his crisis-management skills were singularly inadequate. He would have an international fracas on his hands unless he retrieved the situation fast. He dipped into his backpack and brought out the box of Godiva pralines that Mrs Laughton had given him that afternoon for assisting her husband with some work he was doing for the UN. Anything, absolutely anything, for a bit of peace with Vivian, and besides, he hated pralines.

'I have a little present for you.' Zia smiled his most practised, impossible-to-tell-from-the-real-thing simulation of a disarming smile, and offered her the chocolates.

Vivian stretched her hand out, vacillated and snatched the box.

'It's always Zia this and Zia that,' Vivian began to yell hysterically. 'Look how well Zia's doing in school. He's a mathematical genius.

Absolutely unbelievable the confidence with which he held his own against Noodle or Poodle Devi, beat her at her own game and then generously allowed her to win at the very end.'

Zia laughed. 'Come off it, Vivian. Stop exaggerating.'

But nothing could staunch the flow of Vivian's wrath.

'Even when you were behaving like a moron, stinking up the whole of Cambridge with your unwashed armpits and your unbathed crotch, we didn't give up on you. Just a passing phase, it will pass. This, even as you were about to be thrown out of the country.

'And now that the prodigal has returned, oh, what joy, the bells in heaven are pealing, the angels are singing dithyrambic paeans, and glory of glories, if further proof of a miracle was needed, gee whiz, the light of God has shone upon the boy, he is assisting the Master of Emmanuel. Soon he'll be called to the IMF, UNESCO or some other hallowed congregation of men. Oh, he is the shining light and he is going to lead the multitudes to the promised land, hallelujah, hallelujah.'

Zia looked at the swollen green veins of her vocal cords. It would do the world and him a whole lot of good, he thought, if he were to put his hands around her throat and strangle her.

It was obvious Vivian needed help. She was forever trying to get attention any which way she could. For all he knew, her drug habit, her strange friends whom she never brought home, her indifference to her studies, her temper and her tantrums were merely ways to make herself more interesting. Her sense of persecution and neglect were monumental.

The Doctor of Divinity too was a bit of a puzzle. When you care about the whole world and want to do nothing less than save mankind for Jesus, a few individuals including your daughter, may end up getting short shrift. That was understandable. But it would always remain a mystery to him why Antonia Booth-Langston held him up as the exemplar Vivian was supposed to imitate, and used him as the stick with which she was goaded.

Zia settled down at the original Queen Anne bureau in his room at Aunt Antonia's and worked for an hour and a half. It was then time for afternoon prayers. He cleansed himself meticulously, washing his hands thrice, his mouth thrice, the nostrils twice, the face from ear to ear thrice, the right and then the left arm thrice, passing his wet hands over the head, ears, neck, and finally washing his ankles and feet thrice. He unrolled his prayer rug, faced the Kaaba and proclaimed his intention to pray and the number of prayers he would say.

'Allah is the greatest. All glory be to Thee, oh Allah; and praise be to Thee; blessed is Thy name and exalted is Thy majesty and there is none worthy of worship beside Thee. I betake myself to Allah for refuge from the accursed Satan. In the name of Allah, most gracious, most merciful.'

These days, almost as soon as he started to recite his prayers, something happened to Zia. He had the palpable feeling that the world was falling away from him, that he was abandoned and at the mercy of Allah. No one could rescue him except God. His words would become more and more frantic. But there were also times when the prayers made him giddy with joy. He wanted to do things for Allah, to show Him how madly he loved Him; his eyes, ears, all his senses he dedicated to God; his body, spirit and soul were Allah's; every act and action of his was a votive offering to the One and Only.

'Make me worthy, oh Lord. Make demands on me. Make impossible demands on me. Test me, oh Lord. Try me. Just give me a sign. Reveal to me the task You've chosen me for.'

Then suddenly Zia felt the hand of Allah on his head. It was as though he could hear the Almighty talking to him: 'Have you not knocked on my door day in and day out and asked me to give you a sign? Have you not begged me to entrust you with a task, however impossible? Now go, my son, and defend the honour of your God.'

Zia, brother mine,

If you are early enough, sometimes you can get the pool all to yourself. The water looked black and cold. I thought a few quick laps would get my circulation going and plunged in. There was a fizz to the water, more like the light stinging of ants, which was bracing, and my stroke was soon fluid as a wave rising and falling. What a misnomer the word 'crawl' is. It completely misses out on the speed and grace of the stroke.

My body had become the perfect machine. The feet drummed the water into a fine, shallow spray, the right arm spanned the air like a leaping dolphin, plunged deep and swept the water back, while the face turned sideways to the right a little above the water and quaffed the air.

I had been doing a steady five miles an hour for fifteen minutes when I winced in pain. I thought it was the swimmer's ancient nemesis, a cramp, but was relieved to find it wasn't. A crab, or perhaps it was an angry lobster, had sunk its claws in my thigh and wouldn't let go. Soon the water was crawling with creatures. They came in all sizes, miniature, minor, medium, large and extra-large. A cockroach-like bug was sidling up my face, its whiskers swivelling like nervous antennae near my nose. I wanted to slap it dead but the prospect of its white squishy innards spilling out gave me pause. I tried to flick it away but it had already slipped through and was tiptoeing down my throat. Vomit rose like a full tide but that didn't seem to deter the roach. It carried on downwards into my belly.

Where had all these creepy-crawlies come from? The pool was crammed with them now and there were thousands more sliding in. I stretched my hand and scooped up a fistful. They were restless and vicious. I brought my palm closer to get a better look at them and relaxed. What I saw were not worms and insects and primordial beasts from a cheap horror movie, but words, hordes of them. I knew them. They were my daily companions. I waved out to them excitedly but they seemed to be overcome by a strange lasciviousness. Their fine aristocratic features had coarsened and they seemed to be in an ugly mood. They snapped at each other and got progressively more belligerent. I hollered to them again and this time there was a response. 'Torpor', 'lupine' and 'distemper' looked at me venomously and shoved two fingers in the air.

'Uliginous' was tottering drunkenly over the tip of my index finger while 'intimidate' slashed my left eye. 'Lubricious' lolled on its back while the mast of its 'b' stuck out like a hard-on. An altercation was brewing between 'brio' and 'hubris' but I paid little heed to it. How come after looking it up an endless number of times, I wondered, I still couldn't remember whether that word 'jejune' sitting like a wet slug on my tongue meant dull or youthful?

Catalyst, carbon, monochrome, louche, necrophilia, blister, plodding, puerile, pugnacious, pococurante, xylophone, sanguine, gregarious, teleological and their innumerable companions swarmed threateningly all over me in Century Bold, Times Roman, Garamond, Futura, Bodoni, Melior and Antique. Serifs and sans serifs appeared to be ranged against each other for the final Armageddon, but I was distracted by the tableaux in my peripheral vision. 'Decorous' was perched on my shoulder, her lips pressed primly and her legs crossed over, how else but decorously, and she was doing her best to keep her distance from 'love'. 'Love' had her black patent-leather mini hitched up so I could see the colour of her panties, and the laces of her red bodice were untied casually to reveal her fulsome but sagging breasts. Her lower lip was caught between her teeth and she was gesturing to me to follow her. At last I had found someone who was willing to acknowledge my presence. I smiled and crossed over hoping to negotiate the price of a night with her. She kissed me with her wet tongue. I saw something glint in the lurid lamplight and then the blade in her hand unzipped my belly and my small intestines unravelled.

'Don't you recognize me?' I asked incredulously. 'We are, we are…'

'Sure, I remember you, honey. We are lovers, right?' she replied. 'I'm the one you want to fuck every night.' She smiled then. 'I've offended you with that word. But that's what I do for a living.'

I keeled over and my head hit the stone pavement. Her hand was in my pocket and she was counting the notes in my wallet. The others had smelt blood and were gnashing and sharpening their teeth. I could hear the cornea of my right eye pop and my nostrils had been eaten through till the bone lay exposed. I hollered for help. It was no use. They had clogged my larynx solid.

Words are the only friends I've ever had and now they had turned against me. Was I grieving their betrayal or my inability to make friends with them?

'You are my friends,' I tried to tell them, 'the only ones I've ever had.' But they were not listening. Perhaps words have sounds and meanings but are otherwise deaf. They were piranhas and they would not rest till they had picked me clean.

How are you, Zia? We wait for news of you weekly, if not daily. Ammi, Abba and Zubeida Khaala read and reread your letters so often, I suspect they know them by heart.

Do write.

Love,

Amanat

# 15

Months had passed and he had not yet accomplished the one task Allah had set for him.

'Do not, oh Lord, do not think for a minute that because so much time has gone by, I have forgotten You or that it is not my intent to carry out Your orders. I give You my word, Lord of all the worlds, that, come what may, I will accomplish my mission. But I beg Your patience. The beast has gone underground. Nobody knows its whereabouts. All the heathens and disbelievers of the world have conspired to throw a smoke screen around it. Let them do what they will to protect it but with Your help and guidance, I will locate this evil and annihilate it.

'Look at the map on the wall. Not only London, the whole of Britain is constantly under surveillance. Like Zubeida Khaala, I too have a scrapbook now. Whatever the beast does is covered extensively in the media. I cull every bit of news and gossip and stick it in the scrapbook. I can draw a far more detailed and precise portrait of the beast and its psychographics than Scotland Yard can.

'I've cast myself adrift and entered the soul of the beast. The whole enterprise has been fraught with danger and I have feared that in penetrating its lair, I may lose my own soul. But as long as You are my witness and my guardian, I'm safe and I have nothing to fear. I'm beginning to understand this creature; its rhythms and predilections; its favourite haunts and its need to surface for air, for company and for public approbation; and, most of all, its relentless and inexhaustible yearning for an audience, for continuous applause and for the glare of centre-stage. The beast is an exhibitionist. It needs to expose itself constantly. If even a week passes when it thinks that the world has ignored it or has developed fatigue from overexposure, it will raise the stakes and make some highly provocative statement, beat the tom-toms and sing its song: don't forget me, don't forget me, me, me, me, me, me, me. It is this addiction, this need for attention, that is our most reliable ally. In the end, that is what will give the game away and lead us to it. Slowly, but surely, a pattern of its movements is emerging. Soon a time will come when I'll be able to tell intuitively when and where it's going to show up. I will not disappoint You, Allah.'

Zia had knelt and touched the ground with his forehead when he sensed that someone else was in the room. Not likely. He would have heard if the door had been opened. All the same, he knew that his privacy had been invaded. He opened his left eye a tiny bit and saw Vivian mimicking him. When he stood up, she got up; as he bent down, she bent down; when he cupped his palms together to ask for Allah's blessing, she too held them up side by side. She exaggerated all his gestures without knowing their meaning or purpose.

Something snapped in Zia. He was in a rage and he was at her throat.

'I've taken a lot of shit from you. You've accused me of ruining your life, of working black magic on your mother and stealing her affection. You've bad-mouthed me at every turn. You've wished me ill and prayed that I would slip back into the depression that overtook me when I first came to Cambridge. You've sent anonymous letters against me to the Master of Emmanuel. All this and more I have ignored or borne without comment because I did not wish to add to your misery and sickness. But if you ever, ever again make fun of Allah or of my prayers to Him or anything connected with Islam, I will kill you.'

'Teach me to pray to Allah,' Vivian said to him.

It was not a question of stretching the point a little. Zia knew it was a miracle, clear and simple. Vivian had been saved. She was a new woman. No one can deny God. When He wishes something, it is not as good as done, but done, done, done. She told her mother she was going to Paris for Christmas for a month, and got herself admitted to a detox centre. For the first ten days Zia thought she would not make it. She cried, she begged, she tried to seduce Zia if only he would give her some China white, coke, anything, and when he refused to budge she bit his hand deep and hard, and ran away from the centre. Zia was ready to walk out on her but she came back, and the second time around stuck it out. The two of them went down on their knees five times a day and prayed to Allah to give her the fortitude and strength to overcome her addiction. It had been hell, there's always a price to pay for sin, but she made it. She knew she had triumphed against Satan and it showed. You should have seen her face. It was, how else can one put it, radiant and glowing with an inner light. But the miracle had not stopped there. Vivian had gone back to her studies and her marks began improving.

The measure of a good teacher lies in the quality of his disciples. If Vivian was any proof, then Zia was destined to be a great teacher. They went to the Peterborough mosque every Friday, they took Arabic classes from Maulana Rizvi. They tried to speak Arabic between themselves. Vivian began to read the Koran, slowly and tentatively at first, in the language in which it was revealed to the Prophet Mohammed, and started to unravel its great mysteries. It was a humbling experience and they both laughed at their hubris. How could they possibly have imagined that they could encompass the greatest work on earth when the finest sages and scholars had struggled with it all their lives? And yet when they listened in humility to the words of God, it was like being present at the Creation. One could only marvel at God's Grand Design. And it was present as much in the slow blossoming of a single flower as it was in the movement of the stars, in the formulae of physics and the wonder of mathematical models.

There was nothing Vivian would not do for Zia. She was crestfallen if he did his own laundry instead of allowing her to collect his clothes, separate the cottons from the woollens and blends, the whites from the Indian coloureds that bled. She liked to cook for him, darn his trousers, sew the buttons on his shirts. She needed him to need her.

Sometimes it seemed to Zia that the recent convert was even more passionate about Islam than he was. He wondered if this overheated enthusiasm for her new faith was not in some way related to her feelings for her mother. Zia had no idea what had gone wrong between them. Sometimes he was inclined to believe that Vivian's insecurity and need for attention were so insatiable that Aunt Antonia had given up in despair. Perhaps she had had no interest in having children of her own and Vivian was a mistake. But that couldn't be, devout Catholics don't think of children as errors.

'Didn't the fact that I became a junkie give you an inkling about how unhappy I was at home?' Vivian had asked petulantly.

It did, and then it didn't, Zia wanted to tell Vivian, but kept his thoughts to himself. Vivian would not have been the first child or the last one to blame her mother for everything that had gone wrong in her life.

*

Vivian would have liked to call the ITV and BBC film crews, reporters from *The New York Times*, *Washington Post*, *Newsweek*, *Time*, *Le Monde*, *Die Zeit*, the entire press corps, to the conversion ceremony. She was keen to give warning to the world that Islam was on a comeback trail now that the daughter of perhaps the best-known Roman Catholic woman in England was changing her name from Vivian to Fatima. Zia liked the idea but was against it. He felt the timing was wrong. The mission for which he had been chosen demanded absolute secrecy. Zia tried to talk Vivian out of an orchestrated, high-visibility campaign, but she was adamant. If she went public, Vivian maintained, other Christians too would discover Islam. Besides, she had to let her mother know.

'You are not changing your faith for Allah,' Zia told her. 'You are doing it to spite your mother.'

'No, I'm not. I'm doing it for the greater glory of Allah.' Vivian should have stopped there and Zia would not have been able to counter her argument. But Vivian was not about to let anyone, not even Zia, dictate to her. 'And what if I am?' she asked defiantly.

'In that case I'll tell the mullah at Peterborough about your less than lofty motives and he won't induct you into the faith.'

'I can always go to the mosque in London or Birmingham.'

'That's up to you. But the word will have spread that you are nothing but a Roman Catholic spy for your mother.'

It was a cheap shot but it worked.

Vivian did not speak to Zia for two weeks. He was convinced that he had lost his first and most valuable convert.

'I've looked into my soul and you were right,' Vivian confessed one night. 'My motives were not altogether honourable. I loved Allah but I also wanted to spit at my mother. I'll be Fatima to you and to no one else till you ask me to share the name with others.'

My dear Zia,

How are you, my dear brother? Your letters are, if it's possible, even more cryptic than mine. While you are modestly silent on the subject of your career at Cambridge, we are given a blow-by-blow account of your exploits by the missionary lady. (Beware, my friend, I fear she'll convert you to the Christian faith yet.) Ammi and Abba walk six inches above the ground like the eldest Pandava from the Mahabharata. This is not because they have lived the righteous life but because they are the parents of one Zia Khan who, they believe, will very soon conquer the highest bastions of Cambridge and then become an international star in academia.

Here's news that will gladden your heart. Abbajaan is once again a full-fledged architect and can practise anywhere in India. The judge passed the severest strictures against the National Institute of Architects for 'the unholy haste, the utter lack of evidence and the strong suspicion of prejudice,' the judge's words, not mine, 'in suspending the plaintiff's licence.' The lawyer for the defence had argued that the intent of the institute was not malafide, that they had merely suspended Mr Khan in the public interest and had given him the freedom to clear his name and resume his career. The judge quoted this statement and thundered, he did Zia, he did, there are cracks in the walls of the court if you want proof, 'How would you like it if, God forbid, the august body of high court lawyers on mere hearsay and less than scant evidence and without giving you a chance to defend yourself, suspended you, sir, from the practice of law? It is unconscionable,' he said, 'that a man's career be ruined, his livelihood and his most precious possession, his good name, be destroyed for close to a decade because the governing body of the NIA did not make any effort to ascertain the facts of the case. We will say this to the plaintiff, Mr Zafar Khan: His vindication was long in coming and the court sympathizes with that, but now that it is come, we must ask him to put the bitterness of these past years behind him and contribute to creating a new architectural vision for the country.'

The National Institute of Architects is talking about appealing against the judgement but our lawyer says that's just hot air. The judgement is so strong and precise, the Supreme Court, he feels, will throw out the appeal without considering it.

You will concede, my brother, that I could hardly bring you more joyful tidings.

Yours affectionately,<br>
Amanat

'Why are you monitoring Rushdie's whereabouts on that wall map?' Vivian asked Zia while they were making love. 'Are you planning to bump him off for the Ayatollah?'

Zia's face turned a powdery grey as though someone had injected a solution of concrete into his jugular. 'What are you talking about?' His voice was less than a whisper.

'Come off it. I'm not that stupid,' she said casually. 'I know what you've been up to since the time Mum gave you this room and you put the map up.'

Why was she pretending to be offhand? She had tried to make out that she was unconcerned, but he knew better. She was definitely play-acting. She was a devious one. She had made a sucker of him. She had converted to Islam merely to spy on him night and day. But he would get to the bottom of things. He had to. His life and his life's mission depended on it.

'Who else did you tell about the map? Your mother? Your junkie friends? Or did you go to the police?'

'I haven't told anybody.'

'Tell me the truth, you bitch. Don't you dare lie to me.'

Vivian brought up her knee sharply into his crotch. Zia fell to the ground in agony. It was a long time before he could speak.

'Why did you do that?' Zia had obviously overestimated his first disciple's loyalty to him.

'Nobody calls me a liar and gets away with it.'

Vivian went out of the room without putting anything on. Now he had lost her. He had panicked and overreacted. He should have been smart, played a double game, and wheedled the information out of her. What if she were already on the phone to them? He should get up and follow her, knock her unconscious with a crystal vase, the drawing room had three of them, as she reported him to New Scotland Yard, but he couldn't move. He was paralysed with pain and fear.

The door opened and Vivian came in with a hand towel packed with ice cubes.

'Do you think my junkie friends or I would have waited all this time to report you to the police?' she asked Zia quietly. 'They convert any information to instant cash. If I had gone to the police, you wouldn't be here but in some jail where your interrogators would be playing ping pong with your balls.'

Vivian's tone and high-pitched intensity seemed to convince Zia more than her words. How could she use a word like "balls"? Good Muslim women would not even euphemistically refer to the thing between their own legs, let alone men's legs. He had to re-educate her, make her into a pure and modest Muslim woman. Before she learnt Arabic, she needed to learn manners, social etiquette and, most of all, be taught to respect menfolk and especially her man. She would have to be taught Islamic values. He wasn't sure how, yet, but Vivian's voice intruded upon his train of thought.

'You aren't planning to kill Salman Rushdie, are you?'

'I would appreciate it if you refrained from speaking his name in my presence or discussing the subject.'

'But have you read *The Satanic Verses*?'

'No, I have not. And I don't intend to.'

'How can you condemn a book without reading it?'

'On whose authority do you or I take God? God is not $e = mc^2$, or the quantum theory, that you can check Him out for yourself if you are so inclined. Nor can different gods subsist side by side as Newtonian physics does with Einsteinian. God is faith and must be taken on faith. That is the essence of God.' Zia spoke as though he were hewing the words out of stone. He was giving shape to ideas that he had known in a vague and subconscious fashion but had never articulated before.

'No Rushdie can affect Allah, nor can blasphemy or heresy touch the Almighty. Allah does not need protection from Satan, but a true believer does. It is I who must defend the honour of God or else it is I, not God, who will be defenceless against Satan. If I am to lead my people and perhaps even non-believers to Allah, then I must prove myself worthy of Him. I must vanquish Satan and protect myself and my flock.'

Zia got up and put on his clothes. Vivian sat immobile, hardly aware of what Zia was doing.

'This is the parting of the ways,' Zia spoke simply and without anger. 'It is your creed to question and doubt. All questions cease for me and become irrelevant in the presence of God.'

'Will you take me as your comrade-in-arms in this work of Allah?' Vivian would not raise her eyes. 'I will abide by every word you speak.'

Zia would never have admitted this in public, neither would he have mentioned it to his one and only accomplice, but the Iranian fatwa had not been an astute or effective move. If you want to bump someone off, you don't take out an ad, for that's what the fatwa amounted to, in every journal and on every TV channel in the world.

The fatwa had been Essar's biggest ally. Everybody was impressed with the one-million, or was it two-million? pound reward on Essar's head. That was a bit of a joke. It alerted the culprit and the criminal, it had united the so-called liberal community in the name of the right to freedom of expression; it had forced the British government to commit itself to safeguarding a man they would surely have preferred to ditch, while continuing to sell billions of dollars' worth of armaments to Iran. Now that one of its citizens had been publicly threatened, Britain's prestige as a democracy was on the line.

The fatwa was not the way mature, adult nations did business, Zia reflected. Had Iran talked it over with the people at the British Foreign Office, they would have been only too happy to oblige. A daylight accident or an Indian invention, called an 'encounter' with the police, could surely have been arranged, and the obstreperous Midnight's Child would have been taken care of. The British would certainly have honoured a billion-dollar client state if only the bare minimum of appearances and protocol had been followed.

Instead, look at the fallout of the fatwa. The work of the Prince of Darkness, so aptly called *The Satanic Verses*, was selling in the hundreds of thousands in hardback and millions in paperback. His peers and fellow-artists who hated his bitchiness, gall and guts and who believed – not all, but some of them certainly – that Essar knew exactly what he was writing as well as its consequences, now had to rally around him, sing his praises, write manifestoes to the UN and to each other, egg on the Foreign Office to show that Britain had spunk and little else with which to stand up to a nation of medieval fanatics.

The word was that Essar was being moved like stolen loot from place to place. He had no fixed address and he himself was not aware of where he was going to be the next day. At least that was the rumour New Scotland Yard had put over. Even if Essar had not become a highly mobile local refugee, Zia knew that attempting to erase him in his safe house was an impossibility. The place would be a fortress.

He had, however, always known that his biggest and closest ally was Essar himself. Essar said he came up for light, air and contact with other human beings, and to state his case, but Zia knew that he surfaced from his moving hole every now and then because he was smart enough to recognize that he was dead the moment he was forgotten. He was like the holocaust for the Jews. He would not, he could not, afford to let amnesia take over the people of Britain. And the people of France, Spain, Italy, the USA and the whole world, even if it meant goading his enemies to action. He knew as hardly anyone else in the world did, that the fatwa had made him the greatest living author. No one, but no one, he understood well, would dare to assess the quality of his work till either he or the controversy died.

Zia hung around with the hotheads from the Kashmiri Muslim community in Cambridge and Peterborough and occasionally went to London to pick up any clues about the beast. He spent hours in the library combing through British, American, French, German, Iranian and Middle-Eastern papers and journals looking for precise or vague hints, the stray remark that would throw light on Essar's movements. He read both fiction and non-fiction on Scotland Yard to get an insight into how they protected their high-risk witnesses from hit men, and VVIPs from terrorists.

Now Zia's computer held perhaps the single most comprehensive and detailed file on the traitor in the country, under the apt and brief head, 'Lucifer'. The information was extensively cross-referenced. What Zia's investigations revealed, though, was that the Prince did not travel by train, boat or plane but almost exclusively by car. He travelled in a convoy of cars with plain-clothes policemen. The Prince of Darkness chose to appear at select gatherings and seminars if they dealt with human rights, censorship and the freedom of the press. These were soapboxes where he harangued his audience, scolded Britain and the other Western nations for not isolating Iran. Behind all that highfalutin talk of democratic ideals, Zia saw Essar help himself to a theory of state-sponsored individual freedom that was tailor-made to suit his predicament while promoting the age-old romantic notion that liberty is licence without responsibility. But the sites and occasions that chose him, instead of the other way round, were literary festivals and get-togethers, writers' meets and literary award ceremonies. The Prince was at his flamboyant best, and at his most unguarded and careless, when he was with his own kind.

It seemed to Zia that for a country the size of a silicon chip, Britain had more literary, theatrical and arts events than the entire European continent and the Americas put together. The heyday of the arts was long since over and Thatcherite parsimony had knocked the funding and the bottom out of the cultural barrel, and yet every county, city and toy town had its own writers' conference and literary fest. Even on a conservative basis, there were a hundred and fifty literary events a year across the country. Aberdeen had an Arts Carnival and an Alternative Festival; King's Lynn in Norfolk, a place that even Brits had trouble finding, had three: The King's Lynn Festival, The King's Lynn Fiction Festival and The King's Lynn Poetry Festival. The Edinburgh International, not to be confused with the Edinburgh Fringe Festival, had over a thousand events. The Edinburgh Book Festival, an altogether different kettle of fish from the other two fests, was the world's biggest literary bacchanalia, with over four hundred events and three hundred authors taking part.

The Prince of Darkness was hardly likely to attend a hundred and fifty festivals. The question was which select few he would choose in a year. The problem was further complicated by the fact that he could occasionally choose a minor, out-of-the-way event not simply because it was unexpected and hence safer, but also because the impact of his turning up in a remote location would be far greater.

Zia had done multiple statistical analyses, built probability model after probability model for a simple three-day Poetry Festival at Cardiff, and each one of them had gone hopelessly awry. He had escalated the levels of complexity and of intangibles, and yet had come a cropper every time. For once Zia felt that mathematical modelling was a tool that had limitations; as a matter of fact, it seized up and ceased functioning whenever it had anything to do with Satan.

He had invested not just time but a great deal of money in the project. Almost every penny he had saved was spent on pursuing the traitor. He had seen more of Britain than any politician on a whistle-stop tour of the hustings. He had been to Gwent, Pembrokeshire, Swansea in Wales, to Aboyne, to Perthshire and Fife in Scotland, Bangor and Belfast in Ireland, to Totnes in Devon, to Crowborough in Sussex, to Gosport, Dorset, Rye, Peebles, Shropshire, Eastbourne, the Vale of Glamorgan and a hundred other places in search of the Prince.

The setbacks never seemed to end. Once Lucifer was in the same town as him but at a different event. At other times two festivals would clash and Zia would toss a coin. Needless to say, the devil would skip both. And yet Zia never got disheartened. Allah could easily have told him where the Prince of Darkness was going to be and at what time, but He was testing Zia's faith, fealty and fortitude. Was Zia worthy? Did he have what it took to be Allah's instrument? Would he soldier on in the face of repeated failures?

## 16

Zia was clearing his table when he spotted the gift Amanat had sent three weeks earlier for his birthday. He had put it away unopened. It was bound to be yet another book. It was a novel called *The Arsonist* by Amanat Khan. The flavour of Zia's reaction was something like oh God. He was amazed that his brother, his very own Amanat, was a published author. (When did he get the time? He was supposed to be sick, he was helping his father in the makeshift office at home, soliciting work for himself, designing fail-safe helmets for motorcycle and scooter riders.) Zia also felt uneasy. It was a complicated response. There was a touch of envy, more than a few grains of trepidation, and a desire to protect his brother from those predators called critics.

There was a picture of Amanat (he looked shy and charming) and a blurb about the book on the back cover:

This is the unlikely tale of a weaver. But this is no ordinary weaver. It is a man who weaves God. A work of great ribaldry, exuberance and joy, it is also a metaphysical journey – man's eternal search for meaning and his attempt to make sense of his life and of the world around him.

Khan is a novelist of rare audacity and daring. His protagonist would make the Buddha, Christ and Mohammed sit up and rethink their beliefs and sacred dogmas. *The Arsonist* will shock and alarm the West, as it will the East. It is the story of the camaraderie, love, bickering and friendship between a man and his God: the story of India's great mediaeval Bhakti mystic, Kabir.

It was the usual orotund and inflated hype used by blurb-writers across the world. Oh God, Zia thought, how am I going to read this? What would he tell Amanat? That I thought your book was phoney and pretentious? Why did Amanat have to send his book to Zia?

It was not because he was curious that Zia read the book that night, he just wanted to get over the uncertainty. Nobody knew whether Kabir was a Hindu or a Muslim. Little or nothing was known about his antecedents, his parents or his birth. What was worse, Kabir's verse proclaimed from the rooftops that it didn't make a difference what you were: Muslim or Hindu. Call Him Ram, Rahim or by any other name, God couldn't care less. (This was, of course, blasphemy. Hadn't God told Mohammed that there is no God but Allah and all the others are false gods?)

It was a short book, just a hundred and seventy pages. It was worse, much worse than Zia had expected, but in an altogether different sense. It was full of dark and ambiguous things. It was ambivalent, and it insidiously undermined your faith.

If you had to choose between a woman you had met the day before and God, who would you choose? And the weaver said, The woman. Is there any doubt about that?

And the mullah asked him, If you had to choose between a song and God, what would you pick? And the weaver said, The song, of course.

And the priest from the temple asked him, Weaver, if, perforce you had to choose one or the other, a beautiful sunset or God, what would your choice be? And he said, Isn't it obvious? The sunset.

And they asked him how he could blaspheme so. And the weaver said, Why sirs, God has eternity on his side, he can always wait. Will the woman, the song or the sunset wait for me?

And they asked in desperation, If you had to choose between sin and God, weaver, what would you choose? And he laughed and he said, Sin, always sin. Sin is fun, sin is forbidden; sin is, what shall I say, so sinful. They should forbid God as they forbid sin, then maybe he would become far more attractive and we would all be drawn to him. What a bunch of cretins you have for your devotees, oh Lord, he laughed out loud. The fools would sever you from your creation.

What incensed Zia particularly were the conversations between the weaver and his disciples that occurred again and again throughout the book.

One afternoon when the weaver was taking his siesta, two of his pupils, Ismael and Ananda, rushed into the house and woke him up.

I hope you've found God or something as important, Ananda. For if you haven't, I'm going to beat the living daylights out of you.

Is it true, Ananda was still out of breath, that you were an ascetic and lived alone in the mountains?

Is that why you woke me up, you fool?

Answer the question, Master, Ismael said tersely.

The other apprentices left their looms and gathered around the weaver.

I don't remember. It was a long time ago. How does it concern you, anyway?

No ascetic with any self-respect would ever return to a normal life or go back to his wife and children, Ismael sneered.

I suppose I have no self-respect. Now may I go back to my nap?

Why, why would you come back when you were supposed to be the greatest maharishi in the country?

Can't we talk about that some other time?

Now, the pupils said impatiently.

When I was your age, I set out in search of God. Not small gods and medium-sized gods but the big one, the Almighty himself. I was a pretty persistent sort and over the years I acquired a reputation as a holy man. They called me a sage and a seer. Some said I was a siddhi and I had miraculous powers. I lived in the Himalayas in those days, some fourteen thousand feet above sea level. It was my seventh year of standing on one leg. My eyes were closed and my mind was focused on Brahman. People from far and near, from neighbouring principalities and distant kingdoms, trekked to the mountains to fall at my feet and receive my blessings. Sometimes they would wait for days, even weeks, to see me, for there was no telling how long my devotions and meditations would last.

Why do people go to see holy men? Because they believe the enlightened one can make God bend down all the way from heaven to lend an ear. For them a sage is a go-between, a middleman, and who knows, God may be on the take. But I promised nothing. If I had, as was rumoured, magical powers, I was keeping them to myself. And yet they kept coming, an endless march of pilgrims, the rich and the poor, men, women and children, the lame and the halt and the handicapped; those who needed their lives fixed and those who needed nothing. They came to sit in the shadow of saintliness and be touched by someone who, for all they knew, was privy to God's thoughts.

One day the blacksmith's wife came to see me with her son. He was of an indeterminate age, he could have been twenty-five or maybe he was close to forty. His mouth was open and there was a vacuous smile on his face.

Don't just stand there, you fool. Touch the Master's feet, the mother snapped at him.

He bent down and lay prostrate in front of me, his hands joined prayerfully for a full five minutes.

Bless him, Master, the mother said. I've seven daughters and one son. His name is Suraj. He's a good boy and his heart is in the right place but he's a little simple. He's slow to learn and gets a beating from his father almost every week.

Tell the blacksmith to beat iron and not the boy, I told her. The simple of heart, I suspect, are closer to God than all the subtle scholars of the world. Rise, my son. I put my hand on his head. May God be with you.

Likewise, he said and laughed as if he had said something vastly funny.

He would come by from time to time and watch me from a distance. I would forget him and then hours later realize that he was still staring at me.

It was the beginning of February and a cold nasty wind was blowing, the one they call the Intruder. It whistled inside your bones and froze your blood. The blacksmith's son came up to me and wrapped a shawl around my shoulders.

I thank you for your kindness, I told him, but I must return your gift, for I have vowed that whatever the season, however inclement the weather, I will endure it.

The blacksmith's son looked puzzled. Why would you do this, Master?

A small token, I smiled self-deprecatingly, of my devotion to God.

I have brought you some bread that my mother made and raw chillies. They'll bring warmth to your shivering body.

That is kind of you, Suraj. I'm touched by your concern but I'll not touch food for the next three weeks.

And why would you do this, Master? Are you unwell?

Nothing of the sort, I said. Just another small token of my affection for the Almighty.

Does it give God pleasure then when people starve or freeze to death? he asked innocently. Is that why people scourge themselves?

Oh no, no. The good Lord doesn't ask anything of us. It's just a way of showing my love for him.

Is that why you stand on one leg?

Yes, that is the very reason.

You have a rather funny way of showing your love, Master. For if God wanted us to be one-legged, he wouldn't have given us two.

I smiled at his naïveté but decided to humour him. Maybe you've got a point there.

What else have you given up, Master?

Not much really. I shaved my head, left my young wife and my child of two months. And my elderly parents. They didn't want me to go since I was their only child and the sole breadwinner. Who will run the workshop and who'll look after us? they asked. God will, I told them. He takes care of his own.

What workshop? Are you too an iron-master?

No. I was chief weaver by appointment to the king. All the princesses and queens wore fabrics woven on my looms.

All this you gave up? No wonder they call you maharishi.

Not much really. Just a trifle. I bade farewell to my job as the village mukhiya. The villagers said, Who will save us when the floods come and who will listen to our troubles? And I told them that power is an unquenchable thirst, and high office, a pair of shackles. I will have nothing to do with them. Everything I had desired, I parted with.

Surely then you must part with the Almighty too.

I laughed and asked him, Pray, why should I part with the Almighty?

Because you desire God more than anything else in the world.

I was nonplussed. Was this man just stupid or was he the devil incarnate?

You suggest that I would forsake the most precious thing in my life? I spoke with suppressed rage.

The blacksmith's son fell at my feet and clung to my ankles.

Mercy, Master, have mercy on me. I will not get up till you've forgiven an ignorant man with a loose tongue.

Rise blacksmith, I said, I bear you no ill will.

Your love of God is indeed great, Master. Greater than any other man's, the blacksmith's son said and bowed. I'll take your leave now.

May God be with you, I said.

He never showed up again. The weaver paused. It was I who visited him a week later. He was in the smithy and cleared some cast-iron scrap off a bench to make room for me to sit and asked his mother to get me a glass of buttermilk.

What can I do for you, Master? he asked me.

Will you be my teacher, my guru?

Me? He seemed astounded by the suggestion.

Yes. You have more wisdom than all my years of searching for the Almighty have given me. You taught me that one can get a little too attached to selflessness. You taught me that at the end of the day a man must renounce renunciation itself.

The blacksmith smiled. I taught you, Master? You are pulling my leg.

I'm not, I told him emphatically. I've never been more serious. Be my guru.

He laughed then, a loud guffaw that shook the smithy. You've got to be joking, he said. Do you think I've nothing better to do?

Everybody wants a guru to show them the way, the weaver said. It's not such a bad idea, I suppose. You may not be able to see without a guru. But then, more often than not, you cannot see beyond the guru either. The guru is vision and the guru is blinkers. It is easy to forget that one is not searching for the guru but for God. Once you've found a guru, it's time to think of leaving him and making your own way.

If I could teach you anything, he told his pupils and apprentices, I would teach you irreverence. Irreverence towards your guru; irreverence towards all and sundry, but most of all irreverence towards yourself and your solemnities.

I may have found the true path, if such a thing exists, but the truth, like all of us, has a short life span. Somebody must then find another path, and another truth. And the one will not cancel the other.

No. No more. If I read any more, Zia thought, I'll cast myself into hell. And he read on.

But why is there so much suffering? one of the weaver's disciples, the one they called Gunidas, asked. He was so earnest and solemn in his quest for God, the weaver wanted to kick him down the stairs to get a laugh out of him.

Why does a child of two die of diphtheria? Why do the poor starve while the rich only get richer? Why is there no justice? Why is there pain, Master? There was no stopping Gunidas.

What a silly question, the weaver said. Because God is evil.

Gunidas and his fellow-pupils were aghast. The Master was always being heretical, partly to shock them, partly because he liked to speak in puzzles and enigmas, but today he had gone too far; he had crossed all bounds, even those of irreverence. He had to be taught a lesson. They would all leave him.

Good riddance, the weaver said, I'll have some peace now.

But blasphemy is always tempting. It is, after all, the first expression of freedom. One by one, they came back.

We are here on one condition only. You'll stop being childish and not say something terrible to merely provoke and torment us. Is that a promise?

The weaver gave his word that he would never say anything shocking again. He looked contrite. I swear by Satan I will not be heretical again.

It was pointless talking to him, they said, and walked out.

Is Satan not the creation of God? he shouted after them. Are there departments up there, one for evil and one for good? You, Michael, you are in charge of all plant life. Gabriel, I'm shifting you to the department of plagues and the research institute for new and more horrific diseases. We haven't had anything grand and deadly since smallpox. And you, Lucifer, the portfolio for evil, I'm entrusting it to you. I don't want any dirt to stick to me. You are the bad guy and I'm the good one. It's very primitive and simplistic but take my word for it, good against evil is the best theatre in the world. People will flock to see us. The bishops, qazis and rabbis will philosophize interminably about the tree of knowledge and the doctrine of free will, and how God in his wisdom created polarities and each human being must choose between Him and evil. They'll love it, Lucifer.

Have you noticed something else? the weaver asked. Something bizarre? Satan, I mean Lucifer, has all the time in the world, and I mean quality time, for all of us. He is always available. Not just that, he takes the initiative, he's patient, he's persevering and, most of all, he never gives up on us. He's always there, even when we don't need him. In fact, especially when we don't need him.

How do you think original sin came about? God was sitting on his high horse, acting all mighty and remote and unapproachable while the devil was holding Adam and Eve by the hand in the Garden of Eden and making them feel wanted.

You'll admit that it's a little odd that while the devil is always on call, the good Lord seems a little preoccupied.

Why does God get all the credit for good, the weaver asked, and why is all evil attributed to Satan? If God is the Creator, he can handle both. You must decide who's in charge here, my friends. Only then will you understand that all polarities and divisions are sacrilege. God, if I may use one of these new-fangled academic terms, is the unified theory of the universe. Good and evil, Hindu, Muslim, Jew, Christian, Buddhist are all encompassed in Him. He's large enough and wise enough to accommodate all contradictions.

## 17

There has been a radical change in Vivian's mode of dressing in the past two months. Zia and she were setting out for the mosque in Peterborough one day when Vivian appeared in a burkha with a woven latticed flap that covered the face. He was horrified but he chose to humour her since an adverse reaction from him almost invariably resulted in a showdown and a hardening of her stance. He smiled and made one of those innocuous 'hmm' sounds.

'You like it?' Vivian obviously wanted more than an ambiguous harumph.

He was about to say 'interesting' when he checked himself. A non-committal, faceless word like 'interesting' would send her through the roof. He marvelled at his ability to switch words midstream but even more so at the impromptu felicity of the new word he was about to use.

'Very becoming,' he said and smiled even more broadly.

'You really think so? I'm so glad. I've got three others. One of them is the Saudi sort of chador with a partial mask that goes over the nose like a beak.'

Zia's smile had become a rictus with Count Dracula dentures. Easy, Zia, easy does it, he told himself. 'All set to go?'

'Yes, of course.'

'I'll just see that the back door is bolted while you take the burkha off.'

'Why would I want to take it off? The burkha will be my shield from now on.'

'And what kind of shield would that be?'

'The shield of Islam, the shield of honour, chastity, feminine dignity and virtue.'

'Your virtue has fortunately never been in danger, Vivian. If anybody should presume to sully it, God help him. Come, take the thing off and let's go. Or we'll be late.'

'As a pak and good Muslim woman, I shall henceforth never venture out without a burkha.'

'Viv, I know you want to show off your new dress to all and sundry but not today and not till we accomplish our mission.'

'What's that got to do with my burkha?'

'Because you'll stand out like a seven-coloured totem pole in Cambridge.'

'Nonsense. I've seen women in chadors in Cambridge.'

'I've no doubt you have run across the occasional group of burkha-clad ladies doing the tour of Cambridge, and there may even be a resident female student reading Arabic history at one of the colleges who flits around swathed in black and with her head bowed, but that has nothing to do with you. You are the daughter of a very prominent professor and you live in an area where your garb would make you a freak. The last thing we need is visibility in the eyes of our neighbours and of the policeman who happens to slide past in his patrol car. Now, can we catch the bus for Peterborough dressed like hundreds of other normal people?'

'I'm sorry, I'm not going to change. Take it or leave it.'

'In that case, I'll leave it.'

Zia slammed the door and walked to the bus station in a rage. He was three-quarters of the way there when he realized that people were staring at something behind him. Vivian was running to keep up with him. He had little alternative but to increase his speed. In the bus he deliberately chose an aisle seat just in case she came and sat next to him. She did and he moved to another seat. He thought she would get up and follow him and they would keep hopping from seat to seat till they reached Peterborough. Mercifully, she stayed put.

But Zia's travails were not over yet. 'Zia,' Vivian called out across the bus, 'have you bought my ticket or should I get one?'

Zia pretended to ignore her as almost every passenger tried to locate the person called Zia who, it appeared, had not bought a ticket for his wife or sister.

'Zia,' Vivian called again, this time with a little more drama in her voice, 'what shall I do?'

Again Zia ignored her. Vivian made her way to the driver and asked for a ticket in a stage whisper.

'The gentleman's already bought your ticket,' the driver said.

'He's my husband but he's planning to leave me for another young woman,' Vivian told him in a conspiratorial tone.

Zia got off the bus just as it was about to leave.

As summer progressed, things went from bad to worse between Vivian and Zia. Vivian had said that she was wearing the burkha because she wanted to be a pak Muslim woman. Not merely her conduct but her dress too should become pure as the waters in the gardens of paradise. It should have been an unarguable article of faith except that not even the most unorthodox could have imagined what Vivian did with it. For the true believer, the burkha is restraint and modesty. It is an armour and a bastion. It is the protector of both the one who wears it and the one who might get aroused. The West views it as a shackle, an injustice against womankind, a sign of her bondage, a punishment visited upon the victim rather than on the one who victimizes. For Vivian, it spelt freedom. Under the voluminous black, she had begun to perform Salome's dance of the seven veils. She may have been only half aware of it, but it was a slow, lazy and erotic dance that outraged Zia and drove him to distraction. Over the months, under the forbidding burkha, she shed one item of clothing after another. The sweater was the first to be dropped. The shirt and the trousers were abandoned next. It was the advent of summer that signalled the final stages of the striptease. The mercury rose to 35 one afternoon and the bra and panties were thrown off.

It was not an unusual sight to see a huge black butterfly stuck in the crevice between Vivian's buttocks as she rose from her seat in a bus or the library. Sometimes she remembered to pull the black silk out and free the butterfly. Often it stayed trapped.

Zia had thought Aunt Antonia would become apoplectic and rip the chador into half-centimetre fragments. The least she could have done was to throw Vivian out of the house. As luck would have it, that summer Aunt Antonia was mostly in Nigeria, and even when she was in Cambridge she spent anywhere between ten and twelve hours at work. As with Vivian's conversion, it was more than likely that the sole reason for her burkha was to get her mother's attention.

What was Zia to make of Vivian? And even more to the point, what was he to make of himself? For there was something else, something so shameful that Zia could not even acknowledge it. There was a secret about the burkha that would consign Zia to the flames of hell. It was Spanish Fly, the Nepalese shilajeet, the renowned palangtod or bed-breaker: it was the ultimate priapic stimulant. It transformed Zia till he could no longer recognize himself. He cursed himself and swore never again, never again, and yet in the daylight and in the evening and at dawn, he fell upon Vivian and made violent love to her.

They did not exchange a word, Vivian and he. He did not know whether she was friend or foe, whether this was the tumult of war or the blight of peace. He hated and blamed her but he hated and blamed himself even more. And yet the next time he saw her on the street, at Boots, leaning over the bridges of the Cam, lying on the sloping Backs behind King's College, it took the utmost exercise of his will power not to go on a rampage then and there. 'Home,' he would mutter under his breath, 'home.' She never said no to him. That year, fortunately, Cambridge saw one of the worst autumns in decades, and Viv found it difficult to manage overcoat, burkha and books simultaneously. By the time winter came around, her chador had disappeared.

As expected, Zia topped his final year in economics. Vivian gifted him a seventeenth-century hand-written Koran, James and Deirdre Cambray were throwing a party for him at Cambray Park, and Roy, who was flying in from Boston, was going to meet him at Heathrow and take him straight to Armani's to buy him a three-piece suit. That left Aunt Antonia. She had got him a gold Cross pen and a business-class ticket to India.

His family had called from Bombay. Abba, Zubeida Khaala and Amanat had all taken turns to congratulate him. Since Ammi had been in Simla, she had sent him a telex. It was the longest letter she had ever written to him.

Zia, my darling,

I must have done something good in my past lives (do you think the dear Hindus have got this one right?) to have got you as my son. Oh, how proud you've made us all. People now accost me and ask me if I'm the mother of that young genius from Cambridge called Khan. I was looking at some albums at home the other day and saw pictures of you. Is this handsome young man really my son? I asked myself. Where did he get his brains from? Certainly not from his mother.

I wish I could have been there for the convocation ceremony and watched my baby receive all those wonderful awards and be the centre of attention. Though I'm glad I wasn't. Like a good sentimental Indian mother I might have burst into tears and embarrassed you. But I'm with you in spirit, I always am, my beloved son.

I have one request and one request only to make of you. Come home, son. You have been away so long, don't you want to see your mother? Your father misses you though he won't say it aloud. And so does dear Zubeida. After all you were always her favourite. And Amanat? I think he's been lonely since the time you went to New Eden. Come back and make us all happy.

I love you dearly, my son, and miss you,

Ammijaan

Zia should have been delighted with all the attention he was getting but it had the contrary effect upon him. All the fuss stuck in his craw. It served to underline the fact that while the Almighty continued to shower His munificence upon him, he had still not done Allah's bidding. His guilt was mounting by the day and he kept feeling that he had once again let his God down. He wanted to take the ticket Aunt Antonia had bought for him and board the flight to India if only to escape all the song-and-dance about his success. And yet how could he? That would only mean that he no longer cared to vanquish the Prince of Darkness; that he was admitting defeat and abandoning the idea of being the defender of the faith and Allah's agent on earth.

Vivian hounded Zia to take her along with him when he went hunting for Essar at lit-fests.

'It's not a job for a woman,' he told her.

'How do you plan to terminate him? With extreme prejudice?' she asked him one evening.

'You've been watching too many American war movies.'

'You haven't answered my question.'

'What question?' Zia played for time.

'How are you going to kill him?'

Zia laughed. 'That's between Satan and me.'

'You've never thought about the matter, have you?'

'Of course I have.'

'You plan to kill him with your bare hands?'

'I'm not an idiot, Vivian. I'm going to shoot him.'

'With what?'

'With a pea-shooter, what else?'

'What kind of gun?'

'Supposing I don't want to tell you?'

'You don't really have a gun, do you? You're just making it up.'

'Stop patronizing me, Vivian.'

He was not going to lose his temper. He was just going to put her in her place once and for all. He walked to his cupboard, drew out a gun from the back of a drawer and handed it to her.

'You got yourself a Magnum?' Vivian sounded incredulous.

'Yes, a Magnum 44. It's the one Clint Eastwood uses in *Dirty Harry*.'

'Now who's been watching too many movies?' Vivian laughed. 'Don't you know the Magnum's useless for this kind of operation?'

'Why?'

'It's too big and visible. It's far too difficult to handle. It has a terrible recoil.'

'Maybe for a woman.'

'Have you tested it?'

Nothing incensed Zia as much as Vivian's superior airs. 'Of course not. If I had, the Prince of Darkness wouldn't be alive.'

'Who did you get it from?'

'What difference does that make?'

'Because some illicit sources are more unreliable than others.'

'I got it from a couple of Kashmiri jihadis with whom I got friendly at the mosque.'

'How much did you pay for it?'

'What is this, an inquisition? How come you know so much about guns?'

'Wouldn't you like to know.'

'Answer my question.'

'I just do.'

'Answer my question.'

'I had a boyfriend who knew a bit about them.'

'You have a boyfriend?'

'Past tense. Had. He went to America.' She paused to let this sink in.

'Are you serious?'

'I am serious. How much?'

'How much what?'

'How much did you pay for it?'

'Twelve hundred pounds.'

Vivian looked thoughtful. 'The problem with guns is that they're so easy to detect.'

'What would you do?'

'I don't know.'

She yawned, a lazy cat's yawn, her back arched, her long right arm shot up and stretched out behind her head, her teeth glinted like the dentures on the shelves in Dr Lee's clinic across from Suleiman Mansion. Zia wasn't sure what happened after that. There was an almost inaudible clicking sound, her wrist flicked, a light flared in the air and a dart had embedded a lock of Zia's hair amongst the flags on the map.

'You could have blinded me.' Zia could scarcely breathe.

'I could have,' Vivian said. Another dart whizzed past Zia's right ear and stuck deep into the soft board behind the image of Britain, 'if I had wanted to. I never miss.'

'Are you finished?' Zia asked. He seemed to be trembling in sympathy with the two darts behind his ears.

'There are still a couple of more coming.'

'Spare me the rest of the circus,' he said with suppressed rage.

'We could make a good team, Zia. If one fails, the other can take over.'

Zia had to admit that she wasn't talking nonsense.

'Maybe.'

'First thing we need to do is to go to a shooting range and test the gun. We also need to know whether the Magnum and you are compatible.'

*

Dear Ammijaan,

Someone has to bell the cat. Someone has to tell the truth. If I am the one chosen to do it, so be it. I'll do Allah's bidding.

This is the last time I'll be calling you Ammijaan or writing to you. You are no longer my mother, nor is there any other relationship possible between us. The reason for this is obvious but I owe it to you to spell it out.

As a child, and even when I was at New Eden, I worshipped you. You could do no wrong. Zubeida Khaala may have been my spiritual godmother but you were my universe. If anyone cast aspersions on you or said anything remotely critical about you, I cursed them and put the evil eye upon them. When we left Firdaus, I blamed Abba for all the misfortunes that befell us.

I now know how wrong I was. How blind I was. You were the cause of all our grief. You paid for Altaaf Mamoo to go to Oxford. And when he got into extravagant debt, you got Abba to sell one of his prime properties in Malabar Hill for a pittance to bail out your brother. When Mamoo returned to India, you made sure that Abbajaan gave him a job at Khan Builders. But that didn't satisfy you. Within a few years, you got after Abba to make Altaaf executive director and partner. When he resisted the idea, you pulled out your trump card: 'You don't love me any more.' Abba should have told you, 'You're right. I don't,' and given you a talaaq on the spot and thrown you out of the house. Fool that he is, he gave in as usual.

I still hold Abbajaan responsible but for different reasons. If he had not been so weak, he would never have allowed you to become a whore. For that's what you are, however much it hurts me to admit it. But a whore does what she does for money and for survival. You did it and continue to do so because you are a promiscuous woman and love a life of sin. Horse racing, cards, gambling and good times, that's all you are interested in. You've never had a thought for Allah nor could you spare a moment for your soul. If we lived in a pak Islamic state, you know very well what your fate would have been: you would have been stoned to death in public. Instead of whipping you and holding you to the righteous path, Abba, self-destructive man that he is, indulged your turpitude and turned a blind eye to your fallen ways.

I cannot and will not do this. Pay heed even now. Allah is compassionate and merciful. Change your ways and He may still forgive you. It is up to you.

Do not ever try to contact me or use other people to try and insinuate yourself into my good books. Instead get into Allah's good books. Please remember you are dead for me and I for you.

Zia

The question was where and how Zia was going to learn to shoot. There was an amateur gun club in the University but Zia had no idea whether it was for dilettantes or putative crackshots. Even if it was the latter, Zia would have nothing to do with it. The key word in his mission was secrecy. You could never be too careful. Enrol in the club and your hobby became a matter of public record.

Two months passed and Zia had still not cracked the problem. Then it struck him that he had access to one of the most modern shooting facilities in England. What a fool he had been. James Cambray's guests were always disappearing into a shooting gallery in the basement below the garages.

'Teach me to shoot, Roy,' Zia told his friend the next time he was at the Park.

'Sure. What do you want to shoot? Deer, pheasants, grouse?'

Zia shook his head. 'Not game, Roy. I want to be an Olympic-standard marksman.'

Roy looked puzzled. 'What's up?'

Zia shrugged his shoulders. 'Just want to prove a point to the snobs at the University gun club.'

'You're on. Not with me though, since I'm not a trained teacher. And besides, I'm never at the Park for more than a week. But I know a good teacher.' Then as an afterthought he added, 'Don't go by his name. He's all right really.'

Speed Balanchine. Balanchine as in the Russian émigré choreographer. Roy was right to warn him. The name smacked of bad thrillers and pretentious pulp. He looked every bit as strange as his name. The manic eyes were far too close-set. He was tall but walked with an exaggerated stoop and seemed to live in a drugged haze. He was almost catatonic till he got started on guns.

Speed taught Zia how to load a Magnum and unload it, how to dismantle it and put it back together; how to clean it, how to store it (always, but always, after removing the bullets), and how to operate the safety catch. He talked about the bore, the recoil, the calibre, the comparative merits and demerits of automatic and semi-automatic weapons, the velocity of the bullet and the effect of gravity on its flight path. He said don't ever point a gun at anybody, barring of course your chosen victim, not in fun, not idly, not as a threat, because that's how accidents happen. You may say I wasn't thinking or that wasn't my intention but a dead victim won't be able to appreciate that. One more 'don't'. Don't ever take the safety catch off unless you are planning to kill. It was no oversight, Zia noted, that Speed did not say 'planning to shoot'. If you were going to shoot, it had better be to shoot someone dead. The one person, Speed intoned, who is most at risk from a gun is its owner.

When the hell was the lecture going to end? Zia wondered. And when were they going to the firing range? The first hour was over and Balanchine was still droning on.

The only reason Zia stuck it out was because of what Vivian had said the previous evening. 'The Magnum, Zia, is one mother of a gun. Go ahead, feel it. It gives you an amazing sense of power.'

The gun was lying curled up like a black kitten on top of a shirt in one of the drawers in his wardrobe. It had a dull sheen and Zia hesitated to touch it.

'The Evil One is reading from his satanic book to an audience of a thousand people or more,' Vivian had conjured up the moment that was yet to come. 'He has cocked a snook at the Ayatollah and his fatwa and despite the two-million-pound price on his head, has given the slip to God-alone-knows how many agents of death. The people in the hall gaze at him adoringly. He can feel their adulation, and is well aware that they are in his thrall. His sense of power is a greater intoxicant than any designer drug.

'The reading comes to a close, and there is a roar of applause that will not die down. The power, oh the power and the glory of being Satan. And even as he smiles with his hooded eyes, and graciously accepts the furious clapping as his due, he is unaware that there is a power greater, infinitely greater than his. He knows the Beatles' song "Happiness Is a Warm Gun", but he does not know that you are holding happiness in your hand, Zia. Clap, clap, clapclap-clap. Clap, clap, clapclapclap. No one hears the click of the safety catch as it is released in that rhythmic outpouring.

'You step back, pull out the gun, extend your hands Dirty Harry fashion, take aim and pull the trigger in one swift manoeuvre. The wisps of hair on Satan's head sway as if in a gentle breeze at the lightning approach of the bullet. The lead projectile hits the dead centre of his forehead, the smile fades and his brains explode and scatter like the fireworks on the Queen Mother's birthday. Satan is no more and it is your doing, Zia, even as you get away in all that pandemonium and confusion.'

Zia is entranced as he recalls the live-action commentary that Vivian had whipped up for him. He had not been aware that she had such fabulous bardic talents. Perhaps Homer was a woman, he thinks. He feels heroic as he picks up the gun. The Magnum is heavy in his hand and the steel is cold. Cold as his resolve to exterminate the Prince of Darkness.

'The Magnum is dead on and deadly in the right hands, but it is not a user-friendly piece,' Speed Balanchine rambled on. 'There's no help button on it. If you don't know your way in and around it, just leave it alone. It will not descend to your level of incompetence. You have to take it on its own terms.'

Speed picked up three heavy-duty earmuffs from a shelf, handed two to his companions and put one on himself. Despite the earmuffs, the decibel levels were unsettling. Zia took up position, held the Magnum with extended hands and was about to shoot, when Speed waved to him and corrected his posture.

'Don't keep your arms so rigid. Let there be some give, so they'll act like springs.'

Zia nodded though he couldn't hear a word. He pulled the trigger. Pins and needles coursed through his bloodstream. He was sitting on the ground and his arms felt as though they were plugged into a live socket. Vivian was bent over him, helping him up. He was standing now but his legs could still feel the shock of the recoil. He looked at the dummy cut off at the waist at the other end of the lane. Where the hell was the bullet mark? He looked again with narrowed eyes. Ha, no wonder. It was obvious the Magnum was defective. He went over to Speed.

'Something's wrong with the Magnum.'

Speed took off his earmuffs. 'What? What did you say?'

'The Magnum's no good. It's not shooting straight.'

Speed took the gun from him, went over to where Zia had stood and said, 'Dead centre, forehead,' and fired. 'Left eye,' one more shot, 'right eye,' another shot, 'Adam's apple,' another, 'the heart,' another. The bullets pierced the precise locations he had enumerated.

'Seems okay to me,' Speed said as he handed the gun to Zia.

Zia tried again. Six times. The gun had a will of its own in his hands. It was like a horse in those rodeo movies. It kicked and reared and bucked, he thought, even when he was standing still, arms by his side. He concentrated hard, perhaps a little too hard, and grew more frantic every time he missed and was thrown back. How superciliously Speed and Vivian were watching him make an ass of himself. If only he could shoot straight, Zia would turn around, blow the brains out of Speed, shoot Vivian in the legs, maybe in the liver too, and then mow down the rest of the people in the area. He fired again. That was the last bullet in the chamber and there was no bullet mark on the dummy.

Vivian came over. What the hell did she want? Hadn't she humiliated him enough? She had been right, right from the very beginning. He was inadequate and incompetent and utterly useless.

'You take over.' Zia offered her the Magnum. 'We need someone who'll see the job through successfully. Not a man who's afraid of the gun he's holding.'

She would not take the Magnum from him.

'Can you hear me?' Zia spoke up again. 'Take the gun. I'm entrusting the mission to you.'

'Are you sure, Zia? I wouldn't want you to regret it later.'

'I'm sure,' Zia said. 'Go ahead. Take over. Shoot to kill.'

'Maybe next time.' Vivian lightly bussed him on the cheek. 'Would you like to try your luck with another gun, Zia?'

She held the more compact Luger in her hand.

'You had the Luger with you all along, didn't you?' Zia asked Vivian as they got into bed.

'Yes. Are you angry with me?'

'Hugely.'

My dear Zia,

I will dispense with my usual banter. I don't know how to convey the intensity of my feelings, befuddlement, anger and despair, but this is not the time to quibble about the choice of words.

I am appalled by the letter you wrote to Ammijaan. I've never been shy of being critical nor do I see much merit in not judging people. When people tell you unctuously that they don't want to judge somebody, what they usually mean is that they want to play it safe. They won't judge because they don't want to be judged. But the act of critical assessment does not blacklist anybody nor does it ever mean that it precludes affection or love. I cannot respect Abbajaan's architectural designs or Eisenstein's films without analysing and judging them just as I cannot differentiate between pulp and literature, Grisham and Márquez, without weighing and evaluating their work. So I'm not about to become apoplectic and ask how dare you presume to judge Ammi.

I myself have said harsh things about her often. Nor am I fool enough to think that parents and children always get along. If you've come to the conclusion that you no longer care for your mother, no one is going to coerce you into loving her. If you occasionally run into her by chance, you could say 'hello' and observe the bare minimum of courtesy that a civilized society demands and there's an end to it.

What I cannot fathom is the depth of intolerance and violence in you. Why this need to hurt, Zia? Would you really want Ammijaan to be stoned if, as you say, we were living in an Islamic state? Oh God, Zia, why would you want anybody, whether he or she is an adulterer or criminal, to be stoned, mutilated or murdered by decree? That wonderful old man Gandhi was so right: an eye for an eye will leave us all blind. The trouble with prescribing physical or mental violence as punishment is that they debase and brutalize both parties. I do not presume to comment upon any of the holy books but I believe you cannot have both mercy and retributive chastisement in the same breath. You have to choose one or the other. I truly hope that you will not choose the other.

You could tell me that this is between you and Ammijaan and you would be right but I cannot bear to see our mother suffer. Brave soul that she is, she tries to be cheerful but sometimes when she is not on her guard the hurt shows. Then Ammi sits silently for hours, her lovely face stupefied by something she cannot understand: why would someone she loves so inordinately want to cause her so much pain?

It's not too late, Zia. Will you write to her and tell her you were wrong? Tell her that you love her as only Zia can love his mother. The light will be back in Ammi's eyes and the affectionate mother that she is, she'll not only forgive you but forget that you wrote that letter to her.

Do, do please do that by return post.

Love,

Amanat

1001,

You are your father's son, Amanat. Like Abbajaan you are a weakling. You are unable, or rather are afraid to take matters to their logical conclusions. Like all liberals you want to have it both ways. You want to give it straight from the shoulder but you don't want to be perceived as arrogant and unkind. You don't want anything to sully your nice-guy image. Unlike you I'm not concerned about whether or not I'm a nice guy. All I care about is whether I'm doing the right thing by Allah.

You are intelligent enough to know that you've allowed your mind to become a fetid swamp. There is nothing but confusion fermenting there. Yes, Allah is merciful when you are deserving of mercy. But he is unforgiving when you are unrepentant and not willing to change your evil ways. There is no forgiveness for adultery. Your mother has wilfully transgressed Allah's edicts not once but again and again. She is a nymphomaniac and she rejoices in her adultery instead of shunning it. Besides it's not just sex she's after. She's much more devious than that. She chooses her partners with care. They have to be rich enough to bankroll her expensive habits. Cards, races, the obsessive gambling, the drinking and the good life.... They all come with a heavy price tag. When her victims are bankrupted or get wise to her, she moves on to her next quarry.

The awful truth is that we have had to pay the price for her debauchery. She blackmailed Abba to take Altaaf Mamoo on board and then to appoint him CEO. When Altaaf perpetrated the scam that turned our lives upside down, she blamed Abba instead of standing firmly by his side and fighting the hyenas from the press, other media and the central body of architects. We were left homeless and Abba could no longer practise his profession.

The fool that you are, you do not even realize that you suffered the most. You had to go to a school that was no better than a municipal one. My earliest memories of you are of you working on architectural models of airports, homes, housing complexes and parks. Even your mother said that you were an architect from the time you were in the womb. And yet you abandoned your vocation because you could never forgive or forget the way our father had been betrayed.

We never talk about this but give the devil her due, Amanat. She was responsible for your alienation from your vocation.

No, I do not wish to follow in your and Abba's sorry footsteps. I have been unconscionably kind to your mother. No punishment is commensurate with her crimes.

Zia

# 18

Vivian had met Roy only once, when he had come to Cambridge, and had taken an instant dislike to him. She wanted Zia all to herself but was wise enough to realize that Roy was the only friend Zia had. She understood that there was a strange bond between the two, and Zia didn't take kindly to any criticism of Roy. Fortunately Roy was out of the country most of the time. Her way of dealing with him was to stay away from him as far as possible. She refused to go to Cambray Park for the party.

The celebration at Cambray Park may have been in honour of Zia's achievements at Cambridge, but with the Cambrays, Zia suspected there was always a hidden agenda. (In fairness to Roy, Zia had to admit that he could not bracket the son with the parents.) It was a wonder that World War III did not break out at these parties. Whoever was in charge of the guest list must have had a phenomenal memory. Maybe they had an advanced software program that updated the changing map of the world, the civil wars and the rise and fall of dictators, every half hour. There was no telling which African tribe was butchering which of its neighbours that particular day and who had made up. You had to be on the ball to know who the Americans considered rogue states that week, and you had to be a mind-reader to be able to see through the public rhetoric and posturing to the subterranean swings and realpolitik. The Cambrays never got it wrong.

'May I?' James Cambray pulled his wife away from the Serbs as the band struck up. He was chubby and cherubic and his hands barely reached his jacket pockets. The hairless head was a mini-chandelier reflecting the thousands of lights in the trees, and his behind stuck out like an ample bosom from a Fellini movie. But who would notice these details when James and Deirdre took the floor to do a half-forgotten dance called the Cha Cha Cha.

'Your mother's unbelievable,' Zia told Roy. Then as an afterthought he added, 'But I guess she's supposed to be. Now him, he's something else, isn't he?'

'He is, he sure is.' Roy was watching his parents as intently as Zia. 'Though I can't tell whether he's the joker in the pack. Or the joke's on all of us.'

Zia could not fathom the relationship between father and son. It wasn't as though there was no communication between them. They talked, they laughed, more the father than the son, they went on holidays together and sometimes flew out to London together. But it was a stillborn relationship. There was neither affection nor animosity between them, just a no-man's-land. Zia was not drawn to people easily but he was intrigued by Cambray Senior.

He might act the clown occasionally, but he was nobody's fool. The jolly good fellow bit was real, but it was also a front. You never really knew what was in his mind. He often said there are no blacks, whites, coloureds; no Africans, Americans or Asians. Only human beings. Which means every one of them is different. If you can remember that, and most diplomats, politicians and prime ministers don't, you are going to be okay.

James Cambray seemed to know a lot of people in high places. He might not have been Onassis or the king of Saudi Arabia, but whatever the 'this and that' was that Roy said he did for a living, he must have been good at it.

'Care to dance, my friend?' a woman tapped Zia on the shoulder and asked.

Zia shook his head.

She was twenty-five, maybe thirty, and had eyelashes as long as a peacock's tail.

'You alone?'

'No, I'm with Roy.'

'No, you aren't. You're with me now. I'm going to look after you like no one ever has.'

'I can look after myself, thank you,' Zia said haughtily.

Deirdre was waving trying frantically to catch the woman's eye from across the grounds.

'Not the way I can,' the woman laughed.

'Where's Roy?'

'Let's go, love. Why would you need Roy when I'm with you?'

The woman was rubbing her knee, maybe it was her hand, somewhere near his fly. He looked at his crotch in consternation and attempted to move away. Roy's mother was advancing rapidly upon them. Zia's new companion moved back with him as if they shared a common hipbone. He was panic-stricken and didn't know where to turn for help. He saw a man leering at him. He was hardly a man, more like a colossus, a Brobdingnagian. He was in a lungi, kurta and angavastram. How could Zia ever forget the guru with the Rasputin eyes he had met at New Eden with Roy's mother?

He had his hand on James Cambray's shoulder. They were Chaplin and Fatty Arbuckle, Laurel and Hardy, Arnold Schwarzenegger and Danny de Vito. Roy's father was looking up at the man and listening intently but the man's eyes were still on Zia.

You've got it wrong, Zia wanted to tell him. I'm not up to anything, I swear I'm not. She is.

The giant was smiling at Zia now, with all thirty-two of his gleaming teeth, and the vermilion tikka on his forehead stared at him like Cyclops's eye.

Deirdre Cambray had reached Zia and was speaking to his companion.

'I think you've got the wrong party, Scarlett.'

My dear Zia,

'Cross and Christians, end to end I examined. He was not on the cross. I went to the Hindu temple, to the ancient pagoda. In none of them was there any sign. To the uplands of Herrat I went, and to Kandahar. I looked. He was not on the heights or in the lowlands. Resolutely, I went to the summit of the fabulous mountain of Kaf. There I found only the dwelling of the legendary Anqa bird. I went to the Kaaba of Mecca. He was not there. I asked questions about him of Avicenna the philosopher. He was beyond the range of Avicenna.... I looked into my own heart. In that, his place, I saw him. He was in no other place.'

That's not me, but Rumi, who is suddenly very big in the West. I have been reading the mystic saints, Lalla, Basavanna, Tukaram and Kabir, and I wondered if you approved of them. I'm not quite sure who qualifies as a true believer in your eyes and who's disqualified. Do you have some kind of checklist against which people are assessed? Will you share it with me? Are the Sufis considered deviants or would they find a berth in paradise?

I find the notion of heaven rather colonial, a British club where only the chosen are allowed in. The idea of paradise can only be sustained by exclusion. The more you exclude people, the more exclusive the club.

Why is it that heaven cannot be posited without hell? I'm not particularly fond of the Christian or Dantean concept of hell, nor am I enamoured of the Islamic jehannum. And yet even they are not as misanthropic or mistaken as Sartre's definition of hell. 'Hell is other people,' he says in *Huis Clos*. It is not his arrogance or, irony of ironies, his bourgeois smugness (sure, sure, it's his protagonist talking and not he himself; a likely story indeed) that are staggering, but his ignorance of human nature.

Hell is oneself, as Eliot once said.

Be well, dear Zia,

Love,

Amanat

P.S. You may be right about my being a weakling, but mercy is the first of Allah's virtues. Contrary to your official posture, I know from my own experience and what Aunt Antonia tells us that you are a good man and a warm and caring person. Except when you set out to prove that you are any man's equal when it comes to taking a macho moral stance. All I can hope is that you will miss Ammijaan as much as she misses you and you will forgive her her shortcomings as we are more than willing to forgive our own.

'You must be wondering what was so important that I asked you to come to my office.' Aunt Antonia's secretary was perhaps on leave, for Antonia had a paper knife in her hand with which she sliced through envelope after envelope, arranging the mail in three neat piles. 'I thought we could talk freely here and no one would disturb us.' She went into the alcove adjoining her room and came back with a tray of tea and chocolate biscuits.

Zia was into his second biscuit and wondering if she would ever get down to whatever she wanted to tell him, when she raised the lid of a glass case to her right and brought over some old tome, no doubt a first edition of the King James Bible, or perhaps it was the handwritten and autographed psalm book of King David.

'Tell me what this manuscript is. I'll give you three guesses.'

Zia stared at the strange hieroglyphics on the page. He could not figure out what they were and he didn't care. Something was wrong. Zia couldn't quite put his finger on it, but Aunt Antonia's strenuous efforts to sound offhand failed to conceal her overwrought state of mind.

'Give up?' Aunt Antonia could barely contain herself. 'It's perhaps the world's first book of pornography. My husband got it while he was on a dig in Egypt. The writer is a woman, either the head of the harem or the Egyptian Pharaoh's favourite mistress. I could be wrong but I suspect that the meticulousness of the royal funerary rights comprehends not just spiritual needs and the care of the body, but also bizarre esoteric sexual practices. Isn't that marvellous? Even in the nether world you need your Kamasutra.' Antonia's hand pointed to a painting in the book. 'Can you tell me what those seven are doing? Look. Now I see another leg and pair of hands. Good heavens, there's another figure there. Most intriguing. Perhaps you can throw some light on who's got what where?' Aunt Antonia laid her hand on Zia's back conspiratorially and looked at him for approval as though she herself were responsible for the ancient orgy. 'Phew, can you beat that for sheer acrobatics?'

Zia's eyes had long since frozen into a vacuous stare. He looked at the ceiling, his shoes, his fingernails, the cross on the chain around his aunt's neck. What was the matter with this woman? Did she have no sense of propriety? That was the trouble with this godless civilization. It had no boundaries, no dos and don'ts. No notion that in public, or for that matter in private, decent women don't talk about certain things. He would have liked to walk out of the room, but that, he feared, would hurt her no end. He forced himself to think about the set of proposals he was writing for Dr Laughton on debt waivers for the ten poorest countries in the world. In the last couple of months he had begun to assist the Master of Emmanuel in his consultancy work with the UN almost on a full-time basis. The job paid well enough and he got to accompany the Master to New York and Latin America but, as even Dr Laughton pointed out, he would have to take care not to allow the freelancing to get in the way of his PhD.

'Why Zia, you are blush – ' Aunt Antonia stopped midsentence. She sat down on her writing table as though her legs could no longer take her weight. The three neatly separated stacks of letters slid into each other and some of the envelopes fell to the floor. Zia picked them up and put them back on the table. Antonia's hands were shaking and the blood had sluiced from her face.

'Are you all right?' Zia asked her.

'No, I am not,' she said. 'I have been waiting for this moment for twenty-three years. I've thought about it almost every day. And then when it's here I'm so nervous, I talk foolishly about everything other than what's on my mind.' She got up then and did something she hadn't done for years. She held Zia's face in her hands and kissed his forehead.

'I have no idea where to start or what to say. So I'll just say it. When you were three or four days old, maybe a week at the most, you suddenly collapsed. You were rushed to hospital but none of the doctors could diagnose what was wrong. All they could tell was that one by one the systems in your body were failing. Your stomach was distended with fluids, your kidneys were functioning erratically and your breathing became more and more laboured. They did not want to mislead us, they said. There was no hope, none at all.

'"Can't you get another consultant? Would it help if we took him abroad to get another opinion?" Your father and Shagufta asked the same questions over and over again, but the doctors just shook their heads. Around noon the next day they said another half-hour or hour at the most and it would all be over. Your parents, Zubeida and I, sheer chance that I was there at the time, sat there stupefied waiting for the end.

'You had turned grey-blue and cold to the touch when I asked your parents if I could take you to a church. I have no idea why I suggested it. I hadn't been to church for years and was almost a lapsed Catholic. Your mother smiled wanly and said, "What's the point?" and I said, "None, I guess. But what harm could it do to a baby who's been declared as good as dead?" Zafar asked the physician whether he would permit it and he merely shrugged his shoulders. "Make sure you bring him back. You won't be able to bury him without a death certificate."

'I got into your father's car and told the driver to take me to the nearest church. I couldn't find a priest for ten minutes and when I did, I didn't know why I wanted him. He was a slow, stupid sort of person and he looked at me as if I had either kidnapped you or maybe choked you to death. I couldn't find the right words. He expected me to tell him why I was there, and out of sheer desperation I said, "Baptize him, Father. Give him Extreme Unction." It's strange how phrases from my past that had meant nothing to me for so long, came back unbidden. I'd even forgotten that you don't give Extreme Unction to an infant.

'"Whose baby is it?" he asked. I didn't want any problems and I said, "Mine." And he said, "Looks pretty dark."

'"He's gone blue because he can't breathe. Now are you done talking?"

'Don't ask me what happened,' she paused and shook her head as if she were trying to overcome her own incredulity. 'All I know is that I had a Little Miracle on my hand, and a crisis of faith.' She laughed then. 'Oh, you didn't improve overnight. You were on the critical list for another seven days and the doctors still didn't believe you'd make it. But you are here and that must mean something, mustn't it?' She looked at Zia with such overwhelming affection, he found it embarrassing.

'When I announced that I had baptized you, I don't think Shagufta and Zafar quite took it in. I doubt if I did either. The only one who was terribly upset was your aunt Zubeida. I don't think she's ever forgiven me.

'Nobody knew what to make of it but I was on my way to becoming a born-again Christian, or rather a born-again Roman Catholic. Not overnight but in due time. I was beginning to be convinced that we owed your life to the intervention of Jesus Christ. I felt proprietorial about you. I put it to your parents that you should be brought up as a Catholic. Zubeida, of course, was incensed that I should even propose such a thing. And yet I had been circumspect in my words. Truth be told, I wanted to bring you up myself.'

Zia felt he was being buried alive under a mudslide of words and uncontrolled emotion. He wasn't sure whether it was Aunt Antonia or he who was hallucinating.

'Zafar and Zubeida rarely saw eye to eye but in this instance he weighed in on her side. And so did your mother. At least that's the way I saw it then. But that's not being quite fair to Shagufta and your father. Your parents felt that neither Zubeida nor I should choose your faith for you. You should be the one to decide. "Let him be twenty-one before he hears about his miraculous recovery," Zafar said. I did not wish to give in but I had little choice. After all you were going to be brought up in India and in their home.

'I began to visit India twice a year on my missionary work. From your childhood it was clear that you had a special place in our Lord's heart. He hadn't just saved your life, he had given you unique gifts. You spoke whole sentences before most children learn to walk. You were a wizard at figures and you were modest to the point of being nearly ignorant of your gifts. I watched Christ watch over you and I went on my knees every day and thanked Him for His wonderful grace.'

The onslaught of words now seemed to ease. Antonia looked at Zia a trifle puzzled. 'Aren't you going to say anything?'

Zia shook his head. What was there to say? He just wished she would shut up and let him go.

'I guess this comes as something of a shock to you and here I am expecting you to react or say something when you haven't had any time to take it in.'

'It was you who sent me to New Eden.' Zia's voice was barely audible.

'That was the least I could do for you. Your father's business had collapsed and he was without a job. Both Zafar and Shagufta refused even to listen to my suggestion because they believed it would be very unfair to Amanat. But I argued with them. I could afford to send only one child to New Eden and since I had always thought of you as my baby and responsibility, it had to be you. They gave in very reluctantly.

'I don't want to pretend that it was all smooth sailing. You could be a difficult child at times. There were moments when I felt Jesus had abandoned you and I had lost you forever. But my faith was strong and fortunately I had a little influence with the authorities in New Eden, and you always came through.'

Zia smiled at Aunt Antonia's 'little influence'. He knew now why he had got through every scrape in New Eden, the Muharram flagellation for Hassan and Hussein, and the business with Roy's girlfriend, Sarah Roberts.

'Oddly enough, the one time I nearly lost you was because of my own high-handedness. Like new converts, the "born again" are untouched by doubt. I always knew better than anyone else. I think the good Lord decided to teach me humility then.

'Your parents and I had agreed that I would tell you why you were my "Little Miracle" when you passed your finals. The day came and went. As expected you did brilliantly. I had waited for that moment a long time and yet when it came to pass, I lost my nerve. You are after all a staunch Muslim. I no longer knew how to talk to you and how you would react. Another year and a half have gone by and for the first time I understand why Zafar wanted me to wait. You have to choose what you wish to believe, not I. I think that's the way Jesus would want it too.

'I want you to understand that, whatever decision you take or don't take, nothing has changed between us. Your room at home is, and always will be, yours. I want you to finish your PhD there.' Aunt

Antonia paused. 'There, I've said my piece and I'm feeling the better for it.' She laughed then, a self-deprecating apology of a laugh. 'I can't say that about you though. You look worn out. I've exhausted you with my talk about the past. Shall I make another cup of tea for you?'

'No, thank you.'

'We could go and have lunch somewhere. How about some Thai food?'

'I better run along. I have a third-year student coming over,' Zia told her. 'And then I've got to go to the mosque for Friday prayers.'

15th January: Allah, my Allah. My breath is Yours, my being is Yours and so is my soul. Yours the glory that is creation and Yours the rainbow that spans the heavens. I prostrate myself before You. Shine Your light upon me, oh Lord, for in truth I'm as unseeing as a blind man. I stumble and I fall at every step. Time and again You've stretched Your hand out and steadied me. But never before have I needed You as I need You now.

You had warned Adam and Eve that Satan is mercurial and will tempt them in a myriad forms and shapes. He may come in the guise of Salome, he may come as the Good Samaritan. Why, he may come as a godmother who entices me with the generosity of her heart. Her blandishments know no end. When my family can barely survive, she sends me to the finest of schools. She saves me again and again when I'm about to be expelled. She ensures a smooth passage for me at Cambridge. As if all this were not enough to keep me indebted to her for a dozen lifetimes, she begs my forgiveness for trying to impose her will upon me.

Now she wants me to believe that I have been baptized and am a Roman Catholic. But as long as You are my shield and my scimitar, I know that I am safe.

22nd January: Where are You, oh Lord, why have You forsaken me? The Prince of Darkness is still at large. I have looked for him in every corner of the country, I've gone to more literary events and fairs than anybody else in England. There have been times when I've been a hair's breadth away from him. And yet every time he has given me the slip.

You are omniscient, omnipotent and omnipresent. Won't You give me a hint, Lord, so that I can crush this enemy of Islam under my heel?

Are You listening, Allah? Where are You?

27th March: How long will I keep pretending that I don't know why You have turned your back on me? Why am I fooling myself? I know too well that it is because I've been living in sin with Vivian. But I had every intention of marrying her. Three times I nearly proposed to her, and three times I was forced to stop in my tracks. When she was about to convert, it was not for love of You, but to spite her mother. When I caught her spying on me as I kept a close watch on the Prince of Darkness, she kicked me in the genitals and nearly disabled me. When she switched to the burkha, it was not for reasons of modesty, but to draw attention to herself, at a time when anonymity was critical to us. I must beg You, Allah, to believe that I'm not making a scapegoat of Vivian. She's headstrong and obstinate and doesn't listen to me.

Make me strong, Allah. Give me forbearance. Make me worthy of You. Help me find the Prince of Darkness. How else will people recognize me as the waalee? Only then will I be able to bring the light of Islam to the rest of mankind.

## 19

Damn Amanat. Zia had tried to scotch the book from his mind but the arsonist had installed himself in Zia's head and was lighting fires all over the place. Was Amanat mocking God? Or was he suggesting something profound? Zia couldn't be sure what his brother was up to. There was a passage almost at the end of the book that Zia found outrageous and the most puzzling of all.

The weaver was an old man now. He had announced many a time that he had no intention, none whatsoever, of dying. I plan to carry on, he would say, and get as old and bald and toothless as the Almighty himself. And yet, in his work nowadays, you could see the threads and colours of old age.

His students and disciples smirked and made faces about the half-deaf, half-blind and half-mad weaver who was their Master. He was only half the man he had been, they said. The trouble was, there was no telling which half you would meet. Sometimes if he happened to hear you, he raged and ranted. I am still more of a man, he would say, than all of you young bucks put together. My dong is longer than yours, my hard-ons are harder and they can outlast anybody else's.

They wouldn't have dared to in the past, but now they laughed openly in his face.

Hey, cock-of-the-walk, the troublemaker Inayat sneered, lifting the old man's kurta so that you could see the bulge of his trailing genitals, let's go to the brothel and test the matter.

You think I'm going to pay for your pleasure? the weaver asked, perhaps to put Inayat off.

No, no. We'll all come along and pay for your pleasure.

Well, I'm busy, he said. I get more orders than I can handle. There are so many other weavers but the nawabs and rajahs insist that I design and weave all their fabrics. Just the other day, the Sultan of Persia sent a messenger saying that I must weave the world's most exquisite and expensive cloth for his son's wedding robe next year. I had to refuse. What could I do? I have only two hands and you people are a dead loss. Can't ever rely on you.

Don't give us that cock-and-bull story, old man, Charatram, usually the quietest of the weaver's apprentices, spoke. Why can't you admit that you can no longer get it up?

That evening, all seventeen apprentices and the weaver went to the whores' alley. They took a woman each for themselves and the prettiest, the one they called Sherani because she was a tigress in bed, they kept for the old man. The deal was that at the end of the session, Sherani would give a report to them about the weaver's sexual prowess.

When they were done, the pupils gathered in the courtyard but there was no sign of the weaver. Fifteen minutes, half an hour, two hours. They went and listened at the door. The weaver was still at it. Then there was absolute silence. It sounded ominous after all that panting and heaving. He's obviously overdone it and had a heart attack. Must have burst a blood vessel. We went too far this time, they said, when the door was flung open and Sherani came out swearing at the weaver in the foulest language imaginable. They had to admit that her vocabulary in such matters was infinitely more colourful than their own limited and repetitive oaths.

This is not a man, Sherani screamed. He's a tomcat, a billy goat, a sex maniac. He's done it seventeen times and he wants to do it again. The bloody lech says you guys are paying for it, so why shouldn't he get his money's worth? And what about me? I'm as good as dead. He's done it so often, a bullock cart, even the Maharaja's chariot could pass through. Come on, cough up, each one of you. This is no laughing matter. I'm ruined for life.

That night they had dinner at an open-air roadside café: biryani and tangdi kebabs. The weaver was feeling generous and they ate heartily. He was narrating in great detail his exploits with Sherani when he became short of breath. They made him lie down on a bench. He was pale and a grey shadow was creeping over his face. They wondered if this was the end.

Charatram, the shy one, said, Master, you should have some sense at your age. Couldn't you have controlled yourself? Even we can't do it more than twice, and that too after a break.

The Master could hardly speak but that didn't prevent him from laughing and spluttering. I held Sherani's breasts in my hands. They were full and heavy as papayas and I thought God was finally in my palms. I told her if I sleep with you – and I'm not sure I'm up to it today – you'll earn some money but not much. But if, on the other hand, we lie blissfully in each other's arms for a couple of hours and then you scream and shout that I'm a monster and forced sex upon you seventeen times, all my apprentices will pay you seventeen times as much. Sherani is a businesswoman. How could she not go along with my scheme?

They could have strangled the Master. Instead they laughed, called him a cheat and a liar. Why else would they love him so and follow him everywhere? He was really a child and he never tired of practical jokes. By now, the weaver's pulse was unsteady and his breathing was short and staccato. He looked at them, he smiled weakly and he fell silent. A few more breaths and the soul had flown out of him. They touched his feet and asked his blessings one last time. They sent Charatram to get the wood for his funeral pyre and told him they would meet him at the burning ghats.

But even as Charatram left, Inayat said, The Master is a Muslim and he should be buried. Adil, Rehmat and Suleiman agreed with him. A vehement argument broke out amongst the disciples, but the Muslim pupils were outnumbered by the Hindus and walked away in anger.

Charatram came back with a bullock cart loaded with firewood. The Hindu disciples arranged the pyre and laid the Master gently on it. They performed the last rites, and each one of them lit a torch. They poured the ghee and were about to light the pyre when Inayat, Rehmat and the others returned with a group of Muslim friends. They had knives in their hands. The Hindus and the Muslims were now evenly matched.

If you know what's good for you, Inayat said, give the weaver back to us.

Just you try and take him, Gunidas retorted.

There was only one way to settle the matter. They fell on each other. Scalps broken open, blood and guts, both parties were doing pretty well when the weaver sat up.

Can't a man even die in peace? he asked.

The Hindus and the Muslims froze as in a tableau. What was this apparition? They fled in panic.

Come back, you fools, come back, the wispy figure called after them.

One by one they returned. Some of them stood at a distance just in case the incubus sprang at them.

You won't ever change, will you? For the first time in his life there was defeat in the weaver's voice. Light me a torch, he told them.

They had to help him down off the pyre. He stood unsteadily and took the torch from Charatram.

Come, he said, follow me.

His legs seemed to buckle and he walked drunkenly. He had, after all, just come back from the dead. It was three in the morning when they reached the bazaar. The weaver stood almost at the centre. He was silent for a minute or longer than that. He was not going to make it, they thought, but his voice rang out.

I stand in the marketplace,  
A torch in my hand.  
Whosoever will set fire to his house,  
Come, join me.

Now, he's really gone off his rocker, his apprentices and disciples said to each other.

Bring me the town crier's drum, the weaver said.

Why not, Inayat thought, this might be fun. He went to the peepul tree where the drum rested when it was not in use.

Beat it, the Master said, wake up the whole world and the heavens too.

The townspeople came out of their houses – husbands, wives and children, patriarchs and mothers-in-law, dogs and cats – and soon the whole town was gathered around the weaver. They looked a little eerie and unreal in the light of the torches.

I stand in the marketplace, the Master spoke again. His voice was steady and it seemed to echo off the walls of the houses.

I stand in the marketplace,

A torch in my hand.
Whosoever will set fire to his house,
Come, join me.

What the hell is the old man up to? Ismael asked. What's he trying to say?

Something symbolic and profound, Charatram said sardonically. Something totally beyond you and me.

It slowly began to dawn on the townspeople that the weaver was serious about his invitation. He was always a bit mad but this time he had definitely gone over the edge. They began to close in on him almost imperceptibly, the men followed by the women. There was something sinister about the way they moved as if the weaver's madness had touched them too. The pupils and disciples, all but Inayat, slowly shrank away. The villagers bent down and picked up stones, bricks and whatever they could lay their hands on. Some went back to their homes to get knives, axes, hammers and bamboo poles.

Inayat, they said, move away, lest you get hurt.

He shook his head but was sensible enough to distance himself from the Master. The weaver began to run, his right hand up in the air. The flame of the torch sputtered and quivered. The villagers were not about to let the mad old man burn their homes. They began to pelt him. The Master torched his own house. A stone split open his forehead, a bamboo cracked the bone of his left arm. The weaver did not stop. A boy with a catapult got his left eye. Some of the disciples shouted to the villagers not to hurt the Master but no one paid them any heed. Gunidas and Rehmat flung their torches up in the air, caught them and set their own houses on fire. The haystacks next to their homes crackled and sputtered and turned into fireworks. Sparks rose in the air like fireflies. Three of the houses were burning steadily now, the conflagration making a racket and rising high into the skies.

There was a battle raging between the Master's pupils and the villagers. The disciples were in a minority and even those who had merely stood aside and watched were attacked; some were badly injured. The villagers had long realized that their houses were safe, but that did not assuage their fury. They continued their rampage.

Are you happy now? Inayat asked the Master. Why burn our own houses? Makes no sense.

The wounded weaver said, Fire purifies, my friend. It is our chance to start afresh, to alter the course of our lives. The trouble with men is that the past is always and ever with them, as it was with you, Inayat and Charatram and all your friends at the burning ghats.

You were about to kill each other for the sake of a god who you claim is either a Muslim or a Hindu. But Inayat, there is only one God and Her name is Life. She is the only one worthy of worship. All else is irrelevant.

Is arson, then, the end of all your weaving and questioning, whoring and poetry? Inayat sneered. Or perhaps that is how you conceal your despair.

It needn't have been if even a few of my pupils had changed just a little. We are never fully God's because we are always bound to the world and its ways; to our children, wives, work, pleasures, old habits that don't die; to our pride and sacrifices. Once we are homeless, once we have no past, once there's an end to me, me, me, and there's nothing to hold us back, once we are true orphans, then our only home is God.

And is your work done now, old man?

The weaver laughed, more like a cackle really.

Hardly, he said, now we'll burn heaven and hell and smoke and flush out God himself.

In the guise of writing an updated, postmodernist, swinging biography of a saint, Amanat had written the story of Satan. No wonder it read like a spiritual thriller. It was told with so much energy, it had such an engaging style, that you got carried away. The weaver's relationship with his wife was one of the funniest things Zia had read. It actually made him roll on the floor. The weaver's children saw through their father and were his true heirs. They tried to do him out of his money, his home, and his property. The saint's earlier forays into other careers, especially as a frightened and fast-talking highway robber, then as a pusillanimous soldier and a gravedigger were hilarious and memorable. But behind all that rowdy exuberance and dark humour was a sustained and highly sophisticated campaign to confuse the reader and cast doubts on the goodness of God, and on everything Zia believed constituted the relationship between God and man.

Zubeida Khaala was right. There was only one defence against the allure of Satan. It was the impregnable fortress of the Koran. He had to knit the holy words into chain-mail armour to protect himself from such heresy. And yet, even as he read the Holy Book, the arsonist and his picaresque escapades intruded upon his consciousness.

'Now we'll burn heaven and hell and smoke and flush out God himself.'

What did the arsonist mean when he said that, and more to the point, what did his brother Amanat have in mind when he wrote that?

## 20

Zia disliked long-distance calls, especially those from India. He could see his family standing around the phone, each one waiting to get a turn to speak to him. There were at least four 'how are yous?' If the line was bad they could go up to anywhere between sixteen and twenty. Every question and statement was prefaced by a 'hello' as if it were a mantra that could mend broken telephone connections and, who knows, perhaps even broken lives. 'What's the weather like? Is it cold there?' He would have liked to have asked what difference it would make to them if it were fourteen degrees below zero in Cambridge or forty above. Surely they were not deluding themselves that they could control the climate for him. 'Are you taking care of yourself?' No, I stand naked on the Common in blizzard winds and I don't eat and I don't sleep for love of you. 'When are you coming back?' They were not questions, really. His family members were merely reassuring themselves that four thousand miles away their Zia was still alive and functioning. Or was it the other way round? Were they reassuring him that they were still hanging in there, however difficult or impossible things might have become? We love you, they said, we love you, we love you, we love you. It was like an extended refrain in a teenage song. And he too sang the same song.

When Abbajaan called this time, Zia's first thought was, Is it my birthday? No, that was long past. He wondered whether someone was ill; perhaps something had happened to Zubeida Khaala. He was certain that Abbajaan would, in the usual Indian fashion of easing the shock of bad news, keep stalling with inane preliminaries and then break the truth gradually. He was relieved when Abba said that he had some good news. I'll let Amanat tell it to you, he told Zia, and of course blurted it out himself. The British Council has invited Amanat to attend their Cambridge Seminar starting on 21st June.

Amanat took it from there. There must have been some error, he said. The British Council people in Bombay had mistaken him for someone else and that's how he'd been invited. Or perhaps the person they'd had in mind had said no and they couldn't think of anybody else at the last minute and...

'Amanat,' Zia interrupted him, 'cut the crap.'

Amanat was going abroad for the first time since the Firdaus days. It was his style never to show too much feeling or excitement, for fear that the powers-that-be would become jealous and snuff out whatever he was looking forward to. But Zia knew just how much this trip would mean to Amanat. He asked whether Amanat would like to stay with him at Aunt Antonia's place after the seminar. I would love to spend more time with you, Amanat said, but let's see. If I don't have to get back to work immediately, I may take you up on your offer.

Zia was not quite sure how Vivian came to accompany him to Heathrow. They had not discussed the matter and he had taken it for granted that he would pick up Amanat alone. He found it difficult to believe that he had not met his brother or the rest of the family for close to six years. He was hoping that Amanat's seminar would not extend into the evenings. Surely, he couldn't discuss the drag coefficient of automobile body designs, the ergonomic enhancement of computer screens, or patterns of shock absorption and distribution in helmets, for more than eight hours a day. Zia had gone off to a meeting with the Master of Emmanuel at a little after twelve, to run the outline of the sixth chapter of his thesis by him, and when he got back Vivian was dressed and waiting for him.

Zia was uneasy about what Amanat was going to think of him bringing along a young, striking woman – and she was looking very, very striking today. He had not mentioned Viv in his letters home. He wondered how he was going to introduce her.

Look at her, just look at her. So shy and lovely. And that yellow hat, where had she got that from? Zia had never seen her in a hat before. (Would anyone have guessed that the beauteous Lady Vivian was his partner in a holy crime?)

Zia needn't have worried about Amanat's response to Vivian. Smitten was going a little too far, but he certainly was taken with Aunt Antonia's offspring. He was wearing a jacket two or three sizes too large, must have been one of Abba's old ones. He was still very thin and the jacket flapped on him like a forlorn flag. Zia felt a wave of affection wash over him. He had not realized how much he had missed his brother. Amanat was going to be okay from now on. Zia would protect him.

Vivian was already deep in conversation with Amanat as though he were her brother, not Zia's.

'What's your paper on?' Vivian was asking Amanat as they got on to the bus to Cambridge.

'I am not reading a paper.'

'Not reading a paper?' Zia looked puzzled. The bus made one of those repressed sounds as though it were passing wind.

'Why not?' Vivian asked. 'Zia says you are one of the foremost designers of crash helmets and that you've done more research on head injuries than most trauma surgeons have.'

'You mustn't believe everything Zia says. He's much given to exaggeration when it comes to his family. And besides, this is not a seminar on industrial design.'

'No?' Zia asked. 'Then what's it on?'

'Are you people trying to pull my leg?' Amanat looked at both of them and smiled. 'You are from Cambridge, right? And you don't know what the Cambridge Seminar is about?'

'There are at least three or four seminars a week in Cambridge,' Vivian said.

'Oh,' Amanat looked chastened and overawed. 'This one's on literature, more specifically, on the "British Literary Scene". And it's at Downing College.'

Zia couldn't figure out what Amanat was doing at the Cambridge Seminar. It was hard to believe that he had been invited because he had written that novel about Kabir. Surely it could not have escaped their notice that it was a perfidious book. But Zia was in a forgiving mood today. He was with Amanat now, and nothing else mattered.

Vivian and Zia helped Amanat register for the seminar, saw him to his room on the second floor of the building at Downing and took him to dinner at an Italian place. It was close to midnight by the time they got home but it would be a while before they went to bed.

The British Council Cambridge Seminar. Now, that was a surprise; more like a blow in the medulla oblongata. Zia hadn't even heard of it, and nor had Vivian. Amanat had said it was only for people from different countries who were nominated by the local British Council offices. More like a private, 'by invitation only' affair. Had Satan been invited? Oh, that would be ironic, wouldn't it? Zia spends years, not to mention a tidy fortune, going to every borough and county in the United Kingdom of Regina Elizabeth II, and spends nights in cold, damp, unfriendly bed-and-breakfast places, while the Prince of Darkness decides to visit Zia in his very own town. But Zia would surely have known if the Prince were in Cambridge. On second thoughts, would he really? The press and the media would report the public appearances of the man only after they had occurred and not before.

'Are we going to gate-crash the seminar?' As usual Vivian went straight to the heart of the matter.

'I don't know. We didn't get to see the list of the participants too closely. There were people from Egypt and Turkey. I think there were Muslim names from other countries too. I would think it's a no-no.

'Even if the Prince of Darkness wanted to come, the British Council would very likely discourage him. They couldn't possibly do extensive investigations into the character, religious affiliations and leanings of all the Muslim participants. Besides, his security people and Scotland Yard would veto it as too risky.

'But all that apart, the British Council people are hardly likely to allow in any outsiders.'

'If anyone questioned us, we could always say we'd come to listen to your brother.' Vivian was not about to give up so easily.

'They are bound to make everyone pass through a metal detector, plus feel everybody up.'

'So we drop the idea of attending this thing?' Vivian sounded crestfallen.

*

Doris Lessing read at the first session. Zia had heard her before, as he had heard almost every other well-known novelist, poet, dramatist and critic at all the literary festivals he had attended.

There were others who either read from their work or spoke about it. John Fowles, Rose Tremaine, Hilary Mantel, Fay Weldon, Terry Eagleton, P.D. James, and George Steiner. Vivian listened to all of them dutifully even if she was bored and could not follow what was going on. Dutiful is the right word. She was on duty waiting for Satan to show up. Zia was more cavalier and often slid down in his chair and went off to sleep. He knew that Vivian and he were wasting their time. Security at the event was not lax, it was nonexistent. Anybody could walk in and walk out. When the participants got bored, they went for a coffee or lay on the grass in the quadrangle. Nobody was monitoring anybody or anything. Essar was as likely to turn up here as he was to attend the plenary session of Ayatollah Khomeini's Revolutionary Council. But Amanat was at the seminar and Zia could not endure the thought of being separated from his brother even for a few minutes. This was all very odd for Zia. He had had no idea that he missed home. Or that his brother 1001, who had written that dreadful book about Kabir, could still mean so much to him.

When Amanat did not wish to listen to a particular author, and he had very specific notions about such matters, Zia took him for walks. They went to Emmanuel, King's, Trinity. They went to libraries and museums, and when they went to bookshops, Zia bought dozens of books for his brother. Amanat had been frail and unwell all his life but he could outwalk Zia by a factor of ten; make it a hundred. There was an air of febrile excitement about him. He was tense and agog. Amanat's enthusiasm was infectious and Zia took him to see his old friend Gordon Bowers. It was a droll meeting. Amanat knew more Cambridge lore and trivia than even the historian and tourist guide. Zia had the uncanny feeling that Amanat had come home. Aunt Antonia should have taken Amanat under her wing instead of him.

It was the late afternoon session on the second day of the seminar when some of the non-British writers were to read from their work. Vivian was sitting alone, which was unusual, since there was always a cluster of people around her. She was like a tremulous mirage in her long white dress. The French windows and the doors were all open and the loose skirt rose and fanned out gently as the breeze caught in it. A mile-long silk scarf in savage aquamarine floated around her neck making her the subject of a Manet painting. She looked insubstantial, her whole being a sheath of translucent light as she bent her head forward to read a book.

Zia had little doubt that if they had not been caught and thrown out as intruders, it was because of Vivian's blend of high poise and reserve. It bothered him that he had become aware of Vivian's striking looks mostly because other people, even women, were attracted to her. How could someone who usually went around in a pair of tight jeans and a loose black T-shirt be transformed into a woman so self-assured? Yes, he would propose to her tonight, and with Amanat as witness, he would marry her in the mosque at Peterborough by the weekend. It was long overdue. From the day he had first slept with her, he had known that he was living in sin. He had justified his vacillation, albeit lamely, by saying that Vivian was unstable and unreasonable, but even if there was some truth in that excuse, it was no longer valid. The days when she had been aggressive and defiant were over. She had long since given up the burkha. She was nothing less now than his soul mate.

Amanat nearly didn't read from his work that day. There were five non-British writers who were supposed to participate in a single session and each was given ten minutes to show his wares. (It was, after all, a seminar on the 'British Literary Scene' and not on the literatures of the world.) Amanat's luck being what it was, he was number five. The Chinese-Singaporean was the first. Fifteen minutes after his time was up he had still not finished doing an overview of the different ethnic streams that made Singaporean literature in English such a powerful, wide and vibrant river.

The Singaporean was followed by a poet from the former Yugoslavia. He spoke feelingly about his discovery that most of his former friends had become, unbeknownst to them and him, his enemies. He took twenty minutes, and the other two speakers another thirty-five.

Finally, it was Amanat's turn. He looked a touch raffish and utterly charming as he walked up to the podium in a tweed jacket that Zia had bought him. Frankly, he looked what he should have been: a Cambridge don and scholar.

'We are running a little late,' Amanat smiled sweetly, 'but I'm pleased to tell you that we can all adjourn for tea.'

The seminar director hurried to the podium.

'While it's true that we are running rather late,' she apologized, 'I do think we can manage to survive without tea for another ten minutes and listen to Mr Khan.'

Amanat read an excerpt from *The Arsonist* for seven minutes. He was so good, he was invited to read again that night. Seventy people turned up for the session, even though it was not part of the official programme. They made him read for over an hour. It was an unqualified, altogether smashing triumph.

Zia got undressed, brushed his teeth and came back to find Vivian fast asleep. No wonder the British had such terrible teeth: yellow, full of cavities and jammed with a hundred dentures and bridges. How could she possibly go to bed without brushing her teeth or washing her feet?

'Vivian,' he yelled. 'Have you brushed your teeth?'

What kind of mother would she be to his children? He could see a greenish miasma rising from their mouths as his seven children sat down to have breakfast in the morning.

No answer from Vivian.

'Get up, Vivian,' Zia roared. 'Brush your feet and wash your teeth. I mean wash your feet and brush your teeth.'

Vivian turned on her side but still no answer.

'Will you marry me, Vivian?'

'Yes,' she said sleepily, 'but only if you don't force me to brush my teeth just now.'

Zia considered withdrawing his offer.

'Will you really?' he asked.

'Oh, shut up,' she said, 'and make love to me. Of course I'll be your wife. Who else will marry me?' She smiled with her eyes still closed and turned over.

She woke him sometime around two.

'You don't really want to marry me, do you?' She was sitting up in bed.

'Why would I propose to you then?' Zia asked tetchily. It had taken him a long time to fall asleep.

'Because you wanted me to brush my teeth.'

'Vivian, did you wake me up in the middle of the night to listen to such drivel?'

'Tell me the truth, you were just being kind to me.'

'Do you really believe,' Zia's voice was rising, 'I would marry you out of kindness?'

'You are the only person who's ever cared for me. Till you came, nobody ever scolded me or got angry with me. The only emotion, if you can call it an emotion, I ever knew was indifference.'

'That's not true, your father surely loved you.'

'I was four when he died. I don't remember him. I know,' she jumped again, 'you'll get bored with me.'

'Stop it, Vivian. Don't you have any sense of yourself? You know damn well that you are very attractive and just as bright. The men at the seminar can't take their eyes off you.'

'I love you so much but what if it's not enough?'

'Why will it not be enough?' Zia was getting exasperated.

'Because I don't know whether I can really forget all those years of hating you. You were Antonia's son, her first-born, and I was nothing, nobody. Nothing interested me and I wanted to do absolutely nothing with my life. Now I worry that my only sense of reality is you. What happens if I lose you? Will it be back to the abyss again?'

'You can't hold on to the past, Vivian.' Vivian was sobbing uncontrollably and her snot and tears had wet Zia's pyjama top and run on to his chest. He knew she couldn't hear him or pay attention to what he was saying but he continued to talk to her. 'Besides, your version of the past has nothing to do with reality. Whatever Aunt Antonia considered me, I was never her son. You can't hate someone who doesn't exist.'

'You think you still want to marry me?' Vivian asked him when she had finally quietened down.

'Yes. Before you change your mind again.'

'I won't change my mind. And I won't let go of you ever.'

Two cumulous heavyweights were slugging it out in the sky. The one on the right had a huge purple-blue bruise under his eye, and his legs had collapsed and retracted into his belly, but he wasn't calling it quits. On the contrary, he had got back into the game. His arm lengthened and he made contact with the chin of the other pugilist. Craaaack. It was a deadly blow. The jaw broke and the head and the torso disintegrated. Amanat and Zia had been lying for the last two hours under a willow that trailed its bladed foliage in the Cam.

Zia had disconnected Bombay from his consciousness a long time ago. And yet now he could not stop pumping Amanat for information. It was as though he wanted to catch up with the past six years. They talked about their former home Firdaus and the outhouse where Abba spent all his leisure hours working on his stone and metal sculptures. They talked about The Perfumed Garden and the owner's daughter, Aminara Mirza. There were now Perfumed Gardens in Paris, Geneva, London, Munich and New York. Suleiman Mansion, Amanat told his brother, looked a little the worse for wear. The green paint on the walls of the stairwell was turning the colour of puke. The Sayeds still looked away when the Ahmeds crossed their paths and the Sheikhs on the top floor would not board the lift if the Gelanis were in it. The names of these people had long since faded from Zia's mind and yet now that Amanat had mentioned them, their faces and histories flooded back.

There was an unexpected note of rancour in Amanat's voice when he spoke about Abbajaan.

'Abbajaan,' he said, 'is bent on making up for lost time. But his time has come and gone. This is an odd thing to say about Abba's work since it has always been ahead of its time. But each one of us, if he's lucky, has a time and a season. After that your talent may deteriorate, remain static or burgeon and blossom. Abba's best work may be ahead of him but he has missed the bus.

'Having lost the big opportunity, he now spends his time persuading himself that it is the small, petty successes that give him the greatest joy. He pretends that happiness is the cards fate has dealt you. He is suffering, I suspect, from the final delusion that time will vindicate him, perhaps after he's dead.

'Is there anything sadder than to be told that you may gain recognition and immortality after you are dead? How does it help Donne or Van Gogh that they were discovered and became icons fifty, a hundred, or three hundred years later? What good will a Nobel do a dead man?'

'We both know Abbajaan is an upright man. What you forget is that he's also a martyr,' Zia interrupted Amanat's train of thought.

'I'm not sure "martyr" is the right word. I think Abba suffers from a misplaced sense of honour and an inability to share his pain. I remember you asking me the question that had kept me awake the night Abba was taken to jail: When were they going to come and take us to prison? Did they think we were blind and deaf and unaware of what was going on at home or did they think that we lived in some other city and dropped in only for meals? I wanted to hug Abba when they took away his licence and tell him that I loved his promenade and pavilions. And that more than anything else, I loved him. But how can you tell someone that you'll share his hurt and isolation if he won't even acknowledge that he has been betrayed?

'But there was something worse to follow. Altaaf giving us the slip and leaving us to free fall into an abyss that had no bottom was, in truth, no worse than Abba waiting till the last minute to tell us cryptically that we were going to be dispossessed of everything we had. Did our parents not know that everything was magnified in our childish imaginations? How was one to fight if one did not know who the enemy was?

'Would we be asked to give away the clothes we were wearing and go naked? Would we be parted from our parents? Would I be separated from my brother never to see him again? Were our parents not aware of the ghouls that walk the shadows of the mind?

'It was not the calamitous happenings that had overtaken us that made us cower with terror, it was the kindly silence of our parents. I'm sure that, like me, you too had a thousand questions to ask them. But to ask them would have been to transgress their fragile equanimity and doubt their sacrifice.'

Zia was struck by his brother's bitterness. Amanat had never forgiven himself for not shielding his father. Even today he resented the fact that he couldn't and didn't murder all of Abbajaan's ill-wishers. The only thing he had ever wanted to be since he was a child was an architect. Abbajaan had been sure his son had far more potential than he himself did. But after Zafar Khan's debacle, architecture was a closed subject for Amanat.

'Amanat, I'm telling you again. Join the school of architecture. The same one Abba went to.'

Amanat shook his head.

'Don't worry about the money. All I'll have to pay for is the first term. After that you'll bag every scholarship available.'

Amanat wasn't listening. He had moved on to Zubeida Khaala. 'She misses you terribly but is too proud to say it. She thinks you are never going to return. I am a poor substitute but she makes do with what she has. Over the years she has withdrawn more and more into herself.'

And then Amanat said something truly disgusting.

'Why did the two never have an affair?'

'Who?' Zia asked.

'Why didn't Zubeida have the sense to seduce Abba or Abba to make out with her? Proximity will bring almost any two persons, however mismatched, together. Abba certainly would have had a far more stable life with her.'

Zia could have throttled Amanat. How could he say such terrible things about the one person in their family who did not know what sin was? Frankly, Zia didn't have anything on his father either, but he wasn't willing to swear by it. Was it true what Zubeida Khaala had insinuated without ever putting into words? Or was it just her way of getting back at Aunt Antonia? Had Abbajaan and Aunt Antonia had a little something special between them a long time ago?

Zia suddenly wanted to get away from Amanat. There was something in his brother that needed to corrupt the most simple and innocuous things in life. He was fond of quoting from Graham Greene's *The Quiet American*: 'God save us always from the innocent and the good.' Quite the contrary. It was Amanat you needed to watch out for.

'We should be leaving. Vivian must be wondering what's happened to us.'

Zia rolled off the grass and tucked in his shirt-front. Amanat picked up Zia's leather briefcase.

'Leave that bag alone!'

'Yo,' Amanat put the briefcase down in surprise. 'What have you got in here? Bombs, guns, gold?'

'Nothing.' Even as he said it Zia knew he was in trouble.

'What do you mean nothing?' Amanat shot back. 'Nothing can't weigh a ton-and-a-half.'

'Nothing but books,' Zia tried to deflect the question. Wrong answer again. How could he have been so absent-minded?

'Books? May I see them?'

Amanat was the least nosey of brothers. He did not trespass into your territory unless you invited him in. Except that he did not know how to keep off books. Zia closed his eyes. Please, Allah, I beg You, don't let him open the bag. Too late, Amanat was already fumbling with the clasp. 'Nothing of interest to you. Just books on statistics.'

The clasp clicked open and Amanat was foraging in the bag. '*Don Quixote*?' He had picked up the topmost book. 'I didn't know you were such a reader. *Heart of the Matter*? I wouldn't mind reading that again.'

Don't go any further, Amanat. Stop right there, I beg you... Amanat had moved to the *Pensées*.

'Pascal? Did you come to him through his mathematical writings?' He had Ishiguro in his hands now. 'This is very eclectic reading. *Nine Hours to Rama*? Why are you carrying this mini-library with you? Are you planning to read all these while you are at the seminar?'

It came to Zia with a quiet but unmistakable certitude that if Amanat removed the next book, he would take the gun, put it to his brother's wide forehead and blow his brains out.

Zia had gone back to the shooting gallery first with Speed Balanchine and then on his own. He knew that when he put his mind to something, he could do it better than most people. It wasn't that he was more talented, it was just that when he focused on a task, he concentrated on it to the exclusion of all else.

He had studied the physics of combustion and metallurgy, of thrust and torque and flight paths, and had converted the whole lot into mathematical equations. Once he'd understood the science and the technology behind it, he felt in control. Within the next four lessons at the firing range, he was striking the cutout figure six times out of ten. By the seventh lesson, his score was eight out of ten. After the seventh week, you could call out any part of the body, the little toe of the left foot, the knee, the appendix, the fifth lumbar vertebra, the left ventricle, the right eye, and Zia would pick them off one by one in a matter of seconds. He was as much at ease with a Colt as with a Magnum, but Vivian was right: the Luger was the weapon of choice for what he had to do.

The leather case lay open on the ground and Amanat dipped into it once again and came up with a Steinbeck. You could see the Luger at the bottom of the bag. Zia should have gone for it now. Instead, as Amanat read the title of the book aloud, Zia said, 'I'm getting married the day after tomorrow.'

Amanat dropped the book back in the bag, hugged his brother and grinned. 'What marvellous news, Zia. When is the wedding?'

# 21

Zia woke up in a state of exhilaration. He felt light as an angel. You couldn't see his wings but if he had wanted to, he could have flown straight to Allah. A great burden had lifted from his heart and mind. Starting tomorrow, he would no longer live in sin. Everything, but everything, would fall into place, and Allah would make everything right.

Zia turned on his side and looked at Vivian. He marvelled at the way she lay down to sleep ever ready for a Christian death, her hands clasped below her breasts, her eyes closed and dreamless, her hair a tidy golden nimbus on the pillow and her face at peace with the world. She could lie like this without moving a single limb for eight, sometimes ten hours. She got up as she went to sleep, without a crease on her clothes. How lovely she looked. Why had he put off marrying her so long?

The morning light had begun to creep across the floor like the tide coming in stealthily on the sand. It touched him now and he felt himself becoming transparent. He could see clearly all the way into the future. He was still working on his PhD. The last two chapters were the toughest, no question about that. He had no clue how he was going to see his way through to the one crucial equation that would be the keystone of his thesis and would make sense of whatever had preceded it. He knew he could crack the problem if he zeroed in on it and stayed with it, but there was one other consideration. As long as he was working on his thesis, he could stay in England and hunt down the Prince of Darkness. Once he had got his PhD, the immigration laws would force him to go back to India. But that would no longer be true. Vivian was a British citizen and as her spouse he would have no problems staying in the UK. Besides, all he had to do was take Vivian as his bride before Allah and he had little doubt that Essar would show up in front of him and he would aim and fell the villain once and for all.

He kissed Vivian. She smiled in her sleep and whispered, 'Come in.' He brushed his lips across her eyelids but would go no further. He would abstain from sex this one day and keep himself pure, like a mediaeval warrior before he was knighted. Then he would have her for life.

'Let's call up your mother and tell her we're getting married.'

'It will be night in Perth just now. We'll give her the good news in the evening.'

They got up to dress for the last day of the seminar.

'Think about it,' Zia said. 'The only reason why neither the porters at Downing nor the British Council authorities give a hoot whether anybody carries a Luger or a field cannon and points it at his own head or blows up the college campus is because Satan has no intention of turning up.'

Vivian began to undress while her right hand was unbuttoning his shirt.

'Aren't you coming to the seminar?' Zia asked her.

'Didn't you just say there's no way the Prince is going to turn up? Let's make love.'

'Yes, I did. But if we give up now, it's as good as accepting defeat. That's what the Prince is depending on, our losing heart.'

'So we go on attending these festivals and seminars knowing that it's pointless?'

'If we give up on Satan, we give up on Allah too. The Prince will slip up one of these days, you watch. Or his security will fail. Imagine, if on the one occasion we don't turn up, the Evil One does.'

It was a hot afternoon. Zia had left Vivian with Amanat at the seminar and had gone off to the Peterborough mosque to make the final arrangements for the wedding tomorrow. Now he was back and was whistling softly to Vivian from outside the seminar room.

'I missed you so much,' Vivian flung herself upon Zia.

Zia disapproved of public demonstrations of affection but today all was forgiven. He pretended to disengage himself from her arms.

Vivian's tongue sought frantic refuge in his mouth.

'Can we have some air here please?' Zia was still hamming it, 'I have a marriage to attend tomorrow.'

'You're sure you want to marry me, Zia? You can still change your mind.'

Zia looked puzzled. 'I think there's some misunderstanding.'

Vivian's face fell.

'I'm fixed up with Doris Lessing, Viv.'

Vivian burst out laughing. 'Sure and I'm getting hitched to the Pope.'

Most of the participants inside the seminar room were watching them now. Zia suddenly looked around in panic.

'Relax.' Vivian pointed to her chair.

The bag was sitting on it and Amanat was snoring lightly next to it. Give him time, a few more minutes at the most, and he would be sprawled on the floor.

'Here.' Zia took out his wallet and drew out a wad of notes.

Vivian counted the money.

'What will I do with five hundred pounds?'

'I'm sorry,' he was already dipping into his wallet for more, 'I have no idea what a wedding trousseau costs.'

'Don't be silly, Zia. I mean I'm not sure I'll need even this much. Why don't you come with me to London? You'd know what I should be wearing better than I would.'

'I can't. Somebody has to be here just in case. Just don't buy a nylon or polyester sharara. And no plastic brocade.' He smiled.

Amanat was awake now and Vivian waved out to him.

'It won't take me any time, Zia. I'll be back before I'm gone.'

'You'll do nothing of the kind. We are getting married just this once. So you might as well indulge yourself. Oh, I almost forgot, get some Indian sweets. Amanat has a sweet tooth. I'll wait for you at home.'

'You're sure you won't abscond the moment my back's turned?'

'Viv,' Zia's voice rose an octave.

Arthur Scott was not the most impressive of readers but he was almost soporific that evening. Or perhaps the fault lay with Zia. He wasn't really all there. He had heard Scott often enough in the past but he wasn't sure whether he was reading from *The Last Buck* or one of his earlier novels. Scott was distracted and he kept glancing into the nonexistent wings as though he were waiting for a prompter to remind him of the next line.

Zia had come to know most of the people at the seminar. They fell into three groups. The eager, earnest types sat in the front rows and took notes, who knows about what. When a lecture ended, they crowded around the author with a copy of his book, pen in hand. Then there were those who had come all the way from Turkey or Japan or wherever merely because they wanted a break; they wanted to visit the sights or go shopping. The last lot were the would-be authors and critics from the Third World. They were going to leverage the seminar for contracts and fellowships. They hoped to persuade John Fowles or Martin Amis to write a blurb for their novels.

What about Amanat, why was he here?

'Thank you, ladies and gentlemen,' Arthur Scott broke off and got up as Satan walked in.

All hell broke loose then. No, it didn't. Quite the contrary, it was as if they had been rehearsing for this moment for the last year or more. Everybody in the seminar room rose and gave Essar a standing ovation. They clapped and clapped and clapped. They were never going to stop. Finally the Prince of Darkness waved out to them and raised his hands as though he wanted to quieten them down. As though, as though...as though he could ever have enough of their adulation. Zia took his bag and made his way to the back of the hall where the last two rows were empty. He picked up a chair and set it down close to the French windows. It would not be possible to see Zia now, if you were in the audience, unless you turned a full 180 degrees.

The Prince has begun to read. It's some story about the Queen of Spain and Christopher Columbus. Zia looks at the audience. They are tilting forward slightly, their lips parted as if to listen better. Zia holds the clasp of his bag between his index finger and thumb so that when he clicks it open, there will be no metallic sound. He's only half-listening to the Prince as he sets another chair next to his and places the books from his bag on it one by one. The gun feels light as he picks it up. How quickly one becomes familiar with things. The first time he had handled it, even the Luger had seemed substantial and weighty. He slips it into his jacket pocket and the books go back where they came from, and in the same order as before, barring the last two. When the job is done, he'll drop the gun on the shallow bed he has prepared, and top it with the last two books.

Zia switches off now. Vivian's words come back to him. How prescient she was. 'The Evil One is reading.... He has cocked a snook at the Ayatollah and his fatwa and despite the two-million-pound price on his head, has given the slip to God-alone-knows how many agents of death.... He can feel their adulation and he's well aware that they are in his thrall. His sense of power is a greater intoxicant than any designer drug.'

And then just as Vivian had foreseen, Essar's through with the reading and there is a roar of applause that will not die down. Oh the power and the glory of being Satan. And even as he smiles with his hooded eyes and graciously accepts the furious clapping as his due, he's unaware that there is a power greater, infinitely greater than his. Clap, clap, clapclapclap. Clap, clap, clapclapclap. No one hears the click of the safety catch as it is released in that rhythmic outpouring.

Zia is standing up now, the gun in his right hand. There is metal in his hand but his whole body too has turned to liquid metal and the one flows into the other. When he fires the gun, there will be no transfer of the recoil between two disparate elements, the organic and the inorganic. It will get evenly distributed from his toes to the mouth of the gun.

The clapping is peaking to a crescendo. He's not anxious, he's not tense. He has practised this drill till it's been etched into his genes. He knows his moves and goes through them against a mental checklist. The balding crown of the Prince's head gleams as he bends down to read the next story. The bullet, Zia calculates, will enter the bone of the skull at close to 390 metres per second, deep-dive through the brain like a torpedo raising flurries of grey matter on either side, come out at the nape of the neck, its velocity downgraded but not spent, and strike the wall at the rear. The cerebrum and the cerebellum will explode and splatter on the plaster.

Zia raises his gun, gets the soft middle of Satan's head in the gunsight, aims and fires. He waits for the Evil One's brain pulp to leap out and his body to shudder and gently keel over.

For a moment Zia thinks that he's missed the mark altogether as he'd done in those early days, but there has been no loud report, and no plaster has splintered and burst from the wall. Zia pulls the trigger again. And again. And again. Click. Click. Click but no bullet flies out. He opens the chamber and stares blankly. He feels his own head splitting open. He's going blind, his legs totter and the gun clatters to the floor. People turn around and look at him. He doesn't care. He should bend down and pick up the gun but he's about to collapse. He barely manages to sit on the chair.

Zia tries to take a deep breath to calm himself down but his heart is being squeezed till the pain becomes unbearable. He opens his eyes and looks again at the bullet chamber of the gun lying on the floor. There are no bullets there. Who, who, who? It's an unnecessary and rhetorical question. He knows who it is. It's that whore whom he trusted, though he has always suspected her. He bends down to pick up the gun but he's unable to see anything except a volcano which is erupting and spewing out millions of tons of molten red. The floor, the air, the walls, they are all a vibrant, sizzling red. He closes his eyes and the lava is coursing inside his eyelids. His head throbs and the whole room seems to be see-sawing. He's on all fours now groping for the gun.

He's going blind with rage. Literally blind. He has waited for this day for close to six years. Today he had the Evil One in his gunsight and as sure as the earth under his feet, the breath in his lungs and Allah in jannat, Lucifer was a dead man. Or should have been. Oh the shame and disgrace of it.

Where is that slut and traitor? He'll hunt her down even if it takes a couple of lifetimes. He can wait, he's used to it. That's one thing he owes Satan. But this is not the time to dwell on Vivian. She must have informed Scotland Yard a few hours ago. He senses Amanat watching him and he has little doubt that the other participants are on to him. It's a matter of seconds before the police arrive.

He forces himself to breathe slowly. Easy, easy does it, Zia wills the volcano to subside. He can see again. He's got hold of the gun. He lays it diagonally across *Nine Hours to Rama*, places *The Heart of the Matter* and *Don Quixote* on top of it, closes the bag, goes to the French windows, and slips out.

Zia had to get out of England before the police caught up with him. The bitch would certainly have set them on his tracks, not to mention the people at the seminar. He took the first flight out of Stansted.

It was going to Amsterdam. He had no quarrel with that. It would have made no difference if it had been going to Rome, Paris or Frankfurt so long as he were able to escape the dragnet the police would be spreading around the whole of the UK.

It was a tense night. He had had time to think, and hanging out in Europe did not seem like a good idea. Interpol would have been alerted by now and they would be looking for him. He decided to move on. It was only when the flight took off from Schiphol airport in the morning that he dropped his guard and fell asleep. He was woken up by an insistent knock on the windowpane. There was a long and mournful face outside. This was strange. Zia had thought the plane had taken off some time ago. He looked at the flight information being flashed on the screen. They were at an altitude of 31,000 feet and cruising at 540 mph. What the hell was the man doing out there? Zia wondered whether he was standing on the wing of the plane. No, he wasn't. Absurd as it may sound, he was suspended in midair. He was grimy and sweating like a common labourer. His tunic was made of coarse, dirty brown burlap and he was carrying an unwieldy wooden contraption on his shoulder. He stumbled and tottered and even fell down a few times. He had his face stuck to Zia's window. He looked so piteous, he had to be faking it.

'Let me in, please. It's rather cold here,' the man's beard had turned to icicles and he was shivering violently.

He had the face of the beggar at the junction of Nepean Sea Road and Warden Road near Firdaus. He too had worn a long tunic, slick and shiny with grease, sweat and dust. His head had been tied in a filthy cloth and in his arms he would carry a child. Sometimes the child was as old as seven or nine. Its eyes would be closed with its head lolling limply as if it were unconscious. Every once in a while, the child slid down, its long limbs trailing on the ground, and the beggar would yank it up as if it were a pair of loose trousers, and would come over to your car and tap on the windowpane. He had a perfectly bogus servile expression on his face but was calculating all the time how much he could touch you for. If you didn't respond to his pleas, he would stick his oily cringing face to the glass till you got fed up and gave him some money, or the lights changed.

Zia had always felt acute revulsion for the man. The second or third time you saw the flip-flopping head of the child, you knew something was very wrong. It was perpetually drugged and perhaps brain-damaged by now.

Zia impatiently waved the beggar outside away. He should have known better than that. The man only redoubled his knocking. Zia wanted to complain to the air hostess and ask her to get rid of him, but she was busy serving lunch at the other end. He pulled down the shutter of his window, tamped cotton wool in his ears and closed his eyes.

He must have fallen asleep, for when he woke up, the man was standing in the aisle. How had the stewards and the pilot allowed him in? And how had he managed to get the huge wooden thingamajig through the narrow door? He was blocking the passage to the pantry, and the shorter beam had ripped into the ceiling. He bent down and spoke to Zia in a soft, hesitant voice.

'I don't mean to intrude but, frankly, what happened yesterday was for the best.'

Zia wanted to tell the man that he was indeed intruding upon his privacy, and that he didn't give a damn what he thought. The shame and the impotent rage of his failure to get Satan were back with him. He wanted vengeance. Come what may, he would get that bitch, Vivian. But that wasn't going to be enough. He wanted to kill: kill indiscriminately and kill forever. He had read that Nadir Shah, the emperor of Persia, had captured Delhi and massacred 30,000 of its citizens in a single day. That wouldn't do, wouldn't do at all. No holocaust would suffice either. He would wipe out all of mankind, and yet he wasn't sure that even this would assuage his thirst for revenge.

The volcano had been reactivated, and the hot, bitter bile was shooting like a geyser out into the sky. It scorched him as it pelted down. This is the end, Zia thought.

The beggar had wedged his burden between the roof and the floor of the plane. He ran his swarthy hand down Zia's back and patted him gently.

'Stop torturing yourself, Zia. Did you really want blood and murder on your hands? Thank the good Lord that you didn't succeed.'

Zia got up from his seat. He was unsteady on his feet but that was not going to stop him. He caught hold of the beggar's elbow and propelled him and his wooden cross towards the emergency exit. Passengers turned their heads and looked askance but he didn't care.

He opened the door and pushed the beggar into the blue void. Within seconds he had receded and become a dot. And then you couldn't see him at all.

## 22

Zia came unannounced. He made it plain that he was in Bombay under duress. He stayed at Suleiman Mansion for eleven months. His family had waited to see him for six years. Now he was with them and they wished he had never come back. He was a rabid dog let loose amongst them and in no time at all they were infected with his madness.

He slept. For hours and days. And then he slept some more. He usually got up in the middle of the night and wanted breakfast, lunch or dinner cooked fresh for him. Ammi was more than willing to indulge him, but he wouldn't look at his mother, let alone talk to her. She would catch Zia unawares and be shaken by his desolation. She had no idea what ailed her little child who was no longer so little, or what private hell he was living through. He told Zubeida Khaala what he wanted, and usually it was something complicated like biryani or paya that took hours to cook. It would never have occurred to Zubeida Khaala to ask Zia to raid the fridge and serve himself. While she cooked, he often went down for some fresh air or a walk. When he got back she would serve him his meal but often he said he was not hungry any more.

An air of malevolence enveloped Zia even when he was fast asleep. There was a violence in him, unspoken and unarticulated, which made it even more terrifying. It was the same with his sullen silences. They were hostile and intimidating. The air was so poisoned that instead of closing ranks and ganging up against Zia, Abba and the rest of the family began to dread the sight of each other and were always spoiling for a fight. And yet the most difficult thing to watch was Zia's self-loathing. Amanat spent entire days hating his younger brother. There were times when he wished Zia would have the good sense to climb up to the terrace above the building and leap to his death. He wanted to tell his brother to let go of so much unhappiness. But he never could, because he was afraid Zia would turn upon him and savage him for not minding his own business.

One morning Zia's bed sheet and pillowcase were stained with blood and he had locked himself in the bathroom. Perhaps all of them, Ammi, Abba, Amanat and Zubeida, had seen it coming and were not really surprised. But that only made things worse. Why had they not prevented Zia from doing something terrible to himself?

They stood outside the bathroom and frantically knocked on the door. There was no sound from inside and they finally broke the door down. It wasn't easy. Suleiman Mansion had been built in British times and the wood was solid teak. There was no bathtub in the bathroom in which Zia might lie, immersed, slitting his wrists. The tub had long since been sold to the scrap dealer because of the chronic water shortage in Bombay. But that's what the family had psyched itself into expecting. Instead he was sitting on the toilet seat, a mix of panic and horror in his eyes. His palms were open and there was blood seeping out of them.

Ammi took Zia in her arms and rocked him gently. 'My baby, what have you gone and done?' That was the only time her younger son had allowed her to touch him since his arrival.

The doctor couldn't figure out how to stanch the flow of blood, for there was no abrasion nor was there any wound. There was just enough blood to form a film the size of a rupee-coin at the centre of the palms. He advised Zia to rub an antiseptic cream on the spots and prescribed a mild oral coagulant. The medicine seemed to work for a few days but then the bleeding started again.

It was a painless condition. Barring the unsightliness and the sticky, revolting smell of blood, there were no symptoms. And yet it's doubtful that the discovery that he was suffering from, let's say, leprosy, TB, or even terminal cancer, could have affected him as badly. The bleeding palms made him feel exposed and vulnerable. He started bandaging his hands, though that didn't help much. The blood seeped through and was far more visible on white gauze. Any source of light, natural or artificial, became his enemy. Most of all, he shunned tube lights. The fluorescence turned the red of blood to a lurid sapphirine. Zia now had the look of a marked man. He cowered and hid himself. He became a creature of the shadows.

Things got worse. The beggar he had seen outside the plane had turned up again. He seemed to have only that one tunic. It was doubtful whether he ever took a shower or washed himself. That might not make much of a difference at thirty-one thousand feet above sea level, especially if you had turned into an iced totem pole. But in Bombay, where the mercury stayed at 33 to 37°C ten months of the year, and the humidity gauge fluctuated between 83 and 100, the man was an environmental catastrophe.

Zia couldn't seem to get rid of him. He was there when Zia had meals. He got into cabs with him. Zia deliberately went to five-star hotels to make sure that the bouncers would throw the man out, but it was strange, the swish places didn't seem to mind him. In truth, they didn't even notice him. It was absurd, but he even followed Zia into the bathroom. This was a little awkward as the wooden struts, or whatever they were, couldn't fit into such a small place.

'Get the fuck out of here. Get the fuck out of my life.' The beggar didn't move. 'Do you have problems understanding me?' Zia shoved the man out forcibly and shut the door in his face.

He got into bed with Zia one night. 'Not with those dirty feet of yours, you shitface,' Zia yelled as he tried to push the wretch out. What was the point though, the man never listened.

'Will you, too, deny me, Zia?' the man asked.

He had some gall. 'What are you talking about? How can I deny you? I don't know you.'

Those doleful eyes looked imploringly at him. Zia was never sure whether the man had infinite pity for him or for himself. The beggar put his hand on Zia's head and stroked it. Zia sank his teeth into the man's arm but it was a half-hearted attempt. Who would have imagined that those carapace-hands could be so gentle? Zia's shoulders went slack and after all these months, his eyelids became heavy and he felt he was about to fall asleep.

'Come to me, Zia. Come rest your weary head on my shoulder. There is no sin so great that it will not find forgiveness in my heart.'

'You are pathetic. You can't even tell the difference between a sin and the highest sacrifice a man can make for his God. Besides, you should talk. No mortal sin can compare with yours. How dare you masquerade as the son of God when there is no other than Allah? Stupid bugger, next thing you know, you will be talking about the grandchildren and great-grandchildren of God and a family tree for the first family. You are nothing but a hoax and pretender.'

The beggar, had he had any sense, would have refrained from saying anything more, but he couldn't resist another homily.

'I gave my life to cleanse your sins, my son.'

'Who the fuck asked you to? I don't recall begging you to climb up that cross two thousand years ago. You did it because you couldn't wait to proclaim yourself saviour.' Zia lit into him. 'Do me a favour. Don't tell me day in and day out how much you did for me and the rest of mankind. There's no better way of putting people off than telling them what they owe you. I can look after myself. And even if I can't, Allah will take care of me.'

Zia prayed at home. Sometimes he walked over to one of the mosques in the vicinity of Suleiman Mansion. His prayers were chaotic, full of recriminations and entreaties for mercy. What was going on? What was Zia to make of his life? He wasn't being theatrical. His existence was predicated on one single absolute: dedication. Dedication to the service of Allah and the spreading of His word. And now the whole carefully constructed edifice of his calling was in a shambles. Sometimes he worried that his faith itself was in jeopardy.

How was he going to bring all those who had strayed from the path back into the fold if he couldn't even vanquish the Prince of Darkness? Why had Allah abandoned him? Why hadn't Allah forewarned him? Why hadn't he felled Vivian with a stroke of lightning before she emptied the bullet chamber? And then he thought the unthinkable. And said the unutterable. Vivian might have betrayed him...but it was his God who had let him down.

One day he asked in anguish: 'Who duped whom? Did I? Or did You?'

There were times when he was so wrought up that he bashed his head on the floor of the mosque as he knelt in the prayer position. 'Why won't You rid me of that beggar? He hounds me without let. Have You not tested me enough? Would You rather that my spirit was broken once and for all? I am Your creature. Do what You will with me but the consequences will be on Your head and not mine. Will You not stand up for me when that beggar calls the mission You have entrusted me with, an aberration and a sin against man and God? How can You watch silently and not bestir Yourself when he leaves his stigmata upon me? If you will not watch over me, who will? If You will not take care of your own, who will? I beseech You Allah, save me. Save me from the clutches of that accursed usurper.'

When Zia was at home, and that was most of the time, the Khans lurked around furtively but kept out of his way. He made them feel responsible for his mortification. Ammijaan, unfortunately, was the first one to let her defences down. Amanat attempted to warn her but it was a waste of time. It was not possible for her to understand that anybody could reject her. She knew that her younger son was a man of extremes, but she was sure he would come around. The trick was to give him the impression that she didn't care and he would come around in no time and be begging her to talk to him. Well, she had given him enough time. How tightly he had held on to her that day in the bathroom when he had discovered that he had hurt his palms.

'Why don't you join us at the table tonight? You'll feel much better.' She saw Zia looking uneasy and smiled. 'Frankly, we'll feel much better.'

Zia spoke inaudibly but there was no mistaking his words. 'I would never want to sit at the same table as you.'

'It's Ammi's and Abba's house,' Amanat couldn't restrain himself. 'So if anybody has to leave, it will have to be you.'

'Hush, both of you.' Ammi shook her head sadly. 'Do you know why it's so terrible to be unhappy, Zia? Because you want to make everybody else just as unhappy.'

'I'm not interested in your platitudes. But for you, we would all be living happily in Firdaus instead of this hell-hole.'

'You may well be right, my son. I can apologize for the wrongs of the past, not that it does much good, but I doubt if even Allah can redress its finality.'

'Don't bring Allah into this. I don't know where all this talk is getting us, anyway. Either you leave or I will.'

'We're together after so many years,' Abbajaan said. 'Shouldn't that give us joy instead of unhappiness?'

Zia looked at his father with undisguised contempt. 'What happiness are you talking about? You've destroyed our lives because you could not control your wife.'

'Enough. If it will ease the torment in your heart, I will leave. Just give me a few days.'

'If you go, I go,' Amanat told his mother.

Ammijaan laughed. 'That won't do at all. At this rate we'll all leave and the house will be empty.'

Ammijaan got a reprieve from an unexpected quarter: Zia himself. One evening he came home with Sagari. The change in Zia and, in turn, the mood of the whole family was, not to put too fine an interpretation on it, dramatic. Barring Liz Taylor and a few others, child stars rarely ever make it as grown-ups. Sagari had been no different. She had faded out of public memory so completely, you could easily have convinced yourself she had never been around. It was as though she had set out to peel off layer after layer of herself till she had turned herself invisible. The slightest attention made her cringe and withdraw into her shell.

Dr Pat was one of the few friends who had stuck by Zafar Khan after his precipitous fall. When he too stopped seeing them, Abba was relieved. Pat was a good man, but at some point he had also been bound to realize that it did not help to associate with the Khans.

Sagari hardly said anything for the two and a half hours she was there, but the bad times at Suleiman Mansion came to an end. Zubeida Khaala made tea for everybody and forgot to serve it till it had become cold and undrinkable, but no one seemed to notice. Amanat sat shyly and would not look at Sagari. He wondered when a crack would show up in the unreal calm, but he needn't have worried.

'How's your father?' Abbajaan asked her.

'He's well,' Sagari said, 'at least I think so.' Then by way of explanation she added, 'I no longer stay at home.'

When she left she held Abbajaan's hand and said, 'I've missed you so much.' And no one said to her, 'But we've been here all along.' Then she hugged Ammi and asked her, 'You won't go away, will you?' And Ammi said, 'Of course not, my love.' Ammi turned to Zia then but he would not meet her eyes.

Sagari came often now, sometimes with Zia, sometimes on her own. Zubeida Khaala taught her to knit and Ammi apprenticed her as trainee-cook. It was as though they were back in Firdaus. Perhaps it really was possible to regain paradise. Even Zia must have felt that Sagari was a ring of protection around the Khan family. Amanat was the last to cave in. He told himself he was not going to be lulled into a false sense of security and hope. He did not trust the future. He had taught himself not to expect much from life. It was beside the point that he surreptitiously hoped he would be proven wrong.

But Sagari had an unfortunate effect on Amanat's carefully wrought defences. Try as he might, he could not sustain his cynicism or distrust. It slowly seeped through the walls of his brain that silence can also be a benediction. Sagari's stillness lowered the temperature and the pulse rate of the Khan household. It was a giving and a nurturing. It quietened Amanat till he actually began to think it possible that he was a normal human being.

Then one day the black mood was upon Zia again. Looking back, the earlier one seemed like fun and games. It's hard to say what triggered off the relapse: the letter from Cambridge or the return of the beggar? The palms began to bleed heavily again. The blessed circle of protection too had disappeared, for Sagari had stopped coming. Not that Amanat needed further proof of the malfeasance of fate, but he should have had better sense than to trust Sagari or the good times. He watched helplessly as Zia turned vicious once more. And yet he could see that his younger brother seemed just as helpless. Some unspeakable demon had taken possession of him and he looked pleadingly at his parents and Amanat to exorcize him or to put him out of his misery even as he treated them to another bout of rage.

Zia's self-destruct went into overdrive when he got the letter from Vivian. It was brief.

Zia,

Make no mistake. I'm coming to get you. You know I never miss. You'll never be far enough to be safe from me. Not even if you caught the next shuttle to the moon or Mars.

Look out for me.

Vivian

What was he to make of it? What was she talking about? It was she who had betrayed him. And yet she had the gall to talk about getting him?

Zia became a rod of uranium-238, inflammable with self-loathing and spite. There was enough radioactive toxin in him to contaminate the whole universe.

Amanat could no longer sit and watch.

'I think he needs help,' Amanat told his father. 'Shall we call a psychiatrist to take a look at him?'

'It's no use what you and I think. Unless he wants it, nobody can help him.'

'If we don't do something right away, it could be too late. He's going to destroy not just himself but all of us too.'

'What do you suggest we do?'

'Should we have him admitted into a clinic?'

'Have you ever been to one of our mental asylums, Amanat?'

'Only in the movies.'

'I wouldn't wish the devil such a fate.'

'Let's face it, Abbajaan. Even if he doesn't say it, he's crying out in desperation.'

Ammi was the lucky one. She left.

My dear Zafar, Zubeida and Amanat,

My leaving has nothing to do with Zia. You know my nature, I like to move on. This is not the first time and it won't be the last. I know you will respect my privacy and not come looking for me.

Amanat, take care of your father and aunt. They'll be lost without you. And don't forget, letting go of me also means forgiving your brother's violent outbursts.

I love you all.

Shagufta

'Come to me, Zia.' The wretched tramp, hobo or whatever he was, wouldn't let go of him. 'How long will you shun me?'

'You really want to know, you shithead? Till never. Get that through your thick head.'

'How you torment yourself, my son. Come, let me take the cross off your shoulders.'

It was the first time Zia noticed that he himself was bearing the cross, and not the grimy man. How had this come about? He wanted to fling the bloody thing off, push it right back on to the beggar and hope for the best: that there would be one of those serendipitous accidents and the beggar would lie crushed underneath. But to his horror he discovered that the cross had grown into his shoulder and become one with it.

Late that evening Zia went to the church on Wodehouse Road, the one where Aunt Antonia claimed she had baptized him. It was dark and there was nobody there except two old ladies lighting candles at the back. He located the ladder they used for cleaning the chandeliers and the icons, and carried it to the apse. He climbed it with ease as if he had done this every day of his life. He had come well prepared. He stood on the top step and wiped the wooden saviour gently with chamois leather cloth. That done he took a chisel and desecrated the image.

The next evening, when Amanat was returning from work, Zia was waiting for him on the landing. There was so much pain and hurt in his face, Amanat rushed up the stairs. Zia didn't know what his brother was up to when Amanat embraced him. He was thrown off balance as his knife plunged into Amanat twice.

'How could you, Amanat? How could you?'

*Lucens*

# 23

Lucens pruned the stunted shrubs and sang to them. He was the only one who could make anything grow in this wasteland. Even the tiny plants that occasionally sprang up in the shelter of the buildings were scorched or uprooted by the keening winds. He built screens and fortifications around them and devised windbreakers out of used tin cans and tarpaulins. It was an unequal fight and most of the time the battered and bullied saplings lost heart and gave up. And yet only a week before, Lucens had worked a small miracle. The monks, both ordained priests and brothers, the lay help and even the Abbot, Reverend Father Augustine, stared at it incredulously. It was a tiny bud, a stab of cochineal, a tightly cocooned dark red rose.

They called Lucens Francis II, because he talked to birds and clouds and fish and fowl. In fact, Lucens put even St Francis in the shade. He had conversations with brass doorknobs as he polished them, sang psalms to toilet bowls while he scrubbed them and recited the Gospel According to St Luke as he lovingly stoked a honeyed fire in the gold of the chalice. Whatever he did, he poured his heart, soul and body into it. He was up before everyone else, and opened the doors of the church, swept the floor and lit the candles for Vigils, which began at 2.30 in the mornings. It was the same for the other offices: Lauds at 5.30 and Holy Mass, which lasted until 7.30. He sang the Tierce with the others at 9, Sext around 11, and None at 1 in the afternoon. Vespers was at 4, and at the end of the day, Compline at 7 p.m.

Barring the Novice Master, Father Paul, almost everyone thought Lucens a joy and benediction to the community. He was quiet, self-effacing and always willing to help. He would offer himself for the least pleasant jobs at the Abbey. He cleared the two disused chimneys which the bats had clogged with their droppings and beastly stink over the last thirty years. When the drains overflowed despite Draino and other chemicals, and the suction pump broke down, Lucens plunged his hand in all the way to his shoulder blade, and after hours of failed attempts, dislodged a fat, bloated rat that had split open like a fig with its raw flecked pink flesh, and wedged itself in the shaft of the pipe.

Father Paul was not impressed. The industry and meek nature of the novice left him cold. He thought Lucens had a well-rehearsed act in place but that the real Lucens was bound to show up one of these days, weeks or months. The Novice Master had seen too much of the world to trust first or second impressions.

Life, his previous incarnation as a soldier and entrepreneur, and his current experience of a claustrophobic community had made Father Paul a perceptive judge of character. Which was why the Abbot had entrusted to him the function of initiating, steering and nurturing the novices. Father Paul could see who would fit in and who would not; who was simply enticed by the idea of the severe austerity of the Abbey and who could actually survive and rise above it; who was priest material and who would do better as a brother monk; who was devout and dedicated, and yet must serve our Lord from outside the community. He had to play multiple roles. He was a counsellor to the postulants and the novices, a guide and a disciplinarian, a caring and encouraging companion and yet one who had to continually evaluate the members of his flock and, if necessary, throw out those who gossiped, intrigued or vitiated the air, or who needed to find God in other ways.

No, from day one he had known Lucens was not monk material.

Lucens had arrived at the Abbey one night at a little past 2 a.m. 'Arrived' is perhaps the wrong word; the three cryptic letters of the film noir genre would have described the case better: D.O.A. – Dead on Arrival. He had climbed up the unrelenting 40-degree incline of the tortuously twisting road through deep snow, and was suffering from advanced hypothermia. The Irish carpenter and God's dogsbody, Brendan, had found him a few yards from the old stables when he was driving up to church for Vigils. There was no sign of a pulse in the man, and no I.D. He was wearing torn woollen gloves, a windcheater that could barely have kept him warm on a mild autumn day, and snow boots.

Brendan carried him to the sofa in the visitors' room. Brother Jonathan-Christophe called the Abbot while Father Giovanni raised the thermostat to 100° and lit a fire in the cold hearth. The dead man was a foot taller than Brendan, but Brendan lay on top of him and rubbed his body while trying to give him mouth-to-mouth resuscitation. When he came in, Reverend Father Augustine checked the man's pulse, then asked a novice to get the mirror from the infirmary.

'You may stop now,' the Abbot told Brendan when there was no condensation on the mirror. 'The poor man is no more. Does he have a driver's licence or social security card, so that we can inform the police?'

'No, Reverend Father, nothing I could lay my hands on,' Father Giovanni answered.

'May I have some brandy?' Brendan asked no one in particular.

'Certainly not, you know very well nobody...' Reverend Father was short. 'Oh well, maybe this once. You look done in. Brother Jonathan-Christophe, will you fetch the Courvoisier from the cupboard in my office. It's unlocked. I think you'll find an unopened bottle on the lowest shelf.'

Brendan was still at it, pumping heat and breath into the stiff body. When the brandy arrived, instead of drinking it, Brendan tilted the glass and poured a little into the man's slightly open mouth. It trickled out from either side and spilled on the tartan of the sofa.

'That will be enough, Brendan,' the Abbot spoke sharply. 'I wish to give this man Extreme Unction.'

'But he's dead, Reverend Father,' Father Giovanni said hesitantly.

'Yes, but we are not. And I would like to think that in these unusual circumstances, the Lord will be willing to extend His grace.'

Brendan poured some more of the cognac into the unresponsive mouth.

'Please proceed for Vigils. Brendan, you too.'

Most of the cognac was on the floor and yet Brendan wouldn't stop.

'Get him out. This instant.' The Abbot forced Brendan up by the arm.

The glass from Brendan's hand fell and broke on the wooden floor as a breath and a burp escaped from the dead man's mouth.

One of the brothers found Lucens Kahn's rucksack half way down the mountain. There was a can of tuna in it, a Parker fountain pen, two apples, a pair of jeans and a black polo shirt, a Bible, and a letter from the Novice Master.

'I am pleased that you are planning to dedicate yourself to our Lord Jesus,' the Novice Master had written. 'I need hardly tell you that austerity may, at times, look highly attractive, but the monastic life, especially the Trappist way, is for the very few. Young people often believe they have a vocation in God, but the dropout figures should give you pause. Many are called but not even a handful can stay the course.

'I would urge you to let a few months or even a year pass. The Lord, as you well know, is more patient than any human being can imagine. Consider the various options before you. Please understand there is no shame or indignity in the lay life. Quite the contrary. It is in many ways a harder choice than the monk's way.

'If you still wish to pursue the celibate holy life, write to us. Not a scrap of a note like your previous one, but a candid account of introspection into your choices and your confusions, and an honest assessment of yourself. Do not write to impress, but to share your thoughts, fears, hopes and failings with us. Write about anything you want: your parents, your girlfriends, your desires, the state of the Church, labour unions; anything that gets you worked up or happy or depressed.

'Not a tome, please. Ten double-spaced pages is the outside limit.

'We shall then decide whether you should make the journey to acquaint yourself with the reality of the Abbey and its ways. That will also give us a chance to get to know you personally. Even so, let me emphasize that your visit will not necessarily translate into admission to the Abbey as a postulant.

'May God be with you and help you understand what is best for you.'

It did not augur well, Father Paul said to Lucens as he smiled wryly, that he had not heeded any of the counsel given in the letter. He seemed to have started for the Abbey almost as soon as he had received the missive. Father Paul was willing to appreciate the virtues of youth: impulsiveness, enthusiasm, impatience, the wallop of adrenaline; the quick, perhaps the word was hasty, decision. But in the matter of the Lord and service to Him, he had found that every one of those qualities proved counterproductive.

Later, months later, the Novice Master told Lucens that he had certainly had no intention of accepting him as a postulant, nor was the final authority in the Abbey, Reverend Father Augustine, inclined to entertain any such petition from the brash young man.

But, like it or not, the good Lord had brought the man back from the dead. And as the Abbot said, it was possible that there was a place and purpose in God's scheme of things for Lucens, perhaps in this very Abbey.

The Abbey of Our Lord in Contemplation was crouched precariously on a ledge of the Sierra Nevada range that the locals called Terraferra, some four thousand feet above the river and town of Sweet Waters. The natives said that where the valley was, there was once the ocean. Even today, if you listened carefully, you could hear its heave and swell, and feel the yearning of Terraferra for its companion of ancient times. Perhaps it was because of the mismatched plates in the valley that everything felt transient when you looked across from the mountain head. To say that something was unstable was the same as accepting the oneness of creation.

At Terraferra, matter and antimatter, men and landscape, the elements themselves, seemed interchangeable, if not one and the same, to Lucens. The few stumps of trees looked as gnarled and bent as the spire and buttresses of the church, scarred by lightning. The half-starved monks with beaked noses were really birds wheeling in the sky searching for prey, or perhaps God. The desolate terrain was an echo of the roiling twilight skies. And in winter the snow covered the roof and fire hydrant and chimney stack, the burnt grass and derelict plough in Trappist white.

But it was the wind that was the undisputed master of Terraferra. It shrank and shrivelled the monks' speech, hurled itself onto the flanks of the mountains and tore the stone to ribbons. It was the cook Mac's seven tomcats in heat shrilling across the badlands looking for a night of sex. It spoke in tongues and it held its silence. The simplicity of its arithmetic was daunting. The sky above, the earth below, and betwixt the two, the windy void.

The monks were Lucens's brothers and fathers. He lived in close and continuous proximity with them. He respected them and obeyed them if they were older. They were his family, his only family. And he loved them dearly. But like all families, he had inherited them. They were a given; he had no choice in the matter. It was with the lay workers, the ones who stayed permanently in the outhouses or in the retreatants' homes, that Lucens felt a kinship that he found difficult to explain. They were better adjusted, certainly more at ease with themselves and with God, than people like him and the other monks who spent their entire lives disciplining themselves and seeking that strange virtue: the imitation of Christ.

They were the groupies, the hobos and drifters, the lame ducks and hangers-on of God. They were neither monks nor were they the solid and respected laity of any parish. They were stuck in a grey no-man's-land. He could be wrong but Brendan, Rick, Nelson, Doug and Bert seemed as celibate as the Abbot himself. No sex, no families, no children, no career paths and goals, no life on the fast track, no fun and games, no ambition, no wrenching disappointments, no liquor barring very, very special occasions, no music except the organ and hymns in church, and no social life.

Why did they hang on to this life? The Trappist way is certainly no pasha life, but there is a kind of honour and reward attached to it. You make your sacrifice public, you cut yourself off, you go into lifelong seclusion, but you know, as does everybody else, that you are special. You may or may not have a line to God, but even the atheists suspect that you do.

Had Brendan and Mac, the cook, Bert, the mechanic, and Rick, the baker, felt the tug of God? Perhaps they had been called to the vocation but had failed to make the grade. Perhaps they had intended to leave and seek new pastures but never managed it. Or maybe time had just gone by and they had forgotten to move on.

'"We must first try to define the very concept of the Church. There is too much woolliness, a kind of mystification and obfuscation surrounding it. The Church is the bride of Christ; it is the set of written and unwritten rules by which a Catholic understands how God wishes him to lead his or her life. It is the composite of rituals, it is the Mass and the Eucharist, it is the arbiter in all theological and spiritual matters and sometimes even in our personal lives."' Father Paul, the Novice Master, read from Lucens's assignment on *The Power and the Glory* without revealing the name of the author. '"The Church has always been at the crux of the timeless confrontation between institutional power and individual freedom and choice, organized religion and a need for a personal God. As with the name of our Lord Jesus Christ, which is so often tortured and twisted in theological writing, we need to bring clarity to the concept of the Church. Otherwise the word becomes too vague, too elastic, meaning different things to different people and hence in danger of achieving the opposite effect: becoming meaningless because we want to make it so all-encompassing.

'"Amore Christi, isn't that enough? Why can't we love God without bringing the Church into it?" End of quote.'

Father Paul paused for effect and then repeated the last two questions.

'Do you think, Brothers, that there should be limits on the meaning and power of the Church as suggested by this paper?' The Novice Master cast his eye around innocuously. 'Anybody for an answer?'

The offhand question with its solicitation for candid inputs, Lucens knew, was a loaded gun aimed at him. Fortunately, Lucens was saved. Brother Damien and Brother Jonathan-Christophe were both willing to face the fire.

'Yes, Brother Jonathan-Christophe.'

'The thesis the author of that passage proposes is pernicious. The Church of the Living Christ is, and must be, the supreme authority in matters spiritual. I would go further. Since all temporal matters have consequences in the spiritual realm,' Brother Jonathan was warming up to his subject, 'the Church must, under no circumstance, be fettered or hemmed in.'

'Thank you, Brother Jonathan, for your emphatic views on the subject. Anybody else?'

Perhaps Lucens had been a trifle premature in his optimism. Brother Damien's hand shot up again, only to be ignored. The Novice Master's eyes came to rest upon Lucens.

'And what about you, Brother Lucens? What do you think?'

'Perhaps we could allow faith more free play.'

'Like Reaganite economics and politics, less Church is better governance?' Brother Jonathan-Christophe asked Lucens.

'I wouldn't phrase it quite that way but that would not be a gross misrepresentation.'

'And who is to decide between bad faith and good?' The Novice Master ignored Brother Christophe.

'It's not difficult to tell one from the other,' Lucens answered. 'For instance, there's no arguing the fact that the whisky priest in *The Power and the Glory* has, from the very start, practised bad faith. He has broken the solemn oath of celibacy that he took knowing fully well its implications. He has dishonoured the covenant he made with God by having illicit relations with a woman and then by fathering a child. He is a despicable man deserving eternal damnation and not the sympathy that Greene so insidiously evokes in the reader.'

'Good and bad faith, as you suggest in your paper, Brother Lucens, are not always cut and dried.' There, the cat was out of the bag. Everybody now knew who the author of the dubious essay was. But the Novice Master was no longer needling Lucens. 'You are aware of the Catholic priest in Sri Lanka who not only questioned but rejected one of the fundamental tenets of our faith, original sin. His argument, later supported by many Indian men of the cloth, went something like this: The Church holds that baptism alone can negate original sin. Was one then to condemn entire peoples to hell when they had been exposed to neither Christian dogma nor the scriptures, and for whom baptism was out of the question? Surely, they cannot be held responsible for their ignorance and hence original sin cannot operate in their case. Who is to decide these highly complex and tempestuous questions? Is faith alone enough? Should each one of us have his or her variety or version of the Catholic faith? What is the layman or even the ordained priest to make of the Babel of opinions? Perhaps you have some answers?'

Lucens looked bewildered and shook his head.

'Is it possible then that the Holy Church alone through the living presence of Jesus can throw light on these issues?'

After class, Lucens followed the Novice Master out.

'May I have a word with you, Father?'

'Only if you are not going to tell me how crushed in spirit you are, how remorseful, how abjectly repentant you are for overstating a point that needed to be made.'

'I meant no disrespect to the Church, Father.'

'No, I didn't think you did.'

'But I'm guilty, Father, guilty of hubris and the sin of wanting to be different.'

'But you are different as...'

'I shall endeavour not to be.'

'Will you let me complete what I started to say?'

'I'm sorry, Father. That was thoughtless of me.'

'You interrupted me again, Brother Lucens. The good Lord in His wisdom, generosity and wonderful humour, Lucens, made us all different, unlike the mad scientists and utopian tyrants who would clone us all and make us into photocopies of each other.'

'Yes, Father. But what is my penance?'

'You are one of the more thoughtful novices at our Abbey. Just carry on striving to know yourself.'

'Yes, Father, but there has to be a penance for my sin.'

In the beginning Lucens had talked about the Living Christ, the mercy and compassion of the Mother of God, the complexity of the concept of the Holy Ghost and the mystery of the Eucharist. Now he rarely mentioned them. Had he realized that the senior monks and the Abbot spoke sparingly of God and the rest of the Trinity? It was difficult to say whether he was losing interest in these matters or had simply internalized them. It took time for Lucens Kahn to understand that the monastic experience is a severely dislocating one. He had to unlearn almost everything he had learnt in his previous life. The adjustment was all the more difficult because, while the words and concepts used both outside the Abbey and within were the same, they belonged to two different species. Food, of course, was one of them. The Bible may tell you that man does not live by bread alone, but Lucens thought that the monks seemed to live by nothing else most of the time. Sleep was another such word. It was an understatement to suggest that the monks made do with as little of it as possible. Sometimes Lucens wondered why they bothered with the pretence of sleep at all. The earliest he ever knocked off for the night was at ten, and by two he was up with everybody else.

But perhaps the trickiest unlearning process had been in the realm of time. The monks at Terraferra could give you the time of day, they were rarely ever late for the seven offices or for meals. They knew the days of the week and Lent, Easter, Christmas and New Year, but beyond that time became meaningless. For them, time was a continuum without temporal divisions. As with most early agrarian cultures, time was contextual: when Father Paul fell ill; the day the water diviner located the well; the week the new chapel was consecrated. In time Lucens would begin to talk and think like the Abbey monks. He would telescope time and expand or extend it. He might use words like 'then' to mean two days, two months or two years later.

Before joining the Abbey he had drawn up a list of the things that he was likely to miss most. Sex and privacy had been at the top. To his relief, he had discovered that sex was not as urgent and obsessive a matter as he had imagined it would be. Instead, it was food that tormented him. There were times when he feared that it would oust the Almighty altogether. In a sense it made him a great visionary. Sitting at his desk in the library, he saw rows and rows of apricot cakes and plum puddings where the books were. In the field, the hayricks turned into rich pizzas with shrimps, ricotta cheese and fat lascivious olives. There was no visual logic to the transformation of buildings, cattle, the workers' woollen caps or old shoes into guacamole, tacos and salsa and refried beans spiked with jalapeños. He woke up at night to the ravishment of perfumed rice and Afghani kebabs. There were times when he would have abandoned the Abbey for a single serving of tiramisu, teriyaki chicken or tandoori pomfret. Instead he sat with the other monks in dull silence, barring the vociferous chomping, clacking and chewing of Brother Lionel, over a meal of anaemic cannelloni goo cooked in a lumpy cheddar sauce.

Lucens had the good sense to know that while the monastery was supposed to be an otherworldly place, it was bound to be a microcosm and cousin of the big world in many ways. And yet it never ceased to amaze him how much of the world that the monks had rejected had seeped into this one: the same tics, the same petty jealousies and insecurities. Frankly, for a group of people so small, there were more odd birds here than you would run into on an ordinary day in New York or London. The monastery, Lucens discovered, made him and all the other younger monks clinically and mercilessly observant. Some took a nasty pleasure mimicking the physical and verbal quirks of their brothers, while others averted their eyes uncomfortably. Brother Peter removed his dentures lest they get dirty, and placed them precisely one inch to the right of his plate before starting to eat. Brother George washed all fruit, apples, bananas, grapes, tangerines and peaches, with dishwashing detergent and then wiped them on his field shirt, which was spattered with mud, manure and pesticides. But the most disheartening thing about the Abbey was the abnormal number of elderly monks suffering from advanced Parkinson's. You could hear their wheeled walkers trundling on the floor a mile before they came into the church. Their entire frames wobbled silently as they tried to reach out for a book or a newspaper, and if they did manage to get hold of it, the next instant it would be on the floor. Sometimes they gently dropped their heads never to lift them up again. Your heart went out to them but you dared not touch them lest you catch their disease. It did not matter that Parkinson's was not infectious. You knew it was merely tomorrow, or the day after, that you too would rock 'n' roll to the palsy of old age.

Soon, however, the ancient rhythms of the Abbey took over, and Lucens no longer noticed the tics and peculiarities of his companions. Now, on Wednesday and Friday nights, Lucens looked after Father Charles who suffered from both partial paralysis and Alzheimer's. He took him to the toilet, or if Father Charles forgot that he wanted to evacuate, Lucens cleaned him up and changed the bed sheet. He fed him and coaxed him to drink water, which he seemed to hate with a passion. When he was not too restless, Lucens read to him from the Bible, though he wasn't sure that Father Charles paid any attention or could understand a text that he must at one time have known by heart. On some days, Father Charles would get obstreperous and fling to the floor the bowl of soup, the plate of spaghetti, the Bible or whatever else came to hand. He could be infuriatingly obstinate but Lucens never lost his temper. He will, Father Paul prophesied, he will lose his cool. The habit of obedience will sit askew and Brother Nonstop Good will bare his fangs.

*

For Lucens, as for everybody else at the Abbey, time was divided into 'Before the Storm' and 'After the Storm', or BTS and ATS, as the residents of the place referred to that fateful event. It was the day when life at the monastery changed forever. Storms were not an unusual occurrence at Terraferra. The wind dropped, everything became still and silent, and the air had the feel of dry leaves. It was as though you were entering an area of hypergravity. The pressure was not so much upon your ears and body as upon your soul. You felt crushed, your breathing turned erratic and every moment it seemed your heart would give in and burst.

The people at the Abbey had been through this before, time and again, and yet they did not know what to expect the next time. Every storm had its own bag of cosmic tricks and each struck in different and unknown ways.

The lull before a storm was a term of trial for the brethren at the Abbey. They professed peace, these men of God, they prayed even harder than on other days and they never spoke of it or acknowledged it. But they felt a wild impulse to hit out, to break out of the sham of brother, father and the love of the eternal and living God; they yearned to commit the random act, to perpetrate the crime of Cain, to murder and mow down for no apparent reason, for the sheer mad joy of violence and blood, for the relief and pleasure, however short-lived and delusory, of a purgation and catharsis. They waited in vain for the malaise to depart. And then the floor show of lightning, thunder, wind and rain hit Terraferra and their sins were washed away while their souls rose up to the very doors of heaven.

But the Storm, the Before and After Storm, had been unlike any other. It left no one in doubt that it was a sign from God. Its effects would be felt for years. The family of monks would remember every twist and turn of the crisis, the good and the bad, the courage and the fear, the great hardships that followed and the equally enduring fortitude and grit that helped to overcome them. They would build a monument in memory of the event, a statue of the Mother and Child in marble that had a quality of compassion so nonjudgemental that even the most irreligious of people would feel blessed in its presence.

*

Before the storm, the notion of privacy was alien to the Abbey. The brothers and the fathers slept in common dormitories. The dorms had a muted air even when they were full, but when Lucens wanted to be alone, he went to the church or the library or worked in the garden.

Yet even in the garden, where he felt relaxed and at ease, Lucens sensed that he was an outsider. He had heard the call and had decided to join the Trappist fold, and that too at Terraferra, because he thought only the solitude and solace of God would cure him. He wanted to ponder the mercy of Jesus and His great sacrifice for mankind, and, if he was fortunate, to fall within the ambit of His grace and forgiveness. Yes, he wanted to be alone, but in an inclusive sort of way, not left out. The monks, novices and lay workers were always kind and courteous to him. But so were they to dogs and cats.

It was such a small and closed community, you would think there was no room to keep anyone out. Well, you had better think again. He knew in his heart he was not one of them. The senior monks were lost in their silence and kept mostly to themselves, while the postulants, novices and junior professed monks seemed to gravitate towards Brother Jonathan-Christophe, who was the closest thing to an alpha male in the community. He had been a student at art school when he announced that he had applied to the Abbey at Terraferra. He was tall, boyish-looking and easygoing. He had charm and was not unaware of it, and if that failed to captivate you, his disarming humour and laughter certainly would.

He was good at whatever he did. He worked hard on the Abbey farms at Halfway. If there was a problem with any of the trucks or cars, he was called in to take care of it since he could assemble and disassemble an automobile engine blindfolded. He was always willing to put in a few hours at the carpentry shop or lend a hand at any other job. He was helpful and considerate, and though Lucens found him a trifle superficial, he would have liked Brother Jonathan-Christophe to like him and count him in his inner circle. But it didn't work out quite that way. Lucens could be distant and, at times, puzzlingly unorthodox, and his reputation for humility could be off-putting. Whatever the reasons, the fact was that Brother Jonathan-Christophe and Lucens kept a wary distance from each other.

Why was he skirting the issue? Had his past begun to show on his face in the manner of Dorian Gray? Had the monks detected that he was a moral leper? Had they tied an invisible bell around his neck? Reverend Father liked to say that we were all cripples and only God could make us whole. But that was merely a metaphorical way of expressing our yearning for Jesus and our incompleteness without Him. But what if Lucens were the real thing? What if they could all see that he was a spiritual failure beyond salvation, and had decided to ostracize him?

Oh, how he hated this place. He must have been out of his mind to want to become a monk. Talk about self-delusion. To think that he had claimed to have heard a voice deep inside his soul calling him to the Lord. The only voices he heard now, and he heard them every minute even if he plugged his ears, said: Get out, you stupid fool, get out. Don't become a victim of your own fraud. Get out while you can. Get the hell out of here before you become a solemnly professed monk and are committed to this lunatic asylum for life. The sad truth is that nobody promised you a rose garden. They told you again and again, it's not going to be easy. Yes, they did, but nobody said it's going to be pointless; utterly, totally, unremittingly pointless.

How could he possibly have stomached all the mealy-mouthed things they said? Ask and it will be given to you; seek and you'll find; knock and the door will be opened to you. He had asked till his tongue had fallen off; he had gone seeking in the four corners of the universe and had come up with nothing; he had knocked till his knuckles were bruised and broken but the door had not given and he had been shut out forever. After the hard times, they promised there would be the light at the end of the tunnel. No light and no tunnel, just the dark silence of the grave.'Go into the desert, and I'll speak to your heart,' the voice had told Lucens and he had come to the Abbey of Our Lord in Contemplation. Who was he trying to impress with his virtue, his humility? The Abbot and the monks? A fat lot of good it did him in this deadly place. Was he showing off to God? The Lord had seen through Lucens a long, long time ago. He had gone looking for a pat on the back, the great pat of God, and he had come up against the abyss. He had fallen for the temptation of the desert and all he had to show for his troubles was self-deception and delusion.

He knew he was blaspheming but he couldn't seem to stop. He would regret every word he said but that was tomorrow. Right now he would let the devil in him speak.

Now, 'tomorrow' was here, and after Vigils, Lucens went into the storeroom behind the church. The place was in a bit of a mess; chipped plaster statues of the saints, a few East European icons from which the paint had almost completely disappeared, old chalices and faded vestments. It took him a while to find what he was looking for: a flail with thongs that they had used a long, long time ago when a procession of monks would go down to the village of Halfway on Good Friday to re-enact the stations of the cross, chastising themselves symbolically.

Lucens dusted and washed the flail with care and went into the garage. It was a long, large building that housed the two Abbey buses, three vans with trailer trucks and a fleet of cars. There was no one there at this time. He found himself a middling open space between the trucks and the cars, and swung the scourge in circles in the air. The whipping sound was a miniature variant of the sinister wind that blew across Terraferra when the heat rose in the daytime to 104°. Lucens removed his white robe, black capula, belt, shirt, trousers and underwear, and stood naked and shivering in the cold. How glibly people talk of forgiveness. Even the Abbot. What forgiveness was there for the terrible sins he had committed in another life and on another continent? They were such unspeakable crimes, he could not even mention them in the privacy of the confessional.

He picked up the tentacled flagellum and did not stop whipping himself till he had stripped the flesh off his back. The devil had got into him and the devil had to be cast out. He had to be taught that he would not find a warm welcome in Lucens.

# 24

How long was it since Zia had nearly murdered his brother and vanished? Three years, three and a half, maybe more. Amanat couldn't quite remember. And he didn't want to either. It had taken him months to recover. When he had grown strong enough to move around, he scoured the city.

He went to the YWCA at Bombay Central and the one near Regal Cinema. He enquired at the Women's Hostel on Marine Drive, checked out the Working Women's Hostel next to the Colaba Bus Depot, and finally landed up at the recently built hostel near the Y.B. Chavan auditorium. Sagari was not registered in any one of them. She had come to visit him in the government hospital. He had been a five-line item in the morning papers but the eveningers had played up the incident for lack of any juicy disaster to report that day. She had brought him flowers and went looking for a nurse to ask for a vase. When she came back, Amanat was causing a series of earthquakes, demolishing entire suburbs, bringing down skyscrapers and ripping open highways with his mega-sneezes.

His absurdly ill-fitting hospital pyjamas were rapidly turning an earthen red as his wounds reopened and bled.

'How could I have forgotten that you are allergic to flowers?'

Sagari sat there unable to move, aghast at the havoc she had wrought. Amanat wanted to tell her that it was no big deal, his sinuses needed clearing up anyway and she had done him a favour, but the nurses were wheeling him into the operating theatre.

She did not come again but sent him a Dom DeLillo with just one word written on the flyleaf. 'Sorry.' No 'My dear Amanat.' No signature. Amanat wanted to fling the book out of the window or post it back with a cold 'return to sender', but he had no idea where Sagari lived. He remembered her telling him that she was changing hostels, but then the sneezing had started and he'd been out for the count.

Some months later he had learnt that there were several women's hostels in the suburbs. The Jains had one in Bhandup, and the Sindhis ran one in Borivali and another as far away as Ulhasnagar. Forget the suburbs, the Khojas had one tucked away in a bylane just a few blocks from Suleiman Mansion. Whether Hindu, Muslim or Jain, every caste, subcaste and sect seemed to have its own ladies' hostel. CKPs, Shimpis, Deshastha Brahmins, Marathas of every shade, the Ismailis, the Sikhs, Suleimani Bohras, Pathare Prabhus, they all took care of their own. Soon Amanat had become an authority on women's accommodation in Bombay.

He couldn't figure out why, but there was almost always a sordid air about the hostels. The security guards at the gate were invariably sleazy. And the staff, most of them women, eyed you knowingly. You were not about to fool them. Experience had taught them that the men who came to see the ladies, it did not matter young or old, had dishonourable intentions.

You might have called a few minutes before and fixed to meet your girlfriend, you might have seen her in the window of her room on the third floor, but they told you categorically that you had got it wrong, your friend was not in. Granted, it did not take much to change their minds; all you had to do was to ask them to check again and accidentally graze a few rupee notes against their palms, and usually the missing party was found.

Amanat was glad that Sagari was not in any of the hostels. He swore he would not visit another one as long as he lived, but he was off the minute he learnt of a new one.

He had come to the end of his search and he still didn't know her whereabouts. She was his ring of protection and he had lost her forever.

As a last resort, Amanat was even willing to consider going in for a lobotomy.

Everything, but everything in life, the cliché tells us, loses its edge and sharpness. Not just lust, love, loss and grief, even our sense of grievance and revenge...Time blunts them all. However much you may fear or resist it, the intensity wears off and the fiercest emotions become tepid. So what had gone wrong? Amanat wondered. How come the bitter memories of the stabbing and his stay in the hospital would not fade or blunt? How come they came back to him unsolicited and without let?

The police inspector had had to wait for forty-eight hours before the doctors would allow him to see Amanat. He'd been disoriented, and was still on the critical list but the inspector was not willing to wait any longer.

'Are you trying to tell us you didn't see who attacked you?'

'Water,' Amanat said.

'Can you understand what I'm saying? We need to know who did this to you.'

'Water.'

The nurse held a glass of water to Amanat's lips.

'You've got your water. Now talk.'

Amanat closed his eyes.

'You better leave. He's in no shape to talk,' the nurse told the policeman.

'I'm not leaving till I've got a statement from him. He's pretending, that's all. I've seen enough bad actors in my business to know when I see one.'

He was back the next day.

'Who attacked you, Mr Khan?'

Abbajaan was watching Amanat from a few feet away. Why don't you speak, Abba? You do know what happened, don't you? Or are you going to plead that you were not at home at the time? Do you remember the dog, Sher, Abba? I was lucky. The knife that did me in was sharp. Poor Sher was stabbed with a table knife.

'It was a frontal attack. How could you not have seen the man?'

How do you know it was not a woman? What about you, Zubeida Khaala? Would you like to volunteer information about your acolyte? The waalee and hope of Islam?

'I was preoccupied and looking down,' Amanat croaked.

'Do you have any connections with the underworld?'

As a matter of fact, yes. My brother, Zia Khan, is the supremo. He is the devil incarnate, though oddly enough, he's always looking out for Satan.

'No.'

'Do you know Dawood Ibrahim, the mafia don?'

What you should do, officer, is to alert Scotland Yard, Interpol and the FBI and tell them to look out for one Zia Khan, who's a menace to international amity and peace. He's code Red Alert or whatever you call the ten most wanted criminals in the world.

'Are you connected with any extremist Islamic organization?'

Yes, the worst extremist you can think of. My very own brother's, Lashkar-e-Zia Khan.

'No.'

'Do you have any enemies, Mr Khan? Have you antagonized anybody so badly that they would want to murder you?'

Couldn't possibly be my one and only brother, could it? How about Abba, Ammijaan and why not Zubeida Khaala? All their lives they have shamelessly favoured their younger son over me. They sent him to the finest and most expensive school in India while I got St Paul's and the dirty red tie with the slick, shiny knot that I never untied. And then, good, caring parents that they are, they sent him to Cambridge when they could barely afford to send me to some small-time college in Byculla. I must have antagonized them so badly, they won't stand up for me even today. He hated the self-pity that overtook him every couple of years. And yet he was unaware of the depths of his bitterness against his brother.

'Not that I know of.'

'How about your brother, Mr Khan? He seems to have disappeared about the time you were nearly stabbed to death.'

Tell that to my father, my aunt and the whole world. Oh what was the point, he knew all too well he would never talk to the police or even his family about what Zia had done. He was his father's son. Like him and the rest of them, he would sweep it under the carpet.

There was a week-long Satyajit Ray retrospective at Chitra Talkies that Christmas and he had bought himself a festival pass. He was standing at the bus stop after seeing *Charulata*, the last film of all, when Sagari tapped him on the arm. Amanat was struck by the fact that she too had been at that small theatre the whole week and yet they had not run into each other. Now the fates had slipped up. They had been vigilant for seven whole days and had then looked away. He had met her again by a freak accident and he was not going to let go of her now.

She was staying at the Sisters of Mercy Ladies' Hostel in Versova. It was an old bungalow with a spectacular view of the sea in the monsoons. That was its one and only asset. The Sisters had left a long time ago and the place had been bought by a Punjabi widow with four children. They lived on the top floor while the four rooms on the ground floor had been converted into dorms that would have shamed the shabbiest Salvation Army hostel. The place was coming apart. Even the ceiling had to be propped up with lanky wooden supports every couple of feet. The steel beds and mattresses on which the girls slept had to zigzag around them. There was an egalitarian system at work here. Nobody had a permanent claim to any of the beds. First come, first served. You came late, you slept on one of the mattresses on the floor. The bathroom walls leaked the year round and were velvety with evergreen moss. If you wanted to have a shower you got up at four. Otherwise you had to take a bucket bath, that's if there was any water left in the plastic storage drums.

Sagari was a temporary lecturer in biochemistry at a college in Andheri and the measly salary she earned was rarely paid on time. She did not complain about her accommodation. It was cheap and not too far from her place of work, and that was that. It was a long trudge from Suleiman Mansion to the hostel in Versova, anywhere between an hour-and-a-half to two hours. Amanat had to change trains twice and then catch a bus. He didn't mind the travel but disliked meeting Sagari at the hostel. There were always men hanging out in the compound waiting to be let in, or if visiting hours were over, stealing a few minutes out on the pavement before the gates closed. It was absurd but Amanat felt he was standing, waiting his turn at a bordello. 'Now that's a delightful thing to say about the ladies here,' Sagari said flippantly, 'but I don't really think you can afford our rates.'

Often there was some man or the other waiting for Sagari when Amanat got there but she made it a point not to introduce him. She would look through Amanat and pretend not to know him till the other man had left. This was disconcerting for Amanat the first few times and he would feel hurt. He had never really got used to it but explained it to himself as one of Sagari's quirks.

'Who are those people who come to see you at the hostel?' Amanat finally asked her one day when they went for a walk on the beach.

Two men had been standing outside talking to her when Amanat got there that day. They were both in white shirts left untucked over white satin duck trousers, and wore the shiny white open sandals people from the film world, especially the old-school producers and their lackeys, fancied as a kind of lush statement about themselves. One of the men wore dark glasses while the other leaned against a foreign car and smoked a cigarette with a remarkably long tip of ash that he balanced effortlessly. Amanat went into the compound and waited his turn. Sagari was taking her own time. Obviously she was relishing the conversation, for he could hear their laughter. It was half an hour before she said her goodbyes. One of the men shouted as he closed the door of the car, 'Think it over, Sagariji. Dr Patwardhan wants it and we want it. Now all we need is a "yes" from you and we'll make a big splash in the press and on TV.'

Amanat had by now vowed a dozen times never to see Sagari again. He would not, no, he would not be made to wait and be humiliated in this manner. He was working himself up to a good-sized outburst when she said, let's go. He went along but didn't say a word. It didn't seem to bother her, she was lost in her own thoughts. Savouring the high points of her conversation with those two smoothies, Amanat was willing to bet. He couldn't restrain himself any longer, though he did have the prudence to fiddle with his volume controls and to adjust his query to an innocuous, bland pitch before he spoke. 'Those two men who just left, they must be close friends of yours the way you talked to them.' If Sagari felt that Amanat was being offensive, she didn't let on.

'Papa keeps calling film producers and directors, even ad agencies, asking them to give me work. He plays the same audio tape to all these people and tells them I am Nargis, Madhubala and Ava Gardner rolled into one. His reference points are a little outdated. The first two they may remember as Hindi film actresses about whom their parents still reminisce, but Ava Gardner, now who could that be? But they come to check out what I look like. I guess they are curious to know what happens to childhood memories when those memories grow up and become adults.'

'I thought your father and you don't talk.'

'We don't.'

'So how come he sends all these people after you?'

'He thinks at some point I'll see sense. He's also terribly keen that I get married. At least half the men come with marriage proposals for that "Oh, grow up" girl.'

'Why bother to see them?'

'Because if I don't they come to the college where I teach and that can be embarrassing.'

'Why not tell your father to lay off?'

'You try it. He can't forget my glory days.'

'Maybe I should ask Abbajaan to talk to Uncle Pat.'

'Papa hates Zafar Uncle and your family.'

'They may not meet these days but Uncle Pat couldn't have forgotten how close he was to Abba.'

'How could he forget? When Khan Builders went under it took three-quarters of Papa's savings with it.'

'But I thought you were making big money. The glossies used to call you the Baby Mint.'

'I'm sure I made good money. Nothing compared to what the stars make today though. Besides Papa had heavy expenses.'

'I didn't know he gambled.'

Sagari smiled. 'He did. On his daughter.'

Dr Patwardhan had always been so unglamorous, even a little homely. It was difficult to imagine that he, of all people, would lose his sense of balance. But the glitter and glamour of the Bombay film world had got to him at some point.

He wanted to be thought of not simply as that precocious girl's father, but as a member of the inner circle of Bollywood aristocracy. He gave parties at the Taj, the Oberoi and the Willingdon Club for stars, the husbands and wives of stars, for producers, directors and financiers. The pretext would be Sagari's birthday or the Best Child Star award that she picked up with such predictable regularity. He started to neglect his practice. He also began to get pushy. He wanted Sagari to get more roles even if her calendar was full. She had to be in the public eye all the time. He was constantly after the gossip magazines to cover her, never mind if four-fifths of the stories were fabricated. She was not even twelve but she was supposed to have crushes on the big stars and torrid teenage affairs.

The editors of the trashy film rags, and there were no other kind, saw a whole new field of soft-core titillation and veiled child sex opening up before them. They began to put all the catty and bitchy things they wanted to say in the mouth of that 'horrid little cutie', 'the child superstar', 'the monster-brat', and 'the super-babe', Sagari.

The established stars, the aspiring actors, the starlets and the superstars all have one thing in common: the vulnerability of their image and position. Am I slipping? Is the curtain coming down on me? They know that even when superstars like Rajesh Khanna or Vivian Leigh disappear overnight, they never, never rise out of their long-dispersed ashes.

Very sensibly, they don't trust their luck too much and are sensitive to every whiff and rumour of their fall. Of course they didn't believe that the child star Sagari was saying any of the things attributed to her. But, truth to tell, she had been a threat to them from the day she had got her first break in films. And they would be able to breathe easy only when she entered her teens and became gawky and needed braces. Sagari, the film magazines said, was a born actress, a scene stealer, she could teach the older stars a thing or two, and if they didn't watch out, the 'Oh, grow up' kid was really going to grow up and put everybody else in the shade. As if all this were not galling enough, they said, beware, this lady's going to be one hell of a looker.

It didn't take the stars and would-be stars, producers and directors too long to shun Sagari. Uncle Pat couldn't figure out why the offers suddenly began to dry up but he was not discouraged. He threw more parties, entertained more lavishly and courted the gossip columnists and journalists even more sedulously. And he began to hate Sagari for failing him.

He planned and plotted Sagari's comeback for years so that both daughter and father could return to happier days. He kept on at her to cultivate directors and producers and make sure that they took her in their next film. The day she turned eighteen she walked out on her father. She took whatever little money there was in her bank account and never went back.

Amanat didn't know he was going to get married that evening. Sagari and he had planned to attend the Jazz Yatra at Rang Bhavan the previous night, and he had waited outside for her for an hour after the programme had started before admitting that he had been stood up.

He was on his way to the hairdressers the next morning to get himself a crew cut as always, when he ran into Sagari. Had he seen her in time, he could have slipped into another building or stepped into The Perfumed Garden, but it was too late for that. She could crawl and beg for his forgiveness but he would be obdurate. No one ditches Amanat Khan with impunity. Come what may he would not mention the subject of her not turning up nor ask the whys or wherefores. He would be nonchalant and he would put her in her place. He would have succeeded too except that Sagari talked such nonsense at times.

'Will you marry me?' Sagari asked.

Dr Patwardhan had turned up at her hostel with a young expatriate from the States just as she was about to leave for the concert. The visitor had been an IT millionaire many times over. He had had the charm and self-assurance that early success bestows.

'It's taken a while but I've grown up, as you asked me to from the TV screen when I was a child,' he had said over dinner. 'Now it's up to you to check me out and say "I do".' He had laughed. It was a friendly laugh, confident in the knowledge that it was hard not to like him. 'Your father says you want to go back to acting in movies again. I've no problem with that. Maybe I could finance some of your new films.'

'Sounds like a fine proposal,' Amanat said.

'It is, but my answer's no. I've had my fill of proposals and prospective husbands.'

'So you want to marry me merely to stop your father pestering you?'

'Something like that.'

'I guess that's as good a reason as any other. When?'

'As soon as it's feasible.'

She walked away and then came back smiling.

'I haven't had anyone else in mind for a long, long time. Maybe since as far back as when I came to Suleiman Mansion and you lost at Trade and lost your temper with me. Does that satisfy you?'

'Yes,' he said, and got his hair shorn.

# 25

Brendan, Lucens's brandy-pouring lifesaver, was a broad, short man with a rolling gait, a woollen cap pulled over the ears covering a head of close-cropped hair, and a mouth that had a few forgotten crumbs around it. Brendan hated two things: cooking and washing dishes. He almost never did either. He fed himself on the run, dipping into the leftovers in the Abbey kitchen, stuffing his mouth as quickly as possible lest someone turn up and catch him in the act.

There was an unspoken bond between Lucens and the man who had saved him. It puzzled Lucens that Brendan had not chosen to become a monk. He seemed to observe many of the Abbey's practices far more stringently than they did, and in an atmosphere far less conducive to such things. He was sixty-one, just four years younger than the Abbot. Thirty of those years he had spent at the Abbey and, if one was to believe him, and one had no reason not to, all of them celibate. He stayed at St Luke's, one of the satellite retreat houses, the main one being St Peter's. He woke every morning at 2.15 and was at church for Vigils by 2.30. He might or might not turn up for the other offices of the day, but that was because he worked and often had to go down to Sweet Waters to pick up guests and special visitors to the Abbey.

He was a carpenter. Not the best, but competent enough.

'I learnt watching my father at his trade in the old country,' he told Lucens.

He had left his father's home and Ireland because he had wanted to buy a fast car, preferably a racing model, but he would have been seventy before he could have saved enough to afford it back there. He was still waiting to buy it. He had had his share of girlfriends in the new country, but the Lord's mother had advised him against getting hitched to any of them.

Lucens could never mimic his accent, intonation or turn of phrase, but was spellbound when Brendan reminisced.

'I was in Ottawa in the early days and planning to start a business. I was a little nervous about it since the previous two I had got into had sunk faster than the Titanic. I was passing a church and I thought I might get the Lord's reaction on the subject. My family, my daddy and mam, were not religious, I mean they went to church on Sundays but that was about it. I sat down and I prayed for half an hour. I went home, had some lunch and then the Lord came and seized me. A white light, a blessed light, fell upon me and I was in a trance for two and a half days. I was in a state of exhilaration. The beatitude of Jesus was upon me all that time. It did not occur to me to have a meal or even a glass of water. I knew what heaven was. It was ecstasy. The Lord had given me a preview of it.'

'And then?' Lucens asked.

'It went away just like it came. And a good thing too. It brought me back to earth and told me to get down to work. You want God, you've got to pay for the pleasure. The admission fee is just a prayer, nothing more.'

'What about the business?'

'Out of the window. The Lord said, "Forget it."'

'Did it ever happen again?'

'Yes, it did. Three years after the first time. I remember the date. It was the 17th of March 1956, the time was 7 p.m. I looked up at the clock and I saw the Lord's mother right there in front of me. I sat down and didn't get up for seven days. I soaked in that light, I was afloat in it. It was a gentle thing, that light, the purest of mercy. And I knew that our Lord wanted His mother to intercede on my behalf. He personally put me in Her care. She would look out for me.'

'Did it ever come back?'

'Never. That was the end of them. They had given me an addiction and a thirst that's never gone away. That's how I came here to the Abbey, looking to satisfy my addiction.'

The light of God had shone upon Brendan, he called it a conversion, and he wanted to make sure that everybody else got to share it. He would say, 'Good morning. And how are you today?' and start quoting a hymn to you. God help you if Brendan was reading the scriptures at that moment, or the lives of the saints. He read in an incoherent, stumbling manner but that was all right with him, he would read right through to the end of the chapter or book, never mind if you missed your train or had to go to the loo.

Dates, numbers, memories were all omens to him. Everything was significant and he could read absolutely anything into anything else. He should have become a clairvoyant. He would nod his head and say, 'Get in touch with the three Theresas, they all work together, you know. Tell them you want them to look after you. Talk to them. And they will protect you…'

'I don't need to pick up the phone to talk with Jesus,' he told Lucens. 'I just say, are you listening, Lord? I need to run this thing by you. And you know what, God always gets back to me with an answer.'

It amused Lucens that he himself spent hours, more than a third of the day, praying, but it was Brendan who always got on God's chat show.

Brendan drove Lucens down into Sweet Waters for an appointment with the ophthalmologist.

'What will you do while I wait for the doctor to see me?'

'I'll hang around,' Brendan said, 'run a few errands.'

Lucens was early for his appointment. He hadn't seen a magazine for years and was flipping through *House and Garden* as if this had been daily reading all his life, when he realized that the room was uncomfortably hot.

'Do you mind if I open the window? It's a lovely, warm day outside.'

The two other patients said it was fine with them. Lucens had to struggle a while to disengage the rusty latch but it was a relief to feel the soft, fresh air on his face. He craned his body and breathed in deep. Brendan was on the pavement outside the building pulling out a sheaf of papers from his windcheater. They seemed to have seen some wear and tear and were a little soiled. A man eased his car into the adjoining parking lot and walked up with his wife.

'How are you doing today, sir, and you, ma'am?'

The man hadn't expected a greeting from this short pugilist-type and looked a little puzzled. 'Coming along okay, I guess.'

'I have a message from the Lord for the two of you. Don't do it, I beg you not to kill an unborn baby.'

'What baby?' the man asked truculently. 'We are going to the dentist.'

'And a good thing too. Those teeth can really hurt. Here's something you might want to read while you are waiting for your appointment.' Brendan licked his thumb and index finger, dislodged a single printed sheet and thrust it on the man's wife. She took it almost as a reflex action. One look at its saliva-wet edges and she dropped the leaflet as if she had handled used toilet paper. Brendan picked up the fallen sheet and put it back with the others. He looked around to see if anyone had observed this silent altercation and noticed Lucens. His face flushed in embarrassment.

'God's work. Got to take the ups with the downs.'

Lucens looked at the board on the strip of lawn outside. The Healing Touch, it said, a multispecialty clinic: there was a cardiologist, a urologist, a dentist, a radiologist, an obstetrician, his ophthalmologist, and Mothercare Planned Parenthood all under the same roof.

Brendan was sitting on the steps when a smartly turned-out woman in a banana-peel-yellow pantsuit with a stout briefcase walked briskly towards the door.

'Good day to you, ma'am, and God bless you.'

She nodded and strode ahead.

'No offence meant but you are going to see the obstetrician, right?'

'I beg your pardon. I'll ask you to mind your own business or I'm going to tell the receptionist to call the police.'

Brendan quickly slunk away. Lucens thought that he would call it a day now but he took a turn around the corner and then came back to try his luck again. He had obviously had time to rethink things. You could see the change in strategy when a middle-aged woman walked down the road with a teenage girl and turned towards the medical facility. Brendan doffed his woollen cap at the two ladies and smiled.

'Fine day, isn't it?'

The woman looked around, bemused, as though to check whether the facts coincided with the man's statement.

'Do we know you?'

'No, ma'am, but I assure you, your daughter's going to have a glorious cherubic baby, just like an angel. I've got some literature that you – '

'Heather,' the mother looked stunned.

Heather burst into tears, pummelled Brendan with her handbag, and ran all the way to the end of the street screaming, 'I hate you, I hate you.' The mother glared at Brendan. 'You evil man,' she said and chased after her child.

Sometimes when he wanted to be alone and the wind was not too obstreperous, Lucens would climb on to the gently sloping roof of the refectory and lie down on his back under the sky. This was where you discovered the meaning of silence. Any word, spoken or unspoken, even a prayer or a hallelujah, would be blasphemy. This was the domain of God, the Father, who was sufficient unto Himself. As you lost consciousness of yourself, you heard the rise and flow of Sweet Waters, the mother river in the valley down below. You could hear the drip of a million subterranean springs feeding it. You could hear the crawl of ants moving mountains of food into their hills. You could hear the lapping of polar bears drinking water, the sap in the roots pushing out into grain, the crackle of sun flares, the soft burble of oil under the substratum of the earth, and the shrinking of the substance of mountains as the temperature dropped.

Of the mountain peaks around Terraferra, Rearing Horse was the most forbidding. Its sheer south face, hewn like the thick braids of secondary banyan roots that cling to rock, fell all the way down to the thin gorge into which the river cut. It was a pagan site, the slit of the Earth Mother where the fertility rights of the whole of creation were conducted. It was on the western flank that Rearing Horse rose precipitously, kicking at the very belly of the black crystal sky. It was an amazing balancing act, this mountain peak trying to clamber on to the firmament. But one of these days the hind legs were going to skid and Rearing Horse would keel over and plunge headlong into the valley thousands of feet below.

On Falcon Dive the frisky rivulets that would later become Sweet Waters shone like veins of silver. But the reason for the mad rush to stake a claim on Falcon Dive some ninety years before had been the deposits of mica that glinted in the sunlight like gold. It was a harsh, lethal mountain with brittle substrata that didn't take too kindly to dynamite, and within minutes seven hundred gold diggers had been buried under a landslide. Now, two hours before dawn, Falcon Dive looked benign, and the thin slivers of mica shimmered like silver-foil ribbons dancing on scarecrows. Only the three Bitter Sisters stood apart, silhouetted in a confrontation of hate and hostility that would only end with the death of the planet.

Then the sun rose suddenly, an SOS flare shooting up into the sky. Shards and fragments of light burst into the mountains like mines going off soundlessly in a chain reaction. The black crystal of the sky broke and turned to red velour as the sun began to bleed on it. A lone falcon circled overhead and sat on the head of Rearing Horse.

'You love the Italians, don't you?' Lucens asked Jonathan-Christophe.

'Not really. Just that the Abbey has a book on the Uffizi.'

Brother Jonathan was the resident artist at the Abbey. His paintings, or rather the copies he made of the religious works of the great masters, were hung in the cloisters, the two large and small seminar halls, the refectory, the infirmary, and in the lobby of the church where the monks sold rosaries and crosses, scriptural commentaries and books. Even the portrait of the Lord above the altar was his.

Often other monasteries and cathedrals commissioned him to paint an El Greco, Dürer or anybody else they fancied on their walls. The Benedictine Rule was about the pre-eminence of the interior life in Christ. Extra-curricular activities were frowned upon as distractions and interferences in the pursuit of God. But while the Abbot might not have approved of Jonathan-Christophe's work going public, he did not wish to scotch his God-given talent either.

At first Lucens would stand outside the unshuttered shed Jonathan had converted into a studio, and watch. The two would smile tentatively at each other but they rarely exchanged a word. Jonathan-Christophe had the peculiar habit of working on two or three paintings at the same time, and it was always a challenge for Lucens to predict which masterpiece Brother Jonathan was planning to re-create that day from the book of art works open next to him.

'That's a new one. You've never done Blake before.'

Brother Jonathan looked up not a little surprised. There was no way Lucens could either see the book or make out the painting he had just begun to sketch.

'You know Blake?'

'That's the *River of Life*.'

'I was merely copying that to give myself a break from the Correggio. Can you recognize the other artists?'

'Some of them.'

'Did you study painting?'

'No,' Lucens laughed. 'The usual, can't draw a straight line.'

'So how do you know all these artists? Did a course in art appreciation?'

'No, nothing of the sort. My father liked paintings, and sculpted and painted when he had the time. We always had art books all over the place.'

It was a couple of months before Jonathan-Christophe would finally invite him into his studio.

Occasionally Lucens would speak of one of his favourite paintings and Jonathan would copy it. He suggested Rafael's *The Holy Family with the Lamb* and about a month later Jonathan showed him the completed painting.

'It needs some more work but it's uncanny.' Lucens kept shaking his head. 'Have you ever tried to paint something you really wanted to? A subject that genuinely excited you?'

'Yes, I have.'

'And?'

'I had no ideas. I just stared at the canvas. Or if I forced myself to, the results were drab and less than mediocre.'

'I don't believe you.'

Jonathan-Christophe took Lucens to the loft and brought out a portfolio of about twenty paintings. Lucens went through them one by one.

'You are asking yourself how a man can be such a fine craftsman and so dull and mechanical?'

Lucens blushed.

'No, you are not transparent. It's just that I know my capabilities better than you do.'

Jonathan had put his finger on it. There were several portraits and full-length studies of someone called Lucy in various poses and postures, some skies and landscapes, abstracts and surrealist efforts, all of them competent but bereft of emotion and life and, most of all, of that unique vision and style that marks all the good, let alone the great artists.

'Things change,' Lucens said. 'People mature and suddenly discover their talent.'

'Maybe. I'll let you know if that happens.'

Lucens stood in front of the *River of Life*. It was not an elaborate painting, just a white river flowing towards a big yellowish sun at the back. Angels danced around the golden orb while a muscular, naked young man dived into the water in front of it. Lucens seemed to study it for a long time. Then suddenly he whipped out a pen and scribbled something in the lower left-hand corner.

'What are you doing?' Jonathan-Christophe asked with alarm and anger. He bent down to see what exactly Lucens had done. WB, William Blake's signature with its overarching flourish, rested under the right foot of the woman in white to the left. It was such an inconsequential thing, just those two letters, and yet they seemed to complete the painting.

'God Almighty,' Brother Jonathan whooped and hugged Lucens, 'now it really is the original.'

Like most postulants and novices, Lucens had eagerly sought out silence in the early days. How often had he heard it said in the secular world that silence was the only way to self-knowledge. And only when you know yourself can you know God. He'd learnt the hard way how mistaken that belief was. Silence was a highly unstable quantity. There were times when it made him nervous and irritable, and there were days when it filled him with doubt and self-loathing. But that state of mind too changed. He became introspective and thoughtful. Then for weeks he felt nothing. He went through the motions of being a monk, though in his heart he knew that he was stone-dead. Then that too passed and he was transformed. He felt light and joyous and he walked beside God. In time that feeling of intense happiness slipped away and a quiet crept in on him. Things slowed down. The most pressing of tasks shed their urgency and even a life-and-death crisis seemed to lose its edge. Perhaps he was reading too much into silence. Was it silence that was playing tricks with him? Or was he projecting his mood and state of mind on silence?

It would take him months, more like two or three years really, to admit how little he understood this element that was more pervasive at Terraferra than the air he breathed. There was no point chasing silence, nor could you reject it. You let it be and at some point it would become part of your nature.

An easy silence was a habit the older monks wore more closely than their scapulars and cowls. You did not talk unless there was something that needed to be talked about. Every once in a while, Jonathan and Lucens would spend hours together at the studio. They would exchange a couple of sentences but mostly they kept quiet. Lucens had had the sense of late that Jonathan and he might even reach a stage when they would not need to talk at all. He could imagine a day when the two of them would have silent conversations.

'Maybe you should concentrate on Vermeer,' Lucens suggested to Jonathan one evening.

'Why Vermeer?'

'He's a fine painter. Different from the others in many ways.'

'You're up to something. I can see that brain of yours working overtime.'

'All I'm saying is that he has a very limited body of work that we know of and he's suddenly very big on the art scene.'

'He couldn't have got that good by painting so little.'

'He's an intriguing man. Most painters often use the same model. He certainly does. But there's really a peculiar parsimony in the man.

He also uses the same props. The jackets the women wear, the carpet, the pitcher of water, everything's recycled.'

'So?'

'Nothing. Despite all these self-imposed limitations, there's a big market out there for him.'

'Sometimes I think, Lucens, you've missed your vocation.'

# 26

My dear Zia,

I don't know which is worse, your anger or your humility; your unshakable convictions or your floundering for faith; your zealotry or your relentless repentance. For the last one-and-a-half years there has been an unceasing barrage of letters from you asking my forgiveness. You have pestered, badgered, bullied and begged me to hear your confession and give you absolution. You are like the Ancient Mariner. And I am the hapless wedding guest. Your song never changes. Mea culpa, mea culpa, mea culpa, you scream and breast-beat. But I suspect my forgiving you is not going to give you any peace of mind.

Do I forgive you? Have I forgiven you? It would be a little too pat to say I do.

In the hospital when the pain had subsided but not the astonishment and the shock, I wanted vengeance so badly, I was willing to pay any price for it, paradoxically even with my own life. But I had no idea what shape my revenge would take. I hated you, oh did I hate you. But physical violence has always been anathema to me. At least that's my theoretical position. God knows one's best aspirations often have little or nothing to do with the way we act in real life.

Did I want to stab you as you had stabbed me? Did I want you dead? I don't know now. And I didn't know then either. I was hurt and I wanted to hurt you.

Perhaps time really does help to heal the mind as much as the body. Try as I may, I cannot sustain my anger against you. I might even now cross over to the other pavement if I saw you coming my way but that would be as much out of awkwardness as out of unhappy memories.

You are my little brother. I was barely four and a half when I first held you in my arms. (What confidence children have. I wouldn't dare handle a newborn today.) But you too seemed comfortable with me. That memory must have some kind of hold on me. Is there no getting away from the 'blood is thicker than water' truism? Forgiveness for myself and my own, and vengeful justice for the rest.

When you got back in touch with me I was not unhappy to see you stew in your own guilt. But at some point in time I had to ask myself: between the two of us who betrayed whom? I may like to plead that I stabbed you in the back for a higher moral purpose. I certainly was convinced of that and continue to be so. But so were you. What you were doing was, according to your lights, at the behest of a higher authority, the highest there is. Who is to settle the rights and wrongs of these matters? More to the point, can they ever be settled?

Looking back, how can I deny how catastrophic my visit to Cambridge was for you. If I had not butted in, you would have got Rushdie and at the very least become the greatest hero of Islam of the twentieth century. That's if you had escaped. Had you been caught you would have gained stardom as Allah's favourite martyr and become every extremist Muslim's role model. You would have become at least as well known as Rushdie. Instead you lost your God, your fiancée and, I suspect, you lost your mind.

Paradoxically mine has been a thankless job too. Rushdie owes me one, a very big one. But the man is blissfully unaware of it and will go to his grave without knowing that he owes his life to me. And what did I get for my pains? Two scars in my belly and permanent gastrointestinal problems.

Virtue, one is often told, is its own reward. I'm sure there's some truth to that but I would rather let someone else have the satisfaction next time.

Now that it's all receding in a past that seems to become more unreal as each day passes, I can afford to dwell on some of the tragicomic moments of that last day of the Cambridge Seminar. I got up that morning with a sense of dread. What was I going to do? How was I going to get hold of your leather bag, take possession of the gun in front of all those people in the seminar room and where and how was I going to get rid of it? I could dig a hole in the ground and bury it. Or climb up to the terrace (I wasn't even sure that there was one) and fling it into the blue yonder. Except that with my limited shot-putting prowess, the blue yonder would not stretch even to the buttery. No, I had to admit that getting rid of the gun did not seem like a good idea. Plus there was one other small problem: you did not part with your bag for a second. When you went to the loo, you made sure that Vivian took charge of it.

Everything changed for the worse, infinitely worse, when I reached the seminar room. I was forced to realize that I like to take a lofty moral stance so long as I do not have to act upon it. Vivian said that you had gone to Peterborough to finalize the arrangements for the wedding. Oh, how I wanted you back. Why didn't you ask me? I would have been more than happy to go over and meet the qazi and do whatever else needed to be done. Why hadn't you stayed put? Now I had no choice but to do something about that damned gun.

Normally Vivian needed to go 'powder her nose' or whatever the phrase for these delicate matters is these days, not more than once a day at the seminar. I had no luck that day. She disappeared twice in the morning session alone. The first time around I sat idly and rationalized my paralysis by telling myself caution is the better part of valour. She was bound to come back any moment and catch me red-handed.

The next time I knew it was now or never. Rose Tremaine opened her book *Restoration* and slid her specs up the bridge of her nose and started reading. Vivian smiled and pushed your bag towards me with her foot for me to keep an eye on it. When she was out of sight I placed the bag on my knees and opened it. There it was lying curled up in a foetal position under *The Heart of the Matter* and *Don Quixote*.

That was the end. How the hell was I going to disarm that gun? I had never seen a firearm in real life, let alone handled one. Pick it up, pick it up, pick it up, I screamed at myself but couldn't bring myself to touch it.

What would you know about pusillanimity, Zia, and what a wonderful thing it is. Isn't it ironic that I had to overcome it for your sake? I clasped the gun in my hand and dropped it the next instant. Fortunately into the bag. My hand had got singed. I kid you not. No scalding water, no molten metal could have scarred me so. That icy weapon sank snugly into my palm. Forever and evermore that gun is imprinted into my muscles, bone and skin. It's beyond me how the beepers at airport security gates do not shrill away when I'm within a few hundred metres of them.

But my troubles were just starting. Since stealing the gun was out of the question, all I had to do was void the bullets. All I had to do.... Sure, that's all, whatever 'all' meant. I had no idea whether it was a pistol or a revolver, a semiautomatic or automatic. And I certainly had no clue where the bullet chamber was or how to open it. I propped up the flap of the leather bag and wrestled with the gun under it, hoping that no one would notice what I was up to, but every now and then the makeshift screen collapsed and my groping and fiddling under the leather cover became desperate. Try as I might, I could not pry the gun open. I was frantic and my right hand was doing strange things. It had begun to ricochet on its own. The gun went off. Outside the pigeons scrambled and rose to the sky. The bullet had gone clean through my heart.

Meanwhile, Rose Tremaine read haltingly and kept twirling a lock of hair above her left ear. I wonder if you could spare me a minute, Ms Tremaine. I've got a gun here that I need to unload. Would you please – I must have pressed the right lever for the magazine was expelled. Is this what I was terrified of? It didn't at all look lethal. More like corn on the cob. I spread out my kerchief and plucked out the missiles of death and slapped the magazine back. It was a sturdy piece and showed no sign of the abuse and mauling it had suffered at my hands. I shut the leather case and eased it to the floor.

When Vivian got back, I excused myself and went to the toilet. My hand was still shaking as if I was suffering from the D.T.'s. I took out the kerchief from my pocket and opened it over the toilet bowl. The bullets tinkled down. Under the water they looked different...like the Seven Seas cod liver oil capsules you and I were forced to take as children. When I flushed the toilet I knew that the bullets would stay put as in a bad thriller. And I would keep flushing till the police arrived. Why didn't I have the sense to swallow the lot? Shouldn't have been difficult. I was used to swallowing five to seven tablets and capsules several times a day.

I pulled the flush. They were gone.

To get back, you've done an Agatha Christie on the three years after you vanished from home. They've gone missing, and even after you got back in touch with us, you preferred not to refer to them in your letters. In some strange and unintended way, you are your mother's son. You too took off from Suleiman Mansion without notice. There were all kinds of stories and rumours floating around after you disappeared. You were heavily into debauchery. You were hell-bent on destroying yourself. You had joined some extreme left-wing organization that was into terror and violence in Nepal. You had got AIDS. You had gone to Afghanistan and become a terrorist who often crossed over to Kashmir. Someone had seen you lying drunk in the gutters in Chennai.

What was one to think? Abba was worried sick but as usual tried to put a stoic face on it. I had long since gone off you and yet there were moments when I found myself agonizing about your whereabouts and wellbeing. Zubeida Khaala was the only one who knew, God alone knows how, that however difficult the times were, you were going to make it.

She was right. You did make it, though it was a different God who saw you through. I wonder how she feels about it.

When you go off the rails, Zia, I cannot make head or tail of you. I try to trace its aetiology or provenance but without success. One thing I do know: whatever good there is in you, your energy, your perfectionism, but even more than that, your need to right matters, to seek forgiveness, however belated, are Abbajaan's and Ammi's gift to you.

Love,

Amanat

P.S. Abbajaan must have told you that Aunt Antonia keeps writing, begging him to persuade you to finish your PhD.

# 27

'What is it, my child?' the Abbot asked anxiously. 'Get up, Lucens. Is anything wrong?'

'Don't throw me out, Reverend Father, please don't. This is the only home I have.'

'Why would I throw you out? Get up, son.'

'How will the Lord ever forgive me?'

'That is not your lookout, Lucens. You know well that Jesus came down only to seek forgiveness for us. He will forgive you anything if you truly repent.'

'He won't.' There was no stopping Lucens's incoherent babbling now. 'I can't even recall how many innocent people I killed in Kashmir, Father. People whom I had not seen before and who had not done me any harm.'

'So did most of us who went to Vietnam in the 60s and 70s.'

'I didn't just kill. I tortured my victims.'

'I know. But you have to put it all behind you once and for all.'

'You don't understand, Father. Do you know why I killed? It was to spite Jesus who kept pursuing me with His mercy. The more He begged me to give up my madness, the more bestial I became.'

'But He won out. That's all that matters. How many sinners does He pursue and not let go? I would hardly think any. He certainly didn't come after me or the Novice Master. You must be special, very special to our Lord.'

'But that's not all. I nearly killed my brother because he prevented me from committing my first murder.'

'Don't, Lucens, don't dwell on it.'

'But there's something else that you don't know. I abandoned the woman I was supposed to marry the night before our wedding. She was a good woman, if a little unstable. My walking out on her precipitated a crisis. She's been in a psychiatric hospital several times since.'

Lucens's body was heaving with great sobs. His head was sunk on the Abbot's shoes, which smelt of manure, and his hands were clutching Reverend Father's ankles. The Abbot bent down, raised Lucens up by the shoulders and embraced him. 'Oh my son, my son.' His hands felt wet and sticky. He looked at them uncomprehendingly. There was blood on them. 'Why would you torture your body so, Lucens?'

The Abbot went to his chair and closed his eyes.

'You gave me your word, not once but several times, that you would not flagellate yourself. And every time you've broken it.'

'I'll never again disobey you, Father.'

'If you don't keep your word this time,' the Abbot spoke wearily, 'I'll have little alternative but to seriously consider whether you are worthy of the monastic life. I should have talked to you much earlier but I might as well do it now.

'Why, Lucens, why will you not let go of the darkness in your heart? Why the need for pain? There's a pattern here. Your antipathy towards yourself is so great, no penance or punishment is sufficient for you. You flagellate yourself despite my express orders. I believe you now even have a small school of acolytes.

'You are the most obedient of monks and then suddenly your need to atone reasserts itself and you transgress my wishes and, more important, the will of Jesus. Have you any idea what grievous injustice you do to everything that our Lord stood for? When you tear your flesh to shreds, your assumption is that this will in some way make amends for your past and pacify Jesus. But there's some confusion here. Will you not recall the words of St Paul? "That if thou shalt confess with thy mouth the Lord Jesus, and shalt believe in thine heart that God hath raised him from the dead, thou shalt be saved." Jesus is not, most definitely not, a God of vengeance. He is the God of love.

'I've tolerated your disobedience even though obedience is the first of our vows, in the fond and, as I've discovered time and again, mistaken hope that you'll grow out of your obstinacy and become a good monk.

'God has been good to you in a measure that is rare. You are a warm and generous man and a gifted one. It was not for me to ask why you gave up your promising academic career. There's no explaining who is called by the Lord. What was attractive about you was that you carried your learning lightly. But I was wrong. There is something perverse in your nature. You are bent on disowning your exceptional intelligence.

'You would like to be a simple man like your idealized, or rather much doctored version of Brendan, Bert and Rick or some of the brothers of our Order. Why do you think Brendan's naïveté is a gift from God and not your statistical talent? Why not accept what one is, instead of always seeking to be the other?

'You will not forgive yourself. And you'll not allow God to forgive you. I would caution you, Lucens, do not presume to play at God. If you can be so intolerant of yourself, I fear how intolerant you may be of others. There is no line dividing your self-hatred from your self-righteousness. That can be a very dangerous combination.

'The Abbey is richer for your presence. But we need you whole or not at all. It is up to you to make the choice.'

The fact was, Reverend Father was clueless about the enormity of Lucens's barbarity in his previous incarnation. He was under the impression that Lucens might perhaps have killed a few enemy soldiers in battle, as he himself and other fellow-Americans had in Vietnam. Zia, on the contrary, had been a terrorist. No amount of sophistry, rhetoric or glossing over could obfuscate that simple fact. He had of course killed a few soldiers. But his business, he had thought of it as a duty and a vocation at that time, had been to kill and terrorize the greatest number of people as swiftly as possible.

His troubles, he believed, had begun that evening in Cambridge when Rushdie had turned up and there had been no bullets in his gun. But his life had gone haywire long before that. It was on the day that Aunt Antonia had told him about the strange illness that had almost killed him at birth, and her visit to the church on an inexplicable impulse to have him baptized. He had refused to think about it; in truth he would not even acknowledge that his aunt had had a chat with him. But his mind had been at war with itself ever since that fateful day. From his childhood, from the time he could recall his earliest memories, he had been a Muslim; now it appeared he was a Catholic from a time before memory. Unlike his brother, who seemed perennially mired in it, he had never been given to doubt. He had been decisive and single-minded. Then, overnight, he had lost his ingrained certitude and was in the grip of a dilemma that he could not resolve. Who was he? And who was his God? One thing he knew, come what may, he would not betray Allah. And yet there were moments when he wondered if it was not the Christian God he was betraying.

When he walked out of Suleiman Mansion, he made his way to Afghanistan. He had been far too self-indulgent. A year had passed and all he had done was to beat his breast and feel sorry for himself. He needed to make up to Allah for having bungled the attempt on the Prince of Darkness. The whole of the Muslim world was under siege. He would become a mujahideen, God's guerrilla in the holy war against the infidels.

The madrasa put him through an intense period of indoctrination and trained him for three months along with volunteers from other countries. As with most other professions, what Zia learnt, he learnt on the job. The most critical and lethal fault-line between the West and the Muslim world lay between Israel and Palestine. That's where the fate of Islam would be decided. That's where Zia would go and fight the holy war. But it was not to be. They sent him to Kashmir. He was a soldier and he had to obey orders. Whatever doubts he had about the assignment, they disappeared within the very first week. India claimed Kashmir was an integral part of the country. And yet it was one of the most brutally occupied territories in the world. The residents of Kashmir felt continually violated. Hundreds of thousands of Indian military and paramilitary forces were stationed in that one state and the army interfered and intruded in every aspect of life. Your house, your person could be searched at any time and you could be picked up for interrogation and interned for months, if not years, without legal recourse. You had rights but only on paper. No foreign army could have so successfully alienated the populace of Kashmir.

Zia and his comrades-in-arms would fly the Pakistani flag in Kashmir. They had banded together because, though they were from different parts of the world, they knew that they were fighting for the greater glory of Allah. It was not idle talk. Some of them had given up promising and highly lucrative careers, left their families, perhaps never to see them again. They lived in the Himalayas, sometimes at altitudes of up to 18,000 feet, exposed to thin air and temperatures of –30° and –40°C.

How would any outsider, however sympathetic, know what desperate lives they led? You lived in appalling conditions of filth and deprivation. You went for weeks without showering or brushing your teeth. Your hair was full of lice. You suffered from starvation, infected wounds, acute dysentery, diarrhoea, frostbite. Lung infections like bronchitis and pneumonia were routine. Everybody had a hacking cough. And there was rarely a doctor around. You owned one pair of clothes, the one that you were wearing. There was no question of a salary. If you were lucky on one of your raids, you stole whatever you could: jewellery, money, guns, grenades, water, clothes, sex. You were always on the run, waiting for someone to betray you or for the bullet that would get you.

If you were caught by the Indian army and did not have the time or the gumption to pop the cyanide pill you always carried with you, you were beaten, bruised and broken. You were hung upside down till your head went dead. You were electrocuted repeatedly, but never to death. You would never again have to use nail files or cutters. They pulled your nails out. They shoved hot iron rods up your arse, they said the heat made entry easier. They made you do the usual unspeakable things and then they made you do some unorthodox ones. But if you want an honest opinion, they were a jejune lot without imagination. What would they know of torture? Or terror?

Terror and torture are a competitive business. You always want to be one up and to raise the ante. Your colleagues in the next group of mujahideen butchered fifteen people last Monday, how could you settle for twelve? The least you could save face with was twenty and with any luck add a few children and women. Then you learnt that somebody in Sudan or some other place had managed to bump off 217 people at one go. Well, that meant that you would have to redefine your notions of carnage. There was no ceiling really. You had to aim high. Only then could you break your enemy's morale and bring him to the negotiating table. Look at Ireland or Sri Lanka, that was the only way the IRA or the Tamil Tigers could make any progress. The way Zia looked at it though, razing villages to the ground, pillaging and plundering, the killings and bombings were okay and necessary, but they would not teach a lesson that the victims and their kin would remember for the next seventy generations. What you needed was a sense of imagination and innovation. You had to have a scientist's curiosity in human endurance and you had to be inspired. He wanted to know the melting point of human beings. Was there a difference in the temperature at which men and women became flammable? What was the oil content in the human body? Did it make for better combustion?

Zia may have been fighting for a noble cause. But in a muddle-headed way it was also payback time for all the wrongs he had endured and for every grievance, real or imagined, he had nursed over the years. This was his chance to get even with his brother, mother and father; with Aunt Antonia; with the Prince of Darkness and the British government and the West for supporting him. But most of all, he was settling scores with that beggar whom he had thrown out of the plane. For over four years now he had lived with that man, or rather it was the other way round. He never took a break or a breather. The least he could have done was to stay out of Zia's way. That, however, was never an option. Never mind if Zia was busy planning or was in the thick of a life-and-death skirmish, you could count on the man to interfere. He was unstinting with unasked-for advice. The intention was to dissuade and disapprove. And to put a jinx on Zia. It seemed the only word he knew was 'don't'. What he failed to see was that his persistence only made Zia more perverse and contra-suggestible. Every 'don't' provoked Zia to be more ruthless and wanton in his madness. As Zia reasoned, it was not his fault, not his fault at all; the wretched beggar was responsible for his excesses.

To this day, Lucens can't quite explain why he quit. Maybe he could no longer take it. Perhaps he just wanted to have a hot bath and get rid of the lice and the dirt. Perhaps what got to him was the stoning by the Taliban of the woman who looked like Zubeida Khaala. Maybe he yearned for a breath of intellectual activity. Perhaps he missed Amanat's stupid letters. He had the feeling that a burkha-darkness was closing in upon him and suffocating him. Or perhaps the beggar had worn him down. Why was he lying? He needed forgiveness and his only chance, albeit a very remote one, was that the Son of God might yet find it in his heart to shrive him. 'Remember not the sins of my youth,' Lucens spoke to the Lord just as David had done, 'nor my transgressions: according to Thy mercy remember Thou me for Thy goodness' sake.'

## 28

Then the storm came.

Since noon, black fulminating clouds had been amassing at the edge of the Bitter Sisters. They lent the three Sisters the air and finality of the Fates. They sat in a huddle, their heads bent forward and their eyes hooded theatrically. What the three witches boiled and stirred and fermented was a poisonous and volatile brew that boded ill for the world. There was no knowing why they had become so sour and crusty. They were always egging on the wind and the heat, stacking up pile upon crazily tilting pile of dark clouds, prodding and encouraging the rain to hysterical outbursts. They were always bickering, those three Sisters; but there was something more malign about them today.

The clouds hovered above, gazing malevolently but refusing to move or release their venom. Then, about half an hour before Vigils, the dome of the sky cracked and released a hesitant shower that came limping through the air. It was a hyena of a rain. It slunk towards you on weak and wayward hind legs.

It wasn't quite clear what the role of the lightning was: was it sewing the torn sky together or was it tearing it further apart? Then the rain eased. The monks put on their mackintoshes and walked hastily to the church for Vespers. In the magnetic field of the Sisters, a vast disc of a whirlwind began revving its engines and building up a tremendous torque and thrust. It shot up in the air like a monstrous flying saucer and, shrieking, headed for the distant ocean. There was a fall in the decibel level as it sped away, and the monks could breathe easy again.

Now the wind changed direction. The disc began to close in upon itself and spun out of control. It arced through the air and took a U-turn. Suddenly the piercing high-pitched siren was back and growing by the moment. There was no doubt about it now, the metallic frisbee was headed straight for Terraferra. It had the slant of the concentric rings of Saturn and it was sweeping anything and everything in its path. It was as though the tectonic plates under the earth were exposed as they slid forward, rubbed and crushed each other, withdrew for a while and locked in again. The monks huddled together, their only guide to the mood and intensity of the maelstrom the dread soundtrack.

If only they could see what was happening outside: however great the havoc, they could at least have tried to come to grips with it instead of feeling this nebulous sense of doom. They prayed hard in the unearthly din. The Vigils became a kind of urgent SOS to the Almighty. They stopped praying and looked upwards. The hand of God came down and picked up three-quarters of the roof of the church. The sky was a cobweb of lightning as it pulsed in and out of the darkness. The carpentry workshop was the next to go, then the refectory roof and beams, the garage and the retreat houses. The dormitories were the last to be uprooted and ripped apart. For a second, you could see Brother Damien, who was always late for the offices, cowering with his head between his knees. Then a whole row of beds, along with Damien, was swept up. Two of the beds crashed down but Brother Damien flew like a Marc Chagall angel to the summit of Rearing Horse and beyond.

Five weeks after the storm, they were still clearing the debris from the Abbey. Plates from the kitchen were found lying intact and unbroken in the dorms while one of the large pans sat rakishly over the twisted weather vane above the library. The Abbey had a fine collection of theological and liturgical literature and every single book was laid out on the floor, the tables and the racks to dry. Close to seven hundred books, some of them handwritten originals from the thirteenth and fourteenth centuries, had been damaged irreparably and Brother Henry was working round the clock to microfilm their contents.

Every other day someone from Sweet Waters would come up to Terraferra with the white robes, black and white scapulars and monastic cowls that the wind had deposited in his or her garden. It was in the third week after the storm that a farmer from Cherryfield, which was twenty-seven miles from Sweet Waters, turned up with Brother Terence's split cloak.

Nobody, not even the Abbot or the Prior, had any idea just how much time and effort it was going to take to clean the place up.

Soon they had to abandon the task of clearing even in the library because it was impossible to breathe anywhere on Terraferra. No one had noticed that three of the silos that stored the Abbey's annual supply of grain had lost their covers. The stench of rotting wheat, corn and rice was far worse than wallowing in your own vomit. It took seventeen days for all forty-three monks and seven lay workers with scarves and handkerchiefs wrapped around their noses to load the mounds of fermenting rice and wheat on the trucks.

'How are we doing for money, Brother Lucens?' The Abbot asked him the same question every week, more like every other day. So did the Novice Master, Brother George, Father Lucas, Brother Jonathan-Christophe and any father or brother who ran into him. Yesterday, even the Prior had stopped Lucens on the way to Lauds, patted him on the back and said, 'These days, after "Our Father", I say a prayer to God asking him to make sure that you manage to feed all of us.'

At first, after the news of the storm had been covered by the press, and the TV people had flashed footage of the devastation at Terraferra across the country, there was a good deal of optimism at the Abbey. Money poured in from all over and from all kinds of institutions and individuals. Even the five- and ten-dollar collections at various churches had amounted to more than seventy thousand dollars. The mother and sister abbeys, the Holy See, charities, philanthropic organizations and the big foundations had sent in cheques for large amounts. The final sum had added up to almost six hundred thousand. But soon the insurance money was used up, and the flood of donations had become a trickle, and then it ceased altogether, while the magnitude of the damage began to seep in and the costs of even simple emergency measures kept spiralling higher and higher.

It all boiled down, Lucens thought, to trust. The monks were little children and they were sure that, come what may, God, the Father, the Son and the Holy Spirit would take care of everything. The storm, they knew, was a test, and as always, the Big Examiner in the sky himself would provide the answers and see them through. Yet Lucens had to admit that there was just the faintest whiff, he could very likely be imagining it, of uneasiness these days. Of course God would help, there was no question about that, but what if the help arrived a little too late? What if another storm happened to pick on Terraferra?

Perhaps the Novice Master, who was the unofficial finance director at the Abbey, had sensed the tension of unasked questions or felt the weight of the enormity of the problems ahead, and decided that it was a good time to fall ill with a rare anaemia and pass the reins, or was it the buck, to Lucens. It was a temporary arrangement just as everything else was temporary in the Abbey: the tin roof over the church, the second-, perhaps third-hand freezers in the kitchen, and the Nissen-like huts that were their lodgings. Lucens could understand the anxiety of the monks. Roughing it is fun for a few days, maybe a few weeks, but the transient had begun to have a permanent feel to it, including his finance job, and the temporary measures had swallowed up all the donations.

What was Lucens to tell his brother monks? That everything was all right, it really was?

At some point in time, earlier rather than later, Father Augustine knew he would have to take a decision about rebuilding the Abbey. Forget the money for the construction, there wasn't any to pay the architect's fee. A couple of architects from Sweet Waters had visited the site. They said that they might have done the job pro bono if it had been a question of a building or two. But considering the magnitude of the assignment, they were sorry but they had to beg off.

There was already talk of closing down the Abbey when Lucens decided to intervene.

'My father's an architect,' he told the Abbot. 'If you lay your cards on the table, he might surprise you and say yes.'

Something strange had been happening to Lucens these past few months since the storm. He had become a medium. He could be trimming his nails, having a shower, praying in the church, eating a peanut butter sandwich, which was often the only thing they had for dinner, when something occurred at the periphery of his vision, under his skin or in one of the frontal lobes of his brain. Were they visions, a parallel reality, an extra-sensory perception, a dream like the one Coleridge had when he composed the incomplete 'Kubla Khan'? He had begun to see numbers. Or rather feel them, the kind of digital inputs that can be converted into audio-visual signals; the 3-D virtual models you can rotate, enter, cut into sections, dismantle, configure, rework and rearrange.

Numbers automatically took him back to his childhood. Even then they had been a source of wonderment. He'd been possessive about his toys, the trains, the planes, the fire engines and racing cars, the elaborate puzzles and Trade. But the toys and the games did not intrigue him the way numbers did. He would lie on the Turkish kilim in his room at Firdaus and stare at the ceiling where the numbers had gathered that day. They'd be floating like gas balloons, silent and weightless. He was sure nobody else saw them. They were his secret, the one thing he did not share even with his mother.

He had an instinctive feeling that there was something a little weird about his secret life, perhaps something not quite right, and it was best kept to himself. When people spoke about his facility with numbers, he felt it was safer to shrug off their comments. How can one speak about things one does not understand? Looking back, he felt that numbers were the closest he had come to what people seemed to suggest when they spoke of a mystical experience. These were his moments of rapture, of wordless poetry. Perhaps it was akin to the visitations that Brendan, the handyman, had had twenty or thirty years ago. There was no denying that Brendan was a little touched in the head. The monks raised their eyebrows and smirked at each other when Brendan started on one of his interminable stories about how the saints spoke to him. But did that mean that the Lord and His Mother did not appear to him? Lucens was not about to opine on the subject. If the monks came to know about him and the numbers, they too would find him a little odd.

When he tried to, he could almost recapture the animal joy and the sense of sheer exhilaration that had gripped him as a child. You didn't see them moving and yet without your realizing it they drifted in and out of each other. How did they hang out there, gently grazing the ceiling? The number one was the leanest and trimmest of them all while eight had a big bottom and sat securely like one of those dolls that always righted itself even when its head almost touched the ground. The most stylish, the gay blade, was seven. He stood there leaning precariously to one side. He should have fallen on his back and made a fool of himself. Instead, he extended an arm dashingly in the other direction and looked just dandy. Four, well, four was a bit of a puzzle. There was something aristocratic about him. He had such fine facets and angles, they did not let you notice how unbalanced a figure he had. Now two was a real lady. She knew just how to set herself down on a firm base and gaze at the world from a long swan neck.

They didn't mind Zia because they were not aware of him. They lived in a different universe. All you had to do was watch them without fidgeting. You had to breathe softly; frankly, hardly breathe at all because the faintest draft of air would make them disappear. This was not as much of a problem as you might imagine it to be. Why would he want to breathe, or do anything else for that matter, when he was with them and watching their every move? Everything in his body came to a standstill. If you had felt his heart, it would have been dead. No pulse, nothing.

Numbers, Zia could have told you even then, are the most potent thing in the world, far more potent than atoms and atom bombs, which are so boring in their frenetic energy and ping-ponging and their catastrophic self-importance. Numbers are fixed, more fixed and immutable than the pole star. And yet there is nothing more chameleon-like, more constantly and fascinatingly changing, than numbers. Because. Because. Because numbers are about relationships. Alone they are like anybody else, smart, prissy or aloof. But get them to play musical chairs and no circus or Disneyland is a patch on them. Place a seven after one and you get seventeen. Now just turn them around, the one after seven, and what do you get? Zia had gagged with surprise and delight. He had somersaulted, done cartwheels and figures of eight with his legs in the air and whooped ecstatically. I'll lie down and die this instant, seventy-one.

Forget the seven, just stick to one. Is there anything more upright, whole and indivisible than the great and mighty one? Imagine there's only one of one. You can duplicate it, fake it, but one will always be one. It is truly an attribute of God. And that's just one. You haven't moved to either side of one yet. Now sit down on the floor, fold your legs in a padmasan. Is the back of your head in correct alignment with your neck, backbone and the cleavage of your buttocks? Is your centre of gravity stable so that nothing can rock you? Good. You are about to fall into the void, that truly mysterious thing called zero. This is the vanishing point where everything and nothing, night and day, the future, past and present, here and the horizon, all antitheses, all opposites, the antipodes and all contradictions merge and truly become zero. By itself it is nothing, a nobody and nonentity, but never underestimate it. It is the great annihilator, an abyss where everything disappears. Twenty-three times zero is zero. One million and seven times zero is zero. If you've seen the zero in action, understood even a fraction of its significance, then there's nothing more anyone can teach you. For, truly, there is nothing after and beyond zero.

But there's more, plenty more to numbers than zero. The decimal point and the numbers on the wrong side, and that devious and ambiguous conundrum, the algebraic '*x*'. You can understand now why the child Zia thought that there was nothing greater than numbers. That God himself is a number, an unfathomable one perhaps, but a number nevertheless.

He had followed numbers all these years. Now at Terraferra, they came to him unsolicited, in the form of stocks and securities. There were moments these days when Lucens sensed the market move inside him. He could feel the rise and fall and flux of its topology inside his cells. It was as immediate and real as an ice cube on the flesh or the sting of a bee. He felt the spurt of adrenaline in his veins just before the market rose and rose and rose till there was nothing, not even hot air to support it, and yet it kept rising, and he would bail out when everybody was still on a bullish high because he knew exactly when it would start to slip and take a free fall. He could tell a superstar long before anyone knew of its existence, and ride it all the way to the top, and he would step off a supernova before it shrank into a black hole. When the time was right, he would make his moves.

After Mass one Sunday, Father Augustine called Lucens to his makeshift office. Lucens had recently taken his vows and become a junior professed monk. You needed a two-thirds vote from the community of monks at the end of your two-year term as a novitiate to be allowed to start your juniorate. He had not done badly. There had not been any negative votes, not even from the Novice Master.

'The Chief Abbot is convening a meeting of abbots from all over the world to discuss the future of the Order at some place called Old Mill-on-the-Cam in England. The low rate of enrolment is a matter of serious concern, and many of the monasteries are finding it difficult to be self-sustaining. Since the prospects for our Abbey's survival are even more uncertain after the storm, he wants to be briefed on the measures we've taken. I'll need you just for a day when he and I are talking finances. The other two days, you're on your own. Didn't you say you had some friends in Cambridge? You could look them up and we could fly back together.'

'I don't mean to be difficult, Reverend Father, but I really can't spare the time. There's too much work to be done here, especially since Father Paul is so ill.'

'I think the Abbey can survive without you for five days, but if, with my genius for numbers, I start explaining fiscal matters, the Chief Abbot may well decide to dismantle Terraferra even before I return.'

'You don't leave me with much choice,' Lucens smiled as he turned to leave the room.

'No, don't go yet. There's something else I've been meaning to discuss with you. Your father's been here more than four months and we still haven't discussed money with him.'

'He knows there's no money in this job. At least not for now.'

'But we must at least discuss terms and draw up a contract. All we are giving him is a measly retainer. Anyone else, even a fraction as good as he is, would not have put pencil to paper, or rather switched the computer on, without charging us a packet.'

'I know him. He'll say, let all the buildings come up, then we'll talk money. But certainly talk to him.'

'Yes, I will. The Prior tells me that in all the time your father's been here, you have hardly spent any time with him.'

'He's busy. I don't like to disturb him.'

'Are you worried about insinuations of nepotism even after seeing the amazing work he is doing for us?'

'I would never have suggested my father if I hadn't known the quality of his work. Designing this entire complex, almost a mini-township, in the middle of nowhere, is my father's vengeance on his profession for the way they slandered and abused him and tried to put an end to his career.'

Roy had left Lucens alone after his disappearance from Cambridge, but Amanat wrote to Zia about him from time to time. The two of them corresponded regularly, and when Roy flew down to India every once in a while, he made it a point to visit Amanat and Abba in Bombay. The senior Cambrays were always in the news and Lucens would read about them either in the *Sunday New York Times*, which was the only newspaper the Abbey subscribed to, or on the Internet: James Cambray appointed to the board of directors at De Beers; the Cambrays in the society pages with their new Lamborghini; Cambray Senior exploring oil off the coasts of Sierra Leone and Malaysia. There were, as usual, rumours about James and Deirdre Cambray splitting up, and reports that Deirdre had been to a detoxification centre.

Roy, it appeared, had joined the family brokerage firm and had opened a branch in New York. Cambray and Cambray had not done spectacularly, but in its third year of operations, the SEC had swooped down on the company with much fanfare and had charged Roy with money-laundering and unfair trading practices. From the outset Roy had maintained that his firm had been wrongly accused, but hardly anyone, including Lucens, was buying his story. How could a person whose father was involved in 'this and that' be innocent? The case dragged on for almost two years. At the end of it, the court criticized the SEC severely for running a campaign of innuendo and malicious insinuations against the company in the media, and demanded that the district attorney's office tender a public apology to Roy. But the damage was done, and it looked as though Cambray and Cambray, New York would never recover.

Then, a week before Lucens left for England, he emailed Roy asking whether there was any chance of him being in England at the same time he was. Roy replied immediately. 'Since we never meet though we both live on the same continent, I would fly to England, even to Australia, just to see you after all these years. I'll pick you up from the Old Mill-on-the-Cam on Thursday the 17th at 4.30.'

Lucens had had no intention of getting in touch with Aunt Antonia. That chapter was closed. But as luck would have it, it was not. She was at the Old Mill-on-the-Cam to address the gathering on 'The Cistercian Legacy and the Evolution of the Trappist Order' at the midmorning session. Lucens had spotted her at the tea break, sitting in a corner taking notes. Now she was standing in front of him, and he would have to acknowledge her presence.

What a strong handsome face she had, one that was full of purpose and determination. It was a bit more lined, and there was more salt in her hair than pepper, but she had neither gained nor lost weight. She stood there awkwardly, like most people from his Zia days, unable to decide how to address him. In a sense he owed her everything: New Eden, Cambridge and the fact that he was a Catholic and a monk. He should have been grateful to her but something held him back. He had often asked himself why he bristled when he thought of her, and though the answer seemed to be hovering at the corner of his mind, he had never been able to figure it out. She looked confused when he extended his hand towards her. He could see the hurt in her eyes as they formally shook hands.

'How are you, Zia, I mean Father Lucens?'

'Brother Lucens. I'm well. And you, how are you?'

'I'm well too.'

'Would you like to have dinner with me this evening?'

'I'm sorry, I can't. Roy's picking me up tonight, and then we drive down to Cambray Park.'

'Roy?' She couldn't make sense of that name. 'Roy? Oh, I remember. Your friend from New Eden. Well then, I'll say goodbye to you.'

Aunt Antonia tried to hide her disappointment. They shook hands again, and she was about to leave, when Zia asked her about Vivian.

'Is she in town?'

'Yes, she is, but I don't think she would want to see you.'

Lucens smiled. 'I know, but I want to meet her. I'm free the day after. I could have lunch with you both and then catch the flight back.'

Poor Aunt Antonia, she had such a transparent face. She could not fathom what had gone wrong between them. What was left of their relationship and the years gone by were polythene words that you could chew on forever with no substance or sustenance coming from them. He knew that all she wanted was for him to embrace her; he also wanted to, but he couldn't. It struck him then why he did not care to think of Aunt Antonia. His conversion to Christianity had little to do with her, as she obviously seemed to believe. On the contrary, the knowledge that she had had him baptized at birth had riven his soul and egged him on to greater and greater violence. Only when his brutality had got completely out of hand, and he could no longer bear the burden of his guilt, had he surrendered to Jesus.

And yet even that was not altogether true. However strong the bonds, however loyal the members of any group, chinks would invariably appear. A traitor would rise and ravage all. In Zia's case, more than anybody else, he would betray himself. The beggar with the cross was the outward manifestation of his own gravest flaw. Whenever he set out on a mission, he was haunted by a sense of disquiet. In Allah's kingdom, the righteous can have no guilt. Whence this need for forgiveness then? he asked himself. What a vacuous question. It was Abbajaan's gift to him, a chronic palsy in his resolve: a hairline fracture of doubt in his steadfastness.

If there was a defining moment when his faith could have been said to abandon him, it had been on one of his visits to Afghanistan. It was Zia's last night. He sought Allah's blessings and begged Him to let Borodin keep his engagement, and slept soundly.

Borodin. Zia and his mujahideen friends called him the Waalee of Kabul. He had merely to think of you or put a line across your name in the register, they said, and you had got your despatch orders. You were ready to meet your Maker. He was a nobody as far as the records were concerned and yet even the Soviet administrator of Afghanistan played second fiddle to the KGB man. Borodin knew the colour of every Kabuli resident's stools each morning; if you burped, he could tell its exact decibel levels; if you made love, he could say how long your erection lasted and how hard your wife prayed that the lovemaking would be over quickly and painlessly. And if even the thought of conspiracy crossed your mind, he was over in your hideout before you had time to speak treason. There had been seventeen attempts on his life to date. He was still going strong.

Zia was head of operations in Kashmir. Now he had been recalled to Kabul. If anybody could eliminate Borodin, the mujahideen reasoned, it was Zia.

In the morning, Zia did namaaz and had a full breakfast of eggs and tandoori rotis just in case Borodin kept him waiting. He strapped the explosives around his waist and put on his long and loose Afghani kurta. He was on the terrace of the Noor-e-Islam Girls' School by 6.45. It was the only four-storeyed building in the vicinity and he had a clear view of the road. Five past seven, the girls began to saunter in. At first they sounded like twittering birds, but in another ten minutes when the bell rang they were making a racket worthy of the Bombay Stock Exchange before it was computerized. Zia felt his spirits lift. He had forgotten the sounds of school and the sheer exhilaration and energy of children. It was merely a matter of time before Noor-e-Islam, the last of the girls' schools that was still functioning in the Afghan capital, was silenced once and for all by the Taliban.

The second bell. He looked at his watch. 7.25. A woman in a burkha was crossing the road with her four-year-old. The child was carrying bright pink shoes in her hands. It was a clear day. In the distance, maybe four miles away, Zia saw the car. He skipped down the stairs and out of the school compound. The woman in the shroud-like burkha was trying to coax her daughter.

'Shoes are for your feet, not for your hands. Wear them or they won't allow you to enter the classroom.'

'They'll get dirty.'

'But your feet won't. Your friends are going to laugh at you.'

The third bell tolled. The girls inside the compound grouped themselves grade-wise and when the principal mounted the podium they started to sing the school anthem. Zia walked away quickly and waited at the bus stop. Borodin's car would pass by in exactly forty-five seconds. He was ready.

The Noor-e-Islam rose ten feet, then twenty and then fifty feet into the sky. One of the little girl's pink shoes flew up festively.

Borodin's car was doing a U-turn and then it was gone. Zia had gone deaf and was lying on the ground, a shard of glass lodged deep inside his neck. It was a mesmerizing sight: fourteen- and ten- and five-year-olds, satchels, severed limbs, heads with swaying plaits rising up and coming down. He could have watched the carnival in the sky forever when it struck him that he was a human bomb who had failed in his mission. Borodin had got away yet again. Damn the Taliban for choosing this very day to blow up the school.

When Zia finally managed to stand up, he noticed the mother of the girl with the pink shoes screaming soundlessly. Her burkha was a bloody mess. What the hell was she trying to say? What did it matter anyway? He had to make himself scarce really fast and that's all that he cared about. He was getting a little of his hearing back now. The woman had stopped screaming. She must have died. No, she was merely getting her breath back and now she was dragging herself all the way to where he was. She threw her veil back and clung to his leg. She looked like Zubeida Khaala.

'My baby, Gulbadan. Find her, find her for me.' Her voice was peremptory.

Zia should have run then, run till he had reached Kashmir. Instead he wandered around looking for Gulbadan in the pandemonium of mangled bodies and screaming torsos. If he was caught anywhere near here, they were bound to think he was responsible for the cataclysmic meltdown in the school.

There she was, standing with her left shoe in her hand. 'I want my right shoe,' she said as Zia scooped her up in his arms and handed her to her mother. The police van picked him up along with his new companions. They took them to the hospital for treatment and then to the police headquarters to record their statements. Zia realized this was the end. There would be a body search and they were not likely to buy his story that someone had planted the RDX explosives on him.

There were ninety-seven survivors in the cramped room and by the time the police were done with Gulbadan's mother and Zia, it was past eight at night. But they were stuck in the place because the police had declared a curfew in Kabul. When Zia dropped mother and child at their hut outside the city the next morning, Gulbadan complained to her father, 'He stole my shoe.'

Borodin was not likely to surface for a while and there was not much point in Zia hanging around in Afghanistan. When the wound in his neck healed, he decided to go back to Kashmir. He bought a ticket all the way to the border and waited for the bus. It could arrive in a couple of hours, late in the night or any time in the coming week.

There was a huge crowd gathered in the open grounds from across the bus station.

The voice of the mullah continued to crack on the speakers as he warned of the dire wages of sin. Must be a public flogging, Zia thought. He knew well that nobody could disobey the Koran or the Sharia with impunity. He crossed over to the grounds to witness Allah's wrath.

'Khadija Banu, wife of Imran Banu, has with conscious and deliberate intent committed adultery. Her partner in infidelity has escaped but the vengeance of Allah will pursue him in this and the afterlife. Khadija Banu must, however, be punished here and now.'

Adultery, Zia knew a thing or two about it. His mother had got away with it scot-free. This Khadija woman fortunately would not. He could see her now. She was sitting awkwardly on the ground, her face covered in a veil of shame.

'Her first sin was that she insisted that her daughter be educated.' The stone hit her on the jawbone. Zia looked at the man who had thrown it. He looked familiar. He had four more and was impatient to be rid of them. 'You will refrain from stoning your wife,' the mullah berated the man, 'until I have finished reading the charges and the punishment.'

'That morning she went to drop her child at school and did not return for twenty-four hours. And what was her excuse? There was a bombing at the school, very deservedly I would add, and she was at the police station all night. But her husband Imran knew better. Her lover had the gall to come to their home with his beloved not knowing that Imran would be waiting for them.'

There was no stopping Imran Banu or the crowd now. The sound of stone upon stone cracking Khadija's bones broke Zia's soul, and no God, not even Allah, could mend it.

He begged for forgiveness, not from the One and Only and not from the beggar, but from Khadija and Gulbadan, who stood beside her father and threw a few pebbles at her mother. He begged forgiveness he no longer knew why and for which of his deeds. And he begged forgiveness for all mankind and went back to his work in Kashmir.

Lucens's work at the conference was done by three in the afternoon. After probing him for an hour-and-a-half, the Chief Abbot had spoken to Reverend Father. 'I don't know what kind of a monk he'll make, Augustine, but he knows his figures even better than Paul. I tried to catch him out, but he was on to me.'

'Let me get this right, the Trappist monastery where you're a monk wants to invest money?' Roy asked as they drove down to Cambray Park.

'Is that against the law, Roy?'

'No, of course not. It's a little unusual, that's all.'

'We may be a spiritual institution, but the Abbey, like anybody else in the temporal world, survives on the green stuff. Would you be interested? Or should I go somewhere else?'

'No, of course I'm interested. It's just that your email was so unexpected, not to mention the reason for it. I didn't think I would ever hear from you again.'

'I expect the strictest confidentiality in our dealings.'

'Yes, that goes without saying.'

'But I am saying it because I want no slips-ups, no accidental revelations, no snafus.'

'I take your point. How are you, Zia?'

'Lucens, the name's Lucens now. Brother Lucens.'

'Yes, Amanat did mention that. But it'll take me some time to remember it.'

'That's fine. It's just that if you ever need to call me, ask for Brother Lucens and not Zia. I would, however, like to stress that I will call you and not the other way round. I'm not interested in hot tips. I and I alone will instruct you about what and when to buy and what and when to sell. You'll deal with me and nobody else in matters concerning the Abbey. You have a problem, you talk to me. When I call you and not when you want to. Is that clear?'

'Yes.'

'Good. Let's hope it will be a mutually satisfactory arrangement.'

*

Nothing had changed at Cambray Park except James Cambray's car (the Lamborghini had been replaced by a Maserati). There was no way of knowing whether Deirdre was on the wagon or off, just as there was no telling she had aged a day since Lucens had last seen her, so many years ago. The Cambrays had been Church of England from the time of Elizabeth the First, but if Deirdre and James were discomfited by Zia's Trappist incarnation, their way of dealing with it was to simply query him about the monastic life, and life after the storm.

There were just Roy and Lucens at the breakfast table the next morning. Deirdre liked to have breakfast in bed and Cambray Senior was already at work in his study-cum-office. He had left an envelope addressed to Brother Lucens propped up against a Wedgwood cup and saucer on the sideboard. Lucens was not quite sure if it was good manners to tear open an envelope and read the letter when you were at the dining table at someone else's house, but his curiosity got the better of him.

Dear Brother Lucens,

Here's a small contribution from us towards rebuilding your Abbey. We wish you and all the monks at Terraferra a speedy return to normalcy.

Maybe you could say a prayer for us once in a while.

All the best etc.

Deirdre and James

Lucens looked at the cheque, blinked and read the figure again. It was made out to the Abbey and was for 100,000 US dollars.

'Isn't that a little extravagant?' Lucens asked Roy.

'That's between you and my father.' Roy shrugged his shoulders but his mouth had curled up at the corners in a sour grimace. 'I assure you I had nothing to do with it.'

Lucens was relieved that Roy had had no say in the matter. Whatever Roy's hang-ups about his parents, the money was welcome, more than welcome. Lucens would have been willing to put pressure on Reverend Father Augustine to change the name Terraferra to Cambrayland if James only proved willing to make further contributions of comparable size.

One of James's vintage cars, a 1937 Rolls-Royce, drove in as the two friends were about to leave, Lucens for Cambridge and

Roy for New York. Its windowpanes were tinted and one couldn't see inside.

'We better step on it or we'll be late,' Roy told the driver.

Lucens looked at his watch. What was Roy talking about? They would be at Heathrow at least three and a half hours before his flight took off. Their car was just starting to inch forward when there was a knock on the door and a gigantic shadow fell across Lucens and Roy. Roy must have pressed the button for the window, for it was sliding down on Lucens's side.

'This is a rare honour.' There was no mistaking the hermaphrodite voice. 'I had no idea I would be running into the saviour of the Abbey of Our Lord in Contemplation. Won't you stop for a minute?'

Shakta Muni pulled the car door open.

'Well, well, well. This is indeed a pleasant surprise.' The holy man pumped Lucens's hand vigorously as though it were the long lever of a bore-well pump in a drought-stricken village in India, though Lucens himself had the feeling he was squeezing a two-week-old puppy. 'I'm not sure how to address you though.' He laughed his high-pitched, hysterical laugh as if he had said something uproarious.

'Brother Lucens will do.'

'Who gives him all the dope on me?' Lucens asked as they drove off.

'You'll have to ask him.' Roy answered.

'Isn't Vivian planning to come down?'

'I think she's trying to prove a point, though I'm not quite sure what it is.' Aunt Antonia smiled deprecatingly.

'I'll go up to her room then.'

'I don't mean to interfere, Brother Lucens, but Vivian can be difficult.'

Lucens was struck by how deferential even Aunt Antonia had become towards him because of his monk's habit.

'There was a time,' he said half-humorously, 'when you would have said that about me too. With Jesus by my side, I can manage Vivian.'

Lucens knocked on Vivian's door for a long time, but there was no response. He finally pushed the door open. 'May I come in?'

Vivian was spraying rapid-fire darts at the board as she criss-crossed the floor with manic concentration. The few that had made it to the red centre sat cowering next to each other. Vivian was at the door now and slammed it shut with her foot as she flung another.

Lucens smiled indulgently. If Viv thought he was going to give up on her that easily, she was mistaken. He had wronged her unconscionably, but the irony was that he, and not she, had found Jesus. He could not put off bringing salvation to her any longer.

'You are right to be mad with me, Viv. No punishment is severe enough for the way I disappeared. But after all the months of waiting, I had Rushdie in the cross hairs and I fired again and again and there were no bullets in the chamber. And I asked myself who else knew about the plan to kill him but you. I was convinced you had betrayed me, and Scotland Yard would be on my trail, so I skipped the country.'

Vivian yanked out the darts from the board and went back to throwing them with vicious accuracy.

'I should have known better. You were steadfast in your loyalty. It was Amanat who emptied the bullets from the gun. So it wasn't you who betrayed me, but I who unwittingly betrayed you. After I left you, I did things that were much more terrible than what I did to you.'

It was difficult for Lucens to focus on what he was saying for Vivian had now graduated to lobbing the darts even as she wound round herself like a whirlwind.

'Hear me out, Viv. I've committed crimes no power on earth can forgive. Yet, all through my travails, Jesus did not forsake me. He stood by me even though I spat at Him and behaved abominably with Him. I've come to you today to beg your forgiveness. But I've also come for a greater purpose. I've come to bring you the grace of God. It was I who led you to Islam. I will lead you now to salvation. Come to Jesus, Viv. Come, let me lead you to peace and happiness. Come and embrace the Lord.' Lucens's voice had taken on a hypnotic rhythm. 'Come into the shade of His infinite mercy. Come, bless His creation. Come, Viv, come receive His benediction.'

Most of the darts were arrayed across the board, a couple had fallen, and the cyclone had ceased. Vivian's eyes had turned smoky. Her lips were moving lasciviously and she was panting. Lucens tried hard to lip-read what she was saying as Vivian got rid of her T-shirt. Her pelvis had begun to gyrate. He could make out the word she was chanting now. Come, come. Come. Lucens laughed. 'Are you trying to seduce me? Put your clothes back on, Viv.' The Levis were off and now she had peeled off her panties. The fingers of her left hand were drawing circles around her nipples while her right hand had sunk down and she was stroking herself.

'Stop it,' Lucens snapped at her. 'You're pathetic. It's not going to work.'

It was true. Vivian's simulation of sex only seemed to turn Lucens off. She could try her whole bag of tricks, he knew he would be immune to them. He picked up her T-shirt, her panties and the pair of jeans and offered them to her.

'If you don't stop, I'm going to leave.'

'Come for lunch. I've laid the table,' said Aunt Antonia as she walked into the room.

'Help,' Vivian screamed hysterically, pushing Lucens away.

Aunt Antonia looked from Vivian to Lucens. Her daughter was naked while the monk was in his robes, but it was Lucens who had the air of someone caught in flagrante delicto.

'Hush, Vivian.' Aunt Antonia tried to soothe her daughter. 'You're all right, you're all right…'

'All right? What a hypocrite you are, Mother. Your Little Miracle has ruined my whole life and you say I'm all right?' Vivian bent down and with a graceful flick of her wrist, sent a dart slicing through the air.

'Calm down, Vivian, calm down,' her mother said as she moved towards her, even as the dart pierced her left eye.

Lucens got down to business the day after he returned to the Abbey. He had done all kinds of arithmetic with the Abbey finances after the Novice Master had fallen ill, and every time the answer had been the same. They could carry on for seven or eight months, maybe, by a stroke of extraordinary luck and some windfall at the last minute, a year. After that, the Abbey would have to be closed down and the different members dispersed to other Trappist monasteries. That was not an option as far as Lucens was concerned. He took the plunge. He invested James Cambray's serendipitous gift in the market. Roy's company was the conduit, but it was Lucens who took all the decisions. When most people thought of the countries in Latin America and South Asia as an economic quagmire, he bought technology and pharmaceutical stocks for small change and forgot about them for months, sometimes a year or more, until they turned into windfalls and sometimes into gales. He could see the dance of futures and commodities. He could sense the market a few minutes from now, the market tomorrow, a week away and a few months down the road. It was a stereoscopic, holistic picture that covered the FTSE, the Nikkei, the Dow and the Nasdaq, the DAX and the other European markets, while giving him a hint about what was going to occur in the Asian, African and Latin American stock exchanges.

However, it wasn't as though he made all the money in one go. Hardly. He was cautious most of the time. But every once in a while he went for broke. Went for broke, that awful phrase. Few people in the world would know its terrifying dimensions and implications. On two occasions the market nearly made him insolvent. He had never before known such fear as he felt then. The buildings were all at different stages of construction when he misread what his mind, cells, senses and blood flow were telling him. Perhaps he had grown overconfident, but he had never thought of his financial pursuits as gambling. He was doing God's work. Like Keynes, he had an intuitive feel for the market. So far, he had been scoring seven times out of ten, very occasionally eight. The trick was in providing cushioning for the times when he missed. But what if, in twenty runs, the six misses came together? Frankly four would be enough to finish him, or rather the Abbey. He had nearly gone to the Abbot and told him to file for bankruptcy on one occasion, but the market had suddenly recovered, and the second time he had been rescued by a pipsqueak software company in India in which he had invested more than a year before. It had pole-vaulted on the New York Stock Exchange in four days, making vast gains that bought him a reprieve.

'What's so important that you had to see me in person and couldn't talk about on the phone?' Lucens asked Roy when he came to meet him at the Abbey. You could hardly hear yourself because of the noise of the giant cranes swinging concrete blocks high up in the air and the builders and contractors yelling at each other.

'Can we go some place a little more quiet and private? I had the impression that monasteries were the most peaceful and silent places on earth.'

'Come for a retreat once the work is finished. You'll hear the horses snorting in the stables at Cambray Park and Amanat wheezing in Suleiman Mansion.'

Lucens started walking uphill.

'It's a bit of a climb to the roof of North America. Can you make it?'

Within minutes Roy was ahead of him. How could Lucens have forgotten that Roy walked seventy times seven thousand miles every day, then took a turn around Mount Everest to wind down? It took them an hour to loop around to the other end of Terraferra and come face to face with Rearing Horse and the Three Sisters.

'God Almighty, this is some place. Sorry, I didn't mean to swear, but if Jehovah lives anywhere on earth, it's bound to be here.'

'Do you like it?'

'I'm not sure "like" is a word that would come to mind. It's just so awe-inspiring, it silences you.'

'That's too bad. I thought you wanted to talk.'

'I do. I don't know where to start. I don't mean to sound ungrateful, Zia. Your business has turned Cambray and Cambray, New York around. And I'm grateful for that. After the SEC accusations, people treated me and my company like the leper of Wall Street. I was ready to close shop. Now, slowly, some of my old clients are coming back. Recently some big private investors and philanthropic institutions have been checking us out.'

'So what's the problem?'

'My father, as you must know, has enemies. The only thing Cambray and Cambray, New York owes Cambray and Cambray, London is the name, nothing else. I run a totally independent shop. But I'm an easy target and one of the ways of getting at my father, they think, is to get me. Neither the SEC nor the public prosecutor's office could prove anything against me or the company but the dirt has stuck and I need to tread carefully. Very, very carefully.'

'Then our objectives are the same and you have nothing to fear.'

'Hear me out, Zia. Please don't misunderstand me. I just want to caution you. You are averaging a hit rate of seven, once in a while eight out of ten. Even when you take a bad fall, you rebound quickly. Only George Soros could be that consistent or on the mark so often.

'I frequently take my cues from you and advise my clients but I make sure their batting average is 6. 6 out of ten. What's up, Zia?

You've either got the good Lord as your stock advisor or...no, I don't even want to mention it. I have no problems with either. But if it's the latter, then I must advise you to hire some other trading house before the SEC hauls me to court again. And take my word for it, they'll get you too because they are watching my every move even though the judge asked them to lay off.'

'All I can tell you is that it's not the latter. Besides, I'm not special. Hundreds of people play the market and become millionaires. And I'm not doing it for myself.'

'How come you get it right so often?'

'As you know, there was a storm here a couple of years ago and it razed the Abbey to the ground. We have to raise it anew. Let's just say the Lord is my lucky talisman.'

'I don't know what that means, Zia. All I know is I am your friend and I trust you.'

## 29

The construction work on the different sites was coming along at a good clip. If you were a resident at the Abbey you didn't notice much progress in the buildings rising up all over the place, but anyone visiting after a week or a fortnight was struck by the speed at which the various structures were burgeoning both at Terraferra and Halfway.

Yes, Lucens was doing all right. Yet he had never been so unhappy. There was a manhole in his soul, and he had fallen into it. It was a shaft as narrow as a coffin and the more frantically he clawed to get to the light, the longer it became. Lucens prayed and cried, he begged Jesus to give some sign that he was not alone, that he had not lost his way and his vocation. 'How long wilt Thou forget me, O Lord? For ever?' the words of the psalm were on his lips. 'How long wilt Thou hide Thy face from me? Consider and hear me, O Lord my God: Lighten my eyes, lest I sleep the sleep of death.' The Abbot had warned him about making the mistake of the vertical pronoun, about always wanting to put himself at the centre of things, making himself responsible for all the ills that befell him and the Abbey, so he did not flagellate himself as in the past, but he did other penances. He ate one slice of bread for breakfast, one for lunch and another at dinner, and nothing else. He resolved not to sleep, and to keep himself from dozing off, would lie in bed in his vest, throw off the blankets and shiver all night long. He lost weight, he looked gaunt and haggard, he had fainting spells. But to no effect. Jesus had turned His back on him. Lucens had chosen to go into the desert to find God. Now, blasphemy of blasphemies, he had begun to suspect that God was the desert. Is this, he wondered, what the saints and the hermits, not to mention Christ himself, have called the dark night of the soul?

Jesus had not phased Himself out gradually, nor had He served any notice to Lucens. One day He had been by his side, and the next, He had disappeared. This was intolerable. Why had he come to the Abbey all the way from India? Why was he training to become a monk? Not only that, why would he have become a Catholic, but for Jesus? It was as if the good Lord had hunted him down. He had driven him to the edge when he was in India. In truth, Lucens had gone well over the edge, as his brother and family would attest. And now, Jesus had dropped him. It had not occurred to Lucens that God too was whimsical and idiosyncratic, that He too played games. One minute you were in His good books, and the next you were out. Lucens had waited patiently without losing faith or hope. The Abbot had spoken often about sudden dry spells, long droughts when the ocean of Jesus's love vanished. But it had, he said, only disappeared from sight and would reappear one day fuller and more bountiful than ever. Lucens would have preferred it if Jesus had not stooped to these tricks, but he was more than prepared to indulge Him and serve time. He told himself that God has His reasons and that He moves in mysterious ways.

But the days turned to weeks and the weeks to months. Lucens worked harder, prayed far more than he had ever done. He was kinder, gentler, more forgiving with his brother monks, more humble and self-effacing, and all the while he was certain he would go off the deep end any minute, like one of those crazy people who go berserk and kill everybody at the mall and make headline news.

Things came full circle. In his grief and great anguish, Lucens then asked a question of Jesus that the Son of God Himself had asked of His Father. 'Father, my Father, why hast Thou forsaken me?'

A vow of poverty was no longer a part of the Trappist canon, but they took austerity as seriously as prayer or contemplation of the Lord. They followed literally the injunction of earning one's bread by the sweat of one's brow. The idea was to discipline the mind and body and to make each monastery self-sufficient. The monks worked hard and pushed their bodies to the limit, but even at the best of times the Abbey found it difficult to make ends meet.

The monks at Terraferra had two sources of income. They grew wheat on the terraced fields below Halfway. The land was rocky and unyielding and in the bad years there was barely enough to feed the monks. The other industry, cottage industry would be more precise, was the factory that produced religious artefacts and souvenirs. It had taken some gall and imagination to call the lean-to carpentry shed a factory, but to its credit, its products were established and did pretty well.

When the monks came to look back, some saw Lucens as a visionary. A few were less complimentary and said that nature had abhorred the vacuum created by Father Paul's illness, and Brother Lucens had happened to jump in and fill it. Others were of the opinion that he was the Abbot's blue-eyed boy and was leading the Abbey to perdition with his newfangled ideas, not to mention the fact that the place was turning into a Khan fiefdom. Notice how the young man's father, a Muslim, no less, had been recruited to build the whole Abbey complex. There was no question about it, the Abbot was priming young Brother Lucens to be his successor. Lucens's own view was almost banal and perhaps closer to the truth. When he had taken charge of the Abbey finances, he had had no intention of straying into any other area. But for him, any problem was like the mountain that beckoned; he had little choice but to climb it.

Farming, Lucens was more than willing to admit, was a noble way of life. But unless there were a major earthquake or some such cataclysm, there would be no chance of the Abbey's farmlands becoming fecund in the next few millennia. He turned his attention to the carpentry shop. The Abbey brand had goodwill in the market. It was a religious institution and turned out holy artefacts: crosses, icons, statues and images of the saints, and nativity scenes. Their sales might not have been outstanding but what mattered was that they had a loyal customer base.

Lucens would have been a fool to discontinue these product lines. What he chose to do instead was something simple and yet a dramatic departure for the Abbey. There was no dearth of talent amongst the monks. Lucens decided to move into furniture. Wooden closets, desks, chairs, beds and tables, all of them of the do-it-yourself variety. The keynote and unique selling points would be, 'It's so simple, your 7-year-old daughter can build it,' and 'It's so sturdy your great-grand-daughter will pass it on to her children.'

There were the expected reservations and resistance when the idea was first broached at the Abbey. It wasn't going to work. They were monks. What would they know about commercial manufacture or marketing. It sounded like a cutthroat business proposition. Lucens was good at fielding people's objections. He said he could see their point of view. He was not stuck on the idea, not at all. If anybody had a better proposition, he would support it wholeheartedly. And what if the factory started making profits? Heaven forbid, the Abbot said in exasperation, but isn't that the point of the exercise? Not small profits, they persisted. What if we become a multinational corporation or something like that? A little far-fetched, but Reverend Father had to admit that it was best to clarify all issues at the start. Big, really big profits would go against the spirit of the Trappist way of life. 'If there's any money left over, and it's a big if,' Lucens interrupted the monks' Microsoft-sized dreams, 'how about the Abbey funding a soup kitchen in Sweet Waters?'

This suggestion went down very well indeed. The proposal to manufacture furniture was through and there was no more discussion about what to do with the putative profits.

The new factory building at Halfway was a caterpillar in white taking a slow corner. The idea was that if the business did well, all you had to do was extend the caterpillar on either side. Light, heat and cold were always a problem at Halfway, though not half as much as at the top of Terraferra. There was always too much or too little. But now you could control them, mostly through an ingenious use of sliding shutters on the flanks of the structure and under the skylights. Barring the bays for loading and unloading materials and finished products, the entire surface of the building was a network of solar batteries. There was one other and far more powerful source of energy that Abbajaan had tapped. Behind the furniture factory were seventeen windmills. For once, the violent winds at Terraferra would be put to some constructive use. The Abbey would generate its own electricity.

'If you think of stone, paint, words or whatever material you work with as dead, then what you create will not possess life. It will neither breathe nor will it bite.'

Zia wondered to whom his father was talking. He was climbing the banisterless stairs to the terrace of the unfinished infirmary to check an estimate with Abbajaan. The steady paring away of the chisel at the marble brought back memories of Firdaus to Lucens. The new makeshift studio had the best view of the mountains, and that's where Abbajaan liked to work, under a fibreglass awning, on the friezes for the church. It was decades since they had left their old home and yet even today he felt the acute pain of that loss.

'If you know exactly what you want,' Lucens could see now that Abba was talking to Jonathan-Christophe, 'if you plan to the last detail and stay the course come what may, without making any changes, you may beget the perfect child but the chances are it will be stillborn. At no point will it surprise anyone, including you.'

The Trappist Order at Terraferra, it was becoming increasingly clear, had adopted Abbajaan as its surrogate father. They continued to go for confession, but they opened their hearts to Zafar Khan. They spoke to him of their problems with brother monks, told Abba about their families, and soon they were telling him about their lives and love affairs.

Abba had been at the Abbey less than a quarter of the time Lucens had spent there. Yes, the monks respected Lucens. He was, after all, the one who was responsible for feeding them and furnishing the money for the buildings that would house them. But Abbajaan they both respected and loved. It came to Lucens that he would never be part of any inner circle. He would always be on the periphery. The only conversations Lucens had with his father were about the order in which the buildings were to come up, or other aspects of the work going on at the Abbey.

'When you presented your plans they were for everything together, weren't they?' Lucens asked his father. 'The church, the dorms, the refectory, infirmary, garages, furniture factory?'

'Yes, that's the way one always presents architectural designs. You know that.'

'Then why would you want to build piecemeal?'

'No reason except that I thought it might be easier on the Abbey's pocket.'

'Let me worry about the money. Do it one building at a time, and the construction work could go on for ten years. The dust, the noise and the chaos will also go on that long, and besides, something else may crop up in between and sidetrack us. The money will be diverted and things will remain half-finished for who knows how long. The other issue is, how many years are you going to keep coming back to see that everything's going according to plan and to sort out last-minute problems?'

Abbajaan's left cheek hollowed out into a dimple as deep as an inkpot as he chuckled. 'It would give me a chance to see you once in a while. Maybe I could bring Zubeida Khaala and Amanat with me one of these days.'

'Bring them if you want,' Lucens sounded almost curt, 'but I can't afford to be sentimental at the Abbey's expense.'

'I was being half-facetious, son.'

Lucens smarted at the word 'son' while ignoring Abbajaan's friendly overtures. 'I suggest you go down to Sweet Waters with the Prior or to Portland or Seattle if you prefer, and talk to two or three construction firms. You can hire all of them or just one. You make sure that you get the best work out of them. It's my problem to beat them down to the most economical quotation possible. Is that okay with you?'

'Yes, that seems to make sense.'

'I'm a little confused.' Reverend Father had his arm over Lucens's shoulder as the two of them walked towards the library. Lucens could never get used to seeing Reverend Father in torn, badly patched jeans which he had clearly repaired himself. He always put in the requisite number of hours at the farm, the garage or for whatever manual labour was required, but the new factory had converted him into a macho blue-collar worker. He had become highly competitive and would have a triumphant smirk on his face if he made more cupboards or shelves than whoever else was on the shift that day.

'There was something odd that the auditor said in passing. He said that now that the furniture business seemed to be taking off, we should be able to pay back the bank loan within a couple of years. I thought he had made some mistake and spent some time last night looking over his report.' He smiled. 'Unlike you, numbers are not my favourite pastime. Your father said they invert the phrase in India and call it "timepass", but because I don't like them, I make an extra effort to understand them. The auditor was right. All we owe the bank is seven hundred thousand. Are there two or three zeros missing there, Lucens? After all, most of the buildings are fully ready. It's three months since we moved to our individual rooms and only a fortnight before our new church, the good Lord be praised, will be consecrated.

'Is there some other bank in the picture? Surely we've spent several hundred times more than just seven hundred thousand?'

'Of course we did, Reverend Father. But I assure you there's nothing to worry about.'

'I'm the Abbot of this Abbey, my son. I must know the extent of the Abbey's financial commitments, so that we can gradually pay up our debts and become self-sufficient and independent.'

'Seven hundred thousand, that's what we owe. Nothing more.'

'Humour me, Lucens, and get serious.'

'I'm in earnest, Reverend Father.'

There was a long silence. It was as though the Abbot had got stuck in a quagmire and had no desire to make it back.

'Did you,' he finally asked, in a voice that was softer than death, 'did you make a pact with the devil?'

'No, Reverend Father.'

Lucens wished that like last year, this audit report too could have passed off without Reverend Father looking at it too closely. In the past, Lucens would have been accountable to the Novice Master, who was the Abbey's accountant and finance director, but Father Paul was slowly wasting away and hardly ever dealt with business now. It was not that Lucens felt he was doing anything clandestine, he just didn't want to speak about it. He had hoped that once the buildings were completed and the furniture business was doing well, and the Abbey had built up an emergency fund, he could wash his hands of the market for good, without anybody being the wiser. Till yesterday, no, till a few minutes ago, it had looked as though his wish had been granted. 'So where did the money come from?'

'I don't know how to put this, because whichever way I put it, it isn't going to make sense.'

'Nevertheless, tell me.'

'I felt the market move under my skin, at the very core of my being. I tested it first for fourteen days and then I played.'

'The market?' the Abbot sounded bemused.

'The stock market.'

'And where did you get the money?'

'I borrowed a hundred thousand from the Abbey. Actually it was the hundred thousand that Deirdre and James Cambray gifted us.'

'You obviously must have checked it out with the Novice Master.'

'I couldn't explain what was happening within me. I took the decision on my own. But after that first time, I did not ever touch the Abbey's funds.'

'But you kept playing?'

'Yes.' Lucens sighed. 'By the grace of our bountiful Lord, we are home safely. The construction work is almost completely done. And we have a fair amount in reserve for a rainy day.'

'Were you aware that you were taking a grave risk, a very grave risk, with money that was not yours?'

'My family and I were thrown out of our house once. You know all about that. I was not going to stand still while I lost my second home. I don't know if it was really any graver a risk than the financial bind we were already in.'

The Abbot sat down on one of the piles of rocks outside the church but didn't say a word for a long while.

'I have been blind, deliberately and grievously blind. I must have known at the back of my mind how close we were to being dissolved as a community, and I chose to leave it to you. My feeble defence, I suppose, was you knew more economics than I did, so I should leave it to the professional. If we were in trouble, you would obviously let me know immediately.'

'I would have, Reverend Father.'

'Yes, I believe you would have. I would ask you, how are we doing for money and you would say with your usual British understatement, I think we can get by till tomorrow. And we did seem to. My reasoning was glib. You obviously knew what you were doing and you must have managed by mortgaging the land or the buildings themselves.

'We are all beholden to Jesus for seeing you through what must have been a nightmare at times. But that doesn't in any way let me off the hook. Help me up, Lucens.'

Lucens gave the Abbot a hand. 'Now that the Abbey is on a firm footing, Reverend Father, I assure you I no longer play the market.'

'Oh Lucens, that's the least I would expect of you.'

'How shall I atone for upsetting you, Father?'

'This is not a debit-and-credit account that can be squared. What I'm talking about is an ethical centre that seems to be lacking in you.' The Abbot looked suddenly worn out. There was a terrible sadness in his eyes that Lucens could not understand.

'You've rescued all of us and I'm going to sound ungrateful. Whichever way you look at it, you gambled with the Abbey money. Yes, the gamble paid off. And yes, if you hadn't taken the risk, the Abbey of Our Lord in Contemplation would no longer be around. But you took matters in your own hands. You did not think that you needed to consult your Abbot. I believe you knew that I would not have allowed you to take chances with the meagre money the Abbey had. But you went ahead regardless and did as you wished. I guess you don't even realize that you've abused my trust. I suspect, coming right down to it, you don't know right from wrong. How I've failed you, Lucens. And how I have failed our Lord.'

The new church was consecrated on Easter Sunday, a bit of obvious but not entirely unjustified symbolism. Like Jesus, the Abbey too had been resurrected. The Abbot had wanted a simple, low-key ceremony, with maybe the Bishop of the Diocese presiding, but the Papal nuncio and a cardinal had invited themselves to the ceremony. The church was packed and over a thousand people heard the three-hour ceremony from outside and then filed in for the Eucharist.

Abbajaan had gone over the building, the toilets, the vestry and every other part, inch by inch. He had designed the cross, the altar, the pews, the flooring, the chalice, every single thing, and had himself sculpted the figure of Christ on the cross and two of the reliefs on the walls. Then, the day before the inauguration, he had quietly slipped away and caught the plane to India.

Zafar Khan's church was a paradox and an anomaly. It was built like a fortress to withstand the torments of the elements, and yet it was impossible to think of the building as anchored to the ground. It looked as though it was about to lift off towards the heavens. People seemed to think of the walls as angel wings or as a prayer rising up to God.

## 30

It was a pity Hindus didn't bury their dead, Amanat thought. That way Dr Patwardhan would have been laughing up his sleeve. Sagari had joined the films.

After they were married, Sagari still held on to her post as temporary lecturer, but only just. Amanat landed the odd job now and then, and they got by, albeit barely, on their joint incomes. In the meantime, they continued to live at Suleiman Mansion. Every month Amanat would offer to share the rent with his father, and every month Abbajaan would say, 'Let me think about it.'

'One of these days he's going to say, "All right let's go half and half." What are we going to do then?' Amanat asked Sagari.

'Stop asking him. It's an empty gesture meant to salve your conscience and I'm sure he sees through it.'

'He's not doing too badly, is he? Not big money as in the old days but he has a steady stream of work.'

'Oh, grow up, Amanat, Abbajaan is not going to be your keeper all your life.'

Like a lot of quiet but self-possessed people, Sagari had a mind of her own and she could be ruthlessly honest. She had been critical of a novel Amanat had started after the Kabir book, about a poor family in a remote village in Kutch where it hadn't rained for seven years. She thought it was sparse and austere and relentlessly grim, but there was something missing in it. He was seventy pages into it and reluctant to part with the character of the woman who kills all her daughters, barring the last one, at birth, and lives to regret that she hadn't strangled that one too.

He had moped around a bit and borne a slight grudge against Sagari, something like a low-grade fever that had its rhythms and came and went at will, for creating a vacuum in his life. You could always tell when Amanat was not doing well with a book. He would pretend to be insouciant and not snap at you when he could have swallowed you whole. He would be crabby with himself and not look anyone in the eye. That would be followed by a phase of remorse and apology for his childishness. Still, there was no getting away from the fact that he was a one-book man, a flash-in-the-pan, a has-been who never was. He might as well resign himself to it, this was the end of the line. The best thing for him would be to retire to the Andaman Islands or go into the Andes never to reappear.

The fact was, he needed another room, maybe another apartment; maybe a whole different country or, better still, a new continent. Even then, he would have to make sure that the place had a solid door that no one could break through, for you never knew whether that woman, yes, that very woman whom he had married after having got his hair cut, was watching him secretly. At this point he would crack up, break into manic laughter and hug Sagari, and tell her what a feckless bastard he was, and confess the rotten thoughts he had been having about her.

'Right, I know that you are just waiting to get rid of me.'

'Oh God, it's not true, it's not true.' Amanat would be grief stricken and protest his innocence.

'If I were having evil thoughts about you, and I have no other kind,' she smiled wickedly at this point, 'the least I would do is not tell you about them.' She was thoughtful for a moment. 'You would like a quiet place to work in, wouldn't you?'

'What drivel. I'm fine. You know I don't believe in that artist crap, that they are special, that they are visionaries. More sensitive, more temperamental. More self-centred and spoilt is what they are. They are no different from doctors, engineers or plasma physicists. Besides, every last person in the slums would like quiet and an extra room.'

It was a year and a half or two before he was through with his next book. It was not a big book, a mere two hundred and thirty-seven pages, and Sagari finished it at one go. She found it funny, not smirk-funny but outrageously funny. It was black and uncomfortably close to the bone, and moving, and, strangely for Amanat, full of hope and sunshine. An earthquake has riven the landmass of Bombay and its people, and now the breach between the two halves of the city is so deep, it can never heal. Three young men, however, simultaneously discover a hitherto invisible river in the chasm. Each wants the river for himself, and intrigues and conspires to have the other two eliminated, till they realize one day that no single person can manage the river alone. They join hands and start ferrying people from one side to the other. Split communities and divided families find each other and come together again with strange consequences. The fairy tale will turn nasty and tragedy will strike anew. But the three young men don't give up. Their one failing is their biggest strength: they can't have enough sex, and they initiate young girls as well as the mothers of those young ladies into insatiable libido and riotous whoopee, so that they need new partners from the other side of the chasm, and later from other parts of the subcontinent. There is a remote chance that the city may yet become one.

The novel jumps into action without bothering with preliminaries:

> The island of Bombay, as you know, is thinner than a trickle of pee from a man with an enlarged prostate. In truth, it's almost a straight line. The definition of a line is that it cannot be divided. But that's just what the earthquake has done. It has sundered the line straight down the middle and left a deep and unfathomable and unbridgeable gash. It has cut tables,cupboards, chairs, houses, typewriters, trousers, blouses and shirts into perfect halves. In some places it has run down the middle of families; in others it has divided and sliced even single people along their noses so that the left nostril is no longer on speaking, or rather breathing terms with the right, and the right ear cannot hear what the other does.

Sagari had little doubt that *A River Runs Down Bombay* was going to be a major publishing event. Amanat's literary agent in Britain thought the book was provocative, courageous and timely, and was talking of auctioning it to Chatto and Windus, Bloomsbury, Simon and Schuster, Penguin, HarperCollins and others.

Sagari and Amanat waited. They lived circumscribed lives. They were both loners, shy and withdrawn until they got to know you. After their marriage, they felt even less need for company. They lived in a kind of distorted reality, absorbed in each other and inseparable. They thought this was a good thing, and that this was what love must be. Perhaps it is. But somewhere they were also conscious that it was unnatural, the way they seemed to think and live in each other's minds. The other person was a constant presence, and an overhang that shielded you from the scorching sun but also cut off a part of the view.

It would take a long time for things to come apart, and they wouldn't even notice the first signs. The news from Amanat's literary agent was not good. She mailed him letters of rejection from various publishers while insisting that he should not lose heart. Sagari's college gave her notice that from the end of the academic year, her services would no longer be required. Then she got a message that her father had been removed to hospital.

Abbajaan was at the Abbey when Sagari and Amanat went to visit Dr Pat with a box of Swiss chocolates. They had no idea what he was down with, which perhaps was not such a bad thing.

Dr Patwardhan lay semicomatose with the toxins his liver could no longer process. Amanat fought an intense desire to run. His favourite doctor, the one he had thought of as a surrogate god, far more approachable and accessible than the Almighty, was decomposing and turning to bilious compost. Dr Pat had developed an extremely rare form of cirrhosis and was bandaged from head to toe because he was bleeding from every pore of his body.

'Did you know that he was so heavily into drink?' Amanat asked Sagari, softly, lest the patient hear him.

'I knew he liked to drink, but I had no idea that he was so far gone. How lonely he must have been.'

The box of Lindt chocolates was still there on the day Sagari and Amanat took possession of the dead body. There were just three people at the electric crematorium: Sagari, Zubeida Khaala and Amanat. A small item had appeared in the papers about the death of the father of the child star, but Sagari and Amanat were relieved that none of Dr Pat's neighbours from his apartment building had turned up, nor any of the film people whom he had cultivated and so lavishly entertained.

That night, as Amanat came out of the shower, Sagari clung to him and said, 'Now I have no one but you.' What are you talking about? Amanat said to himself. You and your father haven't spoken for God knows how many years, and all that time you faced the world alone. He recalled the night soon after their marriage when she had said to him, 'Sometimes I think my father would like to be my pimp.' There was such hurt in her at that moment, Amanat did not dare take her in his arms and tell her that they were together, and that no one, not even her father, could do her harm.

Amanat looked at her now and realized how deceptive her voice had been. There was not a tear in her eyes, but it was a face desolate with loss and the longing to make amends. How could this father, whom she had occasionally suspected of almost putting her on the market, mean so much to her? How does one account for the inexplicable ties, ties that are beyond reason, that bind us to other people? Who was he to question Sagari's grief? Had he ever admitted how much he missed Zia, even as he had hated him after he had run a knife through him not once but twice?

Amanat held Sagari tight and would not let her go.

'Promise me you'll never leave me.'

'Yes, I promise.' Amanat rocked her gently till she fell asleep.

On some pretext or other, Sagari had put off going to her father's place for two days. For years after she'd left home, she had fought a losing battle trying to wipe out memories of the past. Amanat and Zubeida Khaala, but especially Abbajaan, had made her feel that she was central to their lives, and the bitterness of the final few years that she'd spent with her father seemed to have receded. She had been in denial so long, she had rejected everything associated with her father, including acting. Slowly, almost without her noticing it, the chiaroscuro and the nuancing had begun to come back to her early years. She could now even laugh and admit that she had been a ham, an insufferable one. That's what her directors and audience had demanded, and she had been more than happy to accommodate them. What surprised her, though, was that even then she had been conscious of the business or art of acting.

She had forgotten how much fun she got out of acting and how she enjoyed being in front of the camera. Acting was almost an involuntary skill for her. The director might not have got the hang of a scene but she knew exactly how to play it. It was an incredible high, a sense of absolute power. She could do what she wanted with her audience. She didn't want to go back to acting. Ever. But she was happy that she had regained a measure of equanimity about her past. Now she was returning to her old home and she was not so confident.

Sagari was worried that her father might have changed the lock during the intervening years, but she had no problem opening the door. Her first instinct was to shut it tight as though she would never open it again. The apartment seemed to have been infected with her father's cirrhosis. A sickening sour miasma wafted out gently like the Union Carbide gas that had killed so many people in Bhopal. The house was fermenting in its own rot. There were empty whisky, gin, rum and country liquor bottles on the floor, on chairs and sofas, on tabletops, on the radio, and balanced precariously on the TV set. Little hillocks of cigarette butts rose in ashtrays, teacups and saucers, and on dinner plates, and floated like shoals of dead fish in the toilet bowls. The kitchen sink was stacked haphazardly with pots, pans and woks in which food had congealed and turned lichen-green or was growing thick acres of white fur. It was in her father's bedroom that Sagari finally broke down. The bed covers and sheets and piles of soiled clothes on the floor were stained with blood. Even the walls on which her father had leaned or supported himself with his hands had the slithering marks of his palms.

It took Sagari and Amanat two and a half weeks to clean up the flat. When he was exhausted and about to collapse, Amanat would sit in one of the sofas with its torn upholstery, the yellow foam stuffing protruding like a roll of fat from under a tight sari blouse, and stare out at the sea. Dr Pat's was one of those old apartments on the sixth floor of a rent-controlled building with four bedrooms, most of them facing the Indian Ocean. The ancient Otis lift had an accordion iron grill that had to be forcefully banged shut. While the landings between the apartments were dim, inside the rooms the light flooded in like a high tide and there was enough air for an army of Amanats.

It was not as big as Firdaus, but it would do, oh yes, it would do. The first priority was to have it painted. They could afford only the cheapest whitewash, one room every few months, and the casements would have to be replaced with new ones. The rent was going to be a problem even though, by current standards, it was a joke, a bare fifteen hundred and thirty rupees per month. They would manage. Amanat would have to bestir himself, knock on every industrial door in Bombay and as far as Pune, and never mind how pathetic and bizarre people's notions of good industrial design were in this country, he would take whatever work he was offered. And he would borrow money from Abbajaan to tide them over the first few months. When Sagari was not around one morning, he arranged a writing table in a corner room with huge windows on two sides and put a chair beside it. He felt good.

'You might want to take a look at these.' Sagari placed a wad of twenty or thirty tiny booklets, and a couple of sheets of loose paper with a rubber band around them, on their bed. She had been going through her father's papers for over a week now.

'No, I don't think so, despite the thinly-veiled coercive character of the Americanism, "You might want to".' Amanat pushed the bundle away. 'Ask me to scrub the floor, rinse the dishes, clean the toilet, that's fine. But your father's papers, no. I don't think he would have liked someone he thought had stolen his daughter to go through his private papers.'

'And what if they are your father's papers?'

'Abbajaan's? What would they be doing here?'

Amanat removed the rubber band and leafed through the booklet on top. 'These are your father's bank-slip books. Why would I be interested in them?'

'Look at the back.'

Amanat did. It was a deposit record of a cheque from Zafar Khan for Rs.7000. So was the next and the one after that and the next. The amounts varied from anywhere between five and ninety-seven thousand, but there wasn't a month in the last eleven years when Abbajaan had not tried to repay his debt to Dr Pat.

Amanat tied the rubber band a little distractedly around the slip books and returned them to Sagari.

'You haven't looked at the two letters.'

Amanat opened the first. It was a letter from Abbajaan.

My dear Pat,

I know you have not forgiven me for Khan Builders going bankrupt. Neither have I. You were the only outsider whose money was invested in our company and I let you down.

This cheque will finally clear the entire amount Khan Builders owed you plus the 15 per cent interest that accrued over the years. But in truth I will never be able to repay the debt I owe you. I remember the time you needed the money and for years after the company folded up, I could not give you a rupee. You were my friend, the closest I have had, and I betrayed your trust.

I may have missed you bitterly at times but the one who felt your loss most was Amanat. The only reason he did not want to become a doctor was because he wanted to be an architect more. He became neither. Time and fate play tricks on all of us. I wish Amanat had not had to pay for his father's sins. And you for a friend's.

I am even more in debt to you now. Sagari is the pride and solace of our family. You should see the changes she has wrought in all of us. She has brought good cheer, good sense and laughter back into our family. But most of all, she has worked nothing short of a minor miracle on Amanat. He was always good at concealing his feelings. Only those who knew him well and long would know that behind that calm and quiet exterior was a tense child full of hurt and doubts about himself. It's unlikely that he will rid himself of all his complexes and the various chips on his shoulders in one lifetime. But he is so much more relaxed and confident these days because of Sagari. Who knows, he may still learn to hope and trust tomorrow.

Why don't you come and see us, Pat? It would make us happy. And it would give Sagari such joy. I think you too may end up being happier than you have been in a long, long time. You don't have to call beforehand. Just come over. If you want, I'll come and pick you up.

Yours affectionately,

Zafar

The other letter was an official one. It was an eviction notice from the Bombay High Court, which had been served two months before. Dr Pat had not paid the rent for over a year and a quarter. In the circumstances, the court order declared that the landlord was within his rights to repossess the flat.

'I thought finally we would have a place of our own. It sounds awful but I imagined Papa's death had not been in vain. You looked all set to write your next novel at that roll-top desk. I was so looking forward to a quiet place with a separate room for you to work in.'

'Large rooms make me feel uneasy,' Amanat prevaricated. 'I feel more secure when I'm at Suleiman Mansion. Besides, I haven't had an idea for years.'

Then the creditors descended upon Suleiman Mansion. Neither Sagari nor Amanat had any idea how they had found out where Sagari lived now. She had not left her forwarding address with the neighbours or the post office. And yet there they were, ringing the bell at six in the morning and as late as 11.30 at night. Brokers, bankers, people from the three clubs of which Dr Pat was a member, servants, friends and even former patients: Dr Pat had borrowed from everyone. He had drawn huge amounts from his overdraft account, and had had seven credit cards with which he'd paid for his gambling debts and liquor, and the expensive presents he bought for his 'friends' in the film industry.

How could one single human being run up such colossal debts? Amanat asked himself, and realized immediately what a foolish question this was. He remembered his father's stricken face when he would open a letter from a bank informing him that his wife had overdrawn some truly ungodly sum. Or the occasion when Ammi mentioned casually that she had had a run of bad luck the whole of the previous month and owed two of the people at her card table seventy-three thousand rupees. But Ammi fortunately did not play the stock market. Dr Pat owed his broker alone forty-seven lakhs; yes, that's five zeroes after the forty-seven.

'I'm going to do a film with the man who made *Sona aur Mona*,' Sagari announced when she came back from work one evening. 'He needs a hit, after three flops in a row, and so do I. I'm going to repay all those predators one by one. And then we are going to buy a flat with a separate room for you.'

# 31

Jonathan-Christophe had a room above the garage, and it was this he now used as a studio. It was a fairly large space, and though

Lucens helped Jonathan move his easels, paints, palettes and whatever paintings that survived the storm, this was the first time that he'd felt relaxed enough to loll on a divan and spend some time there. Lucens couldn't quite figure out how Brother Jonathan's work had changed, but change it had. He was nowhere near charting out his own territory, but what Abbajaan had helped him to do, and Lucens had little doubt that his father was the prime mover in the changes that had been wrought, was to bring clarity and depth to the work. All these years, Jonathan had been in the business of copying surfaces, centimetre by centimetre. Now, for the first time, he was able to get inside the painting, or rather the mind of the painter and the way he saw the world, and to reproduce his inner vision on the canvas.

Jonathan had extended his palette considerably. The secular and the modern were beginning to be as much a part of his repertoire now as the greats of medieval and renaissance times. He was working, as usual, on three paintings: a Douanier Rousseau, a Berthe Morisot and a Paul Klee.

'You are such a precise and remarkable mimic of art, Jonathan, and yet you can't do the simplest of signatures? Doesn't take much genius or skill to sign a Miro or Degas.'

'I can get the signatures right when I'm practising but I lose my nerve when I have to sign on the canvas itself. Tell me, whose name would you put on this one?' Jonathan-Christophe smiled mischievously.

Jonathan holds out a framed painting of a woman who is washing her hair in a basin of water. She is about to pour the water from a ewer in her hand, but someone seems to have called out to her and she looks up enquiringly, twisting her wet hair to the side. Behind her are a chair, and a bed on which a carpet has been carelessly thrown. Lucens is familiar with some of the objects on the wall and in the room. He can also recognize the lips parted slightly to show just a little of the inside of the mouth, and the highlight on the cheeks.

Lucens sits transfixed in front of the painting. He cannot make up his mind whether he is horrified or delighted. His throat has gone dry and he is unable to speak. He wipes his mouth and nose with the back of his sleeve and slowly a smile of such beatitude breaks out on his face that Jonathan's eyes become chinks and he laughs aloud in relief. He has passed the test.

'Jonathan-Christophe, you are nothing short of a genius.' Lucens stood up and sat down. He smiled vacuously, paced up and down and every now and then looked at the painting. 'This is unreal. Jonathan, do you realize what you've gone and done? It's the first new Vermeer in three hundred years. You've got under the skin of Vermeer. You can be a one-man industry now.'

Lucens went over and hugged Jonathan.

'You are something else, Jona – '

He couldn't complete the sentence. Jonathan had his tongue inside his mouth and was kissing him so hard Lucens couldn't breathe.

All day long the police interrogated the monks while two helicopters rose and fell. You could see the pilots and their companions, in their polaroid Raybans, through the glass panels of the church. It was like being at an aquarium, there was no telling who was watching whom. Abbajaan's insulation cut off almost all the frenetic whirring but it was a false tranquillity.

The monks were allowed to take a break for offices and for meals, but they had to return in pairs to the two police detectives who sat in the visitors' room. There was no trace of Jonathan-Christophe's body, but while this was unusual, there had been cases of mountaineers on the adjoining peaks who had disappeared never to be seen again. Those that were found had always had their bones picked clean. Lucens received more attention than everybody else, and had to return three times. The officers wanted to know why Brother Jonathan-Christophe had singled him out for forgiveness in his suicide note. He had, they granted, begged everybody's forgiveness, but no one else, not even the Abbot, had got a special mention.

'What was your relationship with Brother Jonathan-Christophe?'

'We were brothers.'

'Yes, you've told us that before.'

'Do you think the answer would change if you ask the same question over and over again?'

'Did you have a special relationship with him?'

'I don't think so, except that I was a keen observer of his paintings.'

'Let me refresh your memory.'

The officer showed Lucens Jonathan-Christophe's suicide note for the fifth or sixth time. It was not addressed to anyone in particular, a kind of universal message.

I beg the forgiveness of our Lord Jesus Christ as I beg the forgiveness of all of you, especially Brother Lucens. I have proved unworthy and deserve to die.

Jonathan-Christophe

The interrogators beat about the bush for another fifteen minutes and then asked whether there was a possibility that the two of them had had a relationship that was more than platonic.

'We were brothers in the body of Christ.'

'Yes, of course, but were you also sexually involved?'

'Are you aware that when we join a monastic order, we take a vow of celibacy?'

'Vows, even the best of them, are often broken.'

'We would not have needed to break them. If we had wanted the kind of relationship you insinuate, all we would have had to do was to leave the Order. Neither of us had taken the solemnly professed vows yet.'

'Yes, yes.'

Lucens could feel the impatience of the younger officer. He wondered why they persisted with their questioning when Jonathan had had the decency to leave a suicide note.

'You'll admit though that it's not unheard of to want to stay within the Order and yet have sexual relationships.'

'I'm sure that's possible but it's of little interest to me.'

'Is that the reason why he begs your forgiveness?'

'You would have to ask him that to satisfy your speculative bent of mind.'

'We'll let you go for now but we trust you don't mind spending some more time with us again.'

'If I had a choice, I would mind very much.'

Damn Jonathan. He might be dead, but he had certainly made sure that Lucens would not be rid of him that easily. The officers did return, not the next day, but two days later. It was evident, however, that their interest in Lucens was waning.

The monks talked about the suicide note far more than the death of Brother Jonathan. Some had tried to draw Lucens into a discussion about what Jonathan could have meant by his strange words. Fortunately at Mass two days later, Reverend Father gave the homily at which he said that the dead, far more than the living, deserved respect.

'The living can defend themselves if they so wish, or their friends can take up cudgels in their name; the dead unfortunately cannot raise their voices against insinuations and slander. Suicide can never be endorsed by the Church and it is not my intention to defend it in any way either. And yet, let us understand that suicide is a response to what a man or woman found unbearable. Unbearable pain, unbearable hurt, unbearable rejection and loneliness, and unbearable depression. He or she found it unbearable to continue living. All one can hope and pray for is that, like Judas who betrayed our Lord, and Peter who disowned him not once but twice, Jonathan-Christophe too may find peace and succour in the arms of our Lord.

'When someone commits suicide,' he said, 'we need to look into our hearts. Because suicide is about unhappiness. What we need to ask ourselves is whether we tried to lessen or increase the degree of Brother Jonathan's unhappiness. Even if the answer is that we tried to alleviate his unhappiness, did we do enough?'

It was an oddly circumspect homily, heartfelt, but bordering on the kind of platitudes that the Abbot made it a point to avoid. It was as though he were skirting the issue, picking his way and words carefully, so that what was left unsaid raised more questions than those that he had addressed. It was a sermon from which Brother Jonathan was strangely missing. And there was no escaping the heresy of the Abbot's views on suicide.

'We'll pray for Brother Jonathan today and as often as we can. His paintings are a living testimony of his love for God. Beyond that we will treat him with dignity. We will not gossip about him or dissect his motives. We will leave him alone and in peace.'

After that, nobody bothered Lucens.

'Tell me exactly what happened, Lucens.'

There was no preamble or introduction, just a flat statement. It would not brook cavilling, casuistry or evasion. The Abbot had waited over two weeks before broaching the subject with Lucens. Now he would have the truth.

What was Lucens to say? He had tried to shield Reverend Father Augustine from the rot that had set into the very bones of the Abbey; make no mistake, the culprit had confessed as much. What was there to tell, except that the goodness and mercy of Jesus were all-encompassing? The Lord had seen fit to rid the Abbey of this painter who had no face or character of his own, but took on the persona of whomsoever he inhabited at the moment.

Lucens was not quite sure why the Abbot would want to reopen a wound that was just beginning to heal. Frankly, Lucens would have preferred almost any punishment to reliving that awful and unmentionable time. He had staggered to the washbasin in the studio and gargled maybe a hundred times; he had applied soap to his tongue, and the inside of his mouth and lips, and had washed them again and again. Jonathan-Christophe had watched him and laughed his head off.

'Oh, come on, Lucens. I'm not buying this big act of innocence. As if you've never felt the urge to pleasure the body.'

Lucens had begun to shake. His flesh and soul seemed to want to heave out Jonathan's tongue clogging his mouth, his body pressed hard against him, his hand frantically pulling down the zip of Lucens's trousers, grabbing his penis and stroking it even as something in Lucens began to respond. He had returned to the sink and washed his mouth with soap again.

'I'm not impressed, Lucens, not one bit. I know how you get your thrills. I am game for S&M if that's what you want. Giving pleasure gives me one hell of a sexual kick.'

Lucens had stared at Jonathan, unable to comprehend his words and, even more than them, his conspiratorial tone.

'I would not have graduated to any of the finer points, to a really much higher plane of exultation and ecstasy till you showed me the way with that flail of yours.'

Lucens did not know who was more depraved, Jonathan-Christophe or he himself. He kept shaking his head while Jonathan's face turned from smirking complacency to consternation to horror.

'Did I make a mistake, Lucens? Did I get you wrong? Have I hurt you? Oh Lucens, what an appalling blunder I have made. Please forgive me. Say you do.'

All night long Lucens had bathed, swallowed shampoo and brought it all up. In between, when he dozed, he suckled at the stone breasts of the Bitter Sisters while Rearing Horse did a dance of death on his broken body. The river in Sweet Waters had caught fire and was flowing through his penis.

'Please, Lucens, I beg you to forgive me. I'll never indulge in sex again. I know my flesh is weak and I've given my word to Jesus in the past and broken it, but I'll try very hard this time. I'll do anything to earn your forgiveness.'

Lucens had looked away. He spoke so softly, you could hardly hear what he was saying. 'I hate you. I don't want to see your face again.'

'You are right to hate me but can you bring yourself to forgive me?'

It did not seem as though Lucens would ever answer him. But he did, and when he did, his head was still turned away. 'What forgiveness can there be when you've defiled the very body and blood of Christ?'

Now Reverend Father Augustine wanted to know what had happened. So be it. He would tell the Abbot exactly what had happened. Indeed he would not miss out on a single sordid detail. And he would give him a piece of his mind. Reverend Father was lucky that Lucens had not reported him to the Chief Abbot or written to Rome. The Abbot was the shepherd of his flock at Terraferra. He was responsible for their physical as well as their spiritual wellbeing. But what happens if the shepherd himself has eyes but does not see? Hadn't the Abbot known about Jonathan-Christophe? Why had he not thrown him out years ago? The first vow you took, even as a postulant, was the vow of celibacy. It did not matter whether you became a brother or were ordained as a priest, you forswore sex. There were no ifs or buts, as there were no extenuating circumstances. But Lucens was not so naïve as to believe that priests don't transgress the law. Hadn't the whisky priest in *The Power and the Glory* done just that? But he, more than anybody else, is conscious that he has forfeited the right to be a priest. Thomas Merton himself had fallen in love with a woman years after he had been ordained, but knew very well that if he was to have sexual relations with her, he must first give up monkhood.

For Lucens, Jonathan's sin was the unspeakable one, a sin so unnatural that the living Christ and the whole of the Church recoiled at it. And what was Reverend Father's response to it? He was trying to blame Lucens instead of the guilty party. For the sake of argument, and to give him the benefit of the doubt, Lucens was willing to overlook the Abbot's unforgivable negligence. Maybe Jonathan-Christophe had confessed to some other priest, maybe he had kept his vile predilection a secret. To be fair, Lucens himself had not had even an inkling of it, though Jonathan and he had spent hours together. But to excuse suicide, to ask the monks to pray for the soul of one so depraved, to claim that Jonathan's paintings were a living testimony to his love for Jesus and, worst of all, to hope and suggest that a suicide find peace and succour in the arms of our Lord, that was truly abhorrent. There was no other way of looking at it: it was sacrilege, blasphemy and heresy all rolled into one. There was one other question that had so far been unasked and unanswered: how far had the rot spread? Had Jonathan-Christophe infected anyone else in the Abbey with his diseased mind?

'When Jonathan-Christophe asked you to forgive him, you didn't really tell him, "What forgiveness can there be when you've defiled the very body and blood of Christ," did you?'

'Yes, I did.'

Reverend Father shook his head as if he didn't want to believe Lucens.

'Poor, poor Jonathan, how lonely and frightened he must have felt. Why Lucens, you pointed that sad, sinning child straight to his own destruction.'

'Not child, Father, grown-up man and a monk at that. And I didn't point him to hell. He was headed there all on his own steam and by his own depravity.'

'I hope, Brother Lucens, our good Lord is a shade more forgiving of you and all the rest of us sinners than you were of Jonathan.' The Abbot got up and put his hand on Lucens's head. 'I sometimes think that if Jesus had his way, He would welcome the very soldiers who crucified Him and Judas himself to heaven.'

'Why would anybody then bother to walk the straight and narrow?' Lucens was barely able to conceal his contempt.

'So you think heaven is an exclusive place meant only for the select few? You may be right. I'm sure you are. There's a book somewhere in the library that Zafar gave me, it's by one of your countrymen. I can't quite remember his name. When I first read it, it offended me no end. But the more I see of the world and how we all stumble along, sinning and not sinning, making a mess of our lives, I have begun to think there's something wonderfully wise and compassionate about the book. If I find it, I'll give it to you to read.'

'If you think some half-baked, liberal book will change God's mind, you are wrong.'

'I was hoping it would make you a little more tolerant.'

'God forbid that I should countenance the thought of tolerating what is expressly forbidden.'

Reverend Father suddenly seemed to have had enough of Lucens. 'I'm confining you to your room till such time as I think necessary. You'll attend the offices and Mass every day but you will not communicate by spoken word, gesture or in writing with anyone. I suggest that you spend that time constructively to look into your soul and ask what makes you so rigid, and so superior to those around you.'

## 32

My dear Zia,

Let me call it 'the air pocket' for the time being. It's a total misnomer but that's how I thought of it in the beginning. I first came across it at The Detroit Institute of the Arts. Sagari was shooting a song sequence in Michigan and at the Niagara Falls for a Hindi film and I had tagged along with her. I had nothing to do all day and went to see *Double Indemnity* at the Detroit Film Theatre. (Did you know that Billy Wilder wrote the screenplay for it?) The film finished at around 3 p.m. and I still had two hours on my hands before Sagari got back. I thought I would step into the museum and take a look at the Impressionists. It's not an outstanding collection but they have some Corots and Corbets, and a rather lovely Monet on loan. Yes, one of his *Water Lilies* series. I am always happy to see them singly, though I'm afraid more than three in a row makes me want to lop off the heads off the whole lot.

At ten to five the bell rang and the guards came around to tell the stragglers to leave. I was making my way back to the entrance when something at the end of a long passage caught my attention.

A man followed by a woman, both of them naked, were climbing a steep hill. They looked utterly done in; they were almost skeletal and there were deep wounds and gashes on their bodies. And yet their faces, Zia, their faces, were so incredibly lit up with hope and expectation. Where were they going? What had they seen at the top of the hill? There seemed to be light emanating from some strange birdlike figure wheeling in the sky. I was transfixed not so much by the bird as by the intensity of emotion of the two people. No, I'm misrepresenting things and missing the point. It is the fervent eagerness and the yearning on the two faces, their unshakable faith that all those terrible travails, the starvation and the suffering are about to be rewarded, that draws you inexorably to the bird.

What was unsettling was the fluid and unstable nature of the creature. What was it? An insubstantial aqueous being from the deepest depths of the ocean? A nimbus hovering on the edge of the horizon? For a while I was certain that it was Coleridge's albatross, the good and kindly bird, the bird of good fortune, the one that brings back hope and will be killed by the purest evil in all of us. Then I was no longer sure. Now it looked, can I use the word 'unmistakably' about something that seemed to be in flux? like a deadly bird of prey, the kind of vulture we used to see near the Parsi Well of Death on Malabar Hill. Its shoulders were raised almost to its ears, with its long neck telescoped deep between them. It looked old and greedy and there was a leer in its eyes. I thought I saw a strip or shred of raw flesh in its mouth. And then I wasn't so sure again. It looked peaceable now and seemed to have a mellow, calming effect upon me. What was the matter with me? How could I have missed something so obvious? It was the Holy Spirit, the dove that rises heavenward, the symbolic third in the Trinity, the unknowable nature of God himself in Catholic dogma. Perhaps the power of the painting lay in the fact that it was the one and the other and all of them simultaneously.

It was a huge vertical painting and in the middle of the frame at the base was a brass plate with the artist's name: Hectorine Farrel. I had not heard the name before nor had I seen her work. And yet the next moment I was overtaken by a terrible panic, a panic far more frightening than the recognition that the vulture was pecking and gouging the flesh of the couple in the painting even before they had turned to carrion. I suddenly saw the appalling danger that Hectorine Farrel was in every minute, every instant that passed. Below her name were the four digits 1957 followed by a hyphen. After the brief hiatus of the dash was an empty space, the one I thought of initially as an air pocket. The year of birth, the hyphen and the terror of the gaping space were neatly bookended by sharply etched brackets.

'Watch out, watch out, Hectorine Farrel,' I screamed a silent warning. 'One step, one step on an innocent banana peel, just one cardiac arrest, or a sleepy motorist on the expressway, and you are going to disappear forever into that air pocket.'

I stopped trying to warn her. What was the point? She couldn't hear me. Besides, I had utterly misread that hole there. This was no air pocket; you were never going to bounce back from it. How many paintings did Hectorine have on display in the various art museums of the world? There would be a boa constrictor with perennially open jaws under each one of them. The reptile of time would lie still, not for a moment would it exert itself. No, it wouldn't have to do a thing; Hectorine would find her way unerringly into its mouth.

In truth, Hectorine would be inching her way into the boa constrictor's craw from the day she was born. Does the boa, I wondered, have an Adam's apple that swallows or is there a peristaltic action by which, in wave after wave of involuntary muscular contractions, Hectorine would tunnel her way into its alimentary canal? First the head, then the shoulders, the breasts, the stomach would disappear. And all the while the boa constrictor's eyes would be glued to her buttocks; no hurry there, soon, very soon, the soles of her feet would be in, and the vacant space after the hyphen would suddenly be filled with four new digits. Oh the relief, and the feeling of the fullness of things; Hectorine would be no more and the bracket complete and the theorem of her life solved once and for all. Q.E.D.

There is no greater perfection than nothingness. Why else would we worship God. Hectorine too then would have achieved perfection. Her case and file would be closed forever.

And all the while I studiously and pointedly avoided looking at the abyss that followed upon the hyphen under my name. I could see the Great Curator of the world looking disapprovingly at the messiness of the unfinished business in my bracket. I was thrashing my legs frantically. The behemoth snake waited patiently to wrap itself around a banyan tree and crush my bones when I was finally all in.

Dear Zia, how did I manage all these years when you were missing?

Love,

Amanat

# 33

For the first time since he had chosen to become a monk, Lucens felt at peace with himself. In his light-hearted moments, he told himself that a man could get used to anything, including the desert. He missed the Jesus-highs but he was grateful that he was not swinging between manic rapture and suicidal depression. The silence of the monastic way did not automatically translate into the contemplative life, neither did the act of disciplined concentration alone bring you closer to it. All you could do was to create the optimum conditions and wait patiently for God to show up. Frankly, even the notion of waiting was like putting pressure, and seemed to queer the pitch. Oe Tanaka, a Japanese monk who had come to the Abbey for two weeks to teach Zen techniques of meditation, had repeatedly spoken of going with the flow. Lucens understood the meaning of the phrase but he had had no idea how one went about immersing oneself in the act while forgetting about it. Now, sometimes almost without being aware of it, he would find himself floating up with the Holy Spirit.

He had at first been furious with Father Augustine for imposing a vow of silence upon him. The Abbot might claim he was not vengeful, yet of course he was nothing but. Why else was Lucens confined to his room? He was no longer so certain though. The enforced quiet of the solitary cell had begun to affect him. He did not have any visions and he was not struck by earth-shaking insights. What happened was something both distressing and satisfying. He began to enjoy the humdrum and the placid. He did not need to be on a continuously euphoric high.

He was more than a little disappointed when, at the end of six weeks, the Abbot asked him to take care of the former Novice Master, Father Paul. Lucens was suddenly afraid of the outside world. Outside were the other monks, the people who worked at the furniture factory, and the lay people who came to pray at the church and for retreats, plus the weekend tourists, and he felt he couldn't manage a 'good morning' or a simple conversation with any of them. His room had become a womb and he felt insecure and lost outside it. Like the wolf-boy, he would have to be retaught the basic tools of negotiating with his fellow-men. But he had lost the will and didn't see the point of it.

Luckily, the former Novice Master's leukaemia was far too advanced to require much conversation, or anything else for that matter. He lay in bed exhausted and in a kind of torpor between life and death.

The Abbot would visit Father Paul every evening after Compline. The two of them had known each other since the time they were junior monks, and the Novice Master would occasionally make an effort to be alert when Reverend Father came over. On a good day he would manage a sustained conversation for seven or ten minutes while the Abbot checked his vital signs.

'What's the prognosis, Augustine? How long do you give me?'

'Consider yourself fortunate, Paul, that I gave up my practice some thirty-five years ago and Dr Snowden looks after you. Do you know what my fellow-physicians used to say about me? If the disease didn't finish the patient off, Dr Augustine would.'

'Is that the reason why you had to move to psychiatry?'

Reverend Father looked dolefully at the former Novice Master. 'Must you speak about these matters in front of young Lucens? What will he think of his Abbot?'

'Have no fear, Augustine, I have not breathed a word to him about you being the first doctor in the annals of psychiatry to be committed by the inmates of your own hospital.'

It never failed to astonish Lucens that monks too had led normal lives like other people; that they had studied medicine or engineering for years, dated girls, practised their profession, contemplated marriage, often without a thought of joining the monkhood. Who would have imagined that Father Paul and the Abbot were both veterans of the Vietnam war and were still bitterly divided about its merits? Reverend Father thought America had had no business being there, while it was Father Paul's unshaken belief that the only mistake this country had made was to give in to the Viet Cong instead of bombing them all the way to hell. It was odd, but one took it for granted that priests had no past, as if they were born into a habit and a vocation and that was all there was to them.

'I found the novel I spoke to you about, the one Zafar gave me. You could read the whole book, it's quite short really, or just the bit that I've flagged.' Reverend Father handed a book to Lucens one evening while Father Paul was dozing uneasily.

Lucens looked at the title and placed the book on the table. 'It's by my brother, Amanat,' he said softly.

The Abbot didn't quite take in what Lucens had said. Then his face creased into a smile. 'How ridiculous, I keep forgetting that you were a Khan until you joined us. Then you certainly know it well.'

'I read it a long time ago.'

'And you hated it. I don't blame you. Do you remember the bit where Kabir goes to heaven?'

'No, at least not very clearly.'

'I read the whole thing again. It's outrageous how many harsh truths your brother makes us swallow in the name of laughter.'

There wasn't much to occupy Lucens by Father Paul's bedside. Besides, the least he could do, since the Abbot was insistent about it, was to read the bit he had marked out.

Almost at the very end of the book, Inayat says to the weaver:

We were so much better off with you dead. Your reputation would have remained intact. And we would have grown fonder of you. Nostalgia is not just selective memory, it is the reinvention of the past as it never was. We would have romanticized and idolized you. Your crass attempts at attention-seeking and your juvenile desire to shock would have become the stuff of parables and mythology. You were dead. I checked again and again. You had no pulse and you had no breath. Why did you come back?

The weaver patted Inayat's back as if to console him. Inayat shook off the Master's friendly overtures.

It was something of a surprise for me too. I was standing in the queue with thousands of others waiting at the gates for St Peter to check in the Book of Life and tot up and tally my sins and good deeds and decide whether I was to go to heaven or hell. Suddenly, there was a commotion and the doors to God's mansions opened and Michael flew out. It was an amazing sight. The painters and the sculptors have got it wrong. You can't see the angels and yet there's no mistaking them. Their wings are transparent and insubstantial as air and the beatitude on the face...I can see you getting impatient.

Like everybody else I wondered why he was in such a hurry and why he was carrying a beauteous garland of carnations, or maybe they were roses, the colour of dried blood, when lo and behold, he set down where I was waiting and put the garland around my neck and lifted me as if I was as light as breath, and took me straight inside.

People were screaming abuses. You would think that they would behave at least after they were dead but I could also understand their anger.

Welcome Kabir, I heard a wonderfully mellifluous voice speak to me. God got off his bejewelled gold throne and embraced me. We are absolutely delighted to see you here. We must say you kept us waiting so long, we had begun to wonder whether you had given up the idea of dying altogether.

I prostrated myself in front of the glorious presence. I was overawed and speechless. I couldn't believe my eyes. I mean this was the real thing, the ultimate experience.

Rise, weaver. No need for you to touch our feet. He bent down and raised me. I do apologize that you had to stand in the queue with the rest of the crowd, God said. Peter had a bout of shingles and you know what a hypochondriac he is. He still hasn't managed to update the records for the births and deaths and of course while he was recuperating, all was chaos. I'm afraid it's no excuse but that was the reason why you were not picked up directly from earth and had to stand in the queue.

I had the depressing feeling that I was still on earth. Nothing it seemed, had changed. If you were in with the bosses you got special treatment.

Make yourself at home, weaver. This is after all your final resting place, your heavenly abode. Ask for whatever you want, milk and honey; the best fruit in the world; absolutely any kind of cuisine you fancy; wine, women, song. Anything you need, consider it yours. Any time you feel like company, just call or drop by. It would be a pleasure to spend time with you.

It was clear that the interview was over but I must have looked puzzled, maybe even a little alarmed, for God asked me, Is anything the matter, Kabir? You look pale and not entirely happy.

Almighty Father, am I to understand that I have got admittance to heaven?

But of course. Was there any doubt about that?

I don't mean to sound ungrateful but I thought this place had some standards.

He looked at me coldly and I could feel the mercury rising. You haven't been here over a minute, he thundered, and you already have complaints.

You misunderstand me, Lord, I said hastily. I merely wanted to point out that there must be some mistake.

What mistake? His irises had narrowed like a cat's.

How should I put it? My history of misdemeanours would hardly make me eligible for heaven.

Oh, he said, and his face relaxed and a smile broke out like sunlight from a crack on a grey, oppressive day. You mean your whoring and blasphemies, your days as a brigand and a highway robber, your constant lying and your desire to shock and scandalize, anything to be sensational?

I squirmed at this litany of my misdeeds and didn't dare look up.

There's more, much more. He paused. Do you want me to go on?

No, no. I am well aware that you are omniscient, my Lord.

How could we keep you out? You are our annual gesture of forgiveness. Our token sinner and Untouchable. We do not subscribe to that dubious doctrine of equal opportunity, but we have to be careful about our reputation. They call you a saint down there. We don't want to disappoint your constituency, do we?

Then he turned to me and said, Besides, don't forget, as our honorific title says, we are all-merciful and compassionate.

My joy knew no bounds then. This was truly the God of love. I fell on my knees and took his hand in mine and kissed it joyously. Thank you, God. You are truly great. Then all those waiting outside, the good and the bad, the sinners and the pious, the whole and the halt, they'll all find a place in heaven, yes?

He looked at me in consternation. You must be joking. What happens to the promise I made to the chosen people? What happens to heaven and hell? What happens to the concept of dharma? If people do not respect the word and the law, all nature will be out of joint. It will be a free-for-all. The stars and planets will stray from their orbits and crash into each other, spring will follow summer and the sun will freeze us all. He looked at me indulgently then. Enough nonsense, weaver. We know that old habits die hard and you are merely trying to get a rise out of us. He clapped his hands and a hundred houris appeared out of the blue of the sky. Someone give a glass of ambrosia to the weaver. Look after him well. He is one of our favourites.

The cup was at my lips, the elixir of life that would grant me eternal youth and bliss. And a great sadness came upon me.

Tell me that we are all chosen, Almighty God. Tell me that you'll let all your creatures into the kingdom of heaven, the worms and the weevils, the birds of prey and the sharks in the sea, the lion and the serpent, the vines and creepers, the parasitical plants and the great trees, all those who walked the straight and the narrow and the rest who fell to temptation and ate of the apple. Tell me that no one but no one will be left out of paradise. I was breathless but continued recklessly. Forgive me, Father, but otherwise send me back to where I came from, for I cannot bear the thought of a God who will leave behind a single creature of his.

You are an arrogant fool, weaver. We would urge you to think again. Do not cross swords with the Almighty. We may deal in infinities but our patience is finite.

He looked long at me as if to give me time and a second chance.

Let them all in, Lord God, I said again.

I see that your mind is made up. So be it, weaver. You are banished forever to the earth and mankind.

Now, Inayat, you know why I came back from the dead.

'I'm about to meet my Maker,' Father Paul woke up one night and announced to Lucens in a surprisingly firm voice, 'and what do I dream of?'

Lucens had been dozing on the hard, infection-resistant mattress he rolled out at nights, and looked blankly at the priest.

'Take that mask off your face. I want to talk to a human being, not to some sterilized mortician.'

'I have no idea, Father, about what you were dreaming.'

'Naked women, Brother Lucens. They are happy to see me and I'm grateful and joyous.'

Lucens sat there, stoically trying to look as deadpan as possible.

'You think I've lost it, eh? And my mind is rambling? Don't you ever think of sex, Brother Lucens?'

'Not too often.'

'My devils are of the commonplace variety unlike yours, Lucens. I'm finally through with guilt. When I look back I can't believe that I made it as a monk. I owe it to Father Augustine. Yes, the Reverend Father. Did you know he was one of the youngest abbots in our Order? I was a brother then and I was amongst those who voted for him.

'I was five years older than him but he took me under his wing. I became what he later called his lucky cross, the first one he carried on his thin bony shoulders. I joined the monastery rather late, after I had led, what was called in those days, a colourful life. I thought I was ready for Jesus but I was wrong. I went to the Abbot and told him that I loved Jesus but my libido had won out. He said that I was at liberty to leave but did I want to stay on for a short while to make sure that I had taken the right decision?

'One month here or there won't make a difference, I thought. I stuck around and discovered that I couldn't make up my mind. The tug of war went on for some time, we are talking years here. The Abbot said to me, "God belongs to the mind and spirit while sex is all biology and nature. Of course the latter is bound to win hands down." I remember him winking at me and telling me that in some sense God is an unnatural desire. But what matters is whether we feel more incomplete and lost without God or without sex. In my case he seemed to think it was the first. I would keep back-sliding and failing and he kept pulling me back.

'But I had had enough of this seesawing and was all set to leave when Reverend Father appointed me Novice Master. I asked him years later why he had taken such a foolish risk, putting me in charge of the spiritual wellbeing of the novices.

'"It was a chance I had to take," he said. "I had to push you into a corner, test whether you had it in you to hang in there with our Lord. Either you would make it or we would say goodbye to you."'

The Novice Master was becoming breathless again and his speech was getting blurred. 'Give me a glass of water, Lucens.'

'Why don't you rest, Father.'

'I'm about to take the longest rest known to man. Will you get me a chocolate or a sugar pick-me-up?'

Lucens walked over to the kitchen wondering where this biographical confession was leading. It couldn't go on much longer. There was of course no chocolate, not even a cookie in the pantry, just boxes and boxes of peanut butter and some ghastly syrup that one of the retreatants had donated. Lucens ran to the Abbot's office, it was never locked, and got out the bottle of Courvoisier he kept there for Easter and Christmas.

'Good thinking, Brother Lucens.' Father Paul savoured the cognac. 'The Abbot believed Brother Jonathan-Christophe was a possible lucky cross. He had this gut feeling that Jonathan had a special love for Jesus and that his own faith and people's faith in him would see him through. I am, as you know, the arch-conservative in the Abbey. The Abbot and I were always at loggerheads but strangely enough I too thought that Jonathan-Christophe would not fail Jesus.

'When I got to know you though, I told the Abbot you had to go. That was many, many years ago. You have been a godsend and you have saved the Abbey financially. But I haven't changed my mind.

'Augustine had always thought that I was a good judge of character, except in your case. He'll retire in seven years and he thinks he'll be lucky again and you'll be his last lucky cross.

'I doubt it. I've known it from the beginning. You'll be his and the Abbey's cross and nothing else.'

My dear Zia,

Last Monday I got a rather strange call from someone asking for you. When I said that you were not with me, the man told me cryptically, 'Tell Zia Khan (he used your full name) that no one betrays him without paying a price. Assure him that we will not rest till justice is done. I asked who was speaking but the line went dead.

What in God's name is going on, Zia? I hope you are not up to any mischief.

Love,

Amanat

Lucens wondered what was so urgent that Abbajaan had to disturb him in the library. He was relieved that this was to be his father's last visit to Terraferra. The other monks got to see their family and friends just once a year, and that too for three days on the outside. Abbajaan had been in and out of the Abbey so long, hardly anybody remembered that he was not a member of the community.

The only one who was uneasy with him was his son. Lucens had prided himself that there was rarely any fog or area of darkness in his mind about his relationships or what he expected of life. The only exception was Abbajaan. He had no idea how to deal with his father. He had been anxious that people would accuse him of favouritism when Zafar Khan was appointed architect at Terraferra, but whatever misgivings there may have been at the start had turned to admiration and pride. He resented it that the Abbot and Abbajaan had become close, and he thought it rather cheap of his father that he was popular with everybody. He was envious that they were free to approach him while he himself felt inhibited when it came to a simple smile.

He knew that, barring the Abbot and maybe Father Giovanni, hardly anybody at the Abbey or Sweet Waters understood the magnitude of Abba's achievement, its quietness or its true greatness. Abbajaan's work at the Abbey was a vindication of his talent. And yet Lucens found it impossible to forgive or forget that it was Abba who was responsible for the total disruption of their lives, starting from the loss of Firdaus. Plus, he still hadn't sorted out his father's relationship with Aunt Antonia and how he himself figured in it. Not to mention the matter of that bizarre, almost profane, sculpture in the new church.

The Abbot had gone a little overboard in his enthusiasm for Mr Khan's work. It was one thing to leave all the architectural designs and decisions in Abba's hands, and quite another to let him fool around with the icons of the faith. Abba had done four reliefs for the Abbey, all of them familiar subjects, and yet if you looked at them a little carefully, you felt something was askew, if not wrong. It was difficult to put your finger on the specific details, but you felt that his work was making fun of all that was sacred in the Christian faith, even perverting it.

Perhaps the one that was most offensive was the low relief at the entrance of the church, ten-feet high and twenty-feet wide. The stone covering the grave of the Lord was flung aside, and a serene but smiling Christ strode out full of purpose and determination. On the left, towards the lower edge, a kneeling Mary Magdalene raised her head up more in joy than in awe, as though she had been expecting the resurrection. At a distance to the right was the Virgin Mary consoling one of the sorrowing apostles, who knelt near her unaware that Jesus had risen. The rest of the apostles were huddled together.

The key to this shocking relief was not simply the face of the Lord, but both his body and posture as well. There wasn't a trace of the crucifixion left on Jesus. He was no longer mortal but divine. He was not walking on the ground but stepping on firm air. He was naked to the waist, and it was more than clear that while he had not been pumping iron, he was strong enough to have shifted that great big slab of stone over his grave with a flick of his right hand. His eyes were piercing, but their power of penetration came from the light within. The divinity in him shone through his face, and through the sheer reality of his presence.

That reality was, however, fraught with dubious overtones, for what Abba had done could only be termed subversive. The preternatural serenity of Christ owed its inspiration to the Orient. He had insinuated the Buddha of the Gandhara variety into the features and figure of Jesus so that in reality you were worshipping someone other than the Son of God. Mary Magdalene was a study in barely concealed carnality. She exuded an air of eroticism that bordered on the sinful. The only saving grace was the scene with the Virgin. There was something deeply moving about it. She had a heightened air of spirituality and it was apposite that instead of the apostles assuaging Mary's grief, it was she who consoled them.

There was a footnote to all this that only Lucens would decipher and rage at. The Christ in the deep relief was the very image of Amanat. And if that was not outrageous enough, there was worse, unforgivably worse. The Virgin, there was no mistaking it, was Zubeida Khaala, and Ammijaan, the Magdalene woman.

'What is it?' Lucens asked, barely concealing the irritation in his voice.

'I'm sorry to disturb you but I wanted to tell you that Zubeida Khaala just called. Amanat has been unconscious for the last seventeen days. The doctors said that this time there was no hope of his recovering but Sagari wouldn't accept their word. Your aunt said she dug in and told the doctors they had got it wrong. Come what may, she was going to bring him back. It seems she got her way. Amanat regained consciousness this morning.'

Was that the reason Abbajaan had disturbed him in the library? Lucens wondered. What was he fussing about? Anybody who had a passing acquaintance with his brother could have told him that Amanat had performed that routine half a dozen times before and he would perform it half a dozen times again.

Amanat had drawn up his will a long time ago, instructing whoever was around to hand his dead body to JJ Hospital. He said there would be more instruction to be had from his gutted lungs and limbs than all the medical tomes put together. Very amusing. For all his misgivings about his brother, Lucens had to admit that he wanted his own death to be almost as anonymous. As a Trappist, you were austere in life and even more so in death. No fuss, no flowers, just the most muted of farewells. He remembered how simply and starkly the Novice Master had been interred. Lucens bathed him and then spent five minutes trying to decide which of Father Paul's two habits was the less tattered. He pulled the cowl over Father Paul's head. He was not a tall man but he seemed to have shrunk six inches. Father Paul looked so forlorn in that straitjacket of a wooden box, Lucens did not have the heart to let him go. Once he was brought to the Abbey church, the brothers sat in pairs at the head of the coffin and took turns at reciting the Psalter for the next twenty-four hours. After the funeral mass, again nothing elaborate, the Novice Master was taken to the tiny cemetery next to the church. The brothers lifted the body from the coffin and passed it on to Brother Peter who was already in the pit of the grave. Brother Peter placed a pillow under Father Paul's head, crossed the Novice Master's arms over his chest, and covered the face with the white hood of the cowl. One by one the monks filled the grave. Reverend Father stuck a white wooden cross, with the Novice Master's name and date of death carved on it, into the ground to the east. It was a small graveyard. When it came to be Lucens's turn to be buried, it was not unlikely that Father Paul's bones would be gathered in a cardboard box, along with those of other dead monks, and placed under Lucens's head.

'The Abbot's given me permission to call Sagari. Shall we make the call now?'

'You call. I've got a couple of things to take care of.'

## 34

'Amanat, did you really give the film rights of *The Arsonist* to Sahil Thapar and sign a contract with him to write the screenplay?'

'What if I did?'

'No, you didn't. Say you didn't.'

'I didn't realize I needed your permission to earn some money.'

'Sahil Thapar is one of the shrewdest brains in the industry. But do you think he has a clue what *The Arsonist* is about? He makes crass commercial films like almost everybody else. What are you doing with him?'

'You think it's okay for you to work with him but not for me?'

'Yes, because I've no illusions about the film business, the people in it or about myself.'

'Whereas I have delusions of grandeur?'

'Don't twist my words merely to score a point and be hurtful. You have such high standards and you expect so much of yourself. These people are different. The only standard they have is money. You don't want to make compromises at every step. It would kill you.

'Your job is to write, Amanat. Novels, plays, whatever. That's the only reason I don't mind working in movies, so you won't have to worry about money.'

'I can't bear you making sacrifices for me. You make me feel as if I am using you the way your father did. But I won't be your pimp. I can earn my own living.'

Amanat could have predicted every single twist and turn he would take, every blind alley and byway he would trudge, every folly he would knowingly commit, every misplaced and disastrous move he would make, every station of the cross he would linger at on his way to making a mess of his life after Sagari joined the films. And yet he seemed powerless to avoid any of it.

What was the matter with him? Why was he behaving so boorishly and being so self-destructive? What choice did Sagari have but to get back to the movies to pay off her father's debts? How many women or men with creditors on their backs have the opportunity to become film stars? And here was the best part: Sagari believed in him and his work. Nor did she merely believe in him; barring writing his novels for him, she did everything possible to make his life comfortable. She bought an apartment for them where he had a room of his own, a simple but solid roll-top desk to write on, a chair that gave his perpetually problematic back solid support, and reams of paper. And she didn't expect a damn thing of him in return. He didn't have to earn a paisa. All he had to do was to write, and never mind if anybody bought his stuff or not. She didn't care whether the world had the good sense to appreciate his work. She knew he was good and that was enough. Or at least it should have been.

She learnt to handle money and soon became fairly astute at understanding the legalese in contracts as well, and negotiating good deals for herself. Everybody and everything changed after Sagari joined the films, starting with Sagari herself. There had been a transformation in the attitude of her creditors. Overnight they went from being sharks to fawning courtiers who wanted to open credit lines for her that stretched all the way to the moon. It took a couple of years before Sagari was able to buy an apartment near Pali Hill Extension in Bandra. She tried her best to persuade Abbajaan and Zubeida Khaala to move in with them, but this was one of the few times, perhaps the only time, Zafar Khan did not give in to Sagari's wishes. Zubeida Khaala too stayed behind.

'Who'll cook for Zafar?' she asked.

'What nonsense, Zubeida, I can cook as well as you,' Abbajaan told her.

Zubeida Khaala didn't think Abba's comment merited a reply and merely snorted.

'All right, all right, I'll keep a cook. How about that?'

'So you tolerated me all these years only because I was a cook?'

'I give up. Stop being so obstinate, Zubeida. Don't disappoint the children.'

'It's my house, Zafar. Don't you forget that.'

That put an end to the discussion. It was the first time that Zubeida had ever mentioned that the Suleiman Mansion flat was hers. Even Amanat, who sometimes had a sixth sense about things, had not known about it.

'Yes it is, Zubeida. And I never forget it.'

Zubeida Khaala put out her hand and almost touched Zafar but not quite. 'How would I leave you, Zafar?'

There was a terrible silence in the air. They had not got around to talking about Ammijaan all these years and they were not about to do it today.

Sagari was much more reserved and aloof now. Not with Amanat or the family, but generally. She had to be. She was not number one or two or three, but she was a star, and anywhere she went, she was mobbed. She worked eight-hour shifts, though if the film set had to be dismantled the next day, she put in an extra hour or two or sometimes an entire extra shift. Sundays were time off, but she was often out of town on a shoot. If she was going to an interesting place, either in India or abroad, she would ask Amanat to come along. Sometimes he accompanied her, but not often. Wherever she went she got him a gift, at least that was the case in the beginning. She bought him a shirt, the multicoloured sand from Kanyakumari, a book, a chip from the million-year-old bark of a tree from the petrified forest near Jaisalmer.

Wrist watches and fountain pens, as Sagari had learnt over the years, were a no-no. The first he never wore. He had thin wrists and watches, he felt, looked like grandfather clocks on him. He had had a weakness for fountain pens as a child. They'd had a large collection of pens at Firdaus: Parkers, Mont Blancs, Sheaffers, Dunhills, Yves Saint Laurents. He would watch Abbajaan clean them in water and polish them with a velvet cloth on Sunday mornings.

When he lost a cheap ballpoint, Amanat was bereft. He went around moping for days and turning the house upside down searching for it. He'd know he was behaving absurdly but that wouldn't alter anything. One day he couldn't find the Parker Sagari had bought him when they got married. That was the end. He was in a foul mood for weeks. He retraced his steps to all the places he'd possibly visited before he lost the Parker. He went to the Lost and Found offices of the BEST bus service and the taximen's union. After that he forbade Sagari from buying him pens. Soon he ruled out presents altogether. Abstinence would not be his ruling principle in life but it wouldn't do him any harm if he denied himself a few things and lived more austerely. He didn't want to be caught with his pants down if he had to move to Suleiman Mansion again.

The move to the duplex apartment, the view of the sea, the space and the quiet had a quickening effect on Amanat. He couldn't wait for Sagari to leave in the mornings, and went to his table in a state of repressed excitement. He was taking a break from fiction and trying his hand at a play, more like a bawdy, riotous opera. The action takes place at Big Mama's, a bordello whose motto is 'Home Never Felt So Good'. Big Mama's is the place to meet, be seen in and cut deals if you want to do anything slightly, or preferably entirely, illicit.

Big Mama has just one heir, a daughter called Tarangini, Tara for short, who's at a finishing school in Switzerland. The play opens with Tara's return to India. From her bedroom window on the first floor she sings a lusty song. She has been waiting for years for this day, she croons, when she'll be initiated into the family business by being auctioned to the highest bidder. The glitterati, actors, tycoons, politicians, businessmen and the mafia who gather at Big Mama's have known her from childhood and they love her dearly. When Tara enters, there's absolute silence. No one, but no one, bids for her. She's so ordinary, she would make Plain Jane look like a sex bomb. It is a truly tragic moment, an existential crisis when Tara will become wise to the ways of the world. Only one young man thinks she is a houri. He is Popatlal, the son of the mafia boss Pyarelal. It is Popatlal's misfortune that his father detests him as much as Big Mama adores her daughter.

On the advice of Pyarelal and the ancient media tycoon Bhushan Jani, Big Mama sends Tara to study business management at Wharton. Before she leaves, Tara and Popatlal sing a song that alternates between her swearing vengeance and Popatlal passionately confessing his love for her and begging her not to leave. Tara takes an oath to return and lay low every Indian male, good, bad and indifferent. She promises to take the Miss Cosmos title when she gets back. Tara is a woman of her word. She returns to India with an MBA summa cum laude and the biggest pair of knockers known to man or woman. She's ready to compete for the Miss Cosmos crown. She looks like a billion dollars, and she certainly mouths the platitudes and phoney sentiments expected of a Miss Cosmos with more oomph and conviction than the rest of the line-up. But Bhushan Jani, the 83-year-old media tycoon, casts his vote against her, and she's awarded merely the runner-up prize.

This is the last straw. Tara is out for vengeance again, only this time the crown is no less than the mummified Bhushan Jani himself. Popatlal courts Tara assiduously while getting rid of his father and taking charge of the underworld. But Tara seduces Bhushan Jani, marries him and gets him to change his will: his entire estate now goes to her and not to his children. When the tycoon shows no signs of dying, she gets the disappointed Popatlal to bump him off with the promise that she'll marry him. Instead she sends him to jail for her husband's murder and is finally Queen of the Cosmos.

The play went into rehearsals but never saw the light of day. Hardly anybody except the young director and the actors had read it, but the fundamentalist Hindu parties claimed it was a travesty of Hindu traditions and threatened anybody who was associated with it with dire consequences. Muslims were incensed because there was a suggestion in the play that Tara's unnamed father might have been a Muslim politician. Luckily for Amanat, *Queen of the Cosmos* was invited to 'The Other Theatre Festival' in San Francisco. Rehearsals started again, though this time clandestinely in Sagari and Amanat's flat. That was when the media empire that had the largest circulation in the country, and sponsored beauty contests, began to write editorial after editorial in its papers savaging the play and its author. The night before the theatre group was due to leave for San Francisco, the government banned the play.

Amanat thought that he had written a rambunctious piece of theatre that would unsettle people. He was no longer so sure. Maybe there was something perverted about him. He had always traced his lineage to Rabelais, to the now nearly extinct tradition of bawdy Indian folk theatre. Maybe he had got it wrong; maybe he was confusing the ribald and bawdy with his own depravity.

Or the simple truth might be that he never really had been any good. He had a small coterie of loyal readers but he could not draw much solace from that. They could be just as mistaken as he. Maybe he had been deceiving himself all along. Genuine talent can be ignored once, twice, even thrice, but after that you had better do some major introspection and come to terms with the truth: if you didn't amount to much, you might as well learn to live with it.

He started watching movies at home. He would wait till Sagari left for work and then run over to the video shop at the bottom of the hill and pick up five or six films. There wasn't much likelihood of his being able to finish seeing the lot in ten hours, but he was terrified that Sagari's shooting would be delayed and he would be left without anything to watch.

He watched anything and everything. If there was no new English film, he watched Hindi movies. He disliked most of the stuff and loathed himself for watching it, but he couldn't stop. At twenty to six he would call Sagari and ask casually how she was doing, but his only motive was to check when she would be back. If she was on her way home, he would turn off the DVD player and sit at his table pretending to write. He had no idea why he needed to dissemble, for Sagari was hardly likely to ask him how much work he had done that day. Without realizing it, Amanat had begun a life of prevarication with his wife.

What he dreaded most were the times when Sagari sensed that everything was not as placid and hunky-dory as Amanat made it out to be, and tried to cheer him up.

'They are fools, Amanat, utter fools. What does it matter if they appreciate you or not, or recognize your talent? I know that you are a good writer, one of the very rare good ones, and that should count for something.

'I'm so proud of you, Amanat. Ten, twenty years from now, perhaps after both of us are dead, they are going to realize that your work is timeless. You write, Amanat, that's all you need to do.'

He would look at her and put on a grateful smile that was also meant to be affectionate, wondering all the while if goodness of heart, a state of innocence really, made someone like Sagari impervious to ordinary human wants and needs. Get real, Sagari, I don't give a fig for the great rewards that lie in wait for me twenty or thirty years down the road or in the afterlife. I could do with a little recognition and money here and now. Money I earned with my own work so that I don't always have to look to you for it. But there was no way he could ever say it to her. It would devastate her that he thought of money as his and hers. He didn't, honest to goodness he didn't. All he wanted was some notice and acknowledgement of his contribution to whatever; a lunatic take on the lunacies of his people and country and perhaps a chance to laugh at himself and his fellow-men, and what it meant to be living on the cusp of the twenty-first century.

He was too polite to ask how she would feel if four or five of her movies flopped in a row. Though with Sagari it was safer not to probe. She would very likely say, 'It would have been good if a couple had done well at the box office. But that's okay really. I've been missing teaching and now I'll have a chance to finish my PhD.' And she would mean it too.

Amanat and Sagari had two servants at home, one to do the cooking and the other one for cleaning and washing and pressing the clothes.

They were not overtly defiant or disobedient but they did whatever Amanat asked for in an oblique fashion, making it a point to fall just a little short of his instructions. The idea was to make sure that he knew that they were aware of who was the breadwinner in the family.

Sagari's secretary, Rakesh Trivedi, came over around ten in the morning and went directly to the room that served as Sagari's office. He was the de facto boss of the house. The cook gave him breakfast and the account for the previous day's expenses. He paid the servants' and driver's salaries, ticked them off and decided when they could go on leave to their homes in Bihar or Nepal. He was on the phone most of the time, receiving or making calls. He decided Sagari's shooting schedules and gave appointments for script, make-up, hairdressing and photo sessions. He filtered information, requests for donations, appearances and interviews, calls from fans, admirers and cranks. Sometimes Amanat had the impression that Rakesh Trivedi filtered him out of existence too.

It was his way of making it clear that Amanat was of no consequence, an opinion that Amanat shared without reservation.

# 35

The sky had hung out a week's worth of laundry to dry: polo shirts, panties, halters, jeans, windcheaters, shirts, saris and linen. If only the clothes would stop fluttering and making a racket, you would see the apostles and the saints, Jesus and his mother, through the transparent blue, and perhaps even overhear their conversations. When Terraferra was beautiful, it was the next best thing to paradise. You could feel your soul lift up and sing hosannas to God. Two of the brothers, the twins Leonardo and Michael, were actually singing not a psalm but a Bruce Springsteen song as they cleaned the glass panes of the refectory. Lucens looked enviously at them as he entered the church. He didn't give a fig for the picture-perfect day, and if he hadn't been watching himself, he would have wished a pox on the world, starting with the twins. He sat in his pew and tried to pray. The words were bereft of meaning. He took out the Abbot's letter and read it again.

Dear Lucens,

Two months ago I could not have imagined that I would have to write a letter to one of my brothers at the Abbey when I could walk over and talk to him. But there is a gravitas in writing that is lacking in a face-to-face meeting. I hope and pray that this note will bring home to you the seriousness of the subject I'm about to touch upon and make you give it your deepest consideration. The subject is no less than the fate and future of your soul, not just as a monk but even more fundamentally, as a human being.

You have been a blessing to the Abbey, Brother Lucens, but as I've discovered over the years, not an unmixed one. It was nothing short of an unusual grace that Jesus chose you as the instrument for saving the Abbey and building it anew from scratch. But there is, I believe, a pernicious streak in you. It destroys whomever it falls upon, and it brutalizes you. I believe if you do not confront and check it now, it could jeopardize, even destroy, the life and peace of our Abbey.

I suspect, Lucens, that you think of our vocation as a race and you wish to outrun every other monk. Your humility is as overreaching as your need for forgiveness is insatiable. You must pray more, fast more, work more, hanker for God more, deprive and flagellate yourself more than anybody else. The Novice Master warned you repeatedly against the hubris of humbleness but to no avail. Our Lord Jesus is not an Olympic medal that you can wear around your neck, Lucens. He must love us all equally, saints and sinners, or not love at all.

As with all extremes, there is a downside to your goodness; a kind of schizophrenia that pushes you towards evil. There is a pleasure that you take in inflicting pain that is both horrible and terrifying. The saddest part is that you justify all your intolerance and rage in the name of morality. And yet you find yourself unable to tell the difference between right and wrong at critical moments. You abuse trust not because you are devious but because you are not aware that you are doing something reprehensible.

It is righteousness, self-righteousness, I fear more than the sins and follies of a monk like Brother Jonathan-Christophe. Do you know what the Buddha said? Ye must leave righteous ways behind, not to mention unrighteous ways.

Not once but again and again Jonathan asked for your forgiveness. He said he would do anything to earn your forgiveness. And what was your response? What forgiveness can there be when you've defiled the very body and blood of Christ?

Whence this boundless arrogance, Lucens? If you continue heedlessly down this road, you'll end up usurping the privileges and prerogatives of God Himself. It is not up to you to judge or punish anyone including yourself. It is the Lord's right and the Lord's alone to punish. And as He made clear even on the cross, He prefers forgiveness to vengeance.

Do you think that the Pope himself and the bishops are not aware of the fact that many priests today have illicit liaisons? That there are clandestine societies of Catholic priests who have long-term relationships with women? Do you feel that the Church is busy pushing its dirt under the carpet? Or are you even more cynical and think that the Church's attitude is: if you don't acknowledge it, it does not exist? I'm sure there would be more than a grain of truth in that sentiment. And yet I would not doubt that the good Pope himself, even as he reprimands these priests, believes that the business of judging is best left in the hands of God.

The moment of enlightenment, the real breakthrough for a monk as for anyone else, is when you begin to appreciate that God loves you despite your failings and flaws. The mystery is that God loves us even when we are unworthy.

Have you looked at the Resurrection frieze Zafar did for the Abbey closely? Almost half the monks, and not just the ones who are glibly clubbed as the conservatives, have written to the Chief Abbot of our Order and the Holy See to have it removed. They think it is heretical since it is Judas whose grief and perfidy Mary assuages. Perhaps you feel the same way. Some have even asked for my removal just as they did when the proposal for admitting women into our retreat houses was first broached.

I wonder what Jesus makes of people like Zafar and your brother Amanat. They may or may not believe in God and yet can often be more godly than all of us who chant His name and make a song and dance of the flesh and blood of Christ but will not follow His example. How can Jesus not smile and walk in their company?

When you came to the Abbey the first time, the Novice Master and I asked you why you wanted to change your religion, become a Catholic and a Trappist monk. Your answers were lucid enough and yet can words ever explain something as intangible and mysterious as faith?

We know that Paul, the one who hated Jesus, saw a white light and became a disciple. All that the white light tells us is that something happened, something that changed the very nature of his soul.

God works in curious ways, I told myself, and if you had heard the call, who was I to refuse you? But if you think that by joining the monkhood, you'll elude your past, you are wrong. I do not say this lightly: the Abbey is where all your errors, flaws and sins come home to roost. A monk's life has only one dual purpose: get to know yourself and then know your God.

I find ultimatums offensive. Time and again I've asked you to take heed and you've ignored my warnings. There's a point after which leniency becomes counterproductive, even harmful. Now I'm left with little option but to tell you that this is your last chance to stay on at the Abbey.

There are two paths before you. Perhaps I did not understand the needs of your mind. After working all hours trying to save the Abbey, you were suddenly left with nothing to do. It may still be possible to rectify that. The Diocese in Sweet Waters, for instance, has been asking for someone to help them out with their accounting and financial management and you could spend three afternoons a week helping them. The Bishop's assistant, Father Nicholas, keeps the books there, but he's no wizard with numbers and I'm sure he'll be happy to get some expert advice. God willing, the work may help to steady you and give you time to ask yourself whether you are suited to the monk's vocation. God willing, you may yet become a better and more caring monk.

On the other hand your gifts may lie in an altogether different direction. God may have chosen you with your special talents in the field of economics to tilt the balance towards the poor and the deprived, especially in the Third World.

Think about it, Lucens. Reflect. Seek guidance from Jesus. And then come to me with your answer.

God bless you.

Your friend and Abbot,

Reverend Father Augustine

There hadn't been any Pauline white light, but Zia did know the exact moment of his conversion. He had come back a month before to Indian-occupied Kashmir, from Kandahar, all fired up by an advanced course in the Sharia, the Islamic law. It was a freak winter. It had been snowing for eleven days running, the only change now being a blizzard that trawled the landscape for anything still standing – trees, huts and barns, flagpoles and electric towers, cars, buses, fences, air-traffic control posts, men, women and cattle – and uprooted and relocated them within a radius of five to seven miles. When the gale finally died down, everybody ventured out for a bit of fresh air, and to shop for groceries. This was the only chance they had to stretch their legs as a second blizzard came unannounced. All the passes were unpassable. Road and air traffic had long since ground to a halt. The Indian army and the various security forces were marooned in their quarters in the cities and hamlets. The break was good for them. It was a long time since they had had a chance to relax, write letters home or watch TV.

Fat, sleepy snowflakes fell like seamless swathes of lace. Zia wondered how many feet of snow had fallen in the last few weeks. The mountains seemed to sink under its weight as though they might collapse any moment now.

The wind whistled and soughed, twirling the snow around an invisible spindle that flew across the stark wastelands. There must be some word, Zia thought, in Inuit or one of the other Eskimo languages, for snow that had suction pads attached to it. Every step he and his men took was a descent into a bottomless quagmire. Zia was aware that he had blundered but it was a little late to retreat. Going back would mean climbing uphill and that would be far more difficult, if not impossible. Besides, he was not about to admit to that damned beggar, who never left his side, that he had been right.

'How long will you continue on this murderous path, Zia? Come, it's time you made peace with yourself.'

'The only way I'll have some peace, is if I could be rid of you.'

'Don't go, Zia, you and your men are at grave risk.'

'Keep your bloody voodoo to yourself. Every time I set out on a job you put a hex on it. Get it through your head, I'm never going to listen to you.'

Zia had felt no regrets about having ignored the beggar. All he could do at that point was to beseech Allah that his foolhardiness would not cost him the lives of his men.

He discovered that the worst thing they could do was to resist prematurely the drag of the fresh snow. He closed his eyes and let his mind take readings of the tow. There was a pattern to it: plunge, plateau, plunge, plateau. The trick was to extract the leg from the deepening hole just as the foot came to rest for a brief, almost imperceptible moment, and then take the next step instantly.

Visibility had dropped further in the last hour, but Zia surmised that they had nearly reached their destination. The five villages collectively called Puncham clung desperately to the angled ledge of the mountain, always on the verge of slithering into the valley some nine thousand feet below. It was past 2 a.m. They had been out in the blinding weather for seven and a half hours now.

Zia had planned this operation for weeks. The purpose of the endless drills and rehearsals was to eliminate conscious thought from the performance of their exercises. Each move would be as involuntary as breathing. Zia waited for half an hour before doing a count. Thirty-four. Fleetingly he reflected that he would never forgive himself for losing the thirty-fifth man, Yunus, in the snow, but this was not the time for a post-mortem.

'Remember,' Zia said, 'secure the horses first. Whatever the problem, even at the risk of death, do not fire a single shot.'

They knelt down and prayed to Allah to bless their mission, divided into five groups and dispersed. Zia's party of six, the seventh one would have been Yunus, headed for the last of the five villages in the eastern corner of the shelf. When they had safely corralled all the horses they could find, Zia shot a flare into the sky. It was time.

The men bolted the doors of the houses from outside, broke windowpanes, flung lit torches through, and waited. The snow kept coming down while the flames leapt up to embrace it. It was a surreal sight, the sparks and the white flakes interweaving and then fusing into each other. With knives, daggers and swords, Zia and his men took care of the few people who managed to jump out of the windows.

When they finished, they met up once again in the first village. It had stopped snowing. The other men were already busy roasting five goats on spits. They ate well. It had been a good sortie. None of Zia's men had suffered injuries. Not only the Indian media but the international press and TV channels would be sure to cover the story. Three hundred and fifty-three dead including one hundred and sixty-four women and children. Zia sent three men to get the horses, and was checking the ground to see whether the snow had really hardened enough for them to ride home, when the Indian army opened fire. He took two hits, one in the thigh and the other in the chest. He cursed himself as he fell. How stupid, how unforgivably stupid of him to think that Yunus had been a victim of the blizzard. He scanned the faces of the enemy as he lay inert. Yunus had been wise. He had refrained from joining the hunt.

There was mayhem. Thirty-four well-aimed shots would have been enough, but the Indians kept firing for a full ten minutes, maybe longer. Suddenly there was a low, loud unearthly sound, and the peaks and the ground underneath shook. After that everything seemed to Zia to be happening in a drugged stupor. Half the mountain detached itself, hung suspended in the air for a long, long second and then began to tumble and somersault down. The avalanche was gaining speed, racing down unstoppably.

Zia's mind went back to Yunus. He understood now that the army had waited and watched while the mujahideen burnt and slaughtered the villagers. Obviously they must have believed that the Puncham residents were Pakistani sympathizers, maybe even enemy agents.

But how could he, Zia, have got things so wrong, so utterly wrong? His sole source of information had been his right-hand man and deputy, Yunus. Yunus Habib had done the research and the scouting and had chosen the Puncham villages as their target. He might have betrayed Zia and his men, but the blame, Zia knew, was his and his alone.

He deserved to die like a dog at the hands of the Indians. He had no regrets about that. All his anger and bitterness revolved around the fact that he could not dismember Yunus limb by limb before he breathed his last. And here was that wretched beggar again, shaking his long bearded face.

'Zia, Zia why persecutest thou me?'

What Zia hated most was his melancholy eyes and pathetic martyred airs. 'Damn you, you put a jinx on this operation from the beginning.'

'How much more blood wouldst thou spill before thine heart seeks forgiveness?'

'You'd need to give me a second life for that, wouldn't you?' Zia's derisive laughter was swallowed up even as one side of the snowy mountain rolled down gathering together the men of the Indian army, Zia's colleagues and Zia himself.

When he came to, he was lying pinned under a pine tree. Three of his men, the ones who had gone to collect the horses, were kneeling by his side.

'My chest hurts so much I can't breathe,' Zia whispered.

'Allah be praised that your chest hurts. You must have broken a few ribs. The snow-slide took everyone with it, the Indians as well as our people. You were lucky you crashed into the tree. It broke your fall.'

Lucens walked out of the church and ran smack into the panel of the Resurrection. How unobservant he had been. His first error lay in not having scrutinized the low relief closely. But even so, how could he possibly have missed the central, the most obvious and outrageous feature of the sculpture? You had to be blind not to notice the haunted guilt and remorse and fear in Judas's face as he clung to the Virgin's knees. As though that were not plain enough, Zafar Khan had made the rest of the apostles draw away from him, and even from the Virgin, with revulsion, as though his very presence would defile them. You had to hand it to Abba; the beguiling nature of his art was such that even a hostile observer like Lucens had found the most seditious part of the sculpture engaging.

Lucens was going down the steps when something made him turn around and look at the Resurrection again. Nothing had changed. Jesus still looked as if he were about to step out magisterially from the sculpture and stride across the grounds of the Abbey. Dear Zubeida Khaala, Abba couldn't have chosen a more archetypal Virgin Mary. He couldn't figure out what was troubling him; must be the strange frame of mind that the Abbot's letter had put him in, he thought. And then his peripheral vision registered a blur that made him stop. That was no Judas, it was Lucens. There was no mistaking it. Oh, the shock of it. It was not Lucens but Abba who had betrayed his family from the very beginning. He had had them thrown out of their home and reduced them to penury; he had most likely had an affair with Aunt Antonia when he was pretending to be married to Ammi. And now his father had had the gall to petrify Lucens for all time as Judas in his own home and church. Abbajaan would have to pay for this.

He would take care of his father, but not now. Right now, he had more urgent matters that needed his attention. The letter. Lucens had finally figured out the Abbot. It was obvious, the Reverend Father was nothing but a confused liberal. Mercy was certainly one of Jesus's qualities. Compassion, love and forgiveness, those were the great leaps the New Testament had taken over the Old. But Jesus was never namby-pamby or weak. When the occasion called for it, he was severe, wrathful, unforgiving. Recall the dudgeon he was in with the shopkeepers and vendors in the temple, not to mention the priests. He threw them out bag and baggage. He was one against so many but that did not deter him. He was not afraid. He swung into action and settled matters in the most unequivocal manner possible.

It was one thing to be silent about Judas, as Jesus was, quite another for the Virgin to give him succour after what he had done to her son. No wonder the Abbot was such an admirer of Abbajaan and, as Lucens had discovered, of Amanat too. But Father Augustine did not simply indulge in woolly thinking and do-gooding, he was a dangerous monk. He was willing to tolerate homoeroticism in the Abbey. As far as Lucens could make out, he had not even bothered to check whether the rot had spread, whether Jonathan-Christophe had partners in his sin in the Abbey itself.

To think that yesterday, when Lucens had first read the letter, he had been set to grovel before Reverend Father and to beg him for one more chance, just one more. He had blindly believed in the Abbot's greater wisdom and had been taken in by all that Jesus-as-an-Olympic-medal and the schizophrenic rubbish. Now, humility itself was suspect. You couldn't ever be right with this Abbot unless you were morally wrong and openly venal. It was time to mutiny for the sake of the Abbey. Fortunately, Reverend Father himself had furnished him with the wherewithal. Lucens wasn't quite sure why the Abbot had mentioned the bit about Abbajaan's Resurrection. Perhaps it was to garner Lucens's support against the other monks since he knew something about painting. Add to that, and this may have been the primary consideration, the artist was his father, and that would seal his loyalty. But there was one small error in that calculation. Lucens owed his loyalty to none but his Lord God. Clearly it was the will of God working in mysterious ways that had led the Abbot to play into his hands. There was a revolt brewing at Terraferra but it would fizzle out, like previous ones before Lucens's time, when the Abbot had given his okay to two movies a year, a class where

Catholic and non-Catholic authors, some of them highly controversial, were discussed, and of course the business about the women retreatants. But things were going to be different this time.

If the Abbot was to be unseated, then the campaign to oust him would have to be well-planned, orchestrated carefully with other Trappist monasteries in the rest of the country, and executed with tact and finesse. What Lucens had to bear in mind was that it would take time, and a great deal of patience.

2nd April: No religious in his senses would recommend insurgency or dissidence. It goes against the very basis of the monastic life. But what should one do when the canker runs so deep that the shepherd himself is tainted, and morally unfit to lead? The history of the Cistercians, including the Trappists from the earliest times, shows that when the rot in the Order becomes intolerable, the only way to cleanse the community is to rebel and reform.

I will not evade my duty. I will take charge of the good monks and transform them into moral dissenters. I must do this unobtrusively, and shape and sharpen the demand for the Abbot's removal.

It's not going to be easy. It's been attempted only very, very rarely. I know that my brother monks, as usual, will want to back out halfway through. They'll protest that they do not wish to sully the reputation of the Order. But I must stand my ground, for I know that I tread the righteous path. Nobody, however, wants a confrontation, least of all me. All I want is a strong and tradition-loving Abbot, instead of a weak one, as head of the Abbey.

My dear 1001,

It has taken me some years but I cannot be at peace till I've told you the truth, the truth about why Sagari stopped coming over to our place when I was in India the last time and behaving foully with everyone. What I am about to say is shameful but I owe it to you to come clean about it. I want you to understand that Sagari is innocent.

I don't see much point in going into details but will come directly to what concerns you. Sagari knew that I was disturbed and tried to help me in any way she could, though she had no idea about what had gone wrong. To put the record straight, I too was unaware at the time that you were responsible for my state of mind.

I used to meet her off and on, and one weekend I asked her to go to Matheran with me. It was the only hill station I knew in India that does not allow cars and I thought the quiet and the solitude would do us both good. Sagari was reluctant to come but I told her she owed it to me. I suggested that we could go for long walks, commune with the hills, talk freely or be silent and I could gradually regain a sense of equilibrium. Sagari is not a fool but she is trusting and believed me.

It was not a trip I remember with any pleasure. I forced myself upon her. She resisted but I would not let her go until she finally gave in. She did not talk to me after that and we left the next morning.

I beg your forgiveness for the way I behaved and the pain I caused, though you were not in the picture then.

Now you know the truth, I feel much better and a great burden is off my mind.

Yours, etc.,

Lucens

# 36

'What I would recommend,' Sahil Thapar told Amanat, 'is that we keep this under our hat and don't speak of turning *The Arsonist* into a film till it's done. Or at least till we start shooting.'

Yes, yes, yes. See, Sagari had got it wrong. Thapar was not just another Bollywood film producer. Sure, he was a good businessman, Amanat hoped so for all their sakes, but he was sensitive and understood both the nature of *The Arsonist* and Amanat's temperament. He himself wouldn't talk about a book he was working on till he had finished it. And he was grateful that Sahil Thapar wouldn't talk about the movie till it was finished or at least well underway.

Thapar wanted Amanat to ascertain for himself whether the two of them shared the same values and wanted the same kind of movie made of *The Arsonist*. They talked around the subject for a good two months when Sahil suggested bringing Sudhin Sen on board as director. Sen had made several Bengali films that were considered an ideal blend of the commercial and the artistic and had gone on to become blockbusters. Amanat had seen some of them. They were well-intentioned and slickly produced but they were also simplistic and manipulative. Sen, Thapar said, wanted to make an out and out, no-holds-barred, Oscar-entry film now, and thought *The Arsonist* should be the film to earn him an international reputation. Amanat was wary of him but Thapar was persistent.

'He's made compromises, I'm not denying that, but he was making commercial films then. Now he wants to make a clean break from formula films.'

Sudhin was coming into town from Calcutta on the weekend. That would give the three of them a chance to meet and let Amanat decide whether he thought Sudhin was the right man to direct the film. Two days later Sagari came beaming into the bedroom with a heap of Sunday newspapers and flung her arms around him.

'Your picture's in every newspaper.'

The news about *The Arsonist* was either on the bottom half of the front page or had made banner headlines in the movie supplements. 'Sahil, Sudhin and Author Amanat to Make New Kind of Movie'; 'Look out Oscars, here comes *The Arsonist*'; 'Revolution in Indian Cinema'; 'Bollywood Goes Literary'. Amanat was livid. He couldn't understand what Sagari was crowing about. It was Sahil Thapar who had suggested of his own accord that they keep a lid on the filming of *The Arsonist*. He was also on record, well, not in writing, but he had said clearly that he would ask Sudhin to come to Bombay so that Amanat could develop a feel for the man and his commitment to *The Arsonist* before deciding whether he wanted to work with him or not. Thapar must have organized a press conference the very next day.

The phone had been ringing without a pause: Abbajaan and Zubeida Khaala had called to congratulate Amanat; the regular press and film magazines wanted interviews; the Indian publisher of *The Arsonist* was wondering if this was the right time to reissue the book. Even Sagari's secretary, Rakesh Trivedi, felt the need to congratulate sir.

'Have you seen the papers?' Sahil Thapar called at nine. 'We are all over the place. You mark my words, Sudhin, you and I are going to change the face of the industry.

'The problem, Amanat, has always been that we've had good directors, lyricists, composers, even actors. What we have lacked is good, solid screenplay writers. You can't make great movies without great screenplays. I mean original screenplays. It's as simple as that. I'll be the catalyst, Amanat, and give you and Sudhin the wherewithal to make world-class cinema.'

Sahil was talking a blue streak and nothing was going to stop him from making Bollywood, instead of the old and exhausted Hollywood, the centre of the New Cinema. It may have been mostly about Thapar spearheading the revolution, but Amanat was slowly warming up to the idea that he was part of the avant-garde. He was no longer unhappy about the attention the press was according him.

'What are you doing tonight?' Thapar asked.

'Nothing special.'

'Why don't you and Sagari join us for dinner? I've called some people I would like you to meet. Sudhin will be there too.'

Sagari was waving frantically to Amanat to say no but he had already accepted the invitation.

Amanat was surprised at how thoroughly Sudhin Sen and Sahil Thapar had done their homework. They knew their *Arsonist*, and Sudhin's analysis of him had intriguing possibilities. The problem, as Sen put it, was to find the emotional co-ordinates for the intellectual content of the book: how to make the audience feel the breath of the characters on their cheeks and the heat of the arsonist's torch on their flesh; how to make them laugh and yet force them to think about the uncomfortable stuff: follow a guru and let him take all the decisions for you or put the onus of one's life on oneself? In short, what they had to come up with was a narrative strategy that would involve the viewer from the very start.

Amanat would have to wait and watch but so far they had been professional, and he had to admit that he was beginning to enjoy working with them. Thapar could get rather carried away when talking about his contribution to the changes that had occurred in Indian cinema. Sudhin was the dapper type. He had shoulder-length hair that he tied in a ponytail with a rubber band. He was always in black: black T-shirt or button-down collar and black jeans or cords. He was tight-fisted and tight-arsed. He was watchful, always on his guard, wondering whether you were going to touch him for a meal, his light-sensitive Armani glasses, or for the rights to his next film.

They decided to meet in a fortnight to discuss their ideas on the narrative strategy. Three days later Sahil Thapar was on the line.

'We need the screenplay within a month. We start shooting in February.'

'I thought we decided to meet in a couple of weeks.'

'There's been a change in plans. We want to enter the film in the Competition Section at Cannes next year and pick up gold there. There's no time to waste. I suggest you get cracking. Sudhin or I will call you in a week to see when we can look at the first draft.'

Cannes? What were these guys talking about? Only one Indian feature film had walked away with an award at Cannes, Ray's *Pather Panchali*, and that had been almost half a century ago. Thapar couldn't be serious. Besides, what about the narrative voice? Were they leaving it to him to come up with a solution? Amanat was filled with a strange mix of terror and exhilaration.

Amanat did not hear from Sahil Thapar or Sudhin Sen for the next fourteen months. For once, he'd believed, luck was on his side. He had cracked the problem of 'the point of view' and 'narrative voice', and worked steadily at the screenplay for the next three weeks. What he needed urgently then was feedback. He called Sahil Thapar's office. The woman who was the secretary or the manager of the Bombay office, he could never tell which, was friendly and polite. Mr Thapar was abroad; Mr Thapar was at a shoot in Jaisalmer; Mr Thapar was not taking any calls; Mr Thapar was holidaying in Nainital but I'll make sure that he gets your message. He called Sudhin on his cell phone and was informed by a prerecorded woman's voice in a foreign accent that the person he had dialled was unavailable at the moment but he could leave a message if he wanted.

Amanat, as was his wont, kept changing, fine-tuning and revising the *Arsonist* screenplay while he waited for Sahil or Sudhin to show up or call. He refused to talk about either the screenplay or their inexplicable behaviour to Sagari because she would be her bloody decent self and never say 'I told you so'. He could have done with sympathy, actually he wanted to throw a magnum-sized tantrum, but he was damned if he was going to let that woman know how Thapar and Sen had kept him hanging for months without a word, destroying whatever fragment of self-esteem he had left. Their conduct was so alien, he could not come to grips with it. Nor did he know how to cope with it. Should he write them an abusive letter? Should he threaten them? though he had no idea with what. If only they would come back, come back on all fours, he would keep them waiting a few years and then demand some absurdly exorbitant recompense before even considering whether he would go back to the screenplay. Amanat laughed hollowly. He well knew they would not come back.

He closed his roll-top desk and went back to video watching, and his new obsession: party-going. He had not given it a thought, but he knew he would never write again.

# 37

The first meeting between Father Nicholas, the Bishop's assistant at the Diocese in Sweet Waters, and Lucens did not go well. That by itself would not have bothered Lucens. He knew it could be intimidating if his reputation as a genius in statistics and economics preceded him. It would also be perfectly understandable if Father Nicholas was a little exercised about some young twerp from the Trappist monastery at Terraferra coming down to look over his shoulder and explain the maths of accounting to him.

But that was not it. Father Nicholas had not only taken an instant dislike to Lucens, he seemed to mock him with condescension as though he thought Lucens a fool. Where was this resentment coming from? They had not met before nor had they had any dealings with each other. Other priests from the Diocese would come up to the Abbey once in a while; sometimes they would say Mass or spend a week on retreat, but never Father Nicholas. How could the priest detest a man he had never set eyes on?

Well, Father Nicholas was welcome to be as perverse as he wanted, Lucens would not respond. It was possible the Abbot had poisoned the priest's mind with stories about him, but he had obviously underestimated Lucens. When he chose to, Lucens could charm stones, the elements, the rose bushes at Terraferra or his worst enemies. He would take up Father Nicholas as a challenge. He would win him over with one of the oldest and least practised tactics of diplomacy: he had come to proffer advice; instead he would seek guidance. Come what may, he was going to win over this dour and sullen priest.

He let Father Nicholas be. He kept his distance and yet was always within easy reach. It didn't take him long to get a feel for the politics and dynamics of the Bishopric. From Father Nicholas's oblique references to his superior, Lucens gathered that, like many an exalted man of God, Bishop Sanger was rarely in town. He liked to think of Rome as his home and it was taken for granted that the next time the Pontiff spread his largesse, he would make Bishop Sanger a cardinal. It was rather unfortunate, but so far His Grace had not fallen upon the Bishop of Sweet Waters. But the spiritual overseer of the Diocese was not one to lose heart or hope easily, and had redoubled his efforts.

For a while Lucens toyed with the theory that Father Nicholas's alienation could be traced to his boss. It was more than possible that the Bishop was sensitive to the needs of those above him and despotic with his inferiors. But he soon realized his mistake. Bishop Sanger might be ambitious, but it was impossible to dislike him. He was good-natured, jovial and kind; and even more important, he was as much a man of the world as he was a man of God.

Two months passed but Lucens had still not made any progress with Father Nicholas. The priest derailed his every attempt at friendship. Lucens was filled with a strange sense of apprehension. Why had something as routine as auditing the books become so intractable that it impinged on his self-confidence? He could not cope with Father Nick and feared he would slip into the same kind of depression that had paralysed him in his first year at Cambridge.

Luckily, Lucens's clandestine campaign on the home front was more successful. The community of monks at the Abbey, small though it was, represented almost every shade of opinion in Catholic dogma. He knew who stood with the Lord and who sat to His left. But he also knew who his real enemies were in the fight against the Abbot. They were the ones who had no opinion and those who didn't know their minds. His victory would depend on their swing vote. Since he himself would stay in the wings, the rebellion would need a face and a leader, someone who would canvas and convert the vacillators. He found the man in Father Theo who was currently managing the furniture factory.

Father Theo was big and burly with a hail-fellow-well-met, hearty manner about him. He had drive, and the factory was doing well under him. He was, however, not the most popular monk at the Abbey. He was domineering and some of the monks thought he would like to be the Abbot after Reverend Father retired. Ambition was not looked upon kindly at the Abbey, but it was that very quality that made him so eligible for Lucens's purposes. Father Theo did not lean either to the right or to the left. He only tilted towards himself.

'Has there been a change of late in the position of the Church regarding homosexuality, Father?' Lucens asked Father Theo late one afternoon as they were returning from the factory at Halfway, where they met once every month to discuss cash flow, orders and the outlook for the next quarter.

'Not that I know of. I doubt if even the most liberal pontiff in Rome would consider such a step. It would defeat the very purpose of sexual congress, the transmission of life, that the Church has always held sacred. Why this sudden interest in the subject, Lucens?' Father Theo slapped Lucens on the back and a mischievous twinkle came into his eyes. 'Are you about to come out of the closet and declare yourself?'

Lucens ignored Father Theo's little jest. 'I guess Reverend Father penalized me only because he was upset, not for any other reason.'

'Punished you? For what?'

Lucens looked uncomfortable and spoke reluctantly. 'He thought I was wrong to tell Brother Jonathan that homosexuality was a mortal sin in the eyes of our Lord.'

'That's not possible.'

'Do you remember the time I was confined to my room? Everybody thought I had taken a vow of silence for a fortnight to cleanse myself. I had not. Reverend Father had grounded me. He now wishes me to examine my conscience and decide whether I'm fit to stay on in the Abbey.'

Lucens did not pursue the conversation further. The intention was to sow a thought that would fester and ferment for a while, and then, with a little bit of stirring, come to a boil. After that it was to be hoped that Father Theo would take over and the campaign against the Abbot gather momentum.

*

Father Nicholas continued to keep Lucens at a distance. He often made it a point to be away on the three days of the week when Lucens was supposed to visit. Lucens could no longer afford to wait. He could perhaps continue to be evasive with the Abbot when he enquired about how the work on the accounts was coming along, but he could hardly play for time with the Internal Revenue Service. The accounts were due within a fortnight. A delay would cost the Diocese a steep fine, and he would be blamed for it.

Lucens was uneasy about confronting Father Nicholas. If his relationship with the Abbot had been a shade more amicable, he would have begged off even at this late stage. He steeled himself and told Father Nicholas that he wanted to see the books.

'So you've finally decided to stop wasting everybody's time and get down to some serious work?' Father Nicholas sneered.

It didn't take Lucens more than half a day to sense that there was something seriously amiss with the accounts. It was obvious that there was major finagling going on at the Bishopric, but what intrigued him was that Father Nicholas had been so cavalier in covering his tracks. It seemed as though he wanted the fraud to be detected. The question was, who was responsible for the misappropriation of funds? Given the dimensions of the defalcation, Lucens was inclined to believe that the Bishop was the culprit. If that was the case, it made sense that Father Nicholas's only hope was that either the IRS or Lucens would cotton on and he would no longer have to cover up for his superior. It would also explain the priest's bitterness against the whole world. But Lucens was reluctant to jump the gun. Until he had got to the bottom of things, Father Nicholas or someone else in the office of the Bishop were just as suspect.

By the next evening he had gone over the books twice.

'I can't reconcile the books, Father Nicholas.' Lucens was brusque and brief. 'There are glaring discrepancies in the accounts that you'll have to explain to me before I can fill out the IRS forms.'

'If you can't do your job, Brother Lucens,' Father Nicholas said tartly, 'I can always ask the Bishop to get somebody more capable.'

'I'm not sure you understand the gravity of the problem. If you don't come clean with me, I can't balance the books and you'll be behind bars.'

'Do you think, Brother Lucens, that I give a drayhorse's fart for your pettifogging figures and the spurious accounting for which you'll send me to jail? My reckoning is with our Lord. Trappists like you can afford to spend a lifetime in prayer and contemplation and not lift a finger or give a damn if right next door in Sweet Waters unborn babes are butchered with impunity daily. I'd be willing to face eternal damnation, can you comprehend that, Brother Lucens? eternal damnation, if I could only dismember that murderer of foetuses, Dr Cornelius Lester, and thus save a few innocent infants.'

Lucens stared at the priest uncomprehendingly. It couldn't be; he didn't say it; it wasn't possible. No Christian in his senses, let alone a Catholic priest, would blaspheme so and willingly jeopardize his soul and invite damnation. But that was just the point. It had finally begun to dawn on Lucens that Father Nick was not, repeat not, in his senses. Then an even grimmer thought occurred to him: the devil had taken possession of Father Nicholas.

Father Nicholas's satanic profanation, however, had a bizarre effect on Lucens. He knew he ought to report the priest to the Bishop, but he kept putting it off. It was as though he had been felled by a terrible blow to the head, but instead of slipping into a terminal coma, he had come awake for the first time. Sure, he loved Jesus more than anything or anybody else in the world and he had devoted himself to a life of prayer and contemplation of the Lord. But the truth was, it was an extraordinarily accomplished act of self-deception. He might pretend to be, no, he might even believe he was a man of God. But it was not God he was after; everything he did was for himself. His sole concern was his own salvation.

What was it that Father Nicholas had said to him? 'I'd be willing to face eternal damnation, can you comprehend that, Brother Lucens? eternal damnation, if I could only...' He sensed that it would be a mistake to take Father Nicholas literally. It was his way of telling Lucens what the unborn children meant to him. It was a figure of speech, a rhetorical escalation of emphasis. What Father Nicholas had done was to raise the ante of that tepid and much abused word 'sacrifice' and to open up the possibility of making life far more meaningful than it had ever been before. Lucens now realized how mistaken he was in his estimation of himself. He had confused aloofness, a cutting off from the commerce and chaos of life, and severity of discipline, with absolute devotion and surrender to God.

But the scales had dropped from his eyes, Father Nicholas had made sure of that. He could now see that he had been merely muddling along, deluding himself that he knew what he was up to. What Father Nicholas had done was to give him both a compass and the loftiest and most difficult ideal available to man. Even in the darkest night of his soul, Lucens would never lose his way now.

# 38

Amanat started reading to Sagari as she sat at her dressing table, removing her make-up. He was done in two hours. Sagari sat there zombie-like, unable or unwilling to react. He could have strangled her but there was no escaping the banal verities of his life. It wasn't working. It was so bad, she would rather sit in silence than tell him the truth. Well, he had better have a shower and get dressed. It was Anil Kapoor's birthday, and though Amanat didn't know him well, he had been invited to the bash, and that was better than facing up to the fact that he was a burnt-out case. Even the finest authors suffered from it without the good fortune of having a kindly soul tell them to shut shop and not write another word. Sagari had told him now in the most eloquent words available to man or woman: silence.

'Who were you thinking of casting as Rani?' Sagari asked as he was about to get into the bathroom.

'Oh, I don't know. Preity Zinta, Rani Mukherjee? Maybe Kajol.'

Sagari's face fell. 'Oh, I see.'

He had wanted to write a screenplay for Sagari, something that would exercise and exploit her talent, something against the grain, since the time she had joined the movies again, but try as he might, his mind seized up and refused to function whenever he thought of it.

'Don't tell me you want to play the thief Rani,' he said offhandedly and closed the bathroom door.

She was banging on the door now. He took his own time opening it.

'What seems to be the problem, dear?' he asked in a Stan Laurel voice of utter innocence.

'What do I care who acts as Rani?'

'That's exactly what I thought. It's not the kind of role you would be interested in.' He paused a minute. 'Though come to think of it, I did write it with you in mind.'

'Amanat, I'm going to eat you alive for what you've put me through.' She tried to pull his hair out but it was so short you could never get hold of it. 'Did you really write it for me? It's such a lovely caper, so tense and tight and so much fun.'

That night in bed she smiled and said softly, 'I think we are going to be okay.'

Amanat thought so too. How could he ever live without his ring of protection?

On the weekend, Sagari read through the screenplay, *Rani and Regina*, again.

'Regina, that's a tough nut to crack. Who's going to play her? If she's not a strong actress, Rani will fall flat.' They were nearly finished casting excepting the role of the additional police commissioner, Regina.

'We've talked about everything except the most crucial point. We need to find a producer and director who can handle this stuff,' Sagari said. 'A caper is like a comedy, far more difficult to pull off than a straight story or tragedy. It's not just timing, it's style and it's got to have verve. I can't think of anybody here who has a clue to what a caper is.'

Amanat sat quietly for a long time.

'Hello, are you there?'

'You are going to be the producer. And I am going to take a shot at direction.'

'Get serious, Amanat.' She looked at him then and shook her head. 'You are serious. Don't even begin to think about it. This is a completely different ball game. The financiers and distributors are a species apart. They'll bankrupt us before we take the first shot and then file a suit against us for all kinds of breaches of contract. You may be talented, but you don't know the first thing about direction. Stay clear of it, my love.'

Amanat dropped the subject. But he was back at it two weeks later.

'Do you think *Rani and Regina* is a commercially viable subject?' he asked Sagari.

'Yes, it is. It doesn't talk down or make compromises, yet it will work anywhere in the world.'

'Then why won't you produce it?'

'Oh Amanat, please don't make me feel more guilty than I already do. I'm clueless about being a producer just as you don't know a thing about direction. I'll make a deal with you. You go to film school, to New York, LA or anywhere you want, finish the director's course there, the full three or four years, and make three or four short films. In the meantime I'll find you a producer. After that you are in business.'

Amanat laughed. 'You don't really expect me to go to film school, do you? What will you do when I'm gone?'

'I'll stay here and work. We'll meet in the holidays and before you know it, you'll have trained to be a director.'

'Come off it, Sagari. I'm too old to go back to school. Those courses are useless anyway. I've seen enough movies and read enough books on films to know what I'm talking about.'

'Quit deluding yourself. Books can't replace hands-on experience. I'll make another suggestion. Become a second or third assistant to a director, do your apprenticeship for two years, become a first assistant director on a couple of movies and you're all set. How about that?'

Amanat shook his head. 'There are no good directors here. I'll work with the wrong people and learn all the wrong things. That's worse than being ignorant. It'll take me a lifetime to unlearn.'

'I can't win against you, Amanat,' Sagari said in a rare fit of exasperation. 'Find yourself a producer and do what you want.'

'I've found myself a producer. I don't need to look anywhere else.'

Sagari clutched her head in her hands and wouldn't look up.

'Do you have any idea what you've begun to sound like in the last four months? My father. Just like you, he wouldn't let go. Day in and day out he badgered and pestered me. Can't you see what's happening to you? There was a time when you couldn't understand how my sensible and pragmatic father so dedicated to his profession and patients could lose all sense of balance and run after film people. Look at you now, you are no different from Papa.' She looked at his stubborn, unresponsive eyes. 'I guess you're in no frame of mind to listen. I love you, Amanat. You're the most important person in my life. But I won't let you emotionally blackmail me and get your way. I'll give you start-up money but I will not be a producer, now or in the future.'

Sagari got out her chequebook, and signed a blank cheque. 'Find out what our savings are, in the bank, in mutual funds and other investments, and then write the figure.' She extended her hand to give Amanat the cheque, then hesitated. 'No, this can't go on. The money's for us, not for you to squander on a venture that has a ninety-three per cent chance of being canned after you've shot two or three reels.'

'You obviously have a high opinion of your husband's talents.'

'That's the industry average, Amanat, and it comprises mostly seasoned producers.'

'I wouldn't have taken the bloody money anyway.'

'I'm sure you wouldn't have. Listen to me.' But Amanat was already at the door. 'You can sulk and throw one of your silent tantrums after I'm through.'

Amanat walked back sullenly. 'Aren't you finished yet?'

'You remember calling me "precocious brat" without knowing the meaning of that word when we were playing Trade?'

'What about it?'

'I was far beyond precocious. Papa may have tried in his foolish way to secure a future for me in films but he was nowhere as ambitious as I was. I was at the top and I was damned if I was going to part with that spot. I was smart enough to realize that I was good copy only when I said something bitchy. I wanted so much to be liked, I was more than willing to oblige. I could be vicious as only children can be, especially since I was slipping in the popularity charts. What I seemed to have forgotten was that while my mind was still a child's, I was growing up to be a woman. I'm sure I looked like a nymph or worse, a bimbette with all the uncomprehending coquettishness of a fourteen-year-old.

'I remember the Sunday when a script reading of *Aboli* was fixed at the producer's home. As usual, the scriptwriter, the director and the actors were late. As time passed, it became clear they were delayed to the point of not turning up. Who had arranged the meeting? I wondered. Was it Papa, his secretary or the producer? The role of the mute girl, who ultimately brings the whole village together, should have been mine by right, but it was very much up in the air. Papa was hellbent on my getting the role. I had a sense of how much was riding on it and was willing to turn on my charms full blast.

'Luckily I had the producer all to myself. I was far too wise for my years and just as ignorant. He was gentle, very gentle.'

'Very enlightening. Will you stop being so coy?'

'He was gentle. What else is there to say? I didn't get the role and I was done with movies once and for all. I didn't give any more interviews. I just faded. The brat had finally lost her tongue.'

'Why are you telling me all this?'

'Whatever my age, I was complicit in my abuse as victims sometimes are.'

Amanat thought she had finished but Sagari was still trying to extricate herself from the past.

'Never again will I be used by me, you or anybody else. It's a terrific script and if you are willing to wait, I'm sure we'll find a good producer, and a director who has the flair and savvy for a caper. I've as much at stake in this project as you. I know I am Rani. I won't say this again but if you talk about my producing the film or your directing it, that could be the end of our relationship. Do I make myself clear?'

'Tell me when you are through with the sob story.'

Sagari looked distastefully at him and walked out of the room.

Sagari had never been a party animal and on the rare occasions she could not avoid saying yes, she left it to Amanat to decide whether he wanted to accompany her. That was in the old days when she was the main attraction and he was seen as her appendage. Nothing had changed except one thing. Sagari still declined and Amanat still dreaded going and, once there, was as lost as a puppy whose owners have driven fifty miles to abandon it just so it won't find its way back. But he wouldn't miss a film party for all the Oscars in the world.

He could not understand himself. Why this compulsive need to be seen at these bashes? Did it restore his self-confidence because they took desultory notice of him? He suffered when his photograph did not appear on page three of the daily rag that he had scorned all these years. He found himself despicable, and yet the next time he was invited, dared not not go.

There would always be single women at these gatherings, women as lonely and lost as he was: aspiring actresses who had not got their first break and perhaps never would; starlets who wanted to be stars but were now hanging on to the sleeve of some cameraman or assistant director; a one-time star who was now a mafioso's moll, gone to fat and become unrecognizable in the ten years she had been kept out of sight; the beautiful playback singer whose voice had cracked and deserted her, some said because the competition had mixed a drug in her drinks, while others maintained that partying and overindulgence had ruined her vocal chords.

They detected a kindred spirit in Amanat. It was as though they felt they had to protect this boyish misfit in the midst of the lecherous wolves. Maybe loneliness is a kind of leprosy that draws its own together. Very likely it was nothing of the sort and the truth was banal and mercenary: they were so desperate, they made themselves believe that Amanat was a stepping stone; who knows, he might have a say in the casting of the next Sahil Thapar film.

Amanat could not bring himself to sleep with them. Often they suggested it bluntly; sometimes in coy, veiled language. But every time he was about to cave in, he could not get rid of the feeling that he was no better than all the stereotypical but nevertheless real-life directors and producers for whom the casting couch was not a metaphor but a sordid droit du seigneur and a mandatory rite of passage for would-be stars.

He had his affairs elsewhere. Sometimes it was more than sex; there was an emotional and intellectual intimacy. At times there was little more than sex and self-loathing. It was as though these liaisons were the only way he could reassure himself that he mattered. He was like a dog who picked up his hind leg to pee at lampposts, tree trunks, turnstiles and fire hydrants to remind his brethren that he was still around.

Later, when he looked back, he decided that Thapar and Sen had been playing mind games with him. There was a purpose and system to their playing hot and cold. They wished to unsettle him, to keep him guessing about their next move, so that he understood who was in charge, and when it came to making changes in the screenplay, they could manipulate him any which way they wanted without any resistance from him. It was, Amanat had to admit, an effective tactic. But in time he realized he had got it wrong. It was nothing so devious. Sahil and Sudhin did not need to operate on those terms. They simply switched him off when they wanted to. They forgot about him. They knew that if and when they needed him, he could be switched on again. They were right. Fourteen months later, Sahil Thapar was back.

'I don't get you,' Amanat said. 'Don't you want to have at least a couple of script sessions before the film goes on the floor?'

'I've gone over it,' Sahil Thapar said. 'Seems okay to me. The set's being built, so we can't afford delays. Sudhin will be here the day after and by then he will also have read the script. Whatever changes he wants, you'll make them as we shoot.'

Thapar had turned up early in the morning at the apartment.

'I hope you don't mind my coming over without calling. There should be no formalities between friends.'

Seven o'clock on a Sunday, for God's sake, even the servants weren't up yet, and he had been watching videos till five. Shirley MacLaine had got it right in *The Apartment*. 'Some people take and some people get took.'

As the shooting got underway, Amanat hoped perfidiously that Thapar would run out of money and *The Arsonist* would be canned. Later it didn't matter. *The Arsonist* got middling to indifferent reviews in the press. It didn't change the face of Indian cinema but to Amanat's eternal shame it did amazingly well at the box office.

There was no end to the cheap ironies of that whore called fortune.

# 39

Dear Roy,

I'm writing to ask if you would be interested in trading for me once again, though this time around it will not be for the Abbey but for a pro-life organization called The Initiative for the Protection of Unborn Children, IPUC for short. Bear in mind that my name will not figure in any transaction, nor will you mention it in any context, not even accidentally. If you need to contact me urgently, you can send me an email asking me to call you and nothing more.

I will call you within two days to check whether you agree to be IPUC's stockbroker. If all goes according to plan, I should be ready to start investing within a month.

God be with you.

Lucens

Lucens moved swiftly. After taking charge of the Diocese finances and writing to Roy, he talked to the banks, got the debts rescheduled and, to Father Nicholas's amazement, was able to talk the bankers into lending the Bishopric another $70,000. He tracked the market closely, forecast and jotted down where it would go the next day, the next week, the next fortnight, and checked his margin of error. As in the past, when his score had stabilized at seven bang-on guesses on a scale of ten, he plunged in.

Father Nicholas was a taciturn man and it took Lucens a while to grasp that the huge liabilities were not, as Abbot Augustine and the bankers assumed, Diocese debts. The anti-abortion project was Father Nick's illicit baby. Bishop Sanger could not have been unaware of his assistant's involvement with the pro-life movement, but since he did not interfere with fiscal matters, he was in the dark about the priest diverting Diocese funds towards his pet project.

Lucens calculated that he would play the market until he had generated enough money to settle Father Nicholas's outstandings, and to constitute a reasonable corpus for IPUC. He would then lock up the funds in blue-chip companies, government bonds and securities, and the dividends and interest would pay for the activities of the organization. After that he could turn his attention to matters closer to home and oversee the removal of the Abbot.

The turning point in his relationship with Father Nicholas had come after a chance meeting in Sweet Waters. He had rushed out in his work clothes to the Mariposa Mall to pick up a blade for one of the furniture factory's electric saws, when a woman of thirty thrust a handbill at him. It had the ring of a coffee-cup at the bottom and faint traces of tomato paste from a pizza, or maybe it was salsa.

When the woman looked away, Lucens crumpled the paper and threw it into a litter box.

'You killed a child, you just did,' the woman screamed.

'What?'

Never to engage in a conversation with cranks and lunatics was a rule with him, but he had slipped up this time. People were looking at him as though he had committed infanticide right there in public.

'I'll tell you what,' the woman spoke aggressively.

Lucens continued to walk away but she followed him. There was no escaping it, he was in for a harangue.

'If only you had bothered to read it, you could have saved one, even ten unborn babies.'

He was not about to tell her that he was a monk, and that fathering a child was not on his agenda. 'I believe there's freedom of expression in the country, but also the right not to have to listen to every crackpot who wants to save the world.'

The small crowd of shoppers and cinemagoers laughed and began to disperse. Lucens had not expected such an easy victory. He looked at the woman and said, 'Now if you'll excuse me, I have other business to attend to.'

'I'm sure you have.' She seemed near tears. 'Everybody's busy. Nobody reads my leaflets.'

'Give me one. I'll read it this time.'

Read This Before You Kill A Child

Medicine is about the art of healing. That is what every doctor swears when he takes the Hippocratic oath. But some doctors today are in the business of killing and not curing. And who are they killing? Not enemies, not murderers or even anyone who can fight back, man to man, woman to woman. No, they are busy killing unborn babies and making vast fortunes. These are crimes against children, against humanity and against God. Sanctioned by the state and the federal governments.

And pray, who are the collaborators of these satanic doctors? None other than young mothers and fathers mostly living in sin and out of wedlock, 13-year-olds as much as 30- and 40-year-olds. Nights of pleasure and wanton promiscuity. And who has to pay for them? The mother and the father? The grandparents who gloried in being liberal and brought up their children to think that moral values, not to mention Almighty God, were dead? No, they don't pay at all. Or if they do, it's a few hundred dollars to the murderers called doctors. The only one who has to pay with its life is the unborn child.

These heinous crimes must stop. No woman or man of conscience could ever tolerate such criminal behaviour. What are you doing about it? Do you think your disapproval and distaste are enough? Not at all. You too are an accomplice to the crime in the eyes of God. Unless you are willing to raise your voice against the killers and their evil deeds.

Right here in Sweet Waters, at the Mothercare clinic opposite the Mariposa Mall on Chesterton, a millionaire murderer called Doctor Cornelius Lester has a thriving practice, butchering innocent foetuses.

Every Monday at 11 a.m., The Initiative for the Protection of Unborn Children (IPUC), a volunteer organization, holds a demonstration against abortions at Mariposa Mall. Come and join us. Help us save an unborn child.

Stop abortion. Be pro-life.

'Would you join me for a cup of coffee?'

'Why?' She eyed him suspiciously. 'Are you against us or for us?'

'Who's us? I see only you.'

'I knew you wanted to make fun of us pro-lifers. You have that superior look.'

'Forget it.'

'I'm Dawn, Dawn Gold,' she told him as she stirred her coffee at Starbucks. 'I'm doing my PhD in Eng. Lit.'

'Lucens.'

'I'm sorry, I'm tense. I've never done this alone.'

'You still haven't told me how many join you for these Monday morning protests?'

'Many. A hundred.' She looked at him and changed her mind. 'On some Mondays we were fifteen or twenty. Then three weeks ago the police put us in a van and took us to the county jail because we barricaded the door to Dr Lester's clinic and wouldn't let him get out. After that only a few turned up. This time just me.'

'Did the police book you people?'

'No, they let us off after half an hour. But the big honcho there warned us that next time they would be forced to file cases against us. And we could all end up going to jail. Most of the pro-lifers don't have the money to hire lawyers, nor can they afford to lose their jobs.'

'Are they all Catholics?'

'Most, but not all. Five out of twenty must be Lutheran, Orthodox or Baptist.'

'Any men?'

'A couple. Are you from the press?'

'No.'

'You are one of them. The pro-choicers. You want to pump me for information.'

'You are right to be suspicious. How did you join this group?'

'You don't like to talk about yourself, do you?'

'Not much to tell. You can relax. I'm not pro-choice.'

She seemed to be on the verge of tears again. Now what? he wondered.

'I got pregnant. I had to get an abortion. Dr Lester, the one in front of whose office we protested, did it. Now every night the baby comes into my dreams. The priest says if my repentance is sincere, God will forgive me. Maybe God will but I know my baby won't.'

It was nine months to the day since Lucens had written to Roy and started playing the market again. He had kept his part of the deal and stuck to his timetable. He had paid off Father Nick's debts and invested in a manner that would generate enough income to fund the activities of IPUC for years to come. It was now time to concentrate on the business of getting rid of the Abbot.

There was only one flaw in his calculations. He had failed to factor in Father Nick. The priest had taught him that if you really cared for the sanctity of life, then as a last resort, you must be willing to risk your very soul. Now, unconsciously, Father Nick was teaching him his second most important lesson. Idealism was not enough. Passion was not enough, nor was total commitment. What you needed just as much were well-defined objectives, a clear-cut strategy, and the discipline not to give up till you had achieved your aims. Father Nicholas's idea of a plan of action was to improvise haphazardly at the last moment. At the best of times it had a fifty-fifty chance of being effective. When it misfired, as it often did, there was never a post-mortem of what went wrong. There were no lessons learnt and you went back to making the same mistakes again.

IPUC members were an odd assortment. There were the idealists, the professional haters and malcontents; unwed mothers, like the woman he had met at the mall, who could not forgive themselves for having aborted their babies; kind souls like the carpenter, Brendan, who were a little touched in the head; the lonely and the lost who would as willingly join Alcoholics Anonymous or a group of arsonists as IPUC for a bit of company.

The main thrust of their activities was to accost people in front of the polyclinic where Dr Cornelius Lester and his partners ran The Mothercare Planned Parenthood and Auxiliary Services Clinic, to harangue them and try to hand them the much soiled and recycled sheets of paper that he had seen Brendan distribute years earlier. Sometimes they got together at the Mariposa Mall and shouted slogans for half an hour. Without time frames, clearly defined targets or a sense of direction, they rarely acted in concert. They were demoralized and their numbers were dwindling fast.

Lucens had two options: he could quit or he could take charge. The first smacked too much of a cop-out. The second was fraught with all kinds of difficulties and perils. Father Nick was very much his senior. He had vast reserves of bitterness, not all of them, Lucens suspected, related to his animus against the pro-choicers. And he had a temper. There was one other overriding consideration: even if Lucens managed to ease the priest out, he himself could hardly afford to be seen as the strategic planner and the guiding light of the pro-life lobby in Sweet Waters. Trappists were recluses. They did not engage in activism. Indeed, he couldn't think of a better way of playing into the Abbot's hands.

Every once in a while Lucens cannot figure out whether he's short-sighted, blind or just plain stupid. The chalice, the one they called the Holy Grail, had been staring him in the face but he had failed to notice it. Father Nicholas had unsuspectingly given him the key, the creed that would give his staid life meaning and purpose. There was no dilemma and no ambiguity about the course of action he must follow: he had to save the unborn children.

Lucens was grateful that however belatedly, he had seen the light. Was there anybody closer to Jesus's heart than children? Who could forget the Lord's words: Suffer little children to come unto me for theirs is the kingdom of God.

For Lucens, God had always been a search for purity, simple and absolute. How could he have forgotten that children were dearest to Jesus because they were the purest amongst all of God's creatures? From now on till he breathed his last, he would be the defender of unborn children.

On reflection, he realized that the Abbot need never find out about his involvement with IPUC. Lucens's predilection not to be in the public eye would also accord rather well with his desire not to wound Father Nick's fragile ego. If he played his hand carefully, the priest need never know that he had become a mere figurehead.

The first step was to broaden the base of the movement. It was taken for granted that if it was anti-abortion, it had to be Catholic. This was a misconception but it suited the media and, of course, the pro-choicers. They painted the anti-abortionists as a lunatic fringe of Papist extremists. That narrowed the appeal of the pro-life brigade drastically.

What hardly anybody noticed was that at least 65 per cent of the conservatives from any denomination were either for anti-abortion laws or were favourably disposed to them. Lucens made another surprising discovery: a sizeable majority of gays and lesbians, not to mention blacks, came out pretty strongly against abortion. The question was, why had no one thought of putting together a coalition of like-minded people? If the pro-lifers were seen to be more broad-based in their constituency, the movement would be far more widespread, effective and successful. Whatever his personal views about homosexuals, he was going to rope them in too.

He wanted to start with a bang, something explosive, perhaps even shocking, that would grab everybody's attention. He spent long nights thinking about it, went to the Central Library, and scoured the Internet. Nothing. Nothing that came up to his expectations. Then one day he read a notice in the local paper about some medical shorts being shown at the Roosevelt Room in the museum. Lucens thought he would chance it and check whether there was anything of interest. He deliberately went in late so no one would recognize him. He needn't have worried; there were only three people in the auditorium, all of them in the front row. There was a film about a coronary bypass that made him almost pass out twice, once when the surgeon harvested the saphenous graft from a calf and the second time when the palpitating muscle was exposed and leapt about like a red snapper thrashing out of water. The next short was about advanced carcinoma of the liver, its various incarnations, symptoms, diagnosis and prognosis. He was about to leave for the Abbey when the third film began. It was an ultrasound record of an abortion.

Lucens was in business.

Father Nicholas liked the idea of spearheading the crusade against abortion. He called a meeting at the Diocese of Catholic and non-Catholic clergymen and women, leaders of pro-choice and pro-life groups, leading feminists, and lesbians and gays from within a radius of a hundred miles. Bishop Sanger was away and Father Nick had the run of the place. After tea and a rather elaborate spread of small eats, he begged the invitees' indulgence to screen a film. It was a rhetorical request, as the conference room went dark without him waiting for a response from the audience.

The film opened with a lazy opium-like sequence of a foetus smiling in its sleep. It woke up slowly and yawned, its hands outstretched and its fists clenched. It turned to face the viewer, extended its neck and rolled its shoulders as if it was working out, and drew its feet up till the toes touched its forehead, and then laughed, pleased with its own antics. It had all the attributes of a premature infant: eyes, ears, nose, hands, legs, gender, a little heart pumping away at 120 beats a minute, and a brain. It was doing what children all over the world do, sucking its thumb. Suddenly the soundtrack got pumped up and the foetus' heartbeat seemed to rise precipitously. An instrument had violated the privacy and security of its cocoon. The baby's face crumpled as the instrument proceeded to hack, tear, rip apart and dismember it.

Of the seventy people who attended the show, forty-five walked out at this point. Even amongst those left in the room, hardly anyone dared to watch as a pair of forceps grasped the head and crushed it so that it could make its way out through the suction tube. A subtitle at the end said: 95 per cent of all legal abortions occur at the age this foetus was, ten weeks. When the lights came on, all the people who had gone out returned. Lucens had warned Father

Nicholas to expect anger and heated words. What he eventually had to deal with was outrage verging on violence.

'I am, as you can see, a Catholic nun and a committed pro-lifer. Even so, I am in a state of shock at what transpired here this evening.' The first to speak was Sister Elizabeth of the Convent of the Holy Spirit. 'A respected and senior member of the Catholic Church has perpetrated the most revolting trick upon all of us. I cannot state too strongly that you have exceeded all bounds of decency, Father. When you invited us, you had expressly stated that you were calling a meeting in the hope of getting pro-choicers and pro-lifers together for the first time to start a dialogue and see if it was still possible to find some common ground for sharing each other's concerns and views without abusing each other.

'You had other plans for us. You deliberately betrayed our trust and assaulted our sensibilities without preparing us for this nightmarish evening.

'May I make a suggestion to all those who feel violated today? Let us sit down and draft a letter to Bishop Sanger and Cardinal Reginald telling them how Father Nicholas intentionally deceived us and subjected us to this film almost under duress.'

The words may have differed from speaker to speaker but the sentiment was the same. After the fourth speaker, it was decided to take a vote whether the assembled audience wished to follow up on Sister Elizabeth's suggestion and write the letter. Perhaps a copy could also be sent to the press.

'My friends,' Father Nicholas spoke from the back of the room, 'I beg your leave to speak just a few words.'

There was a chorus of nos.

'Your conduct,' Reverend Malcolm said, 'was indefensible and no apology will make amends.'

'I do not wish to apologize.'

That took the wind out of the audience for the moment and the priest pressed on. Lucens had coached him well.

'What I did today was unworthy; unworthy of your friendship, unworthy of the trust you placed in me by accepting my invitation at such short notice, and unworthy of the office that the Church has vested in me.

'I cannot and will not pretend that I did not know what I was doing or of the consequences of my behaviour. I knew that I might even have to face the prospect of being defrocked. If you decide to send the letter to the press, it will make for headline copy and my flock will be terribly disappointed in me.

'But I would do the same tomorrow or at any time in the future. Had I told you in advance that I was going to show such a graphic ultrasound film of the dismemberment of a foetus, would any of you have come? A few perhaps, mostly those who are already converted.

'Both pro-choice and pro-life believers have vaguely felt that there is a degree of sentience in a foetus but none of us had any idea just how alive and capable of pain and suffering an unborn child is.

'Your rage against me may be great, but I would beg you not to make unborn children suffer for it. Write to the Bishop or Cardinal, if you must. But I beg you, let us not kill Christ again in the unborn foetus. The crimes against foetuses will not wait while you vacillate.'

Twenty-seven people became members of IPUC before the evening was over. Another sixteen said they would call back within a week. Of the twenty-seven who had signed up, seventeen had been either pro-choice or undecided earlier.

'It was a triumph,' Father Nicholas said smugly to Lucens the next day. 'Didn't I tell you that a little doctoring wouldn't hurt the cause? Everything went exactly as you and I had planned. You watch, we'll put the murderers behind bars.'

Lucens had the feeling that from now on it was not going to be difficult to handle Father Nick. He had seen the results of a little bit of forethought and planning. And he had got a taste of power.

# 40

My dear Zia,

I had decided to ignore a letter that you wrote quite some time ago, but maybe it's time to answer it. Since you've told me the truth about Sagari and you, I hope you are finally at peace, never mind that thanks to you my peace of mind has been ruined for good and my marriage in its last throes.

I've learnt the hard way (how else but through my own example among others) that people hardly ever change, however cataclysmic the events they have been through. When I re-established contact with you, at your insistence I may add, I had foolishly hoped that you had turned over the proverbial new leaf. What put me at ease though was the fact that you had become a Trappist monk for whom silence may no longer be mandatory but is still a high priority. Even more reassuring was the almost inaccessible remoteness of the Abbey. I believed you were almost cut off from the rest of the world. How mistaken I was. Even if you were stranded on darkest Pluto, you would still be up to some terrible mischief.

How does one make the world safe from you and your tribe who have such infinite faith in the power of honesty? You are like Greene's Quiet American. Your innocence is deadlier than the plague. Somebody should tie a bell around your neck and every time one hears you approaching, the whole town should run for its life. Whatever or whoever gave you the idea that honesty is like the Hindu sacrificial fire that purifies? Honesty, my deluded brother, is hardly ever the best policy. It's a killer virus best kept sealed and put away in an impenetrable ten-foot-thick metal vacuum box lest it infect and devastate ordinary muddling sinners like me.

I don't recall where I had read that the annual turnover of partners amongst young gays is in the region of a thousand, more not less. That's about two and a half or three partners a day. That is a staggering figure, but I was sure that these guys were just not in Sagari's league. The actors, directors, producers, cameramen, the crews of the film she was shooting, her driver, secretary, I was certain she was making out with each of them.

If one were to predicate my wife's sexual appetite on my crazed imaginings, it would take a regiment or two a day to satisfy her. Was I not aware of how absurd I was being? Oh yes, I was. But does that help when you are under the influence of the hydra-headed monster called jealousy? Of course I knew that Sagari was not fickle and loved me enough not to want anybody but me. Oh God, I knew she was innocent, and yet there was nothing I could do to stanch my doubts and suspicions. I may have been operating on a totally fabricated premise but you cannot fault my logic: if she was a nympho, I would out-nympho her. I'm vastly overstating matters, but what difference does it make whether you carry on with one, five or fifty women once you've let down the one woman who loves you?

Are you merely thoughtless, or is it that you can't see beyond your self-interest to the damage you do? Sometimes I'm inclined to think that you are a truly evil person. You profess to be not just a Christian but a Catholic. It is the only faith that understands the unbearable burden and pressure a sinner must live with, and had the good sense to establish the institution of confession. Unfortunately, blabbing to the Father Confessor at the Abbey was not enough for you. You needed to vomit it all over me after God knows how many years.

Like all self-righteous people I bet you thought you were doing me a favour. How lucky you are, Zia. You never have doubts nor are you ever confused. You know what's right and what's wrong. There is only one point of view: yours. Just deserts or poetic justice demanded that I should have gone after you but you were eleven thousand miles away and I did not know how to strike back. I chose Sagari as my victim.

Did Sagari suspect the reason for my suddenly having taken to debauchery? If she did, she must have had a fine sense of intuition. It could not alter the facts. Besides it suited me to keep silent. I felt virtuous sparing her the pain and hurt of knowing that I knew what had transpired between the two of you. Since I could not redress or cure the grievance, I would nurse and nurture it. I could then hold it against her all my life and justify my actions.

Poor Sagari. She knew how childish I could be and it was her wont to laugh off my absurdities as well as my shortcomings. Perhaps she reasoned that if she ignored my waywardness, I would soon come to my senses. But the more forgiving she was, the more I messed around. I may not have done it consciously but I must have been testing to see how far I could go. To the breaking point as it turned out.

I would not presume to question your motives but if you were ever to give in to a moment of self-doubt, you should ask yourself if under the guise of being 'honest', you did not also want to get back at Sagari and me.

And yet I wonder if you were not merely the trigger, the pretext and the lame excuse. Was my relationship with Sagari doomed from the beginning because of me?

When Sagari suggested that we get married while I was on my way to have my hair cut, I had little or no idea what I was getting into. It was as if I was assaying a move, an action or response, testing it out on a 'let's see if it's all that it's cracked up to be' basis or for the sheer adventure of it. The assumption was that I could always retrieve the situation. But the fact is you can't say sorry and go back and play it differently. I liked Sagari, I had turned the city of Bombay upside down, combed its dark corners and pursued her down unknown alleys, but I had not given marriage any thought.

I got along with her; she was bright, intelligent, loved my jokes (that always helps), and gave as good as she got. She had a sharp critical mind, we enjoyed the same kind of music, movies; hell, we enjoyed each other. But that did not entail taking the vows. I said yes to Sagari the way I would have assented to going to the Ajanta caves or to a play.

Call it immaturity, sheer thoughtlessness. Amanat, the apostle of responsibility-for-one's-acts, could not grasp that actions have consequences, that what you say and do locks you into relationships, some of them for life. It's not as if I am an irresponsible person or have no staying power. You cannot be a writer unless you are patient and can bring things to fruition despite false starts, endless rethinks and rewrites and depression; but when you have a chronic illness with a rather melodramatic condition and live from day to day, an ad-libbing quality creeps into your life. You lose your faith in tomorrow and long-term commitments are suspect. The here and the now is the farthest you can see or trust.

Is that a little too pat? I suspect it is. But I'm too much of a masochist to give credence to my own stories. Am I then covering up my inconstancy by making you the scapegoat? I doubt it, but who knows? The price of self-knowledge, I sometimes think, is too high.

I'm inclined to believe now that honesty is an ailing currency that only the petty-minded would trade in. It is heedless and headlong, at least the variety that you practise and hold in such high regard. Perhaps the truth, whatever that is, should be reserved for bigger occasions, like looking steadily and unflinchingly at oneself and then having the courage to act on it.

I doubt if this letter will make any sense to you or have any effect. Maybe we come from different galaxies and can never communicate.

Despite everything,

Love,

Amanat

# 41

Within three weeks of the meeting, Father Nicholas was elected chairman, and Denise Ashby from the Presbyterian parish at Rockford became president of IPUC. The first newsletter followed soon. Dawn Gold, the woman who had accosted Lucens at the Mariposa Mall, was appointed editor. An ex-army colonel, Cameron Masters, was given charge of the task force that was to lay siege to Mothercare Planned Parenthood, which the pro-lifers preferred to think of as a euphemism for abortion clinics in the area.

When you got to know the colonel, you realized that he had no business being outside a straitjacket. He had served with the Green Berets and had been decorated several times. He was dangerous because he had no concept of limits or acceptable parameters for casualties on either side of a conflict. If a job had to be done, it made no difference whether anybody survived to claim victory.

Ideologically, his position lay beyond the outermost reach of the extreme right. And yet in some ways he was a hardcore Marxist. Like Marx, he believed that the state had to be done away with. The lofty language of the American constitution was merely a pretext to curb the freedom of its citizens. He was not for less government, he was against any government at all. He thought Ronald Reagan was a commie agent. According to his deranged logic, the actor-president's aim was to lower taxes for the idle and evil rich, and raise taxes for the rest of the country while working them to death to support the fat pet dogs of the affluent. The first freedom lay in zero taxes. The grapevine had it that Colonel Masters was the leader of a private militia whose goal was to blow up all the offices and records of the IRS. Lucens wondered if Masters aroused unswerving loyalty because he was a man of so few and barely literate ideas. But it was not for the quality of his mind that Lucens engaged him. He was dependable, and once he had accepted your leadership, he took orders even if they went against his philosophical grain.

Father Nick tried to persuade Lucens to become secretary of IPUC or at least a member of the advisory board, but Lucens declined. Lucens said he was grateful for the offer but really, Father Nicholas was running the show just fine, and he himself would continue to oversee the finances.

Lucens dashed off letters in the name of IPUC to the landlord of the building on Chesterton Avenue where the Mothercare Planned

Parenthood and Auxiliary Services Clinic was, and to all the offices in the area. He wrote to the shops and stores in the Mariposa Mall. His pitch to Macy's, Neiman Marcus, Dunkin' Donuts, the cineplex and Yoghurterie was only slightly different from the letters he sent to the families in the neighbourhood. He informed the big chains and the small shops at the mall that a recent survey conducted by the county showed that business had gone down 9.7 per cent thanks to the adverse publicity the Mothercare clinic had been garnering. It was likely to drop even further, now that all major churches and denominations had joined hands under the aegis of IPUC, and protests and demonstrations against Mothercare and its prime abortionist, Dr Cornelius Lester, were going to be intensified. They would be using a new strategy called 'Close the Roads. Paralyze the City.' Conscientious pro-lifers in the hundreds would court arrest by lying down on all the roads near Mothercare. This would not be a one-off march. Concerned citizens, especially the three hundred retirees who were members of IPUC, would obstruct all traffic and activity at least twice a week, without giving notice.

In the circumstances, business was likely to suffer heavy losses. Unless...unless responsible citizens, corporate institutions and commercial houses in the community of Sweet Waters got together and brought pressure to bear to close down the clinic. Think about it, the letter's last line read, can you imagine a better cause for which Christian values and business interests can join hands?

The letter to the homeowners had a more wrenching tone, but the message was similar. The neighbourhood was getting an unsavoury reputation. Property prices were slipping. They had dipped 11.3 per cent in the last two years. And the predictions were that they could dip another 9 per cent unless the cause of the decline in real estate prices, Mothercare clinic, was asked to vacate its premises.

He showed the letter to Dawn and asked her for suggestions.

'Wow. Are these figures for real?'

'Helps being an economist,' Lucens answered obliquely.

'You must have an amazing memory to have all these facts and figures at hand.'

Lucens shrugged off the compliment.

'What's Dr Lester's residential address, Dawn?'

'I don't know.'

'You don't?' Lucens asked disbelievingly. 'Will any of the older members who were active before you know?'

'I doubt it. None of the abortionists list their numbers.'

'Check with the others, just in case. If they don't come up with anything, follow him, will you?'

'How could I follow him? He's not from anywhere near. Who knows, he may be coming in from Denver or Seattle.'

'He can't be flying in every day unless he owns a private Cessna.'

'Takes one of the regular airlines, I suspect. Besides, he doesn't come in that often.'

'He flies down just to kill babies?'

'It's just possible that in his mistaken way, he thinks he's saving the mothers and not doing it for money.'

'A likely story. What happens on the days he doesn't come in?'

'Dr Slater, some expat Brit called Dr Douglas and occasionally Dr Brooke take turns.'

'How come you didn't tell me this earlier?'

'I thought you knew.'

'How would I? You've only mentioned Dr Cornelius Lester.'

'He's the leader of the pack, that's all.'

'So who makes the appointments?'

'There's a nurse there. You don't get an appointment unless you come in personally and she checks whether you really are pregnant. Brother Lucens, can we take a break? You've been at it for hours.'

'I suggest you tail Dr Lester next Tuesday,' Lucens said.

'To the airport? That still won't tell you – '

'To wherever he lives with his family.'

What happens to time in black holes? Lucens wondered. With the compression of matter, does time too get squeezed so tight that at some point it ceases to exist? Something strange was happening to his own time. He had the constant feeling that he was running out of it. Someone had tied a tourniquet around it, and one of these days, its supply would be cut off totally. And yet paradoxically enough, it had expanded too. He was a full-time monk. He helped with the accounts of the Diocese. He kept an eye on the soup kitchen at Sweet Waters that the Abbey was funding. Amongst all the pro-life organizations in America, membership at IPUC was growing the fastest, and so were expenses, which meant that Lucens was again watching the market and keeping in touch with Roy. He was organizing marches and he had successfully transplanted the *rasta roko* campaigns of Bombay on to the streets of Sweet Waters. The name was self-explanatory as he told the shops and stores at the Mariposa Mall: 'Close the Roads. Paralyze the City.' In 1993, Congress had made it a federal offence to attack abortion facilities and to assault and obstruct people who used them. IPUC was a law-abiding organization. It would not block access to Mothercare, it would merely stop the city dead. The tactic was a huge success and was immediately adopted by pro-life organizations in the rest of the state. Lucens had, however, introduced a highly effective variation on the Indian original. Instead of lying supine on roads till they were forcibly dragged away, about a hundred elderly members of IPUC drove up to a busy traffic light, got out, locked their cars and left. Another hundred or so captured the cross street. The tow trucks could handle only so much of a load. Besides, they had a tough time merely making their way through the snarled-up traffic. Lucens had let loose chaos on the streets, and Sweet Waters would never be the same again. IPUC was now making headlines not merely in the local and West Coast press and TV, it was featured in national news broadcasts.

Lucens's article in the *Washington Post*, under Dawn's name, about how men knocked up women for their pleasure while women had to pay not only the biological and psychological price, but even more important, the spiritual price, gave the membership drive another fillip. As surely as God was in his heaven, women who felt trapped and had their foetuses aborted would go to hell. Maybe, the article suggested, it was time men paid for their crimes. All the women had to do was adopt Nancy Reagan's contribution to the English language: 'Just say no.' The feminists loved it. All these years, pro-lifers were the enemy for most of them. Now, they were having second thoughts. It was too early to be unreservedly sanguine, but there was cause for optimism.

Dawn had tracked down Dr Lester to San Diego. Lucens would have liked the neighbourhood to have been more affluent, but it was clear that the man and his family were not exactly poverty stricken. It was a good solid middle-class street with two-car garages and the occasional motorboat parked on the side of the driveway. It was time to stir things up and make life difficult for the doctor.

Colonel Masters was sent to San Diego to co-ordinate the first phase of the campaign. On every lamppost along the road that the Lester children's school bus took on its way to and back from Wishbone Wilson School, were posters showing pictures of Alex and Mirabel Lester. The caption read: Dear Alex and Mirabel, please ask your father, Dr Lester, not to kill children any more. Imagine if he had done the same to you while you were in your mother's womb.

Colonel Cameron Masters may have envisaged his job as a military campaign and talked of targets, tactics and pincer movements, but it was the ladies who were far more effective than the men. The older ones, especially, were more intuitively shrewd and knew just where the advantage lay, and would milk it for all it was worth. The 'Close the Roads. Paralyze the Town' campaign would not have been half the success it was without them. They looked so endearing and made great pictures and copy for the media. Only the policemen, including the pro-life cops, understood how dangerous these sweet old ladies were. They hated them, but they made sure they treated them like glass dolls. One false or careless move and everybody, the judges, the press and the people, would lynch them. Even the normal and natural death of just one woman of seventy-nine or eighty-three at one of their 'Shut-the-city' rallies or in jail would trigger off nothing short of riots.

The police, the mayor and the governor were terrified of taking one of the elderly ladies into custody, and if compelled to, they couldn't wait to release them. Sometimes the judges would take a tough line and put them in jail for a week or even a month for public disturbance. The old ladies didn't mind it. On the contrary, they were delighted with all the publicity it got them.

# 42

My dear Zia,

Do you remember I wrote to you about a year ago, maybe it was a year and a half, that there was a mysterious call for you? The same man called again last night; well, at least the voice sounded the same. 'Tell Zia Khan,' he said, 'vengeance is mine. The traitor who played him dirty has paid for his dastardly crime.' I asked him for his name this time too, to which he responded, 'That's irrelevant. Just inform him that when the time is right, the Afghan will get in touch with him.'

Who is this Afghan, Zia? Do you have any idea what he's talking about? I don't think a Trappist monk would ever hire a hitman. But I wouldn't put it past you. I fear for you, my brother.

Love,

Amanat

1001,

Is this one of your stupid stunts? Are you sure you actually received those two calls? It wouldn't surprise me if you are no longer able to distinguish between reality and your fictions. Maybe you really should see a shrink.

Zia

The past was past. Lucens would not have any truck with it. In an earlier incarnation, when he and his companions had set out in a blizzard to burn five Kashmiri villages, his most trusted lieutenant, Yunus Habib, had indeed double-crossed him. As Zia had lain in the snow, he had brooded over how to dispense exemplary punishment to the traitor. He had wanted every comrade and fellow-warrior to appreciate that neither hell nor Satan himself could devise a retribution so patient and horrific as the one Zia had in mind. In that awful moment, as acres of snow slid down the mountain and engulfed him and his men and the Indian army, Zia continued to work out the nitty-gritty of Yunus's extended torture trip. He would kill him softly and lingeringly, dragging out the agony forever. No lover would be so attentive, so painstaking, so particular about the slightest detail, as he. Shards of glass, acid, red-hot iron, electric currents, boiling oil, ice, water...no, Yunus would never have a dull moment. The possibilities for refinement were truly infinite, since any or all of the options could be played out on that most sensitive of instruments fashioned by none other than Allah Himself: the human body; the human body with its multiple orifices, its tongue, eyes, testicles, nails, flesh. But, of course, it would not stop there. Every member of Yunus's family, regardless of how remote or distant the relationship, would be brought over to his cell with great fanfare, and raped, sodomized and swung from hooks in the ceiling in his presence.

Zia was dead. Lucens had shut the door on him, and on his past. Now some Afghan with a bloodthirsty memory was trying to tell him that Yunus had got his just deserts, but Lucens barely reacted to the news. He just wasn't interested. All he could say was, Amen.

'I tried, Brother Lucens. I put every kind of pressure on her but she won't budge,' Dawn Gold told Lucens. 'She's completely loyal to him. Not only did Dr Lester abort her child, he gave her the job.'

'She's a Mexican immigrant, very likely an illegal one. Tell her you'll report her to the authorities if she doesn't hand over the mangled remains of the day's abortions to you in a plastic bag.'

Dr Cornelius Lester had left the clinic a few minutes earlier and IPUC volunteers were tailing him to the Sweet Waters airport. They would enter the terminal and unfurl placards and banners as Dr Lester stood in the check-in queue. The day had not gone badly for IPUC but Lucens was not happy. There was only one criterion for success in his mind, and that was getting the clinic closed. IPUC had made life difficult for the doctors but they had carried on regardless.

Lucens's patience was running out.

'I can't do that, Brother Lucens. I won't report her to the INS.'

'It's just a threat. Nobody's asking you to actually do it.'

'It amounts to the same thing. She must live on the edge all the time. I don't want to make it worse. Besides, you are so obsessed with getting rid of these doctors, you might just pick up the phone and follow up on your threat.'

'Isn't that the objective, Dawn? Neutralizing the doctors?'

'Many of the people who send me emails and letters about the articles you publish in my name want to know where I get my facts and figures. They accuse me of inventing them.'

'Don't change the subject.'

'Stop dodging. Are you fabricating the figures?'

Lucens laughed. 'I'll see you tomorrow.'

*

Colonel Masters walked into the accounts office behind the cathedral without calling beforehand. The colonel was trying to prove a point. Lucens had cancelled two previous appointments and he was getting impatient. The Abbot's middle path, which the Abbot himself confessed he had borrowed from the Buddha, was alien to the retired colonel. The middle ground, according to him, was for cowards, nincompoops and hypocrites. To your friends, you always gave notice of your intentions and plans. To your enemy, you revealed nothing. You just struck him dead. The IPUC people, according to him, were lily-livered; folks with no backbone. Lucens was aware that this classification included him most of the time. Masters found Lucens too slow, too soft and too indecisive. If I was in charge, he said, I would blow the pro-choice people to hell tomorrow. Lucens didn't doubt it.

Lucens was not avoiding Colonel Masters. He had had no time to meet him, it was as simple as that.

'You've been on my mind, Colonel. I have an appointment with the legal team just now.' Lucens could see that his gambit was having the desired effect: the colonel was about to burst a blood vessel or strangle Lucens. 'But I'll keep them waiting, if need be, for a full fifteen minutes. What's up, Colonel?'

'That's precisely it. Nothing. Nothing whatsoever. The doctors at the abortion clinics and their patients know they are safe and that they can carry on murdering unborn babies without a care in the world.'

'You are an impatient man, Colonel. IPUC's tactics may not meet your demanding standards, but we expect a 30 per cent drop in abortions over the next six months.'

'Don't give me that crap, Brother Lucens. The state's health department report states that they've never dropped more than 7.6 per cent.'

'And you believe in the state? You of all people?'

Even as he sneered and put down the colonel, Lucens knew that Masters was right. The abortion figures had not suffered a sharp decline and had very probably bottomed out. The tide had begun to turn against IPUC and their aggressive stance. This had been bound to happen. Success, especially high-visibility success, invariably begets a backlash. Lucens wasn't overly exercised but he had to admit he had grown complacent. On the West Coast, the pro-choice people were not only better educated and more affluent, they had also woken up to the threat IPUC posed and had begun to get organized and hit back. Anybody obstructing traffic could now lose his or her driving licence for good, and the Freedom of Access to Clinic Entrances (FACE) laws, which made invasions and blockades of abortion clinics a federal crime, had been enforced far more rigorously in the past few months.

'What do you suggest we do?'

'When a ship is adrift, when morale hits rock bottom,' the colonel's voice was rising, 'when the captain abdicates responsibility and neither looks after his men nor guides the course of the ship, the law says a mutiny is justified. I hereby give you notice, Brother Lucens, that I am relieving you of your command and taking over the wheel. More than half the men and women are with me. If you are looking for a show of strength, you'll discover at least three-quarters are behind me.'

'Shall we go for a walk, Colonel Masters?'

'Your cheap tricks won't work, Brother. You don't have either a designation or any official responsibility, so at tomorrow's quarterly meeting I'll be elected policy director of IPUC.'

'I'm going for a walk, Colonel. Are you coming?'

'It won't make a difference.'

The colonel found it difficult to keep pace with Lucens. The sun was a taut, pink-red blister ready to burst. Lucens could not understand why Americans bothered to build pavements. There were never any pedestrians. Bombay, he recalled, had been far more advanced in these matters. There were millions of pedestrians there, all of them jaywalkers. The local authorities felt that if you didn't have pavements, pedestrians would automatically disappear, or perhaps they believed that the solution to the population problem was to let the cars, taxis and buses run down anybody who dared to walk on the streets. The fat palm trees in Sweet Waters, unlike the slim and delicate ones in India, stood like sentinels at thirty-yard intervals down the middle of the road keeping a neighbourhood watch. He wondered why India was making such frequent inroads into his consciousness these days when it had totally disappeared from his imagination and context so many years ago.

'Whatever you have to say, say it quick. I haven't got all day.'

'I am a little puzzled that you switched to maritime imagery today. I hope like me the army too has not fallen out of favour with you.'

'Get to the point.'

'I would have thought you might want to take it easy at your age. Of the three current conspiracy cases against the nation, investigations so far point to your involvement in two: the conspiracy to blow up the Long Island subway hub in New York, and the attempt to destroy all the records, old and new, at the Internal Revenue headquarters with a lethal computer virus. I could, of course, be wrong. It's more than likely that the government has no case or you are not the Colonel Masters they are referring to. After all, Masters is a fairly common name.'

Lucens let his speech sink in while pretending that he was waiting to be contradicted.

'You and your militia colleagues will relinquish your membership of IPUC tomorrow. You will not step into or come anywhere near the IPUC offices or attend any of the demonstrations. You will not contact any staff member by phone or email. Do I make myself clear, Colonel?'

'Are you threatening me? It won't work. You'll be out by tomorrow.'

'The FBI came around to the Diocese a couple of weeks ago and questioned Father Nicholas about you and your activities. In passing they gave us the low-down on you. Father Nick was noncommittal then but he can always call them and bring them up to speed on your pastimes.'

They walked back silently. The colonel was about to get into his car when Lucens spoke. 'Let me repeat, Colonel, that you and your associates will resign immediately.' He paused. 'I will be in touch with you personally to give you your assignments.'

Success. Finally. After all these months of trying every possible means, the Mothercare clinic had shut down. Lucens had become increasingly downhearted in the last couple of months. He had tried one thing after another, he had tried the truth and he had lied shamelessly, he had juggled figures and he had bought transparencies of aborted foetuses from an agent in India and plastered them all over San Diego. The latter campaign had backfired badly. It did not do Dr Lester and his family any good; their reputation had long since sunk to minus zero and was still dropping. But Lucens had overplayed his hand. People were aghast at the crassness of IPUC and their lack of feeling for the sensibilities of the residents of San Diego, especially the women and children. There were editorials in the papers, and a suit was filed against the printer of the offensive posters, the agency that had undertaken to put them up and the management of IPUC.

What had saved the day was butyric acid. It had undone Dr Lester's work and his resolve. Mothercare was closed for good. Or at least for many, many a moon. How and in what words can Lucens sing the praises of butyric acid, a.k.a. butanoic acid, chemical formula $CH_3(CH_2)_2COOH$. Butyric derived from the familiar, delicious and ubiquitous butter that goes on your toast, muffins and scones, and into your cakes and other baked dishes. And which in turn is a mutant of the Latin *butyrum* or the Greek *bouturon*.

Butyric acid is a mere ester, which is nothing but a reaction between an acid and alcohol minus the water molecule. Let us make it even simpler. Rancid butter and vomit make for good butyric acid. As with almost everything in life, there are two ways of looking at butyric acid. Abortion foes toss it off as a mere stink bomb. Now when a skunk squirts on you, they say, the only way to get rid of the smell is to dunk yourself in a tub of tomato juice. Agent butyric has a slightly more lasting effect and there is as yet no known antidote to it. Its foul, choking bouquet is almost impossible to remove even after you've repainted and recarpeted the place. But that's the good news, or the least offensive part of this ester. The other view is that butyric acid is nothing short of chemical warfare. It may be colourless, but it has some very colourful aftereffects and consequences. It can only be neutralized with the greatest difficulty and by expert and highly trained professionals who wear protective clothing. As an extraordinarily effective chemical hazard, it is easily absorbed through the skin and can cause severe burns in the skin, eyes and the mucous membranes. Inhale the vapour and you are sure to suffer from acute nausea, vomiting and severe irritation of the respiratory system. It can cause all kinds of pulmonary problems including chemical pneumonia that may require hospitalization and constant care for two months. Your nails break, you lose chunks of hair and your liver may be permanently damaged.

When Lucens had drawn up the plan of action, Colonel Masters would not discuss it till it had a code name. Lucens was not going to quibble over the man's sense of military protocol and self-importance. He had nearly trephined and lobotomized Masters the last time they had met. If the colonel now wanted not one but two code names, it was okay with him.

'Does Operation Beatitude sound all right?'

'We could do better,' the colonel pondered over the name. 'But it will do. What we must aim for is maximum impact.'

'I can't emphasize enough that you will not leave behind any telltale sign or clue that may even remotely indicate a link with IPUC.'

'I assure you it will be a foolproof operation. You can rely on me for that.'

Lucens thought it wise not to bring it to the colonel's notice that his previous ventures had left enough of a trail of evidence for the FBI to name him as a suspect in various cases.

'I do, Colonel Masters. I trust you will not disappoint me. Please understand that if either you or your men are picked up, IPUC will disown you. As you are well aware, you are doing this entirely on your own initiative. If under duress you claim that you took your orders from me, that, I'm afraid, will not wash. Let alone holding any position with IPUC or being on any advisory panel associated with it, I am not even a member of the organization. The Pavlovian reflex of the abortionist brigade and the media will be quick to point their finger at IPUC. We won't just deny the accusation, we'll condemn the attack in the strongest possible language. We'll point out that IPUC takes its inspiration from Gandhi and Martin Luther King and is committed to nonviolence.'

The colonel and Lucens went over the checklist again. Lucens had to admit that the colonel was thorough and left little to chance. Given a clear directive and goal, you could rely on him to execute things effectively.

'Good luck, Colonel.'

'If I left things to luck, Brother Lucens, we would all be in trouble.'

'True. We'll just leave it to your military training and precision. Incidentally, Colonel, what exactly did you mean when you said you would go for maximum impact?'

'Isn't it obvious? We'll do the job during daytime when the doctor's operating.'

It was obvious, at least it should have been, and Lucens had almost managed to undo all the goodwill the work of IPUC had earned because of his carelessness.

'Not one person, I repeat, not one person gets hurt. It's a night-time operation.'

'Why do it then? Why take all the risks? There's security there round the clock.'

'We want their business closed, not ours. Do you read me, Colonel?'

The colonel read Lucens loud and clear but there was one casualty anyway. The cleaning lady had fallen asleep at her job and ran out screaming when a half-gallon of the acid was poured down the ventilation system and another half-gallon through the slot for dropping mail. She was removed to the hospital with severe burns and acute breathing problems. The fire department was on the scene within minutes and the hazardous materials unit within an hour. Traffic was rerouted and all the medical consultancies in the building were closed till further notice. The parents of the seventy children in the daycare centre across the road were directed to the auditorium of George Washington High for the next week. The damage to the clinic had not been assessed fully yet, but it was estimated to run into tens of thousands of dollars. The IPUC governing body was appalled, and condemned the brutal attack as a barbaric crime deserving the most severe punishment. They seemed genuinely upset. And with good reason. They thought another agency, perhaps one from outside town, was responsible for the vandalism.

Lucens's work was done. It was time to go home, go back to the Abbey. The last time the Abbot had questioned him, he had been not a little incredulous that sorting out the monetary affairs of the Diocese should take so long. Lucens had gone into a convoluted rigmarole about how complicated the financial mess at the Bishopric was: many of the church properties were in dispute; records were missing and the prospect of endless litigation was daunting. Add to that the fact that Father Nick's book-keeping had been a trifle original and inventive, not to stretch a point too much, and the IRS wanted to re-examine the books for the last several years.

The Abbot was not convinced. He ordered Lucens to stop going to the Diocese. Father Nick didn't seem too concerned about his younger consultant withdrawing from the scene, and Lucens was grounded. Eight weeks later the priest made a frantic call to Reverend Father. Lucens alone had any idea of Diocese finances, tax matters and how to negotiate with the IRS. Could the Diocese have him back please? The Bishop would not be very pleased if he were asked to report to the Internal Revenue authorities. The Abbot gave in reluctantly, and Lucens knew that his time with IPUC was limited.

Well, everything was on track now. IPUC was in overdrive and the results spoke for themselves. Maybe it was not such a bad time to call it a day. Besides, he had so much unfinished business at the Abbey. He had not really followed up with Father Theo and was certain that things had not progressed much. He would work full time now on the task of evicting the Abbot.

It turned out that Lucens had been a little premature in his calculations for the future. He was about to learn one of the hardest lessons of his life. Don't count your victories, especially after you've won. In the battle between the two of them, Dr Lester had not merely totally outwitted Lucens, he had made the anti-abortionists the laughing stock of Sweet Waters and the West Coast, if not of the whole country. The only reason Lucens could show his face around was because nobody suspected that he was behind the butyric acid attack. Dr Lester was featured in the People section of *Time*, in the asinine upward arrow section of the Sunday newspapers where the rise and fall of people in the news is noted, and he had appeared on the David Letterman show to wild canned applause from the audience.

A worthy enemy deserves kudos and a pat on the back. Should Lucens say 'touché' or should he wipe the smirk off the doctor's face? His preference was for the latter, though he had no idea how to go about it.

About a month after the butyric episode, the clinic had been boarded up, and a covered walkway appeared on the pavement with a warning to customers about construction work. Nothing had changed three months later except for a notice that had gone up: Centre for Advanced Neurophysiotherapy opening shortly. IPUC immediately swung into action and did a statewide search to find out whether Mothercare was about to shift its location. It soon became evident that hardly anybody in the Valley or elsewhere on the West Coast would want to risk their property by renting it out to the abortionists.

Lucens's job now was to locate other abortion clinics in the state and get the colonel to eliminate them. He was finalizing the plans for an all-out attack when Dawn Gold, the editor of IPUC's newsletter, came to see him.

'May I talk to you somewhere more private?'

'Now?'

She looked tensely subdued as if a time bomb were ticking inside her. 'It's important.'

Dawn had been prone to phases of incipient manic-depression since her abortion and it was a mistake not to pay heed to her moods. Lucens took her to the Bishop's private chapel.

'I'm going to have a baby.'

He could barely hear her. 'Congratulations. I didn't know you were married.'

'I'm not.'

'How can you be pregnant if you are not married?'

'Then it must be an immaculate conception, Brother Lucens,' Dawn Gold said with asperity.

'I beg your pardon. That was thoughtless of me. How do you know you are going to have a baby?'

'I missed my period.'

'I'm told some women have an irregular cycle.'

'I did the test at Mothercare.'

'That couldn't be. What are you talking about?'

'Mothercare's open.'

He wanted to shake her and tell her it was closed, closed for good, and that none other than he was responsible for this kindness, but he kept his head.

'There's an advanced neurophysiotherapy clinic coming up there. But sometime later, not now.'

'I'm pregnant, Brother Lucens, that's what Dr Cornelius Lester told me after the test results.'

*

Lucens was right, of course. The neurophysiotherapy board was still there and it still said 'opening shortly'. He eased his foot on the brake of the Abbey van as the traffic signal turned green. The cars ahead of him moved forward slowly and he saw a girl, who had been crying maybe for over a week, and her mother walk through the covered gangway and turn into the doorway of the former abortion clinic.

Mothercare, he found out the next day, had been functioning for over a month now.

Lucens did not have too many options to choose from. He had to do something decisive and he needed to do it fast. He could bomb Mothercare with RDX, the current favourite amongst terrorist organizations, so long as it was not something that would link it to the colonel's past record. But there were obvious risks in this plan. It would not do, for instance, for the plastic to blow up the whole building or endanger the clinics of the other doctors. They hadn't done anything wrong and he didn't want them to pay for the sins of the abortionists. Besides, amateur and unfocused attacks always had repercussions and the adverse publicity would negate all the good work of IPUC. But even if the bomb were precision-calibrated, and detonated so that only the abortion clinic was wiped out, it would not make a difference. Mothercare would come back to life perhaps even faster than after the butyric episode. That would certainly put a halo around Dr Lester's head and turn him into a martyr. Public sympathy would coalesce around him and it would be well nigh impossible to touch the clinic again.

Lucens had no choice. The doctor would have to go. Colonel Masters, he was sure, would be only too happy to obey orders.

*Tejas*

# 43

In retrospect, Lucens might concede that Amanat's call had been fortuitous. Back then, however, he had viewed things differently. Abbajaan's timing had never been particularly good, but it had been really thoughtless of him to have a heart attack just before the liquidation of Dr Cornelius Lester.

Lucens's final conversation with the colonel had been, as usual, brief and to the point: 'There will be no further demonstrations against Dr Lester or the pro-choice people. No more paralysing the traffic and the town. For the next few weeks we want him and his friends to feel secure and to relax. The police and the FBI must think we're a spent force. Once that's done, two months from now, you can get rid of Cornelius Lester for good. Eight weeks is a long time to prepare.

'Just make sure no one will point the finger of suspicion at IPUC. Don't disappoint me, Colonel. Don't botch it up.'

Abba, doubtless, was to blame, but as was so often the case, the real culprit was Amanat.

'Has Abbajaan asked for me?' Lucens had wanted to know.

'No, he hasn't,' said Amanat, 'but…I think you should come down anyway.'

Had it escaped his brother's notice that he was a little over voting age and could take his own decisions?

'Where did you get the Diocese number from?' Lucens asked suspiciously.

'From you, who else? You gave me two numbers. This was one of them.'

'Give me a couple of days, maybe a week. I need to tie up some loose ends here.'

'I don't think that's such a good idea. I think you should take the first flight out.'

Indians were always confusing sentimentality with love. What would be the point of rushing down, travelling thirty-six hours, or whatever it took with a change of flights and perhaps a change of airports at New York, only to find at the end of the journey that all you could do was stand or, if you were lucky, sit for days outside the ICCU?

'Aren't you overdoing the drama a bit?'

'I hope I am, for all our sakes.'

'Abba is, what, barely sixty-five?'

'Get on the plane, Zia.'

'When you join the Trappist Order, you cease to have parents and family, and your only home is the monastery. I doubt if the Abbot will give me permission to go back to India because Abbajaan is a little unwell.'

'I've already spoken to Reverend Father Augustine. He is waiting for you at the Abbey.'

'How dare you go over my head like that.'

Too late. Amanat had put down the phone.

'What are you doing here?' Lucens asked Roy liverishly when he came to pick him up at the airport in Bombay.

'Same as you, came to see Abbajaan.'

'How did you know he was sick?'

'Am I under investigation?' Roy laughed. 'Abbajaan and I have a deal. I call him twice a week. He got the attack when I was on the phone to him.'

'Maybe that's why he got it.'

'That's a thought.' Roy wouldn't take the bait. He never did.

Lucens looked bemused. Abbajaan was doing it to him again, being a father to everyone but him.

'What do you talk about?'

'I don't know. Nothing. Everything. I never think about it.'

'How is he?'

'Too early to say. If I were you, I would importune your God without delay.'

Abba's eyes were closed and his breathing was laboured. He looked puffy. Had someone pumped all the blood out of him? He had withdrawn to a place so remote, no one could reach him. How could Abba, this man who had hammered, chipped and chiselled away at stone, ten, twelve hours a day, week after week at the Abbey, bending, pushing and twisting it into any shape he nursed deep inside his cortex, have became so fragile?

Lucens found himself looking uncomprehendingly at all the mute digital graphics monitoring his father's bodily functions. The first couple of days, he could feel no grief, no sensation at all, really. He had been emptied out. Roy, Amanat and he took turns staying the night at the hospital. The three of them hardly ever talked, and yet it was as though, in some inexplicable way, Abbajaan had fallen ill to bring them close again. Oddly enough the one subject that they seemed to avoid was Zafar Khan himself.

Lucens was at a loss to understand the violence of his affection for a man who could not control his wife, and might have had a child by his mistress. He had gone down on his knees next to Abba's bed. 'Please let him live, I beg of You,' he'd prayed silently to Jesus. 'Let my father be. Please. You don't need him. I do. I've got to make up to him for all these years.'

'Mr Lucens,' the nurse had seemed to materialize from nowhere, 'there's a call for you.'

'Is my father all right?' Lucens was flustered.

'It's not the patient calling,' she could not keep the irritation out of her voice. 'It's someone on the phone.'

What did Amanat want at this time of the night?

'Where's the phone?'

'In the nurses' office outside the ICCU.'

'Yes? Lucens here.'

'Speak here.'

That was obviously not Amanat. Who could it be? He could think of only one other person who would call, the colonel. Well, he would chew him out for this because he had left strict instructions that, however serious the matter, there should be no telephonic contact between them.

'Sorry to keep you waiting, Brother Lucens.' It was an unpleasantly familiar voice. How could he possibly know that Lucens was in India? 'How's your father?'

'I'm afraid I don't know who I'm talking to.'

'Is your father all right?'

'It's too soon to know.'

'I'll keep in touch. A word of advice before you put the receiver down. Don't give him a hard time with all your pet grievances just now.'

The phone went dead. Shakta Muni. James Cambray's guru. What was he talking about? Why would Lucens give Abbajaan a hard time? It didn't make sense. Lucens had to admit, though, that if the holy man was trying to psych him, he hadn't entirely failed.

Must be morning in the States. Lucens sat on the bench outside the ICCU trying to access the news on the Net from his laptop. Where was the colonel? Had he accomplished his mission or not? How come the papers were silent on the subject?

Three of the patients in the ICCU had died in the last two nights. Abba was bound to be aware of the fatalities around him. Did it demoralize him further? What was going on in his mind anyway? It was still uncertain if he might take it into his head to absent himself forever. The statistics told you that more people died at night than during the day, but they never explained why. Lucens hoped that Abbajaan had had the sense to return to God's fold and beg His forgiveness for having neglected Him so long.

Work and assignments had been pouring in, Amanat had told Lucens, from all five continents. Private sponsors, public trusts and philanthropies, municipalities and national governments had all hounded Abba to take up their projects. Money was rarely a consideration and he had been at liberty to quote his fees, no questions asked.

He was currently working on two projects, each with its own multiple building complexes: The Freedom and Integration Centre for South Africa, and a modular plan for village schools, playgrounds and paramedical centres for an NGO working in the villages of Bihar. Abba had felt it was a race against time: a self-fulfilling prophecy and predicament since he would not or could not stop pushing himself to breaking point.

'I know everything,' Lucens had said to Abbajaan that morning.

'Then you must be Allah.'

'Not funny. I'm sure Allah's not amused either. I mean you. I know everything about you.'

'That's as it should be between father and son.' There was a pause while Abba tried to catch his breath. 'Though I can't say I know much about you. But that's okay. You are my enigma.'

He was off the critical list and had been moved out of the ICCU. The doctors said he was improving but Lucens had doubts about that. His pallor was a shade of dead slate. He was restless and losing weight and still unable to walk to the toilet. But instead of groaning and moaning like the patient across the corridor, he was busy pretending to be normal.

'Thank you for coming down. It's good to see you, though I must have disrupted your schedule at the Abbey.'

Lucens looked out of the window of the corner room. What had happened to Bombay since the last time he'd been here? The pollution was a sepia mezzotint haze that never lifted, and all the people in the world, men, women and children, seemed to have migrated to this one city.

'I know about Antonia and you.'

'And what would that be?'

Lucens shook his head in disgust. 'You could be dead tonight or maybe in the next five minutes and you're still pretending that nothing happened between her and you?'

Was Abba mulling over what Lucens had said, or was he trying to get his breath back? Lucens thought he detected a note of panic in his father, or was it a distant hint of anger? It was curious. He didn't recall Abba ever losing his temper. That was not possible; he had had so much to rage about. But then, he was an Indian at heart; he sublimated everything, not just betrayal and grief, but hope, triumph, everything, into resignation.

'You were cheating on Ammijaan.'

Instead of going red and apoplectic, Abbajaan laughed in Lucens's face.

'You think Antonia, my very dear and overearnest friend Antonia and I were carrying on?'

'Yes. And the proof is me.'

'Poor Zia, my poor, poor Zia.'

'Don't you dare "poor, poor" me.'

Abba tried to sit up.

'What are you doing? For God's sake, no melodrama. Just a straight answer will do.'

Abba lay back. You could feel him trying to control and even out his breathing. 'Where did you get that notion?'

'I got it from the horse's mouth. Antonia told me.'

'What did she tell you, my son?'

'That I was her first.'

'First what?'

'She said she had me baptized when I was barely a week old.'

'That she certainly did.' Abba's voice was petering out. 'You are your mother's son and no one else's. Certainly not Antonia's.'

'Don't quibble. Answer me.'

Abbajaan smiled and mumbled something.

'What?' Lucens asked irritably. 'What did you say?'

Abba had closed his eyes and it was painful to watch him breathe. He was quiet a long time.

What had his father said? What were his inaudible words? Sometimes I think even God can't help you, is that what he had said?

It was not a little droll the way the two Khan brothers tried to avoid Sagari. The hospital had given her a special visitor's pass and, as usual, when she was going out in public, she came every day after visiting hours in a burkha. The day the cardiologist had admitted Zafar to the hospital, Amanat had agonized for a good ten to fifteen minutes over whether he should inform Sagari. He didn't want to worry her. But that was, as with all matters Amanat, only half the story. He had gone back to Suleiman Mansion more than twenty months before, and had neither spoken to her nor seen her since. How was he going to break the ice? He would rather take that long walk off the short pier. Why was he messing about? Zubeida Khaala spoke to Sagari at least once a day and she was bound to tell her. If he didn't make the call, Sagari would think him even more contemptible than he already was.

Abbajaan was her confidant, guide and the closest thing to a father figure. It was not a one-sided affair. Amanat thought at times that Abbajaan viewed her as the family deity.

Amanat had dialled her number.

Now she was calling out to him. 'You won't catch your death from me, Amanat, if you stay on a few minutes.' Amanat hesitated in the doorway to his father's room. It took him time to look her in the face.

'I thought it was the other way round.'

Amanat had written a note to Sagari one morning, and was waiting for her to go to the studio before leaving it on her table.

My dear Sagari,

I can't remember how long it is since we talked. My fault, not yours. I seem to have lost the knack.

I'm leaving. Your innate politeness will not permit you to tell me to get the hell out of your house. I should have had the sense, if not the decency, to leave two or three years ago. But I am shameless and stuck around because I love the place, not to mention its comforts.

I can't afford a flat of my own and must perforce go back to Suleiman Mansion. It's unfortunate that in our country it's almost unthinkable for one's parents to shut the door on their children. Poor Abbajaan and Zubeida Khaala, they'll have to put up with me whether they want to or not.

You've been good to me. You deserve better; far far better than my mendacity and infidelities. I have asked you repeatedly to give me a divorce. You have refused so far. But I hope you will want to make a life of your own. Call me when you want to file for a divorce. The least I can do is to give it to you without any trouble.

Love (how fake that word sounds on my tongue but however warped I may be, I'll stand by it),

Amanat

He had packed his clothes in one suitcase and his medicines and nebulizer in another. He'd read the note again. It sounded self-pitying and expediently self-serving. If he could only be half as forgiving of others as he was of himself, he thought, he might just make it as a postmodern saint. He tore the note up and wrote a two-liner.

My dear Sagari,

I'm leaving. I'll be staying at Suleiman Mansion. I do not have the face to see you any more.

Give me a divorce and you'll be free of me.

Amanat

He was sorting his papers when Sagari knocked on the door of his study and came in.

'I've been watching you for some time now, Amanat. You've been tense and unhappy because you feel guilty. You want to leave but you feel guilty about that too. Let me do you a favour. I'm going to ask you to leave. It will be best for both of us. You can do what you please without feeling resentful and I, I can get on with my life. Who knows, I may even meet the prince on a white steed.'

He hated her, oh how he hated her. How dare she patronize him. He'd been about to leave anyway. Why did she have to pre-empt his move? I can get on with my life, she had told him, as if she had not been carrying on regardless of him all these years. How could she humiliate him like that? It was obvious she wanted the run of the place and hoped to get him out of the way.

'Take your time. Leave whenever you want.'

How could he after she had rubbed his nose in the dirt?

'I'm leaving one chequebook for you to operate the account.'

The nerve of the woman, the bloody nerve. She was welcome to keep her damned money, he didn't want any part of it. No, not on your life. How should he phrase it? Her life? His life? Then suddenly his anger was gone. He felt alone and desperate.

Sagari, however, had not finished with him yet. 'I hope you will be happy. That's the least you owe yourself.'

What a strange thing to say. What had happiness got to do with life, at least his life?

Amanat was certain that there were mafia genes in his family. The Khans were apparently bound to their own rigid brand of omertà. Ammi had not communicated with them for well over a decade. As for Zubeida Khaala, she might not have been a Khan by birth or blood, but she had become more of a Khan than Abbajaan,

Zia and Amanat put together. The code of silence allowed neither Zubeida nor his father to ask Amanat why he had abandoned his wife and home. If they had any questions or doubts, they kept them to themselves. Amanat was grateful to be left alone, and yet he wondered whether it might have eased his conscience had he been able to unburden himself. Unfortunately, the only person with whom he had ever shared his thoughts and innermost feelings was the one person he could no longer talk to: Sagari. Besides, he was not sure how effective a purge a confession really was. Oscar Wilde may have held that absolution lies in the confession and not in repentance, but if one were to believe Coleridge's Ancient Mariner, and Amanat believed him implicitly, then spewing out one's guilt brought only the most evanescent relief. The act of confessing was like an addiction. You needed a fix every few hours.

Amanat withdrew into himself. It was difficult to avoid Abba or Zubeida in such a small flat, so he took to sleeping late and then locking himself in his father's room when Abbajaan went to work. He was ill-humoured and moody. He was turning out to be his brother. His mind had gone as slack as a hammock. He had never cared to talk about his writing, its hows and wherefores. Others were welcome to analyse and dissect the creative process. Some mysteries were best not demystified. He wasn't sure what the connection between Sagari and his writing was but he was convinced he had defiled his muse. If he ever wrote anything again, it would be tainted, sterile and perverted.

'You'll do no such thing.'

'I have no say in the matter, Zia, and neither do you. It was Abbajaan's wish. He left clear instructions in his will.'

'I've seen it and it makes no difference. He was obviously not thinking straight.'

'Christ, have you lost your head?' Amanat was losing his patience and his temper. Don't raise your voice, he kept telling himself, Zia will get the better of you if you do. But it was no use. The brothers were having their first full-blown spat since Lucens had got back from the States.

'Don't take our Lord's name in vain and I would appreciate it if you didn't use foul language.'

'And I would appreciate it if not you but Abbajaan had the final word in matters that concern him and nobody else.'

'Abbajaan's dead.'

'I'm aware of it. I don't think he wanted us to cremate him when he was alive.'

Lucens ignored Amanat's wisecrack. 'The wishes of the dead are paramount.'

Finally, Amanat thought, finally the man's talking sense. But Lucens was not finished.

'The wishes of the dead are paramount so long as they are reasonable. I'm not suggesting that Abba was not sane but he liked to think he was liberal and he tended to get carried away. He was a man of the book and it's unthinkable that we should do anything as uncouth as cremating him. It would be unforgivable if on the day of judgement, his chances of going to heaven were jeopardized because his body was not in a fit condition to be received.'

'I've listened to enough of this nonsense. I'm going to the Chandanwadi crematorium to submit the death certificate. When I get back, whether you like it or not, we'll do what Abbajaan wanted for himself.'

Amanat had no idea how much time it would take at the crematorium. He had been there once before, when Dr Pat had died, but was still apprehensive about the forms he would have to fill and whether he had all the documents that were required. Who would have imagined that Abbajaan would die the day after he was discharged from the hospital? Roy had already gone back to the States. As expected, Sagari was the worst hit. She had burrowed into a hole and refused to come out. He would have liked to accompany her home and share in her silence, but he had long since forfeited all rights to her privacy. He was grateful to Zubeida Khaala that she took it upon herself to spend the night with Sagari, despite her protestations.

In those last few days Zia had begun to behave peculiarly again. Amanat feared that he was going back to his old ways. He wondered if Abba's death would set him back even further. Maybe Bombay didn't agree with him. He was constantly edgy and irritable and spent hours on the Internet combing through the American papers. Amanat had been under the impression that the monks at Terraferra were devoid of interest in worldly matters. The good news, though, was that he would surely be leaving soon. The Abbot had made an exception in Zia's case, but wouldn't he want him back at the Abbey now that Zafar Khan was no more?

Considering that there were three other people in the queue before him, Amanat didn't do too badly for time. Within three hours he was back at Suleiman Mansion. There were about fifty men, maybe more, from the building, and people from nearby, standing outside with their heads covered with crocheted caps or handkerchiefs. Someone else too must have died, he thought, and wondered who it was. He was about to ask a neighbour when he saw the coffin come down the last few steps at a precarious angle. Zia's back was to Amanat and he was directing the pallbearers.

'Careful, it's tilting far too much to the left. Yes, that's better. Mind the step.'

'What the…what's going on?' Amanat pushed his way to his brother and forced him around. 'What do you think you are doing?'

'Trying to give our father a decent burial. Take your hands off me. You don't have to come if you don't approve.'

Amanat caught Lucens by his shirt-front and pulled him down the steps. 'Abbajaan's wishes will be carried out, not yours.'

One push from Lucens and Amanat was on the floor holding his head. The pallbearers put the coffin down on the pavement. Amanat could sense Sagari watching him from the tinted windows of her car. She had come to say her final farewell to Abbajaan.

'Can you believe this?' Lucens asked the mourners. 'My brother wants to cremate our father.' There was a collective gasp from the crowd. They began to close in on Amanat.

'I'll call the police and show them the will.' Even as he said it, Amanat realized how ridiculous the situation was and began to laugh. This couldn't be real. Abbajaan's funeral had turned into street theatre. Two sons fighting over a father's right to dictate his own last rites. The oddest thing was that Amanat was still a Muslim while Lucens was a Catholic. 'You win,' Amanat conceded defeat. He wanted to apologize to his father for letting him down even at the very end but he couldn't allow Abbajaan's funeral to turn into a farce. He wanted to get into Sagari's car and disappear. He wanted not to see Zia's face again. The coffin was lifted again and this time Amanat thrust his shoulder under it.

'I knew you would see sense,' Lucens told Amanat and walked alongside him. Sagari's car rolled off and was gone in a minute.

Nothing, there was still nothing on the Net.

Never again, Lucens vowed to himself, would he employ that stupid unreliable colonel. The news of Dr Cornelius Lester's death should have been headlined at least ten days ago but Masters had obviously ditched him. Unless, unless there was a conspiracy of silence in the media. A little far-fetched considering that *The New York Times*, *The Washington Post* and the *LA Times* had a pro-choice bias, and the doctor's death would surely be big news. Fortunately, Lucens would be back within two or three days and the suspense would be over.

His plans changed 180 degrees the next morning. He wasn't sure yet, but very likely the States and everywhere else on the five continents would be out of bounds for him. He would have to go underground. He must systematically wipe out any telltale clues of his whereabouts. They would be able to track him to Bombay; they would know which airline he had travelled on and the flight he had taken; they would find out where he had stayed and which hospital he had visited daily to look after his sick father; they would talk to his brother, his aunt, his neighbours, even Sagari. But beyond that they must come up against a blank wall. His trail must go dead. Not even Zubeida Khaala or Amanat should know where he is or even whether he's still alive. He must encash the 2000 dollars' worth of traveller's cheques that the Abbot had given him before the FBI or CIA, whoever's in charge of these matters, could alert banks all over the world, but especially in Bombay. He had been reluctant to carry so much money on him, but the Abbot had been adamant. 'You won't need it, I know, but just in case. Anyway, we'll be happy to relieve you of it the moment you are back.' He was sorry, but the Abbot would have to forget about the money.

It was ironic that Abbajaan had drawn up his will barely a month before being admitted to hospital. He had taken it as given that Brother Lucens was going to be a monk at Terraferra to his dying day, and had left him nothing. The money would certainly have come in handy now. Lucens had occasionally been curious about what Abbajaan did with his money once he began to get assignments from all over the world. Why had he and Zubeida Khaala not moved to a bigger apartment? The will solved that mystery. The preamble was addressed to the whole family. It was what you would expect of Abbajaan, simple and direct:

I wish to apologize to my children, Amanat and Zia, to their Zubeida Khaala and most of all to my wife, Shagufta, wherever she is, for the hardships they endured when we moved from Firdaus to Suleiman Mansion. I have heard it said that it is better to be born poor and then become rich than to be born rich and become penurious overnight. The first must be marvellous (don't you ever give credence to what a burden affluence is); no one wills the latter. You have no option when it happens. Shagufta and our family didn't deserve this fate, neither did I. But it did teach me a lesson. I thought I cared for the poor and the underprivileged when I was doing well. It took me time to realize that I could and must do more.

Zubeida and I haven't lived badly. We have an apartment, a fridge, a TV and enough to eat. We've been lucky. Zubeida and I found that we didn't need more than that. And what we haven't needed, we've been happy to part with for what we considered deserving causes. It's been a pittance and could be considered a pointless gesture. If many more people shared a little of their wealth, maybe it would not be such a futile exercise.

Zubeida, there is money enough to last you a long, long time. If you change your mind and want to travel, do not be abstemious. A little indulgence will do you good.

Amanat, there's some money for you too but nowhere near enough for you to live off it forever. Besides, I think you would go out of your mind doing nothing. You have so much going for you if only you would not be so hard on yourself. Perhaps you may decide to go back to your first love, architecture. The world will be a better place because of what you contribute to it.

Zia, or rather Brother Lucens, I owe you one, and Reverend Father Augustine, a very big one. You gave me my second break. I shall never be able to thank you enough. Your Abbot is the best thing to have happened to you, Lucens. One may not demand of others, one can only hope that they will demand of themselves. Don't try to improve on Jesus. Stay with the teachings of the Reverend Father. He is wise but he is also compassionate. You couldn't go wrong with him as your light.

It was a little unusual to have a third son, and that too a grown-up one, as late as we did, but better late than never. No parents could wish for a better son than Roy. You came into our lives almost exactly when Zia left us. I know that the women in the family including Sagari have been shamelessly trying to fix you up with some local houri or the other. I've not participated in the endeavour but have tacitly wished it success. Not such a bad idea, Roy, getting married. I'm no different from any other father. I would like to have grandchildren.

You've always had your eye on my roll-top desk. Did you know that my great-grandfather was a carpenter in Surat and that he made it with his own hands? So it's something of an heirloom, and it's yours.

I miss you, Shagufta. I wish you would come back. I'll miss you all the more if you come back when I'm gone. Zubeida's resources are limited but I'm sure she'll take care of you. You won't do too badly if the gambling doesn't get out of hand.

What can I give someone who knows only how to give? I've almost finished the plans for the home you want to build off the sea, Sagari. There are still a few details that need to be ironed out. If I don't see them through, get Amanat to look at the designs. He has a fine sense of space.

I'm blessed to have all of you. I love you.

Be well. And remember, it's not a crime to be happy.

Shame about the change in plans, but Lucens was not one to indulge in regrets and 'if onlys'. Colonel Masters had finally popped out of the black hole into which he had disappeared. Dr Cornelius Lester, if one was to believe the media reports, had broken his ankle and had been bedridden for a fortnight. Colonel Masters had made his move the day the doctor had gone back to the clinic. The plastic had blown up all right, but in the wrong face. Colonel Masters had lost a couple of limbs and the right side of his face, and was in a critical condition. Dr Lester, notwithstanding the blast, was Captain Courageous himself and had performed five abortions the very day he resumed his practice at the Mothercare clinic. The press reports said he had no plans to stop the good work.

The next twenty-four hours were going to be crucial. If Masters had the decency to die, Lucens would be safe and could head back.

But as any greenhorn strategist would tell you, you don't make plans on the assumption that everything will work out just fine. What if the colonel survived? He might be a military man, one who had seen a good deal of action, had been wounded, and decorated twice for exceptional courage beyond the call of duty, but he was no longer young, he was already the prime suspect in two other cases (read he was guilty as guilty can be), he had lost a lot of blood and was suffering from third-degree burns. He was in exactly the right frame of mind to tell the FBI from whom he had been taking his orders.

Lucens had twenty-four hours to decide what to do with his life. Abbajaan was right. Even though the Abbot had suggested that he might be unfit for monasticism, quitting had never been an option: he was a monk and would die a monk. Now, suddenly, he was faced with the prospect of having to reinvent himself. He would have plenty of time to think about this later. First he would have to settle on where and how he was going to do the vanishing trick. He could take a flight out to Europe, Africa, Australia or South America, but he wasn't familiar with those continents or any of the countries in them except England. England, of course, was out of the question since it was all but a colony of the US of A. The only place where he would blend into the human landscape was India. He could go to Cherapunji in the Northeast where, he had read in school, the annual rainfall was between 400 and 500 inches. But there was a heavy army presence in the area because of Mizo insurgents, and that would make him suspect. Nearer home, there was Matheran, the hill station where he had gone with Sagari. But it was far too close to Bombay, and easily accessible from the metropolis. He was bound to run into someone who would recognize him as Zafar Khan's younger son. There was one other hill station that might just fit the bill: Mahabaleshwar. It rained about 250 to 300 inches there in the monsoons, and barring a few pig-headed locals, nobody ventured there from June 15th to the end of September. A couple of hotels were bound to be open and would be only too happy to offer him a suite of rooms at ridiculously low prices. It was the first week of July. He would have close to three months to sort out his future.

He was not surprised that the news next morning was not good. Colonel Masters had regained consciousness. Lucens knew what he had to do. He would take a shower, get dressed and go to the American Express office near Regal Cinema. The dollar unfortunately was weak at the moment, and instead of a hundred thousand rupees, his traveller's cheques would fetch him barely 90,000. But that was okay. He had appointed a stockbroker the day before, and within a week or two, he would be back in the market.

The phone rang then. It was a call for him.

'Prolonging your stay in this country may not be such a good idea, Brother Lucens.' No 'hello', no 'how are you', nor any condolences, though it had to be said that the first wreath to arrive after Abbajaan's death, and the largest, was from the Holy Man. 'Now if you were to go back as scheduled it could only mean that you are innocent and have nothing to fear. Within a few weeks, a month at the most, the whole affair will have blown over. Keep as low a profile as you can in the next six months. It will give you time to think things over and take some major decisions.' Shakta Muni put the phone down without waiting for Lucens to respond.

Lucens had had his fill of Shakta Muni's phoney clairvoyance. Blast that Roy, who couldn't keep his mouth shut. Though it was something of a mystery how the Muni had got wind of his decision not to go back to the States. Maybe it was no big deal. Anybody who could put two and two together could have worked that one out. What was unnerving was that every time the Muni phoned, Lucens got the feeling that he was losing control over his life. He would have liked to assert himself. But he could not trust himself when he was with that charlatan, never mind if it was on a long distance call.

Well, Shakta Muni was welcome to give uncalled-for advice, make portentous pronouncements, take it upon himself to change the course of other people's lives, but he was underestimating Lucens. The monk had no intention of swerving from his resolve. First stop American Express, then a visit to the stockbroker. When he had said his goodbyes to Zubeida Khaala and Amanat, he would board the night bus to Mahabaleshwar.

# 44

Two FBI agents came to see Lucens at the Abbey the day after he got back. He was dead beat, suffering from jetlag, and would have liked to have scheduled the interview for the following day, but the agents preferred to interrogate him when he was disoriented.

'Jetlag makes people careless, and they spill things they would never dare tell their Father Confessor.' The older man looked down his long nose at Lucens. His colleague thought this remark wildly funny and slapped Lucens on the back. Finally, the Abbot consented to the interview, but only on condition that he was present.

'Where were you when Colonel Masters attempted to kill Dr Lester?'

'I was in India.'

'Rather convenient, isn't it? I thought you were not allowed to leave the Abbey.'

'I don't get you.'

'So that no one would link you to the doctor's attempted murder. Shame that Masters was felled by his own bomb and not the doctor.'

'Are you suggesting that I asked my father to have a heart attack?'

The FBI agent was not fazed by this news. 'Not impossible, is it?'

'No, you are right. Not impossible at all,' the Abbot interrupted the proceedings. 'He must have also instructed his father to die, because that's what happened.'

'I'm sorry to hear that but you'll grant that Brother Lucens does have something of a record. You'll recall Brother Jonathan-Christophe's death.'

'You are wrong, officer. Brother Lucens has no record even if you are trying to insinuate one.'

'The word is that Brother Lucens was the brains behind the strategic planning of the IPUC campaigns. That, as a matter of fact, "Close the roads and paralyze the city" was his idea.'

'I would like to remind you, officer, that if you've come to question a highly regarded member of my Abbey on the basis of hearsay, I must terminate the interview. Brother Lucens went to the Diocese offices on my orders. He's an expert in maths and I asked him to help the Bishopric with its accounts. If you wish to interrogate him again, make sure you come with a warrant or not at all.'

'We just might take you up on your invitation, Abbot. In the meantime, if I were you, I wouldn't let Brother Lucens out of my sight. God knows what other mischief he may be up to. See you soon, Brother Lucens.'

'Nothing but bravado,' Father Augustine remarked after the agents had left. 'They're trying to scare you because they've got nothing on you. What you want to do, though, is to ask your conscience whether it is at peace with God.'

Why on earth had he changed his plans to lie low in the quiet hill town of Mahabaleshwar, and decided at the eleventh hour to catch the flight to the States? As things had worked out, it was even later than that. There'd been a traffic jam at Mahim, and his cab had reached the airport half an hour after the flight was due to take off. But Lucens had been lucky. The flight had arrived late from London, and its departure had been delayed. What he was forgetting was that there was no such thing as luck. The rustle of a leaf, the drift of a cloud, the twitter of a bird, the stirring of the breeze, the systolic and diastolic pendulum of the blood, every birth and death was a grand design called God.

Two weeks later, Lucens went to Sweet Waters and informed Father Nicholas that it was no longer possible for him to work for IPUC. The priest was unwilling to let him go.

'Why this sudden decision to leave? IPUC owes its success as much to you as me.'

'That's generous of you but as you know I was deputed only to sort out the accounts of the Diocese. I've long since exhausted Abbot Augustine's patience. If I don't go back to being a full-time monk, I'll surely be thrown out of the Order.'

'That would not be such a bad thing, Brother Lucens. The Bishop would be only too happy to have you and ordain you a priest. Your vocation and place are with IPUC. When I retire, and that day is not too far off, you'll take over IPUC.'

'IPUC is close to my heart but it's time for me to go back to the ascetic life.'

'You know, if you change your mind, there will always be a place for you here.'

'I won't forget that, Father Nick.'

'I've been wanting to speak to you ever since you got back,' Father Theo cornered Lucens that evening after dinner. His voice sounded excited. 'I'm relieved to hear that you've given up the work at the Diocese.'

Lucens went cold. Had Father Theo got wind of his involvement with Colonel Masters? How much did the monks know? For a place that professed the importance of silence, the speed and range of word-of-mouth communication in the Abbey was staggering.

'We can now get down to some serious business,' Father Theo interrupted Lucens's thoughts. 'You were so right. The Abbot is a bad apple who must be removed before the rot sets in. I've built up a complete docket on him. We've got enough ammunition to take our case to the Chief Abbot and have him removed.'

'Why would you want to do that?' Lucens tried to focus on what Father Theo was saying. He had long since forgotten the campaign against the Abbot.

'Don't you remember? You were the one who pointed out his heretical views on suicide, homosexuality, and the obscene sculptures in the church.'

'Yes, I see what you mean.' Lucens looked away for a moment, trying to marshal his thoughts. 'I realize now,' he said, 'that I was going through a rebellious phase and being perverse. Let him be, Father Theo. He'll retire in a few years, anyway.'

Reverend Father Augustine thought he observed a change in Lucens. Zafar Khan's death seemed to have mellowed him. He had given up going to the Bishopric in Sweet Waters. He was no longer recalcitrant or resentful as he had been for the last two years. But his focus had altered. He seemed preoccupied, even absent-minded. The Abbot wondered whether Brother Lucens had finally begun to look inward, and in the best Trappist tradition, was becoming a genuine contemplative.

The real miracles since apostolic times, the Abbot had always felt, had occurred in the hearts and minds of people. Paul, the unbeliever, was of course the classic example. Lucens was the most gifted of the Abbot's flock, the one who had the capacity to be wholly and unstintingly God's and God's alone. Perhaps the day would come when there would be a stillness in him that really did fall like the first morning light across the Abbey. The Abbot wished the Novice Master had been around to see his prediction going wrong. The Lord be praised, Lucens would surely prove to be the Abbot's lucky cross.

Lucens saw himself in a rather different light. It was true that the Abbot had stood rock solid behind him. If you were in trouble your best bet was Father Augustine. He might reprimand you privately, even forbid you from having contact with the other monks or the outside world for weeks, even months, but no outsider dare cast any aspersions on a member of his Abbey. But Lucens thought he detected a coldness amongst the rest of the monks. Until he had come on the scene, the Abbey had not had visitors in the shape of policemen or the FBI. There was nothing overtly different in the monks' behaviour, and he may well have been imagining it, but he felt subtly excluded from the community.

Lucens had no idea what the future held for him. He had tried to do the right thing by his God, and the hapless unborn children, but he had failed at every stage. Come to think of it, his entire life had been a failure. Not a single venture he had undertaken or supported had succeeded. The Abbot might reassure him that the FBI had no case against him, but they would be watching his every move, and he would have to be exceptionally stupid to continue his association with IPUC. However difficult it was for him to admit it, he had reached a dead end. For the moment, like a tortoise retracting its feet and head at the first hint of the unknown, he retreated into his shell.

For weeks now, Lucens has been gazing at a ship abandoned in the middle of a wasteland unpeopled and uninhabited by any living creature. Grounded forever, it stubbornly tilts to starboard, never quite managing to keel over and rest on its side. Where are the sailors, and what has happened to the captain? Did he refuse to abandon ship? Die of starvation and loneliness? The iron body of the vessel is in an advanced state of disrepair, and is discolouring rapidly. Rust has eaten deep into it and clings to it like barnacles.

For a while Lucens thinks it's a shot from a Herzog film he had seen with Vivian, an image of a crazy man called Fitzcarraldo, transporting a steamboat across the mountains. And then he realizes that it's nothing of the kind. It's something from a BBC documentary on Kazakhstan he had watched on the plane.

Lucens knows the numbers by heart. The boat is stranded in a saltwater lake, the fourth largest in the world, 68,000 square kilometres in size. A lake so immense it's known as the Aral Sea. There's a weird synergy at work between the lake and Lucens. Every step he takes, the waters recede ten kilometres. He figures that if he takes ten steps backwards, a hundred kilometres of the lake will be restored. But the arithmetic doesn't work that way. Any step he takes, in any direction, turns the water to desert. Lucens looks on in horror as sturgeon, carp, barbel and roach gasp for water and air and life, and die in the millions in front of his eyes. What havoc has he wrought? He tells himself that the Aral has been in retreat for fifty years now. It has shrunk into three separate lakes, and if the volume of water today is less than 25 per cent of what it once was, it is because the Soviets had diverted the upper riverine waters of the Syr Darya and Amu Darya into canals for irrigation. But the facts don't make a difference. He knows he's responsible.

Lucens had always envied some of the older monks, especially Father Paul, for their easy camaraderie with God. On his deathbed, Father Paul could discuss sex with Jesus without blushing. It was one thing to claim that the Lord was all-knowing, and quite another to share everything, but everything, with Him. Lucens suspected that the Novice Master had had no secrets from the Almighty. It was as though he had enjoyed what would be a 'tum' relationship in Hindi, or a 'tu' familiarity in French, with his Maker. He could cry on Jesus's shoulder, reveal the most intimate details of his life, laugh with Him about his foibles and unburden his soul.

What would Lucens not give to be on such friendly terms with Jesus? Even when he asked for a favour of Him for the unborn children, the unemployed, and the starving, he could never demand confidently, as any child would of his loving father, 'I want this'. Instead, all he could manage was a stiff, formal tone with the most important person in his life, and as a result there would always be a cold and rigid wall separating him from the Son of God.

He needed to knock on God's door now, if necessary barge in on Him, beg Him to relieve him of his sterility, and not let go till He had answered his prayer. But he knew he could never do that.

God had His dignity, and Lucens's own sense of decorum would not permit him to breach it. Lucens wondered whether he had failed Jesus in some vital way that God must always keep him at a polite distance.

It had been a long, hard winter and the snow had not thawed until a week earlier. Spring would be short, and along with the other monks Lucens had to plough the land even after Compline, sometimes until eleven or twelve at night. It was tough work: the ground at Halfway was like a clenched fist most of the time, and driving a tractor required concentration. Lucens's back, thighs and calves ached, and his arms were about to disengage from their ball-and-socket joints.

As he walks across the dry Aral Sea for the ninth consecutive day, his eyes burn and he has a wracking cough. A sandstorm is raging, blowing across the desolate seabed, carrying with it dust laden with salt, pesticides and fertilizer. Finally, finally, he sees a green island surrounded by water. What balm it is for his eyes. He gets his second wind, he's running now, his chest is about to burst and his legs falter, and even the thought that it might be a mirage cannot stop him. At last, he plunges into the cold water. He's not sure he can swim all the way to the emerald isle, but he needn't have worried. There's a buoyancy to the water that keeps him afloat. He can take his time, lying on his back to watch the hundred thousand and forty-five fluffy puppies snuggling tightly against each other in the sky, between leisurely spells of a backstroke.

He flings himself on the beach. He could be in Krabi, the shady lagoons of Kerala, or Mauritius. Clusters of coconuts hang from the slender tops of palm trees like heavy green udders. There's a muted thud as a ripe fruit falls next to him. He slices it open with his Swiss Army knife and drinks the cool, sweet water.

He walks up an atoll to get a view of the island. There's no two ways about it: he is in paradise. For the first time he really understands what Adam and Eve lost when they disobeyed God. This is a Douanier Rousseau world, pristine and untrammelled, a miraculous blend of tropical and temperate climes. The pomegranates, kiwis, peaches, pineapples and mangoes; the dahlias, hibiscuses, peonies, daisies and crocuses; all the fruits and flowers here are larger than life and so enticingly rich in texture and bouquet, they look synthetic and genetically modified to Lucens's jaded eyes. But he has only to sink his teeth into a forbidden apple and he knows he has tasted ambrosia. His shirt-front and chest drip with juice. The flowers are pure enchantment. He picks marigolds and frangipani, weaves a garland and wears it around his neck. He knows that the blossoms will never wilt or disintegrate. But it's the colours that get to him. This is an altogether different palette from the meagre and colourless hues that he was taught to call VIBGYOR. They are vibrant living things that leap and lunge at him.

His eyes come to rest on a big hoarding on stilts. The paint is chipping and bleached, but he can make out the Cyrillic letters and underneath them the words in English: 'Welcome to Vozrozhdeniya'. He looks out over the water and sees that the mainland is barely ten kilometres away. He can't wait to give the news to his brother monks. He must talk to the Abbot about moving the Abbey to Vozwhatever.

The next day, Lucens swims back to the mainland and takes the train to the airport. The compartment empties as he boards; he tells himself that this must be the main downtown stop. But the same thing happens when he enters the plane: all the other passengers disembark in a hurry, and he's the only one left. When the plane lands in Sweet Waters, four men in full anti-viral protection gear enter the aircraft and escort him out. They inform Lucens that there is a corruption in him. It makes the waters and the land, the amphibian creatures and winged birds in the sky, his fellow-human beings, even his brother monks, flee and shun him. He's a biological menace to America and mankind. Wasn't he aware that Vozrozhdeniya was the former Soviet testing ground for biological weapons like tularaemia and bubonic plague, and that hundreds of tons of live anthrax bacteria lie buried there?

He's put in a glass cage from which he'll never be allowed to leave. He'll never meet or see anyone for the rest of his life.

When Lucens came to, he was lying in the hospital with stainless steel screws holding his left femur in place, and the leg in plaster.

'Jesus must be looking out for you,' the Abbot said when he came to visit. 'Luckily for you, when your tractor rammed into that boulder, the rock rolled down two thousand feet into the valley, but your vehicle merely overturned. What happened, Lucens? Did you fall asleep?'

What happened, what happened, what happened? Why had he begun to see himself as an agent of death? How did this shameful defeatism creep into Lucens's life? He has never had a negative thought all these years. Most of all, he's never been a quitter. Whatever the circumstances, he has always soldiered on. Now, out of the blue, he has begun to think like that stupid brother of his who cannot make a simple statement about the weather without a 'but', three 'ifs', endless 'ahems' and seven conditional clauses. His only mode of operation is vacillation and indecisiveness. But Lucens knows that the devil thrives on doubt. And that doubt makes you ineffective and impotent. His rule is, once you've made up your mind, don't look back. If you do, like Amanat, you'll turn to stone.

Far too long has Lucens been caught up in the affairs of the temporal world: the rebuilding of the Abbey; the urgent and constant need for money and more money; the thrust, parry, feint and cut of market play; then Father Nick and IPUC. Now suddenly, he's confronted with a vacuum. Emergencies, crises, the tension, the constant improvisation and, why not say it? the thrill of living on the edge, are gone, and he doesn't know how to adjust to doing nothing.

The mind is a vessel. If you don't fill it with Jesus, the devil will be only too happy to move in. Lucens wondered whether quiet and stillness scared the daylights out of him now. He had forgotten how to be a monk; to let his mind contemplate the passion and the compassion of Christ instead of being beguiled by the toings and froings of lay life. It's true, Lucens thought, let the devil in and there's the devil to pay.

But enough was enough. He was giving notice to Satan. He would fight the Aral Sea and its barrenness every millimetre of the way. Every monk who had come to visit him had told him that it was a miracle that he had survived the crash against the boulder. But that was not the only miracle. Colonel Masters had told the FBI absolutely nothing. He had refused to enlighten them, or the police, about his associates, their network or from whom he was taking orders. Jesus was indeed watching over him.

That night Lucens woke up thinking that someone had broken into his room. There was a full moon over Terraferra and the coconut-flesh light fell gently on Jesus's face. Lucens could see His thick dark hair, His kind laughing eyes, the high cheekbones and the sharp, strong cut of His chin. He was sitting on Lucens's bed and seemed lost in thought. Lucens had no doubt, none whatsoever, that the Son of God had come to visit him, but it had not occurred to him that Jesus might be clean-shaven.

When Abbajaan had unbearded Him in that central sculpture at the entrance of the church, Lucens had been convinced that his father was being heretical. He was no longer so sure.

Jesus picked up the open Bible lying on the bedside table and browsed through it. 'I find it hard to believe that I said some of the things that are attributed to me. I rather think the authors of the gospels, being eloquent, must have put words in my mouth.'

Lucens wasn't sure why He was here. If He had something on his mind He was taking His time saying it. Ten minutes passed and then thirty. He had been very different in the old days. Back then He hadn't been able to stop talking. 'You could sleep here but the sheets are not fresh. Would you care to lie down in the guest room?'

'No, I'm okay here.'

Jesus might be okay, but Lucens was getting more anxious by the minute.

'I've been wondering for some time now, Lucens, if you've been missing the wood for the trees.'

When he woke up the next morning, Lucens realized that he had been dreaming, but he was convinced there was nothing random or accidental about it. Jesus's words could be construed as a criticism of Lucens, but His tone did not suggest a reprimand. It was as though He happened to be in the vicinity and had dropped by on an impulse and had merely spoken out loud something that was on His mind.

The Lord had intervened through a dream to alert Lucens that He had a mission for him. For months Lucens had been asking the Son of God to show him the way, tell him what he should do with his life. Now, suddenly, the darkness lifted from his mind and a majestic vista opened before his eyes because of a phrase that had lingered from that dream. Of course he had been missing the wood for the trees. The wisdom of God was truly infinite. How incredibly narrow his vision had been when he thought he had finally zeroed in on the purpose of his life, and had decided to put the full moral weight of his being behind Father Nicholas's efforts to save unborn children. He had not been thinking straight, he saw that now. What had he expected to achieve by getting rid of Dr Cornelius Lester? Ten others would rise up to replace him and continue with his hateful work. Besides, that violent act was hardly going to stop people indiscriminately sleeping with each other.

The more Lucens thought about it, the clearer it became to him that he had confused symptoms with causes. For several years he had proceeded on the assumption that abortion was the problem. But if he had looked just a little further, it would surely have been evident that what he had been attacking was an outward manifestation, not the malaise itself.

Was sexual promiscuity, he asked himself, the issue? Lucens found it difficult to give credence to the figures for teenage pregnancies, especially those relating to the very early teens, and for sexually transmitted diseases. He was a statistician by training: how had he missed such crushing evidence? What he had done, he realized now, was to simply take his cues about abortion from Father Nick, instead of checking the facts himself.

He searched out the cold, incontestable numbers: the rate of pregnancies in the US was the highest in the developed world. Four out of five young people had sex as teenagers. One million, yes, one followed by six zeroes, teenagers become pregnant each year. He was even more shocked to discover that over one-third of all teenage pregnancies in the US ended in abortion. A comparative analysis between America and several countries in Europe put things in alarming perspective: the teenage birth rate in the US was four times that in Germany and eight times higher than in the Netherlands; and the AIDS infection rate in the same age group was 11.5 times higher than in Germany.

Yet Lucens had to grant that, notwithstanding the facts, sexual promiscuity was a symptom, just as AIDS and homosexuality were symptoms. It was impossible to underplay their gravity, and they would have to be addressed both separately and in conjunction with each other. But if he wanted to get to the bottom of things, then he would have to cast his net much wider.

The crisis of Western civilization, especially America, Lucens saw with an exultant and absolute clarity, was that it had lost its moral centre. Christianity was under siege, and the siege had been laid by none other than godless Christians themselves. It had become a badge of honour among West and East Coast liberals alike to scoff at God and religion. Americans, hopefully not the majority of them, had only one goal in life: to engage in an unending and ultimately futile search for new sensations and thrills. Hollywood, MTV, sexual promiscuity, the pursuit of Mammon, pornography, the obsession with guns and violence were all, this was obvious, instruments of instant gratification. And since America was the sole superpower around, and since it controlled the most powerful media, American values, or rather its perversions and its consumerism, had become the paradigm for the rest of the world.

Clearly, America was exhibiting the same signs of profligate depravity as the Roman Empire when it hurtled towards dissolution. But the situation, Lucens felt with weird certainty, was not altogether irreversible. What needed to be done was to turn the world upside down. The very nature of the value systems in the country had to be changed. The US had to be taken back, by force if necessary, to a state of innocence and grace.

And who was going to accomplish this? Was it really true that only a madman would think such a project possible? Fine. Call it Mission Impossible. Let the cynics scoff. What would they know of the power of an idea backed by Jesus Himself?

It took just one inspiring monster and mass murderer, only one, to change the nature and future of a people. Call him Hitler or Stalin or Mao. What might not a collective of righteous men of firm resolve, clear vision and fierce faith do? As the first step, these good people would rouse the conscience of the critical mass of middle Americans, who must number in the millions. At the same time, there was no point merely addressing people from the Bible belt. That would amount to leaving out half of America. The issue of teenage pregnancy affected the children of liberals as much as those of ordinary, hardworking, Christian folk. What leftist would enjoy subjecting his 12-year-old daughter to an abortion? And what parent, in God's name, would wish AIDS upon his child?

Lucens reasoned that if you wished to change the way America thought, you would need to exert the kind of clout that the highest lawmakers could ignore only at the risk of losing their office and power. In short, let them delude themselves that they are in charge. Let them hold the gun and pull the trigger, so long as you took aim.

How short-sighted he had been when he was at IPUC. He had been a sniper, and not a very effective one at that. His tactics had crossed over to the wrong side of the law. That was foolish and counterproductive, to say the least. It was amazing what the law could get away with. No mafia don would dare in broad daylight to commit the crimes the police do.

One thing was absolutely clear to Lucens: pro-life would have to remain the focus; but pro-life in a much wider ethical context. With the whole law-making machinery under the control of like-minded people, abortions, same-sex marriages, funding of family planning and other despicable institutions would disappear for good. America would find its soul again, and Jesus would triumph.

He divided his plan of action into three phases: the short term covered the first five years; the second stretched to the end of year twelve; and the last concluded in the twentieth year. He knew what he wanted, and he had a fair idea how to go about achieving his aims.

Nine months after he had returned to the Abbey, Lucens gave up the monk's habit and left Terraferra.

Once again, what he needed was money.

# 45

My dear Zia,

That night the allergy specialist came to see me in my room at the hospital. He said that so far I had been lucky to have been allergic mostly to vegetable proteins but now I had begun to react badly to the standard variety of animal proteins too. There would not only be further restrictions on what I could and could not eat but I would have to get used to foods that appeared not a little exotic. Rabbit and venison, he felt, should from now on be my staple diet.

•

A bit difficult to have access to these meats, especially in Bombay, but Ammijaan, as you well know, has friends in high places and more to the point, can be very, very persuasive when she sets her mind to it. Within a week I had a regular supply of rabbit and venison. Incidentally, my taste buds must be singularly ungourmet-like, for I still cannot fathom why they make such a fuss about deer meat. It's tough enough to dislocate one's jaw and has a raw off-putting flavour. That never got to be a serious problem though: a couple of months later, maybe three at the most, I nearly went into anaphylactic shock due to my new diet.

When I recovered, there was the usual whispered confabulation amongst my pulmonary consultant, the allergy man, the resident internist who's supposed to keep track of the whole picture, and our family physician. The next morning the GP came over and told me that from now on I was to eat lightly cooked cat flesh with a hint of ginger and cardamom and nothing else.

'Sure', I said, 'but you forgot to mention the hyena chutney.'

'This is no joking matter, Amanat,' he replied. 'It's nothing less than a survival tactic.'

'You are having me on,' I laughed, but even then I knew that he was in earnest. 'Cat?' I asked. 'You mean domesticated cats?'

'Anything in the cat family,' he said. 'If you've got access to the bigger cats, they'll do too.'

It turned out Abbajaan had designed a country house for the former manager of Kenyan Airways and the man was now on the board of directors of the airline. It would not be cheap, but at least we were assured of a regular supply of cat meat.

When I look back on those days, I realize how unappreciative I was of the good Lord's mercies, small and big. Leopard or lion flesh may not be everybody's cup of tea but in time I developed a taste for it…till of course things went terribly wrong and cat meat was out too.

I knew then that that was the end of the line for me. I had often asked myself why I bother; why I bother to gasp and grasp for air if every breath takes so much effort and brings so much pain and grief. And yet I was so greedy for life that I had never really come to terms with the fact that it would all end one day. Now that day was upon me and there was no escaping it.

I guessed that it would not be the GP who would come around this time. I was right. The chest specialist, like others of his ilk when they come bearing ill tidings, had the special long and solemn face that he had got out of his winter clothes closet. He turned up at the time the night nurse gave me the last shot of the day and turned out the lights. He waved her out with a 'Good night, sister' and sat down on my bed and patted my hand.

'We both know that your condition is close to desperate but I believe there is reason not to give up hope. The Americans, as you know, are at the cutting edge in the field of allergies and they've had fairly encouraging results with a rare kind of animal protein.'

'I thought I was already on a rather flamboyant variety of animal protein,' I told him, perhaps a little too brusquely.

He was obviously used to such outbursts and didn't lose his cool.

'Let's just say the new food is even more unusual. We should be getting samples of it in the next couple of days. Till then it's best that we continue to feed you intravenously.'

Any unfamiliar food starting from mother's milk is a shot in the dark. Taste, I fear, is overrated. To put it baldly, taste is mostly habit. The first two days are always difficult. After that Komodo dragon meat is just as welcome as cat or coyote flesh. The new food was a new lease of life. I had good reason to be grateful for it.

The pulmonologist told me in the middle of the second month that I had adjusted rather well to the changed diet.

'From now on,' he said, 'you must make your own arrangements to get a regular supply.'

'I could try,' I told him, 'though it would help if I knew what I was to order for my meals.'

He looked at me quietly for a long moment. 'It's human flesh. Not carrion but good, healthy flesh.'

I threw up for days. That was only natural but I had also lost the ability to talk. My tongue had retracted deep into my throat and I didn't seem to mind it. I had no desire to have commerce with the world. The truth is this time around I *wanted* to die.

One morning I felt hungry again. Not just for food but for company, for life itself. It was not that I had overcome my moral scruples, my repugnance. I had merely begun to appreciate that life goes on and God helps those who help themselves.

In the beginning things were difficult. I ate what I could get. Human meat is not easy to come by and costs an arm and a leg. (Unintended pun that, but nevertheless in terrible taste.) Don't get me wrong. There's no shortage of it, especially in a country like ours. But there were no established channels of supply and distribution. Perhaps it was the prohibitive costs that led me to study the market; perhaps I had merely discovered an unsuspected talent for organization and enterprise.

The fatality rate from accidents, not just in the four metros like Bombay, Delhi, Calcutta and Madras, but in cities and towns like Bangalore, Pune and Kanpur, is one of the highest in the world. Add monetary persuasion and once you've established the modalities, it would be possible to organize a fairly reliable supply. All of which meant that with proper refrigeration facilities, we were never short of fresh meat. Frankly, I must confess that I was at times dismayed by the enthusiasm and eagerness of some of the police operatives. There were instances where the accident victim might perhaps have survived if he had been rushed to hospital and given emergency treatment, but the authorities involved preferred to push the injured party into the arms of Hades. I need hardly add, however, that the success of the project would have been inconceivable without the co-operation, some would prefer to call it connivance, of the coroners, hospital staff, judges and other well-meaning people.

It's only with experience and a little bit of imagination that one learns the ropes and becomes innovative. Soon our dependence on accident fatalities went down drastically. I had, as the Americans say, lucked out. I found a new source of supply and even if I say so, the quality of the new product was infinitely superior. It is so much better and tastier, there is now a demand for it, perverse as it may sound, even amongst those who are perfectly healthy. There is a thriving black market for it and it is served by a few select restaurants as a rare delicacy to their most valued clientele.

What I am talking about is human foetuses. India is often categorized by foreign diplomatic corps as a hardship post. Yet even this benighted country of ours can boast of not altogether small blessings. Abortion is legal and available everywhere. If you happen to travel by local train in Bombay, you would find poster after poster promoting safe, hygienic abortions for Rs 75. That's not even two US dollars. The owners of these clinics, mostly seedy doctors, were more than happy to earn money on something that had so far only been a major waste-disposal problem.

Success always engenders imitation and we soon had competition. But it has never posed a serious threat to us. No diseased or unsafe foetus has escaped our quality check. Our foetuses come hot, I use the word advisedly, from the wombs of their mothers. You can literally taste their freshness; something that our competitors just can't match.

I may have spoken a little prematurely when I said that we'll never run short of suppliers. The demand for our product is worldwide and rising, particularly in Australia, which has the dubious distinction of the highest rise in allergy patients. But, as you may have guessed, our biggest market is the West, especially America. I'm already exploring possibilities in Thailand, Sri Lanka, Pakistan, Vietnam and several African countries as future suppliers. The prospects for business look good and we may be going public earlier than I had anticipated.

Our motto: We'll stop at nothing for you. For further information on our activities, look us up on the Internet at http://www.rarefoods.com.

Zia, what a wonderful surprise it was to receive the Graham Greene book. I had no idea that he made it a point to get up in the middle of the night to jot down his dreams. I'm afraid I'm far too lazy and lacking in discipline to do that sort of thing.

No letter from you again. I'm getting to be a nag, aren't I?

Come, brother mine, don't make yourself so scarce.

Love,

Amanat

1001,

You are despicable. How dare you send that ghastly story in the garb of a letter to me? Only a satanic imagination like yours would think of something so disgusting.

From the time that I remember, I've known you to be a very sick person. Sick in the body, that is. Now I know how wrong I was. You are sick in the head. Maybe you always were and your terrible physical ailments are a manifestation of your ghoulish and morbid mind. What is unforgivable is that you make God a party to your depraved ravings. How could you possibly suggest that 'God helps those who help themselves' is validation of your cannibalism?

I'm ashamed to call you my brother. Even hell would be too kind a place for you.

Lucens

My dear Zia,

I had no idea that my last letter would upset you so much. I was hospitalized once again with, as you know, one more lethal food allergy and lay swollen as a porpoise on a full belly, unable to speak, move or turn on my side.

The doctor came by one evening on his rounds and told me that my options in terms of what I could eat were narrowing fast. I must have looked a trifle anxious for he patted my arm and said cheerfully, 'No need to panic, Mr Khan, at least not yet. I must send you an old issue of *Newsweek* that speaks of some patients who are so highly allergic they have to live in plastic bubble-tents and can only eat strange foods like lion or snake flesh.'

When I read the article some days later, I was struck by how wilfully we had ruined our planet, its waters and air, and by destroying the ecological balance, endangered ourselves; and the lengths the sick like me will go to, to survive. But it's not only the sick who are sick in the head. The healthy are no better. You'll be amazed how many normal people who go to the game parks in Africa want to try out zebra, giraffe or cat meat. Besides, have you not heard that 'snuff' movies, in which real people are actually killed, have a substantial viewership all over the world?

I thought I would write an essay along the lines of Jonathan Swift's *A Modest Proposal*. Sorry to have got you so hot and bothered.

Love,

Amanat

P.S. I can hardly think of anything worse than my febrile fantasies and fictions turning out to be prescient. You were incensed by my last letter about unusual foods. Oh Zia, the reality, it turns out, is far, far more dreadful. I was browsing through a British weekly this morning when I came across an article about Russian women who spend a fortune taking injections of aborted foetuses in the hope that they would never lose their beauty and youth.

It appears that this is one of the bizarre offshoots of the stem-cell controversy in the West, especially in the States. There is no scientific evidence, none whatsoever, to support the thesis that these cells would help women retain their youthful looks, but the idea seems to have taken quick and deep root in President Putin's Russia.

# 46

The impulse behind America was utopian. It was a fresh start, an adventure into the possible, a one-off chance to make the normative a reality, a fervent attempt to build Eden. The precondition of paradise, however, is that you must lose it.

Look at the names of US towns, cities and even states, and you sense that America is a continent of homesickness and nostalgia. It is about missing and yearning. It is about memory, myth and lost continents. It's a new world that cannot forget the old. It's a land that nearly wiped out and forgot its original inhabitants and repeopled it with migrants and immigrants. It's a brash new world where each succeeding wave of immigrants bestows legitimacy and aristocratic pedigree on the previous one. It rejects the past and clings to it. It cannot make up its mind whether to opt for amnesia or to remember, and so it romanticizes and reinvents homelands.

You did not set out on the *Mayflower* from Plymouth for unknown lands unless you were persecuted, starving or deeply unhappy and wanted to make a new life at any cost. But once the new settlers were secure, they tried to make an uneasy peace between the old and the new, the past and the present: New York, New London, New Jersey, New Brunswick, New Mexico, New Lisbon, New Hampshire, New England. Having erased the history of the Amerindian natives and turned their backs on their own, the other option for them was to ransack antique civilizations and create semblances of venerable ancient traditions and history: Troy, Athens, Ithaca, Jericho, Rome, Naples, Florence.

By the twentieth century, the new continent thought it was time to flex its muscles and create its own myth: the American Dream. Anybody, but anybody, Americans like to believe, can access the Dream, though it's a little difficult to know what exactly they mean by it. Is it Jesus or is it Mammon? Sometimes the two seem interchangeable. To be an American is to be riven by polarities: puritanical intolerance is companion to monumental greed and the pursuit of the sybaritic life. It is a lucky continent; they have everything in excess and extremes.

Lucens too will dream the American Dream and hunt for the Holy Grail. He will settle in a small town called Sparta on the border of Pennsylvania and New York state. He will try to transform this faceless, colourless, odourless place, like the 99,999 others suffering from interminable suburbia, into a powerhouse of moral energy, inspiration and influence.

He has chosen Sparta, Penn. after long and careful deliberation. It is a God-fearing, closely-knit community that has the third lowest crime rate in America. Most Spartans work as lab technicians, nurses, parking-lot attendants and administrative assistants for a major hospital facility called Glades some fifteen minutes to the west of Lake Santa. Twenty-five miles from Sparta are the twin towns of Concord-Ashton. The latter was at one time a flourishing dairy-produce centre, while Concord was once the shoe capital of America. The shoe factories have all closed down now, and but for the Glades Medical Center, so would the airport.

The first thing Lucens did after settling down in his motel in Sparta was to go to the county office and register a trust in the name of The Guardian Angels. Reverend Father had loaned him three thousand dollars to start his new life, and almost all of it was gone in lawyer's fees and on the deed paper. It was a small place and by the evening word was out that there was a new man in town who was going to start a trust.

Lucens and the team he built, and the people who joined them, aimed to become the guardians of the Living Christ and of a reborn moral America. In time, nobody would remember the name Lucens Kahn. He was the Angel and would always be that for the people of the three counties of Sparta, Glades and Pylon.

Lucens had been trying to get through to Roy for five days but was first told that he was travelling in Europe, and was now informed that there had been a change of plans and Roy had left for India and would not be back for ten days. Lucens couldn't help a wry smile floating up to the corners of his mouth. He had thought that he had factored in all the things that could go wrong. Well, he had better think again. The timing of the setback was unfortunate. He was out of the game before he had made his first move. What he had hoped to do was to touch Roy for $20,000 to be returned within a fortnight at 30 per cent interest, and to move into the market. Now, by the time the week was over, he wouldn't have the small change to buy a hamburger or a hot dog. He would check out from his motel tomorrow before 12 p.m. and go to the campsite on Lake Santa and wait for Roy to get back.

The next morning he was surprised to hear the phone ring in his room as he was about to leave. He had a bus to catch and was running a little late. Must be the Gujarati owner's daughter at the reception checking to see if the room was free to be cleaned. It was a woman's voice, but not the Gujarati woman's.

'Mr Lucens Kahn, my name's Honor Lockman. I'm the manager of the First Penn Bank in Sparta. Would it be convenient for you to drop by at the bank? Or would you rather that I came over and we met at the motel café?'

'I was about to leave. May I know in what context you wish to see me?'

'Yes, of course, but I would rather not talk on the phone.'

'I'll be at your office in half an hour.'

'I've instructions from the head office to hand over a draft for $100,000 to you,' Honor Lockman said to Lucens, after he turned up at the bank and introduced himself, 'and to be of assistance to you in any way I can.'

Lucens laughed. 'The money would be most welcome, Ms Lockman, but you've got the wrong party.'

'I doubt it. I checked at your motel and they told me that your previous address was listed as the Abbey at Terraferra. Isn't that so?'

'Yes, it is.'

'Then there's no mistake.'

Lucens was having a difficult time deciding who was making an ass of him. The only person who knew his whereabouts was the Abbot, and he was not into juvenile pranks.

'Who's the cheque from?'

Honor Lockman pushed a printout across her table.

My dear Lucens,

Congratulations. Few people hurt for others. And even if they do, they will rarely do something about it. You are different. You care and you are a man of vision and action.

I join Shakta Muni and Deirdre in wishing you the very best in the work you are setting out to do. We hope that the good people in the world will support you in your endeavour and contribute to it in any way they can. I'm pleased that we are the first to do this. Shakta Muni is of the opinion that it's the best investment we are likely to make in this lifetime.

Regards,

James Cambray

After leaving India the last time, Lucens had said to himself that he would never again have anything to do with the Muni. As a matter of detail, he never had. It was Shakta Muni who poked his nose into Lucens's affairs and offered advice gratis when none was asked, though it had to be said that on the last day in Bombay, Lucens had indeed followed his counsel and returned to America. All things considered, it had not worked out too badly. Even if he hadn't formally broken off from the Muni, that chapter was nevertheless closed; frankly, the book too. In metaphorical terms, and in reality, he was turning a new leaf, starting a new life.

Get up, Lucens. Say thank you to Honor Lockman and walk out of First Penn Bank. Ten days won't make a difference. Roy will be back then and you will be trading in no time. And what if Roy said no, he couldn't lend him the money? Don't be absurd, Lucens. Roy had not said no to him in all these years. Not once.

The money, however, was already here. Ten days was not a long time, but it would give him a head start. A hundred thousand, he had to admit, was eighty thousand more than he had planned to ask for from Roy, and the windfall was not to be scoffed at. Besides, Shakta Muni himself was looking at it as an investment. James Cambray had said as much. Lucens was obviously confusing things. He was doing them a favour and not the other way round. He would return the money at 30 per cent interest within a month, make it 40 per cent. Where else in the world was either the Muni or James Cambray likely to get that kind of return? The debt would be cleared and he would be free of the obligation once and for all. Besides, the last time he had taken a cheque from Cambray senior, for the reconstruction of the Abbey, he had not had any qualms, and the thought of paying the money back had not occurred to him then. This time he most certainly would, no question about it.

'Would you like to withdraw a part of the money or all of it just now?'

'I aim to trade in the market, Ms Lockman.'

'Call me Honor.'

'My stockbrokers are Cambray and Cambray, New York. I'll be asking them to liaise with you from now on.'

*

It's a moot point whether Lucens was merely the latest in the long line of American conservatives, starting from Washington, Jackson, John Foster Dulles and McCarthy, down to Nixon, Jerry Falwell, Pat Robertson, Rush Limbaugh and the Bush cabinet. He may well have been, but he didn't fit the arch-conservative template too well. He was a Catholic, not a Protestant or a born-again evangelist. He was an extreme ascetic and still followed the monk's routine of seven offices a day. He did not indulge in sexual peccadilloes and there was not a whiff of financial finagling about him. The conservative anthem of less taxation for the rich was anathema to him, as was the Republican travesty of compassion. Christ was not a smoke screen. He was the reason why life was worthwhile to Lucens.

His first two initiatives for the Guardian Angels were testimony to the fact that his vision had tapped into something fundamental in the American psyche. In time, the Angels would number in the hundreds of thousands.

The first was called Zero Orphans, and the second, Pledge of Purity.

The key argument against the pro-lifers had always been that they were good at making lofty pronouncements against abortion, but they didn't really ask why so many women were forced to go down that road. Part of the reason for clandestine abortions was, of course, the stigma attached to illicit pregnancies. But there was no denying that young girls, especially teenage girls, simply couldn't face the terrifying responsibilities of motherhood, in most cases without money or support. State-run orphanages were hardly the answer, since they almost always turned out to be breeding grounds for future criminals.

The tone at IPUC had been one of Old Testament retribution: an eye for an eye and vengeance is mine. The focus was on individual villains, and the objective was to eliminate them. The ethos behind the Guardian Angels would be far more mellow and life-affirming.

The plan was ambitious. The Angels would buy or rent houses that would be called Homes for the Children of God. Unlike orphanages or charitable institutions, each Home would have a Mother and Father and ten children. The idea was to give personal care and attention to each child till he or she was sixteen. There would be separate homes for boys and girls, and the Angels would look after all the child's needs, including education at a parochial school. The test of how well a Home was faring was pragmatic in its simplicity: the Children of God would have to do better at studies and sports than children from middle-class families. A committee of educationists, paediatricians, psychologists and other specialists would supervise the performance of each Home.

11th Jan: Sent cheque for 150,000 to James Cambray. Goodbye Shakta Muni. Goodbye forever.
14th Jan: Cambray Sr. wrote to say: 'You shouldn't have really. It was a donation to a good cause.' But he kept the money nevertheless. There was another note along with James's. 'Happy to hear you are doing well and your projects are about to take off. If you want something, get in touch. Or come to see me. Wishing you and the Guardian Angels the best. Shakta Muni.'

Lucens caught Honor Lockman as she was going home from the bank.

'You helped me get my place and you've introduced me to most of the people I know here. Now I'm about to ask you a much bigger favour. It's for the Children of God. I don't know much about parenting or about children. I would prefer to trust your judgement and instincts in this matter. Will you help me interview the 53 couples who have applied for the job of foster parents and choose the ones you think will care for the children as much as they would for their own? Before you answer, let me tell you that I can't afford a no from you.'

Honor laughed. 'Why ask if you've already made up your mind for me? I'll be happy to help you in any way I can.'

By April end, Honor and he had short-listed two pairs of foster parents, the Prestons and the Burgesses. The former couple was childless, while the Burgesses had lost their only son in a car accident when he was seven. Both couples were lonely and eager to start new families. Father Raymond was willing to vouch for the Prestons' integrity, but it was Honor's word that shifted the balance in favour of the Burgesses. It took another three months to buy a suitable home, and furnish it.

*

23rd May: Have been boning up on Roe v. Wade. The shame, the terrible shame of it.

The blackest day in American history, one that hardly anyone noticed or mourned, was January 22nd 1973, when Justice Blackmun and six of his colleagues in the Supreme Court decided that it was legal to murder unborn children.

Roe equals Jane Roe, real name Norma McCorvey. In 1970 she filed a federal suit against Henry Wade, then district attorney in Dallas County, challenging the Texan law that decreed abortion illegal, except when the mother's life was at stake. Roe claimed the law itself was unconstitutional.

She shouldn't have won. It was a Nixon court, and Henry Wade had never lost a case.

But Wade and team failed to see that the real enemy was not Roe, her attorney, Sarah Waddington, or liberals in court, but conservatives on the bench. A fatal miscalculation. Majority decision written by Justice Henry Blackmun, right-of-centre Nixon appointee. Chief Justice Warren E. Burger (also a Nixon man) voted along with Blackmun and four others. Siding with Roe, they struck down the Texas statute on grounds of right to privacy, purportedly implicit in the 14th Amendment to Constitution.

Observations: The actual amendment did not imply any such thing. But even if, for the sake of argument, the right to privacy was indeed explicitly granted by the 14th, the 9th Amendment already stated that all such rights cease to operate when they impinged on the rights of others. Did Blackmun, Burger et al. stop to consider for a moment the inviolable right of the foetus?

When six million Jews are killed, it's called a holocaust. When Hutus wipe out hundreds of thousands of Tutsis, the word is genocide. But what is one to call the murder of over 42 million foetuses at the rate of 1,365,000 a year, all of them legally sanctioned by the highest court of the land?

The situation, however, is much more hopeful today. Norma McCorvey, the former Jane Roe, has repented of her misguided act and is now a totally committed pro-lifer. She is running the Crossing Over Ministry, a non-profit anti-abortion organization. The other great hope is the Supreme Court itself. Its colour and complexion have changed radically over the past few years. The Angels must take a much more proactive stand on the issue, and work side by side with like-minded groups. If the case is argued cogently, there is a very good chance of getting Roe v. Wade reversed.

Lucens sat in the third row of St Peter's between Honor and Dr Som Puri and his wife Revati. In the front row were the mayor of Concord-Ashton and the other trustees of the Guardian Angels. Honor had decided to make the baptism of the first of the Children of God a community event, and the church was packed.

Father Raymond was in full flood this morning. 'As we celebrate baptism in this Christian assembly, let me ask you: can anyone dare call the Children of God, orphans? Most children these days are lucky if they have a single set of parents. The Children of God are a hundred, nay, a thousandfold more fortunate. Every couple here, every single man and woman assembled here today at St Peter's is a parent to the Children of God. Why else would you all be here? Surely it is because you, who share a serious commitment to the spirit and mission of Christ, will take personal responsibility for the wellbeing and welfare of this child as he begins his journey into a life of faith and as an honest and upright citizen of our country.'

Som Puri winked as he caught Lucens raising his eyebrows and grimacing at the priest's inflated rhetoric. Apart from Honor, Som Puri was the closest thing to a friend Lucens had in Sparta. It was curious how Americans took the trouble to distort even the simplest names if they were alien and unfamiliar. Almost everyone, including Honor, called the doctor, Sam.

Lucens had met Som Puri some months ago, when the Angels were looking for a paediatrician for the Children of God. The doctor had walked into the office with a copy of *The Guardian Weekly*, and the sight of the British newspaper filled Lucens with an uprush of longing for England: the brash and blustering sea at St Ives, the lore of Sherlock Holmes at the Baker Street Underground station, for fish and chips, for the Orchard where Lytton Strachey, Virginia Woolf and John Maynard Keynes had had tea and scones. Dr Puri, it turned out, had studied at Cambridge, and had got his MRCP in London before immigrating to the States. He was older than Lucens, but the two men had more in common than nostalgia for the British Isles. They were lonely and starved for company.

Som started sending Lucens back issues of *The Guardian Weekly*, *The London Review of Books* and, for reasons best known to him, even the *Lancet*. All through the years that Lucens had spent at the Abbey, he had taught himself not to think of what was on his plate, but merely to swallow it. Now he found himself looking for excuses to visit the Puris so that they would ask him to join them for an Indian meal. He began to drop in at Som's place on the slightest pretext: the latest Harry Potter book for the Puri kids; the copy of *Prospect* he had forgotten to return; a packet of the purest Spanish saffron for Revati.

There were times when Som reminded Lucens of Abbajaan. Like his father, the doctor was interested in everything: architecture, philosophical concepts, politics, history, art. He was also an unrepentant liberal, and he and Lucens could rarely see eye-to-eye on any subject. The two of them almost stopped talking to each other because both had such strong and diametrically opposite views on abortion.

'Pro-life is fine for a rich country like America. But thank god you are not minister for family planning in India. With your kind of extreme anti-abortion stance, we would be two billion there by 2015 and three billion by 2025. And probably resort to cannibalism for want of food.'

Often, Lucens would decide to break off from Som. There were times when he didn't see the doctor for a full five days, but then Som would invariably take the initiative and call him.

'Where have you been all this time? Don't tell me you're sulking because of that little tiff we had.'

'What tiff?' Lucens would make a show of not remembering.

'Good. I'm glad it's all forgotten. Sometimes I tend to go overboard. Why don't you come over for dinner tonight?'

Somewhat unwillingly, Lucens would get out of his apartment, and return in good cheer three or four hours later.

If Som had his moods, they were certainly never on display when Lucens was around. He was guileless, and what he had to say, he said to your face. Maybe that was not such a good idea in the hothouse of intrigue that Glades Medical was. Many of his colleagues envied his rapport with children, and resented the fact that parents made no bones about asking for him even when some other paediatrician was on duty. The problem with him, they suggested, was that he got too involved with his patients, and far too often crossed the line between professional and personal. 'Sure I get personal,' Som would bristle, 'how else can you behave with a child?'

*

Gladys and Alfred Burgess were standing at the font alongside Father Raymond now. Lucens wanted to holler at the Catholic priest as he poured a thin thread of water over the child's head. He was convinced that unless the whole physical body of the baby was immersed in the water, the baptism would be incomplete: the head cleansed of original sin, and the torso suspended in purgatory till Judgement Day. Lucens heard his name being called out then and was about to get up, when the whole congregation started clapping.

'Lucens, I baptize you in the name of the Father, the Son and the Holy Ghost,' Father Raymond intoned in a clear voice.

'How does it feel to have your first-born named after you?' Dr Puri ribbed Lucens.

For once Lucens was at a loss for words. 'I don't know whose idea it was.' He turned to Honor who looked like a cat pretending it had not eaten the family parakeet. 'It was you, wasn't it?'

'Nothing to do with me.' Honor wrinkled her nose and shrugged her shoulders theatrically. 'Ask Father Raymond. I must say it's not such a bad name though.'

It was time, Lucens decided, to open the second front. Zero Orphans was a necessary idea, and a step in the right direction, but there was no escaping the fact that it was wisdom only after the event. It ignored the injunction against premarital sex. And tragically, it did not address the problem of AIDS. What was needed was something far more fundamental, something that went to the very root of the problem.

It's taken almost as a manifest truth that adolescents today are so much more worldly-wise, plugged-in and sex-savvy than any previous generation. Lucens begs to differ. They might have a certain sophistication, they might be a tad more knowledgeable, but as extensive studies have shown, most of the time, ignorance is king, and misconception his consort. Twelve- and thirteen-year-olds have only the vaguest idea of the mechanics of sex. Some of the notions they have would be droll if they did not lead to such serious consequences.

The fact is, they are children, immature, scared, confused children. Whatever little they know is from the perpetual bump-and-grind, soft-core pornography that the nexus between the music industry and channels like MTV parlays into gold and platinum albums and multi-million-dollar profits. But the main culprit is peer pressure. Jane, Roger, Soledad, Tracy, X, Y and Z are doing it. If you want to be perceived as a regular guy or girl, then you do the sex thing whether you want to or not.

But what if the trend could be reversed? What if abstinence could be made more desirable, even sexy? The only way anybody could pull that off would be to make rebellion tempting; to put a premium on being different; make Jesus far more irresistible than all the wiles and seductions of the devil.

This was the most challenging task the Angels would undertake. Lucens tried his hand at TV commercials to promote abstinence.

20th July: 20-second TV spot. Girls and boys in punk hairstyles and clothes dancing mechanically to mechanical music. Cut to girls with the same hairstyles, same kind of clothes and same kind of look, and the same for boys coming out of school. Cut to sheep.

Voiceover of a young girl sneering: 'Just look at them. They look the same, they think the same, they talk the same. Give me a break, how boring can you get?' A long shot of a clean-cut girl in jeans and a simple top. Camera closes in on her. Voiceover: 'Takes guts to be different. And be numero uno.' (Pause) 'Are you different?'

Legend at the bottom of the screen: One million teenagers get pregnant every year. Will you be different? Or end up being girl number one million and one?

TV spot for parents. Shot of parents and 12-year-old daughter watching an adult movie together; mother admiring the daughter as she puts on a mini, and showing her how to apply lipstick.

Voiceover: 'You think you are such a hip, cool parent, you treat your 12-year-old daughter as an equal and give her all the freedom you never had? Children need love, openness and a clear framework of right and wrong. Not some fake notion of equality.'

Legend at the bottom of the screen: 'One million teenagers get pregnant every year. Your girl's going to hate you if you don't parent her right. Be a parent, not a false friend.'

Would this do the trick? Of course not. It was the next step that would be crucial: the Pledge of Purity. The idea was to get young men and women to promise before the living Christ, to abjure sex until they got married. This was not an entirely new concept. Organizations like The Ring Thing were already doing something similar. But anybody could take off the ring and forget the commitment to abstinence that it implied. Lucens could not guarantee that the Pledge would be honoured either, but he intended to make certain that the ritual, and the oath that accompanied it, would be indelible.

The crux of the ceremony would be a discreet tattoo of the cross on the body, together with the words 'Pledge of Purity'. But the real tattoo would be on the soul itself. Lucens conceived the ceremony as a journey in imitation of Christ, where the young aspirant would follow in the footsteps of the Lord as he visited the fourteen stations of the cross. It would be an intense and unforgettable experience.

Wearing a crown of thorns and carrying a heavy cross, the young postulant would finally stumble up a simulated Calvary to the roar of boos, catcalls and jeering from the rest of the gathering. But the traumatic moment was yet to come. Defenceless and utterly shaken, the aspirant would now be hoisted and tied to the cross. It would be a terrifyingly lonely moment; a time to remember the Lord and understand what He had suffered for mankind. That one long minute would be imprinted forever on those who participated in the ritual. Every time they were tempted to break the Pledge, they would know that they were personally responsible for crucifying Jesus all over again. And because the tattoo would stay for life, they would think twice before indulging in adultery after marriage.

23rd July: What does one do with these gutless and blundering liberals? In Michigan and some other states, if a teenager steals or drinks, the parents are held responsible and must pay damages. It's time the same law applied to the parents of children who become pregnant or get sexually transmitted diseases. I can't wait for the day when the Angels will be so powerful, we'll get legislation passed that will condemn guilty parents to years of hard labour.

Amanat forwarded a letter to Lucens of which he couldn't make much sense. It was friendly enough, but it left Lucens with a sense of unease.

Dear Friend,

We live in strange times. Neither you nor I can afford to reveal our true names. We are God's little soldiers, a term I believe you coined, and must perforce live incognito till we have achieved our objectives. But I have long felt that I know you better than my family or my closest friends.

The sins of fathers visit their sons, and however innocent the sons may be, they must suffer the opprobrium of others. Yes, even their most honourable acts are sullied. Sometimes it takes a lifetime to erase the stigma.

This I assure you: I will prove myself worthy, and above all suspicion.

For the time being, let me remain,

Your nameless comrade-in-arms.

# 47

That morning, soon after ten, the Abbot called Lucens.

'I wanted you to come over to Terraferra today for a fortnight's retreat, but I'm told that all flights have been temporarily cancelled. Can you hear me, Lucens?'

Silence at the other end.

'Talk to me, Lucens, I don't want you to do anything foolish. Just hang in there. I'll speak to Father Raymond at St Peter's and get him to look in on you. Are you all right, my son? This has nothing to do with you, do you understand that? Nothing.' All Father Augustine could hear was Lucens's breathing.

'Listen to me. I want you to hold the cross with both your hands and pray for all those who died this morning. In the name of God Almighty, say something, Lucens. The moment flights are resumed, I'll come to Sparta and bring you back with me. You are in my thoughts all the time. Your brother monks here and I will pray for you. May God be with you. I'll call as often as I can.'

Father Raymond rushed in within twenty minutes of the Abbot's call. As always, the door to Lucens's home was unlocked. When Honor had located the small three-room home for him, he had named it 'Open House'. He meant it. Anybody without a roof over his head could park himself there.

'You seem perfectly okay to me.' Father Raymond sounded breathless and not a little aggrieved. 'I don't know what your former Abbot was making all that fuss about. You are not the only one stressed out, we all are. These are apocalyptic times. For all we know, it is the end of the world and Judgement Day is nigh. The important thing is not to go to pieces.' Father Raymond continued babbling, but Lucens was past hearing him. He had gone back to his first love, numbers, and was working frantically on an algebraic equation that had to be solved before time ran out.

'Sixes and sevens, sixes and sevens, we are all at sixes and sevens. I can't tell whether I'm coming or going today. Your Abbot seemed to think that you need looking after. Who doesn't? I'm on the verge of a nervous breakdown myself. The phone hasn't stopped ringing. What am I supposed to do? Are you listening, Lucens? Get yourself together. I've no time for laggards.' Father Raymond lost his patience and tried to snatch the pad on which Lucens was working. 'Will you stop this ridiculous doodling and pay attention to me? You should be helping me look after my flock, instead of wasting my time. I'm warning you, I refuse to be responsible for someone who doesn't even have the decency to put his pen down when I'm talking to him. I'm going to call your Abbot and tell him plainly that if he's that worried about you, he's welcome to come and look after you himself. Or ask Dr Sam Puri. Not that I can see that there's anything the matter with you. Doing some high-school algebra when all hell's broken loose, indeed.'

'I did it.'

Father Raymond looked flummoxed for a moment, then turned away from Lucens in exasperation. 'Sure, you did whatever it was that you did.'

Som Puri watched Lucens as he worked on his mathematical problem without saying a word. He felt his pulse, pulled his head up sharply by his hair and shone a torchlight into his eyes. Lucens went back to work. The doctor walked into the bedroom, stuffed a few changes of clothes into a Kmart bag and came out.

'I did it,' Lucens told him.

'I'm taking you home.'

That first evening, when the Puri boys turned on the TV to watch the news, Som immediately switched channels, but Lucens walked into the kitchen and tried to stab his eyes with a table knife. The doctor followed him just in time to snatch the blunt weapon from his hand. After this, all news channels were banned from the living room TV, and for the next five days Som did not let his friend out of his sight. When the doctor was exhausted, Revati kept Lucens company. Lucens was docile and came obediently enough to the dining table; he even watched *A Fish Called Wanda* with the Puris, but he made sure his pad was always in his line of vision. Most of the time, he worked obsessively on whatever problem he was trying to solve.

Lucens seemed happy to see Reverend Father Augustine, but would not speak to him.

'How long will this last?' the Abbot asked the doctor when they were alone.

'Can't say. A fortnight, a month, even a year.'

'Would you advise admitting him to a psychiatric facility?'

'I'm not a psychiatrist, but a colleague of mine at the hospital examined him and has prescribed some medication. He believes that Lucens is in a state of shock, and that the chances of recovery would be much better if he's with people with whom he feels secure.'

The Abbot hesitated before speaking again.

'Has he been talking?'

Dr Puri looked quizzically at the monk as if he was trying to read his mind.

'I was his guardian and Father Confessor for many years. You may be frank with me.'

'Sometimes, when he dozes off, he mutters or screams. Hallucinating, I think.' Dr Puri smiled. 'Besides, I'm partially deaf.'

'I don't know how to thank you for taking care of him.'

'Aren't you going to do the same?'

'I will do everything I can. And leave the rest to God. You are a good man, Som Puri. I hope Lucens learns to appreciate what a fine friend he has in you.'

*

The Abbot took Lucens back to the Abbey with him. By the end of the third week, he decided to make Lucens attend offices, and took him for long walks in the evenings. He got Father Anthony to read the Bible to Lucens whenever possible: this seemed to quieten him.

At one of the Monday morning Introspections, Father Augustine took a calculated risk and spoke to his flock, all the while keeping an eye on Lucens.

'9/11 has come and gone. But it will always remain a lesion on the psyche of our country. We will never be able to get over the horror, outrage and fear. But at some point we must consciously resist a Pavlovian reflex to the tragedy. What we need to strive for is a thoughtful, nuanced response.

'Loss is always individual. It is the face of a loved one, the way someone cocks his head when listening intently, the infectious, carefree sound of a particular laugh. It is impossible to assuage the grief of those who have lost a mother, son, daughter, wife, father or friend. And how is one to ever grasp the sorrow and pain of our Lord who must hope against hope that the appalling carnage will stop? But the slaughter of innocents never seems to end. Already there is talk of retaliation.' The Abbot looked at Lucens but it was like staring at an opaque glass wall.

'Many of you have come to me and asked that we fly the American flag. I know you mean well and wish to show solidarity with the people of our country. But the flag of God is not that of America. He does not fly any flag but the flag of all those who are good and compassionate and will eschew all forms of violence.

'We are monks, and our flag is prayer. Let us fly it high so that both men and God will heed it.'

'Why don't you stay a little longer?' the Abbot asked Lucens the day before he was due to leave the Abbey.

'Seven weeks is a long time, especially when the Guardian Angels are still in their infancy.'

'Will you be all right?'

'God forbid that I should be all right after what I did in Afghanistan and Kashmir.'

'That was a long time ago. You are not, I repeat, not, to blame yourself for 9/11.'

'What you forget, Reverend Father, is that it's the kind of thing I was entirely capable of doing. Right up my alley, to use one of Amanat's phrases. Anybody can execute a plan. But I was the one who came up with the ideas, the one who conceived more and more audacious schemes. As strategy, striking the World Trade towers compares with Hannibal's inconceivable decision to cross the Alps in winter and attack Rome. It's only the third-raters who do the same thing over and over again. The ones with the brains and the imagination are like auctioneers. What they are selling is terror. They goad themselves to raise the bid continually. And the prize always goes to the one who can shock the most, do the most damage. What we are dealing with here are technical matters. Strike rates. Percentages.'

'Lucens, 9/11 is not a technical matter. And it's not percentages. It's people. Real people with real lives. There's nothing heroic about killing the innocent.'

'Yes, yes, that's what I mean.'

'Is that what you had in mind? I thought for a moment you were missing those exciting times, the adrenaline rush to the cortex.'

'I deserve to die. If only Jesus would permit me.'

Late that night Lucens awoke with an idea for the Children of God ad campaign. The agency he had hired had come up with good ideas, but not for the job at hand. He had suggested they avoid treating spirituality and God as cold abstractions. If you wanted people to buy into these concepts you had to sell them like chocolates or computer games. The creative director had not articulated it, but his expression had certainly conveyed that Lucens was nuts. He scrambled for a pen and jotted down his thoughts for two TV spots.

Script idea: A baby no mother can resist cuddling, gurgles and smiles on the screen. (Screen-test the first of the Children of God for the role.)

Voiceover: 'We would love to have your baby. Please don't abort it. Please.'

Legend at the bottom of the screen: 'Call your local Guardian Angels and give your baby a loving home.'

The second spot will be broadcast a month after the first. It will ride piggyback on the goodwill created by the earlier ad.

Script idea: The same baby as in the first film. Voiceover: 'There are no orphans. Only Children of God. Save a child. Give generously. Anything between 20 and a million dollars will be appreciated.' Line at the bottom of the screen: 'Zero Orphans. It takes time. But we're getting there.'

The Children of God ad campaign seemed to have caught a cynical and blasé nation at one of its rare emotional moments. Instead of 9/11, serial killers and school shoot-outs, the death penalty, reality TV and endless talk of zero taxes for the super-rich, the baby on the TV screen offered Americans a chance to feel good about themselves.

The money poured in. School children, single mothers on welfare, the jobless on social security, blacks and chicanos in their ghettos, the middle classes from suburbia, the philanthropists, corporate America, everybody, but everybody seemed to be in the giving mode. It was not quite Bob Geldof's Live Aid, yet, over the weeks, it built up into a considerable corpus.

As in Hollywood, if an idea worked, everyone wanted to clone it or hop on the bandwagon. National channels like CBS, ABC, FOX and NBC offered to show the TV spots for free. And better yet, the state government appeared keen to fund the Homes.

Media experts and marketing gurus, daytime and late-night talk shows were busy analysing how a film that cost next to nothing to make, had clicked in such a big way. Lucens could not understand what all the fuss was about. Once Jesus stands behind you, even Mission Impossible can work.

Som and Lucens had had one of their usual heated arguments, but it seemed as if this time around, Som was not going to make the first move towards a rapprochement. Ten days had gone by and there was still not a peep from him.

Later that week, Lucens had a meeting with his lawyers in Manhattan. On his way back he made a detour to Jackson Heights and picked up a box of Indian jalebis, those foul-looking orange wheels sprinkled with pistachio and almond slivers, and dripping with syrup that Som was so fond of, he would hide them from his children and polish the lot off at one sitting in his study.

The sky was still a deep twilight blue as Lucens headed home that autumn evening, and the chimneys in the three counties were miniature Vesuviuses emitting angry wisps of smoke. Lucens drove down to the lakefront, turned left at Madison, left again on Hamilton, and parked in the visitors' lot at Glades. The days no longer phased out gradually. Night fell like a high-speed shutter in a single-lens reflex camera, and suddenly all the lights at Glades were blazing. Many of the staff were on their way home. More than likely, Som Puri had left too. But now that Lucens was here, he might as well run up to the paediatric clinic on the fourth floor and see if he was there. The room was empty and neat except for the piles of multicoloured building blocks, toy fire engines, a wide assortment of cars, plastic rattles, three Barbies and a Cabbage Patch doll hurriedly thrown into a corner. Lucens was on his way down when an elderly nurse recognized him.

'Are you looking for Dr Puri, Mr Kahn?'

'Yes, I am.'

'He's in Ward B with a patient.'

'What are you doing here?' Som's voice sounded hostile. He had shaved that morning, but not too carefully, and kept scratching the grey stubble under his jaw. There was no body odour, but he smelt of fatigue and exhaustion and spite.

'I came to say hello. I didn't mean to disturb you. I'll catch up with you some other time.'

Som looked at Lucens with something like hatred. 'You're a man of God, right? So why don't you talk to your God and use your good offices with him to save this child who hasn't responded to treatment for the last fifteen days.'

'Go home, Som. You're dead beat and you're itching to pick a fight. I'll pray for the child if you tell me his name. As for the rest, I suggest we leave it in God's hands.'

'Oh, you smarmy prig with your superior airs. Don't you dare lecture me.'

Lucens wanted to give the box of jalebis to Som, but decided against it. It might start the paediatrician on another tirade. He threw the sweets into a litter bin.

'His name's Philip,' Som hollered as the lift opened its doors.

*

The next time they met was on Saturday night at the supermarket. 'Where have you been?' Som called out to Lucens from across the aisle. It was as though he had forgotten how obnoxious he had been on the previous occasion. He dragged Revati and the children to where Lucens was selecting an economy pack of fruit muesli. 'You must be some guy. Obviously the Big Honcho listens to you. Philip is recovering just fine and should be home by Tuesday.'

'What would you have done if Philip had not survived?' Lucens asked.

'Who knows, killed you first, and then all two hundred and thirty of my regular patients.'

'Do you know how oases form in deserts?' Som asked Lucens.

That was an odd question, all the more so because it came on perhaps the first real summer's day after a long, hard winter. The subzero degree temperatures had stretched all the way into May. There had been barely seven days of spring, and now, overnight, summer had come to the three counties. Som and Lucens had got out their bicycles and were riding at a leisurely pace around Lake Santa. They had come here in snow boots, muffled in Alaskan parkas, every weekend in winter to ice-skate with the boys. Why would Som think of deserts on a day when the good Lord Himself had swathed the land in the most intoxicating green Lucens had seen?

'Haven't a clue.'

'An oasis takes shape whenever two people are lucky enough to find a common language and are able to communicate with each other without having to use it.'

Lucens had not heard Som speak in such a sentimental vein before.

'I left England because Glades offered to finance my research on preemies, sorry, premature babies. They kept their word for three years. Then they got new management, and the new management brought in consultants who told them that the business of medicine was business, and that every minute had a dollar value. That was the end of my research. Every day for the past seven years I've lived in a desert so dreary and barren, my only consolation has been my patients to whom I'm now forced to give less and less time, and certainly no affection. I cursed my foolishness for leaving England. Then you came along, and things no longer looked so hopeless. Imagine meeting someone who actually believes, all evidence to the contrary, that he can make the world a better place.'

The ice on the lake had begun to heave with pain. It was as if a leviathan was waking up in its depths. The waters under the thinning ice floor undulated and rumbled as the beast stretched its muscles. Lucens no longer tried to make sense of his friend: how could a man fight so hard to keep alive a child, and yet believe in abortion?

They cycled for eleven miles and stopped at the Pylon Yacht Club for breakfast. In the years to come, Lucens would begin to see his hothouse friendship with Som, which might soon come to a precipitate end, as the Lord's way of testing him. But today was another day, a perfect day, for over scrambled eggs, toast and fresh ground coffee, Som asked sheepishly: 'Do you think Revati and I could adopt one of the Children of God?'

'But you already have two of your own.'

'Yes, but Revati's always wanted a girl, and the boys think this is the right time to get a sister.'

Lucens had grasped an elementary fact that most politicians and leaders forget as they become powerful: without a solid base and a constituency, you are a nobody. And you will never be able to attract like-minded people from across the country. He had honed his strategy in advance: establish your bona fides with financial institutions like First Penn, and the leaders of society were bound to hear of you and come calling on you. Side by side with his duties as a Guardian Angel, the launching of Zero Orphans and the Pledge of Purity, Lucens's other priority had been to make himself indispensable to the people of his new hometown.

First, Lucens Kahn supported local talent against high-powered outsiders. When Honor Lockman told her bosses in Philadelphia that business would be up by 50 per cent in her branch that year, they thought she was fiddling the figures. After all, even the locals made fun of the place: 'Sparta who when what where?' A head-office team came to take a look and were impressed by what they saw. They told Lucens that they would appoint a much more senior person now that First Penn in Sparta was on its way to becoming their fastest growing branch. 'Honor's just fine,' Lucens was adamant. The bank was resistant, but he would not budge. He was the customer, their most important one in this part of the state, and they couldn't refuse him.

Honor was Lucens's first convert and partisan. He had appointed a high-profile agency to project the image of the Guardian Angels. Its team was good, and made the Guardian Angels a household name, but they couldn't match Honor's enthusiasm, energy or loyalty.

The revival of the twin cities was central to Lucens's game plan. He knew that grass-roots support for him and his projects would come only from economic rejuvenation and prosperity. Once people understood that he had taken the initiative to kick-start the dead economy, he need never again worry about their loyalty. He was sure they would blindly follow him wherever he went.

Lucens had to wait almost one and a half years to be nominated to the Committee to Revive Concord-Ashton. But even after he became a member, he got the feeling that he was stuck on a time treadmill. The committee members were good people but they had been around too long. They were complacent and resisted new ideas.

He waited till it was time for the annual meeting and gala dinner at the town hall that the committee threw for luminaries from the area and the press. It was customary for the youngest member of the committee to address the invitees. Lucens droned on and on, safe jokes, safe subjects, noncommittal prognostications for the future, till he came to his peroration: 'Ladies and gentlemen, let us understand that there is no hope of reviving the Twin Cities...unless we make Satan our guide and master.' What followed was the proverbial deathly silence. It was clear that the committee was mourning the premature demise of their newest member. 'The only cure, the only panacea for our ills and problems is temptation.'

The last word was the cue: the door was flung open and seven veiled women swept in belly-dancing to seductive, lascivious music.

At the end of the three-minute performance, the women removed their veils and smiled shyly to reveal that they were the daughters of six Protestant clergymen. There was silent shock till the mayor guffawed loudly and began to clap. Then you heard a sigh of relief and everybody joined in.

Lucens spoke quietly now. 'Ladies and gentlemen, let's understand clearly that the survival of our twin cities is at stake. If we want to attract new businesses and new industries, we must tempt them. Tempt them with tax holidays and benefits, incentives, competitive medical insurance packages and other deals. Yes, like the Mafia dons, let's make them an offer they can't refuse. Once you've got the first five industries to move, word-of-mouth will do the rest. I suggest that we go for a mix of traditional and unorthodox industries with a high growth potential. Let's do it first thing tomorrow morning. Concord and Ashton have waited too long and our unemployed can't wait any more. Let's show them that when we want something, we'll go get it.'

You may call it a juvenile stunt, but it worked. Word about the tax holiday and other benefits got around. Three start-ups showed interest, and the second largest air-compressor manufacturer commissioned a feasibility study for setting up a plant in the area. With any luck, at least one, maybe even a couple of projects would come through.

The campaign against the Puris had started with a letter to the editor of the *Concord-Ashton Tribune*, titled 'Al Qaeda in the Three Counties?'. The missive began innocently enough, and then, through innuendo, insinuation and hyperbole, it culminated in a purported plot that threatened the very existence of the United States of America.

The crux of the letter was a conversation that the writer, 'An Ever-Vigilant Patriot', had overheard by chance while sitting with his son at the cafeteria at Glades Medical. It had chilled his heart. A doctor, a paediatrician to be precise, who had been responsible for the care of children in the three counties for over ten years, told a colleague that America had it coming, that 9/11 was an act of overdue justice. And if that wasn't treasonous enough, he had gone on to say that if the demands of the terrorists were not met immediately, America could expect a 9/11 every year, who knows, even every month.

Hardly anybody, including Lucens, noticed the letter for the first four days. On the fifth day a completely unrelated event took place: the Penn State Media Association published circulation figures for all local newspapers. The *Concord-Ashton Tribune* had dropped from seventh-last position the previous year, to second-last this year. Over the weekend, the owner-publisher of the *Tribune*, Duncan Leacock, decided it was time for drastic action. The next morning, an editorial headed 'Shame! Shame! Shame!' appeared on the front page of the *Tribune*. It berated the appalling apathy of the local population to the deadly peril facing the country. Duncan Leacock promised not to rest until he had roused the FBI, the CIA, Homeland Security and every patriotic citizen to act against the cataclysmic dangers that confronted the most powerful nation on earth. He swore to expose the vipers in the breast of the Stars and Stripes, even if it cost him his life. The *Tribune*, he announced, would open a Patriot logbook. The denizens of the three counties now had the opportunity to stand up and be counted as loyal Americans by signing up.

There was a half-mile-long queue in front of the paper's offices for the next week. Som Puri called Lucens and said he was damned if anybody was going to coerce him to sign up. Revati had tried to coax him, he said, but had ultimately gone to register at the *Tribune* on her own. What was Lucens planning to do? the doctor asked.

'I haven't made up my mind yet,' Lucens replied.

He was grateful that Som had made it clear where he stood on the issue, but felt uncomfortable talking to the doctor over the phone. The whole country seemed to have gone paranoid with weekly red alerts, and the super-patriotic fever might well extend to tapping phone lines. He had told Som that he didn't know his mind yet, but this wasn't entirely true. The moment Som said he would not sign, Lucens knew that he himself would have to. Som could afford to be principled (could he really?), but Lucens certainly could not. If the truth about his past ever surfaced, the whole of the Guardian Angels project would be in jeopardy. Why not say it? The Angels would be finished.

On the following Monday, the *Tribune* proclaimed a scoop. It drew the attention of its readers to the letter written by the Ever-Vigilant Patriot, and said it had tracked down the doctor at Glades Medical to whom the traitor had spoken. An exclusive interview with the doctor, his name being withheld on account of the grave risk to his life from Al Qaeda and other terrorist groups, followed.

Recalling the discussion, the doctor said that in his colleague's opinion, '"Terrorism does not breed in a vacuum. If you want to eradicate it, then it is necessary to address the grievances that are at the root of it." "So you support terrorism," I said, "since you are willing to give carte blanche to any Tom, Dick and Ali who has a grievance, real or imagined."'

'Would he reveal the name of this man?' the interviewer had asked. 'I have no desire to tell on a colleague,' the doctor replied, 'but in the national interest, I will reveal that the Muslim doctor is from the Indian subcontinent. I leave it to you and your readers to draw your own conclusions.'

Not much room for speculation there, Lucens thought, since there was only one Indian paediatrician at Glades. The doctor who was interviewed seemed to have got one minor detail wrong, but neither the *Tribune* nor the people in the three counties were likely to quibble about it. Besides, what difference did it make whether Dr Puri was a Hindu or Muslim?

The *Tribune* had a field day publicizing the fact that while Mrs Puri had signed the Patriot logbook, her husband had refused to do so. Lucens felt sure that good sense would prevail, and the people of Sparta would realize that Som Puri was being framed. And that even if they didn't, the entire medical community at Glades would stand behind the paediatrician. But no one at the hospital was willing to comment on the issue, let alone defend Dr Puri. Instead, Lucens learnt that one by one, Som's patients, or rather the parents of his patients, were deserting him and asking to be referred to other doctors. Among the few who stuck with him was Honor Lockman. She thought the allegations against him were ludicrous and entirely fabricated. The *Tribune* now began hinting at forming a patriot commission to investigate Dr Puri and look into the threat he and his clandestine cell posed to the community. It was not long before Glades had advertised for a new paediatrician. The hospital management had pulled off a coup of sorts: even if Som Puri had wanted to take them to court, he would not have had a leg to stand on. They had brought no charges against him; there was nothing in writing. They had quietly neutered the man by ignoring him.

For weeks Lucens had dreaded Som calling him, dropping in at his house or at the Angels' office, but he need not have worried. It soon became clear that Som had no intention of imposing on him or asking for his support. Revati had called Lucens once, to tell him that while Penelope (the new parents hadn't changed the name given by the Burgesses to their adopted daughter) was lucky because she was too young to start kindergarten, her brothers were being ostracized by their classmates and were refusing to go to school, but Som had interrupted their conversation. Revati was not herself, he told Lucens, she was seeing things out of perspective. On one occasion, Lucens had run into Som at Sears, and on another at the Paper Clip, where he had gone to buy ink and toner for his computer, but the doctor had smiled from a distance, and had left without saying a word. Lucens was relieved, but resented the man's innate pride. If only he would bend and beg and plead, not his innocence, but the sin of hubris and self-composure in the face of such calamities, the people of Sparta, Lucens was sure, would forgive him and take him back into the fold.

The Abbot had told Lucens how Som had nursed him after his strange reaction to 9/11, and had kept a watch on him even as he slept. Father Augustine had remarked that the doctor would be good priest material. His lips were sealed even when the confessor blurted out something in his sleep.

The least Lucens could do was to stand by Som. He was a born crusader. If he decided to, he was sure he could expose the *Tribune* and its editor, prove that the attacks against the paediatrician had dubious motives; that the first letter itself was a fraud, and that Som could take the editor to court for libellously persecuting him for no greater offence than exercising the most fundamental of American rights: freedom of expression. But Lucens had to perforce hold his tongue, and hated his friend for making him feel impotent and utterly inadequate. Som had nothing to hide. Lucens, on the contrary, could not risk anybody prying into his past.

The moral universe Lucens inhabits is a severe one. There's no room for doubt or human frailty in it. The mujahideen experience helped reinforce a siege mentality within him: you are at odds with the world. You fight for a righteous cause but against infinitely superior forces. The only friends you have are your comrades-in-arms. Your own life as well as that of your brothers depends on one single factor: loyalty. Which is why there is no greater crime in your book than letting someone down.

Now Lucens finds himself trapped. It is a new kind of crisis for him. He's caught in a dilemma he cannot resolve. He must wilfully go against his conscience: he must betray his friend Som Puri. The doctor is neither a fellow-traveller nor a brother-in-faith. He and Lucens have little in common, and if they never talk to each other again it will not be an irreparable loss. The only thing askew in these computations is that the paediatrician is innocent. Lucens is clear that, according to his own strict and absolutist ethical code, he must stand up for Som. He has agonized over his choices. He has weighed one man's future against the fate of unborn babies. In the end he has always come to the same conclusion: there's no contest. The foetuses win.

Some time back, Lucens had read about a cameraman who was shooting a film with the German film director, Werner Herzog, in the tropical jungles of Brazil, when he was bitten in the foot by the deadliest snake in the valley. The man had exactly twenty seconds before he suffered a fatal cardiac arrest. In the sixth second, he picked up a machete and hacked his leg off.

It is an act Lucens comprehends totally. He has that kind of presence of mind and the willpower to translate it into action. The question is, he has no idea which limb he must sever to free both Som and himself.

When the trustees of the Guardian Angels passed a motion terminating Dr Puri's services, Lucens did not demur.

At times, Lucens even managed to convince himself that he had behaved not just rightly, but heroically. And yet he knew in his heart that he had betrayed a friend who could have easily saved his job and his reputation by ratting on him but never did. Never again could he expect loyalty from anybody, not even from Honor. He was despicable, and no reason, however valid, could condone what he had done. He had hated his father for using his face for the Judas frieze at the church at Terraferra. Now the thought struck Lucens that Abbajaan may have been prescient and had seen a facet of him that he himself had kept denying. But Abba's Judas was not so fallen that he could never be redeemed. The Virgin had held him to her breast and seemed to give him hope of forgiveness and salvation. However, the Mother of Jesus, Lucens was well aware, would not mediate on his behalf and seek absolution for him. There was no getting away from it: he was damned, and one of these days he would have to pay for it.

Six months after the Puris had adopted Penelope, they were gone. Lucens heard that Som had got his old job back at London General. He had not even had the decency to wish Lucens goodbye. He and his family had disappeared like felons. Didn't that prove their guilt and complicity?

# 48

In his lighter moments, Amanat was inclined to think of his new career as Abbajaan's revenge. (How many centuries was it since his father had died?) One morning Abbajaan, who should have known better, had walked into the drawing room, which doubled as his older son's bedroom, a trail of apologies following in his wake.

'I don't mean to disturb you but I'm a little pressed for time and I was wondering if you could help me out with a couple of drawings.'

Why was Abbajaan stooping to such mean tricks? He didn't need help, he just didn't want a couch-cauliflower in his house. He was doing the fatherly thing by Amanat, getting him out of bed and on the way to normalcy. Oh, these do-gooders who wouldn't let you be. He had to admit though that Abbajaan was looking a little pale under the gills. Anyway, how do you say 'forget it' to Abbajaan?

In the old days, Abbajaan had had a large architect's office with six or seven junior architects and the full contingent of draughtsmen, model-builders and clerks. Then the move to Suleiman Mansion had meant that he no longer had a separate office, let alone staff. Business had picked up considerably over the years, but Zafar Khan had burnt his hands badly once. He held himself responsible for thirty-five people who had lost their jobs one morning. Now he took a limited number of assignments and kept his staff to the minimum, with just one junior architect to assist him.

Once Amanat had done the job, there was respite for a week, and he was ready, willing and eager to forgive his father for having intruded on his time. Then Abbajaan was back with a lame and, very likely, phoney smile. If one was to believe him, he had spread himself far too thin and wasn't able to cope. Would Amanat please...Amanat was getting used to Abbajaan's unfinished sentences. Soon the apologies and the askew guilty smile ceased, but not the work.

Amanat decided that if he were going to be working, he might as well get paid for it. He started showing up regularly at Abbajaan's office. That was not a wise move. He found that Zafar Khan's seven assistants worked eleven to twelve hours a day, often even on weekends. Amanat expected them to crib and complain when his back was turned about the absurd hours, but the fools seemed to enjoy working with his father. Apparently they had had a peon once, but Abbajaan had got him interested in draughtsmanship and model-making and he was always the first to arrive and the last to leave. Now the former peon supervised the new recruit's work and occasionally helped him out. As an industrial designer, Amanat had depended heavily on software to work out his products, but that had been many years ago. He was a little rusty now and it took him some months to catch up with all the advances.

'I want to make something clear. I'm coming in as a temp, nothing more,' Amanat told his father. 'The moment the workload eases, I'm out of here.'

'But of course. You have far better things to do.'

Amanat was not quite sure if Abbajaan was being sarcastic, but he let it pass. Ten months went by and Amanat was still there. It was ridiculous but there never seemed to be any end to the grind.

Late one night, Abbajaan started briefing Amanat on the new library for the Abbey in Sweet Waters. When he was done, Amanat said, 'I don't understand what you want me to do.'

'I don't know, I was hoping you would work out the basic concept and we could take it from there.'

Amanat was finding it difficult to control his temper. 'You mean you will do the design and I'll take it from there?'

Abba had reverted to his sheepish, off-centre smile. 'I've got to catch the flight to Johannesburg tomorrow. I'll be away for twenty-five days and by the time I get back, the date for presenting the drawings to the Abbot will be only a week away.'

'Why do you take on new work when you can't handle what you've got already?' Amanat was startled to hear his own voice. He sounded insufferably peevish. How could he, oh how could he? And that too with Abbajaan who had to this day never scolded him or ticked him off for his endless follies.

'You are right, so right, but I couldn't say no to the Abbot. He gave me my first big break after my licence was reinstated.'

The fool that he was, Amanat was so full of contrition now that, instead of shutting up, he blundered into a still worse predicament. He said, 'I'll try,' when he meant, 'Not on your life. Get real, Pop. It's a few billion years since I pretended to help you out. Sure I scribbled and fiddled around and built toy models of bungalows, airports and museums. And Ammi and you praised me because I was your son and you wanted to encourage me. But you knew and I knew that I was messing around at your expense; reproducing whatever you had visualized at some earlier date and passing it off as mine. And most of the time you would redo whatever I had done because it was unsound and just too childish.'

But the die had been cast, the Rubicon crossed, the milk spilt, and so on.

Amanat had known terror for a long, long time. The terror of the disease that struck him whenever it fancied and tried to switch off his breathing apparatus. He had learnt the labyrinthine terror of no-exits, sitting at his writing table while it slowly crept in upon him, after his third draft of four hundred and seventy pages, that there was no novel there, never had been and never would be, so what the hell had he been pretending to rework and rescue for the last three years? He was a pathetic fake and a fraud who had pulled the wool over Sagari's and Abbajaan's eyes, and had then made the one mistake no author or artist should: he had bought into his own lies.

And yet what had he known of terror before his father tricked him and stood him against the wall and shot him dead. The tragedy was that Amanat now died every night, only to be reborn the next day, ready once again to be slaughtered and sacrificed to the caprice of his father.

Amanat felt ill. His heart collapsed. He couldn't even say goodbye to Zubeida Khaala. He was so sick, he just disappeared. He would never be able to face Abbajaan again and here's the best part, now that he was dead, he would not have to do the job. Abbajaan was welcome to do whatever he wanted, hire somebody else, do it himself or skip town. Now that was an idea, why hadn't he thought of it before?

Three weeks passed and he had nothing to show for himself. He felt bitter. He loved his father and had hurt so much for him that he had disowned his first love, architecture, many, many years ago. He had betrayed him then and he was about to betray him again. He didn't care. He was exhausted. Three more nights and Abbajaan would be back. He was going to let him down. So be it.

He got up that night and sat at the computer as he had done for the last three and a half weeks and tried out four different approaches to the library building. Now came the part where he was weakest: the engineering and the materials. It stuck in his craw that he was dependent on others for this basic skill. 'Like many painters and artists,' Abbajaan had always maintained, 'architects too believe that basics are for dullards and plodders. I think it's the reverse. If you don't know your fundamentals, it's going to cripple your imagination, your concepts and your architecture. Not you but somebody else will pronounce whether something you want can be done or not.'

Damn Abba, he knew what he was talking about. Fortunately, this was the last time the spineless Amanat would cave in to his father and do his bidding. He buried his nose in Abbajaan's collection of civil engineering books and tried to bone up on the principles of stress, metallurgy, bonding resins. Forget it. He was not going to make the grade. And anyway, who needed this noise? Besides, Abbajaan was not going to buy his concept; not at all. And if he were fool enough to do so, then he'd better straighten out the engineering. Still, he hated the fact of his dependence.

Abbajaan went over Amanat's plans, chose one, made a few seemingly inconsequential changes and added a couple of things, then handed it back to his son. Amanat could no longer recognize his own work. With just a few touches and a minimum of alterations, Abbajaan had reconfigured the total structure and look, and had taken the work to a different plane.

For the next five months, Amanat didn't have time either to feel trapped or to swear at Abbajaan. The man was overworked but refused to take it easy or listen to anyone. What choice did Amanat have but to pull his weight? He had the uneasy feeling that he might even be enjoying himself. What was worse was that he was also feeling the occasional urge to get back to writing. Then that foolish man, who had almost willed his own death, was no more, and Amanat's worries were over. He wrote to the Abbot informing him of his father's demise, and that from now on one of Abbajaan's junior colleagues would liaise with him and supervise the work.

Dear Amanat,

I had thought that after Zafar finished the last of the buildings at Terraferra over ten years ago, the Abbey would not see a bulldozer, crane or earthmover for the next fifty years. But two of our monasteries in the States were forced to close down for lack of funds and, what is more disheartening, fewer and fewer people are choosing to become monks. The brothers and fathers who came over from our sister abbeys are barely thirty in number but the books that have migrated with them number over 190,000. It was natural that we asked your father to design the new library complex. He was an overworked man and a very busy one but he couldn't say no to his old friends. He was a few months behind schedule but the drawings and perspectives he sent us were not just functional but hauntingly apt for our Abbey. When we approved them within a week, Zafar wrote to say that he would like to take the credit for the designs but it was you who had conceptualized the library buildings from start to finish. So there we were, stuck with another Khan and much the happier for it.

When we accepted your drawings for the new library at the Abbey, we were aware that you had not got your architect's degree. But it is time you asked yourself one question: how long do you plan to be a dilettante? After a point the amateur wonder-kid pose begins to wear thin and one is led to ask if it's only a way of avoiding responsibility. Going by your books, you are a perfectionist, not an amateur. So please get the degree and in the meantime you can work at the Abbey with the help of a local architectural firm.

I miss your father. Every window, every sculpture, the church, the factory, the cloisters, all are his gift to us. Did you know I've read *The Arsonist* twice? So you see I've known you a long time and take a paternal, if rather severe interest in your wellbeing. I pray for both you and Zafar. May God be with you.

Yours affectionately,
Rev. Father Augustine

Amanat had taken it for granted that he was merely helping his father out and that the work would go under Abbajaan's name. He should have known better. You couldn't trust Abba. Was it just his desire for fair-mindedness and the need to give credit where it was due? Or was it something more devious, a Machiavellian plan to draw Amanat back to architecture? After all, it was a family tradition to let death blackmail the heir-apparent. Abbajaan's father had tricked his son into taking over the construction firm, and now it was Amanat's turn to be ambushed.

Amanat might like to blame his father for bamboozling him from beyond the grave into studying architecture, but he was not being entirely honest. He was congenitally insecure and had to face up to the fact that unless there was a dramatic change in his fortunes, he would not be able to live off his writing. He could have gone back to industrial designing but his heart had never been in it. That didn't leave him with much choice but to hunker down to architecture. There was one other rather mercenary benefit: he was the sole inheritor of a ready-made and running office, which was no mean plus point in the city of Bombay where real-estate prices were even higher than in Manhattan.

So many years had gone by since he had last studied, he was sure he would not be able to go back to the routine and the discipline. The first couple of months were grim, but then to his horror, his old flame began to seduce him again. Instead of drudgery, he seemed to have embarked on an adventure. Abbajaan was right. Without realizing it, the new knowledge about materials, technology and engineering percolated into whatever projects the college assigned to him.

For three years now, while he has been trying to get a degree in architecture, Amanat has been nursing a secret. He likes to think of himself as a rational animal for whom all superstition is as risible as it is dangerous; but he's nevertheless sure that if he so much as confesses to himself that he's trying out an idea for a novel, he'd be inviting the evil eye upon it and it will be doomed before it got started. Besides there was no novel till you had written the last word.

Well, the last word was in place now.

He didn't have a title for the book yet and was stuck with the initials of his protagonists, R and R. It was an unhinged rumination on that collective Indian obsession and mythos called the Hindi film, and the people behind it. No sensible man or woman, no one with any self-respect, would sit through most Hindi films to the end; frankly, just one was enough for seven lifetimes, but they narcotized your senses and, like a sleepwalker, you went back to them.

Amanat's new novel was the story of Rajan and Roger, two young men who have set their hearts on becoming stars. It is uncanny how often they have appeared with superstars who charge 80 or 90 million rupees. And how they have starred in at least six or seven times more movies than the matinée idols. Surely you must remember them? Rajan was seventh from the left in the third row behind Aamir Khan in that marvellous dance sequence against the dark black clouds in *Lagaan*. And Roger was the fifth of the hoods who attacks Anil Kapoor in the ninth fighting sequence in *Pukar*.

They are the extras of the film world. And of life.

It took him three months of procrastination, teeter-tottering between yes and no to gather the courage to show the novel to Sagari. Or rather to put the manuscript in her mailbox along with a note:

My dear Sagari,

I know I've no right to ask anything of you any more. But you've always been my first reader and my talisman. Will you read whatever this new thing is?

I'm a rat. I didn't have the courage to come over and ask you personally.

Amanat

Sagari visited Suleiman Mansion two days later at six in the morning. She was going out of town on a shoot for ten days and didn't want to keep Amanat on ice. He could keep you waiting for two or three years for a new book, this one had taken longer, and then he wanted your reaction within minutes, preferably in an instant.

'Do you want the good news or the bad first?' she asked as they sat at the kitchen table over a cup of tea, while Zubeida Khaala roasted semolina to make upma for Sagari.

Amanat's heart sank. 'Just the good news. Nothing else.'

Sagari laughed and clutched his hair and shook his head from side to side. 'This is about the closest you've come to a classic, Amanat. I could go back to it again and again, and discover new depths and insights. It is hyperactive. Your imagination has gone berserk even as it is on a tight leash. It is Keystone Cops, broad farce and a rattling good yarn, though you are never sure whether you are rolling on the ground with uncontrollable laughter or with the pain of having glimpsed the worst and best of life. Most authors would be happy with half of what you've managed. You can let it go at that and you would still make the A grade and the four stars. But it's your novel and it's not enough. You've put in an incredible amount of work in it and you are going to want to kill me for it but this novel can't afford to sag or lose its tension. I've made notes, as usual. You don't have to listen to me but I know you will.'

He hated her then, her smugness and self-assurance, her ability to tell him off so casually. Did she know that he had worked at it while he was studying for his architect's degree and designing for clients and supervising unfinished buildings? What does it take to say: do a rewrite. He had already rewritten the novel three times. He was through with it and that was that.

Amanat stayed away from the novel for a week, then another. But he knew all along that Sagari had got him pat. He would resist as long as he could, then cave in and rework the book based on her comments.

It was Sagari who sent the book, it was called *The Extras*, to the publishers. They scheduled its release for the following October. Amanat had no choice but to chew his nails and wait for another fifteen months for the verdict on *The Extras*.

However dimly and occasionally, he now began to sense that he was condemned to work in two disparate disciplines. He knew that he was not one of God's chosen ones. Unlike many a novelist, he would never know what it was to be in full flow. Nothing would come easy to him, not even by fluke or by mistake. He would always have to labour over his fictions, write and rewrite every sentence six or seven times and yet end up being unhappy.

Artists like to think of themselves as the inheritors of Prometheus. Like the Greek hero, they too have stolen the fire, the prerogative of creativity, from the gods. Amanat has a rather less lofty notion of his job (he wouldn't dream of calling it a vocation). He sees himself as a lowly version of Sisyphus, condemned for eternity to push an enormous boulder up the steep slope of a mountain only to see it roll down again.

He is aware that his fiction is nothing but what the word suggests: inventions, febrile imagination, stories, the licence to lie, licit mendacity; in short, fictions. And yet he also views it as an attempt to grasp that highly unstable thing called the truth. It is the fate of man to query and question, knowing full well that there are no answers. He has no option; he must ceaselessly continue the quest to understand the point of pain and suffering, the purpose of life and laughter, the meaning of all that is meaningless. Every time he completes a novel or an architectural project, the boulder will roll over him and break his spirit. And every time he starts on a novel or an architectural assignment, he is condemned to nudge that impossible rock up again if he is to live with himself and make momentary sense of life.

## 49

There was a game that Lucens used to play as a child at Firdaus. What you did was to call out 'Statue!' just as Abbajaan was tucking his shirt into his trousers, Zubeida Khaala was chopping onions in the kitchen, or Amanat was brushing his teeth, and they had to stop dead in the midst of whatever they were doing and not move till you snapped your fingers and said 'Start!' It seemed as though somebody had hollered 'Statue!' to Concord-Ashton, but forgotten to say 'Start!' and release them.

The twin cities were a two-dimensional Hollywood set. A designer had sat at his table and created the prototype of a bustling township from the first half of the twentieth century. It was so close to the real thing, it was almost a caricature: the two-storeyed shops on Main Street where the owners and their families lived on the top floor; the Greek restaurant called Parthenon; The Bride, which sold frothy, hand-stitched wedding gowns; Tony's, the barbershop, with its rotating red, white and blue striped cylinder, and unshaven Tony himself who had cropped the hair of every male child since the Depression; the art-deco cinema Rivoli, which had opened with *Gone with the Wind*; the elegant, neo-classical façade of Hudson's at the corner of Jefferson and Main, where the local aristocracy shopped.

Having built the township from the ground up, the set designer had then got down to planning, to the last detail, the slow but meticulous dilapidation of the place. He had peeled three-fifths of the paint off the railway station façade; tilted the name board of the Concord-Ashton Town Hall to the left, so that from a certain angle the building itself looked askew, and made sure that the clock on the water pumping station had stopped at 2.30. Any moment now, the meeting of the Ladies of Charity would end, and the women in their bouffant skirts and lacquered hair-dos would trip down the steps of St John's Church and step into Desotos, Studebakers and Dodges.

If the twin cities were going to seed, they were slipping gently, a quarter-notch at a time, trying desperately not to let go of their genteel graces.

Lucens did not question his judgement in choosing Sparta as his base, but after Som's departure, there were occasions when he bitterly regretted his decision.

Small-time America is testing Lucens's mettle as even his mujahideen days hadn't. Sparta is his home and yet he has the feeling that he's marooned on some other planet. The people of the three counties and he share a common vision of Christian America. The Bible and the living Christ bind them together. His brethren, however, are untouched by the great metaphysical questions and dilemmas that the faith raises. Indeed, in the beginning was the word, but sometimes Lucens wonders if the word was stillborn on the new continent. Even the most mystifying and shattering moment in the Bible, Christ's last cry, 'Father, Father, why hast thou forsaken me?' does not rouse them from their apathy.

There are times when Lucens believes he's braindead. On the becalmed and dead sea of the three counties he can see his soul listing and sinking into oblivion.

He remembered a poster from Abbajaan's study in Firdaus. He had understood its import only after he had grown up. It was a downtown New Yorker's map of the world. Three-quarters of it was Manhattan; the rest of America was squeezed in at the back. As for Europe, Asia, Africa and Australia, they were islands, mere flotsam nearly edged off the horizon. That was Saul Steinberg, the cartoonist, poking good-humoured fun at Manhattanites. But substitute the three counties for Manhattan, Lucens thought, and that was the way Spartans saw the world. What concerned them, whatever impinged or intruded directly on their lives, was their universe. The rest just didn't figure. There was, however, more to Lucens's sudden bouts of loathing for these people than their smugness and narrow views. They had hounded out his friend Som Puri instead of standing up for him. He despised them, but nowhere as much as he despised himself.

He started going to the library and collecting the most vicious quotations about America and Americans he could find. He agreed with de Tocqueville about the country's 'perpetual utterance of self-applause'; with Arnold Toynbee's comment that 'The worst country to be poor in is America'; and thought Mark Twain had hit the nail on the head when he claimed, 'There are many humorous things in the world, among them the white man's [replace 'white man' with 'American'] notion that he is less savage than other savages.' Truman Capote remarked, 'It's a scientific fact that if you stay in California you lose one point of your IQ every year.' He should have come to Sparta; you lost ten points a day if you were fool enough to read even the headlines in the local newspapers. A single conversation with one of the residents convinced you that you had been lobotomized. They were the compendium, the definitive encyclopaedia of ignorance and prejudice. An impenetrable Teflon glaze came over the eyes of Lucens's neighbours when he talked of Kyoto, Isfahan or Benaras. They thought Indira Gandhi was the daughter of Mahatma Gandhi. They believed Avicenna was a town in Italy, Marie Antoinette, a character from a Hollywood romance. And that Jefferson had coined the phrase, 'Liberty, Equality, Fraternity'.

There were times when Lucens caught himself using phrases like 'irreconcilable differences' to describe his relationship with his neighbours. What did he have in mind, a divorce? The only gratifying feature about his unconscious choice of words was that at least he thought of his commitment as a marriage to the community where he lived. He had to keep reminding himself that they were good, decent people who shared his values even if they did kick out his friend Som Puri. People who were not only loyal friends and practising Christians, but who also abhorred abortion, homosexuality and same-sex marriages. They were his people for better or for worse. In health and in sickness.

'Mr Khan?'

'Speaking.'

'Mr Zafar Khan?'

'No, this is his son, Amanat. My father died over a year ago.'

'And your mother, Shagufta Khan?'

'Who's speaking?'

'My name, Mr Amanat Khan, is Sujeet Nambiar. I'm the commissioner of police. I would appreciate it if you would come over to the directorate of police near Crawford Market.'

'Why do you want to see me?'

'Some things are best not discussed on the phone.'

The man sounded reasonable enough but Amanat did not care to meet him. He had had one brush with the police when Zia had knifed him and that would suffice for the next few lives.

'Do you remember the twin explosions, the one at Zaveri Bazaar and the other at the Gateway of India?'

Zia, Amanat thought, he must be connected with it; that's why I've been asked to come over. He realized he was being absurd. Zia was in Sparta and had long since changed his ways.

'That was close to three months ago.'

'Yes. Many people were killed at the Gateway. Some torsos and limbs were flung far into the sea.'

'Why are you telling me all this?'

'A few bodies were recovered. In the trouser pocket of one of the men in the sea, we found this.'

The commissioner laid a thick, misshapen passport on the table.

'Open it.'

Amanat took the passport reluctantly and opened it at the wrong end. Many of the visas were illegible but whoever owned it had travelled considerably. He was on page one now. The salt water had erased the picture of the owner but you could still read her name: Khan Shagufta Zafar.

Ammijaan's story had finally come to an end. Not Zia but some other terrorist had got her. Abbajaan hadn't talked about it but Amanat knew that he had kept looking for her almost until the time he was hospitalized. It had been an article of faith with him that whenever Ammi disappeared and for however long, she always came back to him.

'If you are thinking what I think you are,' the cop's voice was curiously characterless, a timbre deliberately cultivated to discourage any emotional response, 'then I must caution you not to jump to conclusions. At this moment we have no idea about your mother's fate. Unfortunately, not finding her body is no guarantee that she's alive. But neither does it mean that she is dead. The Gateway area is full of tourists, Indian and foreign, and a favourite with petty thieves. The man who stole from your mother must have thought it was his lucky day. Mrs Khan's passport case had eleven thousand rupees in one thousand rupee notes and four hundred Euros. Pickpockets, like all of us, are superstitious. They believe in the goddess Bhavani who's responsible for a good start to the working day. In that case he may have hung around after your mother had left the scene, scouting for his next victim. What we know for certain is that his luck ran out then. I can only hope that Mrs Khan was more fortunate. We checked with the Taj hotel across the street to see if she had been staying there. She was not registered at the hotel.'

The commissioner looked at Amanat with the first hint of sympathy.

'I'm sorry we took so long to get in touch with you. But it has been a taxing time and we didn't want to call you prematurely and discover we had got things wrong.' The man was not curt but it was obvious that the meeting was concluded. Amanat should have got up but he couldn't move. He was still waiting for the policeman to casually trap him with a query: Isn't it odd, Mr Khan, that neither you nor your family registered a missing person case with the police?

Instead Sujeet Nambiar opened a dusty file and began to read from it.

'I used to know your mother when she was a regular at the Willingdon Club. A natural gambler and one of the most charming people I've come across.' The commissioner still did not look up from the document he was perusing. 'I assure you Shagufta was not registered at the Taj under any other name either.'

Amanat felt he was being stripped naked by this man. Were there no secrets of Ammijaan to which the commissioner was not privy? Sujeet Nambiar was being the soul of discretion but Amanat wanted to break open the glass case in which some twenty-odd antique rifles were housed and bayonet him.

Sujeet Nambiar had gone out of his way to call Amanat and brief him, but what was the point of the exercise? Amanat was none the wiser about the whereabouts or fate of his mother. He was grateful that Ammijaan might still be alive but he was resentful that she had been resurrected only to be consigned to a police-limbo called 'Case unsolved. File closed.'

Amanat debated whether he should tell Zia and Zubeida Khaala about his meeting with the commissioner. He finally decided against it. The fact was Ammijaan had been missing for a long time now. She was like the picture in that salt-soaked and twisted passport: a blank, a total blank; the emulsion of memory having come unstuck over so many years. This is what we do to those who have left us, Amanat thought. First death betrays them and then we betray them, despite all our protestations to the contrary, by letting go of them daily, hourly.

It was all over. Lucens and the Guardian Angels were wiped out. The money had decamped, taken to its heels, vamoosed, gone, fled, khatam, evaporated, cut and run, made a quick getaway, sloped off, split and bolted. You could put it a hundred different ways, in any language you cared to, but the sum total would amount to the same: zero, nothing, nil, naught, the void. How could such vast amounts have disappeared before he knew what was happening?

It had taken God six days to create the world. On the seventh He had rested. Lucens was faster. It took all of five days to polish off the totality of the Guardian Angels' funds. By the end of the third day he knew he had to stop just to retain the bare minimum to keep the Homes for the Children of God running for another thirty days, and continue with the Pledge of Purity programmes that were scheduled in the next three weeks.

He had always made it a point to work out alternate scenarios, and had contingency plans and back-ups for everything in life. If the regular plumber was out of town, he had the telephone numbers of two others. Honor Lockman and First Penn were his first choice, but he also had accounts with two other banks. The Concord-Ashton City Council had drawn up the names of fifteen companies and corporations to whom they were going to make a pitch. Lucens was not going to be so measly or complacent. He played it safe and had compiled a roster of forty likely candidates. Time had proved him right. Only one of the council's roll of fifteen companies had shown interest in the region. The rest had come from his own list.

The only subject about which he would not allow himself to think, the one area for which he did not have a back-up plan, was where luck deserted him. No, that was not true. He had never thought of it as luck, but as a gift from God. It was amply clear in the three days that had gone by, that both the gift and his God had abandoned him.

He was still doing God's work, wasn't he? What had happened then? What had gone wrong? No longer could he summon up the next movement of stocks on the NYSE, DAX, FTSE, Nikkei, BSE or any other exchange. Currencies no longer spoke to him, nor did forward markets yield their secrets. For five days he had tried to persuade himself that he was not reading the stellar messages right. Or perhaps he was so exhausted that his mind was no longer receptive. He drove into Concord-Ashton and bought a whip. He would have liked to buy a zanzeer, the scourge with the superfine steel blades that he had used when he was in New Eden, but he doubted that he could locate one in the state of Pennsylvania.

'I know You are testing me, Lord, as You tested Job and Abraham and the other prophets. Don't get me wrong, I'm not comparing myself to them. How could I? They were worthy and righteous and I'm a bottomless pit of sin. Test me, test me as far as You want to, abandon me if You will and I will deserve it, and every punishment You send my way, but Almighty God do not forsake the Children of God, the Guardian Angels or the Pledge of Purity.

'Give me leprosy, give me AIDS, make me a cripple, condemn me to the most painful cancer, but don't victimize the unborn children because of my crimes. Let me finish Your work on earth, let me gather the best possible people, let me enlist the most devoted and dedicated men and women, let me appoint the most capable to take over my mission. Honor Lockman is already in charge. If he shapes up, Mervyn Fontaine could gradually be trained to be the second-in-command. But as You know, that is not going to be enough. Unless the Guardian Angels become the most powerful lobby in the country and can dictate to Capitol Hill, we will not be able to make the living Christ the law of the land. I give You my word, O Lord, that I will work night and day, and twice as hard to expedite the process of finding the right people to take over from me. After that do what You will with me.'

Roy too must have stayed up the whole night, for he called every half an hour and left message after message on the answering machine; but Lucens would not interrupt his prayers. Lucens called back the next morning before going for a shower. Roy picked up the phone on the first ring.

'Where have you been, Lucens? You had me worried sick that you'd gone and done something to yourself.'

'What do you mean done something to myself?' Lucens asked brusquely.

'I thought you might be depressed, perhaps desperate...'

'I'm a Roman Catholic, Roy. Suicide may be an option for you but never for us.'

'I'm vastly relieved to hear that. Please don't get discouraged. You know better than I that George Soros lost millions time and again. I don't remember the date, but the last time he took a beating, I think he lost close to a billion dollars. Give it a rest, Zia.' Roy was so overwrought, he was oblivious of regressing to the earlier name. 'You are overworked and you've never taken a break. Switch off, Lucens. For a week, maybe a month. Recharge your batteries. When you get back refreshed, you'll get your touch back too.'

'Are you done, Roy?'

'Don't do this, Lucens. Don't go cold on me. I'm your friend. If you don't lay off for a while, you'll end up damaging the prospects of the Angels and hurt yourself no end.'

'Are you suggesting that you are no longer interested in my business?'

'Of course not. I would not be where I am without you. You are my best client. You've taught me things about the market that I would never have learnt on my own.'

'Good. In that case you do your job and let me do mine.'

Lucens was not sure how he could possibly have had a dream when he was unable to doze off, let alone sleep. But the dream was as vivid and real as his inability to make a profitable trade in the last five days. He had been climbing up the mountain with his son Isaac when Isaac asked him, 'Why do you need an axe to pluck melons, Pappy? They are ripe and delicious and come off easily.'

'Your mother wants me to cut wood for the fire while you pick the melons.'

He was short of breath and would rather have aborted the trip, but Isaac was leaping around like a frisky young goat impatient to get to the top.

'Come on Pappy, at this rate we won't reach till evening.'

'May we never get there for the rest of eternity.'

'I can't wait forever for you.' And Isaac was off.

Spoilt by his mother, what the boy needed was a good hiding. 'Get back here this moment, son.'

Isaac knew well when not to cross his father and clutched his hand. When they reached the summit, Isaac said, 'Give me that sack, Father. I'll fill it up with melons.'

'Later. We'll pray first to our Lord.'

'But we've already recited our prayers at dawn.'

'I'm going to teach you a new prayer. Kneel down and rest your head on the stump of that tree and tell our Lord God that whatever he does with you, you'll welcome it with an open heart.'

'Why do I need to tell him? He already knows that.'

'Don't argue with me, boy.'

Isaac rested his thin neck on the stump of the tree and asked one last question: 'Should I close my eyes, Pappy, or leave them open?'

It was an innocuous query but for some reason Lucens lost his temper with the boy.

'One more word out of you and I'll lop that head of yours off with this axe. Remember, whatever happens do not turn around.'

Lucens stood behind the boy and removed the axe from the sack. 'You don't need proof of my devotion to You, my Lord. I'm Your slave and servant. I know that You are a just God and a merciful one and You love my little Isaac.'

'No charade this, Abraham,' Lucens heard the Lord thunder at him. 'Now will you do as you promised or will you renege on your word?'

'Thy will be done. May the Lord have mercy on me for obeying Him.'

Even as he brought the axe down, he was sure the Lord would stay his hand. Just then the boy turned his head around and looked at his father. The axe sliced through the scrawny neck and the head was already on the ground. The eyes were still gazing at Abraham trustingly.

'I'm troubled by that dream though I cannot fathom its meaning, Lord. I'll neither swerve from my purpose nor vacillate. You can reject me but You can't get rid of me. You are all that I've got and I'm not about to let go of You.'

By the fifth evening, the game was over. Lucens had lost everything. On the eleventh day, Lucens took an overdraft of a $100,000 from First Penn. By late afternoon there was not a trace of it. Poor Honor Lockman, she had given Lucens the money in good faith, but the Guardian Angels' account was a windsock through which the moolah had whooshed away.

## 50

'You had said that if I ever need anything I should come to you.'

'You shouldn't believe everything people say. They just want you to think well of them.' Shakta Muni laughed his cackle. 'Maybe I'm no different. Did I not also tell you that sometimes I can help and sometimes I can't? I wish I could offer you certitude but all I can do is try.'

Lucens had landed at Heathrow three days before, and as in the old days, there was a car waiting to pick him up. The driver had put his overnight bag in the boot and given him an envelope with his name on it. Lucens took the thin paper packet with the Cambray crest and twirled it in his fingers. Don't tell me, he said to himself, James now hands over cheques even before he meets me.

Dear Lucens,

Delighted to have you at the Park. I have to apologize for a slight change of plans.

A Chechen delegation has arrived out of the blue with rather urgent business and we are likely to be caught up for a couple of days.

Make yourself at home. Use the gym, the billiards room, shooting gallery, and the swimming pool. Order whatever you fancy for meals. The car will be at your disposal 24 x 7. If you want to see a play or a show, just inform Derek Stafford, Deirdre's secretary, and he'll arrange for the tickets and take care of whatever you need.

Will catch up with you later. We are keen to hear about the progress of the Guardian Angels and your new plans.

Warm regards,

James

P.S. Deirdre is away for a few days. So I'm afraid she too won't be around to look after you.

Lucens was troubled by a vague misgiving as the Jaguar sped towards Cambray Park. Why hadn't they called him in Sparta and asked him to postpone his visit by two days? Even if the Chechens had not given much notice, surely they could not have just dropped in on the spur of the moment. Did Shakta Muni and James Cambray have any idea how far beyond desperate his plight was? He had long since run out of time and money and all his projects were at a standstill. In the meantime, Honor was in despair over whether he would ever make good on the overdraft and whether she would lose her job. There was another possibility, though, which was more likely to be the case: the Muni and Cambray Senior knew exactly how ominous Lucens's future was, and wished to impress upon him that he was at their mercy.

After lunch, Lucens sent for the car. Might as well go to the nearest church and calm down, he thought, instead of getting frantic with worry. He looked out of the window. Shakta Muni and James Cambray were walking in the distance amongst the oaks in the Park. As far as Lucens could make out, there were no Chechens or any other visitors around.

The nearest Catholic church was three miles away, and though it was pretty and quiet in a sedate British way, he seemed unable to pray or even seek guidance from the Son of God. He had been overwrought and tense for weeks, but things had got seriously out of hand since he had phoned James Cambray. He had not been quite clear why he was calling, or why he wanted to go see Roy's father and Shakta Muni. Now he was in England and he was in foul humour. He might be overreacting, for all he knew he might be getting paranoid, but he couldn't help thinking that the equation had somehow changed. Shakta Muni had tried to psych him all these years but this was the first time Lucens had come over as a supplicant. If only he had not listened to the Muni when he had last been in Bombay, and had disappeared into the hills, or better still into the mountains, he would not be in such dire straits now.

Lucens wondered whether he should go back to Cambray Park, pick up his bag, which he had not yet opened, and head back to Sparta. What then? he asked himself. Roy was right, of course. Hadn't Lucens known from the day he started losing money that his options had narrowed down to one? To the one remedy which Catholics were forbidden? Well, the fact was, he was already at the Park. He would eat crow for a couple of more days and then remove himself from life.

The next day turned out to be far grimmer than his last trading days had been. He might have blundered and bankrupted the Angels then, but at least that had left him not a single free moment. Now he had nothing but time on his hands, and he had no idea what to do with it. He had never been keen on the idiot box, nor could he bear to open and browse through economic journals, or the *Jane* annuals on aircrafts, munitions and ships in his room. He tried to sleep, but his jet lag wouldn't allow him to. Not that he had managed to knock off in Sparta either in the last couple of weeks. Some time around two o'clock at night he surprised himself by going for a walk in the Park. He ran into rabbits, foxes and a couple of startled deer, and on his way back saw the Muni and Cambray Senior alighting from the Rolls. They waved to him and went into the house without exchanging a word with him.

Lucens was no longer sure he could last out another hour.

In the morning James gave Lucens a cheque for US$ 20 million. The Angels needed vast transfusions of money, but now that Lucens had it in hand, he felt only a sick, sinking sensation. He would naturally pay back Honor and First Penn, and it would tide the Angels over for a while, but if that was all the twenty million was going to do for him, then he might as well close shop and bid goodbye to all the Guardian Angels programmes and the Homes for the Children of God. What was the point of borrowing such a huge sum unless it was going to multiply, if possible exponentially? But he knew that if he played the market now, this money too would be gone in a week. The sad truth was that numbers no longer spoke to him, gambolled in front of his eyes and rafted down the rapids of his bloodstream. There was no converse between them: the market was as uncommunicative as a nameless gravestone.

'Correct me if I'm wrong but I was under the impression that you were undergoing a liquidity – '

'Yes, I am,' Lucens cut Shakta Muni short. He had the feeling that the Muni was playing cat and mouse with him. 'James was willing to offer the Angels a loan of fifteen million without any security. He ultimately stretched it to twenty.'

'And you don't think that's a fair deal?'

'It's twenty million more than any bank would lend me considering that my market value is less than zero today. But it does not address the problem.'

'And what problem would that be?'

'What do I do once the money is spent?'

'The cheque will go some way to tide you over the current crisis and take the pressure off you for a couple of months. But of course its chief purpose is to let you get back to the market.'

'And lose everything once again? I can't. The market's gone dead on me. I've lost the touch.'

'You can't let fear get the better of you.'

'One hundred children depend on me. I can't take a chance and let them become orphans again.'

'In that case the only alternative is to abandon the Angels, and give up the good work you're doing.'

'Over my dead body.'

'Good. I'm glad you're not a defeatist. But we're back to square one again. How are you going to finance your multiple projects?'

Lucens bridled. 'I don't know.'

'Obviously you must have some ideas.'

'If I had I wouldn't be here. Do you?'

'You could try coming to our ashram.'

'If you think you are going to convert me, you're much mistaken.'

'The concept of conversion does not exist in Hinduism, Lucens,' the Muni smiled mischievously. 'You are the one who's into saving people. Allow me to point out a few facts. You came here of your own free will. You are just as welcome to leave as you are to stay. You seem to have a rather simplistic notion of my ability to negotiate what lies beyond the ken of man. I'm not selling anything, nor is your choice of religion any concern of mine. Unlike many another faith, we do not need to exclude others to feel that we are chosen.'

'How can you possibly help?'

Shakta Muni chose to ignore Lucens's disparaging tone. 'You'll need to do the impossible.'

'And what would that be?'

'You'd have to put your trust in me,' the Muni laughed. 'Sometimes I can empower people. Restore their gift. Sometimes.' He paused to let the words sink in.

'You can restore God's gift to me?' Lucens sounded incredulous.

'Why else are you here?'

'Then why do you want me to come to the ashram?'

'You are confusing things. The ashram has nothing to do with recovering your gift. The yogic aim is to awaken the energy lying dormant within you. We do not ask you to give up anything because our aims are very different. Yogic practices seek to heighten and intensify your receptivity, beliefs and experiences. They are first and last a discipline and a way of life. Yoga opens doors and becomes a voyage of discoveries. It frees you and allows you to apprehend that there are skies beyond the one you perceive and that the human potential for growth is infinite.'

'Maybe it's all these things and maybe it's just hot air. What I know is that I can't possibly take weeks off at a time to be introduced to your arcane practices when the entire edifice of the Angels has come crashing down.'

'I've always admired the clarity of your mind, but this minor crisis seems to have fried your brains.'

'You call this a minor crisis?'

'A hiccup, nothing more. Isn't it de rigueur for any self-respecting player in the market to lose all his money and rebuild his fortunes at least seven or eight times over?'

'I'm answerable to someone else, the highest authority there is.'

'Quite. But that shouldn't prevent you from making the trip. We may still be in the Stone Age in many ways in India, but I assure you that if you come to Delhi, we will be able to rustle up a laptop and you can access any market in the world.'

'Help me, Mother of God, I beseech you. Give me back the gift, otherwise both the children and I will be orphaned. Not just that, spreading the message of the Pledge of Purity has become more urgent than ever before. As you know, all the talk of safe sex is nonsense. Cardinal Trujillo has published the latest scientific findings that show that condoms are fuelling the AIDS epidemic. The HIV virus is much smaller than sperm, and can pass through them. Needless to say, the Brazilian government is ready to fly in the face of scientific evidence, and is trotting out what I'm sure are false figures.

'As Bishop Cifuentes points out, condoms are not the solution, but the problem. Trying to prevent AIDS with condom use is like trying to put out a fire with petrol, he says. The Pope himself has declared that condoms lead to indiscriminate sex and the spread of HIV.

'The Guardian Angels, Virgin Mother, are the guardians of both the physical and moral health of America. Please do not let the Angels down.'

A few weeks after Lucens got back, the Angels were already down by three million. This despite the fact that all plans for expansion had been put on hold. Four months, six at the most, and it would all be over. He had just far too many irons in the fire and every one of them singed him: the Homes for the Children of God, the Pledge of Purity programmes, the radio stations, staff salaries, rentals for auditoria, advertising and PR expenses; the money seemed to go up in smoke in front of his eyes. If he didn't do something drastic to reverse the trend, he wouldn't even be able to repay James Cambray and the Muni. He had the vague feeling that the Muni would not take kindly to that.

He took the plunge and went back to the market. Before a week was over, he had lost two million. He would have to fly to Delhi to the Muni's ashram. He loathed the thought, but he had no choice. Shakta Muni's words were his only hope: 'Sometimes I can empower people. Restore their gift.'

'Welcome home,' Shakta Muni said to Lucens as he showed him around The Shakta School of Yoga.

'I hardly think of this country as my home.'

'Isn't it curious how we look forward to the future but want to deny our past?'

'The past hasn't been very good to me. I wanted to make the world a better place, fight for justice.'

'Yes, I remember you wanted to save the world. You've now decided to save America, a continent that's either beyond saving or does not wish to be saved. Didn't someone say, I can look after my enemies but God save me from the good guys. Tell me Lucens, are black children welcome in the Homes for the Children of God?'

'For me there is no them and us.'

'That is laudable if a little facile,' the Muni commented acerbically. 'You'll grant that the powers-that-be have divided this little earth of ours into three worlds, and we are not the First or the Second but the Third World. Would you be surprised if many in our part of the world feel that the West cannot count beyond one and two?'

The vagina mouth smiled with a set of teeth that was so perfectly fashioned, it had to be artificial, and the Muni's hand rested on Lucens's back. The serpent in the Garden of Eden would have been more welcome. The hand was warm but that was, of course, a satanic trick. Lucens felt his blood freeze in the veins, as though somebody had introduced a cryogenic needle into his system. And yet the Muni's hand had a bewildering effect on Lucens. It reminded him of his father's soothing touch, though it was much more than that. It seemed to lower his pulse, and his heart, which had been tight as catgut, eased up, and he heard the vice of unbearable anxiety around his head crack open and fall to the ground. The Angels would make it, he thought, and so would he.

But that was the devil trying to seduce him. He must buy a reprieve and run for his life.

Lucens had no way of knowing whether Shakta Muni was a fraud, a blend of charlatan and saviour, or the real thing. He was an astute and canny man of the world, that much was evident. It was hard to tell whether his spiritual powers made him something of a diviner or whether he merely understood human nature better than most.

There was no way of gauging how big Shakta Muni's ashram was. Even when you were shown around, you could not form an idea of the size of the place. There were various buildings with huge airy classrooms for teaching yoga; meditation halls; state-of-the-art-laboratories; guesthouses for visitors and hostels for students; quarters for the two-hundred-odd male and female resident disciples; several playgrounds and two swimming pools; acres and acres of woods, and gardens with streams. On a hill in the west was a temple, and there were several areas where access was forbidden. Lucens was impressed. It was not ostentatious but tastefully appointed. A great deal of care and planning had gone into the ashram. It was run with military precision and discipline. Security was ever-present but unobtrusive. Shakta Muni himself had 'Z' security clearance, the highest protection available in the country. Nobody could get into the premises or leave without a body search. And every student member and temporary resident was given an identity card with his photograph and other details on it. Each night some foreign dignitary or the other drove in for an audience. Sometimes it was a Hollywood film star, and on two occasions the prime minister himself came over for blessings and consultations.

Where did the money come from? Did the politicians, the stars and celebrities and industrialists finance Shakta Muni's activities?

Perhaps he was a wealthy man in his own right. The Muni seemed to know a lot about Lucens while Lucens was almost entirely in the dark about him.

'I've a question to ask of you.'

'Fire away.'

'You've been tracking me since I was at New Eden.'

'You exaggerate your importance.'

'Maybe, but you are dodging the question. Why have you kept an eye on me and cultivated me for so many years?'

'I guess I want to know you because you are so earnest and don't care for the likes of me. Some people think of me as a holy man while you are certain that there's something dubious about me. That I'm a Hindu is not the issue since most Hindus too are uneasy with the tantrik arts. Like you they too suspect that I'm a fraud, a blend of charlatan and supernatural powers; that I dabble in the black arts and my disciples and I have orgies every night. And like you they too have a deep-seated fear of tantriks. They believe that if they cross me or displease me in any way I may do them harm, put them in the path of untold grief and ruination.'

That was the trouble with Shakta Muni. You had no privacy, no secrets and ultimately no freedom of thought. He saw through you and could read your mind as though he had invented a scanner far more powerful than ultrasound, computerized axial tomography or magnetic resonance imaging. He could access your thoughts.

'Why don't you get to the point?'

'I intend to, if you give me a moment. You need to demonize all that is unfamiliar and difficult to comprehend. But while others may hold their tongues out of politeness or fear, you are a real Tarzan when it comes to speaking your mind. Does that make you a fool or are you one of the angels? Perhaps there's no difference between the two. We are beholden to you for making us more self-aware and self-conscious. Maybe it even keeps our excesses in check. So you see,' the Muni smiled indulgently, 'you too have your uses. And who knows, one of these days we might even find some common interest. You are in the wrong line, Lucens. You should be in business.'

'Hatha yoga,' Shakta Muni had said in his introductory lecture, 'we do hatha yoga, not yoga.' His social persona, even in daily converse, had nothing in common with that of the teacher. Outside, he was never anything but civil and courteous. In the classroom, he was sarcastic, cutting and savage. He was choosy about who qualified for an apprenticeship under him. Even so, within the first couple of weeks, five out of ten aspirants would drop out.

'I'm going to be long-winded today, just this once,' he said. 'I will not waste my breath on outlining the basics again. People are always talking of pranayam, the art of breath control, as the centrepiece of yoga. It is, make no mistake, but pranayam too is a step to something more, to a state of heightened consciousness where matter and mind, the physical and the insubstantial interflow. We could go further in the pursuit of supreme consciousness, allow the body, that is the physical body, to disappear altogether; even the breath. That would be the enlightenment called nirvana. It is a goal and state of realization that is considered the Ultimate. I would urge you to look at it long and carefully. You may think that you know what it's all about and what your choices are. Maybe you do.' He paused. 'Then what are you doing here? Because you've already attained a state towards which we are all striving. What I'm advising is caution and a depth of introspection that may take months, years.

'Alongside enlightenment there is another choice. This is the choice those who aspire to siddhi make. It is an inferior state of being; different, substantially different from nirvana. Now, those who attain siddhi gain extraordinary powers. They're clairvoyant and telepathic. Their sexual prowess is legendary. They can cure incurable diseases; they can even alter your fate. But understand this clearly: the powers that siddhi bestows are earthbound. Nirvana is above all that.

'We respect the white light of enlightenment, maybe it's green, blue or a colour that we've never seen, for we're trying to describe the indescribable; but if you want to put it baldly, we want it all. Body, mind, breath, sex, soul, consciousness. The trouble with greed is that you may end up with less than nothing. You are all bright, well read and knowledgeable. You have a fairly clear idea about tantra and hatha yoga. We'll graduate through the six chakras or centres of the kundalini starting with the muladhara at the anus and then move on one by one to the seventh one, the sahasrara, where the semen is transformed into nectar and you gain immortality. That's what you are here for, am I right?'

All the would-be disciples nodded their heads vigorously and said yes.

'Good. You are ready then for a fifteen- or twenty-year haul at the very minimum, maybe thirty, who knows, thirty-five. And at the end of it you may discover that you've dried up so totally that let alone ambrosia, you can neither get an erection nor have a drop of semen left. So I suggest let's skip all that exotic talk of throwing your semen into the air like a lasso and then drawing it all back without spilling a single sperm.

'There is only one thing you are going to do day in and day out for hours on end every day. Knead your body, your brains and your breath. You are going to knead them till they are putty. You'll make them so pliant and flexible that the one flows into the other.'

The kneading was not metaphorical. The masseurs employed by the house turned you to pulp first, and then when you were semicomatose, the Muni made you do yoga followed by elementary meditation, both of which were closely supervised. Lucens, who had not done any exercise since the New Eden days, except for the time when he was at the Abbey, and that was physical labour and not yoga, had a body cast in concrete. There was no give in it and he was convinced that apart from his bones, his muscles too would break like dry twigs. The oil helped but only up to a point. Yoga was only part of the routine. In the evenings you did traditional Indian workouts. He had improved in the last few weeks. He could, for instance, bend forward till his palms were flat on the floor, and he could stand on his head for a minute, though not without a wall to support him. Some of the other contortions, which his peers could manage as though their bodies were made of string, were beyond him, but Shakta Muni assured him that if he didn't get the hang of them in time, he would be happy to snap his spinal cord or any other recalcitrant part of his body.

'Why are you surprised that you are confused? Anybody in his senses would be. Don't get anxious about all the abracadabra. For the moment, just go with the flow. In time things will begin to fall into place.' Shakta Muni was in an expansive mood. 'Let me start with an analogy. The verb "take" in its transitive form has 33 different meanings in *Webster's Dictionary*. It gives eleven separate meanings for the noun "mind" and the transitive verb of the same word can be interpreted to mean at least ten different things. It's the same with Shiva. The word is rich with multiple meanings and it's up to you to choose one or all of them. Shiva is the destroyer in the Hindu trinity. Now let me add to your confusion because in another sense he is also the creator.

'I could continue in this vein for another couple of hours and yet have scratched only the surface. Bear in mind that word "surface". It is the banana peel on which most outsiders slip and fall. The "surface" will cease to confuse the moment you grasp the essence underlying it. The essence is the One, the Supreme Being, the Ultimate Reality.' Shakta Muni smiled when he saw the perplexed expression on Lucens's face, and patted him on the back.

'It gets even more complicated. Now we are about to enter a hall of mirrors, an echo chamber of paradoxes. Anchor yourself to the Supreme Being, the One and Only, and you will never get lost.'

'What about tantra, how come it doesn't figure in any of this?'

'I'm coming to that. For tantriks like us, Shiva is the fount of knowledge and wisdom. He is the great ascetic, the master at whose feet the sages study and learn. The white ashes on Shiva's skin are a mark of his asceticism. Let's move one step forward. If Shiva is the masculine principle, then Shakti is the feminine. Some schools of tantrik thought will focus on Shiva, the father, to the exclusion of all else, and vice versa for those who see Shakti as the end-all and be-all.'

'That's an untenable position,' Lucens cut Shakta Muni short. 'The Absolute, you've told us, is nirakar and nirguni, without form and without any attributes and qualities. That precludes qualities like gender or any other attributes.'

'You are right, of course. But if you stay firmly on the surface-essence axis, all contradictions will be resolved. The two aspects, Shiva and Shakti, cohere in one another as One Being. Shakti cannot be separated from Shiva, nor can Shiva be decontextualized from Shakti.

'I must caution you at this point that I'm simplifying a great deal. As you become familiar and go deeper, your understanding of the issues will take on a more complex hue. Trust your intuition, Lucens. The West prides itself on its rationality. But it is doubtful if Aristotle or Descartes can help you negotiate the mystery of the Holy Spirit or the divine and the human in Jesus Christ. It's the same with Tantra.'

You had to hand it to Shakta Muni; he did not treat you like the ignoramus you were. Even when explaining the most recondite concepts, he spoke in easy and colloquial language and unpeeled layer after layer of meaning and symbolism. Finally, you thought, finally you had got your hands and arms around the central mystery of the mystical cult. Then you went back to your room and realized that while the wrapping had come off, the dark tropical flower of tantra had shied away and closed its petals and turned to stone.

'I wouldn't worry about the other students doing better than you,' Shakta Muni told Lucens when he came to see him on the day he was leaving. 'You will overtake them soon enough. I know you'll work twice as hard when you are away. Their motivation cannot compare with yours. The stakes are disproportionately high for you. A word of caution. Don't overdo the yoga, the pranayam or the meditation to the point where you wreck your backbone. Remember, excess within limits. As time passes, you'll burn even more incandescently, Lucens.'

'When should I come next?'

'That's up to you. Try your hand at the market when you get back to Sparta. See if you can get anywhere with it.'

# 51

Lucens was back. The same Lucens and a different Lucens. He was more self-assured, more dynamic, more capable and more cautious. He was playing the market again. And numbers were once again doing a jig for him. He spread himself wider to reduce risks. He stayed up nights so he could catch the Nikkei in Japan, the Hang Seng in Hong Kong and the Sensex in India. He had the feeling that both the Angels and he were going to be okay. Shakta Muni still made him uneasy, but like it or not, the Muni had saved him by the skin of his teeth. Mission Impossible was back on track.

Lucens called Honor Lockman over to his office for a working dinner.

'Are you ready for the big step up, Honor?'

Honor looked bemused. 'I don't quite get you.'

'Will you give up your job at First Penn and take over the Guardian Angels?'

'You know I can't. I need a regular salary to bring up my two children.'

'State your price, Honor, and the Angels will be happy to pay you that sum plus any perks you care to name.'

'This is very sudden, Mr Kahn.'

'Not really. I've been grooming you for the job for a couple of years now.'

'I'm not sure I'll be able to cope with both the Homes for the Children of God and the Pledge of Purity campaigns.'

'I don't expect you to be involved in the nitty-gritty of everyday work. You'll hire capable assistants, delegate work and supervise them. Your primary job is to help formulate policy and make sure that the targets you set are met.'

'Where will you be?'

'I'll be there to guide you in important decisions. But from now on finance will be my major responsibility. And I'll be travelling a lot in that context. But I'll be in touch with you daily both on the phone and by email.'

'I'll need to give two months' notice to the bank.'

'That's been taken care of. They were reluctant to part with you but they don't wish to lose the Angels' business.'

'What kind of pay package should I ask for from the Angels?'

Lucens laughed. 'I'm the employer. I'm supposed to beat you down to the lowest possible salary.'

'I know you won't do that.'

'Quite high, Honor. Err on the side of too much rather than too little. You are worth it and will do a far better job if you feel you are appreciated.'

6th April: Things have come to a strange pass. When she was working for First Penn, Honor would advise caution, while I was the impatient one. Now I want to consolidate our earlier gains before taking the Homes or the Pledge to other states, whereas Honor's raring to go national with the Pledge of Purity. We've reached a compromise. She'll test the waters in Michigan, Ohio and Illinois. If the response is good, she can try her luck in two of the most difficult territories in the country – New York and Washington DC.

1st May: Shakta Muni was right. I drive a hard bargain with my body. As far as yoga's concerned, I can do most of the asanas better than many of his older disciples who've been at it for ten or fifteen years. My pranayam and meditation skills are a little better, but there's much room for improvement. I now know how mechanically I must have been performing the offices in the past.

I'm nowhere near that state where the mind is totally blank. As a matter of fact, I'm told it disappears altogether, and what remains is the still centre that is the essence of all meditation. At present when I meditate, my head is abuzz with random thoughts, and I'm caught up in all the things I need to do that particular day. But every once in a while, the traffic jam in my brain clears up a bit and I can manage a fleeting moment or so when my mind is at rest. But imagine the day when I draw near to the ideal: my entire consciousness will be Jesus and nothing more.

5th May: Tunnel vision, that's what I'm suffering from. Did I really think the Pledge was going to work in a vacuum? Everybody has to pull together. We convinced the parents, we won over many of the teenagers. But we forgot the third most important element in a teenager's life. School.

19th May: Hallelujah. How shall I thank You, Jesus, and Your bountifulness. For the next sixty days, I will forgo both breakfast and lunch. It's so unexpected. I thought it would take at least another year or two for us to have a say in this state. But already we've received calls for endorsements. And here's the best part: state elections are in the offing, and it's the Democrats who want the Angels on their side. Dear Jesus, rest assured, we'll exact our pound of flesh. The party's local wing's promising to introduce a bill to make the Lord's Prayer compulsory in schools, and another one which will hold parents responsible if their teenage children become pregnant. It's a long, long haul but with the Democrats on our side in the state, which Republican dare go against us?

'The first nine months are some of the toughest,' Shakta Muni explained to Lucens. 'Now that you have survived close to eleven, you are ready to enter a new phase of hatha yoga. But before that, we must give you a new name.'

'Thanks, but I'm happy with my own.'

'So am I.' The Muni was not fazed by Lucens's brusqueness.

'I'm not about to part with it.'

'You'll always be the light for us, as you were for the Abbey, and before that as Zia. Only this time your light will shine in Sanskrit.'

'Actually, I was thinking of discontinuing my visits to Delhi. I've got back my touch with the market. And I've far too much on my plate in Sparta.'

'Certainly, if that's what you want,' Shakta Muni responded amiably. 'I had a thought the other day. Do you remember how paralysed with fear you were when you'd lost your gift?'

Lucens stared at the Muni with a sense of growing terror. He could feel his heart fibrillating, zigzagging wildly like a plane with an engine malfunction.

'Are you all right, Lucens?' The thin, clear voice was solicitous. 'You look as if you're about to pass out.' Shakta Muni felt Lucens's pulse. 'Maybe you should lie down. I'll call the doctor.'

Lucens clutched the Muni's hand as though he would break it. 'Are you going to withdraw the gift?'

Shakta Muni disengaged his hand. 'It is not mine to take or give. Is this why you're looking so pale?'

The colour found its way back slowly to Lucens's face, and he smiled weakly. 'The thought crossed my mind.'

'Uncross it swiftly. What I was about to suggest, by a strange coincidence, was an antidote to your irrational fears, how shall I put it? a kind of back-up measure, so the Angels won't be dependent on only a single source for funds. Let's for a moment imagine a worst-case scenario: the market no longer shares its secrets with you. What happens to the Angels, the Homes for the Children of God, the Pledge of Purity, the fight against Roe versus Wade? Will you abandon them all? Or, should I ask instead, can you bring yourself to abandon them?'

Lucens looked at the Muni suspiciously. 'What did you have in mind?'

'Maybe it's not such a good idea, after all,' Shakta Muni hesitated. 'It will unnecessarily complicate your life.'

'Let me be the judge of that. I'm quite capable of making up my own mind.'

'I've no doubt about that.' The Muni paused. 'What I was thinking was that you could join James's company. He's no longer young. And he could do with some help. I'm sure the two of you could work out a mutually satisfactory arrangement. That way, you'll never have to worry about the Angels' future.'

Lucens was back in the ashram at the end of the month. As he explained at length to Jesus, 'I don't want to seem ungrateful; the Muni did come through at a critical moment, and who knows, he might be of use to us once again. And what is it he wants from me, anyway? Nothing, except to call me Lucens in Sanskrit. Believe me, oh Lord my God, the change in my name is not going to diminish my love for You. In You alone can my soul find forgiveness. You are my rock, my salvation, my fortress on high, and my everlasting peace.'

In the garbha garbham, the womb of wombs, time ceased. Shakta Muni had warned him that however poetic the metaphor of a rebirth sounded, the triply enclosed womb of wombs would be the most terrifying time of his life. The Muni could have written a four-hundred-page tome giving a blow-by-blow and minute-by-minute account of the terror of the experience and made it compulsory reading for his disciples, and it would still have proved pointless. Dante and Milton, theologians, not to mention clergymen from the pulpits of their churches, had used all their powers of imagination to flesh out and evoke hell and its horrors. You may believe in hell and the terror of hell but hardly anyone today would give credence to the fire and brimstone, the boiling cauldrons, the rack, iron maiden, thumb screw or other marvels of the auto-da-fé, except as images of torture. You can read all the books in the world on the Nazi concentration camps and the gas chambers, and yet reality will dawn upon you only when you are put through them yourself. It is a law of God, or nature, if you prefer, that pain, suffering and grief cannot be transferred or known by proxy. Neither empathy nor sympathy but experience alone is the valid currency of affliction. It alone makes you a card-holding member and allows you to join the club of the wretched of the earth. All else is counterfeit.

Lucens was about to experience the real thing. He could scream himself hoarse, he could weep all night, but there was nothing but night down there: nobody was going to respond. The cell, cave, room, call it what you will, was more than a hundred paces long and seventy across. You could stand on your toes and stretch your hands up, or even jump, but you would still not touch the ceiling. And yet he might as well have been nailed inside a coffin, for the fourth dimension of all space is the imagination. There was a rope along the wall which led you to the toilet and bathroom, and a dumb waiter brought down water. You would think that he would hardly need to use the facilities since he was on a liquid diet but he seemed to spend the greater part of the day there.

The preparations for the naming ceremony had started with a drink of milk from the soma plant in a solid gold cup. It was generally believed that the secret of soma had been lost and nobody could identify the plant. But that was not entirely true. People in the know said that Shakta Muni had discovered it on the eastern flank of Mount Kailash. Soma was the great purifier. It cleansed both your body and your soul. It was destroyer and creator, the end and the beginning, for it started you on a new life. Lucens was soon to discover that it was nothing of the kind. Hemlock, arsenic and cyanide would all have been preferable to soma, for they were known to kill you quickly, in the most efficient manner possible. Soma turned his substance and even his soul to liquid. It was the most drastic of emetics. He had no idea how often he threw up or evacuated his bowels. By the first evening he could no longer make it to the toilet. It should have been the death of him a long time ago but he was wrong. It was becoming obvious that the idea was not to kill him but to prolong his agony forever. His hair had begun to come off in clumps and his scalp showed through as though he were undergoing chemotherapy. His skin was peeling and his nails were falling off. It was a good thing he was not eating anything because his teeth too had become loose and shaky. He had the feeling that he was coming apart. Soon his hands and legs would drop off and all two hundred and sixteen or whatever number of bones there were in his skeleton, would clatter down on the black marble floor. It was not such a bad thing, perhaps, that there was no light around and he couldn't see himself. Frankly, if this was a process of rejuvenation, or rather rebirth, he would any day skip it. He had always thought that the womb was supposed to be the most serene place on earth. The garbha garbham, which should have been thrice as secure, seemed instead to have been devised as the most hellish way of destroying a human being. Besides, he couldn't quite comprehend the point of the exercise. Surely there were easier and saner ways of reinventing the self. The purpose of corporal chastisement, as Lucens knew, was punitive. It was a sign of heartfelt repentance. But pain and torment could not be the agents of enlightenment. Every minute of his waking hours he wished to end his suffering. All he had to do was to ring the bell and someone would come and fetch him. No more solitary confinement, no more claustrophobia, no more lying in your own waste, no more darkness. Oh, for the light. What saved him in the end, ironically, was the soma itself. He was so exhausted and frail he was dead to the world most of the time.

Then, almost unbeknownst to him, he ceased to mind the retching and purging. He began to understand that the difference between light and darkness is one of weight. Light is transparent, darkness always a dead weight. But now the solid, immovable black lost its density, and became a medium through which he could perceive what lay beyond. 'Beyond' was no longer a spatial concept; it had turned into a continuum of space and time. 'Beyond' lay on either side of the present. He seemed to have arrived at a state of clairvoyance that had left the orbit of time. Its essence was not so much the ability to look into the future, as serenity. Perception, he realized, had always been, for him, an attribute of light. Now, for the first time, he could apprehend the world with any of his senses. The curious thing was that the sense of touch was no longer limited to his skin. His ears or nose would do just as well, and it was the other way round with the rest of the senses. He was well aware that in theory this could all be the hallucinatory effects of soma, starvation and dehydration, but he knew it was more than that.

'Your name is Tejas from today, Tejas Nirantar,' he heard Shakta Muni's voice. 'The light eternal.' It hadn't occurred to Lucens so far how sweet the human voice was, even Shakta Muni's. He had been in the dungeon for three days. It had seemed like three months.

He was nursed back to health as though he were a newborn baby. They rubbed him with sandalwood oil and let him lie for hours in a tub of warm perfumed water. Slowly they reintroduced him to a diet of nourishing soups and fruit juices. His hair began to grow and he had a new epidermis. It was unbelievably soft and there were times when he thought it glowed in the darkness. There could be no rebirth without the gift of eyesight. He was taken to a room where a soft, fuzzy light was allowed to stream in. He could not read or walk confidently but he knew he was on the way to recovery. Finally Shakta Muni took his hand and led him into the sun.

'I notice that you are still using the vocabulary of the past, Tejas,' Shakta Muni said to him a couple of days later. 'You think you've regained your health and your life. Let me tell you that nothing of the sort has occurred. The past is dead. That is the purpose of soma. It starts you from day one. And with a tabula rasa.'

On the day he left for the States, the Muni gave him an envelope. Perhaps the tantriks give you a cheque after the naming ceremony, he thought.

'What is it?'

'If you open it you may just find out.'

Lucens tore the packet open. It was a diplomatic passport in the name of Tejas Nirantar. 'What am I going to do with this?' Lucens tried to hand it back to Shakta Muni.

'The disciple is supposed to honour his teacher with a gift. In this case it is the other way round.'

Never again, never again, never again...Lucens chanted those two words like a mantra. Yes indeed, he would never allow the coffers of the Guardian Angels to run dry again, but the words were far more than that; they were a searing reminder of the fact that he had put all his eggs in the free-market basket instead of spreading his risks.

It was time for him to try his hand at 'this and that'.

'Just walk me through this, will you, James? I've been going through the order books, and there are a couple of puzzling entries. A party in Lebanon placed an order for a thousand items a year and a half ago. You sent the same consignment twice within a period of four months. Why is that?'

'Don't worry about it.'

'I'm not worrying. I'm asking because if I am to work with you, then I must understand the complexities of the business.'

James considered Lucens's question for a moment and then said, 'Here's what happened. The first consignment went on a Greek vessel which ran into trouble and was confiscated. So obviously we had to send the consignment again.'

'Yes, I see, but the Lebanese party seems to have paid only once.'

'Naturally. They are not about to pay twice for the same order.'

'But you did.'

'We are responsible for the goods till they arrive at the customer's location and the party verifies that all the orders have been honoured.'

'How come we take all the risks and yet bear the liability?'

'Because it's a buyer's market, especially at the lower end. The competition is so cut-throat that I had no choice but to resupply if I was not to lose the customer.'

Then maybe we shouldn't be at the lower end of the market, Lucens thought, but held his tongue. He would have plenty of time later to maximize his options. For the time being he was here to learn and not to show what a smart alec he was.

Whenever Lucens visited Cambray Park, or they met at the ashram in Delhi, James put him through his paces. He showed Lucens how deals were cut, how commission was calculated, divided and distributed between different parties; where the money was deposited, how it hopped and toured through many ports of call before it was deemed valid currency. He taught him the ins and outs, he drew flow charts and alternate scenarios. He familiarized him with the topology of continents and individual countries, outlined the areas of tension, and the specialized needs of each terrain and ethnic group. He briefed him on the dos and don'ts, on who the competition was; on marketing strategies, on euphemisms and indirections; on disinformation and on never calling a spade a spade; on complicities with government agencies and on silences. And finally he introduced him to suppliers and clients as his partner, Tejas Nirantar.

*

My dear Zia,

Do you remember my favourite four-line fable from Camus' *The Fall*? It is perhaps the shortest, most succinct and definitive example of the existential concept of choice that life, God or the devil presents us. Let me refresh your memory by quoting the passage:

'Do you know that in my little village, during a reprisal operation, a German officer courteously asked an old woman to please choose which of her two sons would be shot as a hostage? Choose! – can you imagine that? That one? No, this one. And see him go.'

If I may be pedantic and extrapolate, what Camus is suggesting is, that's how much of a choice we human beings have. In short, no choice at all. And yet as he and others of his ilk will tell you, you have no choice but to choose. Because in a meaningless world, only by consciously making a choice, can you imbue life with meaning.

Camus and the other existentialists had to make desperate sense of life after having been through the horrors of WW II, the concentration camps, the holocaust and the final solution.

I arrived on the scene decades after the end of WW II. And on a different continent. Existentialism is long since passé. But I have a rider to add to Camus' concept of choice. I've asked myself whether I was being smart-arsed, cynical or posturing when I came to formulate it. I wish so. That would make it much easier to live with. But it started out as an impression, a view of life when such things are but vague misgivings or premonitions. I was merely a child when a deliberate cynicism or sense of irony were quite beyond me. It has crystallized, however, only in the last few years. It is not an axiom. But enough preluding and prefacing.

Here it is: 'In any given situation, the choice you don't make is the right one.' Naturally, it follows that if you had made the other choice, the one you've opted for just now would have been the right one.

I suspect what this amounts to is that whichever choice you make is the wrong one. Is that opening a whole Pandora's box and the possibility that if every choice is wrong, then there is no ethical right in the universe and we may, like Ivan in *The Brothers Karamazov*, justify any evil act? No, I'm not suggesting anything of the sort and I certainly am not proposing a universal system. It's not even a system that I adhere to consistently.

The staple diet of Hindi cinema is a triangle: a woman must choose between two equally attractive and decent men, or the other way round. If there was any integrity or honesty in our films, they would admit that it is an impossible dilemma. Whoever the woman chooses, her lot in life is regret. The trouble with life of course is that we are constantly confronted with multiple choices when things would be so much easier if there was no choice; or if a guru or our parents made the choices and took decisions for us.

There's a parable that Merlin tells King Arthur in *The Once and Future King*. A man runs into Death in a souk in Damascus. He is struck by the surprise and puzzlement on the ghoulish countenance. Panic stricken, the poor fellow consults a wise man who advises him to flee Damascus post-haste since Death has most likely come to fetch him. All night long, the man rides hard, stopping only to change horses and have a drink of water, and does not rest till he reaches Aleppo. He heaves a sigh of relief at eluding Death, for no man has ever covered the distance between the two cities in one night. All he wants to do now is to lie down in a caravanserai and recover for a week. Just then someone taps his shoulder. It is Death.

'But I thought I'd escaped you because I saw you in Damascus yesterday.'

'I must confess I was shocked to see you too, because I was supposed to pick you up in Aleppo today.'

I don't mean to sound pat but the fable exemplifies my thesis rather neatly.

The formulation may sound mathematical but like all neat propositions, it needs to be distrusted. I'm aware that my little maxim is open to charges of despair and nihilism but I tend to turn it inside out and see it as liberating. If whatever I do is likely to be the wrong choice, then it is incumbent upon me to make as sensible and optimal a choice as I can according to my own lights and not because some book, theory or received wisdom says so.

I wonder what's come over me. Why am I bombarding you with letters these days? Perhaps it has something to do with Abbajaan not being around any more and Zubeida Khaala becoming more and more of a spectral presence. I see Sagari once in a while but she's busy and I can't seem to get over my guilt. The only family who I can talk to just now is you and I'm sorry that you have to take the brunt of my letters. If I were you I would never open them. But never, never make the mistake of telling me that.

How are you, my brother? What an up-and-down, love-hate relationship the two of us have had. But there must be something cussed in the foundations for it to have survived such buffetings and batterings.

Look after yourself, brother mine,

Love,

Amanat

19th August: Glades Medical Center is furious with me for stealing Zac Forbes, their top business manager. I had been eyeing him for some time to take over as our interface with Capitol Hill, ever since he suggested that he wanted to do something more meaningful with his life than make obscene amounts of money for the hospital. He's been with us three months and already we're making headway in the corridors of power.

24th August: The more I see of James Cambray, the more I find him an amiable but officious ass. He's totally out of it. The business has changed dramatically but he's caught in a time warp. He likes to make believe that he's the only civilized man amongst a pack of rogues. When was the last time you came across a gentleman in business? It was no different twenty-five or thirty years ago when he started out. It's just that he's bone-lazy and has lost touch with reality. What's needed is a total change of direction and emphasis and some very hard work. After that we'll be in a different league. An altogether different league.

27th August: The Angels are a big organization now. It's no longer practical to rent office space for our staff in Sparta and for our other activities from the Glades Medical Center. Must have a place of our own. It makes good economic sense to take a long-term view and put up a complex of complementary buildings called The Guardian Angels Center: office space, part of which we rent to the new companies in the area, a Pledge of Purity temple, a convention centre, a Christian art museum, an American heritage centre and one of the best libraries in the country, a sports centre, etc.

When I was at Cambridge, I had proposed to Amanat that if he went back to school and studied architecture, which not just Abbajaan but even the gardener at Firdaus would have told him was his vocation, I would give him his first real-life assignment. I failed to persuade him then. I have no idea why he took it into his head to go back to school after Abbajaan's death, but the good news is that he stuck it out and should be a full-fledged architect within a few months. It's time I kept my promise to him. His first assignment will be The Guardian Angels Center.

## 52

The boy was not well. Nothing serious, Gladys Burgess had told Lucens when she called around 8 in the evening. She just wanted to keep him informed. A bit of a fever and a chill. The doctor had asked her to give him paediatric Tylenol and assured her he would be leaping about tomorrow. A change in the weather and you know how children instantly catch a bug. Why was Mrs Burgess bothering him with these details? Did she intend to call him every time one of the Children of God got a cold or a headache?

He did not have much to do with the Burgesses. (They usually met on Sundays in church.) But he had a good feeling about them, especially Gladys. She was solidly dependable if also a little stodgy. But she cared for the children as if they were her own. At the time he had appointed the Burgesses, he had told them that neither he nor the trustees would interfere in their work or question their decisions unless they were irresponsible or guilty of misconduct. Corporal punishment was not an 'option' but he would back them all the way on the issue of discipline. Honor's instincts about the Burgesses had proved right. They were now the role models for the parents at other Homes, including the Prestons who had been hired immediately after them.

Was it possible that Gladys Burgess had called him only because it was 'the boy' and she felt she was answerable to Lucens for him? And because they shared the same name, he was supposed to feel a special affinity for him? Well, he didn't. There was not much occasion for Lucens to visit individual Homes or to think about the first of the Children of God, but for reasons that were not clear he couldn't get himself to call him by his name. If and when he had no choice but to refer to him, he called him 'the boy'.

The Angels were opening a new chapter of the Pledge of Purity at Delacroix, a hundred and thirty miles from Sparta, and for the next three days Lucens was busy training the new Apostles for The Pledge of Purity who would spread the message of 'Zero sex till marriage'. When he got back the next afternoon, there was a note posted on his door: 'Lucens Jr admitted to Glades, Paediatric Ward B. Alfred Burgess.' Lucens couldn't decide whether he was ill-tempered because he was hot and exhausted after three days of intense work with barely three hours of sleep each day or that something about the note irritated him. What did Alfred Burgess expect of him? Was he supposed to make a mental note that the boy had not recovered as the doctor had prognosticated, but had to be admitted to hospital? Was he expected to go to Glades and see how the boy was faring? Or was he supposed to take charge of him and relieve the Burgesses who had nine other kids on their hands?

He showered and went to the Angels' office where there was enough of a backlog to keep him occupied till late at night. It was time for his nightly call to Roy to discuss the mood of the market and instruct him about the next day's moves. Then he thought of the boy.

He drove to the Burgess home. It was past 11 p.m. and it took a while for Alfred Burgess to come down. He switched on the porch light and fiddled around with the latches for a minute and finally managed to open the door.

'Is this any time – ' he stopped short when he saw Lucens.

Lucens was contrite. 'I'm so sorry. I hadn't realized it was so late. I'll drop by tomorrow to check about the boy.'

'The boy?' Alfred Burgess looked confused. 'Oh, you mean Lucens Junior. If I were you I would go and see him now, Mr Kahn. Gladys is with him. He has a high fever and is sleeping fitfully, and has been asking for you.'

'Asking for me? He doesn't know me.'

'Oh, he does. He wanted to know how he got to be called Lucens when his father's name is Alfred, and Gladys told him about you and how he was called Lucens Junior because he was our first-born and we wanted him to be as good a Christian and as outstanding a citizen of America as you.'

'Thank you, Alfred. I'll send Gladys back.'

'I doubt it. She's an obstinate woman and Junior is very attached to her.'

'We'll see.'

Lucens sat still in the car. He was beginning to understand finally why he referred to his namesake only as the boy. He did not want any more Lucenses after him nor any Zias. He was the last of them. No other child should ever have to carry the burden of his name, fate or lineage. Not even an adopted child. He did not wish the sins of the father to be visited upon the son. Honor, he was sure, had meant well but she would have had second and third thoughts about naming the boy after him if only she had known about Lucens's past. He turned the key in the ignition and headed for Glades. Alfred and he had talked a good five or seven minutes but he had forgotten to ask what the matter was with the boy and how he was faring now.

Lucens had been here before. If he walked twenty paces and turned left, he would be in Ward B and see Som Puri sitting at the fourth bed to the right with his back to Lucens, murmuring softly to his five-year-old patient as he gave him an intravenous injection and then took the boy's pulse. Lucens could hear him as he approached.

'I'm not going anywhere, Philip. I'm going to keep sitting right next to you. We are going to break this fever together. As you are beginning to see, I don't know much of anything, least of all what's going on in your body at the moment. But your parents and your brother and sisters don't want to hear that. They just want me to tell them that you're going to be all right. So I'm asking you Philip, man to man, don't let me down. Don't let them know that I'm ignorant and helpless.'

Yes, Lucens was standing at the fourth bed now and the boy's cheeks were the same flaming scarlet and his forehead was radiating as much heat as Philip's had. Gladys Burgess got up from her chair and stood near the boy.

'Lucens. Lucens, look who's here. The one you were named after, the one who gave you to Daddy and me has come to see you. Everything's going to be all right now. Open your eyes, my sweet one.'

It took five minutes, maybe it was ten. Perhaps not more than a minute passed. The boy opened his eyes and smiled.

'You are Lucens?'

'Yes, that's my name.'

'I'm Lucens too. Just like you. Mommy says I'm going to grow up to be just like you.'

'Better, you'll be a much better person than I am. But first you are going to get well, yes? Will you promise me that?'

The boy smiled again and nodded his head.

Lucens found it difficult to reconcile this three-year-old with the baby whom Father Raymond had baptized and who had later become the face of Zero Orphans. Where had the intervening years gone? How could the boy have grown so much when his attention had been diverted for barely a few moments? He thought of the boy's eyes. Despite his high fever and the fact that he had lost four pounds in the last five days, they were full of intelligence and curiosity. How could it be, he asked himself, that during all the years he had spent on the anti-abortion campaign, the one thing missing was the children themselves? He had fought for an abstraction, a dry theoretical principle, and forgotten that children grow at the rate of three inches per second and their minds are the largest sponges on earth. They can fit in the entire universe in that greedy, insatiably absorbent mass of nervous tissue called the brain and then constantly invent new ones. What a fool he had been not to observe the most exciting series of geometrical progressions. When the boy got well, he was going to spend time with him and get to know all the other children in the different Homes.

Early next morning Lucens went to St Peter's and had a Mass said for the boy's recovery. He prayed to the Virgin to intercede on the boy's behalf with her own son, the Son of God.

'I beseech you, Mother, let the boy live. He's innocent and so young. Who would know the pain of losing a son better than you? He's our first-born and the first of the Children of God. Please don't let my sins be upon his head merely because he shares my name.'

Forty-eight hours later the boy was sinking into unconsciousness.

Lucens will sit up day and night by the child's side. He will not, as he has vowed, touch any food. Gladys and Alfred Burgess, Honor, the nurses and later even the doctors, plead with him to go home and rest. He will not budge. One thing is certain. Come what may, the boy must live. Lucens will stake his own life for him. Literally. He does not know why but the boy has assumed a pivotal, almost iconic significance for him. The future of the Angels, of everything that is good and worthwhile, the very regeneration of America in the image of Christ hinges upon the boy's fate.

As the child's condition worsens, Lucens becomes desperate and at times incoherent. He begs the doctors to do something, anything; apply a cold compress, cover his chest with a poultice that will draw out the toxins, give him a cordial that will rejuvenate the cells within him so that he can combat the unidentified infection. He cannot bear to see the boy suffer. He tells them to fly in the best paediatricians, neurologists, nephrologists, whoever they want, the Angels will defray all costs. Surely there's bound to be somebody out there in the United States of America, if need be in England, Japan or Russia, who can diagnose what this fever of unknown aetiology is and start the correct medical treatment instead of groping in the dark as they are doing now and using a scattershot approach in the hope that something will work.

The consultants at Glades and the director himself assure Lucens that they would not hesitate to call in for a second opinion if there was the remotest chance that someone else in the field had a better idea of the nature of the patient's illness. But they've done every available test, yet none suggests a specific infection, viral or bacterial. If they may be candid, only the Almighty can cure the boy now.

Lucens calls the Abbot: would he and the other monks pray for this child? The Abbot tells him that the monks will plead for the child's life through every office of the day and pray for him at Mass in the mornings because he means so much to Lucens. But he also cautions his former disciple that he must ultimately leave the decision in God's hands and accept whatever He deems fit. Even as he speaks he senses that Lucens is no longer listening.

The fever zigzags. When it comes down by a couple of degrees Lucens's hopes surge, he's sure the boy has turned the corner. Then it shoots up and he sinks into a depression. And yet from the beginning he has known that there is only one man who can heal the boy. It is Som Puri. He calls up London General and is told that Dr Puri has left the hospital and gone back to India.

*

One by one the vital organs began to fail. The next day the boy became delirious and was semiconscious. Lucens had a vague recollection that Aunt Antonia had told him that he too had suffered from similar symptoms when he was born. That was when she had taken him to the church at Wodehouse Road and got him baptized. He wondered whether the boy too would start recovering if he was rechristened. He spoke to Father Raymond but though the priest didn't say it out aloud, he thought Lucens was behaving a little oddly.

'He's already been baptized. What he needs is Extreme Unction.'

'Why are you in such a hurry to end the boy's life? He will live to a very old age.'

Father Raymond thought it best not to argue. 'Call me if his condition gets worse.'

That night even Lucens had to admit that the boy was dying. He had known all along whose fault it was. He had betrayed Som Puri when he knew perfectly well that he was innocent, completely innocent. But now instead of Lucens having to suffer for letting down the only friend he had had in the three counties, the boy would have to pay with his life.

He called Father Raymond and asked him to come over for the last rites. Then he knelt down by the boy's bed. A long time ago when he was a child, Zubeida Khaala had told him a story about Babur, the founder of the great Mughal dynasty and the grandfather of Emperor Akbar, the one whose attar Aminara had rubbed on his wrist in The Perfumed Garden. When Emperor Babur realized that his grown-up son and heir apparent, Humayun, was on his deathbed, he walked thrice around the sick man's bed and prayed to God to spare his son's life and take his. And that is what God did. Babur's health declined as Humayun started to recover. Then Babur was no more while Humayun became Emperor of India.

Now Lucens too prayed to his God to take his life and let the boy live. He walked thrice around the child's bed, knelt down again and touched his forehead to the floor in utter abnegation.

'I started the Guardian Angels, the Children of God, Zero Orphans, the Pledge of Purity to save the unborn babies. Now the blood of the very first of the Children of God will be on my hands. Do not do this, Lord, I beg You. Take my life as You took Babur's and let the boy have a full long life in Your service. He will take over my unfinished work and reverse Roe versus Wade. Spare him, Jesus.'

But the Lord would not bargain with Lucens nor heed his prayer. He struck down the boy early in the morning and orphaned Lucens.

# 53

In the course of his dealings in the arms business, Tejas came to three not very original but pragmatic conclusions. He had not intended to be cynical but that was the nature of the beast. His observations would lead him to a radical change in the marketing objectives of James's company, International Strategic Security Systems. Or 'I-triple-S' for short.

One of Tejas's first insights was that it was a myth that production was dictated by need. He was of course overstating the case: the Palestinians might genuinely require ordnance and weapons of all sorts to combat Israel, as had the Viet Cong to fight infinitely superior American firepower or the Afghans against the Soviet Union. But all this was chickenfeed compared to what the major powers spent. The incontestable basis of the weapons trade was keeping up with the Joneses and one-upmanship. This is why in the old days when they didn't indulge in euphemisms and political correctness, they called it an arms race.

In the pursuit of a ludicrous notion of deterrence, both America and Russia had spent trillions of dollars and built up arsenals large enough to nuke the whole world a thousand times over. The sole engine of the appetite for more and more arms and higher and higher levels of technical sophistication was the stranglehold that the arms industry-cum-military nexus had on governments and politicians. How else could anybody in his senses commission something as insane as the Star Wars system of defence?

Tejas's second observation was really a rider to the first. Technology and arms acquisition ultimately tend to become ends in themselves without any reference to reality. The armed forces turn into gizmo freaks. It was not just the developed and affluent nations that were vying with each other. India and Pakistan, Iran and Iraq, and many other good neighbours were busy doing exactly the same sort of thing. Tejas was reminded of an Indian guru, the late Bhagwan Rajneesh, the one who was called Osho. He had ninety-seven Rolls Royces in his ranch at Oregon. One RR made sense; maybe even two if the rationale was to always have a back-up. But how could one account for the remaining ninety-five except in terms of some bizarre concept of status and power?

The closest parallel to the Osho excesses in the 'this and that' business was Saudi Arabia. The largest-ever British contract to date was the first Al-Yamamah deal brokered by Wafic Said with Saudi Arabia. Al-Yamamah was signed in 1985 and was worth over 29 billion US dollars. Think about it, 29 billion.

The Saudis seemed to have bought everything in sight including Tornado and Hawk aircraft. What were they planning to do with all that hardware? It was doubtful whether they had enough trained pilots to fly these highly complex aircraft. And who were they planning to fight? The Israelis would have polished them off faster than breakfast cereal. Besides, no Saudi head of state would go to war with Israel when the US was patron saint to both. Maybe they saw Iraq as the potential enemy. But there too, they would never take the Iraqis head-on. They would leave the job to the US. The only reason the Saudis spent such monumental sums of money was because they had it and those fighter planes in their hangars made them feel like cowboys. Or, to be even more precise, because like most grown-ups, the Saudis too are children. They love toys.

And here's the best part. The first Al-Yamamah was followed by a second one. It was not that big a deal but try sniffing at $7.25 billion.

Tejas's last reflection was that the keystone, the core of the arms business, was not technological advances, nor was it war or freedom. It was the commission, the siphoning off of money into the private pockets of generals, middlemen and politicians. Their avarice, Tejas reasoned, would form the cutting edge of his strategy.

He now had a clear idea about what his aims were: International Strategic Security Systems must move into the billionaire league. He knew the weaknesses of his client-states. These were his greatest resource. He must exploit them to the hilt. Al-Yamamah would henceforward be his role model.

'Here are the figures, James. The size of the pie, the total size of the pie worldwide, is 60 billion dollars. After close to twenty-five years in the business, what is your share? 450 million dollars and that only because I got into the act and recently earned 50 million. Add to that another 3 or 4 million because I've streamlined operations and made the most of the loopholes in the law.

'I've been studying our product mix, and it's strangely skewed. We spend 85 per cent of our time on the lower end of the product range, which accounts for 15 per cent of our earnings. It's the reverse for our big earners. We barely spend 10 or 11 per cent of our time on them and yet they fetch 70 to 80 per cent of our income. What if we spend 50 or maybe 75 per cent of our time on the high-end customers?'

James smiled patronizingly. 'Do you think the thought had not crossed our minds?' James was always using the plural personal pronoun. Was it a pontifical 'we' or did James include the Muni in matters of business?

'That market is like Fort Knox. You may knock on it as much as you want, the entrenched multinationals are never going to let you get a peep at it.'

'But you did get a peep at it. You even pilfered some of their business.'

'It took twenty-five years and it wasn't worth it. Take my word for it. Those big guys are not nice people.'

'We are under no compulsion to be nice either.'

'You are missing the point, Lucens. At the end of the day, we must be able to live with ourselves.'

Lucens had had enough of James's posturing.

'Here's what we are going to do. We're going to phase out the small-change business and devote 85 per cent of our time to the up-market segment. The clientele is exclusive, return on investment is far higher and our visibility much lower. We make the changes from the first of next month.'

'I don't know,' James said. 'I'll have to check with Shakta Muni.'

'You do that, James. Consult anybody else you want including QE II. But make no mistake. Come the first of next month, we are going to be a different kind of company. A leaner, meaner and hungrier company.'

Like Shakta Muni, Lucens too was wary of using words like shakti, kundalini or chakras. Both native Indians and Western dilettantes and hoaxers tossed them around without any idea of their complexity or implications. But once you had even a distant glimmer of their power and the metaphysical apparatus behind them, the subject was closed. It was the same with pure maths. You could intuit it, explore and plumb its depths, and exchange notes with fellow-travellers, but you could not explain it. There was, however, little doubt that Lucens had tapped into an energy source within himself that was an eternal spring. He could now go for days on end without sleeping or resting and not feel fatigued or lose his concentration.

The curious fact, though, was that he could not rid himself of the feeling that Amanat's anaconda of time was swallowing him rapidly. Those round brackets under the paintings that he had spoken of in his letter about his visit to the museum in Detroit had trapped Lucens between them, and were pressing in upon him. His first and only priority was to put the Angels and their various projects on a financially secure footing so that the Guardians could steer America back to the living Christ.

Most of the time these days Tejas was shuttling around the world on business. The diplomatic passport, he was discovering, made travel and life much easier, especially in these post 9/11 times. There were other external changes in his lifestyle. He now dressed in the most conservative designer suits; he stayed in the best hotels. In the interest of fairness and good business sense, he made sure that his next meeting was almost invariably with his previous customer's arch-enemy and nemesis. He would also brief this person on what the other party was buying, without letting on that he himself was the supplier, and would quietly analyse how it was going to affect him. He didn't need to say anything more. The new customer was bound to place an order that would be at least one up.

What Tejas and his clients had in common was their need for secrecy and subterfuge. Tejas did not take any notes; he filed them in his head. Only when the deal was finalized would the country's embassy in London get in touch with James's offshore office and place an order.

There was a missive waiting for Lucens at the ashram in Delhi.

Dear Friend,

The time for our meeting is nigh. I seek no favour of you, nor do I intend to engage you in idle talk. My purpose is business, and yet I cannot deny that it will allow me an opportunity to fulfil my lifelong desire of seeing you in person.

My sources tell me that you are in a safe haven, at the ashram of Shakta Muni. I shall call you there.

I trust we will not be nameless for long.

Your comrade-in-Allah

It took Lucens a minute to place the nameless writer. It was the same man whose letters Amanat had redirected to the Abbey.

'You've fallen short of your monthly target again, this time by 50 per cent.' Tejas could see that James Cambray was already squirming. He had no sympathy for the man. He was Tejas's senior by at least thirty years. He had started the business and had run it all these years. Yet now, while James was still the MD of International Strategic Security Systems, Tejas had clearly taken charge of operations, and planning and development. The first five minutes James would sulk and become resentful, but he wanted the extra income as much as Tejas did. He was an amiable man by temperament, and the figures Tejas conjured up as profit margins would restore his good humour. 'Let me refresh your memory, James. You set the targets, not me.'

'I know but Deirdre has been in detox once again. I'm not making excuses but I have been a trifle distracted.'

'Very touching, no doubt. But you only went and saw her twice in the six weeks she was there. Mind you, I don't blame you, not for that. After a person goes off the wagon the twenty-third time, one tends to lose interest. What's up, James? I'm pulling more than my weight and I'm earning your share of the money. Your business has gone down by 50 per cent, mine's up by 125 per cent. The Free Kashmir Brigade's order was as good as finalized. I had got them to sign on the dotted line. All you had to do was despatch the goods and collect the money. But you didn't even do that.'

'We have a code of conduct. We have our principles. We don't sell to the enemies of India.'

'What a hypocrite you are.' Tejas burst out laughing. 'How are Indians different from anybody else? The Free Kashmir Brigade is our customer and it's our duty to satisfy our clients. I don't recall your having any qualms about selling stuff to the IRA and other friends of Britain. Next time you pull that number on me, you won't get your share of the commission.' Suddenly Tejas's eyes softened and he looked sympathetic, 'You aren't planning to retire by any chance, are you?'

'Well, I wouldn't mind really. I'm no longer young, you know,' James said with half-hearted self-pity. The fool had taken the bait and Lucens pounced on him.

'Don't be stupid, James. With Deirdre in tow, you'll never be able to live within your means, and you'll once again have to put the Park in hock. You have no choice: get down to business.'

James's firm, International Strategic Security Systems, had been suffering from stasis for nearly ten years. There could be two reasons why both turnover and profits had stagnated: James had lost his drive or the industry had changed radically. Lucens reckoned it was probably a combination of both. Cambray Senior belonged to an older school of businessmen whose marketing genius consisted of little beyond the old boys' network. He was congenitally affable, and despite his family tree and coat of arms, was never condescending, or intimidating. Africans, Arabs, South and Southeast Asians, Latin Americans, he put everybody at ease and they all thought they could get the better of him. That ploy had paid good dividends for many years. But by the eighties, the arms business was no longer a seller's market and James was stranded like a silent movie star unable to make the transition to the talkies: he could not adjust to the changed circumstances.

Lucens had imagined that he himself had joined the business because he didn't want the Angels' future to be dependent solely on the stock market. But of late he had begun to wonder if James, or rather the shadowy figure behind him, the Muni, was playing a more devious game: roping him into the business because he was younger, hungrier, and had the capacity to jolt the business out of its inertia with new marketing techniques and systems, and the nerve to go after much bigger game.

Tejas had been, at first, a patient and sedulous student under James at I-triple-S. Whatever his own reservations and doubts about the company's marketing policies, he had kept them under his hat. But even after he had learnt his trade hands-on, had enough field experience and decided to aim at the upper end of the business, he was still not ready.

He had zeroed in on the greed and avarice of clients as his most valuable assets. They would gain him new customers and make sure they stayed with him.

The obvious way to outgun the competition and rope in new business was to cut into I-triple-S's profits and give higher and higher commissions. It was a solution that he found contemptible. Short-sighted fools resort to that kind of tactic. Tejas's strategy would be different. Despite all the talk of offshore banking and tax-free havens, the 'bleaching' of money involved considerable losses. Unless…unless you knew all the ins and outs and the loopholes in tax laws and banking systems. Any client of I-triple-S would get this advice, absolutely gratis. The percentage game may seem negligible at first sight but consider the sums involved and the savings add up. Let's say that the Uzbek PM saves a million and a half because of a little help from Tejas in laundering the money. That money's going to buy him a Lear jet and it's going to work wonders for his self-confidence and status when he flies over to Azerbaijan in his private plane to meet his counterpart who still uses a hand-me-down from the Russians.

Few people understand numbers, economics and finance as well as Tejas. Now he must apply that knowledge to tax laws, test the legal boundaries of tax evasion and money transfers, get to know laundering hothouses like the Bahamas, Luxembourg, Swiss banks. Money, Tejas believes, is like water. It takes time but unerringly finds the most invisible cracks and slips through it. His job is to detect these hairline chinks and interstices and facilitate the filtering of currency.

When Tejas sets his mind to something, he won't just wet his ankles, or a part of his torso, he'll immerse his entire self, body, mind and soul, and will not surface till he has mastered the subject. In the coming months, he'll have a killing timetable: studying, researching, getting to know the similarities and differences between the tax systems of different countries, consulting with tax lawyers and experts and having extensive tête-à-têtes with small, medium and big-time money-laundering agencies. It's not going to happen overnight, too many laws and bylaws, subclauses and sub-subclauses, but he's slowly beginning to recognize the fundamental design behind seemingly chaotic tax structures and the tiny labyrinthine spaces that too much legalese always allows.

But there are further bonuses Tejas will offer every once in a while to his clients. The PM, defence minister or chief-of-staff who'll be retiring in a year or two will get a hot investment tip that will help him put aside a tidy nest egg. Tejas will tell you that all animals stop eating once they've had their fill. All animals except one, that is. There's no such thing as enough for human beings. The more they have, the more they want. Especially the very very rich.

21st March: All these years I've preferred to be in the shadows. It's no longer a question of preference. If one is going to be in the 'this and that' business, it's mandatory to turn anonymous.

25th April: Next time I'm at the Abbey for a retreat, I must persuade Reverend Father to become a trustee. The board is too parochial just now. Needs outsiders with weight and vision.

29th April: Patience, I keep reminding myself, hasten slowly. Revolutionary changes have short lives, whereas incremental ones last. We are building a coalition of the righteous, regardless of a person's political hue. Once we have the power, we'll bend the government to our wishes and programmes. Rest assured we'll change the complexion of this country. No abortion, no gays and lesbians, no same-sex marriages, no child sex, no sex shows, no dirty art. We are going to build fine, upright, God-fearing citizens from scratch. You will see a change at home, in school, in every aspect of life. But we won't stop there. We will move into South America. We will take Europe. We will remake the world in the image of our Lord.

James and Tejas are barely on talking terms with each other. Actually it's a little more asymmetrical than that. The former diplomat is, as usual, his compulsive, convivial self, though you can never really get to know him. Tejas has wondered at times whether the man was a bottomless question mark, or whether there was no riddle to him, just a hole without the doughnut around it. Of late, however, James seems to have lost some of his effervescence. Fact is, he's afraid. He's afraid to open his mouth. And he's mortally afraid of Tejas. He senses a violence in him. He's aware that it will never spill out but that makes Tejas all the more dangerous. He would do anything to become invisible when Tejas is around. But through it all he still tries to maintain his good spirits.

It is Tejas who is silent; a bristling, try-me, make-my-day, Dirty Harry kind of silence. He's a pressure cooker without the steam-escape valve. And what's cooking inside is Tejas.

Tejas had done his homework on the 'this and that' business. He was sure the change in strategy that he had recommended to I-triple-S was the right marketing move. That's where the big money was. But it was one thing to theorize and quite another to pull it off in real life. All this while he had held James responsible for his own lack of success. James was not pulling his weight; James was being deliberately uncooperative. He had badgered and harangued the man. He had called him lazy, obstructive, out of touch with the times. He had pressed him to use his legendary charm; deploy Deirdre to throw a magnificent party for the senior Japanese ministers visiting London; focus on the Taiwanese, take them on a cruise on his luxury yacht (they are threatened daily by the humongous landmass called mainland China, they are insecure and desperate, and best of all they are one of the few nations to have a surfeit of hard cash in their treasury); send free first-class air tickets to the Indian cabinet ministers, generals, air marshals and admirals, they love these free junkets, wine and dine them, get them drunk, shouldn't be difficult, they drink only to get smashed out of their minds, take them shopping for their mistresses, wives, children and grandchildren and extended families, all at the expense of I-triple-S; target the Iranians, the Pakistanis and anybody else you want just so long as you can get them to order hardware in ten figures.

James had introduced Tejas to his guests. Tejas Nirantar, he told them, was a whiz with money. They should talk to him; he could do things for their money that nobody else could. Sometimes, a few of them had even contacted Tejas and took his advice and fattened their investments. But forgot to place the orders for arms.

Tejas was now beginning to wonder whether James had been right in the first place: that the Big League was impregnable. For a time he'd thought that Shakta Muni was playing one against the other. He had grown paranoid and imagined that James was keeping a watch on him. In fact he was, but that was because Tejas had made him a nervous wreck and he was waiting fearfully for Tejas's next repressed outburst. What Tejas had to remind himself about was that James too had fallen victim to the dream of the golden calf that he had conjured up.

James must have still believed in Tejas, for he continued to look up to him. Not Shakta Muni though. In recent times Tejas had seen a look of scepticism in the Muni's eyes. It was as though he had misjudged Tejas. As far as Tejas knew, Shakta Muni was not a partner in International Strategic Security Systems. Nor did he have any official status within the company. He was not on the board of directors nor was he a cosignatory on any contract. Which meant that whatever Tejas's suspicions about the Muni's involvement in James's business, they would never amount to anything more than conjectures. Tejas might not have any proof but he was almost certain that James would not make any critical moves without the Muni's consent.

It was possible that Tejas had become oversensitive and was projecting his own disappointment on to the Muni. But he doubted that. Shakta Muni was as shrewd as they came. He was always ten moves ahead of his opponents as well as his closest associates. If he had brought Tejas on board, it was because he thought that he was young, highly motivated and aggressive. He would rethink tactics and catapult the company into an altogether different league, to the stratosphere where politics and business were inseparable. He would be the 'Open Sesame' to the only club worth belonging to in the arms trade. He must have been pleased with Tejas's progress at the beginning: his quick grasp of the mechanics and machinations, his total reorientation of the company's marketing goals and strategies. Then his performance had levelled out. The plans remained plans and failed to translate into results. The Muni had good reason to have second thoughts.

The Muni be blowed, Tejas told himself. All he cared about was how to hit the Big League. There was far too much riding on it.

# 54

He met Tejas for dinner at Green Banana Leaf, an exclusive South Indian restaurant in Delhi. He wouldn't come to the ashram because he was sure there were hidden surveillance cameras and microphones in the guest rooms.

'How would you know there aren't any here?'

'Because I got one of my men to check the place out, and then choose a corner that's secluded,' he said smugly. His voice belied his age. It sounded as if he was forty-five, and had the same self-conscious ersatz timbre that the ageing Hindi film superstar Amitabh Bachchan had made popular in the subcontinent; but he was twenty-seven or thirty at the most. Tejas wondered if he practised and polished that imitation-mahogany tone early every morning in the mountains, and then stood in front of the mirror to cultivate insouciance of manner.

His name was Nawaaz Irfan and he was trying a little too hard to sidestep his youth. He had a patchy intermittent beard that no amount of massaging with goat's butter had been able to turn into a uniform and respectable Afghan fur. Poor Nawaaz, Tejas thought, even when he was fifty, that's if he made it past the next year, the next month or the next day, he would not be able to convince Tejas to take him seriously.

If one is to go by first impressions, Tejas had not taken a shine to Nawaaz Irfan. The man had been cocky on the phone.

'I believe you only talk to big fish with big money.'

'So are you a big fish?'

'Big fish too usually start out small.'

'I'm beholden to you for this gratis insight but perhaps you would consider getting to the point.' Tejas had enough and more on his mind just now. A prospective client always meant an additional investment of time, and a chancy one at that. But even if the meeting concluded in a sale, he was generally not interested, unless there was the possibility of a long-term relationship with jumbo monetary benefits attached.

'It might be a good idea for us to meet.'

'What makes you think that?'

'Because if we don't and one of these days you discover that I could have been your biggest client, you will never forgive yourself.'

'Your self-confidence is admirable and your concern for my wellbeing touching, but we must, each one of us, find our own way of seeking forgiveness.' Tejas had had his fill of this oblique smart talk. 'Let's cut to the chase, shall we? When and where would you like to meet?'

Tejas had tried to make discreet enquiries about the young man. Given the clandestine nature of the 'this and that' business, the only source of information was the grapevine. The arithmetic was basic: the murkier the background of a rebel leader, a warlord or a tyrant, the greater the volume and persistence of hearsay and gossip. Some of it was on the Net, occasionally the second attaché or the intelligence officer at an embassy could be persuaded to part with a few titbits; at times you tapped the business community, at other times you chatted up the people from a neighbouring country's consulate. The one thing you almost never did was to trust American intelligence. CIA operatives in most parts of the world still continued to think of their profession as a desk job. Their local contacts were almost always people who had been educated in the West, especially in some American university. They were infrequent visitors to their own countries, and you would be wise to ignore most intelligence coming from them. They always had their own agenda. The diplomats in the American embassies were even less reliable. They insulated themselves from the life of the local community except when promoting American business or other interests. The food they ate, the water they drank, the toilet paper they used, all came from back home. They were on a hardship posting, notwithstanding a phalanx of lackeys, a Rockefeller expense account, and a standard of living undreamt of in their small-town homes back in Kansas or Nebraska; and the only event they looked forward to for nine or ten months of the year was their annual vacation. They did not learn the local language, they did not study local customs, food habits, festivals and taboos. They did not mix with the denizens of the country, let alone get to know them well. They were the only superpower and God's gift to mankind; why would they be interested in lesser human beings?

The reports about Nawaaz Irfan's early life were conflicting. One version said he had had a falling out with his father, and had left home. The other theory was that he was a foundling. But what was clear was that he was dedicated, some called him obsessed; he was ruthless and he was a marathoner in a culture where people did not see or plan beyond tomorrow. He had a big mouth and, what was worse, he was able to live up to his big talk. He was that rare bird: he was in a tearing rush and he was willing to wait as long as it took to realize his objectives.

Mirza Rustum, one of the most feared and respected leaders of the Afghan warring factions, who had outlasted every regime since the 1970s and outwitted both his foes and friends, had taken Nawaaz under his wing when the boy was seventeen. Within a couple of years, Nawaaz had made himself indispensable. A culture of perpetual hostilities and war is like the tropics. Everything's accelerated: you mature faster, you've seen the worst by the time you are four or five; sometimes you miss your teens and youth altogether. If only Mirza Rustum had not spotted the promise in Nawaaz Irfan so early, and had let him enjoy a few more heedless years, going down to Peshawar to visit the prostitutes, or to kidnap a couple of rich young boys from the families of affluent Sindhi landowners and industrialists for the going ransom rate, the boy might have turned out to be a little more average and aimlessly sadistic, but also far less dangerous. It was impossible, however, to ignore Nawaaz Irfan's gifts. He had rare organizational talents and could command loyalty even at that age. Brute firepower was important to him, but not as much as understanding how his enemy's mind worked. The Afghan ethic had always put a premium on bravery; strategy was not of much consequence. Nawaaz seemed to think otherwise. Losing face was not as critical to him as living to win another day. He was a master of the disappearing trick. The enemy would have two hundred-per cent-sure information about Mirza Rustum's whereabouts and within minutes they would be whirring overheard in their Apache helicopters, but there would be no trace of him or his men. Yet whatever Nawaaz Irfan's ambitions might have been, he could never succeed Mirza Rustum since the chieftain had a son called Diler, a volatile and vicious young man, whom the tribe feared and loathed, but who was his father's choice for his successor.

Then some years ago Mirza Rustum had died and Nawaaz had disappeared with a third of the Mirza's men.

The fight between the new tribal chief and his rival would be to the death. Time was running out: the question was, for whom?

Nawaaz Irfan was the first to blink. He tucked his tail between his legs and sued for peace. Might as well have slit his own throat. The other tribal leaders laughed up their sleeves. Did the fool really think that the barbarous and brutal Diler was going to forgive him and offer his sister to him in marriage?

They met on neutral ground. Nawaaz Irfan surrendered unconditionally, handed over his men and his cache of arms and murdered Diler that night.

Now Nawaaz Irfan had come to see Tejas with a shopping list. Tejas couldn't quite place the man sitting in front of him. Nawaaz was ordering his third helping of rice idlis and sambar. A little unusual, Tejas thought, for an Afghan to be so fond of vegetarian food. He kept thinking he had seen him before.

Tejas glanced fleetingly at the piece of paper and memorized it. Sometimes a man's grocery list told you much more about him than an exhaustive curriculum vitae. Nawaaz Irfan's choice of hardware was certainly revealing. It suggested that, unlike most ambitious young bucks, he was not motivated by notions of one-upmanship. He seemed to have a clear idea of what his military needs were and to go about satisfying them with as little fuss as possible. What he lacked in experience he more than made up for in native cunning and intelligence. Apart from the usual ammunition replenishments and ordnance, like anti-aircraft guns, he was shopping for advanced electronic warning and detection equipment. His focus was not so much on the latest gadgetry or speed as on accuracy of payload or warhead delivery. But the most intriguing item on the list was the one with the question mark at its side: supergun.

Had Gerard Bull, Tejas wondered, completed the design for the new and bigger supergun before he was bumped off?

It was interesting, Tejas thought, that young Nawaaz should know about the supergun that Saddam Hussein had been trying to build before the first Iraq war of '89. Hardly anyone today remembered this strange relic. Gerard Bull had initially conceived of it in the '60s and '70s as a much more economical satellite launcher, after which it had gone through various incarnations. The Chinese had bought it at an intermediate stage of development and had used it as a long-range gun that shot-putted its lethal charge across 350 or 400 kilometres. What the Iraqi dictator's intentions had been when he hired Bull to design and deliver it, is anybody's guess. Had he wanted a super-long-range gun with a conventional payload or had he been aiming to build a nuclear gun? Even a major British government enquiry had not settled the controversy. And why was Nawaaz interested in the supergun?

Why was he getting into all this? Tejas wondered. He was a supplier and nothing more. The whys and wherefores were not his business. Besides, what did it matter what Nawaaz wanted? He was not going to be his dealer. It was not impossible that tomorrow Nawaaz Irfan might end up as a big player, but right now his business was negligible. Make one exception, and you might as well reconcile yourself to being a small-timer in a dog-eat-dog business where almost everybody is fighting for crumbs and peanuts. It had taken considerable patience and bullying to persuade James of the logic of getting out of the small-change side of the business. Tejas was not about to fall into the same trap.

'Please don't take this amiss,' he said. 'Your business is valuable and I wish you all the best, but as of now it's not worth my while. If you wish I can put you in touch with some other people.'

'No thanks. I know a few people in this trade.' Nawaaz was trying to put up a brave front but not doing well at concealing his disappointment or hurt. He had obviously set his heart on doing business with a big arms dealer. He might even have hoped that the right connection would impress both his enemies and his backers, and make them take him seriously.

'No hard feelings, please,' Tejas said, and asked for the bill, but the young man wouldn't hear of it.

'I'm the supplier,' Tejas tried to make a joke of it, 'and the custom is that I pick up the small tab while you pick up the big one.'

Nawaaz Irfan didn't see the humour in the remark. 'That's not how it works with me. I called you, so I'll pay the bill.'

Tejas shrugged his shoulders in a have-it-your-way fashion and got up. He liked Nawaaz Irfan even less now than he had at the beginning.

'Does my face look familiar to you?'

'Should it?'

'A straight question deserves a straight answer.'

Tejas looked at the man closely. 'No, it doesn't. Are you disappointed?'

'Quite the contrary. I've passed my first test.'

Lucens had the feeling that his life was losing body, girth and heft. It was as if its substance had attenuated. He was like a thriller waiting to get to its denouement, spill its beans, say its bit and then be put to rest. His life had only one meaning. The innocents must be saved and the sinners had to be brought back to innocence. He realized that he had spread himself far too thin. What he had to do was to pare his involvements down to the barest essentials.

1st September: Amanat's here. I've told him that he has a free hand in employing whoever he wants but come 7th September next year, The Guardian Angels Center has to be ready and functional. The Pledge of Purity Temple can be completed the year after. He thinks the deadline is unrealistic but I'm trying to get, at the very least, the governor, but preferably the Vice President himself, to inaugurate the place, and I can't afford to miss the deadline.

The equation between Lucens and the market is good. Honor is doing an excellent job. He has no doubt that she'll soon be CEO of all the Guardian Angels projects. Things are beginning to look up for Concord-Ashton. The word about the tax holiday and other benefits is getting around. Four start-ups are showing serious interest and the second leading air-compressor manufacturer in the country has commissioned a feasibility study for setting up a manufacturing plant in the area. With any luck at least one, maybe even a couple, of the projects may come through.

It's almost four years that Lucens has been here. He's no longer regarded as an outsider. All kinds of people, and not just businessmen, consult him. There's even talk that within a couple of years Glades Medical will co-opt him on their board of directors. Lucens has every reason to be happy. But something's amiss.

Tejas was not used to failure. Intractability, yes; superhuman effort, yes; false starts, patience, yes: he took all those in his stride. You had to know how to frame a delinquent problem, a real brain-teaser; if necessary, change the coordinates and perspective altogether.

Get your head around it and it would unlock its own secrets. He had learnt never, never to stake his pride or self-esteem when he was trying to crack a tough nut; or bring into play concepts like honour and justice. They would only cloud the issue.

He would never have been able to see the Abbey through its worst crisis and find the monies to rebuild it if he had become emotional and lost his head. It was the same with IPUC: he could not have made it into such an effective organization if he had got drippy and dewy-eyed about it or turned it into a personal vendetta.

What you had to focus on, to the exclusion of all else, was that you were grappling with a technical matter, like Fermat's last theorem. It was a job. And it had to be done. It was as simple as that. At least it should have been. But what if...what if you knew the solution, you had all the answers, and yet failed to decode the Sphinx?

Now Tejas had begun to doubt his judgement and was losing faith in himself. Was it all over then? Should he admit that James had been right all along and I-triple-S would never hit the big time? Tejas laughed bitterly to himself. Defeat was never an option. Other people could walk away from a job, not him, not even a remote statistical possibility of that happening. Come what may he would have to gate-crash into the High Flyer's Club.

My dear Lucens,

I remember the day you took on Nandini Devi, the Maths Machine. You were the studious type, I thought, and that automatically made you a nerd for me. As class prefect, I gave you a hard time but that didn't seem to bother you. Then you ran away from school, something I always wanted to do, and came back a bloody mess. While the principal and teachers took care never to say or suggest anything explicitly, it was taken as read that Christianity was better than Islam, Hinduism and all the other religions of the world. And there you were, giving notice that you were willing to stand up for your beliefs. You didn't give a damn what the school authorities or the students thought of you. You just did the right thing by your God.

I decided I wanted to be your friend. It was perhaps the most sensible thing I did. It has paid me rich dividends. Abbajaan certainly treated me as his third son and after you joined the Trappists, Amanat has been my closest friend. I owe them to you as I owe the success of my business to you.

I was the butt of everybody's jokes at New Eden because they thought you had walked away with my girl. If only they knew the truth. I was looking desperately for a way to distance myself from Sarah Roberts. I was terrified that she would discover what my father's business was and detest me. Ammijaan and Sagari too tried to hitch me up with someone or the other. It's never going to work. I don't want to bring children into a world where my father has been responsible, indirectly, for the death of thousands of people.

Now you've joined hands with my father in his business, and I have no choice but to break with you.

I'm sure you know the arms business well by now. Nevertheless let me put down a few facts in black and white. The arms trade is worth US$ 60 billion worldwide and growing at an unsettling pace. The range of products is staggering: tanks, armoured vehicles, guns, Kalashnikov rifles, assault rifles, grenade launchers, missiles, missile launchers, lethal barbed wire, mines, antitank guns, daisy cutters, bunker busters, all kinds of ammunition and a couple of hundred more lethal etceteras. In Uganda AK-47s are so popular, parents often name their children AK. The population of Mogadishu is 1.3 million; the population of assault rifles there is fast catching up: 1 million and steadily rising. The local market sells them alongside grains, headscarves, vegetables and dresses.

For sheer volume though there's nothing to beat small arms and light weapons. Over 640 million guns, pistols and light arms are around today, enough to arm one in every ten across the globe. In Iraq right now there are 24 million guns, one for every man, woman and child in the country. Small arms kill about 500,000 people a year. According to the British-American Information Council, 90 per cent of all wartime casualties are civilians. This is what Kofi Annan had to say about this variety of arms: The death toll from small arms 'dwarfs that of all other weapons systems, and in most years greatly exceeds the toll of the Hiroshima and Nagasaki bombs. In terms of the carnage they cause, small arms can well be described as weapons of mass destruction.'

Surely you don't wish to be party to this slaughter. You are a good man, Lucens, even though you are way too extreme at times. What are you doing with my father and that guru of his who has such a hold on him? Sometimes I really think he is the devil incarnate. As you would know better than I, tantrik gurus have had mysterious powers over some of India's prime ministers. They are not mere spiritual figureheads or advisors; they wield enormous political clout. In Indira Gandhi's time there was that chap Dhirendra Brahmachari. The rumour was that she consulted him on all important matters. He became so influential a figure that he acquired huge estates, had a private plane and his own TV show. When Narasimha Rao took over the reins of government, he too got himself a tantrik. The odd thing is that both gurus had connections with the arms business. Bizarre as it may sound, the brahmachari even had his own gun factory.

Isn't the word 'brahmachari' supposed to mean 'celibate' or 'ascetic'? It has always intrigued me why a celibate, an ascetic and a guru-figure was busy acquiring so much wealth, property and, to top it all, a gun factory? Like Dhirendra Brahmachari, and Rao's tantrik guru, Shakta Muni is also a conundrum. Any relationship with the Muni will always be an unequal one. The equation between him and others is one of power, and the power lies only on one side: Shakta Muni's.

I beg you not to underestimate the tantrik. You may think you can outsmart him. Do not delude yourself, my friend. He's a patient man, and takes a long view of matters. But most of all, he plays a dodgy game.

As I recall, you bet your last hundred thousand dollars in an endgame in the market, and lost all. The Guardian Angels were penniless.

What happened then? All I know is that you went to Cambray Park, and that my father lent you some money. But that also you began to lose. Then you visited the Muni in India, and when you returned, you had got back your old touch. How did you do it, Lucens? How did you regain your gift with numbers? What kind of Faustian pact did you make with the Muni?

There are no zebra crossings in a minefield, Lucens. I would urge you strongly to cut your losses and run for your life. You may think you've got the better of Shakta Muni. You haven't. And you never will. Period.

Bye, Lucens. I'll miss your business. But more than that I'll miss your friendship.

Roy

Lucens's reply was curt and to the point.

Dear Roy,

I will not stand in your way if it goes against your conscience to have me as a client. You go on at some length about small arms and the number of people they kill. I wish you had checked with James before you got on your high horse and told me off. I'm the one who's trying to persuade your father to move out of the small-arms business.

One last remark. The arms trade is like any other business. This is why universities, local authorities, trade unions, NHS trusts, charities and churches in Britain continue to invest in it. County councils as well as boroughs, Cancer Research UK, the British Pension Fund and others invest in many of the top seven British arms companies.

You may not agree but I think we are in good company. Since you seem to have done substantial research on the subject, I am sure you are well aware that the higher end of the arms business works mainly as a deterrent to violence. Saudi Arabia bought billions of dollars' worth of arms including fighter planes. I don't recall them using these except to train their armed forces. If the rulers of flush nations want expensive toys, I've no problem supplying them. If I don't, someone else will. And the boys and girls in the Homes for the Children of God will starve. I cannot permit that.

Even when Gandhi was alive, his disciple, Nehru, did not disband the armed forces in India. Nearly sixty years after the great man's death, do you believe either India or anybody else in the world is going to stop stockpiling? Gandhi thought the answer to Hitler was nonviolence. Do you think Churchill, Roosevelt and Stalin could have won World War II by laying down their arms?

Yes, I'm in it for the money. But unlike you, your father or almost anybody else in commerce, it's not for myself. Every cent I earn goes to the Angels. As for Shakta Muni, you exaggerate his murky prowess. You forget I walk with Jesus, and am well protected.

Baker and Lee are the Angels' stockbrokers now. They are eager for our business and don't pry into my private affairs.

Yours, etc.

Lucens

Roy wrote back within a day.

My dear Lucens,

I'm grateful that you're persuading my father to get out of the small-arms business. But you are being specious, and you know it, when you claim that the top end of the business is mainly a deterrent. Bush Sr and Jr have bombed Iraq to submission twice. And yet the casualties of the so-called peace there are even more gruesome. The dead number in the tens of thousands. But they are the lucky ones. It's the crippled survivors who are living witnesses to big firepower. Successive American presidents have taken it upon themselves to bomb Vietnam, Cambodia, Panama and other unlucky countries to perdition. Israel does it daily, so do the Tamil Tigers and the Sri Lankans, not to mention Indians and Pakistanis. But why am I belabouring the obvious?

Roy

# 55

'You've been cooped up for days. Would you care to join me for a walk?'

Tejas was not sure if Shakta Muni was the best of hosts or the worst. He certainly was the most invisible. He was obviously a busy man, but Tejas had no idea what he did. His ashram was really a hotel, except that there was no tariff. How did the Muni support such an establishment? It must cost a packet to run. Was there a charge for the counsel given by the holy man? Tejas thought that there must be an abacus some place keeping a tab on his stay, the meals he had, the guests he entertained and, most of all, his introductions to some of the most influential people on the Asian continent. And one day an astronomical bill would be presented to him and when it became clear that he wouldn't be able to reimburse the sum in a couple of lifetimes, the Muni would exact a price no man could ever pay.

'Yes, I'd like that.'

In the distance you could hear a thousand generators kick in as the power went off again. All the palatial mansions, a.k.a 'farmhouses', of the rich on the outskirts of Delhi have them. Like the shorn Hindu widows and menstruating women at the end of the nineteenth century, they are stowed in a separate enclosure as far away from the house as possible, but you could not block out their repressed, resentful hum.

It was late and there was more than a nip in the air. It was a freak night. The seven-vertical-mile Delhi smog had parted and the sky was a-quiver with sequins.

'How many of the stars that we can see,' the Muni wondered aloud, 'are but memories and traces of galaxies long dead? Imagine you are going home to your star one night and find that it's no longer there. Will a new Newton or Einstein turn up in the next fifty or hundred years and explain the universe to its last detail? That would be truly tragic. Might as well kill the imagination, perhaps God himself, for the mystery would have gone out of life once and for all.

'There's no dividing line between animate and inanimate matter, between the stars and us, that's how I see the world sometimes,' Shakta Muni said softly. 'There's a school of ancient Indian thought that goes even further. Not just that the substance of rocks and fish, birds and humans is the same, but that they share the same life. Einstein didn't quite say that but perhaps the energy and matter equation may suggest something similar, that everything is interchangeable and a loop, the converse of what you see. Imagine where it would all lead. Matter and antimatter would be the same and so would past and present. Wouldn't it be wonderful if the cosmos was one and we all shared the same soul?'

Here it comes, Tejas thought, the avalanche of platitudes, the pearls of wisdom, the pop metaphysics of Hindu thought: a universal syncretism devoid of all meaning. But Shakta Muni had nothing more to say. It was as though he were talking to himself really, a private reverie. This was a strange holy man; there was no mumbo jumbo, no ash miraculously drizzling from his palms, and at least so far, the whole gamut of Hindu Chicken Soup for the soul, the pancreas and the testes was happily missing.

The road was visibly uphill and winding now. Where had this hill turned up from in the flatlands next to the capital? There were gravel and loose stones underfoot and Tejas had already slipped a couple of times.

Tejas had done a Google search on Shakta Muni before the naming ritual, but he hadn't been able to come up with much. His name occurred often enough at high-profile birthday bashes, charities, and international conferences of world religions, but it also cropped up in unexpected contexts. Four hundred and fifty-one of the thousands of entries on him mentioned that he was one of the world's foremost alchemists and ran something called 'The International Academy of Science and Alchemy'. It got more and more curious. The Muni had written several papers on the alchemical properties of mercury and a couple of other metals, and had been published in respectable journals like *Discover* and *American Science*. There was more. He had edited a book called *Towards a New Definition of Longevity: The Role of Mercury in Cell Regeneration,* published by none other than New Frontiers. Imagine taking the scientific community in America for a ride.

The Muni traced his lineage to Anand Nath, the head priest of the monastery at Jakhbar in Punjab in the seventeenth century. Even Muslim emperors like Aurangzeb, he pointed out, consulted tantrik gurus on alchemical matters. He quoted a letter the fanatical Mughal had written to his ancestor: '"The letter sent by Your Reverence has been received along with two tolas of quicksilver. However, it is not so good as Your Reverence had given us to understand. It is desired that Your Reverence should carefully treat some more quicksilver and have that sent, without unnecessary delay. A piece of cloth for a cloak and a sum of twenty-five rupees, which have been sent as an offering, will reach you. Also a few words have been written to the valiant Fateh Chand to the effect that he should always afford protection."

'Shall we go into the temple? It's peaceful inside.'

What temple? They had taken one more turn around the winding road and had suddenly reached a small plateau, and at the farther end of it was a pillared structure. So this is what that innocent walk was leading up to.

'I'm a Christian, you know that.' Tejas was nonplussed at his own knee-jerk reaction.

'In that case we shouldn't risk it.'

Did he see a smile flit across the Muni's face? What had prompted Tejas to say something so idiotic? How many times had Shakta Muni told him that practising yogic disciplines did not bind him in any way to the Hindu faith or its rituals? Was his Catholic faith so feeble that a mere visit to a temple would threaten it? The Muni, it seemed to Tejas, must find him hugely amusing, for he was always laughing at him without bothering to move a muscle in his face.

Temples made Tejas uneasy and claustrophobic: the plangent clanging of the bells; the crowds; the smell of spilt oil; greasy and grasping half-naked priests with rinsed but unsoaped dhotis and pitambers; the animistic gods, some of them with three and four heads, brandishing ancient weapons and riding vehicles from the animal and bird kingdom; the goddesses with eight, sixteen and twenty-four hands and necklaces of skulls.

'With Hinduism you are at the birth of time and the cosmos. All is chaos. What you see are the very first negotiations of primal man with the mystery of nature and the terror of death.' Shakta Muni was at it again. He had read what was in Tejas's mind and was able to articulate it far better than he himself could. 'Everything is intimidating. The unknown, dangerous and lethal, lurks on all sides. The predatory beasts, the dark rumbling clouds gathering in the western sky, the lightning and the thunder, the deluge, fever, scorpions and snake poison, drought and famine. This is where the first gods arise: the earth mother, the sun, moon, water, wind and fire. And the demons.

'Can you think of anything more exciting and exhilarating than the Hindu gods, or the Greek ones for that matter? They are so alive and real. They love, they hate, they are jealous, and they are duplicitous just like us. Isn't it something of a wonder that Hinduism, of all the ancient faiths, is still so alive and that the faithful number close to a billion people?

'You can argue, reason and have a dialogue with most other religions. You don't stand a chance with Hinduism. You are defeated before you utter the first word. Your only hope is to flee before the tropical jungle with its rampant trees, parasitical creepers, poisonous mushrooms, strangler vines, stifling foliage and carnivorous flowers traps and sucks you in, never to be seen or found again.'

And here he was, Tejas Nirantar, having to decide, consciously and of his own free will, whether to step into chaos and anarchy.

He walked up the steps to the porch and then to the open mandapam. What a fool he had been. It was late at night and both the ante-chamber and the sanctum sanctorum of the temple were locked and he need not have worried about the stark, ever-open eyes of an ancient god looking through him even if his own eyelids were tightly shut. He sat on the low parapet between the pillars of the open hall where the visiting priests, mahants and swamis usually congregated for kirtan. The black kadappa stone polished to a mirror-finish chilled his bottom. The lights of Delhi flickered in the distance and a Boeing 747 cut its engines before gliding down the runway. Shakta Muni, the tantrik, sat down on the floor in a perfect padmasan. Size didn't seem to make any difference, he had the casual ease and flexibility of a reed. Tejas leaned back against the flat of a pillar and closed his eyes.

'You are already so suspicious and unfavourably disposed to Hinduism,' Shakta Muni broke into Tejas's reverie, 'I fear what you must think of tantriks.'

For a time Tejas had been taken in by Shakta Muni's candidness and his willingness to own up to the aberrations that had occurred in tantrism over the centuries. One of his favourite ploys was to pre-empt all criticism of tantriks and the occult arts by talking about them before you did. He made it a point never to offer an apologia or say anything in defence of them or of himself. His tone was thoughtful but not without a touch of lightness and ironic self-deprecation. All of which led you to discount your own gut feelings about the pseudoscience and the man.

By appearing reasonable and open, he calmed your distrust and deflected your attention from everything that was problematic.

'What difference does it make what I think? The whole world seems to think highly of you.'

'A slight overstatement there,' the Muni laughed. 'Don't you know we humans don't like nay-sayers? There was a time when I was no different from you. Since you've boned up on me, you must know that I started out as a student of science and came to tantrism with a fair amount of scepticism and cynicism.

'How can any modern scientific man or woman not scoff at it? Tantrism is supposed to be the stepbrother of Hinduism: a shadowland of black magic and occult practices; a dark and phantasmagorical frontier of orgies and sexual aberration and experimentation. Its provenance is the forbidden, the repressed and the decadent. The tantrik predilection for the bizarre, the left-handed and the esoteric deteriorates into satanic rites, rituals and sacrifices. It may at one time have had lofty ideals like self-knowledge and enlightenment but the general belief is that the business about waking the kundalini and its seven chakras is hogwash and even if it isn't, it is best to stay clear of it. Why else has Hinduism rejected and shunned tantra?

'It's a snake pit that people want to peer into and hallucinate about. People are always telling me in vivid detail what tantra and the tantrik arts are. I am fascinated by their overwrought and rampant imaginings. It is amazing how often their version of tantrism is nothing but their own undisguised subconscious.'

'Are you trying to tell me that the scientist in you has found that the premises of tantrism can now be proven?'

'I'm afraid I'm still ambivalent. I'm certain after all these years that there's more than a kernel of truth in tantra and that it has a tremendous power for good. But how does one retrieve the diamond core when there's no simple or easy way of unravelling the accretions and distortions from the essentials?'

'The power for good that you mention seems to have gone mostly unnoticed, if it ever was there. You'll admit that there's no smoke without fire. The tantriks must have been up to a lot of hanky-panky to have got such bad press over the centuries.'

'That's not quite true. The bad notices are a fairly recent phenomenon, mostly after the British turned up. The alien always threatens and intimidates the outsider. Look at our own discomfort and unease in the presence of African witch doctors. I am not denying the hanky-panky as you call it, but who's to define hanky-panky?

'What is central to tantrism is the stilling of the senses and the mind till they reach a state of perfect equilibrium so essential for enlightenment or nirvana.'

Just before Tejas left for the airport, Shakta Muni came to say goodbye to him.

'Call me if you need anything.' His voice was almost inaudible.

'Is it true that you have one of the finest private chemistry labs in the country?'

'It serves its purpose, though one is always out of date with any equipment one buys.'

'Is it true that the CIA finances you?'

'Not that I know of but I've heard it bruited occasionally that there is a "foreign hand" behind the enterprise. But that is only partially correct. There are many foreign hands that support the research. Have you not heard that dying is no longer in fashion? They've recently discovered that tantrism can offer them the life everlasting.'

'What about the alchemy and the gold?'

'You are going to miss your flight. Next time you must conduct your inquisition a little earlier in the day.'

'Well?'

'Alchemical conversions to gold in labs through the agency of mercury are not a problem. Large-scale production still is. Sometimes we seem close to the exact formula. And sometimes it seems like a wild goose chase. Any more questions?'

'And what if you find you are able to manufacture gold on a commercial basis?'

'Haven't got to thinking that far yet. Maybe that will finally end the Indian fixation with gold.'

'Some other rare metal will surely replace it.'

'You are missing the point. Monism or the essential unity of the universe precludes the primacy of any metal or any order of living things including man.'

'But that is the gateway to chaos.'

'Maybe. Do I detect the fear of the unknown in you too, Tejas?' The Muni laughed. 'I take it you know that if your clients desire any modifications in the products they want, our research laboratories can help out at times. If need be we can supply some very rare biochemicals also.'

'We are middlemen. Why would we want to get into research or manufacturing?'

'It was just a thought.'

Tejas had, by now, a fairly good idea that there was no such thing as 'just a thought' with Shakta Muni. This was a mind where the waters ran so deep there was no way anyone could plumb them. What, for instance, did he mean by 'very rare biochemicals'? Shakta Muni, Tejas believed, was 'the butterfly effect'; barring one crucial difference: a butterfly does not know that the gossamer flapping of its wings as it alights on a flower in the rain forests of Brazil will trigger a hurricane off the coast of Hong Kong a week or month later. Shakta Muni, he was sure, always knew what he was up to. And he was patient. He would sow a thought in your mind and wait for months, more likely years and decades, for the reaction to set in. What was he up to now?

My dear Zia,

I have been meaning to write to you about Zubeida Khaala's death for some time, but did not get around to it because I wasn't quite sure whether you wanted me to talk about it. It seems likely now that I was projecting my own reluctance to speak or even think about her on to you.

I do not know how to come to terms with Zubeida Khaala's life or death. She did not die (let me not get melodramatic or portentous, but

I must tell you that she did not die a natural death), she gave up on life. Just as at some point you gave up on her. Was there a reason for it? Was there a precise moment to that rupture? I'm not about to hazard a guess about what makes two people who have been close, pull out of each other's orbits. You are well aware of my wariness of explanations, not because I don't believe in their validity but because they can never be sufficient.

She would make a pretence of eating dinner, that was the only meal for which I was at home, because she knew that her slow starvation upset me.

'We all have to let go of those who are dear to us. Did you not let go of Sagari?' She was contrite the moment she said that. 'Oh, Amanat, did I say the wrong thing? I didn't mean to hurt you.'

She could be so clear-eyed, this woman, and see right through things. Then how come she hadn't let go of Dilip Kumar? Surely she couldn't have had any illusions about the actor or where her obsession with him was headed? What a silly question that is. When did awareness prevent one from being foolish or self-destructive?

Talking about fate, did I ever tell you about a strange encounter I had, actually it was a non-encounter, when I went to meet a potential client on Pali Hill? It was the rainy season and I had to take a three-wheeler from Bandra station. Perhaps the auto driver was deliberately going round in circles but I was getting impatient and a little nervous that I would be late. Suddenly I thought we had passed someone who looked familiar even though an umbrella covered the person's face. We drove on some two hundred yards when a cigarette vendor told us that we had overshot the mark. This time I recognized her easily. Zubeida Khaala was standing at the corner of the road where the auto turned in. I had no idea how long she had been there. She was oblivious of her surroundings and the constant splash and spatter of water from the potholes on the roads as cars and autos lurched past. Her eyes were fixed on a two-storeyed bungalow with green window frames and shutters. My first impulse was to stop the auto and ask her if she was all right. But I was running late and dropped the idea.

An hour into the meeting with my prospective customer, it became evident that I was not going to get the job since he was undecided whether to build a shopping mall with a multiplex, a high-rise apartment block or a multistoreyed parking lot with a helipad. I was at the door when I asked him about the bungalow with the green shutters.

'You can't be that ignorant. That's Yusufbhai's place.'

'Yusufbhai?'

'Dilip Kumar.' He sounded peeved. 'You really are very ignorant. Actually, he doesn't live there any more. He moved out a long time ago because of some dispute with his family.'

'Is he out on the road then?'

He looked at me to see if I was being smart-arsed and realized that I was merely stupid.

'He stays right here in our compound. Or rather, we stay in his wife's compound. That bungalow next to this multistoreyed building, can you see it? That's Sairaji's.'

It was raining heavily when I finished my meeting and hopped into a cab. Zubeida Khaala was still gazing at the white and green bungalow. I did not have the heart to stop and tell her that she was standing in front of the wrong house.

A couple of weeks before she died, we switched the TV on and guess which movie was showing? *Deedar*. Yes, the same *Deedar* which she had seen as a teenager when she flipped for Dilip Kumar. As you remember it's an absurdly romantic movie with an emotional, cringe-making twist in the tail that passes for tragedy. But if one is in a mellow frame of mind, there's an innocence and naïveté in the black-and-white Hindi movies of the 1950s that can be quite disarming. I got up to switch off the TV when Zubeida said something. I had to bend down to catch what she was saying.

'What if one waits all one's life for God and then discovers there isn't one?'

Was she talking about God or about the man in her life? Or about both? I wanted to hold her to my heart then and tell her it's okay, it's okay; I'll try and make it come out right even now. (Is there anything more nauseous than almighty delusions?) How I hated Zubeida Khaala for making me feel useless.

'I've upset you.' Zubeida Khaala patted me on my cheek and kissed my forehead. 'You take everything so seriously, Amanat. I was joking.'

Three days later, her temperature was 104° and in spite of her protestations, I called the doctor. It was pneumonia, he said, and pumped her with antibiotics. Sagari and I were with her all the time and I found myself taking to surreptitious prayer. It's difficult to tell whether she didn't care to recover or God was in no mood to listen to a need-based devotee.

When I was younger, I used to hold Zubeida Khaala responsible for you becoming a fanatic. I can see that I was being ludicrous and grossly unfair to her. I was looking for a scapegoat, someone to blame, and she came in handy. She was a God-fearing Muslim and wanted you and the rest of the family to be good Muslims too. She did not wish anyone ill and did not do anyone harm. You became an extremist all on your own steam. 9/11 taught the world many things it should have known already. One of them was that terrorists can also come from moderate and well-educated families. Extremism, I suspect, is as often a bent of mind as it is something in the air.

Will Zubeida find Dilip Kumar ultimately? Or God for that matter?

Love,

Amanat

The last time the triple counties of Pylon, Glades and Sparta had suffered such agonizing birth pangs was when the glacier had dug 3,500 feet deep and scooped out the 51-mile-long Lake Santa three million years ago. Now Amanat's earth-movers and bulldozers gouged out huge lumps of the earth's flesh and left cavernous holes in it. All day long and sometimes late into the night, monster-shovels tore into the unwilling ground and ripped it open, crunching boulders and rocks and churning up 40-foot geysers of dust and sand. Once in a while, when Lucens was in town and flew over the area in a chopper with Amanat and the civil engineers, he saw the land along the shoreline of Lake Santa cross-hatched with steel bars, beams and girders, and clusters of concrete mixers rotating around an internal axis like so many planets, every now and then vomiting their cement stew into columns and pillars.

If he had time, Lucens liked to trudge alongside Amanat, letting him explain what was happening in each location. It was a mystery to Lucens how his brother would ever be able to turn this colossal mess into the temperate and serene buildings of The Guardian Angels Center. He was in Sparta only five days in a month, how did his assistants know what had to be done next? How did he manage to keep the project on schedule? Whenever they ran into the townspeople or the heads of the new businesses in Concord-Ashton, Lucens introduced Amanat as the architect of the new century, the one who was responsible for The Guardian Angels Center. Amanat blushed scarlet every time and tried to shush his younger sibling knowing well that it would have little effect.

Lucens was not given to nostalgia, but he kept remembering Terraferra after the storm had laid into the Abbey and razed every structure to the ground. How unobtrusively and without fuss or self-importance Abbajaan had rebuilt the place. How much thought and care had gone into each niche and corner. The Abbot, Lucens had learnt, had named the big seminar room the Zafar Khan Hall, in memory of Abbajaan.

The Abbey was often in Lucens's thoughts these days. He couldn't say what he missed most, the silence or the peace. Only now he was beginning to realize that at the Abbey they were often one and the same and reinforced each other. The brotherhood of the monks had been his safety net. It was their prayers and their simple, warts-and-all and selfless goodness that had kept his soul afloat. Contemplating the Virgin Mary at the Abbey was really the same as communing directly with the Lord.

The letter was short and accompanied by a cheque and a first-class air ticket.

You fill in the figures and I'll tell you what I want in return.

Nawaaz Irfan.

P.S. Let me know the date and time of your arrival at Kabul, and I'll send one of my men to pick you up.

Tejas had done it. He had broken in.

For close to two years, he had used all his guile, talents, charm and cunning to inveigle I-triple-S into the Big League. He had tried to bribe the big guns and the underlings. He had hired a PR agency to lobby for the company. He had spent months learning the byways and bypasses, detours and diversions, back roads and subterranean passages of various tax systems, and had become something of an authority on how to negotiate them so that his clients could make more money on commissions than they had ever done before.

The only problem was that there were no takers for his skills. The Billionaire Arms Club was in no mood to listen to a would-be gate-crasher and his big promises. Now without doing a damn thing, the doors to Fort Knox were opening of their own accord and Tejas was being invited in. Hallelujah. Praise be to God. Jesus, he had to admit, did smile every once in a while on mere mortals like him.

How wrong he had been, he had completely misjudged Nawaaz's potential. Or was it that in reality he had got the measure of the man in the first meeting itself? Had the rebuff provoked Nawaaz to pursue him? He had to prove to Tejas, to his Afghan peers and the world that you could ignore him only at your own risk.

Nawaaz had waited till the time was right to impress upon Tejas who was boss. Six months after their first meeting, he was ready. He had long since declared himself the alpha male of the tribe by bumping off Mirza Rustum's son, and was considered a dangerous pariah by the other Afghan clansmen. Now he was in a hurry to prove that he was not a mere usurper, but a man of principle with an articulate agenda. The Taliban leadership, he believed, had nothing to offer Afghans and other Muslims. Their leaders talked up a storm of religious fervour but discriminated against any Afghan who was not one of their own Pashtun tribe. Their intolerance had no parallel in Islamic history. Their one and only ruling passion was hatred. They abhorred universal education, religious enlightenment, peaceful coexistence even within Islam. Women were nothing but slaves and chattel for them. While their rank and file lived in extreme poverty, the leaders were very well looked after and lived in a world of their own. They were openly partial to Kandahar, and the rest of the nation could starve for all they cared. What was tragic was that they had no vision, no plan, no strategy. Their version of the Koran too was very different from that practised all over the world. They were village bigots and bereft of all culture and compassion.

Nawaaz Irfan, as anybody could see, practised what he preached. Puritanical and austere, he abstained from all worldly comforts and pleasures. There was no one who could touch him when it came to self-control, self-discipline and self-denial. He lived and breathed the Koran but unlike the Taliban it did not make him narrow-minded and brutally dogmatic. Nobody could accuse him of double standards. He starved if his men starved and partook of every hardship they did. They might complain, he never did. He had just one hobby: collecting old Afghan knives, daggers, swords. He had put every Afghan warlord, tribal chieftain and the international community on notice that the future belonged to him. His message never varied: the Americans and the rest of the world could make-believe that, if they had a mind to, they could strike out from Kabul and subdue the rest of Afghanistan with sheer firepower. They were mistaken. They could dump all the bunker busters, cluster bombs, missiles and ammunition they wanted in Afghanistan; for a while they might even take control, but in the end the mountains and the mountain people would overcome them.

He reduced everything to the bare essentials, including his combat strategy. He needed sponsors with very deep pockets, and there was only one way to get them to back him: success. Whenever he hit a target, sabotaged an oil pipeline, struck at enemy encampments, or his suicide bombers blew themselves up in the middle of a busy city junction, he got double and then triple the money. As word of his exploits got around, he gradually became the symbol and rallying point of the Islamic jihad and began to attract people from across the world: plastic-explosive experts, marksmen, authorities on conventional warfare, antitank and anti-aircraft virtuosos, electronic guidance-systems hotshots. The best of them he appointed as teachers. The students' training was intensive and specialized. When a pupil was ready, he was sent to his own country, to a location he was familiar and comfortable with, and told to attack at a time and place of his electing. He had better do his homework with care, for it was his life on the line and nobody else's. If he were caught, he might of course reveal who his bosses in Afghanistan were but, as he knew, if he talked instead of swallowing the cyanide capsule every one of Nawaaz Irfan's men carried, his family, his clan, his village would be wiped out.

Tejas did not wish to raise his own hopes. If the man wasn't bragging, and things worked out, he could be a gold mine for the Guardian Angels. And yet the truth was, Tejas would rather have sent James or some other employee of International Strategic Security Systems to Kabul. He could not pinpoint the nature of his misgivings. But the bottom line was that he did not care for the autopilot single-mindedness of Nawaaz Irfan.

On his last few visits to the building site, Lucens suddenly found that out of the rubble, the prestressed concrete columns, the underground sewage channels and the acres of reflecting glass, Amanat had conjured up the Guardian Angels' headquarters.

Stretching all the way from The Guardian Angels Center to Lake Santa were a series of thirty-foot-wide marble terraces and pavilions that seemed to quiet the spirit and induce introspection. For a moment Lucens was sure he saw his father in the furthest pavilion. It was Amanat with his cheek against the flat of the slender marble column. Lucens was familiar with the sight. At his studio in Firdaus, Abbajaan would do the same, rub his cheek against the marble of one of his sculptures to test the fluid smoothness and undertow of the stone. The older his brother got, the more like their father he looked and acted. Sometimes his turn of phrase, his gestures and mannerisms were so incredibly like Abbajaan's, one was caught in a time warp where father and son merged.

Lucens walked down the terraced steps and sat next to Amanat.

An erratic wind was blowing and the buildings had puckered into narrow fluid pleats in the water. For once Amanat had allowed his hair to grow long, but it could not be trained to lie flat on his scalp. It was immune to the gusty breeze now and standing up straight like a brush with steel bristles. Lucens flopped down next to him and tried to smoothen his mop of hair but without much success. It was as if the two brothers were back at Firdaus, sitting on the ledge of the bay window in the living room as children, watching the ships on the Arabian Sea being tossed around in the monsoon. Amanat put his arm around Zia and for a while neither brother spoke. Then Lucens looked up at the blue heavens and started singing, of all things, a Hindi film song.

'*Har koi chahta hai, ek mutthi asmaan*.'

'I had no idea you had Abbajaan's singing voice. It's uncanny how you remember these oldies. That song is so right. Each of us spends his entire life looking for a fistful of sky. You were lucky, you found your patch of blue early.'

'You've found yours too, though it took a long time. Two blue patches actually. You write and now you are going to be a wonderful architect if the Center is any proof. I wish Abbajaan had been around to see it.'

Unlike Zia to be demonstrative, Amanat thought. He wondered whether his brother would have his mother back if she ever decided to show up again. As usual, when he was being paid a compliment he switched the subject.

'No nostalgia today and no melancholia. Just happy memories.'

'You never did finish the story of the boy from whose head a sapling sprouted.'

'Didn't I? That's strange. You know what tamarind trees are like. Give them an inch and they'll take the whole sky. It grew and grew and grew. And it became home to a hundred thousand and one birds. And there's a story to each one of the birds. Have you got the time for a hundred thousand and one stories?'

Lucens laid his head on Amanat's lap and sprawled out on the long marble step.

'All the time in the world, 1001.'

# 56

The driver of the SUV was taciturn to the point of being mute. He did not ask Tejas whether he wanted to rest at one of the hotels at the airport and start the next day, but just drove through town. Kabul had changed. Landscape, real estate, the electronic goods in the shops, and the grains, fruits and vegetables in the souks, the people...everything changes when the Americans arrive.

For years Kabul had had the look of Dresden towards the end of the second world war. It had been bombed, rebombed and bombed again to rubble. Whenever the curfew had been lifted, people had scrabbled in the debris and dirt for scraps of food, sandals, tyres, parkas, old clothes, anything that could be reused or resold. Now the airport was functioning and there was a fair amount of building activity. Some of the ministries had their own separate headquarters, and the majority of the embassies had already risen from the ashes. Many of the NGOs were back and so were the international journalists. There were areas of the capital where you got the impression that you were in the thick of a boom. But however hard Kabul tried to gull you, it could not get rid of its shabby, tacky, lean-to air.

Half of it was a devastated shanty town, with entire floors of buildings hanging precariously like broken limbs, which nevertheless had a high occupancy rate. But even in the other half of the town where the plush suburbs were, Tejas was convinced that all it would take was one heavy downpour for the colours to run and the cardboard and plywood to start rotting and falling apart. There were new colonies coming up, along with diplomatic enclaves, apartment blocks for foreign residents and a few new hotels, some of them rather fancy.

When Tejas had last been here, many, many years earlier, 80 per cent of the men had guns. If you hadn't killed a few, you were not a man. All the chemists' shops had been closed and doctors were a mere memory. There were hardly any tourists then, and the few hotels had been taken over by different groups of mujahideen. They sat on the steps in front of the plate-glass doors, their Kalashnikovs leaning against them within reach. And reach for them they did, as casually as picking up a pea-shooter, and if the mood was upon them, they shot someone dead.

Now, once again, a few chemists were back, many of the schools were open, and there were women at work, some of them with only headscarves rather than burkhas. The outsider was being persuaded to think that things were back to normal. Tejas thought Kabul was trying a little too hard, protesting a little too vociferously that it had changed. But there was no escaping the new international brigade, the brotherhood of the war-crippled at every street corner: boys, girls, cattle, men, dogs and women with an eye, a leg or an arm missing; the mangled aftermath of landmines, bombs, friendly fire, hand grenades and guns. Let the Americans retreat, and in their wake the Europeans and the UN and, the next thing you knew, the Taliban or one of its cousins would take it right back to the Middle Ages.

Once out of town, everything seemed to become familiar. All was apocalyptic chaos and the end of the world. You would have had to be singularly heartless to wish hope on anyone here. Almost nothing had survived the continual battering from field cannon, surface missiles, and the encore after encore of carpet bombings. The fruit and vegetable orchards stood forlorn, with an occasional dry yellow tendril still coiled around a splintered stake. Entire villages had been flattened, and the rare hut that still stood its ground had either a roof or a wall missing. Sometimes you saw children playing outside, or a heavily veiled woman washing clothes at a stream, but there were no men around. They had joined their militias. So much for peace. Who was going to till this battered, beautiful land and grow wheat and start producing the world's most delicious and juicy plums, peaches and apricots? Fifty miles down the road, you saw endless fields of poppy plantations. Heroin was the new power engine of the Afghan economy. They were stopped at the checkpoints, but Nawaaz had taken care of the permits, so nobody delayed Tejas with serious questioning or a search for contraband.

Tejas had forgotten how cold it was in these mountains. It was a crippling, spiteful cold; it turned your bones to dry brittle sticks that crumbled with the slightest bump. Not that he was unfamiliar with subzero temperatures. Terraferra was a frozen wasteland in winter and so was the North Pennsylvania of the triple counties. But this was different: the air here was so fine, it seemed to have hair-thin rotating blades in it. Every breath you took, your lungs were in shreds.

It was a mercy there were no vehicles ahead or he would have choked on the exhaust fumes and the trail of thick dust. He had a theory about drivers from India, Pakistan and Afghanistan: they'd all been to the same driving school. It did not matter whether there was ice on the road, they were taking seventeen hairpin bends per minute, or that the road was a ten-foot ledge that dropped straight into a ravine some 11,000 feet below. The drivers barrelled through, lurching, hurtling and spinning at breakneck speeds. It appeared to be a daily dare to the fates and to the mountains: let's see if you can kill my passengers and me today.

They were climbing up now and the jeep grumbled and complained every time the driver changed gears. The air was getting rapidly thinner and, as in the past, Tejas had begun to feel light-headed and nauseous. They must be eleven thousand feet above sea level now. By the time they climbed another couple of thousand feet, the pressure on his lungs would become unbearable and he would get a headache that would become progressively worse and he would be in no condition for the tough negotiations ahead. Why had he been so foolish? He should have insisted on getting acclimatized gradually. Unfortunately, despite the pain and discomfort, the past was beginning to crowd him and he found it difficult to stanch the flood of memories. No, he told himself, the Afghan–Kashmir chapter had long since been closed and he wasn't going to allow a brief visit to undo the long years he had spent forgetting it. In future he would make sure James would take over the job of looking after Nawaaz. That's if there was money in it.

Every now and then there were chinks in the darkling skies and you saw low-intensity fires burning behind. Occasionally the clouds sparkled and crackled like a TV set on a wet monsoon day. Then suddenly the cloud cover splintered and sunlight cascaded down. This was the moment that made the stark and pitiless landscape of Afghanistan an unpromised benediction. You could see the mountain peaks with their myriad ridges and accordion folds for a hundred, maybe a hundred and fifty miles. The valley below seemed to rise up on the golden tide of light till you could hear the tinkle of bells of the grazing cattle and almost touch the veils around the faces of the women.

The four-wheel-drive braked suddenly and the driver spread out a prayer rug by the side of the road and knelt facing Mecca. Tejas too went down on his knees and prayed to a different God. He thanked Him for the gift of the mountains and the sunset. He was caught up in work, and had forgotten the handiwork of the Lord. He begged Jesus now to give him the eyes and vision to see the wonder of His creation.

Nawaaz Irfan tapped him on the shoulder. 'It is a four-and-a-half mile walk from here. Unless you would rather ride on a donkey.'

Nawaaz must be joking. He wasn't. The only way Tejas could make it was on a stretcher.

'No problem,' Tejas said. Nawaaz, he suspected, was testing him. He was not about to let the cocky young man know that he was done for. Tejas's overnight case was tied on a donkey's back and they set off. In spite of the regular yoga, for the first mile or so Tejas had to pretend that he needed to pee or tie his laces to prevent his breathing apparatus from collapsing upon itself. But after that, strangely enough, the steep trekking seemed to make life a lot easier.

'Doesn't it strike you as odd that I chose to invite you to my hideout and thus reveal the location of our camp?' Nawaaz Irfan asked over a late breakfast.

'I'm touched that you repose such confidence in me. But I doubt if even an experienced tracker could find this place again. Besides, you are far too wise to have just one hideout. There must be at least four or five others.'

'I see that you haven't lost your touch. Have you had a chance to look at any of those?' Nawaaz Irfan pointed to several framed calligraphic texts on the walls. 'The frames are expensive collector's items but it's the words that are priceless.'

'The Prophet's words?'

'A different kind of prophet, but a prophet nevertheless. You might find the quotations interesting.'

Coyness was not a quality Tejas would have associated with Nawaaz. He wondered why the young warlord was so keen on seeking his good opinion. But he was his host and Tejas did his bidding. He was surprised to find that the quotations were not in Arabic but in English. He went closer and read them out aloud.

We are the mujahideen, the guerrilla warriors of Allah and Islam. We fight not for private gain but for justice and our way of life. Which is why we fight for our brothers in Palestine, in Kashmir, in Croatia, in any place where Islam is threatened. The resin that binds us is Allah. The infidels in the West do not know this but we are the new Crusaders. We will vanquish them.

Most of us leave so much to chance because we believe that Allah will make it come right. Allah will do nothing of the sort. He helps only those who help themselves. The secret of success is endless rehearsals and training till you drop dead or get it perfect.

Put your trust in Allah but first tether your donkeys. The donkey is our lifeline. Treat him well. Remove him from the scene and we are dead.

'Recognize them?' Nawaaz asked.

Tejas froze.

They sat out in the sun on folding chairs. Everything in the camp was light, portable and could be dismantled within a minute. Everybody including guests slept in sleeping bags. The cave they had spent the night in was invisible till you were directly in front of it. Considering that there was at least 250 feet of solid rock above it, the enemy would need a few hundred Raytheon bunker busters to have any effect; maybe more. You couldn't see any gadgetry, but Tejas was certain that a highly skilled operative was monitoring the skies on radar round the clock. Perched high up was a lookout scanning the dirt tracks and the surrounding countryside, and keeping a sharp eye on the herd of donkeys grazing on the slopes. Tejas felt the quote on the donkey was incomplete. Eliminate the beast from Afghanistan and the fighting would come to a standstill. All that advanced American technology couldn't help them negotiate this terrain.

Tejas moved his chair into the shade. He knew he would have to move it back within minutes. It got unbearably hot in the sunlight but you started shivering if you sat in the shade. The only response possible to the flawless day was silence. Perhaps something in Tejas's mood had infected Nawaaz. He too was quiet for a long time.

'You are my hero. I can quote you chapter and verse from your time in Afghanistan. "Don't fool yourself. Anger and rage are luxuries no Islamic warrior can afford. They make you feel good and lead to instant and ill-thought-out action. No enemy could want more of you. Focus on the foe and stay focused. That is much more productive." You were never afraid of the truth and you put things in perspective. Here's another sobering quote from you. "The Americans are our friends. So are the Israelis. They never make any bones about hating us and being our enemies. Now the Europeans, they cluck-cluck sympathetically but haven't done a damn thing for us. But if you want to know who the real enemy is, all you've got to do is look within the family, the family of Islam, especially in the Middle East: Saudi Arabia, the Emirates, Libya, Yemen, Egypt, Iran. They throw us crumbs but not once have they been able to stand united on any Islamic cause. They are the infidels. They sup with the devil and pretend to be with us."

'Even today, you are remembered by many as the bravest guerrilla fighter of the twentieth century. What few people know is that you also wrote a textbook on strategy and guerrilla tactics, going right back to the Crusades, remember? No other Islamic leader I know of, not even Bin Laden, has bothered to formulate the military and political philosophy of jihad. I take it this was one of the first things you did when you became the leader of your organization. It reads as a "how to" as much as a meditation on the quandary of modern Islam and the way out of it.'

Tejas was good with clients. He knew his business. He could reel off a battery of figures, the calibre and range of anti-aircraft guns, the comparative strengths and weaknesses of different missile systems; he was adroit at cutting through the hype and jargon of arms manufacturers and explaining things in simple language. And he could tell his clients just how much they were going to make on commissions and kickbacks because of his creative ways of siphoning money. Most of all, he could win them over by flattering their perceptiveness in choosing what he was selling them. But today, the traffic seemed to be going in the reverse direction. A prospective customer was holding forth on his virtues. Even an experienced operator like Tejas was not immune to hero worship. He had to remind himself that he hadn't flown ten thousand miles to hear about his long-forgotten past. Why wasn't Nawaaz getting down to business?

'I have had more than my share of success in Turkey, in Saudi, and other places. Part of the reason is that I followed your primer to the letter.

'How wise you were when you said, "The Americans and their lackeys, the British, never tire of repeating that we are envious of their values and their lifestyles. May they continue to delude themselves. Who amongst the warriors of Islam would choose their degenerate and debauched life over the life of Allah?"

'Do you know that I searched for you for eight years before discovering your new identity and making contact with you?'

'When you called my brother, or wrote, you gave no name.'

'Do you like to hear stories?'

Nawaaz Irfan, Tejas was beginning to realize, was truly an odd bird. 'My brother used to tell me stories when I was a child. Now I never have the time.'

'Let me tell you one anyway, while we have a moment of peace. There was once a devout Afghan fisherman, almost a contradiction in terms, since there is no sea anywhere near this country. He had heard that there was a sea which was larger than his home town Kabul, larger than all of Afghanistan, bigger even than the entire continent of Asia. He had wanted to see this wonderful thing called the ocean, and had travelled to the west coast of India and settled there. Now he had a small boat, a wife and three children: two older girls and a boy. There was hardly any money, so only the son was sent to school. They had big plans for the boy: he would study and go to college, and own a fleet of trawlers. It was taken for granted that he would make so much money, he would build a palatial home with a hundred and one rooms, and paint the dome of the village mosque with real gold.

'One day a maula from Jammu visited the village. The preacher spoke movingly of the plight of Muslims in Kashmir, of the brutality of the Indian army, the daily desecration of women, the sudden searches and continual curfews, and the great jihad young men of Islam from all over the world were fighting to liberate the state from Indian rule.

'A week later the fisherman disappeared. It was said that the sea had got him. But the Muslim community knew that he had left to join the holy war against the infidels. Some months he sent money home, but mostly the family made do with what the mother and sisters earned as servants in the houses of the rich. The only one whose life did not change was the young boy. Every day his mother exhorted him to study hard and make certain that the sacrifices of his father, sisters and mother would not be in vain.

'Years passed. The boy's father was lucky. He had been recruited by the most successful mujahideen leader in Kashmir. The man was a brilliant tactician. He had a higher success rate than any other troop leader; his raids caused untold damage; he often orchestrated simultaneous attacks which resulted in chaos in the enemy ranks; and he almost never lost any of his men. The fisherman became an expert tracker, and soon became the leader's most trusted assistant.

'Then something went wrong. He became a eunuch. He didn't let on, but he began to get nightmares. He had spilt the blood of hundreds of innocents, and he felt that instead of the promised jannat, there was a seat reserved for him in jehannum. He was wracked by guilt, but dared not talk about his dilemma to anyone for fear of being branded a coward.

'The next attack planned was a major one. When all life came to a standstill in a snowstorm, they would wipe out the five villages called Puncham. The boy's father helped plan the attack to the last detail, and then informed the Indian army headquarters. The deal was that all 350 innocent Hindu and Muslim villagers would be evacuated in advance. To his horror, the Indian army did nothing of the sort. They watched while the five villages were incinerated, then gunned down most of the boy's father's comrades.

'When my father, Yunus Habib, returned home, he said he had come back because he missed his family, especially his son. He hated the mountains and the snow. He yearned for the salty sea, and the storms that carry fishermen to their death. But most of all, he hungered for forgiveness. He wanted Allah to weep so that his crimes could be washed clean.

'We were a marked family. They were looking for him, the few comrades who had escaped death that fateful day. We moved, always in the middle of the night, chased by ragged dogs. We caught trains, we fled in buses, we came to Bombay, and even then we were pursued as much by former friends as by my father's phantoms. My elder sister became a prostitute; the family, including my father, had to eat. My second sister, the one with the thick, knee-length hair and the inquisitive eyes, ran away, never to be seen again; and my mother committed suicide. And all the while my father waited for the one man he had admired, loved, followed blindly and betrayed. But Zia Khan never did come.

'So now it was just the two of us, my father and me. I knew Zia Khan was testing me and my loyalty. He wanted to know if I was worthy of his trust.'

What was Tejas to make of Nawaaz Irfan? There was something about his childlike faith in Zia that was chilling. How could anyone impose such a burden of expectation and responsibility upon another? Tejas listened in horror to what the Afghan had to say.

'I knew that I had to commit the only act that would absolve the honour of our family. I had rehearsed the scene countless times. I thought my father would plead with me for his life. He didn't. What he said was, "Do it quick, son. I've been waiting for this moment so long." It was odd, I too had waited for this moment for so long, yet now I found myself paralysed. He patted me on the back. "A good deed should never be delayed." I did it then.' Nawaaz Irfan paused, as though he was reliving that day. 'I knew that I could now join my mujahideen brothers in Afghanistan, and that I would meet you one day.'

What would it avail a man to have a clean conscience, Tejas asked himself, if the blood of his comrade-in-arms was on his hands? Oh Lord God of mercy and forgiveness, he cried in his heart, will You not rid me of my past?

Nawaaz Irfan locked his intense eyes with Tejas's and would not let go of them till his unwitting teacher had acknowledged his great quest. It dawned on Tejas why he had been so loath to come to Afghanistan. He had not wanted to meet his twin.

'I'm flattered,' he said finally, 'and overwhelmed by your single-mindedness.'

Nawaaz smiled. It was a child's smile, a smile full of assurance that its parents recognized what a bright and brave son they had.

Tejas's gaze wandered. The donkeys were no longer out there grazing, nor were the men who had been cleaning their firearms in the sun. It was quiet and peaceful. Fifteen or eighteen peaks to the southeast he could now see a sprinkling of dots in the sky.

'Might be a good idea to go in,' Nawaaz said casually.

They went inside and one of the assistants brought tea thick enough for water buffaloes to float on, and Parle's Monaco biscuits.

'Three biscuits?' Nawaaz pulled up the man who had served them. 'Don't disgrace me in front of our guest.'

The assistant bent down and whispered in his chief's ear: 'That's all we've got.'

Nawaaz gave him a dirty look and offered the biscuits to Tejas.

'I don't like salty biscuits,' Tejas lied.

Nawaaz smiled at him. 'You don't know what you're missing.' He gathered all three biscuits and bit into them.

You could hear the planes approaching like mosquitoes boring into your ears, and then the caves shuddered as a dozen bunker busters in one go tried to excavate and pulverize the flank of a mountain.

'Who are they targeting? Us? Or some tribal neighbours a few peaks away?'

Nawaaz shook his head. 'They will never be able to find me or my people, not in this lifetime nor the one after that, the bloody fools. Our American friends are, as you know, terrified of body bags, so we rarely have face-to-face combats. That leaves them very little choice but to pretend that they can wipe out our resistance by bombing alone. Sometimes indiscriminate carpet bombing. That puts their Pakistani collaborators in a bit of a spot. They must come up with intelligence about the whereabouts of the Afghan troublemakers. They are rather good at it. When they don't have it, they fabricate it. The next morning the American planes fly out to the precise co-ordinates given by their friends in Islamabad and blast every stone, worm, snake and chameleon in sight. It's a useful exercise. The Pakistanis claim that they've done their job and the Americans can happily report to the Pentagon that they've destroyed a whole settlement of mujahideen. But I keep telling my men never to forget your maxim: "The one day you are not on your guard, the enemy will zoom in on you and mow you down." We never take a chance. We treat every overhead visit as if the Americans know exactly where we are.'

Ask a silly question, Tejas thought, and get a mile-long answer. Nawaaz had still not got around to business. Then suddenly Tejas's animosity drained away. He no longer felt impatient. Nawaaz was lonely and starved for good company. Tejas remembered his own days in these parts. There were times when he would walk for miles just to scream his head off for lack of company and stimulating conversation. Nawaaz Irfan had gathered a loyal band of men around him. They were good in their area of expertise and not much more. Besides, knowing his reputation, they must be wary of him. And he too had to make sure that his men never got familiar with him nor detected his utter isolation.

Nawaaz spoke almost in a whisper. 'I would be insulting your integrity if I mentioned that our conversations are confidential. However great the torture, you never broke your silence in the past.

'At the very end of your handbook, you speak of co-opting the nuclear option.' He was thoughtful for a minute. 'We are about to do that. You understand now why I had to meet you.'

Zia-Lucens-Tejas had finally met his nemesis, his perfect pupil.

'We have two objectives, an immediate one, and the more critical one which will follow later; not an amorphous and indefinite "later" but one that is clearly deadlined. What we are looking for at the outset are half a dozen dirty bombs. After that we want the real thing, WMDs.'

Tejas tried to look nonchalant but he had the feeling that his life would never be the same again. He wondered why he was so shocked. Hadn't he known all along that someone or other was bound to place an order for these items, if not today then a week hence? The only problem was that it was not 'someone or the other', it was a man who metaphorically sat at his feet, was inspired by him and followed his every word as though it was from the holy book.

With the dissolution of the Soviet Union, the media had gone to town about the hundreds of nuclear warheads lying around in the former Soviet states and the weapons-grade uranium and plutonium that would soon be available on the black market. But after 9/11 all notions of sanity and responsible journalism had gone for a toss. The name of the game was let's see who can scare the daylights out of their readers or viewers more. Sure, the threat was real, but so was the fact that the American president's ratings were linked to stoking the psychosis. Now it was taken for granted that some Johnny-cum-lately mujahideen leader or an old chieftain would get his hands on a dirty bomb and let loose a new era of terror. It was a self-fulfilling prophecy.

It would take a while for Tejas to fully grasp the significance of what Nawaaz was saying. For the moment, his whole objective was to buy time. 'I'm sure you know that the destructive power of the dirty bomb is mostly a creation of the media and of the fear the word "nuclear" arouses almost as a programmed reflex in the public mind,' Tejas said. 'One estimate says that an RDD, or a radiological dispersal device as the scientists call it, would kill around 760 people in a town of 15,000 people. But the expert view is that its effects will be no worse than that of a radiation accident. A scientist from the University of Rochester calculated that more people would be killed in car accidents as they fled the site of the dirty bomb blast than from the actual radiation.'

'Yes, I'm aware of that,' Nawaaz answered. 'But the same studies will also tell you that the public perception is that the radiation risk is a thousand to ten thousand times higher than the real danger. It's a "weapon of mass disruption" rather than of mass destruction. It's a psychological bomb that will induce hysteria and chaos across America. Just the kind of atmosphere in which to drop the big ones.

'But we also aim to make the dirty bomb dirtier. If we wish to enhance the radioactive fallout from the dirty bomb and thus increase its lethal effectiveness, the main requisite is superior dispersal technology. That's the first parameter I want you to bear in mind. The second is that what we are looking for is a cocktail of components inside the bomb. It may be interesting to lace the nuclear payload with a heavy dose of biochemical WMDs. I don't doubt that this is going to require some experimentation, but it should be possible for you to deliver this device in what, five months? For the real thing, you have more time. Two years.'

'It's not going to be that easy to put together "the real thing". You underestimate the problems and the risks.'

'Why would I offer you a blank cheque if I believed it was easy? Your company's motto is "When nobody else can deliver, we will." Both you and I know there are enough people in Pakistan and North Korea who are more than sympathetic to our cause. It's just that they would prefer someone else to do the dirty job for them.'

When he was about to leave at 4 a.m. the next day, Nawaaz Irfan tapped Tejas on the shoulder and said, 'Ziabhai, may I call you that? you haven't told me the numbers yet.'

'The goods you want are not available off-the-shelf. I'll have to make some enquiries.'

'You do that. Money is no consideration. The deadline, however, is not negotiable.'

There was a pattern to Nawaaz's behaviour. He had spent the previous day ingratiating himself with Tejas. Now, just in case the supplier had got confused about their roles, he was clarifying who was in charge.

'The supergun, what did you want that for?' Tejas asked as a parting shot.

'The president of Pakistan used to be our friend. He has had a change of heart. We thought we would give him a wake-up call, both in Islamabad and Karachi, with the supergun.'

Amanat sent a rash email:

Tell me I've got it wrong. Tell me it is not true. Tell me you are not financing the Guardian Angels with money made from the sale of arms. Please reply immediately.

Amanat

The governor had come and gone. Half the town was there for the inauguration of The Guardian Angels Center. The federal government had promised millions and so had private philanthropies. As finance manager, Lucens had planned, in typical fashion, to stay in the background and let the trustees and Honor and the others do the talking. But he was not even around. He should have been rejoicing. But he had a white leprose spot growing at the dead centre of his soul and he was rapidly losing all sensation. What was he going to do? Time was running out and for the first time in his life, Tejas felt like a zombie. He was unable to think or act. This had never happened before. Even in Cambridge, his way of dealing with his great depression was to go into overdrive and disown his academic career by doing the most menial job in the world. Now he refused to go to the office, deal with his clients in the arms business, or take phone calls, and when Honor and the others from the Angels' office started visiting him at home, he left town and checked into a motel some thirty miles away. He didn't get out of bed even when the cleaning woman was vacuuming the room. He was waiting, waiting to be put out of his misery.

What should he do? Who should he turn to? He had told Roy some years ago when he had lost all the Guardian Angels' money that Catholics do not commit suicide. So what was he planning to do? Become a Hindu or a Jew now?

How simple and lethal the ironies of life were. How long and hard he had tried to join the Big League. How desperate and demoralized he had become. Now finally he had got entry into the Club, the money was within reach, and yet he dared not touch it. He had never felt so abandoned and forlorn.

What was he going to tell Nawaaz Irfan?

It was months since Tejas had met him in his hideout. He could postpone the next meeting by a week or ten days at the most, but not a day after that.

All these years Tejas had held that introspection was nothing but self-indulgence. It was one of his older brother's pet hobbies. But there was no reverse gear to life. To dwell on the past was a barren exercise. And yet now, like it or not, the chickens had come home to roost. The past had finally caught up with him.

Those were his private jottings Nawaaz had quoted, meant only for his own eyes. He was always making notes. At no time had he intended them to be a textbook or primer for terrorists. Now he was being held responsible for what he had said a long, long time ago in another existence. He had moved on since then, there had been a major upheaval in his life. You could say he had joined the enemy. He was still on the side of justice. And yes, he thought the Palestinians' cause was just, but there was a fundamental difference: He had changed his faith.

But it was a little more complicated than that. He had a commitment to the Guardian Angels. They were his atonement for the past. And they were the reason why he had got into the arms business in the first place. Nawaaz Irfan was giving him a blank cheque worth close to two billion. The Angels could do with the money, more money than James and he had ever earned.

Whatever Nawaaz did now, it was Zia's doing. Tejas was in a bind and he couldn't see any way out.

My dear Zia,

The last time I listened to my conscience, you accused me of having stabbed you in the back. An unhappy turn of phrase to say the least. This time around I intend to give you notice and stab you up front.

I wrote to you a month ago but you have not bothered to reply. Am I to take your silence to mean that you indeed are an arms trader? That, notwithstanding the fact that you are the inspiration and the driving force behind the Guardian Angels, you are actually an angel of death?

I'm going to backtrack a bit. I was upset when you left the Abbey. Reverend Father Augustine was perhaps the best thing that ever happened to you. He is catholic in a way that most intensely religious Catholics are not. And however critical he may be of one, it does not affect his generous and compassionate nature.

In one of your sudden switches, 'sudden' to the outsider though for all I know you may have mulled over it for a long time, you moved to Sparta and started the Guardian Angels. As is often the case with you, your intentions were mostly laudable. I can think of few causes more worthy than Zero Orphans or the Homes for the Children of God. I would even go along with the concept of the Pledge of Purity, but with a few serious reservations. The rate of teenage pregnancies and AIDS is truly frightening and I do believe that sexual intimacy because of peer pressure is a very bad idea. Cyberculture, digital media, Hollywood and its hypocritical cousin Bollywood, not to mention tabloid journalism, which unfortunately includes most mainstream papers, posit that we must continually seek sex and new sensations. It is a search that quickly degenerates into the bizarre and may sometimes have dangerous consequences.

Having said that, I would part company with you on other issues. Abortion, for me, is a last resort, but proscribe abortion and family planning, and I think India is doomed, and in the long run, the world too. I abhor your stance on gays and lesbians. I find it both inexplicable and reprehensible. But the really alarming aspect of the Guardian Angels' agenda is that it can so easily be interpreted to reinforce the neoconservative programme. I am aware that on a personal level you do not share many of the neocon views. I know how strongly you feel for the Palestinians and that you were totally opposed to the invasion of Iraq. You care for the poor and lead a life of austerity whereas the neocons may talk of conservative compassion but all they are interested in is the rapacious pursuit of wealth. But as things are, the Angels are seen as being to the right of the extreme right, which is why the conservatives from both the Republican and the Democratic parties gravitate to you for endorsement.

What depresses me even more about the Guardian Angels' agenda is the numbing aridity of its hopes and aims for a better future. Is your crusade against Roe v. Wade and homosexuals, the sum total of your vision? What petty and negative ambitions you have for mankind. Look to the Son of God, Zia. There is no greater visionary than Christ. What would He make of your organization, and of all the good Republicans who want to reinvent America and, in time, the world itself, in the image of Christ, and yet have no thought for those who were closest to His heart: the dispossessed and the marginalized? Don't you think the least they deserve is a second New Deal? Democracy, like charity, must begin at home, instead of in Iraq or Cuba. How about restoring civil liberties in the US?

Yet, even all this is beside the point. What good are your philanthropic activities if you are going to fund them by dealing in death? You claim to be pro-life, but all you do is leave behind a trail of destruction.

A leopard does not change its spots. You may have switched your religion or whatever 'ism' you subscribed to but you remain true to your nature. Arthur Koestler, Dos Passos and the others from the 'God-That-Failed' brigade, not to mention Mussolini, were card-carrying Marxists who turned into the most rabid conservatives. Like them you too turned apostate and like them you remained faithful to your religion, the religion of extremism.

I will give you three months to wind up your operations, to opt out of your commitments and to resign from I-triple-S. If you still persist, I will go to the press and onto the Internet with this terrible story.

For better or worse you are my brother. I love you. Don't make me do this.

Amanat

Three days before he was to meet Nawaaz Irfan, Tejas finally saw his way through the thicket of problems, dead ends and paralysis that had immobilized him as firmly as the nails that pinioned Jesus and the two thieves to the crucifix. What he'd forgotten was that the Virgin and Jesus take care of their own.

The first complication was his very own blood, Amanat. He should have known better than to ask Amanat to design The Guardian Angels Center. He had got the fat assignment, and as repayment had been meddling in things that did not concern him. How could Tejas have forgotten that Amanat was trouble, the worst kind of trouble. He had appeared once before at a critical juncture in Tejas's life, and he was assuming that role again. Did the fool have the foggiest idea how much work, time, money and planning had gone into the Angels' project? Halfway through, the whole enterprise had come to the brink of collapse. Tejas did not care to recall the panic attacks. Or relive the fear that his beloved Jesus had abandoned him. He had lost everything and had been about to file for bankruptcy. Then, out of the blue, surely the purest blue of the Virgin's robe in a Raphael painting, he had been rescued and the Angels reborn.

Did Amanat have any idea how much it cost to run the Homes for the Children of God, an idea that he supported wholeheartedly? Lucens had discontinued the project for some time because of a lack of funds, and then realized his folly. Now once again the Angels were committed to starting more Homes. Would Amanat or Roy like to take over the responsibility of funding them? At the moment Lucens and his top executives were putting together a team of the best legal brains in the country. Their aim: to appeal Roe v. Wade, overturn the pro-abortion judgement of 1973. Once abortion was illegal, the pressure on Lucens to finance the Homes would ease up and then he would not have to trade in arms. It was not going to be easy, even the legal team had its doubts about whether they could reverse a Supreme Court verdict. But Lucens had no reservations. God was on the side of the Angels. They would overcome. That's if that dangerous and interfering brother of his did not put a spoke in the wheel.

It was something of a mystery where Amanat had got his information about Lucens's second life. Or was it? It could only be that rat Roy. He had been up to his tricks from the very beginning, pretending to be holier-than-thou. They could try as hard as they wanted to ruin all the work Lucens had put in, but it wasn't going to work. He was no one's fool. He had covered his tracks every centimetre and inch of the way. What Amanat had on him was nothing but rumour and hearsay. Vivian was locked up in a psychiatric hospital, and the Salman Rushdie story sounded as far-fetched as one of Amanat's or Salman Rushdie's own novels. Barring Shakta Muni, James Cambray and a few select clients, nobody knew about Lucens's double life. They could of course betray him but if they knew what was good for them, they would keep their mouths shut. Tejas was not just their arms supplier, he was the conduit through whom they diverted their stash into numbered accounts. And Lucens knew all the numbers. It was what they so felicitously called a symbiotic relationship. 'Mum' was the word.

Amanat had given him three months' notice. Time enough to sort out matters with Nawaaz Irfan. And take care of his brother.

The second complication was James Cambray, who not so long ago had been making peanuts and was gloriously happy, till Tejas had given him his first glimpse and taste of the super-bucks. The bumbling fool who was once terrified of Tejas, and wanted to resign because he couldn't contribute to the new marketing strategy, was now acting boss-man, tracking his every move, checking back with Tejas's clients if they were having problems with him, and hounding him for not delivering. Tejas would have to cut James down to size. Maybe even cut him out of the loop altogether.

Right now though, his first priority was the meeting with Nawaaz Irfan. Nobody would go wrong, or make a false move, if they had access to hindsight before the event. Yes, Tejas should have gone by his instincts and given Nawaaz the cold shoulder from the beginning, refusing to meet him at the Green Banana Leaf restaurant. Yes, he should have torn up the blank cheque and said no, thank you. But that was spilt milk. He could still excuse himself and not meet Nawaaz. Just one minor caveat. As Tejas had tried to explain to Roy, he was not the only arms dealer in town. If he said no, the Afghan would go to somebody else and get what he wanted. The least Tejas could try to do was to stop Nawaaz from following the dictates of a misguided and deluded teacher, a man who, as it happened, was long dead: himself.

What foxed him, though, was why he had got the willies and worked himself up into such a state that he had lost over three months. It was unlike him to overreact. He had forgotten one of his own rules. The one mistake most people make is to think they are Superman and can solve their own problems, especially the intractable variety. Instead, all you have to do is pass the buck on to Jesus. The moment you do that your worries are over. It's his problem from there on and you are free to shake a leg or climb a mountain. Tejas had finally managed to knock some sense into his own head. He had spent the last three days praying, fasting and chastising himself, and it had paid off.

He had a clear strategy now. One, don't lose it ('it' in this instance being his head). He must calibrate his responses, so that at no time would he allow himself to be hostile or to give the game away. Or to give up hope.

Two, put your best foot forward with Nawaaz Irfan. The Afghan mind was not an urban one. Irfan and his people might live alongside contemporary artefacts, cars, airports, even computers and cellphones, but their psyche was deeply rooted in their nomadic origins. They owed loyalty not to a region, class, sect, or the nation itself, but to their tribe. It was the primary fact of their lives. Their traditions, rituals, hierarchies and relationships, their world-view, had all evolved from the tribe and were circumscribed by it. You wore your heart on your sleeve. Their palette had no shades of grey, just black and white. And everything was painted in broad, bold strokes. Everything boiled down to emotion. And everything got converted to high-voltage drama: love, enmity, affection, anger, vengeance, friendship. That was the nomadic convention; all your responses were excessive. But that didn't mean it was all fabricated, fake and phoney. It was some of that too, but there was a lot more to it. The Afghan heart was as big and capacious as it was generous, just so long as you were perceived to be a friend. If Tejas could hit the right note at the very start, something that would rapidly translate into instant rapport, he would do swimmingly.

Three, and this was perhaps the most important factor he had to bear in mind: Nawaaz Irfan was his best ally and it was he who would win the game for him. Nawaaz hero-worshipped him, he had said as much not once but repeatedly. Tejas had to merely tap into this reservoir of goodwill and he would be home. There is only one crime in the Afghan book: it's doubtful if even God, the good Allah Himself, could save you if you made an Afghan lose face.

# 57

The idea of giving gifts in order to put Nawaaz Irfan in an amiable frame of mind was a stroke of pure luck, or perhaps of genius. Tejas had couriered a hundred packets of the Monaco biscuits Nawaaz was so fond of, all the way from India to the Carlton Hotel in London.

'You remembered.' The Afghan was beside himself and did an impromptu jig on the carpet as though he had just been declared the victor in a game of bouzkashi. He looked different today. He was clean-shaven and wore a three-piece suit.

When the waiter poured the tea Nawaaz became apoplectic.

'I want tea, not horse piss.'

The waiter looked alarmed. 'But this is horse piss,' he said in an aggrieved tone. 'I mean it is tea,' he corrected himself sheepishly.

Nawaaz shoved a twenty-pound note in his hand. 'Now run for your life and ask an Indian or Bangladeshi waiter to brew some Indian chai, strong and thick.'

A few minutes after the tea ceremony was over, Tejas took out a small packet from his jacket pocket.

'Yes, let's get down to business,' Nawaaz said.

'Why don't you open it?'

Nawaaz tore open the watermarked white wrapping paper. Inside was a miniature Nepali kukri in its leather sheath. He pulled out the six-inch knife, indispensable for hunters and fighters alike, which looked like a distant cousin of the American Bowie.

'How come there's still blood on it?' Nawaaz shook the kukri like a thermometer but the bloodstone stayed put. Nawaaz seemed mesmerized by the stark simplicity of its design, with its unerringly placed ruby at the very tip.

'I'll be damned, I really thought…What's this?' He noticed the inscription on the tiny handle. 'Death to your enemies. From the King of Nepal to the King of Afghanistan, H.H. Ahmed Shah Abdali.'

The young warlord tested the sharpness of the blade on his index finger. A drop of blood popped up like an echo of the ruby and then there was no stanching the flow.

'I thought it was a toy knife.'

'I'm glad you didn't try it on your throat. It is a toy knife but the blade knows its business,' Tejas told Nawaaz Irfan as he tied his kerchief around the finger. For some reason the Afghan found Tejas's comment apoplectically witty.

'How did you know I collect knives?'

'You are not the only one with a network of spies.'

'How much?' he asked after the blood had finally clotted.

'How much what?'

'How much do you want for it?'

'How much are you willing to pay?'

'Anything unreasonable.'

'Spoken like a true connoisseur.'

'You haven't answered my question.'

'It's a gift.'

'Are you trying to bribe me?'

'There is only one bribe,
My dear friend.
His name is Allah.
Since you are already
Rich in Him,
What can I
Offer you
But empty pockets
And that sorry thing
Called my life?
Take them both
And let's be
Done with it.
Beggars deal in
The currency of time.
Friendship knows only
Eternity and the

Grace of Allah.'
Nawaaz had a ready rejoinder:
'Allah is a thief,
the biggest there is.
He's stolen my all,
Hearth and home,
Wealth and volition.
He hath purloined
Wife and father,
Children and my mother,
Peace of mind
And concubine.
Whatever's mine
He has taken.
Now he has the gall
To tell me,
I've come
To collect my dues.
Beggars in Bokhara,
He adds witheringly,
Have more change
Jangling in their pockets
Than you.
What choice do I have,
You foolish bankrupt,
But to repossess you?'

They were on a roll now, the couplets were tossed back and forth and grew like a stack of Afghani rotis at a wedding feast. Tejas was amazed to see it all come back. It was true then, he thought. Urdu and Persian poetry were like cycling or swimming. Once you learn it, you never forget it. This was a twilight zone for him. He was Abbajaan's son, the classical and the austere were his inheritance. He gagged on the banality and hyperbole of the Urdu sher; its narrowness of subject matter; its predilection for the cloyingly florid and ornate; its recurrent soggy images and themes. And yet there were times when the daring, the abandon and the uninhibited emotion of mystic poetry left him breathless. It touched him as few things could, and humbled him. In that instant he knew he was in the presence of an all-embracing God.

When they were done, Irfan stuck the Nepali knife back into the clot and thrust his finger into Tejas's face as the blood welled up.

'Drink of it,' he said.

Tejas knew better than to ignore Nawaaz's bidding. He hated the smell of raw blood but he loathed the taste even more. This too shall pass, he told himself and drank. Imagine not reciprocating Nawaaz's sentiment. He would make an unforgiving enemy of him for life. He took the knife and stabbed his forefinger with it. Nawaaz sucked deep and then took him in his arms and hugged him for a long time.

'Now we're blood brothers. No man or woman can come between us. Death alone shall part us.'

The easy part, the mediaeval tribal ritual, was over. Tejas now braced himself for the arduous climb to he didn't know where.

'I'm going to play the devil's advocate. I use the word "play" advisedly. It will be my role to question, probe and pick holes. And yours to dispassionately rethink and reconsider everything you believe in passionately. Let me start by being heretical: One of the qualities of leadership is to have the courage to reverse decisions. Whether you retract or decide to proceed, either way you are the winner. The idea is to make sure you are doing the right thing. Will you then listen to me in good faith?'

'On our blood, I will.'

'Some years ago, Amartya Sen, the Nobel prize-winning economist, wrote an article. Its thesis was that for years, perhaps from the time the two countries won independence, India was militarily superior to Pakistan. It had double the armed forces of Pakistan and it was better equipped in every sense. When India went nuclear followed immediately by Pakistan, Sen argued, it sacrificed its military superiority for good and from then on the two countries would always be on par.'

'Where is this leading to?' Irfan was running out of patience already.

'Bear with me.' Tejas ignored the interruption. 'If you acquire nuclear weapons, you will naturally not be in the same situation. And yet there will still be substantial similarities. At the moment, Afghanistan is the underdog. Not an enviable position to be in but the world's sympathies are with you. Admittedly they are not of much use at the moment but one can't ignore them either. Explode a nuclear device, even a tiny "dirty" bomb, in the US and instantly you are the villain. Within hours, they'll retaliate by dropping a dozen, maybe many more, megaton bombs and will claim justification for their actions by citing an unprovoked attack on their country.'

'What difference will that make?' Nawaaz asked. 'As if the Islamic underdog has anything to look forward to or live for. The Palestinians are viewed as subhuman. The great majority of them are without jobs. Most of their children, I doubt if you know this, suffer from the same degree of malnutrition as children in the worst parts of Africa. Their water supply is controlled by the Israelis. Often they have no drinking water.'

'I know the tragedy by heart, Nawaaz. They have no access to their own fields. They are bombed and pulverized at the will and whim of the Israelis, which is sometimes twice or thrice daily.'

'So why don't you do something about it? The Israeli motherfuckers and their American cocksuckers like to propagate the myth that the reason we become suicide bombers is because Islam promises its martyrs instant transportation to paradise and its houris. If that was the case we would all commit mass martyrdom tomorrow. But the truth is nobody in his senses wants to commit suicide. Our children, men and women opt for it because they have nothing to live for. That's the Israeli gift to us.'

Tejas knew that the anger was genuine and so was the sense of impotence, but if he didn't cut in now, it would be impossible to have a sane discussion.

'Everything you say is true but you are missing the point.'

'And what the fuck would that be?' Nawaaz screamed. He was standing with his feet apart and arms akimbo. His face was flushed scarlet and there was a concussed, glassy look in his eyes. He was receiving his instructions from some remote astral source. One wrong word or move and he would implode.

'I'm not the enemy, Nawaaz,' Tejas said softly.

The Afghan's face clouded. 'Why are you baiting me then?'

'I'm playing the devil's advocate, remember?'

A smile broke on Nawaaz's face. 'You are doing a bloody good job of it. The Americans should hire you as their PR agent.'

Tejas locked his eyes with Nawaaz Irfan's in a deadpan stare.

'Sorry, no offence meant. Go on.'

'They'll nuke Afghanistan and not Palestine. And nothing will remain of its beautiful people and their civilization.'

'So they will. But let me quote you. "The children of Allah are all identical twins and share the same nervous system. Gouge the eye of an Iranian," you said, "and I will go blind. Deprive a Kashmiri of a job and I will starve. Bomb the homes of the Palestinians and I'll be homeless."' Nawaaz's voice was devoid of emotion now and sounded all the more ominous. 'I don't mind if they kill every single one of us, just so long as at least once, just once, I can make the Americans and the Israeli dogs taste what it means to be kicked around, starved and humiliated when you are already down and helpless.'

'Well spoken even if they are my words.'

The Afghan smiled and Tejas heaved a silent sigh of relief. If you have had your back against the wall for decades, Tejas knew too well, all you have is impotent rage, and it can torch everything in sight.

'The Americans need to be taken care of. I'm not denying that. There's much that's wrong with them. They've become insufferable because of their arrogance and hubris. They tolerate gays and abortion. Their decadence is bottomless. They treat the earth as if it was their private resource. But let's come closer home. Do you remember the adage, healer, heal thyself?' Tejas suddenly shifted gears and used the inclusive pronoun 'we' instead of 'you'.

'Should we not first heal Afghanistan before looking abroad? You plan to spend an astronomical sum on nuclear weaponry. Can you imagine what that kind of money could do for the people of Afghanistan?'

'You can pour ten billion, twenty, thirty, into the coffers of the country and nothing will come of it.'

'Why is that?'

'You damn well know why. Every bloody Western country, not to mention Russia, China, India and God alone knows how many others, has an eye on that oil pipeline and will play one tribe against the other.'

'True. And not true. Yes, they want the oil. But they can be made to pay a hefty price to access it. What's the point of building that pipeline if it's not going to be safe and secure from sabotage and constant fighting? The precondition of that pipeline functioning is peace. Maybe that's why most of the tribes and groups in Afghanistan don't want it. Because they abhor peace more than war.'

'That's not the reason,' Nawaaz Irfan gritted his teeth as he spoke, 'and you know it. All they are busy doing is smuggling drugs, making money and squabbling. And stabbing each other in the back. It's each for himself and let the country be damned. We can no longer be in the same room and at the same table without being at each other's throats.'

'Is it possible then that that's the role Allah had in mind for you?'

'What role?'

'To bring the warring tribes together and bring peace to the land?'

'Sure,' Nawaaz sneered. 'Nobody has been able to pull that one off. You are pulling my leg, right?'

'I've never been more serious. No other Afghan leader has your drive, will and charisma. When you took charge, the other Afghan leaders gave you six months at the most. Now they look to you for leadership and vision. Of course, it is mission impossible, I don't doubt that. So was Ireland at one time. Until a few people made it possible.'

'I don't know what you are talking about. All you've done since you've come today is to run circles around me. First you tell me you are going to play the devil's advocate, then you insinuate that I drop the idea of acquiring the bombs. Now suddenly you want me to be the Afghan saviour. Are you playing mind games with me, Zia Khan?' Nawaaz was closing in on Tejas menacingly. 'Because if you are, there will be hell to pay and not even Allah can help you then. You don't know what Afghani retribution is.' The young chieftain's hands were around Tejas's throat now.

'I know something more now, Afghani stupidity. Take your hands off, Nawaaz.' Tejas's voice was lethal in its coldness. But it was the look in his eyes that held Nawaaz back. It wasn't just contempt, it was as if Tejas had written the man off.

'You will have your dirty bombs within two months. And the rest after that as per the schedule. Keep the cheques ready.' He was up and already at the door. 'No pupil of minc, I thought, had the spark you had. Nor your grasp of the issues.' He paused. 'I was wrong.'

# 58

Lucens had neglected business for over three months and the backlog of work was intimidating enough to paralyse him for the next year. But he was through with dithering and procrastination. He met Honor, Zac, the ex-Glades administrator, and the rest of the Guardian Angels' staff and listened to their woes and whining and realized that there was a good deal of overlapping in the subjects they handled, which allowed for ambiguity and finger-pointing while no one took responsibility. The governor's visit had also done more harm internally than good. An L.A.-smog of complacency had settled over the office. Everybody was behaving as if they had already reversed Roe v. Wade and the fight against the gays had been won.

Lucens cut through the fog and the crap.

'We could of course appoint a committee for co-ordination amongst the various activities and then another committee to oversee the work of the previous committee by which time none of us will be talking to each other. But we are not the government and though we may be working in different areas, they are not mutually exclusive.

'Anything and everything to do with pro-life issues is the responsibility of Honor and her group. Zac and his people, on the other hand, will be responsible for formulating strategies and legislation to ban homosexual marriages and ultimately the disease of homosexuality itself by making it illegal.

'Every Monday morning, we'll all meet to review the previous week's activities and chalk out the next week's. If anything gets left out or there's a new development, don't pick up the phone and don't write memos. Walk over to your colleague's office and discuss it. And if you have a small, big or brilliant idea that's going to improve our performance, even if it's not from your own area of operation, let's hear it. The Angels will benefit from it. Now, if you don't mind, I've something far more important to do: attend the board of trustees' meeting as a special invitee. I have to smile, be obsequious and thump the trustees hard on their backs so that they will cough up more. Bye for now.'

Lucens put all his papers in his attaché case and then spoke again. 'It would appear that all of you have forgotten one important matter. I am the figurehead here, you are not. If I'm not around or am

AWOL, you know our aims and objectives. Think, deliberate amongst yourselves, though not forever, and take wise decisions. Once in a while things will go wrong. So what? We'll rectify them with the help of the Virgin and Jesus.'

Tejas had expected it would be his other job that would take up all his attention and effort. But as things turned out, he had little or no catching up to do at International Strategic Security Systems. James, it appeared, had trespassed into his territory and taken charge. It was true that he had gone slack for three months. But James had been unproductive for much longer and yet Tejas had taken a lenient view of it instead of sacking him. Tejas was miffed about it at the beginning, but not for long. No point picking a fight about it. Besides, James was allowed a few whims and privileges. After all he was the older and founding partner of the company. Tejas would start from scratch and develop a new client base. He would have to work like a maniac. He would need to rebuild the business, plus make up for the two thousand million worth of orders that he had shelved. He had no regrets. He knew he was good and he would make up for lost time and money.

He recalled that day in London when he had walked out of Irfan's room at the Carlton. It had been touch and go. He'd taken a colossal risk and he knew it. But he couldn't stop. It had been his call and he had had to take it. He hadn't been getting anywhere and he'd thought, what's to lose? and had pushed his luck. The door had closed and he'd walked to the elevator with a heavy heart. Had he really thought he had a chance?

He was leaving the hotel when he found Nawaaz waiting for him at the entrance; he must have jumped out of the balcony or crashed down the staircase. Tejas thought Nawaaz was having trouble speaking because he was out of breath but that was not the case. Afghans, like most Indians, have trouble with certain words.

'I'm sorry,' he spat out the apology and was relieved to be rid of it. 'Did you really mean what you said?'

'I said many things.'

'That I had vision and I could bring my people together.'

'What would I gain by lying to you? Don't forget I'm going to be the poorer by two billion dollars. But yes, if anyone has a fighting chance of pulling it off, I would bet on you.'

It was dark by now and raining. Nawaaz and Tejas walked down to a Pakistani take-out place and bought a couple of biryanis with extra helpings of pickles and chilli powder. Back in the room, Nawaaz spread a towel on the carpet and placed the food on it. They sat cross-legged and ate from the same plate.

'I'm going to tell you a story, Nawaaz, a story I've never told anybody else.' There was a job to be done and Tejas pulled out all the stops. 'In my last year at school, I became a father. I don't know if it was a boy or a girl because I never saw the child. I have no idea what the mother did with it because I never saw her again. Some years later I took a vow of celibacy, so I shan't have any more children. I have a brother who was married once but the fool doesn't have any children either.

'In the last couple of months I've begun to think of you as my lost son. You are older than him but that doesn't make much of a difference. I see you and I'm reminded of myself as a young man though even then I didn't swear the way you do. I've always believed that there is nothing random in the universe, that we are all part of God's Grand Design. It may appear a coincidence that we met but I'm sure there's a purpose to it.

'I'm a statistician by training and my science tells me that the chances of our meeting were on the wrong side of zero. I did my best not to meet you, but it was written and I could not escape it. Imagine my astonishment when I heard you quote from my diaries, which I lost so many years ago. Some bonds cannot be broken however hard one may try and however adverse the circumstances. All I can tell you is I'll support and help you in any way I can if you embark on the great endeavour to unite your country.'

'And if I don't?'

'I'll deliver the goods and collect my cheque. And you won't hear from me again.'

Nawaaz kept shaking his head as if he couldn't fathom what was going on. 'I wish we hadn't met. I don't know if this is the worst day of my life or the most important. I have always known my mind. I've never been troubled before, not even when I killed Mirza Rustum's dastardly son. I don't know anything about the Grand Design. All I can say is you've come into my life and all my certitudes and self-confidence are gone.'

'I would think that's a good sign. It's difficult to contemplate such a crucial step in your life without being shaken to your roots. Your whole system is going to be churned up and you are going to feel battered. Fortunately you don't have to make up your mind today. You have almost two months to think things over.'

'What about the stuff I ordered.'

'That's the least of your worries. It will be there.'

Nawaaz Irfan was still shaking his head when Tejas left.

'I don't know. I no longer know anything.'

# 59

Tejas had memory lapses about what happened on the night of the Shivratri festival. Was it the previous night, or the night before that, when Shakta Muni had invited him to join the celebrations? Tejas couldn't remember and he couldn't get the sequence of events right. He was sure he had been hallucinating.

'Where have you been, Tejas?' Shakta Muni had called out to him as he walked into the open grounds of the ashram that night. 'Deirdre and James have been looking all over for you. It's Shivratri today. The great Shiva was born at the stroke of midnight. Someone give thandai to our friend here.' There was an epidemic of hugging, embracing, clasping and cuddling amongst the ashramites and guests.

'We never get to see you, Tejas. Even when you come to the Park, you go into a huddle with James and never come up to see me.' Deirdre's eyes were unnaturally bright and excited. The fine-china face was still intact except that the skin was stretched tauter than before. There had always been a touch of the deliberate or, if you prefer to be unkind, of the artificial about Deirdre. Which in a way made it impossible to tell how many face-lifts she had had. Tejas was a little wary of this sudden bout of affection, but it seemed genuine enough even if it was very possibly drug-induced. Her lips brushed against his cheek and then she touched his face.

'Such a good-looking boy and in such perfect shape too.'

'Hardly a boy, Mrs Cambray. I'm as old as your son.'

She was not listening. 'You would have made a good ballet dancer and we could have danced *Giselle* or *Swan Lake* together.'

James was even more effusive in his greetings.

'Tejas, my better half in business, I thought you had gone underground for good. How are orders for this quarter? Sorry, wrong question. Shakta Muni's warned me, no shoptalk today. Heard from your friend Roy in New York? Ready for a night of wild partying and carousing?'

Before Tejas could respond James was already talking to somebody else. It appeared no one was really interested in replies today.

A woman poured him a glass of ice-cold sweet milk laced with bhang leaves in it.

'No, thank you. I'll pass.'

Shakta Muni laughed. 'The whole of India drinks thandai on Shiva's birthday, Tejas. It's an ancient tradition, that's all. We are not asking you to give up your religion or deny your Lord.'

Tejas hesitated. He was also embarrassed. Why did the Muni expose his thoughts in front of the others?

'Forget it. Just wanted you to let your hair down for once. But that's okay. I wouldn't want to do anything to upset you.'

That was true. The Muni didn't try to force anything down your throat. Tejas emptied the glass and then had one more. He watched himself slipping imperceptibly into another dimension. He asked for one more thandai.

He noticed that time had developed cracks and there were bits and pieces missing from it. He crouched on the floor and looked for them under the beds and in the cupboards; he went into the kitchen just in case someone had forgotten them there; he went to the terrace, but they were nowhere to be found. He sat in the corner with his head in his hands. He was in charge of time and he was unable to account for it. What was he going to do? From the beginning of the universe, time had run in a straight line like a tightrope stretched across infinity. He lay down on his belly on that quintessential Euclidean proposition, a line so pure it was without breadth or width, and inched forward till he reached the first hiatus and peered down. Shakta Muni, James, Deirdre and the others were at the bottom of the abyss on the other side of the earth. There was a carnival going on, the revellers were a blur as they gyrated and swayed like snakes in a fog of cannabis.

A cosmic drum, the drum of Shiva, was pounding as though at the creation of the world. Or maybe it was an apocalyptic beat and Shiva was dancing an ecstatic dance of death. That was the puzzle of tantra. Everything was simultaneous in tantrik time: life and death, creation and destruction, male and female, violence and stillness, matter and antimatter. The drum punched, beat and bludgeoned him into numb submission while drawing him into a hypnotic trance. The revellers were waving to him to join them. He looked a little more closely. Shakta Muni was eating from the green stalk of time, the time yet to come, and was passing it on to others. Tejas couldn't possibly permit that. He leaned over as far as he could to snatch the broken line of time. And then he was falling, falling, falling...till Shakta Muni caught him in his arms.

Tejas thought he caught glimpses of ritual fires and occult rites and sacrifices. Bodies were writhing on the floor. He closed his eyes because he did not wish to be tempted.

'Open your eyes,' the Muni told him, 'only then will you stop projecting your private fantasies on others.'

'You've stolen time. I've come to take it back.'

'Yes, of course, but before you do that, wouldn't you like a bite of immortality?'

Tejas was missing for two days. The police picked him up wandering naked in the countryside. Shakta Muni drove down to the police station with some clothes and a shawl and brought him back to the ashram. He slept right through for forty-eight hours.

'Thank you,' Tejas joined Shakta Muni in his study.

'What for?'

'Thank you for rescuing me. All night long I could hear the prisoners screaming in agony. When they brought them back to their cells, they had been beaten almost to death. They were threatening to work me over to get at the truth about who I was.'

'We take care of our own, Tejas.' Then almost as an afterthought Shakta Muni added, 'One way or another.'

'Would you remember what I was up to on Shivratri night?' Tejas asked sheepishly. 'Did I conduct myself honourably?'

Shakta Muni smiled wryly. 'What antiquated language you use sometimes, Tejas. What exactly do you have in mind when you use the word "honourably"?'

'Did I break any commandments?'

'You are free to think the worst of yourself. But I don't recall you doing anything I myself didn't do.'

'And what did you do?'

'I'm not the one with the guilty conscience. So I'm not sure I'm eligible for a cross-examination.'

It was obvious that the subject was closed. But Tejas had other matters on his mind.

'Something strange happened while I was missing. I was on a lightning guerrilla raid on Tel Aviv when I was taken prisoner. Sharon, the Israeli prime minister, took me back to my village in Galilee and told me that if I led them to Arafat, they would let me go. I took them to the home of Mary and Joseph and waited till Jesus came out of the carpentry shed and I pointed to him. "That's him, that's Arafat."

'"Can't be," Sharon said, "he looks very different." And I told him, "Of course he does. He's had cosmetic surgery so that no Israeli could identify him." Can you believe it? I betrayed my God. And don't tell me my mind was playing tricks with me.'

'You are not the first and you are not the last to deny your God. Peter did it and so did the others. I doubt if any of the disciples loved Jesus half as much as Judas. Have you ever wondered what would have happened if Judas hadn't betrayed Jesus? What would have happened to the arithmetic of the prophecy? Imagine the moral pressure on the apostle not to give the lie to a divine prediction that said he'll nark on his God. Has anybody ever bothered to understand the tragic bind Judas found himself in? Sometimes I think Judas was a victim of the Almighty's Master Plan and it was Christ who let him down. He could easily have told Judas not to give him away. Or the least he could have done was to remove himself from the scene and everything would have been fine.'

Tejas had gone red in the face and was glaring at the Muni. 'If you persist in speaking heretically, I will leave.'

'No need to get so worked up. I have little doubt that one of the lost gnostic gospels must have dealt with the dilemma of Judas and his tragic fate, and would have clearly shown how Jesus chose him instead of Peter to be the first amongst equals.'

'I see that you have no intention of desisting. I'm off.'

'It was just a thought, Tejas; a philosophical speculation, that's all. For instance, it's possible to see Judas as the exemplar of all the principled betrayers and traitors like the Cambridge dons, Kim Philby, Burgess, Maclean, and Anthony Blunt, the art historian who passed British secrets to Moscow.'

Tejas sneered. 'Judas did it for money, not for any principles.'

'You mean the thirty pieces of silver? That was a cheap storyteller's gimmick and below the belt. He damns Judas as a villain and allows us to feel morally superior to him. First you announce in public that the man's going to betray you. And when he actually does it, do you really expect people to believe that he did it for that paltry sum?'

'You are perverse. You distort everything.'

'What would you do if you were the judge in the matter of Judas versus the Roman Empire?'

'Torture him after yanking out his sinning tongue. And then crucify him, what else?'

Shakta Muni looked at him thoughtfully. 'The same for the good traitors? The ones who do it for a cause?'

'Why should they deserve any better?'

'And you? What do we do about you, now that you claim you too have betrayed your God?'

'Death, if it was for real.'

Tejas scoured the flea markets in Delhi and Bombay and met almost every important antique dealer but he couldn't find anything he liked. Someone said Agra was the place for the genuine collector, but that you had to know the right people and you had to be there at the right moment. It was the kind of safe and inane proviso that would work just as well if you were looking for any kind of collector's item: cars, paintings, cameras, furniture, antique anything and everything. Agra was a dead loss. He went down to Hyderabad. No joy there either. He flew back to Delhi the next morning. At lunch, for lack of anything to talk about, he asked Shakta Muni.

'I guess you wouldn't know any good antique dealer?'

'Why do you say that, am I not an antique myself?' the Muni asked. 'I see that my lame humour's lost on you. What are you looking for?'

'I'm not quite certain. I'm sure I'll know it the moment I see it.'

'That's very helpful. How much time do you have?'

'I leave early tomorrow morning.'

'Let me call someone I know and see if he can be of any help.'

It took Tejas two-and-a-half hours to find the shop and fifteen minutes to find what he didn't know he was looking for: a sixteenth-century scimitar that had belonged to Sher Khan, the Afghan chieftain who had evicted the second Mughal emperor, Humayun, from the throne of Delhi. The short sword was an exquisite piece, sturdy but graceful, studded with twelve emeralds, one for each month of the year, and seven rubies for the days of the week. 'Is it sharp?' he asked.

'It is not a decorative piece, sir. It was meant to be deadly and it still is.' It was beyond Tejas's budget, far, far beyond it, but there was nothing else there that caught his fancy and would be worthy of the occasion. It was a small price to pay for a clear conscience.

Commissions had always been the mainstay of the arms business. The majority of clients wanted hard cash deposited directly into their offshore accounts. But many wanted gifts that were status symbols in their own countries. In Tajikistan, the preference generally was for a BMW, a Mercedes or, even better, a Jaguar. Some of the African rebel leaders wanted the latest digital movie cameras to shoot their love-making, the funerals of their loved ones, and their atrocities. Nawaaz Irfan, on the other hand, had not asked for anything, and it was unlike Tejas to overdo the gifts bit. But there was a good reason for it. The scimitar might have had a cutting edge only on the inner side, but it was a double-edged weapon as far as Tejas was concerned. If the Afghan leader bought into Tejas's suggestion to spend the two billion on his people instead of a nuclear arsenal, then Tejas would be off the hook and the price was well worth it. And if he didn't, then the scimitar would come in handy for other reasons.

For a while Nawaaz and Tejas couldn't see eye to eye on the venue of their meeting. The acolyte preferred his hideout in the mountains, but Tejas pleaded that he had a slipped disc problem and was in a great deal of pain. He would find it well nigh impossible to trek the last four or five miles or, worse still, ride on a donkey. Any place else was okay with him so long as it was on flat ground. Two days later Nawaaz had called to bow graciously to Tejas's request.

'How about the same place as last time, the Carlton Hotel?'

'That would suit me fine.'

*

Till the end Tejas had the feeling of unfinished business.

He sat in the plane and went over his plans, step by step, for the hundredth time. There were two possible scenarios: one, Nawaaz took the bait of accepting the challenge of uniting the warring factions of his country and gave up the idea of the bombs. It would be nothing short of a miracle but that's why Jesus was called the Son of God. He could swing that kind of thing. Who would have imagined twelve or fourteen years before that Zia Khan, the terrorist whom Nawaaz had appropriated as his role model, would walk out on Islam one day and join Jesus? If, and he was aware that it was a big if, the miracle occurred, then he would slowly begin to work on the young warlord. It was a bit late in the day but he now understood why Aunt Antonia had felt compelled to tell Tejas about the Little Miracle that Jesus had wrought for her. And why she then took it upon herself to share her good fortune with the rest of the world, especially those who had endured unspeakable hardships and deprivation. You don't keep the news of salvation to yourself. You go out there and share the largesse of the Lord with every single person on earth. Who knows, Jesus might take a shine to Nawaaz, and then Nawaaz and Tejas could bring the word of the Lord to godforsaken Afghanistan.

Tejas was too much of a realist, though, not to have Plan B in place. Why else had he insisted on not meeting on the Afghan's home ground? He wanted to be on neutral territory, some place from which it would be possible to make a quick getaway. There would, of course, be Nawaaz's personal secretary-cum-security guard in civilian clothes with whom he would have to contend. But that was a far better option than being surrounded by hundreds of his people, not to mention that he would be utterly at sea in that maze of mountain peaks.

Nawaaz stared at the scimitar for a long time. He removed it from its sheath, weighed it in the palm of his hand, held it by the handle and thrust it back and forth to test it for aerodynamics and the flow of movement.

'Did it really belong to Sher Shah?'

'It's written on the handle. He got it made specially for his ascension to the Delhi throne.'

'It's uncanny, I feel a current pass through me when I hold it. I can feel Sher Shah's presence in it. Allah be praised, it is a beautiful piece.'

'It's a delight to the giver when one's gift is truly appreciated.'

'People are always giving me money. The parents of children whom we kidnap and ransom. And the arms dealers are always trying to bribe me. Nobody has ever given me the kind of gifts you pick for me.'

'I must confess that it takes considerable patience and perseverance to find just the right gift.'

'I used to be a random collector of knives, daggers and swords till I met you. But it's no longer a mere hobby with me. I'm contemplating becoming a serious collector.'

'In that case you might find the background information valuable. If you ever wish to sell it, it will help to establish its authenticity.' Tejas gave Nawaaz the papers from the dealer dating the scimitar, and detailing its provenance and its history.

Nawaaz examined and studied the information avidly. 'I've no intention of selling a single item from my collection. What I intend to do is to build a museum for these art objects. It will be a place of national pride that will draw people from all over Afghanistan and give them a sense of their past.'

That last comment might have been a giveaway, but Tejas was not going to count his chickens before they hatched. He picked up the scimitar to take a closer look at it and left it on the table next to his chair just in case. 'Shall we get dinner out of the way and then talk business?' Nawaaz asked.

They did not walk down to the Pakistani take-out place this time. Nawaaz's assistant opened a large vacuum-sealed tiffin carrier, the kind that was at the centre of a mammoth food-distribution network in Bombay, and was the subject of so many Western and Japanese documentaries and studies. He laid the piping hot food on an Afghan tablecloth on the carpet. It was a minor feast, albeit a little greasy. Four varieties of Afghani kebabs, roasted chicken stuffed with dry fruits and peaches, saffron-scented rice, lentil curries, rumali rotis, fresh salad and pickles.

'For weeks I mulled over what you had told me. It was all very new to me. It also seemed presumptuous to view myself as the leader chosen by Allah to bring the various Afghan tribes together. I was forced to look beyond myself and my immediate concerns and ask myself: what is the future of my country? Would we all pray to the same God and yet fight each other till Judgement Day? Where do I fit in all this? They were troubling questions. I'm not, by nature, a reflective person and I couldn't understand why I should torture myself in this fashion. But in the end I was persuaded of the wisdom of your counsel. I started to think in terms of calling a secret meeting of all the tribal leaders and drafted a letter to them. That's when I received a visit from a colleague of yours.'

'A colleague of mine?' Tejas forgot to conceal his surprise.

'His name is James Cambray. He mentioned that he was a trifle concerned about you. You were behaving strangely, he said, and letting down the company's most valued customers. He hoped that was not the case with my order. I told him things were fine between us; that I had checked and rechecked with you and you had never expressed any doubts about delivering the goods on time. "May I speak candidly?" he asked me, but didn't wait for me to say yes. "There is no order from you in our books. I'm afraid he has no intention of honouring your contract." "That couldn't be," I told him. "Zia Khan is like a father and philosopher to me and I am beholden to him for opening my eyes and guiding me through some of the most difficult times both for my country and me." The Britisher got a knowing look in his eyes then and shook his head sadly. "I may have come just in the nick of time. He intends to dupe you of two billion dollars. We have information from reliable sources that he is an American agent."'

Tejas looked at the table next to his chair. The scimitar was no longer there.

'"One thing I solemnly promise you," James told me. "We may have to shift the delivery date by a couple of months but we will not let you down. We take care of our customers, come what may." "You mean you don't want to let go of two billion dollars?" I said to him. "Absolutely. We are businessmen. Which is why we never let a customer down. We have our own advanced laboratories and testing facilities. And we have contacts all over the world. What we can't manage at our place, we can get elsewhere."

'I don't think I grasped the gravity of what he had just told me. After a while I asked him what he wanted me to do when you came to see me. He said, "You are the best judge of that. We don't care for anybody who betrays the trust of our clients, even if he's our partner. Actually, especially if he's our partner."

Nawaaz tried to gauge the effect of his words on Tejas but there was no telling what was going on in his mind.

'Do you remember what you had written about traitors when you were one of us?'

Tejas said, 'How could I forget?' but it was as though he was not listening any more. He was intrigued by the phrase 'to take care of someone'. How often had he heard it said that God takes care of his own. He himself had sworn to 'take care of Amanat' when his brother had threatened to reveal his arms-trade activities to the media. James had told Nawaaz, 'We take care of our customers, come what may.' And when Shakta Muni had picked him up from the police lockup he had assured him, 'We take care of our own...one way or the other.' Now Nawaaz Irfan, his devoted disciple, would take care of him.

It was odd, but the last thing he recalled was something Amanat's Kabir had said towards the end of his book: 'There's only one God and Her name is Life. She is the only one worthy of worship. All else is irrelevant.'

# 60

My dear Zia,

This is not one of my overwrought stories nor is it 'Ripley's Believe It or Not'.

The sole extant speaker of a language that is spoken no more, is a parrot. Its current keepers are clueless about what it's saying. And its original owners have long since disappeared. Can you imagine the loneliness of that parrot? And the tragedy of that language and its people? I want to cosset that bird and hold it to my breast and tell it that my brother will find both its parents and its lost language.

Patrick Nudjulu and his sister are the only two people who speak an Aboriginal language called Mata Ke. Two is better than one, you would think, but tribal culture disallows a brother having converse with a sister after she reaches puberty. The siblings, one assumes, have the freedom of their land and the sky above, but Patrick Nudjulu and his sister, like the parrot, are condemned to permanent solitary confinement.

Figures and statistics are your speciality. And yet every now and then an innocuous number gets stuck in my coronary artery and I begin to sink. About 6,000 spoken languages still survive today but the number is fast diminishing. Every two weeks one of those 6,000 gives up the ghost. There's no knowing how many languages have atrophied and vanished over the centuries because of conquests, natural calamities and the civilizing hand of the explorer and the missionary. You know as well as I that when you lose a language, you forfeit an entire way of life: a way of feeling, seeing and thinking. We count, imagine, suffer, dream, hurt and love in a particular language. The full quantum of our experience and culture exists and is preserved in it.

The saddest part is that it is another language that's threatening every other language in the world. I speak of course of English. The colonizer's tongue was the currency of power since around 1830 in India. The colonizer left in 1947 but his language stayed behind. From the periphery and the margins, it has now moved to the centre as the language of privilege. I would hate to lose English just as I find the thought of life without Bengali, French, Swahili or any other language intolerable and life-threatening.

Where are you, Zia? In one of your notations before you moved to Sparta, you said, 'A few good men with determination, patience and vision too can change the world for the better.' You were so right. If anybody could alter the fate and fortunes of people, it's the likes of you. If Marathi, Assamese and our local languages are to survive, if language diversity is as important as biodiversity, then they need someone like you: single-minded, dedicated and unswerving. You are disciplined and organized, you have a game plan. And you don't give up. You are the one person I know who will deliver without any thought for yourself or your safety.

On second thoughts, maybe it's not such a good idea. The little bird with its strange tongue and the siblings may be better off dead than have any truck with you. You may be a saviour but one who's always accompanied by the Four Horsemen. God alone knows, and sometimes I wonder whether He can keep pace with you either, what blights and pestilences will follow in your wake.

Where are you, my brother? I had given you three months to get out of the arms trade or I would make your sordid double-life public. It's now five months and nobody knows where you are. Have you given up the death business? Or have you gone underground in order to continue to finance the Angels with gun money? Honor and Zac haven't heard from you either. I checked with Roy and he asked his father. But James Cambray too is in the dark about your whereabouts. Has something happened to you? You keep such dubious company, I've been uneasy about it for a while now. There are all kinds of rumours about that Muni of yours and that he too is connected with your line of business in some way. I have no idea what kind of Faustian deal you made with him. Has he done something to you? I suffer, as you are well aware, from a hyperactive imagination and keep thinking the worst: that you are lying crippled or dead somewhere. Some of your arms-trade clients must be involved in genocides and ethnic cleansing. And even those who aren't would not have any compunction bumping off people. Has one of them done you in? I want to go to the police but I'm afraid of overreacting. Prove me wrong and surprise me. Show up tomorrow. Better still, tonight.

My favourite memory from childhood is of your visits to the attar shop across from our building. You haunted that place for months, stood mouth agape in front of the window displaying the bejewelled perfume vials from Mughal times. One day out of the blue you were ushered in by the owner's daughter, Aminara, and a hint of Mirage, the very perfume that Emperor Akbar used, was dabbed on your wrist. Do you remember what you said to me when you got back home? Your hand had stretched all the way back four hundred years and touched Akbar.

It was one of those moments when a door opens for a split second and you get a whiff of something mysterious, how shall I put it without sounding pompous? about the meaning of life and what we are doing here. What you had tapped into was a continuum: your hand didn't merely stretch out to the visionary Akbar, who tried to bring the different peoples of India (with their rigid loyalties to their religions) together in a new faith called Din-e-Ilahi or the Religion of God, but extended all the way back to the Prophet, to Jesus, to Emperor Ashok, who forswore violence after the carnage of Kalinga, and then to the Buddha. They are lodged in your DNA. You are heir to a shared history. Which is why there can no longer be us and them for you, no dividing line. What you had glimpsed, along with the endless atrocities and the holocausts, the ignorance and the inquisitions, was an obdurate determination in our blood not only to survive, but to overcome. To pick up the pieces and reinvent ourselves. To let the light come through, write King Lear, build the Taj Mahal, compose Beethoven's Ninth, attempt The Bill of Rights, and nurture that strangest of God's gifts to us, hope.

What went wrong? How could you turn your back on that ambrosial life-affirming insight, Zia? How did pro-life become so rabidly pro-death?

'Evil' has become such an emasculated word these days, a handy stick with which to beat your enemies. It is used to describe anything from comic-book images of the Evil Empire in *Star Wars* to big dams, stem-cell research, Salman Rushdie and GM foods. And as for George W. Bush, all dissent is evil.

True evil on the other hand requires vision, albeit a deranged vision. It takes staying power and a scorched-earth mind: Hitler, Stalin, Pol Pot and Saddam had it, and doubtless they won't be the last. I think of evil and the men and women who have come to symbolize it as the sins of God. Unlike them you espouse the most honourable causes. And as time passes you unfailingly subvert them. You are an alchemist, a reverse alchemist. You turn gold to dross and good to the purest evil. Perhaps you too are one of the sins of God. One of these days someone's going to write the story of the Angels and discover your role in the anti-abortion campaigns and then in the death business. Some stories, Zia, are best not told.

As an author I am expected to write closures to my stories or novels that really bring all the strands and themes to a satisfactory end. Unfortunately, that flesh-blood-and-chance romance, misadventure, tragedy or comic interlude called life rarely permits the luxury of QED endings.

First Ammijaan went AWOL; Abbajaan was next, followed by Zubeida Khaala. And now you've disappeared, God alone knows where. You tried to kill me, Zia, but without you I feel lost and orphaned. If this is one of your ploys to avoid my barrage of aimless and maddeningly meandering letters, it is a misconceived one. I don't intend to stop writing to you because you are not around. Actually I am contemplating writing more often. How does a letter a day sound, maybe two, merely to make you feel guilty and flush you out from wherever you are hiding.

I have news of sorts for you. I had another anaphylactic episode because of some allergenic food I had in a restaurant without knowing it and had to be admitted to hospital. When I was allowed to go home after eighteen days, Sagari insisted on taking me to her apartment saying that it was too risky to let me be on my own. Neither she nor I have any illusions about my errant ways but I've been wondering whether I stage-managed my illness this time because I wanted Sagari to take me back. The lengths to which some people will go to be with the ones they love. Just keep your fingers crossed and pray that I don't mess it up this time.

Come home, Zia. I'll call Roy over. Let's put up our feet and talk about old times. About Abbajaan, Zubeida Khaala and Aunt Antonia. And yes, of dear Ammijaan too.

Love,

Amanat

# Acknowledgements

'Keep it brief, Mr Nagarkar,' a critic once told me. 'That way we might even read your work instead of merely panning it.'

Sound advice, but as you may have noticed by now, I've failed to take it.

But here's the good news. I'll limit the acknowledgements to a mere hundred words.

First, the Abbey that took me in, a little tentatively at first, and then embraced me as if I was one of their own. God bless you, Reverend Father, Father Gerard (Brother then), Brother Paul and all the other good monks. There was no Lucens there, nor Jonathan-Christophe.

Rebecca Gowers, the novelist, who went through the manuscript thrice, corrected my flawed grammar and English, and made invaluable suggestions.

I've met few editors as painstaking, perceptive and meticulous as Ratika Kapur. Even I can get lucky sometimes.

Nancy Fernandes, who typed out *God's Little Soldier* a mere 11,597 times, lost her patience more than once, but stuck by the book.

My friends Pervin Mahoney, Peggy and George Dardess, Debjani M. Dutta, who gave me wise counsel about the book, about Christianity and Islam, and guided me through tricky waters.

The city of Munich, which allowed me to stay at the Villa Waldeberta for three months and rethink my book. And Paul Smith of the British Council who gave me a travel grant.

Last of all, Tulsi Vatsal. The book got nine lives (more, not less) because of her. Every time I strayed and lost sight of the main objective, she brought me back on course.

However inadequate this sounds, thank you, thank you, thank you. I owe a debt of gratitude to all of you, and to those who read and supported *God's Little Soldier*.

Peace be with you, Zia, Amanat, all my friends, readers and non-readers.

*Further praise for Kiran Nagarkar's earlier work*

No recent book has the strength and complexity of *Cuckold*, and none offers such rewards. By choosing the husband of Mirabai as his protagonist, Nagarkar is able to fashion a dazzling narrative infused with multiple layers of philosophical, historical and spiritual meaning. The book contains many moods and registers...Here is writing so immediate and sensuous it leaves the reader with almost physical memories. This is not all, for the book explores in a deeply personal, introspective vein and with great subtlety and intelligence the place of love, hate, good and evil in human life. Nagarkar crowns his achievement with a stunning, illuminating ending which raises the novel to another plane and opens the reader to new possibilities. This is a very important book, one which is deeply relevant to the contemporary world and yet will undoubtedly stand the test of time.

**Dr Susan Daruvala**, University of Cambridge

[Nagarkar's] work can only be described as dauntingly imaginative, a feast for the mind, a virtuoso performance in the art of using language like a paintbrush to fill the eye with colour, the ear with the rhythms and cadence of poetry only thinly disguised as prose...I loved Kiran Nagarkar's *Cuckold*.

**Carol Andrade**, *The Metropolis*

Those who mourn for the alienation of the English language as and when applied to native images and attitudes, should get up and dance naked in the rain at the levels of natural fluency in Nagarkar's *Cuckold*. Language in *Cuckold* is not just a means of communication. It isn't even a mediator between readers and plot. It acquires an almost invisible status. What we see and hear are the characters and their thoughts, nothing more, nothing less.

Miraculously liberated of all linguistic obstacles, unfettered by inhibitions of sacrosanctity, *Cuckold* is controlled by a truly renaissance imagination.

**Subhash K. Jha**, *The Hindustan Times*

[Nagarkar] is a born story-teller, thinker and has a way with words uniquely his own...You enjoy, you learn and you are made to think. What more can you ask for from an author? *Cuckold* is historical fiction at its best.

**Khushwant Singh**, *Sunday Despatch*

[*Cuckold*] is a work of substance that exists on many levels and has much to say about our own times as it has about the past. It is an exploration of the nature of kingship and statecraft. It offers a fresh vision of sainthood. It questions sexual identities. It contains graphic depictions, deftly drawn, of the confusion and mayhem of the battlefield. It is a panegyric to the power of music. It plays on the theme of cuckoldry with many a variation.

In the course of events, remarkably compelling personalities come to the fore. They love, hate, manoeuvre, conspire, engage in intrigues and deceptions...Each character – no matter how minor – is distinct, unpredictable, capable of surprising us, and fully rendered...

And finally, a word about Nagarkar's language. He employs a distinctive yet unobtrusive narrative voice which comes as a welcome relief from recent novels whose styles call attention to themselves and trivialize the material in the process, whose relentless quirkiness soon becomes a bore. Likewise we have to thank him for the absence of magic realism, a device that has been flogged to death by every writer aspiring to be another Marquez or Rushdie.

**Jacquelin Singh**, *Indian Review of Books*

Let me say it right away: [*Cuckold*] is a fascinating and brilliant book, a colossal epic, which devours the reader just as the reader devours the 704 pages without stopping.

**Gabriele Venzky**, *Die Zeit*

[*Ravan and Eddie* is] insouciant, savage, disarming and profound...[Nagarkar's] imagery has the quality of switch-blades flickering in the dark alley of the narrative. [His] humour is dark, but passionate.

**Manjula Padmanabhan**, *The Asian Age*

[*Ravan and Eddie* is] one of the wittiest, bawdiest, most perceptive books in contemporary Indian English literature.

**Prem Panicker**, *The Sunday Observer*

Kiran Nagarkar is totally unpredictable, and reading his books is like taking a roller-coaster ride for the imagination...[His] use of language recognizes no barriers, and flows over through and around the reader, engulfing him in a torrent of fantastic images...[His] lively imagination is like a force of light, touching now this problem, now that. His digressions [in *Ravan and Eddie*] are perhaps the best part...

**Usha Hemmadi**, *Indian Express*